DESTROYERMEN: UNKNOWN SEAS

Books by Taylor Anderson

DESTROYERMEN

DESTROYERMEN

UNKNOWN SEAS

INTO THE STORM & CRUSADE

TAYLOR ANDERSON

SCIENCE
FICTION

INTO THE STORM Copyright © 2008 by Taylor Anderson
    Publication History: Roc Hardcover, June 2008
                                 Roc Mass Market, February 2009
CRUSADE Copyright © 2008 by Taylor Anderson.
    Publication History: Roc Hardcover, October 2008
                                 Roc Mass Market, November 2009

First Science Fiction Book Club Omnibus Edition: July 2011

Published by arrangement with
The Penguin Group (USA), Inc./ New American Library
Roc
375 Hudson Street
New York, NY 10014

Visit the SFBC online at www.sfbc.com
Follow us on Facebook: www.Facebook.com/ScienceFictionBookClub

ISBN 978-1-61129-768-3

Printed in the United States of America.

CONTENTS

INTO THE STORM

For my darling daughter, Rebecca Ruth.
Everything I do is for her, after all.
In return, I get her humor, wit, companionship,
inspiration, and unqualified adoration.
Not a bad trade.

ACKNOWLEDGMENTS

First, I must thank my parents, Don and Jeanette Anderson, who tolerated my various early eccentric pursuits—albeit sometimes with dubious, strained smiles and rolling eyes. Parents always want the best for their kids, and many of the paths I chose in life were untrodden, dark, and overgrown. At least they didn't have to worry that I was running with the "wrong crowd," since I spent most of my formative spare time in the woods with a flintlock and a bedroll. They didn't just sit back and watch, though, and therefore must take a measure of responsibility for the example they set. My dad taught me about old radios, Fort Worth Spudders, flying—and honor, of course. My mother taught me strength of will and character. I might sometimes feel compelled to substitute "stubbornness and obstinacy" for those more noble-sounding traits, but which is, after all, more virtuous and practical?

I have to thank MMCPO (SS) Tom Postulka, USN, a good friend I miss a lot and who, even though a submariner, sparked my interest in four-stackers a dozen years ago. Erik Holland, USN (ret.), is a quintessential "snipe," and his stories of engine-room life on diesel-electric Fleet submarines have kept me laughing and learning for years. SCPO Jeff Fairchild, USN (ret.), may be a "Nukie Puke," but he's helped me out of a few jams too. Lt. Col. Dave L. Leedom, USAFR, and Mark Wheeler reminded me how fun flying can be. (Bad) Dennis Petty, Jim Goodrich, Col. Alan Huffines, USAR, and Lynn Kosminski convinced me that maybe I could string a few words together after all—in spite of the harm many of my professors did by stifling all literary allusions in my earlier, purely historical work.

Other people who've helped me in so many ways include (but are certainly not limited to) Robin and Linda Clay, Mark Beck, Brad Fisher, USMC (ret.), Dennis Hudgens, Michael Dunegan, Walter Baldree, Sgt. 1st

Class Dex Fairbanks, USA (ret.), Riqui and David Wartes, Preston Furlow, and Cortney Skinner. Special thanks to Dr. David Bererra and all the nurses and staff at Harris Southwest Methodist Hospital, and of course, to my long-suffering, beautiful bride, Christine.

Last, but certainly not least, I have to thank Russell Galen and Ginjer Buchanan.

Ginjer is the best editor I know and has always been gracious, friendly, and supportive. She and her staff are a pure pleasure to work with.

Russell Galen is the best agent in the business. His patience, professionalism, encouragement, and friendship truly are the steam that moves this ship through the water. To say "I couldn't have done it without him" is ridiculously insufficient praise. I rarely find myself at a loss for words, but I simply cannot express how much I appreciate his help. Thanks, Russ.

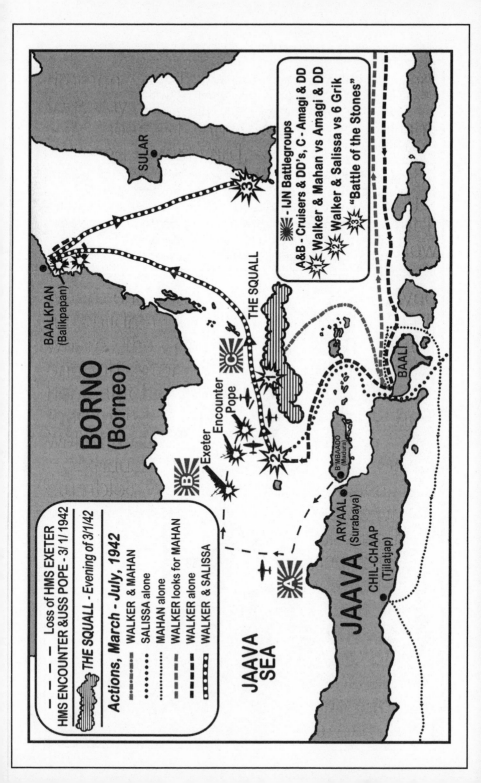

Ceylon

Madagascar

Africa

Arabia

U.S.S. WALKER   DD-163

NAVIGATIONAL CHART FILING LABEL

M.S.N. No. 6293-58-56   Date August 6, 1942

--- Possible Meaning of Grik Map Symbols ---

--- (On Dark Tone) Extent of enemy conquest.

☾ ---- Lemurian territory.

⚬⚬⚬ --- Lemurian population centers.

▲ --- Closed Triangle - Single grik ship?

▲ - 3 grik ships?

△ - Blood Smudge - A place of battle.

〰〰 - Lemurian Home

◯ - Patrol/area for grik squadrons

Lt Cmdr Matthew P. Reddy H. Cmdr Matthew P. Reddy
Commanding

CHAPTER

1

hey were running. There was no other word for it, no comforting euphemism to make the sting less sharp. In fact, it seemed impossible to wring the slightest sense of purpose from the confusion, privation, terror, and bone-numbing weariness they'd endured since the very day the war began on December 7. Now, three months later, they were running away ("limping" might be the better term) and they hadn't even had a chance to lick their wounds. The tired men and elderly ships of Destroyer Squadron (Des Ron) 29 had hurled themselves repeatedly at the implacable juggernaut that was the Japanese Imperial Navy while their numbers were ruthlessly slashed by disaster and disrepair. It was a tragically lopsided contest, a feeble gesture of defiance against overwhelming odds. In the end, a gesture was all it had been. Now all that remained was to flee—and it was probably too late.

Lieutenant Commander Matthew Patrick Reddy, USNR, the captain of USS *Walker*, stood on the starboard bridge-wing and tried to maintain at least a semblance of dignity in his rumpled and sweat-stained shirt. His left hand clutched his hat to his head against the thirty-knot breeze while his right tried to keep the half-filled mug of lukewarm coffee from slopping onto his uniform.

Red-rimmed eyes squinted from what was normally an almost embarrassingly boyish face, but at the moment a general covering of brown stubble and a fatigue-slacked expression made him look older than his thirty-two years. Not quite thirty-six hours earlier, he and his exhausted crew had participated in the largest surface action of the war to date: the Battle of the Java Sea. For once, the forces were evenly matched—in numbers, if not quality—and they thought they'd had a chance. But from the beginning, nothing went right. The battle finally ended sometime in the night with the ruthless slaughter of virtually the entire force under Admiral Doorman's command. While the enemy grew ever stronger, the scattered Allies were picked off in ones and twos.

Walker wasn't there when the poor old *Houston* and the staunch *Perth* were surrounded and hammered to the bottom. All the destroyers had been ordered to Surabaya to refuel and had thus been granted a short reprieve. *Edwards, Alden, Ford,* and *Paul Jones* departed for Australia as soon as their bunkers were full, and nobody knew if they'd made it through the gauntlet or not. The remaining destroyers were ordered to wait for the British cruiser *Exeter,* the only capital ship to survive the battle, and escort her to Ceylon after she completed temporary repairs. Matt spent that day of short intermission sending out parties to scrounge anything they might use, but little turned up in the bombed-out remains of the Dutch naval yard. The searchers discovered some belted .30-cal, eighty rounds of four-inch-fifty for the main guns, two condemned torpedoes, a little food. It wasn't much. All the while, emergency repairs to *Walker* were under way. Even if Matt had found the time, he couldn't have slept through the racket.

Now, standing on the bridgewing, he allowed a huge yawn to escape and hoped it made him look calm instead of just worn-out. The morning sun was bright, and the beauty of the vast, calm, almost violet sea was marred only by the distant hump of Bawean Island and the tiny cluster of American and British destroyers guarding *Exeter*'s wounded flanks like battle-weary army ants escorting their injured queen to a new home. As far as Matt knew, he was looking at all that remained of the Allied Forces in the American, British, Dutch, Australian—or ABDA—defensive area. He knew they'd been the last ones out of the tangled mass of wreckage and half-sunken hulks that Surabaya, Java, had become. ABDAFLOAT's initial force was composed of two heavy cruisers, seven light cruisers, twenty-three destroyers, and about thirty submarines and assorted support vessels. Now all that was left were three battered, Great War–vintage U.S. "four-stacker" destroyers, one British destroyer, *Encounter,* and the badly damaged heroine of the River Plate, HMS *Exeter.* The massive Japanese fleet that destroyed or chased off the rest of their comrades now had them alone to concentrate on. USS *Pope* (DD-225) and HMS *Encounter* screened *Exeter*'s starboard side, while USS *Mahan* (DD-102) and Matt's own *Walker* (DD-163) screened to port.

He glanced up at the lookout standing in the little tub near the top of the mast. Rodriguez, electrician's mate 3rd class, appeared transfixed, staring through heavy binoculars at a point far astern. From where he stood, Matt couldn't see anything yet, but he knew the two Japanese heavy cruisers and the destroyer that had pursued them since 0700 were still behind them. Rodriguez could see their smoke and they were getting closer.

When they'd slipped out of Surabaya the night before, they intended to run the Sunda Strait into the Indian Ocean and make a dash for Ceylon. Blocked by the enemy, they reversed course across the Java Sea to run east along the Borneo coast. Their quick about-face gained them breathing room, but the enemy cruisers launched observation planes. Two circled even now, high above and beyond reach of their meager antiaircraft defenses. All they could do was watch while the planes kited lazily overhead and reported their progress to every Japanese ship within range of their radios.

The convoy was limited to twenty-seven knots by *Exeter*'s damage, but Matt knew *Walker* couldn't steam much faster herself. The daily litany of mechanical casualties plaguing his ancient ship read more like a shipyard inventory than a morning report. *Pope* and *Mahan* were in no better shape. The stress of constant steaming and frequent combat—in addition to ordinary wear and tear—had placed a heavier strain on *Walker*'s machinery and equipment than she'd endured in all her twenty-three years of service. *Walker* had gone beyond her design, and Matt was very much afraid that she, as well as her crew, was being pushed beyond their capability.

He hadn't commanded her long, only four and a half months. As a reservist, even one from the Academy, he'd been treated pretty rough by the Navy. He'd worked his way into the exec's slot on a Benson-class destroyer (a major step up in the peacetime Navy), but he'd lost the posting to an older regular officer and found himself on the beach. He knew it wouldn't last and he was right. War was brewing all over the world, and it was just a matter of time before the United States got involved. When he got the letter, he expected—hoped for—a posting to one of the new Fletcher-class destroyers, possibly as gunnery officer. That would have suited him fine. Much to his surprise, he was given a command. But not of one of the sleek, lethal, modern destroyers he yearned for. No, he was to command one of the decrepit and almost defenseless antiques with which he was familiar, but found far from satisfying. Even more disheartening, his "new" command was attached to the Asiatic Fleet.

USS *Walker* had toiled with the Asiatic Fleet for more than six years and in that time she'd never been back to the country of her birth. She was 314 feet long and not quite 31 feet wide. Her long, sleek, needle-shaped hull and the four slightly raked funnels that provided the unofficial moniker for her class gave an impression of speed. And she was fast—by the standards of 1919—having made thirty-six knots on her trials. Even now she wasn't what one would have called slow, but the effort required to maintain her maximum speed was . . . excruciating.

Her ancient boilers were choked with sediment, and her steam lines sprouted leaks with unpredictable capriciousness. Her wiring was so corroded that most of it didn't do anything anymore. Much had been spliced or bypassed, and unidentifiable bundles of wires ran all over the ship. Her hull plates leaked rust through cracked and peeling paint, despite constant work by her crew to keep it chipped and touched up. The plates themselves were only two-thirds as thick as they once had been. She stank of sweat, smoke, grease, paint, fuel oil, steam, and strangely, hot linoleum. Her round bottom made her roll horribly in anything but the calmest seas, and she rattled and groaned and vibrated so badly you could feel it in your teeth. Her blowers produced a loud and decidedly asthmatic wheeze, and the general cacophony of abused machinery made hearing difficult in the remotest areas of the ship.

Her main battery consisted of a meager quartet of four-inch guns— only three of which could possibly bear on a single target—and none of which could elevate high enough to engage aircraft. There was one little three-inch antiaircraft gun on the fantail, but its range was so short it was used mostly for firing illumination star shells. The only even marginal antiaircraft defenses she had were two .30-caliber machine guns on the fire-control platform and two .50-caliber guns on the amidships deckhouse. Hanging over the fantail where it tapered sharply to a slightly rounded vee were two old-fashioned depth-charge racks. Her real teeth consisted of twelve 21-inch torpedoes carried in four triple-tube mounts between the number four funnel and the aft deckhouse. The torpedoes, and her once-respectable speed when delivering them, had been the reason for her creation so long ago. But like everything else in this new war so far, the torpedoes had been a grave and costly disappointment.

Matt had always heard that new captains often overlooked the shortcomings of their first command. But the first thing that sprang to mind when he saw her riding at anchor in Manila Bay, besides a general feeling of dismay over her apparent condition, was that the white-painted letters "163" on her bow seemed much too large.

Matt had been to the China Station and the Philippines—the Asiatic Fleet's area of operations—only once before. He'd been an ensign aboard another four-stacker during the buildup over the *Panay* incident, when the Japanese "accidentally" bombed and sank an American gunboat on the Yangtze River. Even then, the men, ships, and conditions of operation in the Asiatic Fleet made quite a negative impression. Equipment- and personnel-wise, the station was the abused, ugly dog of the Navy. The men were considered the dregs of the service, and the ships were third-rate obsolescent relics that, it was joked, were kept in the Asiatic Fleet because they weren't worth the fuel to steam home to scrap. When he assumed command of USS *Walker* he'd studied the log and fitness reports of his predecessor, Captain Simmons. As expected, the crew's reputation for hard drinking and carousing was confirmed on the pages he read. But to his surprise, there was also a subliminal thread of tolerance, amusement, and even protectiveness among the author's words. Discipline had been strictly maintained, but it was quickly clear that Captain Simmons had liked his crew. Judging by the initial reserve with which Matt was received, the feeling was mutual. He wondered at the time how difficult it would be for him to "fill the Old Man's shoes" and how much trouble he'd have making the men conform to his own expectations. Even on more agreeable stations, change often provoked the most friction when a new captain took command. And he hadn't "come up" in the Asiatic Fleet.

Despite his apprehension, there was little friction after all. Perhaps it was his quiet competence and uncomplicated, black-and-white sense of duty that left no doubt among the crew where they stood. Or maybe it was his quick discovery that these men were not dregs—at least most of them weren't. Ever since the Depression, the Navy had been particular about the recruits it accepted. A fair percentage of the misfits may have gravitated to the Asiatic Fleet, but for the most part, the men were at least as professional as their counterparts on other stations. They just led an entirely different life than was the norm in the rest of the Navy. They were forced to cope with worn-out equipment and keep their ships combat ready with little more than the proverbial baling wire and chewing gum. It was only natural that they might vent more steam than their peers on stations with less stress, a better climate, and fewer "diversions" than had been the case in China or the Philippines. He could discipline and punish them for their rowdiness and debauchery during a night on the town, but in his heart he couldn't condemn them for it. Their ability to fix anything, or at least make it "sorta" work, in difficult circumstances appealed to his sense of independence. Whatever the reason, much quicker than he'd expected, he'd been elevated to the exalted status of "Skipper," and he realized he liked them too.

Now, captain and crew together had been tested in the cauldron of combat, and Matt's black-and-white concept of right and wrong had come under serious assault. They'd dodged air attacks and experienced the unexpected exultation of "victory" in the Makassar Strait. They'd seen the senseless waste of lives in the Badung Strait caused by confusion and miscommunication. They'd lived through the frustration and horror of the Battle of the Java Sea, while their comrades on other ships and in other navies died for a purpose that began to elude them. No one questioned the War; it came without warning or mercy. It was real, it was all-consuming, and it was here. Why they were fighting it here was the unfathomable question.

Leaving the Philippines was tough. A lot of the guys had Filipino wives and sweethearts, and to them it was home. Some planned to retire there. But after the Air Corps was slaughtered in the opening days of the war, the only things left that had wings had red circles painted on them. Clearly, if the air belonged to the Japanese, remaining in the Philippines was suicide. No one wanted to leave, not even Matt, who still hated being stationed there. But he hated being "run off" even more. Maybe it was his Texas upbringing, or the "Spirit of the Alamo" or something like that, but he'd been perfectly willing to fight to the last even though the withdrawal made good sense.

Shades of gray appeared when *Walker* and Des Ron 29 were redeployed south to defend the Dutch East Indies. It was clearly a hopeless cause. Air cover was still nonexistent, and there weren't enough ships to stop what was coming. The Dutch oil fields were the Japanese objective, but leaving a few old ships to try and slow them down would only provide them with target practice. If they had to make an Alamo-like stand, why couldn't they have done it in the Philippines? Their "home" waters, so to speak?

Java belonged to the Dutch, and it was understandable that they'd want to keep it, but it was impossible. Reinforcements weren't coming. It made more sense to Matt to pull everything out and save the men and ships until they had enough to knock the Japanese on their butts for a change. Of course, he wasn't an admiral or a politician, and the very condition of the Asiatic Fleet proved that its survival wasn't a priority to those who were. He admitted he might've felt differently if Java was his home. The Nazis had Holland, and Java was all that was left. He *had* felt differently when the Philippines were at stake, and he hadn't even liked it there. It was all a matter of perspective. He knew he was relatively young and inexperienced, but he couldn't shake the thought that if it was strategically wrong to defend the Philippines, it was wrong to defend Java too. Maybe he was just bitter. The same people who expected them to fight to the last in the Dutch East Indies hadn't lifted a finger to support the United States in the Philippines.

After the disaster in the Java Sea he thought even the Dutch would realize it made more sense to fight their way back in than be destroyed getting kicked out. As far as he knew, they hadn't sunk a single Japanese ship during the battle. Except for *Exeter* and the aged destroyers, ABDA-FLOAT had ceased to exist. He was mistaken. Word was that Admiral Helfrich, the Dutchman who'd replaced Tommy Hart as ABDA's commander, still planned offensive action even after Admirals Glassford and Palliser told him they had nothing left. The Dutch had no monopoly on stubbornness; the British hadn't showed much more sense regarding Singapore, and thousands of Americans were trapped in the Philippines, cut off from any support. But it was past time to leave. ABDA had done its best with what it had. There'd been willing cooperation, but no coordination. Without air cover or reconnaissance, or even a common language, they'd been like blindfolded kids running around on tricycles with a steamroller bearing down. It was a disaster.

He often reflected on the certainty he'd felt regarding an eventual war with Germany, and he admitted that before he got out here, he'd never given much thought to the Japanese. Evidently nobody had. Now his entire consciousness was devoted to preventing that underestimated foe from shredding his ship and her crew and sending them to the bottom of the Java Sea.

With a gauging glance at the stately *Exeter* off the port quarter to ensure that *Walker* was holding proper formation, he stepped into the pilothouse. The gunnery officer, Lieutenant (j.g.) Greg Garrett, looked anxiously from the port bridgewing and Matt waved him back. The tall, lanky young officer nodded solemnly and resumed scanning the sea toward the dark smudge in the north that was Borneo. A good kid, Greg. He was conscientious and industrious, if just a bit intense. They were still at general quarters, as they'd been since the morning watch, and Garrett's battle station was normally on the fire-control platform above the pilothouse. Matt had told him to rotate himself and his team out of the wind and sun periodically. The main battery was useless against air attack, and it would be a while before they were in range of the Japanese cruiser's eight-inch guns. Longer still before they could hope to reply. Even so, when it was Garrett's turn to take a break, he merely descended to the pilothouse and kept doing what he'd done above—watching and waiting. Matt understood how the younger man felt. The atmosphere of anxiety and tension was thick. Everyone anticipated the cry warning of enemy ships or planes.

The stocky, broad-shouldered form of Lieutenant James Ellis clomped metallically up the ladder from the main deck below, and Matt arched an eyebrow at him. He liked Jim Ellis, and they were as close to being friends as their rank difference allowed, but Jim was much farther from his battle station at the auxiliary conn on the aft deckhouse than Garrett was from his.

"Yes, sir, I know," Ellis said, anticipating the reprimand as he maneuvered Matt out of hearing of the others in the pilothouse. "But those nurses and their flyboy chauffeurs want to know if there's anything they can do. That Army captain"—he tilted his nose up with unconscious disdain—"actually tried to come up here and bug you. Chief Gray said he'd have to wait your convenience." Ellis grinned. "That wasn't good enough and Gray offered to sit on him—physically. Then he sent for me." Matt smiled in spite of his jitters.

Before they cleared Surabaya, they'd taken aboard a rather motley assortment of passengers. First to arrive was an unkempt and harried-looking Australian, a Mr. Bradford, a construction engineer for Royal

Dutch Shell. He introduced himself as a "naturalist," but paid his passage by intervening on their behalf with the harbor officials, who didn't want to fill their bunkers. They'd argued that the fuel would be better used by Dutch ships, staying to defend Java. Courtney Bradford countered with the fact that there was only one Dutch ship left, a destroyer, and she was getting the hell out just as fast as she could. Perhaps it was their lingering respect for a corporate superior, or maybe just the final realization that everything really was falling apart. Whatever the motivation, *Walker* left Surabaya with her bunkers overflowing.

Next to come limping aboard was a sergeant from *Houston's* Marine contingent. He'd been wounded by a bomb that had killed dozens and wrecked the old cruiser's aft turret. Left ashore in a hospital with a lacerated leg, he missed her final sortie. He didn't intend to become a guest of the Japanese. Upon his arrival, he was roundly scolded for bleeding on the deck and sent below to the surgeon.

Finally, motoring out to catch them in a "borrowed" boat just as they were preparing to get under way were six Navy nurses and two P-40 pilots who'd escaped the sinking of the old *Langley* the day before. *Langley* had been ferrying P-40 fighters in for the defense of Java, but she was caught fifty miles short. Bombed into a smoldering wreck, she was abandoned, and one of *Walker's* sisters, *Edsall*, was forced to finish her with two precious torpedoes. The majority of *Langley's* personnel shipped south on the oiler *Pecos*, but in the confusion, the nurses and airmen were left behind. They persuaded the driver of a Dutch army truck to take them to Surabaya, and they arrived just in time to come aboard *Walker*.

Matt hadn't seen them. He'd been aboard *Exeter* conferring with Captain Gordon's executive officer. When he returned, he was informed of the ship's newest passengers by a leering Jim Ellis and a scandalized Lieutenant Brad "Spanky" McFarlane, the engineering officer, whose strict observance of Navy custom—if not always regulations—filled him with a terrible conviction that women on board would certainly doom the ship. That Army aviators accompanied them would probably send them to hell as well. Matt was inwardly amused by the diverse reactions, and it never occurred to him to set them ashore under the circumstances. He only wondered briefly where they'd be kept. Since then, he hadn't seen them and they'd been forgotten.

"What's his name?"

"The Army captain? Kaufman, sir."

"Very well, send him up, but by himself. And, Exec," he added ominously, "we don't need the distraction of women on my bridge. Clear?"

Lieutenant Ellis grinned hugely and went to fetch their visitor. Matt stepped onto the bridgewing as the Air Corps captain clumsily appeared.

He prepared to return the salute he expected, since they were technically out-of-doors. It didn't come. His eyes narrowed slightly and the other members of the bridge crew exchanged shocked, knowing expressions.

"Lieutenant Commander Reddy? I'm David Kaufman, Captain, U.S. Army Air Corps."

The man stuck out his hand and Matt took it briefly. His initial impression was that the lack of a salute and the use of his specific rank instead of the appropriate, if honorific, title of "Captain" were due to ignorance. A Navy lieutenant commander was equivalent to a major in the Army. But the emphasis Kaufman applied to his own rank warned Matt that his guest didn't see it that way and might try to intimidate him if he could.

"What can I do for you, Captain Kaufman?" he asked, placing emphasis on the "Captain" as well, but in a way he'd address a subordinate. Kaufman glanced at the hostile expressions of the seamen on the bridge and modified his tone. His next words were less condescending.

"I just thought if there was anything I or Lieutenant Mallory might help you with, why, just let us know." He smiled smugly, and the patronizing inflection returned as he spoke. He acted like he'd granted a favor.

"What can you do?" Matt asked simply. "Besides fly airplanes. I assume you can fly airplanes."

Kaufman's face reddened, and he realized he might have overstepped. "Yeah, I can fly airplanes," he said with a quick, brittle smile. He held his hands out to his sides. "But I'm fresh out. You don't have one I can borrow?" His attempted joke fell flat and he just shrugged. "I can fire a machine gun."

Matt turned to Garrett, observing the exchange with wide eyes. "Mr. Garrett, perhaps the captain and his lieutenant might assist your crews on the thirty-cals on the fire-control platform? If we come under air attack they'll need to be supplied with ammunition." He grimaced. "Since we lost most of our mess attendants when we left the Philippines, it's hard to spare men for that chore." He looked the aviator square in the eye. "Thanks for the offer. You're dismissed." With that, he turned and peered out the pilothouse windows at the number one gun down on the foredeck. He sensed Kaufman's furious presence behind him for a few moments more, but with an audible sigh and a few muted chuckles, the rest of the watch relaxed and he knew Kaufman must have left. *I shouldn't have let him rile me*, he scolded himself, but he made a quiet snort of amusement anyway. Then he spun—"Exec!"

Ellis's head popped back into view. "Skipper?"

"Those women are nurses, you say?"

Ellis leered again. "Absolutely."

Matt shook his head. "If they want to help, send them to Doc Stevens in the wardroom. And spread the word! They'll be treated with respect.

Any man who inflicts himself on them will go overboard for the Japs. Understood?"

Ellis nodded, his leer now slightly wistful. "Sir."

"Very well. And, Exec?"

"Sir?"

"Keep them off my bridge."

Ellis slid down the ladder, firehouse style, and caught up with Kaufman, who was striding purposefully through the amidships deckhouse. His handsome, square-jawed face was clouded with anger. Ellis touched his sleeve and Kaufman spun. He recognized Ellis and forcibly composed his expression. He stood six inches taller than the burly exec, but Ellis was more muscular. A tolerant smile never left his face. Fitzhugh Gray strode up, adding his pudgy but powerful presence to the group. He handed each man a Coke, already opened, and slipped a church key onto the cap of the one in his own massive paw.

In a service where everyone had multiple "names"—real name, nick-name, and sometimes multiple titles—Gray had the most. He was the chief boatswain's mate, and the highest-ranking NCO on the ship. Al-though he was technically subordinate to the most junior officers, only the captain and the exec would have dreamed of giving him an order. Time in grade, as well as personality, made him the "senior" chief aboard, and he was usually referred to as just "the Chief" by the crew. The other chiefs and of-ficers often used the outdated but still honorific "the Bosun." Only the cap-tain or the exec ever used the respectful diminutive "Boats."

"Going to be another hot one," Gray said, wiping his forehead with his sleeve. "Course, if the goddamn Nips get us, I guess we'll be swimmin'. Them that can swim. I think I'd rather be sweating than swimmin'. I guess you fighter jocks don't give as much thought to swimmin' as destroyermen do." It was just a friendly jibe, but Kaufman was still annoyed by Gray's earlier threat, and what he perceived as the captain's humiliating treat-ment of him.

"What's that supposed to mean?" he demanded hotly. Gray looked at Ellis and rolled his eyes. At that moment, Lieutenant Benjamin Mallory joined them. He was already drinking a Coke and he held it up.

"How about this, Captain?" he said. "These destroyer pukes have a Coke machine! Far as I can tell, it's the only thing that works."

Rebuffed by Kaufman, Gray began to bristle. Ellis recognized the lieutenant's friendly banter, however, and turned to him. "That's right, boy," he said with a grin, "and if you airedales had done your job in the Philippines, we'd still be sitting fat and happy going up and down with the tide in Cavite. Nothing to worry about but keeping the Coke machine stocked while the yard-apes worked on these worn-out boilers." He stomped his foot on the deck for emphasis, indicating the forward fireroom below.

Mallory didn't laugh. "I'm afraid you got me. I wasn't there, of course, but I heard the fellows didn't do so good." Ellis saw Gray take a breath and prepare his tirade about the ineffectiveness of the Air Corps, a topic much discussed. The Japanese air cover and the American lack thereof had been an extremely sore subject since the war began. Ignored now, and glad to be, Kaufman strode away. Mallory started to follow, but Ellis stopped him.

"By the way, Captain Kaufman asked if we could use a hand, and the captain said if you could keep the ammunition flowing to the machine guns it would help."

Mallory nodded thoughtfully. "Sure thing. Not much else we'd be good for on a ship. Show me where you keep the bullets and I'll haul as many as you need." He looked wryly at Ellis and gestured over his shoulder with his chin. "He didn't like that much, did he?"

Ellis smiled and shook his head. "No, son. I think he expected us to put him in charge."

The corner of Mallory's mouth quirked upward. "Kaufman's really not such a bad guy, but I guess he is sort of—" He caught himself and shrugged sheepishly. "I'll do anything I can to help."

Ellis slapped him on the back, and the powerful blow nearly knocked Mallory into the Chief. "I know you will. Boats, have somebody show this man where we keep the bullets. I better get back where I belong."

Nurse Lieutenant Sandra Tucker pushed aside the pea green curtain and led her entourage into the wardroom. She was petite, measuring only five foot three, and her long, sandy-brown hair was coiled tightly about her head. When it came down, it framed a face that may not have been classically beautiful, but was striking in a pretty, "girl next door" sort of way. Her large green eyes projected an impression of naive vulnerability, but anyone making that assumption would have been mistaken. At twenty-seven, she'd been a Navy nurse since '35, and in that time she'd encountered every excuse, pickup line, real and imagined ailment, injury, and malingerer's complaint possible in a bored but active peacetime Navy. She was smart, confident, and even tended toward an arrogant streak when in her realm of expertise. Her mild conceit was understandable, since she was an outstanding nurse and often made a better doctor than the doctors did. She'd assisted in a variety of surgical procedures and performed everything from appendectomies to amputations by herself, since many of her postings had been in remote areas where emergencies were handled on-site. When war loomed, she and her companions volunteered for the Philippines.

She had friends there, and that was where she figured nurses would be needed. She knew she was good at her job and genuinely wanted to be where she could make the greatest contribution. That was why she'd become a nurse in the first place. Right now, although she was the highest-ranking officer in the wardroom, it became quickly obvious that she wasn't in charge.

The ship's surgeon, "Doc" Stevens, was a tall, cadaverous man in his mid-forties. He and Pharmacist's Mate 3rd Class Jamie Miller were sitting at the green-topped wardroom table with the Marine sergeant, Pete Alden, playing dominoes when Sandra entered with the five other nurses.

The wardroom was the officers' dining room, but it also served as a surgery when the ship went into battle. The long dining surface became an operating table, and a large light hung above it by a fixture that could be lowered near the patient. Except for the dominoes, all superfluous articles had been stowed, and various gleaming surgical instruments lay neatly arranged and ready at hand.

The pharmacist's mate looked to be just a boy, like most of the crewmen Sandra had seen, but the Marine was a large, well-muscled, and deeply tanned thirtysomething. He regarded the nurses with a frankly appraising eye. The imposing surgeon grimly played a domino and glanced at them as the nurses crowded through the opening.

"I sort of expected to see you . . . ladies here." His Massachusetts accent was strong and nasal. "I bet you nurses want to be nurses, right?" He shifted in his chair and rubbed his chin. "I never had a nurse before. Not counting Jamie here, of course. Tell me, Sergeant," he said, addressing the Marine, "have you ever had a nurse?" Alden looked at him, astonished. The nurses were, after all, officers. Stevens shook his head. "Never mind, Sergeant. Of course you have. You're a wounded hero, after all. I'm sure you had nurses all over you." Sandra's face clouded and she began to snap a reprimand. Doc Stevens's look momentarily silenced her protest. "I know you're officers and I'm just a lowly Warrant. I don't give a damn. I know about you nurses; wouldn't even give me the time of day if I came squirming into your nice, clean, modern hospital. Well, this is *my* hospital! If you want to stay here and help, that's fine. There'll probably be plenty to do. But if you want to give orders or get in the way, you can turn around, climb that ladder and go play dollies under the depth charges because I don't need you." He stopped long enough to smile at their expressions. "I've got Jamie. He makes a pretty good nurse, even if he looks dreadful in a dress."

Sandra's eyes narrowed, and for an instant she hesitated. She'd faced this kind of attitude all her life and it was particularly pervasive in the military. Her father had perhaps been the worst, refusing to accept that she might do something with her life other than wait for "the right guy" to come along. His restrictions and expectations might have been couched more gently than Stevens's, but they were no less corrosive and condescending. And wrong. She'd proven that. She straightened her back and forced a smile.

"Surgeon's Mate Stevens, is it not?" she asked, and her voice held an icy calm. Stevens arched an eyebrow, but jerked an aggressive nod.

"Your captain asked that we report to you and that's what we've done. I know this is your 'hospital' and I'm prepared to defer to you." Her voice took on a dangerous edge. "But since you insist on wallowing in your 'lowly Warrant' status I'll remind you I'm a LIEUTENANT in the United States Navy. My ensigns might not pull rank on you, but I SURE AS HELL WILL! You're clearly not a gentleman, so I won't appeal to you as one, but as a superior officer I insist you get up off your skinny ass and show the respect due my rank or by God, I'll have you up on charges for insubordination!"

Her voice had risen as she spoke, until her final exclamation was uttered as a roar that her small form seemed incapable of producing. Jamie Miller's chair hit the deck as he rocketed to attention. Even the wounded Marine struggled to his feet, his face a study of embarrassment mingled with respect. Doc Stevens remained seated a few moments more, but finally he stood also, an expression of mocking insolence on his face. He threw an exaggerated salute.

"Your orders, ma'am?" The question dripped sarcasm, but Sandra smiled in anticipation of his reaction. She looked at Jamie. "You!"

"Pharmacist's Mate Miller, ma'am."

"Mr. Miller, stow those dominoes and disinfect that table this instant. We could have casualties at any moment." She looked at the blood-soaked bandage the Marine wore. "Are you even fit for duty?"

"Yes, ma'am."

"Hmm. I doubt it, but we'll see. We'll have a look at that leg presently, circumstances permitting."

Stevens cleared his throat. "And what about me?" he demanded, surly. Sandra was sorely tempted to upbraid him again, but instead she smiled sweetly and indicated the rest of the nurses.

"You, MISTER Stevens . . . will tell us what you want us to do next. This is your 'hospital,' after all."

Matt had already forgotten his encounter with Captain Kaufman. He had far more important concerns. A Morse-lamp message from Captain Gordon was composed of only three words: "Enemy in sight." *Exeter's* lookouts had a higher vantage point than Rodriguez, but just a few moments later Garrett held his earpiece tight against his head and looked up.

"Sir! Rodriguez sees them too. Still dead astern, but coming up fast.

They must be making thirty-five knots!" He sounded incredulous. Matt nodded. Even without *Exeter* slowing them down, *Walker* couldn't outrun them. Not anymore.

"Very well, Mr. Garrett. Return to your station. Mr. Rogers?" he said to the first officer. "Relieve Rodriguez in the crow's nest, if you please. If we can see them, they can hit us. Lieutenant Flowers"—he addressed the navigating officer—"take the conn."

Flowers spoke to the man holding the brightly polished wheel. "I relieve you, sir."

The seaman relinquished his post. "Mr. Flowers has the conn," he responded and looked around, at a loss. Matt motioned for him to put on a headset.

"Sound general quarters again. We've been at battle stations all morning, but somebody might be fooling around in the head."

The rhythmic, ill-sounding *gong, gong, gong* of the general alarm reverberated throughout the ship.

In the aft fireroom, Brad "Spanky" McFarlane, the engineering officer, wiped sweat from his narrow face and shook it off his hand to join the black, slimy slurry on the deck plates. In the space containing the number three and four boilers, it was at least 130 degrees. He barely heard the sound of the alarm over the thundering blower and the roar of the burners as atomized fuel oil was consumed at a prodigious rate.

"Gotta get back to the forward engine room. That's the second time they've sounded GQ. Maybe they mean it this time."

Firemen Isak Reuben on the blower control and Gilbert Yager on the burner nodded, but paid him no further attention. They were both entirely focused on their tasks. Their two jobs, and that of the water tender, required careful concentration. Too much fuel and not enough air, and black smoke billowed from the stacks, earning an instant reprimand from the captain and the scorn of their fellow "snipes." Not enough feed water in the lines, and white steam rose overhead. Too much water, not enough air and fuel, and water instead of steam sprayed into the turbines. That could damage the delicate blades. Isak and Gilbert were magicians at their jobs and the very best he had, but McFarlane didn't know what to think of them otherwise. They were inseparable, but rarely talked to anyone else. They were both wiry, intense little men, and neither seemed to mind the hellish temperatures in which they worked. Even off duty, they lingered in the vicinity of their posts—which annoyed the men on watch. They never caused any trouble, but they didn't make friends and they didn't play on the ship's baseball team. They just kept to themselves. The other snipes called them the White Mice, or just the Mice, because of their similar, almost rodent-like expressions and because they never went above deck if they could help it. Therefore, their otherwise perpetually sooty skins had an unhealthy pallor. The only explanation McFarlane ever got was that if they spent too much time in the "cool" air on deck, they'd lose their tolerance for the temperatures in the fireroom. McFarlane shrugged and stepped to the air lock. They were squirrels, sure enough, but they were his squirrels.

He cycled through the air lock into the forward engine room. He was shaped much like the Mice, and he barely had to squat to step through. The large compartment was filled by the big turbines and a maze of steam lines and conduits, but he moved among them with practiced ease to the enclosed intercom by the main throttle control. "Throttle manned and ready," he said into the mouthpiece. The talker on the bridge acknowledged, and Spanky looked at the other throttlemen. They looked back with almost pathetically hopeful expressions. They were all so young, and the faith they placed in him and their "new" captain made him feel uncomfortable.

He wasn't much of a poker player. He disliked games of chance. He felt at ease only when he was totally in control of everything it was his business to control. Right now his business was the engines, and cantankerous as they were, he could handle that. He couldn't influence the outcome of anything beyond the confines of his engine room, and in a way he was glad. Deep inside, however, was a feeling like the one he hated whenever he did play poker: knowing that his destiny, or at least a portion of his pay, was at the mercy of the cardboard rectangle held carelessly in the dealer's hand and knowing that luck alone would dictate how it affected him. He understood the sense of frustrated helplessness plaguing the young sailors nearby. It gnawed him too. But he couldn't let it show—just as the captain couldn't. All he could do was hope for an ace. Somehow, they'd drawn the right cards so far, in spite of their deficiencies, but the Japanese kept stacking the deck. He hoped Captain Reddy had some card tricks of his own, because that was what they'd need to survive this call.

Matt squinted ahead against the sun. It no longer streamed directly through the windows, but it was bright enough to make everything washedout and fuzzy. Suddenly, exactly where he looked, two closely spaced geysers of spume erupted directly in their path, two hundred yards ahead. This was followed by the superfluous report of his talker that the enemy had opened fire. The columns of water thrown up by the eight-inch shells were at least as tall as the mast. Matt glanced at his watch and took note of the time. He was glad to see that his hand was steady. His carefully hidden anxiety of a few moments before had subsided now that the first shots had been fired. Large, grayish-brown clouds enveloped *Exeter* as her own eight-inch guns replied to the Japanese salvo. The overpressure of the report shook the pilothouse windows. The waiting was over, and Matt felt a surge of exhilaration edge out the anticipation even further. It was much like the baseball games of his youth, he reflected. He sometimes got so keyed up for a game that he felt physically sick. He didn't know why, but he suspected he was afraid he would screw up somehow. He played third base, and in his mind's eye he always saw himself missing the critical catch and thus allowing the other team to score the game-winning point. The idea of such humiliation was worse than enduring the real thing, and always, as soon as the first pitch was thrown, his nervousness was forgotten. He supposed this wasn't a dissimilar context, although if he screwed up here much more than a game was at stake.

Exeter's salvos came faster than Matt would have expected, and he noticed with a sense of admiration and vicarious pride that Captain Gordon had replaced *Exeter*'s naval jack with an enormous battle flag, much like the little destroyer *Electra* had done in the Battle of the Java Sea when she charged the enemy fleet all alone. That action saved the crippled *Exeter* from destruction by forcing the enemy to maneuver to avoid *Electra*'s torpedoes, but the resulting fusillade of enemy shells obliterated the gallant destroyer. It was one of the bravest things Matt had ever seen, and he'd seen a lot of courage in the last few months. Unfortunately, he thought bitterly, most had been futile.

The enemy shells became more concentrated, and the great plumes erupted continuously around the veteran cruiser. The impacts seemed to have increased in number as well.

"Sir, *Exeter* has sent a radio message. I guess they don't think we'll see their Morse lamp through the splashes." It was Petty Officer 1st Class Steve "Sparks" Riggs, the comm officer, who had scampered down from the fire-control platform above.

"What does she say?" asked Matt impatiently.

"Two more Jap ships, heavy cruisers at least, and three destroyers bearing two one five! The heavies have opened fire. *Exeter* says her fire control is out—no hits yet, it just quit. They've gone to local control of the main battery." Matt's sense of exhilaration turned to dread. Without her fire-control equipment, *Exeter* was nearly as helpless as her escorts. "Captain Gordon wants us to take formation with the other destroyers astern and make smoke."

Matt nodded. "Acknowledge. Confirm *Pope* and *Mahan* received as well. Make the adjustment, Mr. Flowers," he said, addressing the helmsman. "I'm going topside for a look. You have the deck."

"I have the deck, aye, sir."

Matt turned and climbed briskly up the ladder to the platform above.

Now, except for the mast and the four slender funnels beyond it directly astern, he had a full 360-degree view of the panoramic drama of which *Walker* was, so far, such an insignificant part. Garrett stepped from the range-finder platform.

"More Japs, sir! They just popped out from behind that squall. Do you see? There!" He raised his long arm and pointed far astern, off the port quarter. "There's more and more rain squalls," he added hopefully. The deck tilted as *Walker* heeled into a sharp turn to starboard. The blowers lost their intensity briefly, as Flowers reduced speed to join *Walker*'s partners forming in *Exeter*'s wake. Off to the west-northwest, a number of indistinct ships were visible to the naked eye, not far from the coast of Borneo. That landmass appeared as a hazy smear, but it was actually closer than it seemed. The shoreline was obscured by the same squall that had concealed the Japanese ships.

"I see them, Mr. Garrett," he said in what he hoped was a confident tone, but he felt like he'd pronounced their death sentence. There were now two distinct battle groups in pursuit and far above in those loitering planes he knew even more forces were being called. It would probably not be long before attack aircraft arrived as well. He leaned over the speaking tube. "Let's make a little smoke, Mr. Flowers."

Immediately, his orders were relayed to the torpedomen, who sprang to activate the smoke generators. At the same time, in the boiler rooms, the burner batters exchanged the sprayer plates to increase the flow of oil through the burners. Slowly at first, but building rapidly, a huge column of sooty black smoke gushed from the funnels and piled into the clear morning sky. It was joined by the smoke of the other three destroyers, rapidly creating an opaque wall between them and the enemy. The incoming fire began to slacken, and Matt stared aft at the huge cloud they were creating. It seemed to blot out the entire western horizon. Lieutenant Garrett glanced at him when he chuckled quietly. "I always get a hoot out of doing that."

They continued east-southeast under a black pall. The enemy barrage was less accurate, but it didn't stop. The cruisers were in direct radio contact with the spotting planes overhead, correcting their fire. The Allied squadron tried to zigzag subtly, to increase the correction error, but they couldn't deviate much from a straight heading because the enemy was already faster and zigzagging slowed them down. All they could hope for was a squall of their own to hide in, to stretch the chase until dark. Then they might change course unnoticed and lose their pursuers. Matt had little hope of that. It was now only 1100. Whatever fate awaited them, it would certainly unfold before the sun went down.

Lieutenant Rogers's excited voice screamed from Garrett's headphones. "Surface target! Starboard quarter! Four Nip destroyers out of the smoke. God, they're fast!" The ordnance strikers on the platform swung the gun director.

"Gun crews, load!" Garrett shouted into his mouthpiece.

"Fire on the nearest target as soon as you're ready, Mr. Garrett," Matt said, and stepped back to the speaking tube. He looked to see how the other destroyers, in line abreast, were maneuvering. "Conn, starboard ten degrees."

At this speed, *Walker*'s range finder was useless because of vibration, but Garrett estimated the range to target. "Fire up-ladder. Range, nine five-double-oh!" The shouted commands came rapidly and Matt heard the tinny replies of the gun crews leak from Garrett's earphones. He couldn't help but feel a surge of pride in his crew as they went about their duties with calm, well-drilled precision. After the range, bearing, and apparent speed of the target were fed into it, the mechanical fire-control computer reached a solution.

"Surface action starboard. Match pointers!" Garrett instructed the three crews whose weapons would bear. He listened as they reported their readiness and looked at Matt. "The guns are ready, Captain."

"Commence firing."

"Three rounds, salvo fire. Commence firing!" He leaned forward and stabbed the salvo buzzer button. The nerve-racking, jangling *raaaa* sound was almost instantly overwhelmed by the simultaneous concussion of three 4-inch guns. Even before the first rounds fell, the buzzer sounded again and the second salvo was on the way. Splashes kicked up beyond and astern of the closest enemy destroyer, but seconds later more splashes rose among the ships when their friends opened fire as well. The third salvo seemed to have the range, but it was still behind the enemy.

"They're even faster than I thought! I guess I didn't lead them enough," Garrett said apologetically. He fed corrections into the computer. Somebody got a lucky hit with the first salvo, and the third Japanese destroyer belched black smoke from her curiously raked 'stack and slowed out of line. Men cheered and even Matt felt like pumping his fist. It looked like the hit came from *Pope* or *Encounter*. The remaining enemy ships continued the charge. They opened fire from the twin mounts on their foredecks, all three shooting only at the damaged British cruiser.

"They're making for *Exeter*. Get on them, Mr. Garrett!" To Matt, the enemy strategy was clear. They were trying to get in a few licks on the primary target and slow her down still more. Her escorts would then be forced to leave her or stand and fight. Either way, the result would be the same. Another salvo slammed out from *Walker*, and this one looked on target, but there were no explosions. Either they were still shooting long, or the shells were passing through the thin-skinned Japanese ships without detonating.

"That's it!" shouted Garrett into his comm. "No change! No change! Rapid fire! Let her have it!" The geysers erupting around the advancing enemy now resembled those that had bracketed *Exeter* a short time before, if not in size, then surely in volume. The Japanese couldn't know that *Exeter*'s fire control was out, and Matt had to admire the courage of their approach. They began to angle for *Exeter*'s starboard side. Knowing their gunnery was in capable hands, Matt realized his place was in the pilothouse. Without a word of distraction for Garrett, he dropped to the quarterdeck below.

"Captain on the bridge!" somebody shouted.

"As you were. I have the deck, Mr. Flowers. You keep the conn."

"Aye, aye, sir. You have the deck. I have the conn."

"Skipper." PO Riggs spoke up. "Captain Blinn on *Pope* sends to execute a starboard turn in column and prepare to fire torpedoes." Blinn was senior to both Matt and Captain Atkinson on *Mahan* and had authority over the three American destroyers.

"Very well, acknowledge. Mr. Flowers, bring us in behind *Mahan* when she makes her turn."

Ensign Bernard Sandison, the torpedo officer, stood on the starboard bridgewing and adjusted his headset while an ordnance striker fiddled with the connection linking the antiquated torpedo director to the two mounts on the starboard side. As the four destroyers accelerated to block the enemy thrust, his eyes burned when they turned into their own smoke screen.

"Sir," commented Flowers, "*Exeter*'s firing torpedoes." He pointed at the cruiser, now off their port bow. Puffs of smoke drifted aft from her amidships tubes, but the splashes when the weapons hit the water couldn't be distinguished from those of enemy shells. Then, as they looked on, there was a small reddish flash between *Exeter*'s two funnels. A column of black smoke rocketed skyward and a cloud of escaping steam enshrouded her amidships. Except for the racket of the blowers and the wind, there was stunned silence in *Walker*'s pilothouse, broken only by someone's soft, pleading murmur.

"No, oh, no . . . no."

Matt didn't know who said it. It might have been he. Somebody cursed. *Exeter*'s speed dropped to nearly nothing, as if she'd slammed into a wall. Shells rained down and more began to hit as she wallowed on helplessly at barely four knots. The Allied destroyers executed another turn, in column, and ran up *Exeter*'s starboard side, placing themselves between the doomed cruiser and the oncoming enemy ships. Through the thinning haze of the smoke screen, the Japanese cruisers were visible, much closer than before. At the head of the line, smoke and steam spewed from

Encounter as her torpedoes leaped into the sea. The two American destroyers ahead followed suit.

"Engage as they bear with the starboard tubes, Mr. Sandison."

"Aye, aye, sir!" he replied, and cried into his microphone: "Torpedo action starboard! In salvo! Fire one, fire three, fire five! Fire seven, fire nine, fire eleven!"

Matt peered around the chart house. The amidships deckhouse was in the way, but he saw the cutoff-looking muzzles of the pair of starboard triple launchers angled out thirty degrees from the side of the ship. As he watched, the first three 21-inch-diameter, 2,215-pound MK-15 torpedoes thumped out, one after another, the sun shining on their burnished metal bodies as they plunged into the sea with enormous concave splashes. They disappeared, but a moment later dense trails of effervescent bubbles rose to the surface in their wakes. There were only three, however.

Sandison looked at his captain with an apologetic, frustrated expression. "Sir, there's a casualty on the number-three mount. They don't know what it is yet, but the torpedoes are secure."

Matt swallowed a curse. It probably wasn't anybody's fault, just worn-out equipment. "Very well, Bernie. Let me know what you find out. Light a fire under it, though. I want those torpedoes!"

"Captain!" cried the talker. "Lookout reports torpedoes in the water!"

Matt looked at him blankly for a second. Of course there were— Then realization struck. He ran to the bridgewing and shouldered Sandison aside.

"JAP torpedoes!" he yelled over his shoulder. "Right full rudder!" *Walker* heeled sharply. "Signal to all ships—torpedoes inbound! Lots of torpedoes! Am evading!" During his brief glance, he saw over a dozen wakes. He looked back at the incoming streams of bubbles, which contrasted sharply with the dark, deep water. They should be relatively easy to avoid in daylight, but there were so many. They might blunder into one while maneuvering to miss another. *Walker* was only thirty feet wide, and Matt instinctively turned directly toward the oncoming weapons to present the smallest possible target. The rest of the column of destroyers disintegrated into chaos as they maneuvered independently as well.

"Lord, looks like the Nips just flushed a covey of quail," said Flowers as dryly as he could manage.

"Rudder amidships!" With gratifying alacrity, *Walker* steadied, and the cant to the deck disappeared. *She may be old*, Matt thought with an unusual sense of proprietary satisfaction, *but she still handles like a rum-runner*. Nimbleness wasn't a trait usually associated with four-stackers, but Chief Gray had told him an extra three feet of depth had been added to her rudder as an experiment. It worked, but there were objections to the added draft and, as far as Gray knew, only a couple of her sisters were ever altered.

"Here they come!" someone yelled. Almost everyone in the pilot-house but the helmsman rushed to the bridgewings and looked anxiously at the water as a pair of torpedoes raced by on either side of *Walker's* frail hull. The one to starboard passed less than a dozen yards away. A young seaman's apprentice named Fred Reynolds, a boy who looked all of thir-teen, grinned at Matt with a pallid expression and then vomited over the rail. The malicious wind made sure that most of the spew wound up in his close-cropped hair. The salvo buzzer rang again, and the number one gun fired alone. The report stirred the bridge crew from the momentary relief of having dodged the torpedoes, reminding them that they were steaming directly toward the enemy.

"Where the hell do you think you are? Watching toy boats in a duck pond?" bellowed Chief Gray as he ascended the ladder. He gave Reynolds a malevolent glare and pantomimed dumping a water bucket on the deck. The boy wiped his mouth and staggered back to his station. The rest of the bridge crew followed suit. Matt winced inwardly. He'd been as guilty as the others, but Gray just winked at him and sighed theatrically when no one was looking. Matt nodded grimly and turned.

"Left full rudder! Helm, tack us back onto the tail of the column as it re-forms!"

There was a loud *clang* above their heads, and Lieutenant Rogers's voice blared from the crow's nest speaking tube. "JESUS CHRIST! A shell just took a notch out of the mast about two feet under me!"

The salvo buzzer rang and three guns fired again. Matt looked down at number one and was surprised to see a young man in Army khakis carrying four-inch shells from the wardroom below to replenish the ready-lockers.

"That's Mallory," said the Chief, reading his mind. "He came aboard with that other officer. *He* seems a decent sort." Matt nodded his under-standing and noted Gray's obvious opinion of Captain Kaufman.

The column shook itself out. But their relief over evading the torpe-does was shattered when they were brutally reminded of the one member of their group that couldn't evade anything. A towering column of water spouted directly under *Exeter's* aft funnel on her starboard side. She heeled hard to port and then rolled back into a pronounced starboard list. A heavy secondary explosion sent debris and smoke high in the air.

The salvo buzzer rang. *Wham!*

They couldn't worry about *Exeter* now. Waterspouts were rising around *Walker* again, and there was another loud noise somewhere aft.

"Damage report!"

Ellis's voice came over the intercom. "Nothing serious, Skipper. A new hole in the aft funnel. The shell didn't explode. It must've been armor-piercing—and it's not as if we have any armor."

Raaaaa! Wham! Cheers erupted from fire control when a big explosion rocked a Japanese destroyer. It veered hard out of formation, smoke obscuring the bridge. The other two enemy destroyers finally broke off their attack and retreated behind a smoke screen of their own, toward the protection of the remorselessly approaching cruisers.

"Skipper." The grim voice was Riggs. "Signal from *Exeter* to all ships. Captain Gordon says thanks for the help, but he'll take it from here." Matt strode to the port bridgewing and stared at the once-handsome ship that had seen so much action in this war before the United States was even involved. She'd hounded the *Graf Spee* to her doom, but past glory meant nothing now. Lifeboats were in the water and men were going over the side. He took a deep breath.

"Acknowledge. And send, 'Good luck, *Exeter*. God bless.'"

Shells still pummeled the helpless cruiser as *Walker*, last in line, sped impotently by. Matt slapped the rail in frustration. "God help them," he muttered. *God help us*, he added to himself. Another huge explosion convulsed *Exeter*, and she rapidly rolled over onto the boats and men in the water. He could see the red paint of her bottom come up on the far side as her superstructure disappeared into the sea. And still the shells fell. The number one gun was silent now, no longer able to bear on their pursuers, and he saw the grim expressions of its crew as they watched *Exeter* go down.

"Skipper . . ." It was Riggs. "Signal from *Pope*. She says to resume line abreast and continue making smoke. She also wants to know if we can increase speed."

"Acknowledge, and tell her we'll try."

The next hours were like a feverish nightmare. They gained some distance on the cruisers, but they never moved completely out of range. Periodic savage salvos churned the sea around them, and all the destroyers were damaged, mostly by near misses. An eight-inch shell detonating close aboard made a hell of a concussion and *Walker*'s riveted seams leaked in a dozen places. More enemy aircraft arrived, and they finally cut the smoke, figuring it just made them easier to spot from the air. Only fighters had appeared so far, but they were carrier planes and they strafed the lonely ships repeatedly. They soon decided to wait for the bombers and cruisers to finish the job after one of their number fell to the destroyers' machine guns. It narrowly missed *Mahan* as it plunged into the sea.

A few tantalizing squalls marched across the horizon, but it seemed they could never reach them. Matt vigorously rubbed his eyes and looked at his exhausted bridge crew and their haunted expressions. The trauma of watching *Exeter*'s destruction—the most powerful member of their group—had etched itself on their faces, and he knew they believed it was only a matter of time before they all met a similar fate. One by one.

Encounter's turn came next, and with appalling suddenness. Another ranging salvo of eight-inch shells screeched in, the sun glinting off the projectiles in flight. Geysers of spume marched across the sea—and across the British destroyer. In the blink of an eye, for all intents and purposes, she was gone. When the spray cleared, all that remained was twisted wreckage, already awash, and a few men scurrying about on the buckled deck, throwing anything that would float into the sea. The three tired greyhounds raced on. There was nothing they could do. Matt knew it on a rational level, but deep down he felt an overwhelming sense of shame. His jaw muscles tensed, and he ground his teeth as he forced himself to watch what was left of *Encounter* slip farther and farther astern. Chief Gray stood beside him, watching too.

"I'm getting sick of leaving people behind," he growled.

Matt nodded. "It could just as easily have been us. And we wouldn't want them hanging around to get slaughtered picking us up." The Bosun shook his head, but Matt would have sworn there was a damp sheen in his eyes.

"With your permission, sir, I'll see if Spanky and his snipes need a hand with anything, like patching holes, or keeping the screws from falling off." Matt felt the corners of his mouth twitch upward by themselves. Gray must really be frustrated if he was willing to descend below his holy deck and help engineering do anything. He shrugged at his captain's look. "Hell, Skipper, if they sink the bottom half of the old girl, the top half goes too."

"That's true, Boats, but Spanky's keeping up with the problems below for now, and I'd rather have you up here to direct damage control for the deck divisions if need be."

"Yes, sir."

Rogers's voice piped down from above. He was still in the crow's nest, where he'd been almost all day. "Skipper, there's a promising cloud off the starboard bow. Looks like it's working up to rain pretty good." Matt raised his binoculars.

"Sir, signal from *Pope*," supplied Riggs. "Make for the squall."

"Acknowledge. Helm, right ten."

The cloud hung before them, growing darker by the moment. A new flurry of enemy shells kicked up spray as their pursuers noticed their course change.

"Jap planes! Bombers! Six o'clock high!" came the shout from the crow's nest. "Three pairs of 'em! I thought they were those observation planes, but they're comin' right in!"

Almost immediately, there came the *thump thump thump* of the little three-inch gun on the stern, throwing up shells in the path of the oncoming planes. Matt craned his neck upward and saw them, dark specks growing larger fast. Two angled for *Walker* through the small black puffs of smoke. He looked toward the cloud and saw it had started to rain. Harder and harder it fell, only a couple of miles away. They'd never make it. He looked at the planes, trying to judge their angle of attack and praying he could predict their release point. "Steady as you go, helm!" he ordered tersely. "Make them think we're easy." He waited. He couldn't see the furtive glances exchanged around him. *Wait. Wait! NOW!*

"Left full rudder! All ahead flank!"

Walker heeled so sharply it was difficult to stand, and she surged forward with an audible groan. Two small objects detached themselves from the pair of descending planes. They grew rapidly larger until it seemed they'd fall right on the ship. Two thunderous explosions ripped the sea less than a hundred yards off the starboard beam and fragments spanged against *Walker*'s side. The heavy bellow of the .50-cals and the lighter clatter of the .30s sent tracers chasing the fat-bodied dive bombers as they pulled out and thundered away. Their ungainly fixed landing gear seemed only inches above the water. Glaring red circles clearly contrasted with the white-painted wings.

"Damage report!"

The machine guns stuttered to a stop as the planes flew out of range.

"Just some scratches in the boot topping."

"How about the other ships?" Matt asked, looking for himself. They seemed okay as each emerged from the spray of bomb splashes.

The squall was closer. Still at flank speed, *Walker* strained with every aged fiber to reach the camouflaging shroud of the torrent ahead. To starboard, *Mahan* labored to keep up. Farther away, her interval doubled since the loss of *Encounter*, *Pope* blurred as she dove into the opaque wall of rain.

The bombers were re-forming and Matt urged his ship forward as she stretched her tired legs. Suddenly the bow disappeared as it parted the edge of the storm, and within seconds the windows were blanked out and a heavy drumming sound came from the deck above. Water coursed onto the open quarterdeck behind them, and small smiles of relief formed on several faces.

"Secure from flank, all ahead two-thirds. Come left ten degrees. The Japs can't see us, but neither can our sisters. Let's put some space between us."

"Jesus," muttered Sandison, and dabbed sweat from his face with his sleeve.

Lieutenant Garrett, along with the rest of the fire-control team, was soaked to the bone and water poured off his helmet, obscuring his view. No one had any idea where their consorts were. They'd altered course several times to accomplish the dual necessity of staying within the squall and continuing in a general direction away from the enemy. Garrett and his division did their best, straining their eyes to spot another ship or warn about upcoming "light" spots, but realistically they would probably run into one of their sisters before they saw her in time to turn. It was growing lighter ahead, however, and there were no "dark" areas to advise the bridge to steer for. He huddled over the speaking tube when he raised the cover to prevent too much water from pouring in.

"Bridge. We're breaking out of the squall."

With almost the same suddenness that they'd entered it, they drove out of the squall and into the afternoon sunshine. They all blinked their eyes against the glare, and the water on the decks and in their clothes began to steam. Then, less than five hundred yards to port, *Mahan* emerged and seemed to shake herself off like a wet dog as she increased speed. Men immediately scanned for enemies.

"Oh, my God, Skipper! Look!" shouted Sandison. The Bosun swore and Matt shouldered in beside him on the starboard bridgewing. He felt like his heart had stopped. There, about four miles off the starboard beam, *Pope* was enduring her final agony. She wallowed helplessly, low by the stern, while aircraft swirled like vultures in the sky above. Massive waterspouts rose around her as the spotting planes summoned the cruiser's fire upon their carrion.

"Skipper! Can't we . . . I mean, is there . . . ?" Young Reynolds clamped his mouth shut, realizing the pointlessness of his appeal. Then he looked at his captain's face and was shocked by the twisted, desperate rage upon it. With an audible animal growl, Captain Reddy spun back into the pilothouse. Ahead, about seven miles away, another squall brewed. It was huge, and darker than the last one, almost green, and it blotted out much of the horizon. For some reason, it seemed to radiate an aura of threat nearly as intense as the force that pursued them so relentlessly.

"Make for that squall!" ordered Matt in a tone none of the men had ever heard him use. It was the voice of command, but with an inflection of perfect hatred. "Signal *Mahan*. We'll keep this interval in case we have to maneuver. Helm, ahead flank!"

Another squall, lighter, was a little to the left of the one they were heading for. It was dissipating rapidly, though, as if the first was somehow draining it, sucking its very force. As it diminished, two dark forms took shape.

"Holy Mary," muttered Gray, crossing himself unconsciously.

Before them, racing to prevent their escape into the looming rainstorm, were yet another destroyer and a massive capital ship. There was a collective gasp.

After a moment spent studying the apparition through his binoculars, Matt spoke. "That, gentlemen, is *Amagi*." His voice was harsh but matter-of-fact. "She's a battle cruiser. Not quite a battleship, but way heavier than a cruiser. I know it's her"—he smiled ironically, but his expression was hard—"because she's the only one they have left. Built in the twenties, so she's almost as old as we are"—he snorted— "but they've spent money on her since. Major rebuild a few years ago. Anyway, I remember her because I was always impressed by how fast the Japs could make so much metal move." He sighed. "I guess it's fitting, after everything else, she should show up here. They *really* don't want us to get away."

He turned and spoke to Riggs in a voice that was white-hot steel. "Signal *Mahan* to prepare for a torpedo attack with port tubes. Mr. Sandison, speak to your division." He crossed his arms over his chest and his hands clenched into fists. "We can't go around her and we can't turn back. That leaves only one choice."

Gray nodded with grim acceptance.

"Yes, sir, we'll have to go right through the son of a bitch."

Blowers roaring, haggard destroyermen performing their duties in an exhausted fugue, the two battered, venerable old ladies slightly altered course and together began their final charge. Matt noticed that even Captain Kaufman was on the foredeck now, hauling shells. Lieutenant Mallory and two ratings scurried up the ladder behind, each festooned with belts of .30-cal. It was clear to everyone that getting past the two ships ahead and disappearing into the strange, ominous squall was their only hope. It was equally clear that it was impossible.

Ahead waited *Amagi*: 46,000 tons of cemented armor plate. As they watched, she began a leisurely turn to present her full broadside of ten 10-inch guns. Her secondary battery of 4.7-inch and 5.5-inch guns was entirely superfluous. The sleek new destroyer at her side was all but forgotten despite her guns and deadly "Long Lance" torpedoes. The additional threat she represented was almost laughably insignificant under the circumstances. She could have taken them by herself.

The shriek and splash of incoming shells proved the cruisers behind hadn't forgotten them either, and the growing drone of propellers indicated the bombers had seen them too.

"Looks like every Jap in the Java Sea's in a race to sink us," mumbled Gray.

Five miles away, *Amagi* opened fire. She pulsed with flame from one end to the other as she salvoed her big guns. Seconds later, the rattling roar of ten-inch shells thundered toward them. They sounded deeper than the eights, Matt reflected absently. Then he stepped into hell.

The first salvo fell short, but it threw up a wall of spray that drenched Greg Garrett and his team and probably soaked Lieutenant Rogers way up in the crow's nest. Rogers had fallen silent, and Garrett tried to adjust the fire of the number one and three guns, but he couldn't bloody *see*. *Walker* pierced the spume raised by *Amagi*'s main guns, but the splashes from the secondaries and the cruisers behind were uninterrupted. He thought of all the times he'd shot turtles in the stock tank behind his grandmother's house—now he knew how they must have felt. There was a loud *bang* behind him and he twisted to see chaos on the amidships deckhouse.

A roar overhead made him turn to see a dive bomber pull up and blow by, its wingtip a dozen yards from the mast. An enormous explosion convulsed the sea to port and bomb fragments whined off the rail and the range finder. Tracers rose to meet the plane and something fell off it. Another mighty salvo rumbled in, the splashes seeming to concentrate on *Mahan*. He half expected to see a twisted wreck as the spray fell away, but somehow she staggered out of the trough and shook herself off. Water sluiced from her. Her aft deckhouse was wrecked, and her number four funnel lay on a crushed lifeboat davit. The searchlight tower had fallen as well.

Something went *crump* forward, and a 5.5-inch plowed a furrow in the starboard bow and ricocheted into the sea. The big anchor chain that normally disappeared into the well trailed over the side from the bollard. Another salvo bloomed ahead, less than three miles off. *Damn we're close!* he thought as the shells almost sucked the air from his lungs as they passed—just barely—overhead to thrash the sea astern. He peered through his binoculars during a momentary respite.

"There they are! Right there!" he shouted into the speaking tube. "I mean, surface target! Bow! Estimate range five five double oh!" The salvo buzzer sounded more shrill than usual before the pathetic report of their own guns. Greg held on tight as *Walker* turned sharply to starboard. *Amagi* seemed almost motionless, the destroyer tucked under her skirt like a timid child. Beyond them, much closer now, the squall beckoned. Dark and alive with a torrential green rain.

Another salvo slashed out from *Amagi* just as six torpedoes chuffed from their tubes and lanced in her direction. Black smoke poured from the stacks again and Garrett felt a sense of anxious elation now their torpedoes were on the way. With any luck . . . A thunderous crash and a fiery cloud of hot, black soot and steam swept him to the deck.

Walker heaved when a ten-inch shell on a virtually flat trajectory punched through the forward fireroom. It didn't explode, but the sudden decompression of the compartment caused the burners to fireball. The flames didn't kill the men, but the steam from ruptured lines did. The destroyer's speed dropped and Matt turned to Chief Gray, but he'd already left. His gaze returned to the shattered pilothouse windows, sweeping past the speaking tube that led to the crow's nest. Blood dripped from it to join a widening pool. Electrician's Mate Janssen's blood was there too, as well as Rodriguez's. Rodriguez had been carried to the wardroom. Janssen was dead.

"Sir, forward fireroom's out of action! Mr. McFarlane bypassed with the main deck valve. He says our speed should be restored—almost—momentarily."

"Very well."

Mahan emerged from the smoke and spray astern cutting a wide, looping turn to port. Back toward *Amagi*. Matt stifled his instinctive command to signal her when he saw the reason why. The gun on her foredeck stood vacant and exposed, the splinter shield shot away. Behind it, the entire bridge superstructure was askew, torn and shattered and gushing smoke. After a single horrified glance, he doubted a soul had survived inside it. Her port torpedo tubes were rigged out, so at least maybe she got off her salvo, but otherwise she was a wreck.

More men lost. His men now. Since Captain Blinn was lost to them with *Pope*, he was senior. He'd ordered the torpedo attack—it made no difference that there wasn't any choice. Those men now steaming blind and helpless at flank speed directly toward the enemy were under his orders. But what of *these* men? Chances were, with *Mahan* headed straight for her, *Amagi* would concentrate on the helpless destroyer. The fire aimed at *Walker* had already slacked. She could almost certainly slip into the squall. He rubbed his forehead vigorously and looked into the wide-eyed, expectant faces of the men around him. They wanted him to do it: to give the order to turn back. They were willing it. Didn't they understand it was death? They had a chance to live—all they had to do was abandon *Mahan* to *Amagi*'s fury.

No, they couldn't live like that and neither could he. They'd run far enough. It didn't matter anymore where they were. The fight was here and they would face it. Shades of gray no longer existed. Everything was a stark black and white once more. Was that what it all boiled down to? Had the entire Asiatic Fleet been sacrificed just because it was there? The salvo buzzer rang and numbers one, three, and four let loose, but he didn't even hear. Finally his gaze fell upon Reynolds. The boy was the youngest and most junior crewman on the bridge. The look he returned was . . . pleading.

"Come about! Bring us as close alongside *Mahan* as she'll bear." He gestured at the bombers above. Three of them flew lazy circles, watching, as if afraid to descend into the line of fire. "Maybe we can at least keep them off her."

"Skipper, the Jap cruisers behind us are out of the squall. They can see us now."

"Good. Let 'em watch," Matt snarled. Some of the men giggled nervously. "How much longer for the torpedoes, Mr. Sandison?"

"Ten seconds."

Walker finished her turn and sprinted after *Mahan*. The sea frothed around her with the strikes of enemy shells. She staggered from another impact forward.

"Time?"

"Three . . . two . . . one . . ." Sandison looked up from his watch with a wretched expression. Damn! More duds—or whatever it was that had been wrong with the torpedoes since the war began. They were nearly even with *Mahan* now. Her speed was dropping off.

"See if—" Matt was interrupted by a bright snap of light, and he looked up in time to hear the detonation of the single massive explosion that disemboweled the Japanese destroyer. The ship hung, jackknifed, her bow in the air and her stern already slipping. The flames were bright against the dark squall beyond. Wild cheering erupted and Matt cheered too—but they'd missed *Amagi*. She was turning toward them in case there were more torpedoes in the water, and therefore, for a moment, she couldn't fire. Shells fell in earnest from the cruisers behind, but *Amagi* suddenly blurred. The squall was moving over her. Toward them. They were a mile away.

"Skipper! Get a load of this!" shouted Flowers. He was looking to his left, at *Mahan*. A column of spray collapsed on her deck and a man struggled through the cascade. He pointed at them with his right hand and held that arm up. Then he patted his chest with the left and brought it from below, across the bottom of his elbow and up alongside the other. Then he vanished in more spray.

"What the hell?" muttered Sandison.

Mahan dropped back and they saw men on her wreckage-strewn deck heaving on the exposed steering cables. She sheared to the right and narrowly avoided colliding with *Walker*'s stern. With a burst of speed, she lanced forward along the starboard side. The same man as before stood between the two torpedo mounts, still rigged out. He pointed at them exaggeratedly.

"My God, they're still loaded!" shouted Sandison. Matt ran onto the bridgewing and held up his own right arm. Then he took both arms and brought them up, diverging on either side of where his arm had first been. The man on *Mahan*'s deck held up an "OK" sign and scurried away.

"Left twenty degrees!" Matt shouted. "We're going to run up both sides of her! We may not have any torpedoes, but the Japs don't know that!"

Amagi had crept out of the squall, but just barely. It was almost as if the storm followed her. Now she was pointed directly at them and water peeled from her bow as she surged ahead. They were so close and the angle was such that only a couple of her secondaries would bear. *They're still plenty big,* thought Matt, *and as soon as we come alongside, the entire secondary broadside will come into play.* It would happen in less than two minutes.

Mahan moved farther and farther to starboard. With the loss of her forward fireroom, *Walker* could barely make twenty-five knots. *Mahan* looked like a wreck, but she was keeping up. The roaring bombers swooped to attack in spite of the incoming shells. Machine guns clattered above and behind. The salvo buzzer rang. Antiaircraft rounds raked *Walker*'s bridge as the two four-stackers streamed past *Amagi*'s bow. Lieutenant Flowers spun away from the wheel and collapsed to the deck, and Matt jumped into his place. The maelstrom of fire and the kaleidoscope of images were beyond anything they'd experienced yet. *Amagi*'s side was alive with flashing muzzles, and *Walker* drummed with impacts as numerous as the raindrops of the previous squall.

Simultaneously, *Walker* heaved with the close impact of a pair of bombs, and the plane that had dropped them slanted unnaturally toward *Amagi,* trailing smoke. It impacted with a monstrous fireball directly atop her amidships turret. Two more explosions rocked *Amagi* from the opposite side and she heeled sharply toward *Walker* with the force of the blows. The salvo buzzer rang. *WHAM!*

Another bomb detonated and shells from the other cruisers still fell. Some even struck *Amagi.* Amid this tempest of fire, smoke, overpressure, and death, they were finally consumed by the squall.

*E*lation surged in Matt's chest as the green deluge—tinged with the reflection of explosions and flames—descended upon them. In spite of himself, a shout of exultation escaped. Instead of the comforting, drumming rain on the deck above, however, a shocking . . . silence . . . stunned his senses. He heard surprised shouts on the foredeck and then confused murmuring of the bridge watch, but for a moment there was nothing else. He spun to look past the chart house. As the rest of the ship . . . materialized out of the greenness behind them, he began to hear it—the ship itself. The reassuring thunder of the blowers as they roared into being, the shouted obscenities of the number two gun crew amidships. On and on, until he heard the tumult as far away as the fantail. But other than the increasingly alarmed voices of his crew, the normal sounds of his ship, and the loud ringing in his ears caused by the din of battle, there was nothing.

But there *was* rain. The rain he'd expected to pound his ship at that very moment was there—but it wasn't falling. It just hung there, suspended. Motionless. He raised his hand in wonder amid the pandemonium, waved it through the teardrop shapes, and felt their wetness on his hand. He moved out from under the shelter of the deck above and felt the rain as he moved through it, saw it wet his ship as their forward motion carried them along. Just as his initial shock began to give way to an almost panicky incredulity, the screws "ran away," like when they left the water in really heavy seas. The sound lasted only seconds—at least. Spanky was on the job—but it drew his gaze over the side. He blinked in uncomprehending astonishment. The sea was gone. Down as far as he could see, past the boot topping, past the growth-encrusted red paint of the hull, into the limitless greenish-black nothingness below, were only uncountable billions of raindrops suspended in air. Before the enormity of it could even register, the deck dropped from under his feet and a terrible pressure built in his ears. He grabbed the rail and pushed himself down to the wooden strakes of the bridge—anything to maintain contact with something real. What he'd just seen couldn't possibly be. His stomach heaved and he retched uncontrollably. He heard the sounds of others doing the same as the sensation of falling intensified. Then there began a low-pitched whine, building slowly like a dry bearing about to fail. It built and built until it became torment. The pressure increased too. He dragged himself back into the pilothouse, careful not to take both hands off the deck at once. He scrunched through broken glass and blood until he reached his chair, attached to the angled right-forward wall, and he slowly climbed up the braces.

His eyes felt like they were being pushed into their sockets, but he saw that everyone else on the bridge was down. Reynolds met his gaze with an expression of controlled terror. Riggs sat on the deck with his palms over his eyes. Matt looked through the shattered, square-framed windows and saw men on the foredeck crawling amid empty shell casings, or trying to hold on to something as if they, like he, felt they would fly away from the ship like a feather if they let go. And all around there was nothing but the wet, greenish void. The screeching whine continued to grow until it drowned the noisy blowers. He held his hands over his ears with his arm linked through the chair, but it made no difference. The sound was inside his head. Again he fought the urge to vomit.

Abruptly, with terrifying suddenness, the deck swooped up beneath him like a roller coaster reaching the bottom of a dip and rocketing upward. With a thunderous roar, the raindrops that had remained poised for what could have been only moments, plummeted down and became the deluge they should have been from the start. Exhausted from straining against the impossibly contradictory sensations of weightlessness and gravity, he collapsed into his chair and stared numbly out at the now perfectly normal squall. *Walker* coasted along, her engines stopped, losing way on the rain-stilled sea.

Matt gathered himself while the men picked themselves up and stumbled back to their stations. In their confusion, they sought the comfort of their responsibilities. He didn't know what had just occurred, but he knew that, for now at least, he must do the same. Later the time would come for questions. He still had a crew and a ship to save, and to fight with, if need be. The cries of alarm began to grow again, but then, with unspeakable gratitude, Matt heard the booming voice of the Bosun rise above the tumult.

"Stow that girlish gab! Where do you think you are? You! Yeah, you,

Davis! Secure that shit! Form a detail and clear these goddamn shells! Look at this mess! LOOK AT MY BEAUTIFUL DECK! You'd think a bunch of goddamn hogs or even *snipes* been rootin' around up here. You think you've been in a battle? I've had scarier fights with the roaches in the wardroom! Quit pukin', Smitty. You sound like a frog!"

Matt listened as Gray's abuse moved aft. He cleared his throat and rubbed his lips with wet hands. He tasted blood. Riggs stood, shakily, holding the wheel, and Matt nodded at him. "Damage report," he croaked, his voice a harsh rasp. He cleared his throat. "Damage report!" he demanded more firmly. "Why've we stopped?"

The blowers didn't sound right. Sandison was on the bridge phone, listening intently as reports came in.

"Lieutenant McFarlane shut down the engines," he reported. "Water's coming in, but the pumps can handle it—when we get them back. Forward fireroom's out of action. Fires are out in the aft fireroom. It's full of smoke from raw fuel on the burners and they're venting it now. As soon as they can get in, they'll relight the fires. Should be just a few minutes." Sandison's voice had a cadence to it as he repeated the information he heard.

"We took a lot of hits forward and there're lots of casualties," he added grimly. "Doc's dead. He was working on Rodriguez when a shell came through and just . . . took him apart. Lots of the wounded were killed in the wardroom. One of the nurses is dead." His face turned ashen. "She was standing next to Doc. The other nurses have been helping out. Mr. Garrett reports one dead and two injured on the fire-control platform and he thinks Mr. Rogers is dead. There's . . . blood running down the mast from the crow's nest. He sounds a little rough." Sandison replied to Garrett and then listened to other reports, nodding as he did as if those making them could see him.

"There's water in the paint locker, but"—he shrugged—"there's always water in the paint locker. Probably mostly rain. We were real lucky with the hull—at least below the waterline. Most of the leaks are coming from loosened plates, from near misses. A lot of the shells hit us on flat trajectories and just punched through the upper hull. A few lighter shells exploded. The number three gun's out of action with four men killed . . . but all the big stuff must've been armor-piercing and didn't hit anything substantial enough to make them blow."

He listened a little longer and then looked at Matt. "Jesus, Skipper, we have a *lot* of holes."

"Anything on the horn? Anything from *Mahan*?"

Sandison shook his head. "Radio's out of whack, sir. Radioman Clancy just reported there hasn't been a peep since we entered the squall. Before that there were lots of distant distress calls, merchant ships mostly, under attack and begging for escorts." He cleared his throat. "Just static now. Something probably came unplugged."

Matt took a breath. "Casualties?"

"Don't know yet, sir, but . . . a lot."

The captain removed his hat and ran fingers through sweat-matted hair. "Torpedoes?"

The ensign shook his head guiltily. "No sir. Just the ones in the three mount, and with everything that's been . . . I'm sorry, sir, I just don't know."

"Very well. Secure from general quarters. There's too many men just standing around with so much work to do. But keep the crews on the guns and a sharp lookout. See if we can get some hot food into these guys." He stifled a jaw-racking yawn that wasn't quite an act. "And I need more coffee. Also, as soon as Lieutenant Ellis is able, have him report to the bridge." He paused and added in a softer tone, "Ask the Bosun to detail some men to bring Mr. Rogers down."

The rain continued and Matt yearned to be under way, making as much distance as they could under cover. There was no way of knowing *Mahan's* fate. They'd taken as much pressure off her as they could, but he didn't know what to think about how that turned out. Evidently *Walker* had returned to help *Mahan* while she was making a suicide charge to let *them* get clear. Hopefully, the confusion saved them both. But even if *Mahan* had made it, she would be in bad shape. Maybe even sinking. Then again, she could be miles away by now. Either way, there was nothing he could do for her. *Amagi* was badly hit, that much he knew. How badly was anybody's guess. Enough to retire? Hopefully. Enough to sink? That would grant his fondest wish. But whether *Amagi* swam or not made little difference, because the other cruisers were still coming. He didn't think they would give up, not when they still had spotter planes to guide them. They couldn't be far away.

When *Walker* regained steam pressure, she must press on. All they could do was pray that *Mahan* had escaped. Matt suddenly wondered if the other destroyer had experienced the same phenomenon *Walker* had. He shuddered, and glanced quickly around the gloomy pilothouse. He didn't think anyone else had seen what he had, and he couldn't completely banish the suspicion that he'd been teetering on the brink of madness. It had to have been a hallucination, brought on by exhaustion and the stress of combat. The motionless raindrops were certainly explainable, he assured himself. They'd passed into the most intense squall he'd ever seen. Squalls were by nature extremely unstable. Who knew what sort of strange winds might exist within one? Sudden gusts that could capsize a ship weren't unheard of. Why not some freakish updraft? His nervous fingers tried to reshape his sodden hat. That still didn't explain what he'd seen when he looked over the side. Nothing could explain that. It couldn't have happened—must not have happened.

"Skipper, Mr. Garrett says the squall's passing."

The volume of rain had diminished and it was perceptively lighter. Matt stirred and turned to see a woman's face peering at him fearfully from the ladder at the back of the quarterdeck. All that was visible was her rain-drenched hair, head, and shoulders. Her big brown eyes widened in surprise when they met his and her mouth formed an O of alarm. The white of her uniform blouse was stained and sooty, her cheek smeared with grease and blood where she must have wiped it with her hand. Immediately, and without a word, she raised a shiny coffee urn and placed it on the deck. She gave it a tentative shove in his direction as if it were an offering to a terrible god and then vanished down the ladder.

"Coffee's here," he muttered, then blinked and shook his head. He moved from his chair and was surprised his legs supported him. "Get Spanky on the horn. I want those engines *now!*"

They were fully exposed to the midafternoon sunlight by the time they had steam to move, and then only with the starboard engine. The water beneath the fantail churned and foamed as the screw began to turn. The deck vibrated horribly and pieces of broken glass fell from the empty window frames. The pressure was rising on number four, and soon Ensign Tolson, who'd replaced Bob Flowers, wouldn't have to fight the unbalanced thrust of a single screw. The squall still raged astern, but it was dissipating. They all expected the menacing forms of Japanese cruisers to emerge at any moment, and every eye watched the sky for spotting planes or bombers. If only they hadn't lost the boilers, they'd have been long gone by now.

Jim Ellis was on the bridge. There was blood and soot on his uniform, and his eyes were puffy and swollen. His customary ebullience was tempered by the horror he'd seen, and he spoke in a soft, somber tone. "The ship's a wreck, Skipper. Just about everything topside is shot to hell. We're in better shape below, if you can believe it, but we're still taking water, and the faster we move, the more we'll take. Hell, most of the water's coming in through holes above the waterline. Waves slopping in." He sighed. "You know, my granddaddy was at Manila Bay. His brother was at Santiago Bay. He always said there'd be days like this, only he always made it sound more fun."

Matt nodded wearily. "Dad was on a can just like this in the North Atlantic, during the last war. They chased a few subs, but they never saw anything like this. Somehow I think his stories may have been closer to the mark. He didn't have fun. I can't imagine many things more miserable than one of these four-stackers in the North Atlantic. At least I couldn't until the last couple of months." He paused. "And today, of course. Especially today."

They'd been talking quietly, but Matt glanced around the bridge to ensure that no one could hear before lowering his voice still further. "What did you think of our . . . experience, right after we entered the squall?"

Jim looked at him with a hesitant frown. He clearly didn't want to talk about it, and his expression seemed to accuse Matt of breaking some unspoken compact by even mentioning it. "Yeah, well, that was different," he managed at last. "I'm, ah, thinkin' it was an updraft or something."

Matt nodded agreement. "Me too. In fact, that's how I'll instruct Mr. Tolson to enter it in the log. But . . . did you ever happen to look over the side?"

Lieutenant Ellis pulled back, as if recoiling from a slap. The look on his face was sufficient to confirm he had indeed seen the same thing as the captain, and Matt's guts twisted.

"Just a little," Jim whispered.

Matt glanced around again. "How many of the crew, do you think, might've seen it?"

"Not many. Hell, probably none. They were pretty busy at the time. Then with the screwy raindrops . . . I figure most everybody was looking up."

Matt massaged his temples. "Damn. I only asked because I hoped you'd confirm my suspicions that I *didn't* see anything." He took a deep breath. "Well, whatever it was, it's over now. We're back in the real world where all we have to worry about are the Japs."

The corner of Jim's mouth twitched. "Yes, sir, but if it's all the same to you, I'll—"

He was interrupted by Quartermaster's Mate 2nd Class Norman Kutas, who'd replaced Sandison as the talker. "Mr. Garrett reports surface target, bearing one seven zero! Range five five double oh!"

They rushed to the starboard bridgewing and brought up their binoculars. A dark form was taking shape behind them as the squall dispersed. It was bows-on and listing to port. Smoke poured from amidships and slanted downwind. Even at this range, tiny figures were visible on the foredeck, wrestling with a fire hose.

"Oh, my God, Skipper," breathed Jim. "It's *Mahan!*"

Walker made a wide, slow turn to avoid having more water pour through her perforated sides. Once pointed at her sister, she sprinted to her. Everyone was at least secretly terrified by the prospect of turning back. But one man dressed in dark khaki, standing on the foredeck, silently cursed the ill luck that showed them *Mahan*. If they hadn't seen her, hadn't known she was there, they could have continued on. That would have salved his conscience—not seeing her—even if he knew she was there. But there she was, in obvious distress and at the moment with no enemy in sight. He fumed. Of course that upstart on the bridge would risk all their lives. He'd been safer in Surabaya! And the way he'd been treated was an outrage! He was an officer, by God, a fighter pilot! And to be forced to perform manual labor—and be physically threatened to do so—alongside common sailors was beyond the pale. Heads would roll for this, he decided. He had friends and he'd remember. Now if they could just *go*! But there was *Mahan*, damn it. They were all going to die for the sake of a ship that was already doomed. He shoved an empty shell casing savagely over the side with his shoe.

What Captain Kaufman didn't realize was that most of the destroyer-men on DD-163 wouldn't have cared if *Amagi* still stood between them and their sister. They hadn't expected to last this long, and the deck was stacked against them whether they went back or ran away. They might as well die doing the right thing.

They ran down on *Mahan* and hove to upwind. Jim Ellis took the conn and kept *Walker* poised forty yards off the other destroyer's beam. Matt went on the bridgewing with a speaking trumpet and stared at the other ship. She looked doomed. She was low by the bow and her forward superstructure was a shattered wreck. Smoke gushed from the ventilation hatches above the aft fireroom and men directed hoses into them. More smoke still wisped from the first two funnels, so the forward fireroom must be okay, but her aft deckhouse and auxiliary conn were wrecked, so her only means of maneuvering was still the exposed steering cables. The number four funnel was gone, probably rolled over the side to clear the deck, and the searchlight tower had fallen across the number one torpedo mount, crumpling the tubes. Men on the amidships deckhouse manned the guns, but everyone else seemed too busy trying to save their ship to even talk to Matt.

He glanced at the sun, nearing the horizon, and he willed it to move faster. He looked up at Lieutenant Garrett's disheveled, blackened form on the platform above, and the younger man returned his glance with one of confusion. The squall had finally spent itself and all the lookouts were tense and alert, but so far there was nothing. Matt wasn't about to complain, but he couldn't believe the Japanese had simply given up. Even if the cruisers had turned away, the aircraft would have continued to search. Of course, some were carrier planes. Maybe they were low on fuel, or didn't want to land at night. The spotting planes might have returned to their ships as well. He frowned. Even so, they'd mauled *Amagi* badly—at least he hoped they had. He thought two of *Mahan*'s torpedoes had struck her at the end. She at least should still be near, unless she'd continued on at full speed, and he didn't know how she could have unless she was even tougher and faster than he thought. Maybe she sank. Now that was a happy thought.

All these considerations came in an instant, just before he turned back to *Mahan* and raised the speaking trumpet.

"Is your fire under control?" The trumpet projected his tinny voice across the intervening distance. "Will our hoses help? Can you steam? Where's Captain Atkinson?" He thought he already knew the answer to his final question. A bedraggled form moved to the rail. It might have been the same man who had helped coordinate their charge, but it was impossible to be sure. The man cupped his hands and shouted.

"I'm Lieutenant Brister. Engineering. Captain Atkinson's dead. The whole bridge crew's dead or badly wounded. I think we've about got the fire licked and we can steam, but I had to use the men on the steering detail for damage control. If you can spare some men, I think we can get under way."

The entire bridge crew? "Who's in command?"

"I guess I am, sir."

"Lieutenant Brister's a fine officer," commented Matt as he and Ellis watched the whaleboat motor across the short distance between the ships. They'd sent half a dozen seamen under Bosun's Mate 1st Class Francis "Frankie" Steele, of the second deck division, as well as Signalman Ed Palmer, with one of the portable Morse lamps. None of *Mahan*'s lamps had survived the destruction of her bridge and auxiliary conn. At least now they'd be able to communicate.

Jim nodded. "Yes, sir. He deserves a commendation for keeping his ship afloat, not to mention fighting her so well. He's gonna have his hands full, though."

"Yeah, he's not a navigator or a bridge officer. I hate to lose you, but maybe you better go across and assume command."

Jim frowned. "Well, sure, if you say so, Skipper, but we've got damage of our own."

Matt waved away his objection. "Lieutenant Dowden can handle it. He knows what to do, and the men like him. Besides, he's the assistant damage control and repair officer. With Richard dead, it's his job." He looked at Ellis with a sad smile. "Go on, Jim. *Mahan* needs you. We have to get her under way as soon as possible, and if anybody can speed that up, it's you."

Jim quietly watched several ratings sweeping and mopping debris. "Aye, aye, sir. I guess I just hate to leave the old girl in such a shape." He smiled wryly and looked at *Mahan*. "I never expected my first command to be the best ship in the Navy, but this is ridiculous." Matt barked an unexpected laugh at how closely his exec's thoughts mirrored his own when he first assumed command of *Walker*. Of course, *Mahan* was in worse shape than *Walker*, and *Walker* had taken a terrible beating. Comparatively speaking, Jim had more right to complain.

"I'll just run down and get some things and as soon as the boat returns, I'll go." He stood awkwardly for a moment, then thrust out his hand. "Take care, sir . . . Matt."

Matt shook his hand and squeezed his friend's shoulder. "You too. Report as soon as you have a handle on what shape she's in. Holler if you need help."

Jim grinned. "Same here." He looked around. "Even money who hollers first." They both chuckled, and then Lieutenant Ellis stepped back a pace and saluted. Matt returned it and after Jim left the bridge he sighed and sat tiredly in his chair. "Pass the word for Mr. Dowden."

The whaleboat returned and the coxswain, Tony Scott, was unhappy to learn he had another trip to make. He was strangely uneasy. The water didn't seem quite right. He was wrung out, like everybody, and the weird experience of the squall had left him unnerved. But what had him on edge right now was how many things kept bumping into the boat. He was accustomed to the occasional thump of a fish, or a shark, but they were out in the middle of the ocean and things wouldn't stop bumping his boat. It was constant. Nothing big had struck it, and occasionally he glimpsed a silvery swirl alongside, so he knew they were just fish. But why the hell were they bugging his boat? It was like the bright white bottom paint was attracting them. He shuddered with a premonition that it might draw other, larger things as well. Jim Ellis tossed down his seabag and swung over the side, descending by way of the metal rungs welded to the hull. As soon as Ellis was aboard, Scott advanced the throttle and steered for the other destroyer, hoping to make his second run as fast as he decently could.

"Skipper," reported Sandison, "lookout sees something 'screwy' in the water, dead ahead, about two miles. Wait a minute! He thinks it's a submarine!"

"What's the status of the whaleboat?"

"Alongside," supplied Riggs. "They're hoisting it aboard now."

"Very well. Signal Palmer on *Mahan* we're investigating a possible submarine. Sonar's still out?"

"Yes, sir," said Lieutenant Dowden, puffing up the ladder. "Jim, I mean, Mr. Ellis, had us working on it, but . . . We still might get it working if—"

"Just put it in your report." More worn-out equipment.

"Sir, Mr. Garrett sees it too, and damned if it don't look like a sub to him," said Kutas. "He says there's debris and people in the water around it. Might be a sub taking on survivors from that Nip can we sank."

"The whaleboat?"

"Secure, sir," said Riggs, standing on the port bridgewing, watching the work.

"Sound general quarters! All ahead full. Maybe we'll catch 'em on the surface."

Spanky was inspecting the damage in the forward fireroom. Eight bodies had been removed, and he shuddered at the memory of the scalded men. Men he knew. Machinist's Mate 2nd Class Dean Laney and Dave Elden, shipfitter, trailed behind him with clipboards. Dwindling daylight seeped through the two holes made by the ten-inch shell, one on either side of the compartment. The boilers had escaped destruction, but steam lines and conduit were shredded.

"It's a miracle it didn't hit a boiler," observed Laney. McFarlane grunted. "Yeah, but a wrecked boiler'd be the least of our concerns. It probably would've exploded if it had, and blown the bottom right out of the ship." The other men nodded solemnly.

"Not much we can do right now, Spanky," said Elden. "She needs yard time bad."

"I know. Let's see if we can get at least one back on line as a spare, though. I don't like steaming on two boilers. 'Specially if one's number four. I don't trust it. Anyway, if either of the boilers in the aft fireroom craps out, we'll be down to one, and we'll be a sittin' duck for the Japs."

The general alarm shattered the relative quiet of the ravaged compartment.

"Jesus H. Christ!" groaned Laney when the grating beneath his feet tilted and the ship surged ahead. "Not again!"

"Didn't they tell you?" McFarlane growled, as he hurried for the air lock. "There's a war on."

"Surface action, bow!" shouted Garrett over the comm. "Estimate range two two double oh. Target is stationary. Match pointers!" Most of the soot had washed away, but the back of his neck still hurt where the steam scalded him when the fireroom was hit. Fire control was still a mess, but it was back on line. He watched a dark shape, barely on the surface, like a flooded-down submarine, ease slowly through a group of men in the water. He didn't feel good about firing on helpless men, even if they were the enemy, but he was about to give the order when a strange thought occurred. He leaned over the speaking tube without taking the binoculars from his eyes. "Skipper, something's not right."

Matt snatched the headset from his talker and spoke into it. "What do you mean?"

"Sir, something *is* screwy. The sub's moving a little, but there's no conning tower. And the men in the water seem to be trying to get away from it. I see splashing. There're not many men, sir, just a few, but they look . . . upset." For several moments, as they drew closer to the object, no one said anything. "Skipper . . . ? Do you think it's one of our boats? Maybe that's why the Japs don't want to get aboard. I've heard they won't surrender."

"I don't think so, Greg. I'm looking at it too. It doesn't look like any sub I ever saw. We have quite a few boats out here, but none look like that."

Reynolds was in the crow's nest and his voice suddenly crackled on the line. "Holy *shit* . . . Sir! That's not a sub. It's a great big stinkin' *fish!*"

Garrett blinked. He'd seen a submarine because he expected to see a submarine. As soon as Reynolds spoke, he realized the young seaman was right. "Jesus Christ! Skipper, it *is* a fish, or whale or something and it's . . . I think it's *eating* those Japs!"

"Commence firing!"

"Aye, aye, sir! Gun number one, range is now, ah, one four five oh! Match pointers! Commence firing!" He was so distracted by . . . whatever was swimming lazily about, snatching the struggling sailors, he didn't press the salvo buzzer. The gun on the foredeck boomed, and a split second later, a geyser erupted a little beyond the target.

"Gun one, correction! Down sixty, three rounds, resume firing!" Three shells slammed out as fast as the breech was opened and another round loaded. A tight group of waterspouts erupted on and around the creature; a tinge of red intermingled with the spray. The thing heaved itself from the water and in the gathering gloom Garrett got an impression of a long, pointed flipper, like a right whale. But he also saw an elongated, tooth-studded snout like a crocodile's, snapping viciously at the spume as the beast slapped back into the sea. Two more large flippers churned the surface and propelled the monster beneath the waves.

"God a'mighty."

As they drew near the few remaining men, clinging desperately to floating debris, the surface of the sea churned again with hundreds of silvery shapes schooling around the survivors. Garrett watched in horror as the fish struck. They looked like tuna, but acted like piranha. They were close enough now he could hear the screams.

"All back two-thirds! Right ten degrees rudder!" Matt yelled. He leaned through the shattered window and shouted at the foredeck below. "Boats! Get those men out of the water!" He looked at Tolson and spoke in a more normal tone. "Rudder amidships. All stop. Keep them in our lee." He looked down from the port bridgewing. The sea churned with a horrifying frenzy that brought to mind an old reel he'd once seen of a cow carcass thrown into the Amazon. He'd been fascinated as he watched the voracious fish reduce the carcass to a mere skeleton within moments. Now he fought to control his stomach as hundreds of much larger fish attacked the struggling Japanese in much the same fashion. What were they? He was no expert on marine life by any means, but he'd never seen such a thing. By the expressions on the faces of his men, neither had anyone else. Only Chief Gray seemed immune to the shock. He went about his assigned task with a single-mindedness that Matt could only envy, as though huge sea monsters and man-eating fish lurked in the water every day. Which they did, he supposed, but not like this.

In spite of Gray's efficiency, before he could assemble a party to throw lines to the survivors, there was no one left to save. A froth of flashing fins and teeth marked the spot where the final swimmer had disappeared. The rest of the swarm began to disperse or snatch tiny morsels drifting here and there. Alone upon the gently rolling sea, an overturned lifeboat bobbed with two forms precariously balanced. One seemed unconscious, and the other hovered over the first with a split and badly gnawed oar in his hands. He now regarded the destroyermen with inscrutable Asian eyes. His stoic face hadn't changed expression since he had battled the carnivorous fish and the submarine-sized cross between a whale and a crocodile. *We're just different enemies,* Matt thought. He turned and saw another face peering anxiously from the ladder, aft. This one belonged to the Australian engineer whom he'd only briefly met.

"May I, ah . . . come up there, sir, for a word?" Matt nodded, and the tall, portly man puffed to the top of the ladder. His sparse, graying hair was plastered to his skull with sweat, and he ran his left hand over it as if feeling for the hat he held in his right. Noticing that everyone on the bridge wore a hat or helmet, he plunked his back on his head. He glanced at the foredeck, where men were throwing lines to the enemy seaman on the boat and trying to convince him to take one.

"Oh, dear. Unimaginable. After what that Jappo's been through, he still won't surrender. I don't suppose you have anyone who can speak to him? No, of course not." Matt looked at him and quirked an eyebrow. He'd noticed before the man's strange habit of answering his own questions.

"Actually, Mr. Bradford, we may surprise you. Quite a few old China hands aboard this ship. Some may have learned a few words."

"Indeed?"

In the end, their translator was not a "China hand" but Lieutenant Mallory, the Army pilot with Captain Kaufman. He spoke a few terse phrases in what could have been Martian for all Matt knew, but the stubborn Japanese sailor finally let his oar slip into the sea and caught the rope. Matt looked up at Garrett. "Get some weapons to those men before they hoist those Japs aboard." He raised his voice to be heard by the men on the deck below. "Where'd you learn Japanese, Mr. Mallory?"

The young officer shouted a reply. "I grew up in Southern California, sir. My folks ran an orange plantation. Lots of Japs in the citrus groves."

"Why wouldn't he take the rope?"

"He said his family, his ancestors, would be ashamed if he surrendered."

"That's nuts! Didn't he see what happened to the others?" Matt shook his head. "How'd you talk him into it?"

Mallory hesitated. "I didn't, sir. But he agreed to let us 'rescue' his officer since he's unconscious and can't decide for himself. I told him we'd let him kill himself later if he wants."

"Jesus," someone muttered. Chief Gunner's Mate Sonny Campeti arrived on deck with several Springfields. He quickly passed out all but one, which he kept for himself. The others stood back, their rifles ready, while three men pulled on the rope. The burly Japanese sailor held the other end, bracing himself upon the keel as best he could. Occasionally a jostling wave caused him to glance anxiously at the unmoving man beside him. The supine form's uniform was dark blue. The boat bumped against the hull, and another rope was lowered. Quickly and professionally, the man tied it around his officer's chest under his arms and then stood back, balanced precariously, as the destroyermen hauled the unconscious man to the deck. Without another glance at the men above, he sat down on the boat and put his hands on his head, lacing his thick, powerful fingers together in his hair.

Chief Gray looked up at Matt with an expression that said, "Now what?" and the captain raised his speaking trumpet. "Is he alive?" Gray felt the man's neck for a pulse and nodded. Except for a small gash on his head, there were no obvious injuries. "Take him to the wardroom, under guard."

"Aye, aye, sir."

"What about the other one?" Mallory asked.

"I don't know. Maybe we can lasso him, or something. We can't just leave him here—Jap or not."

"Goodness gracious!" exclaimed Courtney Bradford. He stood next to Matt, looking into the sea. The captain looked at him, then followed his gaze. The dark blue water became much darker directly beneath the boat. Suddenly the creature they'd driven under, or one just like it, rose to the surface, and its gaping, crocodilelike jaws snapped shut on the capsized boat. The thing was enormous! Matt knew the boat must be twenty-five or thirty feet long, and the jaws were very nearly that long themselves. As the boat splintered, Matt heard a shriek and saw the terrible jaws close on the Japanese sailor's legs. Even then, it sounded more like a scream of pain, not terror. He shuddered. The roar of the machine gun just above his head deafened him and an instant later, the bigger .50-cal, amidships, joined in—as did a couple of men with rifles. He hoped a few thought to finish the stubborn Jap, but amid the geysering splashes he couldn't tell. The creature writhed and slammed into the ship hard enough to make him grab the rail. With a huge splash and a swirl of flippers, it disappeared from view.

"Goodness gracious," said Bradford again, his voice subdued by awe.

Matt stood transfixed, but for only a moment. Then he bellowed to the men below. "Boats, get somebody down there to check the hull for damage. Whatever the hell that was, it bumped us pretty good." For a moment nobody moved, but finally the Bosun stirred.

"Get the lead out, you miserable girly saps! The Skipper gave an order! Ain't you never seen a sea monster eat a Nip before? Shit!"

With that, Matt turned, walked woodenly back to his chair, and sat. Out there, off the port bow, the sun finally vanished entirely beneath the blackening sea, and he removed his hat and plopped it on his lap. He felt like the reserve of adrenaline that was supposed to last his lifetime had been completely tapped out that day. He was so tired. Finally he sighed and rubbed his face.

"Mr. Tolson, take us back to *Mahan*. Hopefully, she's ready to move. Secure from general quarters, but keep men on the machine guns for a while." He yawned tremendously and glanced at the men looking at him, still stunned by what they'd seen. "It's been a hectic day," he whispered.

hey ran south all night at twenty knots. The two operational boilers on each ship could have carried them
faster, but with all their damage, twenty knots was a
sufficiently hair-raising speed. Repairmen labored on,
exhausted, trying to accomplish tasks while under
way that ordinarily required a yard. Shoring timbers
pushed warped seams together and shipfitters welded
them instead of waiting for rivets. They had too far to go. Matt briefly considered returning to Surabaya, but with all the enemy activity, they'd probably wind up trapped. Ceylon was still within reach, fuel-wise, but the only
reason that had been their original destination was that its yard facilities
could handle *Exeter*. With the British cruiser lost, there was no reason to
go there. Wiser to make for Perth, Australia, where some of their sisters
had gone.

It was a cloudless night, but the moon was the merest sliver. It provided just enough light for *Mahan* to follow their wake. Matt pitied her
shorthanded, exhausted crew. *Walker* had lost more than twenty killed
herself—almost a quarter of her complement—and another eight were
seriously wounded. But *Mahan* had more than sixty dead. She was a floating
morgue. Most of her casualties occurred when a ten-inch shell destroyed
her bridge. Other men were lost in the aft deckhouse and fireroom.

It was a miracle that either ship had survived. The only things that
saved them were getting in close where *Amagi*'s main guns couldn't
engage . . . and the Squall, of course. Matt shifted uncomfortably in his
seat at the memory. The Squall had been unusual in itself, but then a
whole string of strange events followed. The ravenous fish, the "sea monster" (he couldn't think of anything else to call it). Then there was the odd

lack of radio traffic. The radiomen and electrician's mates had studied the equipment carefully and found nothing wrong, but everyone was exhausted and they must've missed something. It was that simple . . . Matt's eyelids fluttered open again, and he shook his head to clear his blurry thoughts. Instead, his chin slowly drooped until it rested on his chest.

The midwatch would be coming on soon, he thought muzzily. *At least some of the men could sleep. Poor Richard. Up in the crow's nest all day long, only to die when they were so close to safety. He'd done his duty, but he'd missed the sea monster. Jim missed it too, as had everyone on the other ship. They were lucky. At least it won't swim in their dreams. It's already in mine and I'm not even asleep.*

He was snoring lightly. Garrett, his neck and hands covered with gauze, had the deck. He stepped quietly over to stand beside his captain, lest he fall from his chair. He caught the eyes of the other tired men and held a finger to his lips.

Matt came awake in a blurry, gray dawn. He blinked, rubbed dried grit from his eyes, and looked around. Lieutenant Dowden was nearby, conversing in quiet tones with the Bosun. Matt felt a surge of irritation at being allowed to sleep, but it was immediately replaced by a vague sense of guilt at having done so. Wry acceptance followed. At least now he could face this new day without dropping from exhaustion.

"Coffee?" he croaked.

Almost before the word was uttered, Juan Marcos appeared at his elbow, steaming mug in hand. Juan was the officers' steward and the only Filipino who hadn't—understandably—jumped ship when they left the Philippines. He beamed as his captain took the cup and nodded his thanks. Raising it to his lips, Matt took a tentative sip. "That's good," he said, and sipped again. "Very good, Juan. Best coffee you've ever made."

A wounded expression clouded the Filipino's face. "But Cap-tan Reddy, I did not make it!"

Matt glanced at Gray, who suddenly looked away. "Well . . . of course I just woke up and it's my first cup. I'm sure it just tastes so good because I really needed it."

The Bosun coughed to stifle a laugh. Juan took good care of them, given his limited resources, and no one would have dreamed of hurting his feelings. But his concept of good coffee was . . . different from everyone else's.

"No, Cap-tan Reddy. I'm sure it is very good. Better than mine." Juan spoke with brittle formality. "One of the nurses made it. The *señorita* nurses," he added darkly as if to say it might taste good, but would probably poison him. "Now you are awake, I will bring you a breakfast I doubt they could match!"

Matt chuckled. "I'm sure you will, Juan. I'm starved!" The Filipino summoned all his dignity—a most impressive quantity—and left the bridge. Matt raised an eyebrow at Chief Gray and shook his head. He then turned in his chair to glance astern.

"She's still hangin' tight," Gray said, referring to *Mahan*. Matt could just make her out in the grayish pink morning half-light. He stood, stretching his arms over his head. He felt like he'd been thrown from a horse, but except for minor cuts from broken glass, he'd escaped the previous day's battles without injury. "Where are we?"

Dowden stepped to the chart table, and Matt and Gray joined him there to peer at the map. "Here, sir," Dowden said and pointed. "Just about exactly."

Matt looked at the indicated position and then stared out the windows. It was difficult to tell, but he thought he saw a landmass ahead. "I'm not enthusiastic about running Lombok or Bali Strait in daylight," he said. "If the Japs are here ahead of us, it would be simple for them to put a stopper in the bottle. There're only so many holes in the Malay Barrier. Even after all the running around we did yesterday and last night, we're only about three hundred miles from where we started. They could easily have beaten us here."

"Yes, sir," agreed the Bosun. "And they don't even need ships." He pointed at the map. "A couple of planes patrolling here, or here, and they'd have us. They couldn't miss us. We're in no shape to dodge dive bombers."

Matt rubbed the stubble on his chin and nodded thoughtfully. "What's this?" He pointed to a sliver of land off the northeast corner of Bali.

Dowden leaned closer. "Ah . . . Menjangan Island. It looks like it's only about two and a half miles long. The chart shows a narrow channel between it and Bali that's about a mile wide."

"What if we eased in there and hunkered down for the day, and then ran Bali Strait tonight?" Matt mused aloud. Dowden looked unconvinced, but Gray was thoughtful.

"Looks like plenty of water. The channel shows a hundred forty feet. There's about three fifty all around. The currents look okay." He looked at Matt. "Bali Strait wouldn't be my first choice in the dark; it's so narrow. But the Japs might think that too. It sounds good, Skipper."

"Yeah, but we know there's Japs on Bali," added the captain darkly. "After the fiasco in Badung Strait, there was nothing we could do about it. That should have been different." He sighed. "It all depends on how far they've advanced. We know their force wasn't very big and they'll be concentrating on securing airfields." He deliberated. "Bali's pretty big and they went ashore on the far side of the island. Worst case, they might've sneaked a few observers in to watch the strait, but I can't imagine they'd waste their time watching that little gap beside Menjangan. It doesn't go anywhere." Dowden was nodding now. Their only other option was a daylight run through a very confined stretch of water.

"We lie doggo for the day," Matt decided. "It'll give us a chance to patch some holes. Besides, I'd like to get with Jim. I need a real report on *Mahan's* condition, as well as our own." He stared at the map a few moments more. "I wonder what kind of cover Menjangan has. A lot of these little islands are just jungles poking out of the sea. That'd be perfect for our needs. Some are barren volcanic rocks too." He looked around the pilothouse questioningly. "I've never been there." Dowden and Gray were both shaking their heads, and no one else spoke up. "Send for Mr. Bradford. Maybe he knows."

"Aye, aye, sir."

The Bosun followed Matt to the bridgewing, where they stood silently staring aft at *Mahan*. Matt grimaced. "By the way, Boats, how are our other 'passengers' making out?"

Gray arched an eyebrow and then snorted. "Well, Skipper, I've been a little busy, and they might've strayed from my immediate presence a time or two . . ."

Matt chuckled. "But, Boats, you're not just a chief, you're *the* Chief. The Bosun! You're supposed to know everything that happens on this ship."

Gray grunted noncommittally. "Yes, sir. Lieutenant Mallory pulled his weight. He helped out a lot hauling ammo and if it weren't for him, I guess we'd've had to leave the Nip. He'll live, by the way." He glowered. "On the other hand, Kaufman's a wonder. He ran around all day, gettin' in the way and tryin' to tell everybody what to do. Finally, Campeti got fed up. He handed him a four-inch shell and told him he could carry it to the number one gun or he'd cram it . . . down his trousers . . . and throw him over the side."

Matt started to laugh, but the humor was replaced by anger at the self-important idiot who'd harassed his men during battle. He forced himself to maintain a placid expression but was shocked by how quickly his outrage flared. "What about the nurses? I heard one was killed."

Gray nodded. He put his hands in his pockets, but quickly withdrew them. When he answered, his voice held genuine regret. "Yes, sir. She was a pretty thing too. Leslie Runnels, or Ranells, or something. She was helping Doc with Rodriguez when they got hit. Rodriguez'll be okay, though. The cut on his leg wasn't very big, but they nearly didn't get the bleeding stopped. Cut an artery, I guess." He was quiet a moment, but when he continued, he was shaking his head. "The shell that got Doc and the nurse couldn't'a missed Rodriguez by a foot. The other nurses took over and did just fine. Their lieutenant—Tucker's her name—just jumped right in. I looked in a time or two, bringin' guys in, mostly, and there she was, shells slammin' through the ship, smoke and blood all over the place . . . and her stitchin' and cuttin' and giving orders as calm as you please, and her no bigger'n a button. I don't know what we would've done without her. Would've lost more men for sure." He stopped. "They went through hell, though, all of 'em, and that's a fact. We had a lot of wounded—and them losin' one of their own . . ."

"I'll have to thank her. Thank them all." Matt took a deep breath and let it out. "I have a rough idea of our casualties. I want the specifics, names and such, when I take a report from each division. A lot of letters to write . . ."

Courtney Bradford chose that moment to ascend the ladder and present himself. "I understand you need a pilot for these mysterious seas? Of course you do, and I'm just the fellow! The marine life around Menjangan is exquisite! Simply exquisite! There are no shallows, you know, just a sheer underwater cliff with all manner of fascinating creatures clinging precariously to it! Once I lowered a net and dragged it up the side and was amazed by what I found. Amazed!"

"Yes, well," replied Matt, taken aback. "I'm afraid we won't have time for sightseeing. I'd forgotten, though. You said you were a naturist?"

"Naturalist, actually. It's a hobby of mine. I planned to write a book one day." He shook his head wistfully. "This confounded war has certainly inconvenienced me, let me tell you!"

"What exactly does a naturalist do?"

"A naturalist, dear boy, is one who studies nature. It's a dreadfully inclusive term, but I'm a dreadfully inclusive naturalist. Most of us tend to have a specialty, but I have broader interests, shall we say. I'm not really an expert on anything, but I know a little about quite a lot. In fact, my book wasn't to be a treatise on any particular thing, per se, but more a general discussion of the various fauna of this region as a whole, don't you see? Of course."

They'd moved into the pilothouse as they spoke, and the rest of the watch were surreptitiously straining to listen to the strange Australian.

"Tell me, Mr. Bradford," asked the captain in a serious tone, "in your studies, did you ever happen to hear about that . . ." He hesitated, searching for a term. Somehow "sea monster," however appropriate, didn't strike him as a responsible description. He finally settled for "creature" regardless of its inadequacy. "I failed to ask you last night before you left the bridge."

Bradford looked pensive and glanced at the others within hearing and lowered his voice. "No, Captain. Not ever. And that school of fish! Abominable! I've never even *heard* of such a thing. Unless, of course . . ." He paused and removed his hat, fingers massaging his brow. "Have you ever heard of the plesiosaurs?" he asked hesitantly. Matt blinked, and Gray just shook his head. "They're quite fascinating, actually. A particularly formidable specimen of a type of plesiosaur was once found near Queensland. It's called kronosaurus, I believe, and its head is nearly eight feet long!"

With an audience including the entire bridge as his voice began to rise, Bradford warmed to his subject. "Quite horrible, I'm sure! Great long fins, or flippers, you might say, and a long mouth full of unusually terrifying teeth! Consummate predators, not unlike killer whales, I should think. Surely you remember hearing about them now?"

Matt shook his head and smiled. "No. I'm glad somebody has, though! That must've been what we saw. You sure described it well enough. They must be awful rare, or you'd hear more about them."

Chief Gray looked at Courtney Bradford with the skeptical expression of a man who's been told a fish story. "I been in the Navy almost as long as this ship," he rumbled, "and I never heard of 'pleezy-sores,' or whatever-the-hell-you-called-its."

Bradford stared at them, astonished. He resembled nothing more than a paunchy owl that awakened hanging upside down from a limb it knew it had been standing on. "No! You don't understand! It cannot *possibly* have been kronosaurus! They've been extinct for tens of millions of years!"

Matt looked at Bradford and took a deep breath. He shifted his shoulders uncomfortably. He definitely didn't need this endless procession of mysteries. He'd hoped that Bradford could sort them out.

"Extinct, as in all gone?" muttered Gray in an ominous tone.

Bradford was nodding. "Precisely. Extinct means precisely that. I didn't mean to imply . . ."

"Hmm. Well. Boats, I assume you have duties? Very well. Mr. Bradford? We're going to hide out between Menjangan Island and Bali until nightfall. I hope you'll be available if we have questions. I'm going up top for a while." With that, Matt nodded at the two men and stepped to the ladder.

As he climbed, he heard the Chief mutter, "Real cute. If I ever hear you call the captain 'boy' again, I'll toss you in the wake!"

In spite of his concern, Matt couldn't help but grin as Bradford sputtered and protested and apologized at once. *Gray thinks he was spinning an educated fish story,* he thought, *but I'm not so sure. We definitely saw* something *eat those Japs, and it was damned real. Every now and then, something turns up that scientists thought was extinct forever. Maybe this*—he didn't even try to pronounce it—*is one of them?*

On the fire-control platform, he exchanged greetings with the morning watch and peered ahead at the landmasses looming before them. The flanks of both islands were shrouded in fog, but it wasn't too dense. It was unusual in these seas, but it shouldn't hazard navigation and it might help conceal them from planes. After a while he returned to the pilothouse.

Mahan followed closely behind as they crept carefully—with just a few suggestions from their guide—into the narrow, hazy strait that separated Menjangan Island from Bali. On the foredeck, the Bosun bellowed commands at the special sea and anchor detail. The anchors were dropped, and several men from each ship motored ashore on Menjangan with a heavy hawser. The bridge crew watched anxiously as the boats became vague shapes in the fog.

"You did instruct them to stay out of the water, I'm sure?" asked Mr. Bradford in a nervous tone. Matt glanced at him.

"You don't think there might be more of those fish here?"

Bradford shook his head. "There shouldn't have been any where we saw them."

Matt grunted agreement. "I wouldn't worry. After yesterday, I doubt anyone wants to get wet."

The anchors held well enough and they could have stayed right where they were, but Matt wanted to snug up as tight to the bank as they could and camouflage their ships with foliage from shore. It was strangely quiet. The roar of the blowers had faded to a steady rumble. There was only the slightest breeze, and the gentle swell of the strait lapped innocently against their battered hull. Men brought thin mattresses from below and spread them on deck to sleep away from the stuffy berthing spaces. Others continued making repairs. As always, Matt was struck by the contrast.

His destroyermen were capable of amazing feats of courage and endurance while on watch, but only because when they weren't, they could sack out anytime, anywhere, and in any situation. Many of the men shuffling about looking for a place to stretch out had been awake for thirty-six hours and more. Most who were busy had managed at least a little sleep during the night. He watched as two "snipes" emerged from below, squinting, as if even the fog-filtered morning light hurt their eyes. Beneath the grease and sweat-streaked soot covering them, he saw their pasty skins and realized they were the two firemen everyone called the Mice. He didn't remember ever seeing them above deck. They looked around, very much like mice that had just chewed through a wall into an unexplored room. Finally, they climbed the ladder onto the amidships deckhouse and crept to the ready ammunition locker behind the number two gun. They lay down on the bare deck and were probably asleep before they'd even finished moving. Of all the men, the damage-control parties and the engineering division had suffered the worst, he thought.

He joined Lieutenant Dowden, staring intently in the direction the boats had gone. They were visible in the thinning fog, tied to the rocky shore, but there was no activity. The island beyond the landing faded into haze, but they had the impression it was covered by dense brush and stunted trees. A prickly sensation of apprehension crept into his chest, but he shook it off. They would be searching for trees large enough to secure the hawsers to. Perhaps it was taking longer than expected to find any suitable ones. From the island, they heard a muffled shot. Then another. They both raised binoculars and tried to pierce the haze. Three more shots thumped from shore, and without lowering the glasses Matt shouted up at the plat-form above. "Make ready on the starboard .30-cal, but hold your fire until I give the word!" The canvas cover on the gun was snatched away and a new belt of ammunition prepared.

Gunner's Mate 2nd Class Dennis Silva, ordinarily gun captain on num-ber one, was on the trigger. He was probably the best they had and would have been a credit to the ship—if he weren't more often an embarrassment. He was tall and powerful and kept his hair burred so short he might as well have shaved it. Aboard ship, he was usually competent and professional, but ashore he was completely unable to behave. He always reminded Matt of a quote he once read: "Maleness gone berserk." That described Dennis Silva to a T. Matt would have restricted him to the ship for life, but he'd just go AWOL (he'd done it before) and wind up in more trouble than he could be rescued from. He was *Walker's* Hercules—a valuable man, but he re-quired . . . supervision. Now Silva peered at the boats like the rest of them, his hands on the weapon, but the muzzle was pointed up and away. One of his minions, Tom Felts, held the belt of linked cartridges.

"I see them!" exclaimed Dowden, pointing. Emerging from the gloom were several men. Two were helping a third. They reached one of the boats and piled in, pushing off from shore. There were a couple more shots and then the rest of the shore party ran down and hurriedly cast off the second boat. Matt heard the motors cough to life, and then the boats were speed-ing back toward *Walker.*

"I don't know what they're shooting at, Silva," Matt called above, "but keep that shoreline covered."

"Aye, aye, Skipper."

A few minutes later, both boats bumped alongside and the men climbed out, sending the injured crewman ahead. Matt was surprised to see a couple of the nurses waiting for him on deck. Bosun's Mate 1st Class Carl Bashear, who'd commanded the party, lingered over the wounded man and spoke to one of the nurses. Then he puffed up the ladder to the bridge.

"Skipper, we couldn't secure the hawsers," he said. He was breathing hard and his black hair was plastered to his skull. Even with the haze, the temperature was already over eighty degrees and the humidity was hor-rible.

"I can see that. What happened? Who got hurt?"

"Lizards, sir! It was *lizards.* Big ones."

"Impossible!" snorted Courtney Bradford.

Matt shot the Australian a look that silenced him. "What do you mean? What lizards? What were you shooting at?"

Bashear's breathing began to slow. "Damned if I know what I mean, Skipper, but there *were* lizards. We'd split up and were looking for some good trees to tie off to, and a couple more to drop in the water to make a pier. All of a sudden, Leo Davis takes to hollerin' that somethin' had ahold of him! Me and Vernon and Scott ran over there, and sure enough, this big-ass—'scuse me, sir—this dern big lizard has chomped down on Davis's leg and is draggin' him off."

Bradford was about to burst. "But—but—" he stammered. Matt held up his hand and motioned Bashear to continue.

"Yes, sir, thank you, sir. Anyway, ol' Davis is carryin' on that he's bein' ate, so we took to shootin' at the lizard. Me and Scott had rifles." He stopped a moment, and thankfully took a long gulp from a Coke the Bosun handed him. He smacked his lips. "Well," he continued, "it turned him loose and come at us." He shrugged. "We shot it some more. I'm pretty sure we killed it. Anyway, we grabbed up Davis and headed back to the boat. All of a sudden, there's *more* lizards, so we shot at them too. I guess we nearly didn't make it. All we had was the shells in the guns. And like I said, Skipper, those lizards was *big*."

"Preposterous!" sputtered Bradford. "The only 'lizards' that might attack a man are on the island of Komodo. That island, sir, is two hundred nautical miles from here. The great reptiles inhabiting it are found there and on a couple of small neighboring islands. Nowhere else. Certainly not Menjangan! My God, man! I've been here myself, and there are no such creatures! I don't believe there are even the smaller monitors."

Bashear eyed the Australian coldly. "You callin' me a liar?"

Gray interrupted. "These Komodo lizards—"

"Dragons, sir. We in the scientific community call them Komodo dragons. *Varanus komodoensis*, to be precise." Bradford sniffed.

"I don't care if they fly and blow fire out their ass," Gray growled impatiently. "Are they poisonous? One of my men was bitten."

Bradford blinked, his contention forgotten. "Oh, dear. Yes indeed, they're extremely poisonous—or rather, their bite is highly septic. We believe it has to do with bacteria in their mouths—" The Chief merely glanced at Bashear, who interrupted Bradford again.

"Skipper, with your permission . . ." Matt waved him on and Bashear hurried away.

Bradford turned and walked onto the starboard bridgewing and peered at the island, which was becoming more distinct. Suddenly he stiffened.

"Oh!" he exclaimed. "Oh, look! Someone lend me a glass, I beg you!" The assistant gunnery officer, Ensign Pruit Barry, shrugged and handed him his binoculars.

"There! Oh, there! There are *two* of them!" Matt joined him and raised his own binoculars for a look. On the beach, in the dwindling mist, was a pair of extremely large lizards. They appeared to be ten or twelve feet long from their blunt-nosed snouts to the tips of their whip-thin tails. They crept down almost to the water and seemed to stare at the pair of destroyers, their beady eyes fixed on the ships. "Oh, my goodness, they *are* big!" chortled Bradford excitedly. "They're the largest I've ever seen. And their color! Green and red! Amazing!" Then, as they watched, one of the lizards raised itself onto its hind legs until it gained a nearly entirely erect posture. It stood with its head bobbing up and down as if testing the air. Bradford gasped.

"My God! Oh, Captain, I must go ashore! Look at that! It's standing up! My God! This must be an entirely new species! Never before seen! Just think of it!" Matt lowered his binoculars and turned to the man. "Captain," Bradford continued, oblivious to Matt's stare, "I insist you allow me ashore! I must have a closer look!"

When Matt spoke his voice was quiet, but he couldn't hide his incredulity. "Mr. Bradford, have you entirely forgotten yourself?"

The Australian wrenched his gaze from the beach and regarded Captain Reddy. His mouth hung open as if to protest, but then it clamped abruptly shut. With a mournful expression, he nodded. "Of course, Captain. Of course." He sighed. "I apologize. It's not every day a man of my interests observes a new species, particularly one this important." He glanced wistfully at the island. "Just one more debt I owe those miserable Jappos."

Matt nodded understanding. "I think we're all keeping score." He turned to Dowden. "It doesn't look like we'll be able to secure to the island. We'll remain at anchor here. Every pair of eyes not otherwise occupied will watch for aircraft, and I want to be ready to move in a hurry."

Matt suddenly reflected with surprise that he'd already begun addressing Lieutenant Dowden as *Walker*'s executive officer. With Jim gone and the other senior officers dead, he was the obvious choice. He'd been Jim's assistant and he'd filled in for him often enough. In many ways, execs had the hardest job on any ship, and this wasn't the time to appoint somebody unaccustomed to the role. He was just a "jay gee," and very young for the job, but with a war on he'd likely be a full lieutenant by the time they got to Australia anyway. He would do fine. Besides, the only other possibilities—within the chain of command—were Alan Letts, the (j.g.) supply officer, Garrett, and Spanky. Spanky and Garrett were essential where they were and Letts was . . . a disappointment. He was a good guy and knew his job, but he wasn't very industrious. *Walker* needed a go-getter right now, and the willowy, blond-haired lieutenant from Tennessee certainly fit that description.

Matt mentally shook his head and continued. "Chances are they won't spot us, though. They'll be looking at the strait. Signal *Mahan* and ask Mr. Ellis if he's comfortable coming across for an hour or so, or whether he'd prefer to report by Morse lamp."

Matt sat on the bunk in his small cabin and tested his freshly shaven chin with his fingers. It had been difficult negotiating the razor around the painful glass cuts scattered across his face. Satisfied, he finished dressing and looked in the mirror over his desk. *Better,* he thought. The quick shower he'd indulged in had helped. His eyes were still red and there were circles underneath them, and he was still so tired that when he blinked it seemed his eyelids moved too slowly and then tried to stick together. He sat back on the bunk and listened to the growing conversations in the crowded wardroom. If only he could lean over and lie down. Just for a minute. The cramped, uncomfortable bunk was the most inviting thing in the world at that moment.

Someone knocked on the doorframe. "Sir?" said Garrett hesitantly. "Everybody's here." Matt sighed and rose to his feet. Squaring his shoulders, he stepped through the doorway and down the short corridor into the wardroom. Most of his officers and department heads—many new to their jobs—were there. Ellis and a bandage-swaddled ensign named Tony Monroe had come from *Mahan*. Monroe was assistant navigation officer and aside from Perry Brister, her chief engineer, the sole surviving officer. Brister remained on *Mahan* to continue repairs—and so there'd be at least one officer aboard her if they had to move in a hurry.

Three of the nurses and the Army pilots were also in the room. Courtney Bradford leaned against the far bulkhead since there were too few chairs, and Juan circulated through the crowd filling coffee cups from the two carafes in his hands. Everyone was sweating in the stifling heat, and cigarette smoke eddied and vented away through the punctures in the hull that made up two of the wardroom walls. In the general hubbub, the captain wasn't immediately noticed. Garrett shouted over the din:

"Captain on deck!"

Everyone came to attention, with the exception of Captain Kaufman, who continued leaning against the bulkhead with an expression of hostile disdain.

"As you were, gentlemen . . . and ladies," Matt added for the nurses' benefit. Even exhausted, he noticed that the nurses were young and attractive, and he recognized the one who had brought coffee to the bridge and made a small nod of appreciation. One of them, though, the lieutenant, returned his gaze with a frank appraisal of her own.

What Sandra saw was a very tired young man who'd been violently forced to shoulder extraordinary responsibilities under very stressful—and unusual—circumstances. They all knew their predicament, or at least thought they did, and it was no secret that there'd been strange goings-on. She detected uncertainty beneath his veneer of confidence, but whether that reflected the situation, the unusual events, or the heavy burden of responsibility for two badly damaged ships and all their people, she didn't know. Instinctively, her heart went out to him. She was a nurse, and she knew when a man was suffering, even through gritted teeth. Though his injuries were superficial, the wounds to his ship and her people were reflected in his eyes.

Matt had the uneasy feeling, looking into her green eyes, that the nurse lieutenant saw beyond his facade of calm, and he quickly turned his attention to the room. "First, our own condition: I don't have all the details yet, but I have some idea. We can steam, our leaks are under control, and we have fuel for a twenty-knot run to Perth. Since our plans are contingent upon *Mahan*'s capabilities, however, I think Mr. Ellis should start."

Jim nodded and cleared his throat. "Thanks, Skipper." He looked around the compartment. "*Mahan* took a hell of a beating. She's not sinking, but everything topside is a wreck. Half her crew is dead and there're twenty wounded. Some seriously." He looked at the surprise on the assembled faces. "Yeah, that's a pretty lopsided number," he said grimly. "Most of the casualties were on the bridge and in the aft fireroom. Everybody in the pilothouse or on the fire-control platform was killed. She has no fire control at all. Guns two and four are okay, and we can use them in local control, but that's it. Number one might be repaired, but we haven't really even checked." He sighed wearily. "The machine guns amidships are okay, so we're not totally helpless from the air, but all torpedoes are expended and I'd rather not push her past fifteen knots. She can make that, the forward fireroom's fine, it's just . . . well"—he gestured at the beams of light entering the wardroom through the holes—"you know.

"Anyway," he continued, "*Mahan*'s shorthanded as hell—only about forty effectives, not counting the guys I took aboard—but she's not finished yet. Whatever you decide, Captain, we'll do. We might just want to take it a little easy. I also really hope we don't have to fight again." He chuckled wryly. "At least not as briskly as yesterday." His last comment drew scattered chuckles, but the mirth was tempered by the realization of what that fight had cost.

"What's the status of your wounded?" Matt asked.

"Mostly stable, but we could use a hand. The pharmacist's mate is dead, and the surgeon's run pretty ragged."

Matt nodded, and glanced at the nurses. They were a study in contrasts. The one who'd brought coffee—he'd learned her name was Karen Theimer—seemed nervous, jittery, almost fragile. She blinked constantly as her eyes quested around the compartment and her hands squirmed against one another on the table. The one beside her, Pam Cross by her name tag, was almost as short as Lieutenant Tucker and outwardly as self-possessed, but her eyes told a different story. The other two nurses, Beth Grizzel and Kathy McCoy, weren't present. The sandy-blond lieutenant was still watching him, which was understandable. Everyone was. But once again, her expression of appraisal left him uneasy. Besides, she was a knockout. He managed to smile at her. "You must be Lieutenant Tucker."

She stood from her seat at the table. Since the captain didn't sit, she wouldn't remain seated while speaking to him. "Lieutenant Sandra Tucker, sir."

"Lieutenant, I apologize for not greeting you when you came aboard, and I'm sorry I haven't had a chance since, but I'd like to thank you now for all the help you and the other nurses have given us. I'd also like to extend my deepest regrets for the loss of Ensign Ranell." Several heads bobbed, and there was a general murmur of condolences.

"Thank you, Captain Reddy. I'm sorry too. I'm sorry for Leslie, and for all our losses. My nurses and I stand ready to help any way we can."

"Thank you, Lieutenant. As a matter of fact, that raises my next subject, and that's to ask if you'd feel comfortable detaching a few nurses to *Mahan*."

"Of course, Captain. I'm willing to go, but I'd ask you to allow my nurses a choice." She smiled ironically. "Not that there seems much difference in the relative seaworthiness of either ship, if you'll forgive my saying so."

Matt smiled back at her amid the ensuing chuckles and good-natured indignation. "Absolutely. They can choose, but you may not. The needs of the service, not to mention the needs of my crew, dictate that I break with tradition—as well as virtually every regulation I'm aware of—and appoint you acting medical officer. Under the circumstances, we'll consider it a separate department."

"Yes, sir." She grinned. "I wouldn't enter it in the log, though, if I were you." Matt grinned back.

"Perhaps not." He paused, watching her sit, admiring her poise and apparent calm. *Gray was right,* he thought. *She's something else.* He cleared his throat self-consciously and addressed the others. "Next on the list, Lieutenant Dowden is acting exec in Mr. Ellis's place, for as long as he commands *Mahan*. Rick Tolson is acting navigation officer. Larry? You

and Rick better pick assistants. Think hard about it, but give me your rec-
ommendations as soon as possible." He turned to Chief Gray. "How about
the deck divisions?"

Gray's brow furrowed, and he tucked his hands behind the belt encircling his ample girth. "Like we talked earlier, we're still afloat. But I'm running shorthanded too." The deck division's noncombat occupation was
general maintenance, and it served as a labor pool. He glanced at Lieutenant
Ellis, who now had some of his men, but it wasn't an accusation, merely a
statement of fact. "All the leaks are under control. We welded a lot of seams,
which'll have the yard-apes throwin' fits, but there's no way to replace rivets
out here. The big holes are all above the waterline. If we don't run into heavy
seas, we'll be okay. We're workin' on covering those holes too, but it's slow.
Some are pretty big and there's nothing for it but to patch 'em." He cocked
an eyebrow. "Not a lot of plate steel just layin' around. If we had time, we
could cut patches out of *Mahan*'s aft deckhouse, but for now we're sort of
working our way up. I figured the stuff close to the waterline had priority."

Matt was nodding. "Very well. Anything to add?"

"Nothing big. About a thousand little things are in my report. Mostly
the same stuff the old girl throws at us every day, times ten."

"Mr. Garrett?"

Lieutenant Garrett now wore a real bandage on the back of his neck
to protect his scalded skin. Thankfully, his injuries weren't more serious.
He fidgeted and cleared his throat, and Matt suppressed a smile. He'd
been the personification of cool professionalism during the action, but
now, in this setting, he was more like a schoolkid than a naval officer.

"Uh, main battery's operational and responding to fire control." He
paused and shrugged. "The range finder's wrecked. A big chunk of shrapnel just about chopped it off—but it wasn't any good anyway. The ready
ammunition lockers have been replenished. There's something wrong
with one of the .50s, but Gunner's Mate Silva says he'll have it working by
this afternoon."

"Tell him to get a move on. That one gun represents a quarter of our
antiaircraft defense. What about torpedoes? Ensign Sandison's working
on them now, correct?"

"Yes, sir. He still doesn't know what the problem was. A connection on
the mount, maybe? He was drawing them out of seven, nine, and eleven,
and intended to put them in one, three, and five, unless you'd rather disperse them."

"No, that's fine. What's the status on the two torpedoes we picked up
in Surabaya?"

"They're not sure what's wrong with them. They were condemned.
Hopefully it's something we can fix. One looks pretty beat up, though."

"Thanks, Greg. Have Sandison keep me informed about his progress. Now, let's see. Engineering? Spanky, let's hear from you."

"Yes, sir. Well, we took a beating, sure, but it looks like most everything's under control. We might even get number two boiler back on line. We'll keep her going if the water stays out. Twenty knots, at least." Matt smiled at Spanky's qualifier and started to ask a question, but the engineer wasn't finished. He shook his head and continued in a quiet tone. "Honestly, sir, I don't know how we made it. This old girl'd had enough before the war even started, but I guess she's tougher than we thought. She deserves a lot of credit." He shrugged. "God should get the most, I guess. I didn't see it, but there's talk of a weird squall . . . Anyway, I'm not real damned religious, but that's where most of the credit should go."

Matt controlled a shudder at the thought of the Squall. Somehow, he didn't think God was responsible for that. But who knows? He looked at McFarlane and saw the engineer staring back.

"A lot of credit should go to Captain Reddy."

There was a general murmur of agreement to the unexpected compliment, and Matt felt his face heat. He didn't think he deserved much credit at all. Spanky was a good officer, though; he knew how important it was for the crew to have confidence in their captain. For the captain to have confidence in himself. Deserved or not, he appreciated Spanky's gesture.

"Thank you, Mr. McFarlane." He paused to sip coffee from the cup Juan handed him, breaking eye contact with the engineer. It was his own white porcelain cup, the one he always used in the wardroom. He had another just like it on the bridge. As always, his eyes strayed to the black printing around the side: CAPTAIN—USS WALKER—DD-163. With mixed feelings he took a breath.

"We'll stay here for the day, at anchor, and make whatever repairs are practical." He looked back at McFarlane. "Maintain full steam, but I want no smoke. We'll keep double lookouts and the machine gun and three-inch crews will remain at their stations at all times. I know the three-inch isn't good for much, but a puff of black smoke in the air might make enemy planes think twice. I intend to run the strait tonight, as fast as we can manage. Hopefully, we'll have some torpedoes by then. Jim, I know you'd rather go slow, but I want every turn you can make, at least through the strait."

Ellis nodded. "We'll keep up, Skipper."

"Good. Once again, we'll lead. Stay close, though. There'll be almost no moon, so it'll be dark. Sonar's still out, but we won't waste time zigzagging. The strait's too tight for that anyway. I think, even with all our problems, we have a good chance—if we make it fast and sneaky."

He took another sip of coffee and looked at the faces in the room. He'd rather just ignore the next subject, but he didn't have that choice.

"That brings us to the last item of business." He noticed several people shift uncomfortably. "Everyone knows, in addition to our other problems, there've been . . . strange events. The crew's talking about it, and they have enough to worry about without a bunch of mysteries." He let that sink in for a moment. "On the other hand, if you discourage the talk it'll just make them worry even more. You must all assure the crew by your words and actions that we're taking care of the problem, whatever it is, and it's not something to concern themselves with. Do I make myself clear?"

There were nods.

"That may be easier said than done." Captain Kaufman spoke for the first time. He stepped forward and put his hands on the table. "What's the dope on the radio?"

Matt gritted his teeth. "It's still not working."

"That's not what I hear. I hear it's working fine, but we're not receiving anything but static. Have you tried to transmit?"

Matt looked at him incredulously. "Of course we haven't tried to transmit! We might as well paint ourselves pink and steam through the channel in broad daylight. It's obvious the Japs have carriers between here and Australia. The reports before we left implied they did, and we've since seen carrier planes. That means they're ahead of us and behind, and can easily triangulate our position. It's equally obvious, despite what you've heard, that the radio can't be working—otherwise we'd hear something. They don't know what's wrong with it, but there must be a problem. Checking the radio by giving away our position seems sort of counterproductive, don't you think?" Matt's voice rose as his annoyance grew. "And frankly, Captain Kaufman, as to your earlier statement, if you find it difficult to suppress your fears in front of the men, I prefer you not go around them."

Kaufman's face turned purple. He looked around, surprised to see almost everyone, even the nurses, regarding him with hostility. Only the bandaged ensign from *Mahan*—Monroe—seemed sympathetic. He barely heard Gray whisper to Lieutenant Garrett: "Ought to be in the chain locker with the Nip." He was practically sputtering with rage, and he started to reply, when they all became aware of a commotion on deck. It might have been going on for a minute or two, but with the confrontation the wardroom hadn't noticed. Now they heard running feet and rising voices.

Bernard Sandison burst into the wardroom, wide-eyed and gasping. "Beg pardon, Skipper, but you better come on deck."

"Are we under attack?"

"No, sir. Not under attack, but . . . just please come and see."

As one, spurred by the ensign's cryptic statements, the assembly crowded for the passageway. "Make way!" the Bosun bellowed. "Make way for the captain!"

All the officers, including Nurse Tucker, scrambled up the ladder to the pilothouse. Everyone else climbed onto the amidships deckhouse to join most of the crew already there, or along the port rail below. In fact, the port side was so crowded that *Walker* was heeling noticeably. As soon as he gained the bridge, Matt heard Gray bellowing for the men to return to their duties before they capsized the ship. It was no use. For once, even the Bosun's legendary wrath was wasted. Matt snatched his binoculars from Ensign Tolson and looked toward Bali—the direction everyone was pointing and staring. He adjusted the objective slightly.

The fog to the south had almost entirely dissipated and he clearly saw the northeastern coast of Bali less than a mile away. It was a scenic view, about what he'd expected from descriptions he'd heard and pictures he'd seen. Beyond the dark volcanic beach was a rocky shoreline, choked with a lush hedge of vines or brush. Beyond this boundary, a broad coastal plain rose steadily upward to the flanks of a distant mountain. He'd read the slope was terraced and had been for hundreds of years. Mr. Bradford had commented on it as well. He saw no terracing, but everything else seemed as it should. Except one thing. Upon the plain before him, in the middle distance, was a small herd of what could only be described as dinosaurs, grazing slowly along.

Ridiculously, the first thing that popped into his mind was that they were smaller than he would have thought, about the size of Asian elephants. But the long necks and whiplike tails protruding from the otherwise quite elephantine bodies were exactly what he'd have expected of an artist's rendering of, say, a brontosaurus. He heard a small sound and glanced aside.

"Somebody grab Mr. Bradford. He's about to faint."

Jim Ellis leaned close and whispered nervously in his ear. "We're *damn* sure not in Kansas anymore, Skipper."

Matt grunted distractedly as the amazing creatures ambled unconcernedly along, much like cattle feeding on grass, except these animals took as many leaves from the trees as they did grass from underfoot. "Personally," Matt whispered back, his voice shaky, "I liked the black and white part of that movie the best. Everything that happened once it went to color gave me the creeps."

The Mice filed tiredly back to their stifling lair. There was way too much commotion on deck to rest. No good ever came from leaving their boilers. One of the water tenders looked up as they entered.

"What the hell's going on up there? We run aground or something? Why are we heeling over?"

Isak looked at him with bleary, disinterested eyes. "Dinosaurs on

Bali," he said simply. Then he and his friend lay down next to the hull, where the water outside kept the plates slightly cooler. They wadded up a pair of greasy life jackets for pillows and promptly went to sleep.

All over the ship, men slowly returned to their duties or tried to rest. Some talked nervously among themselves, and others said nothing at all, pondering the implications of this latest mystery. A few might have panicked if not for the steadying influence of the older hands, but mostly the destroyermen took it in stride. It was just one more thing. What was one more thing after all they'd been through? They didn't know what was happening and they knew it wasn't right, but most were too tired to care. Men from Mars flying by on giant blue chickens would probably not have elicited a more prolonged response—but they probably would have been shot at if they came too close.

Dennis Silva was thinking just that. He manned the .50-caliber machine gun on the port side of the amidships deckhouse. He'd been almost finished putting it back together when the commotion began, and he'd been one of the first to see the creatures. Now he stood, still watching, with just a few others. The first group of "bronto-sarries" had moved along, but there was a steady stream of other, equally improbable animals. A smaller group resembling the first ones they'd seen appeared.

"Boy," exclaimed Silva, "I'd sure like to shoot me one of those!" Tom Felts and Paul Stites looked at him.

"What the hell for?" Stites asked incredulously.

Silva shrugged. "Ever'body and ever'thing's been pickin' on us lately. I feel like pickin' on somethin' myself for a change."

Felts shook his head. "I wouldn't pick on one of those damn things. Hell, Dennis, what if they can swim? You'd have prehistoric monsters down on us too! Ain't the Japs enough?"

Stites peered over the side at the water speculatively. "You think them things are really dinosaurs? I mean, there ain't supposed to be dinosaurs on Bali, is there? I thought they all died off."

"Course there ain't *supposed* to be none here." Silva guffawed. "There ain't supposed to be none anywhere! All that's supposed to be here is a bunch'a nu-bile young native girls runnin' around without shirts."

Stites and Felts both looked at the island. "Well, where the hell are they?"

"Better ask the Skipper, fellas." Silva's grin went away, and when he spoke again his voice was uncharacteristically subdued. "I bet he don't know either."

For the first time since she could remember, Sandra didn't know what to do. She didn't have an answer or a solution or even a suggestion. That hit her almost as hard as anything else. Seeing the creatures on Bali did something to her that nothing else had ever accomplished: it shook her sense of pragmatic self-assurance to its core. She was still on the bridge, although she doubted she was supposed to be, but no one asked her to leave. There were no more critical patients to treat, and the seriously injured had been transferred to their berths, where the other nurses and their shipmates fussed over them and tried to make them comfortable. If not for the possibility of air attack, she would have already asked to have them moved on deck for fresh air. *Maybe I should move them up,* she thought, but the latest shock left her unable to concentrate. She'd always prided herself on her ability to adjust to any situation; that was what good nurses had to do. But this! What was going on?

She looked at the captain. He was deeply involved in a whispered, serious conversation with several officers. After the initial excitement, the ship grew eerily quiet. She looked aft. Now the mist had cleared and the sun beat down once more, and most of the men had resumed their duties, or the perpetual quest for shade. Now and then, however, she saw men glance furtively at the island as if to confirm they'd actually seen what they thought they had. She looked again herself. Sure enough, the bizarre animals were still there. The place was teeming with them. She shuddered. She was *not* imagining things. If she was, so was everyone else.

She looked back at the group of officers and saw the fatigue in their expressions—the tired, bloodshot eyes and haunted looks as they too glanced nervously toward Bali now and then. Captain Reddy looked little better than the others, but she admired the way he hid the fear and uncertainty he must feel. He just stood there, listening attentively and nodding occasionally. When she heard his murmured words, she was encouraged by how calm he sounded. She found it ironic and unsettling that, shortly before, she had been evaluating his steadiness from a perspective of self-confidence. Now she looked to him for reassurance.

Courtney Bradford had recovered himself, and now leaned against the port bridgewing rail, oblivious to the concerns of others and staring in rapt fascination through binoculars. She moved beside him.

"Are they truly . . . dinosaurs?" she asked in a quiet voice.

He nodded vigorously. "Of course! They do seem rather small, compared to what we were given to expect by the scale of most assembled fossils. But indeed, there can be nothing else to call them. Obviously, they shouldn't be here! I've studied the charts, and I've been here before. That island *is* Bali. The only difference is the lack of agricultural terracing and, well, the dinosaurs, of course! The terracing is strange enough. It hasn't been very long since my last visit, and I can assure you that even with a concerted effort and heavy machinery, the terraces couldn't possibly have been removed so thoroughly as to leave no trace they ever existed. As for the dinosaurs?" He shrugged and smiled happily. "I have no explanation."

"But surely . . . what could've happened?" She pointed across the water. "Those things have been gone for millions of years! You don't think . . ." She couldn't finish.

"Once again, I have no idea," Bradford replied cheerfully. "Perhaps that disconcerting squall had some unusual effect beyond what we experienced? Perhaps. Time travel?" He snorted. "Hardly. If the Squall did something to us, it didn't send us back in time! Time travel is, of course, impossible. Besides, during the age those creatures"—he waved toward land—"roamed the earth, the shorelines were shaped quite differently. Warmer temperatures, higher water . . . These islands are frightfully volcanic. They might not have even existed!" He pointed shoreward again. "That *is* Bali! So whatever is afoot, we're in the *now,* if you follow my meaning? Of course you do."

"But if this is now, *where* is it now? And where is the now we should be in?" Her voice was almost pleading. "Dinosaurs on Bali are impossible too, aren't they?"

"Precisely."

They didn't run the strait that night. Instead, they remained at anchor and continued repairs while the officers pondered what to do. It was clear now, beyond doubt, that something extraordinary had befallen them. Bradford's argument that they hadn't been transported back in time was gratefully accepted, for the most part, but that left the burning question of what *had* happened. Was this simply some bizarre phenomenon localized in the vicinity where the Squall had occurred? Or had they been transported somehow to an entirely alien world? No. That couldn't be. The stars were right, the sliver of moon did exactly what it should as it traversed the heavens overhead, and the charts showed them to be exactly where they were—anchored snugly between Bali and Menjangan Island.

But that couldn't be. Nothing that had happened since the fight with *Amagi* and their subsequent entry into the Squall had been normal. The moon, the stars, the sun itself, and the very air they breathed—the smell of the sea upon which they gently rocked—all testified to their senses that nothing had changed. But there were monsters in the water and giant lizards on the land, and that couldn't be.

Despite all their planning in the wardroom that day, no one knew how to proceed. If they'd been transported to another time or place, what about the Japanese? Were they still in danger from attack? If they went to Perth, would it even be there? Like any good destroyer commander, even in the face of such profound questions, Matt immediately began to worry about fuel. What if the phenomenon extended to Australia? Where would they get fuel? If it was even possible that Perth was gone, should they risk wasting all their fuel to get there? These were the questions he pondered now. The immediate concerns. What they would do in the long run hadn't even entered his tired mind.

Like most destroyermen in the Asiatic Fleet, Matt had no family back home, besides his parents, to concern him. A lot of the old hands left wives and sweethearts in the Philippines, but most of them had already resigned themselves to the fact that there was nothing they could do for them while the Japanese ran unchecked. Even when they steamed away from Cavite that last time, Matt was struck by the stoicism of most of the married men. They knew they might never return. If they did, that would be good. If they didn't, they'd keep fighting until they did. It was all very matter-of-fact. Whatever had occurred when they entered the Squall had created a whole slew of distracting implications, and he wondered how the men would react to leaving their whole world behind? He wasn't yet prepared to deal with that. Right now, his primary concern was for the safety of *Walker* and *Mahan* and their crews—and how best to use their fuel.

Utter fatigue finally forced him to turn in, but before he did, he ordered Jim to shut down one of *Mahan*'s boilers. *Walker* would keep both hers lit, just in case, but henceforth, they would conserve fuel any way they could. It was all he could do. Perhaps after some sleep he would think of something. Maybe he'd wake from this terrible dream and find that all he had to worry about, once more, was the Japanese. He stripped off his sweat-sodden uniform and lay on his bunk. The small, rattling, oscillating fan on the bulkhead labored to move the dank, stifling air. He was so very tired, but a vast tension clutched his chest. Even as he reached to turn off the light, the ghosts and monsters of the last few days began to gather around.

Captain Reddy was sitting in his chair on the bridge when the forenoon watch came on at 0800. The familiar routine of the watch change had a soothing effect that helped dispel the unpleasant aftereffects of unremembered nightmares that had plagued his sleep. Lieutenant Garrett relieved Larry Dowden, who immediately went in search of a cool place to rest. Garrett looked like he'd had a difficult night too, and he acted for a moment as if he had something to say. But then he stepped onto the port bridgewing where Courtney Bradford stood. The Australian was waiting impatiently for the morning fog to disperse so he could view Bali's wonders once more. Matt stood and stretched, and then went back to stare at the chart. He heard the sound of someone climbing the ladder at the rear of the pilothouse and checked his watch. Right on time.

"Morning, Jim."

"Morning, sir," Jim Ellis replied.

"Sleep well?" Jim made a wry face and stifled a yawn, theatrically. Matt chuckled. "Look, I've made a decision you're not going to like, but I don't see any alternative." Matt's former exec looked at him questioningly. "I'm going to take *Walker* to Surabaya and have a look around. If everything's as it should be, we'll still have fuel for a slow run to Australia. If the . . . phenomenon has affected Surabaya like Bali, we can only assume the same is true for Perth, if not the whole world. If that's the case . . . Well, we'll figure out what to do. If Surabaya's unchanged, or we run into Japs, we'll turn around and collect you. *Mahan* will remain here until then. I'll leave three of the nurses and all the most seriously wounded with you." He grimaced. "I know you're shorthanded, so I won't leave you the prisoner to guard, but I will inflict Captain Kaufman on you. Maybe you can get some work out of him. I think his lieutenant will be a help, at least." He motioned toward Bradford. "I don't know whether to leave him here to gawk at the animals or take him along. He might prove useful again if we have to scrounge for fuel."

"I don't like you leaving, sir, but it sounds like as good a plan as any. *Mahan* would just slow you down and give you something else to worry about in a fight." Jim grinned. "As for Mr. Bradford, I'd just as soon you take him. I'd have to watch him constantly to keep him from swimming ashore, sea monsters or not. As you said, if I don't have men to guard a Jap, I sure can't keep up with him."

Matt chuckled. "Very well. We might as well get started. If we're not back in three days, proceed to Perth alone. Alor will be our rally point. If we don't meet you there . . . we're not coming."

The unusual mists had mostly cleared by the time the personnel were transferred and *Walker*'s anchor chain clanked and rattled through the hawse and into the well. The special sea and anchor detail directed a spray of seawater from the fire hose on the chain as it came aboard. Matt stepped out on the starboard bridgewing and peered at the enigmatic Menjangan. He noticed the wind had begun to swing the bow toward it, now that the anchor had cleared the bottom.

"Starboard engine ahead slow." He spoke quietly, but his voice carried to the helmsman.

"Starboard ahead slow, aye," confirmed Tony Scott. Matt sighed. The routine of ship handling soothed the tension of their predicament. The anchor came aboard as the ship twisted to maintain her position and the men on the fo'c'sle leaned against the safety chains to hose the mud and weed off the anchor. It was a procedure he'd witnessed many times, but for the first time he truly appreciated the efficient and matter-of-fact way the deck-apes accomplished it. He was glad to see that no matter what happened, some things never changed. Things like duty.

Suddenly the intercom buzzed, and the bridge talker opened the circuit to the lookout, Alfred Vernon, in the crow's nest.

"Bridge! I have a surface target! Bearing three five zero! Range . . . damn! It's hard to tell. The mist is still heavy in the strait. I make it six zero, double zero! Whatever it is, it's *big!*" Vernon's voice was pitched high with excitement.

"Sound general quarters!" shouted Matt. "Signal *Mahan* to head for the rally point. We'll . . . distract whoever it is and catch up tonight!"

In the aft fireroom, Spanky had just returned the coffeepot to its place near the burner when the general alarm sounded. Then the bells rang up AHEAD FLANK and all hell broke loose. He dropped his cup reaching for something to hold on to, and it shattered. The stern crouched down as the big screws bit and *Walker* surged ahead. The Mice and the water tender worked frantically to keep water out of the turbines. The blowers roared and raw fuel gushed straight into the stacks. Isak swore when the coffeepot fell to the deck, sending scalding liquid sloshing across his legs. Men scampered about, sliding the loosened deck plates back where they belonged as the ship picked up speed, but began settling back into a relatively normal and only slightly nerve-racking acceleration.

Spanky looked around at the aftermath of chaos and wiped sweat from his brow as he checked for blown gauges. "Bloody hell!" he muttered. "I guess the Skipper didn't take the hint when I asked him to take it easy."

C hack-Sab-At was sulking. High in the air, at the very top of the first great wing—almost a hundred fifty tails above the main deck of *Salissa* Home—he could concentrate on nothing but his rejection. He should have known. Selass had flirted with him only as a means of attracting Saak-Fas, first son of the clan chief controlling the center, and most prestigious, of Home's three wings. He realized now, with a measure of embarrassed bitterness, that he'd fallen for her ruse, as had his rival. Her pretense of favor easily convinced Saak-Fas to take her to mate before it came Chack's turn to choose. No matter. He was young and not without prospects. He had a wide choice of eligible mates. He was a first son also, and though his sister was older and closer in line to succeed their mother as clan chief of the forward wing, he expected to go far. He was the best wing runner on all *Salissa* Home and when a new Home was built in a season or two, he would climb to the top of its center wing and become fas chief himself.

Or maybe not, he corrected himself glumly.

Selass might truly dislike him enough to see to it that her father, the High Chief of *Salissa*, did not grant him that honor. It wasn't unheard of. The hereditary nature of the wing "nobility" was rarely interfered with, and each of the three wing clans of Home was virtually autonomous. Except, of course, in how they cooperated with the other clans to move Home from place to place. If a clan chief were incompetent, or unable to agree with one or both of the other wing clans—or the Body of Home clan, for that matter—the succession could be altered. High Chiefs always rose from the Body of Home clan and were supposedly impartial to the bickering among the wings. They had the power to confirm or deny all successions and, indeed, the power to banish.

Keje-Fris-Ar was sovereign over them all and literally held the power of life and death. If he began to dislike Chack, life—which until that very morning had seemed so full of promise—might reveal progressively more disappointment as time went by. Subconsciously, Chack knew Keje was a good and benevolent ruler. He would not countenance any personal vendetta based on a scornful daughter's whim. But Chack felt sorry for himself, and he was in no mood to limit the depths of his misery. It didn't help that, try as he might, he couldn't shake the vision of Selass's soft silver fur and green eyes from his mind.

He glanced far below at the surface of Home and saw the many Body of Home people performing their daily chores: salting fish from the morning drag or tending the plants that grew from under the protective overhangs ranged entirely around *Salissa*. Life went on as it did every day, day after day, during fair-weather times. The People were happily heedless of his puny disappointment, for the People *were* happy, for the most part. Few water monsters were a threat to anything as large as Home, and only the worst storms were noticed. The only threats were the rare mountain fish, land, and of course, the Grik.

Mountain fish were few and encountered only in the deepest regions of the Great Seas, where Homes of the People rarely ventured. Land was easily avoided. The Sky Priests, with their mystical instruments and scrolls, saw to that. If weather hindered the path they decreed, the sharp eyes of the wingtip watchers—the post that Chack stood—would see danger in time for the Body of Home clan to deploy the great fins that could move them against all but the most furious sea. If even that failed, then they had the huge copper feet, two at each end of Home, that could be dropped into the sea attached to a great cable. There had never been a blow—not even a strakka—that could conquer the feet.

The People really feared only the Grik. The Grik were the Ancient Enemy, who cast them from paradise long ago. So long had it been that even to the Sky Priests, it was just "Long Ago." But the People escaped the Grik, and it had been so long since any had been seen that they'd become creatures of legend, of myth, of nightmare—boogeymen to frighten younglings into performing their chores. If they did exist, they dwelt safely across the Western Ocean, upon which no vessel could pass. That was what the People believed for generation upon generation—until the Grik came again and an ancient, almost instinctual dread was revived.

They hadn't been long in these waters, but there were more of them all the time, and they were liable to appear anywhere in their ridiculously small and fragile Homes. Homes that only a few hundred could travel upon, but Homes that were amazingly fleet and maneuverable and had very sharp teeth. Homes that always attacked. In Chack's first seven seasons, he'd seen only one of their tiny Homes, and it had attacked them—only to be beaten off. But the shock of that day lingered still. That such a small thing with such frightening creatures would attack without thought or warning—and with such dreadful ferocity—still troubled his sleep. The next seven seasons carried him into young adulthood, and he'd seen no less than six more Grik Homes. Each time one appeared, it attacked without fail. They never managed to do more than inflict minor damage, but always a few of the People were slain repelling them. One such had been Chack's father. It made no sense. The Grik had to be at least a little intelligent, else they couldn't have built the fast little ships. But to attack Homes of the People from their much smaller craft was like flasher-fish against gri-kakka. They could wound, but nothing more. The priests taught that Grik were creatures of the land. Perhaps that explained their madness.

Chack didn't pretend to understand them, any more than he understood the treachery of females. He glanced at his sister, Risa, on the wing support a dozen tails beneath him. She watched him with concern in her large amber eyes—and impatience. He knew Risa loved him; she was his very best friend. But she also thought he took things much too seriously. She made a joke of everything except her duty, but there was a difference between giving and taking a joke—and becoming one. Her body language told him more than words ever could: he was acting a fool. He blinked rueful acknowledgment and resumed scanning the skyline. They were in a confined area and as good as the priests were at laying a course, it was instilled in wing-tips from birth that they could never be too careful. Besides, it was in confined areas that the Grik usually chose to attack.

He was studying the hazy shoreline with just that thought in mind when he first saw something strange. A large puff of black smoke appeared above the haze that lingered between the small island and the large one. There was a sudden impression of rapid motion and a white froth grew on the water. A smallish shape, advancing impossibly fast, appeared atop the foam, under a diminishing cloud of smoke. He clung to his perch for a few moments more with his jaw hanging slack. *Nothing* could move that fast! He blinked his eyes. Of course it could. He saw it. He reached over and grabbed a line.

"The Grik! The Grik come!" he shrieked at the top of his lungs, and dropped down the rope toward the surprised and alarmed upturned faces.

"I can't tell yet!" answered Vernon in the crow's nest to another urgent query. "There's too much haze," he continued excitedly. "It's big, though. God, it's big! Bigger than that cruiser we tangled with!"

Dowden clambered up the ladder to the pilothouse, wiping sleep from bleary eyes. "What is it, Captain?"

"Don't know yet, Larry. Something in the strait." Matt smiled grimly. "Sorry to wake you. I have the conn, Mr. Garrett. Take your station, if you please. Torpedoes?" Ensign Sandison scrambled to his position at the starboard torpedo director.

"They're ready, Captain."

"All stations manned and ready, sir," supplied the talker.

Matt brought his binoculars to his eyes. The haze in the strait was still thick, but it was thinning rapidly under the combined assault of the fully risen sun and a freshening breeze. Even on the bridge they could see a large dark shape, and it did appear larger than *Amagi*. Matt knew then that all their toil, sacrifice, and suffering, the gallantry and heroism of his fine crew, had been for nothing. Whatever lay ahead could only be a very large Japanese ship, and as soon as it saw them they would die. His only plan was to gain the attention of the enemy, fire *Walker*'s last torpedoes and run like hell under a cloud of smoke back in the direction of Surabaya. Maybe they could distract it from *Mahan* and the other destroyer would escape.

The talker asked the lookout to repeat himself. "Captain?" he said hesitantly. "Vernon says he's a little above the haze now and he can see a fair amount of the target, which is also above the haze. He says it ain't no Jap warship he ever saw. It ain't nothin' he ever *heard* of."

"Explain!" snapped Matt. Every eye in the pilothouse was fixed upon the talker.

"Sir, he says it's got sails."

All binoculars were instantly in use as the bridge crew scrutinized the apparition more closely. Sails. Whatever it was, it was *huge* and it had *sails*. Lieutenant Garrett's voice came over the comm, calling out range estimates and instructing his gun crews. "Range six four five oh. Bearing two five oh. Speed fo—four knots? Captain, I have a solution. Request permission to commence firing."

Captain Reddy tore his gaze from the ship that was rapidly resolving into something . . . remarkable, and strode to the intercom himself. "Negative, Mr. Garrett. I repeat, *negative*! Hold your fire. Continue to track the target, but hold your fire!" He looked at Sandison. "You too, Bernie." He returned to stand beside his chair and raised his binoculars again. Wind rushed in through the empty window frames and threatened to take his hat, but he didn't even notice. It was a ship, all right. Bigger than a battleship. Bigger than a carrier. Hell, it was bigger than anything he'd ever seen. And rising high in the air, at least three or four hundred feet, were three huge tripods that each supported enormous semi-rigid sails much like those of a junk, but bigger than any junk's that were ever conceived.

"Engines slow to two-thirds. Left ten degrees rudder. Let's see what we have here."

The great ship was threading the channel—with evident care, considering its size—on a heading taking it into the Java Sea. There was silence on *Walker*'s bridge as she drew closer and details became more defined. Matt didn't even notice Sandra Tucker and Mr. Bradford join him to gape at the leviathan. It was double-ended, sharp at bow and stern, and looked like a gargantuan version of the old Federal ironclad *Monitor*, except the straight up-and-down sides reared a hundred feet above the sea. Instead of a turret, there were three large structures with multiple levels, like wedding cakes, forming the foundations for the great tripod masts. In a sense, they looked like the pagoda-style superstructures distinctive of Japanese warships, except they were larger and were, like the rest of the huge ship, evidently made of wood. Bright-colored tarps and awnings were spread everywhere, creating a festive air, and from what he could see of the deck from his low perspective, the space between the structures was covered with pavilion-like arrangements of brightly striped and embroidered canvas.

The ship was easily a thousand feet long, but most outlandish of all were the hundreds of creatures lining the rails and in the rigging and leaning out windows in the "pagodas" to stare right back at them.

"Bring us alongside, Mr. Scott." Matt's voice sounded small, and he cleared his throat, hoping for a more authoritative tone. "No closer than a hundred yards. Slow to one-third." He glanced at the talker. "Try to raise *Mahan* and tell her to hold her horses." Perhaps they'd repaired her radio. Jim was optimistic.

"Sir!" cried Sandison. "What about the Japs? Won't they hear us transmit?"

An explosive giggle escaped Tony Scott, but he managed to compose himself. Matt let out a breath he must have been holding and gestured out the windows with his chin. He smiled hesitantly. "Mr. Sandison, I don't believe there are any Japs. Not anymore."

The chattering voices grew progressively quieter as the strange vessel approached. Excited exclamations and panicky activity all but ceased. Chack and Risa were on the catwalk above the gardens that ran around the ship. They squeezed through to the railing for a better view. The thing was close now, less than a hundred tails distant. Though small compared to Home, it was longer than any Grik ship ever seen, although maybe not as wide. There was a single tall mast toward the front and a much shorter one at the back, but neither carried a wing of any sort! It had checked its mad dash and now matched their speed, moving parallel to their course.

The white froth it threw aside as it dashed through the waves diminished to a whisker.

No wings—and yet it moved effortlessly in any direction, regardless of the wind! As it kept station off their beam, Chack had the impression it was going as slow as it possibly could and strained to surge ahead against some invisible bond. Four tall pipes, or vents, towered from the middle, and occasional wisps of smoke curled away. Perhaps the pipes were wings? He couldn't see how. If so, must they light fires in them to make them work? When he first saw it, there was much smoke and it went very fast. Now it was slow, but there was little smoke. Perhaps. He felt a twinge of superstitious dread. Fire was another thing the People feared, and only the cookers and lighters were allowed to use it. All it would take was one careless moment and all of Home might be consumed. To harness fire and use it so made him feel uneasy. The thing boasted few colors, except for a tattered, striped cloth that fluttered at the back. Other than that, it was dull, like a stormy sky, with brownish streaks and smudges here and there. It also looked like it had been bitten by a mountain fish, as there were holes, large and small, all over.

Chack's thoughts were interrupted by the arrival of the Guards, who arrayed themselves along the railing every five tails or so, pushing spectators away. Most hadn't bothered to don their light armor, but all had their axes and crossbows, which they strung when they took their positions. Chack felt a twinge of guilt. He was in the reserve Guard, as was every ablebodied person on Home. But he hadn't even thought to arm himself, so anxious was he to get a look at the stranger. He thought about fetching his weapons now, and even started to leave, when the chattering grew louder again. He squeezed back through the people that packed the rails. Risa grasped his arm. "They are *not* Grik!" she shouted over the growing clamor. "Not Grik!"

He blinked rapidly in surprise and stared back across the water. He'd been so preoccupied by the strange vessel, as had everyone, that he'd failed to notice there were people on it. Well, not *People*, of course, but not Grik.

"What are they?" Risa asked, barely heard.

"What the hell are they?" Matt said softly, barely aloud.

"They look like monkeys! Or cats! Or . . . hell, what are they?!" blurted Sandison.

"Quite like lemurs, I should think," said Bradford in an excited tone, "although they do have a strong feline aspect as well."

"I don't know what a lemur is, or a feline neither. They look like cat-monkeys to me," grumbled Scott.

"Silence on the bridge!" Matt said softly but forcefully. "Tend your helm, Mr. Scott."

Keje-Fris-Ar stepped to the rail, surrounded by his personal guards, and waited for Adar, the High Sky Priest, to join him. Keje was short, even by the standards of the People, and he tended toward a mild plumpness common among the Body of Home folk. His arms were massive, however, as they'd been since his youth, when he'd been the greatest lance hurler in living memory. In his fortieth season, he was still among the best. When the People hunted the great gri-kakka, or "lizard fish," for its flesh and the oil from its fat, he still often found a place in the boats. His short fur was reddish brown, now salted with white, but his eyes—a much darker reddish brown—sparkled with youthful curiosity, along with a natural concern. As he gazed at the amazing visitor, one of his clansmen-guards dressed him in his war tunic, made of gri-kakka skin and covered with highly polished and beautifully chased copper plates. At his side was his scota, a long, broad-bladed sword used primarily for hacking gri-kakka fat but also a formidable weapon in his practiced hand.

Adar arrived, shouldering gently but firmly through the gathered people. His long purple robe hung from his tall, thin frame and billowed as a gust of wind breathed softly across them. On each shoulder was an embroidered silver star, much the same color as his pelt, which was the badge of his office. He stared intently at the unbelievable ship, but more specifically at the creatures upon it in their outlandish white, blue, and light brown garments. Creatures doing nothing more threatening than staring back at them. They were bizarre, to be sure, and taller even than he. They had virtually no fur at all, just little tufts on their heads covered by strange hats. A few had fur on their faces, but not very many. The most shocking difference, however, at least at a glance, was that the beings had no tails. At all.

Most looked back with as much apparent astonishment as the People displayed. Others evidently communicated with one another in some animated, alien fashion. Generally, though, their reaction to the meeting seemed to mirror that of the People. There was no fear in his voice when he spoke to his leader and lifelong friend. "Tail-less mariners," he said quietly. "How very strange indeed. Could it possibly be?" He shook his head. "Demons from the East, most likely."

Keje glanced at him and blinked questioningly. "The Scrolls speak of demons from the East? Specifically? The People are harried sufficiently by demons from every other direction. These must be distinguished demons indeed."

Adar allowed the slightest smile to appear on his perpetually stoic face.

"Not specifically. Not in the Scrolls. But there is wisdom passed down among the Sky Priests that is not always written, my Brother."

Keje huffed. He noticed that some had seen the exchange and several blinked with alarm. He heard the word "demons" whispered and saw the effect ripple down the rail, fore and aft. He huffed again, in annoyance. "Watch your tongue, my gloomy friend. No one doubts I rule the minds and bodies of all the People of Home, but your words carry weight in their hearts." He gestured at the thing that lingered with such unnerving precision and spoke louder. "They're not Grik. They're very strange folk, but they haven't attacked. I doubt they can. I see no weapons. No swords, axes, or crossbows at all. Their Home is very fast. If our Home was as fast, we would not need weapons either!" He laughed.

He watched as his words quickly spread to counteract the unease that Adar's comment had inspired. Adar inclined his head and lowered his ears in respect.

"You are wise, Keje-Fris-Ar. That's why you are High Chief of all the clans of Home, and I am merely a humble servant of the Heavens." The sarcasm was thick, but those nearby recognized the customary banter between their two leaders, and the mood lightened still more.

"I wonder what we should do?" Adar whispered in his ear.

"If they do nothing," Keje whispered back, "I will continue to stare at them. It has worked very well so far."

Captain Reddy moved onto the bridgewing, closely followed by Sandra and Courtney Bradford. He saw Gray standing with the number one gun crew on the foredeck, his hands behind his back. He too was looking at the huge ship, but by the expression he wore, he might have been watching an empty San Miguel bottle bobbing alongside in Cavite. The gun crew traded nervous glances, but they had themselves under control. The Bosun's presence probably helped, and Matt was certain that Gray had stationed himself there to hearten or intimidate the crew—whichever was required—in case the gun was needed.

Cigarette smoke wafted back from the gun crew, however, and Matt was amused that Gray had, at least momentarily, relaxed the prohibition against smoking on duty. With a start, he saw a cigarette dangling from the Chief's lips as well. He looked aft and saw that the transgression was universal. Even the unflappable Dennis Silva struck a light to a smoke with slightly trembling hands. The big gunner's mate never smoked. He preferred chewing tobacco, because there were no sanctions for safety reasons—as long as he remembered to spit over the side. Sandra Tucker seemed in a state of shock. She said nothing, but her expression of amazement was even more profound than when they had seen the creatures on land. He didn't recall exactly when she'd come onto the bridge, but he realized he didn't object to her presence. Courtney Bradford merely stood, beaming with joy and mumbling to himself.

Matt didn't know how he felt. Shocked, amazed, even terrified perhaps. Not surprised, strangely, that a new impossible thing had occurred, just that it manifested itself in such a way. He felt a bizarre sense of relief, in fact, knowing with complete certainty that nothing was certain anymore. Nothing. At least now he could plan accordingly. He looked once more at the creatures staring back. He knew what a lemur was—Bradford wasn't far off the mark. Crude as it was, neither was "monkey-cat." They had tails like monkeys, he could clearly see, and they were furred in a wide variety of colors. Their faces did look very feline, though, and just like cats, he couldn't tell what they were thinking. All was silent, fore and aft, when he finally spoke.

"Any word from *Mahan*?" he asked over his shoulder.

"Nothing, sir."

"Very well. Mr. Scott, right full rudder. All ahead two-thirds. Let's see if we can pick up her trail." Even over the rising whine of the blowers, Matt heard the chattering exclamations of the creatures when *Walker* surged ahead. On impulse, he raised his hand palm outward and waved at the inscrutable faces.

"Upon my word!" Bradford exclaimed when the gesture was hesitantly returned by a few of the creatures as *Walker* peeled away.

"Unusual," commented Adar as the strange ship receded with magical swiftness. "Not only did they not attack, but that one gave the Sign of the Empty Hand. That's encouraging, at least." The Sign of the Empty Hand was a common greeting among the People, to show they held no weapons.

"Perhaps it was just shielding its tiny eyes from the sun." The crowd began to disperse, chattering excitedly. "Despite what I said, I don't think they were helpless. What was that long thing on the front of their ship if not a weapon? And there were three others just like it. I think they must be weapons."

"That possibility did not escape me, lord," Adar whispered back. "But if they were weapons, they did not use them, did they? Never before have we met others than our own kind that did not attack. I, for one, find that encouraging."

Keje huffed noncommittally. "I find it encouraging when I do not encounter strange beings that move faster than any Home ever has—and do not even have wings—before I have eaten my morning meal. Join me while I do, and we will talk more of what we've seen."

———

Virtually every surviving officer had gravitated to the crowded pilot-house. The petty officers, warrants, and division chiefs were there too, or gathered aft by the ladder behind the bridge. None abandoned their posts without proper relief, and all stations were manned, but nearly everyone who was responsible for other men had come. They hadn't discussed it, hadn't planned it in any way. It was as though they instinctively knew it was time to go to the captain and hear what he had to say. Matt wasn't surprised. He wasn't worried about mutiny, but he knew a threshold had been reached. The men had been through hell even before everything became so strange. When it had, they took it in stride, determined to carry on to the end. Only there was no end. Somehow, for some unknowable reason, nothing was the same anymore—and if Matt had learned anything about his destroyermen, it was that they didn't welcome change.

As he looked at them standing respectfully but expectantly nearby, he reflected that this might actually be harder on some because they were Asiatic Fleet. Many had been on the same ship, on the same station, and with the same shipmates for years. One of the fundamental characteristics of the Asiatic Fleet had been that nothing ever changed. Some would call it ossified; the ancient ships and obsolete equipment certainly supported that, but an all-pervading, decades-long routine had been established and until the War, there'd been no reason to disrupt it. The men with Filipino wives had expected to serve their time and retire in the Philippines, where they'd grown accustomed to the routine of life. The War destroyed that life, but they'd fallen back on the routine of the Navy and their duty. Many hoped that by doing their duty, they could restore everything to the way it had been before. Now even that hope was gone. All that remained was their ship, their duty, and each other. That would have to be enough. For now, that was all they had.

They'd gathered to hear what he had to say. To draw strength and purpose from one that they hoped—since the Navy thought he was smart enough to lead them—would be smart enough to figure out what to do. Matt didn't know what to do, as far as the "bigger picture" was concerned, and it was no use pretending he did. Inwardly, he was at least as scared as they were. But he had faith in these rough men, and to cross this threshold and move beyond it he knew he must appeal to their strengths—their independence and their industry. More than anyone else in the Navy, they were accustomed to surviving on the fringe. If anyone could do it, they could—if they stuck together. Only then could they protect their most immediate, most comforting routine of all: their life on USS *Walker*. With that as a foundation, they could meet the bigger challenge together.

"Shipwide," he said, wondering what he would say.

"Now hear this!" he began, repeating the preparatory phrase that would have been used for any ordinary general announcement. He turned with the microphone in his hand and stared out the windows forward, past the fo'c'sle, into the far distance where the hazy sky met the sea.

"A few of you may have noticed some strange goings-on." He smiled wryly and waited for the nervous laughter to die, then continued in a serious tone. "I don't know more than any of you about what's happened. When I find out, I'll tell you. That's a promise. I won't lie to you, though. The situation's grim. We're a beat-up tin can that's been through a hell of a fight. We have limited stores, ammunition, and fuel." He paused for emphasis, then hammered it home. "And I can't tell you where, or from whom, we can resupply. My immediate plan is to collect *Mahan* and then begin searching for a source to fill our needs. Once we do, we can worry about the big picture and decide what to do next. That's the bad news."

He sensed a flicker of humor over the profound understatement. "The good news is, nobody's shooting at us. The charts are correct, and we know where *we* are; it's just everyone else who has disappeared. Fortunately, that seems to include the Japs. We'll secure from general quarters."

He started to hand the microphone to the talker, but changed his mind. "One more thing," he said, looking now at the faces of his crew. "Whatever happened to us, you can look at it a couple of ways. You can say it's strange, and I sure can't argue. Weird? I'm with you. Bad? We'll see. You might also look at it as salvation, because we were dead, people. Whatever else it was, it was that." He watched the thoughtful expressions and saw a few nods.

"Wherever we go, whatever we do, no matter what's happened— whether we're still part of Des-Ron 29 or all by ourselves, we're *Walker*s! We're destroyermen! And we represent the United States Navy!" The nods became more vigorous and he sensed . . . approval. He hoped it would be enough. He sighed and glanced at his watch. "Return to your duties. Damage control and repair has priority. Funeral services at 1300. That's all."

As always, encouragingly, were the muttered replies: "That's enough!"

Lieutenant Tamatsu Shinya sat on one of the chairs beside the table in the wardroom, his hands cuffed together in his lap. A chain extended down to a pair of leg irons encircling his ankles. The bandage around his black-haired head drooped and obscured his left eye. The compartment was filled with cigarette smoke, but occasional gusts of fresh air reached him through a large hole in the side of the ship. Sitting across from him, leaned back in evident repose and busily creating the smoke, was the American Marine who'd been watching him since he regained consciousness.

He wasn't fooled by the Marine's apparent ease. Nor did he think the bandage on his leg concealed a wound that would prevent him from using the .45 holstered at his side if given the least provocation. His attitude implied that he would welcome an excuse. Together, they'd listened to the captain's words from a speaker on the bulkhead, and although he pretended not to understand, Shinya honestly didn't know if he felt like laughing or if he wished the terrible fish had gotten him after all.

He wasn't a career naval officer, but a reservist, the son of a wealthy industrialist. He'd spent several years in the United States and attended UC–Berkeley. He entered the Japanese Imperial Navy because he was supposed to, not because he was in favor of his country's China policy—although his father glowed with the prospects of a Greater East Asia Co-Prosperity Sphere. He entered the Navy because he was a patriot, and that was what his family did. Besides, the war in China was an Army operation. In the Navy, he would be among cooler and more thoughtful heads.

When preparations for war with America began, he couldn't believe it. He'd been there! He'd seen! He knew as well as anyone how dangerous war with the United States would be, not to mention—according to his sense of honor—wrong. He admitted it was difficult to be objective. He liked Americans, and he'd enjoyed California. It was possible his perceptions had been influenced by people he'd known and, yes, friends he'd made, but only to the extent that he better understood the vast cultural chasm that separated the two peoples. Despite the rhetoric on both sides, he understood the root causes of the war and that nobody was blameless, but the chasm of misunderstanding prevented any reconciliation. The alliance with Germany and Italy might have made war inevitable—and maybe even winnable—but he couldn't ignore his sense that the way it started was wrong and sure to provoke American fury.

Without question, the war was going well so far. The relic he was imprisoned aboard was an example of American unpreparedness. But he'd been at Balikpapan and saw what they could manage, even with what little they had. He feared the outcome if the war dragged out and new and better weapons reached these determined men. Then came the lopsided fight when his destroyer screened *Amagi* against the two old American ships. He'd been amazed and even proud of their bold charge. They'd had no other choice, but it was stirring all the same.

Of course, when two torpedoes exploded against his ship and it vanished from under him, all considerations except staying afloat became secondary. He didn't remember what struck him on the head, and he didn't remember being fished from the water. He did remember a bizarre, stomach-wrenching sensation when the Squall engulfed him, but nothing else until he woke aboard the American destroyer. He'd heard things, though, whispered by men who didn't think he understood.

And then he saw it, through the shell hole, just a while ago. The enormous ship. In that moment he knew all the rumors were true.

He didn't know how or if it would affect him. He was a prisoner of war, he supposed, but what did that mean? How should he act? His situation wasn't often discussed in training. Surrender was not considered an option by his instructors, so how to behave in enemy hands was never mentioned. Despite his "Americanization," he felt vaguely guilty for having survived, although there was nothing he could have done. The man who saved and surrendered him was dead, and he would never know why he'd done it. In any event, whatever he'd expected to happen to him as a prisoner, being shuffled from compartment to compartment but otherwise ignored wasn't it. No one even asked him a question. They had no idea he spoke English, but at least one of them, the young aviation officer, knew Japanese. It seemed unnatural they wouldn't care what he knew of the Imperial Fleet's dispositions. He'd resolved to tell them nothing, but no one ever came and he grew nervous—and wary.

Possibly they'd been so preoccupied with repairs and flight that they'd forgotten they even had him. He hadn't seen the captain, even though he knew the wardroom was where the officers ate. As he overheard the rumors of the crew, however, he began to suspect it wasn't just neglect that kept them from questioning him. Perhaps the relevance of what he knew had diminished to insignificance. Then, not long ago, as he gazed through the hole in the side of the wardroom, it became blindingly clear that whatever information he might have no longer mattered to his captors at all. So they sat, each alone with his thoughts, listening to muted machinery noises.

There was movement behind the green curtain leading to officers' country, and a head poked around it and looked at them, surprised. The curtain slashed back in place and a retreating voice reached his ears. "Shit. The Jap."

The Marine smirked slightly and rolled his eyes. Then he looked squarely at Tamatsu. "That's the new exec. Somebody finally remembered you. Maybe he'll remind the captain." He grinned darkly. "I hope he throws you to the fish."

Thirty minutes later the curtain moved again and two men entered the compartment. One was younger than the other but had a brisk, businesslike demeanor. He had brown hair, but unlike everyone else Shinya had seen, there was no trace of stubble on his cheeks. His dark green eyes betrayed fatigue, but they were alert and curious. The other man was older, shorter, with a noticeable paunch. He looked tired too, and disheveled, but his expression wasn't curious. It seethed with predatory hostility. The guard jumped to his feet as rapidly as his injured leg allowed.

"As you were, Sergeant—Alder, isn't it?" said the first man.

"Alden, sir," he replied. "Sergeant Pete Alden. Marine contingent, USS *Houston*." He said the last with a grim glance at his prisoner.

"Glad to have you aboard, Sergeant. I apologize for not speaking with you sooner, but"—he allowed a wry expression—"I've been preoccupied."

"No apology necessary, sir."

"Nevertheless, I appreciate your taking charge of the prisoner in spite of your injury. How's the leg?"

"Fine, sir."

The captain accepted the lie. The injury didn't affect Alden's current duty, and there were plenty of wounded at their posts. Matt gestured at the Japanese. "Has he behaved?"

"No trouble, sir. Mostly he just sits and looks around. He does what I tell him, and I keep the crew from beatin' him to death."

Gray snorted, but Matt just nodded. He pulled a chair out at the table across from Tamatsu and sat with his elbows on the green surface, fingers intertwined, looking at the prisoner. The man looked back, unblinking, expressionless. Matt took a deep breath and exhaled. "What am I going to do with you?" he asked himself aloud.

Tamatsu felt a surge of adrenaline. He knew he should keep his mouth shut and pretend not to understand, but suddenly he couldn't see the point. From what he'd seen and heard, the war he was part of was gone, as were—evidently—their respective navies and probably even countries as well. He was overwhelmed by that possibility, and when he'd first heard the rumors he suspected some ploy to get him to speak, if he could. Dinosaurs on Bali, indeed! Then he'd seen the ship and, through his shock, he realized that now was the time. If they later, inevitably, discovered he'd been listening to their conversations, they would never trust him—difficult as it might be anyway. No matter what he thought of the war, he was no traitor, but he wanted them to trust him. Whatever happened, wherever they were, they might be there a long, long time.

Hesitantly, he cleared his throat. To the astonishment of the man across from him, he spoke in excellent, lightly accented English. "Captain, I am Lieutenant Tamatsu Shinya. I am your prisoner. Japan did not ratify the Geneva Protocols, but I give my word of honor I will cooperate every way I possibly can, short of treachery to my people or government. Under the . . . unusual circumstances, I find it unlikely that the cooperation I offer will cause harm to my country. If you are willing to accept it, Captain, I offer my parole."

There were a variety of expressions in the room. Tamatsu's face remained impassive, but Gray's clouded with anger and the Marine's eyes widened in shock. Matt leaned back in his chair, shaken by yet another surprise, but he gathered himself quickly. If there was anything he'd learned about himself lately, it was that he had a growing ability to flow with assaults upon his preconceptions and adapt quickly. He only wished the assaults were less frequent.

"Lieutenant Shinya," he said, "that's ... a generous offer. I'll take it under advisement. I suppose you heard what I said on the comm a while ago?" The prisoner nodded. "Then you understand we're in a tense situation for which there are no guidelines or regulations to refer to. Technically, you're a prisoner of war, and somewhere, I assume, that war still rages. It's my duty to present you to my superiors. Since I have no idea when or if that will ever occur ..." He spread his hands out on the table. "I'll consider it. I hope you won't find it inconvenient, at present, if you remain under the protection of Sergeant Alden?"

Matt heard Gray grumbling as they worked their way aft. He'd decided to take a quick walk around—and be seen doing it—and look at repairs while getting a feel for the mood of the crew. He also wanted to talk to Spanky. The engineer was the only department head who hadn't heard his comments in person. Gray continued to growl under his breath as they climbed into the open air on the main deck and stepped into the shade of the amidships deckhouse. Men formed a line leading to the open-air galley and snatched sandwiches from the counter as fast as the cooks put them down.

It was unbearably hot. That, at least, was the same. He changed direction and went back into the sun and stooped at the drinking fountain on the back of the big refrigerator next to the number one funnel. A stupid place for a refrigerator, he reflected again, but a great place for a drinking fountain. He pushed the button, and the cool stream rose to his lips. He drank, savoring the refrigerated water. Gray joined him.

"You seem annoyed, Boats," Matt observed without preamble.

"That Nip. You ain't gonna let him go, are you?"

"If he behaves, I might. Christ, we've got enough to worry about without guarding a Jap. He offered his parole."

"So? They were making all nice before they bombed Pearl too. We wouldn't *have* to guard him if—" Gray shifted uncomfortably and glanced around to make sure no one was within earshot. "We ought to just get rid of him. He's a Jap, for cryin' out loud!"

Matt looked at him. "Get rid of him? You mean kill him?" He shook his head and stared at his crew for a long time while they talked and ate their sandwiches. He sighed. "No. We won't. You know why? Because we're Americans and we don't do that." He was quiet a moment longer and then strode aft again. "Wherever we are, we're still Americans," Gray heard him mutter.

The sun had just touched the sea when Spanky McFarlane stepped toward the rail near the number two torpedo mount. For the first time since their run from Surabaya, the deck was almost deserted. It had been a hard day in more ways than one, and with the most critical repairs complete, it was as though the crew had breathed a collective sigh of relief and then just collapsed. The only men he saw nearby were Dennis Silva and some of his hoodlum friends in the ordnance division, talking on the amidships deckhouse. Spanky ignored them. It was a moral imperative. If he paid too much attention to what those jerks were up to, he'd probably have to put them on report.

He took a dingy rag from his pocket to wipe sweat and grunge from his eyes. They burned like hell. He pitched it into the churning wake that scoured the side of the ship. Was it just his imagination, or had something actually snapped at the rag as it fluttered to the surface? He sagged against the safety chain. *Starting to get jumpy,* he thought, and fumbled for his smokes. With the ease of a practiced hand, he lit one in spite of the breeze and inhaled deeply. Yeah, it had been a hell of a day.

They'd buried their dead in the time-honored fashion soon after the Skipper came to talk. All those men—nearly a quarter of the crew—slipping over the side as the captain gruffly read the prayer. Spanky shuddered, wondering how deep the shrouded corpses went before being shredded by the piranha-like fish that seemed to be everywhere. The Old Man was thinking ahead, though. Instead of the customary four-inch shell sewn into their fart-bags to carry them down, they'd been sent to their graves with whatever wreckage or heavy piece of debris Spanky thought they could spare.

That was what the captain came to talk about, to tell him to discard nothing that might have any conceivable use. So Spanky detailed some men to sort the scrap pile they'd started and find the most worthless junk. Then he checked it himself to make sure he couldn't think of any use for it either. Only then was it passed on—a piece of *Walker*—to accompany her dead sons. He snorted ironically. At least a few of the men went down with the customary projectile, even if they'd been Jap shells pried from *Walker*'s hull. He was glad the Skipper was starting to think about the long haul, though. He'd seemed kind of overwhelmed the night before—and that was before they saw the ship. His speech helped a lot, and it came at just the right time. Spanky suspected the Skipper needed to hear the words just as bad as the crew did.

The sun dipped below the horizon and it began to grow dark. At least the day hadn't been all bad, he reflected proudly. He didn't know what difference the strange creatures on the big ship might make, but after the shock wore off, the fascination and speculation among the crew had done much to take their minds off their troubles. Also, they'd managed to get the number two boiler back on line. There was no hope for number one.

The concussion had broken most of the firebricks. Besides, the lines and seals were shot, and he'd cannibalized it to revive number two.

He heard Silva's booming laugh and couldn't help but smile. It took more than a funeral and a battle and being transported to another world to get the big gunner's mate down. He could find humor in anything. For a moment, Spanky listened to the conversation. He couldn't help himself.

"I say they was more like monkeys than cats. Did you see them tails?" argued Tom Felts. "We ought'a call 'em monkey-cats!"

"Cats have tails too, you idiot," countered Paul Stites. "And their faces looked more like cats. Besides, 'cat-monkeys' sounds better."

"What do you think, Marvaney?" asked Felts of their friend, who stood by the rail above Spanky. Mack Marvaney only shrugged and stared into their wake. Felts started to ask again, but Silva rapped him on the shoulder with his knuckles and shook his head. Mack had a Filipino wife in Cavite. It was bad enough when they'd left the place to the Japs, but now . . . he was taking it hard.

"I have decided," Silva announced in a lofty tone that usually brooked no argument. "We'll call 'em monkey-cats!"

Stites, grateful that Silva had kept him from pestering their suffering friend, rounded. "Hell, Dennis, that's what the snipes are callin' 'em! We can't let that stand!"

"The snipes are callin' 'em monkey-cats?" asked Silva darkly. "Those bastards didn't even *see* 'em. They were all creepin' around belowdecks the whole time we were there. Hidin', I bet! Critters could'a looked like three-legged hippos for all they know." He brooded in silence for a while, then stepped next to Marvaney to spit over the rail. He glanced at him, then turned to face the others. "I have decided!" he repeated grandly. "From this point on, they're cat-monkeys! We discovered 'em. We'll call 'em what we want!"

Spanky shook his head, then sucked the rest of the cigarette to the tips of his fingers and flicked the butt into the sea. By tomorrow the whole crew would be locked in the "cat-monkey-cat" debate. Still smiling, he patted one of the empty torpedo tubes. Even with only three boilers, this tired, shot-up ship that he hated and loved so much was probably the fastest thing in the world, if all it had to offer was big lumbering tubs like they'd seen that morning. "There's humor for you."

For the next day and a half, *Walker* steamed east, searching for *Mahan*. The other destroyer hadn't had much head start and she wouldn't be making full steam. They should have caught her in a few hours, but so far there wasn't a trace. Everyone was worried, not only because of her damage but because she represented the only other thing in this very strange world that was familiar. That was as it should be. Besides, some of their own shipmates were aboard her.

Captain Reddy wearily climbed the ladder and returned to his chair. He waved the men back to their duties at the warning: "Captain on the bridge!" He hadn't been gone fifteen minutes. A rising tension knotted his chest, and though he thought he hid it well, his concern over *Mahan* was making him almost ill. He had a terrible choice to make.

The windows had been replaced, and once again he could look at the sea ahead without the wind stinging his eyes. Larry Dowden had the watch, but Matt couldn't stay off the bridge. He knew it looked bad, like he didn't trust Larry, but he'd hardly left at all except to go to the head.

"Report?"

"No contact, Skipper."

Matt nodded and resumed his silent brooding. They should have seen her. The weather was fine, the sky clear. The northeast tip of Alor Island was sharp and defined ten miles off the starboard beam. They'd reached the rally point. It had been agreed that they would meet here, or if *Walker* didn't make it *Mahan* would cut northeast around Wetar and drive south between Timor and Moa Island. *Walker* had cruised at twenty knots, but Matt was certain Jim wouldn't have pushed *Mahan* so hard. Even if he somehow beat them here, he would have lingered, and should have been visible on such a clear day. That left only the inescapable conclusion that she hadn't come this far. They must have passed her somehow, maybe in the dark, but she must be behind them. Unless something had happened to her.

That thought haunted him. It was his order that sent her away and led to this wasteful chase. He couldn't have known separation was unnecessary, but that did little to console him. Now the specter that haunted all destroyermen could no longer be avoided. *Walker*'s fuel bunkers were down by a third. He had no choice. He spoke with a heavy heart.

"Mr. Dowden, bring the ship about. Reduce speed to one-third."

Larry sighed. He knew how painful the order was. He wasn't sure he could have made it. Maybe the other ship really was behind them, but it felt too much like giving up.

"Aye, aye, sir. Helm, come left to a heading of two eight zero."

Matt stood and looked at his watch. "Pass the word, Mr. Dowden. All officers in the wardroom at 1630." He paused. "Better see that our 'guest' is moved elsewhere." He turned to leave the bridge but stopped. "I take that back. Have Sergeant Alden escort the enemy officer to the meeting." Dowden's eyebrows rose. "Also, ask Mr. Bradford if he'd be kind enough to join us."

"Aye, sir."

Cigarette smoke swirled and eddied in the breeze from the open portholes. The shell holes had finally been patched. Captain Reddy sat in his chair at the "head" of the table, all his surviving officers ranged down either side. The table was crowded, with representatives from each division. Larry Dowden, Chief Gray, Rick Tolson, Bernard Sandison, and PO Riggs sat on his left. On his right were Sandra Tucker, Spanky, Mr. Bradford, Garrett, and Lieutenant (j.g.) Alan Letts, the supply officer. The chair at the far end of the table was unoccupied. When Sergeant Alden escorted the Japanese officer into the compartment and seated him there, a hushed silence fell on the group.

Tamatsu sat with dignity, eyes fixed upon the captain. Alden leaned against the bulkhead behind his prisoner until Juan brought him a chair. He thanked the little Filipino and sat, his leg out in front of him. The room was charged with an electric hostility, and all eyes were on the enemy officer.

"This is Lieutenant Tamatsu Shinya. He's offered his parole and I've decided to accept, conditionally. He'll be treated with courtesy and allowed freedom of the ship—within reason. For now, however, he'll be accompanied at all times by Sergeant Alden. Sergeant? Is that acceptable to you?"

"Aye, aye, sir. There's not many places I can go now, though."

Matt nodded expressionlessly. "Lieutenant Shinya, allow me to present my officers." He named the others at the table, and they each acknowledged him with a nod, but most were clearly displeased. The reaction wasn't lost on the captain. "Gentlemen . . . and lady, Lieutenant Shinya's country and ours may still be at war—wherever they are—but that can no longer affect us. That's what we have to talk about. We must make plans based on the assumption that we're completely on our own and the United States Navy can't support us. At the same time, we must remain conscious of the fact that, no matter what, we're still part of that Navy. No relaxation of discipline will be tolerated, and there'll be no change whatever in the way we run this ship. Lieutenant Shinya is here because he is, literally, in the same boat we are and he is subject to the same rules and regulations as anyone else. There'll be no special treatment"—he looked at his officers with a grim expression—"or abuse. Mr. Dowden?"

"Uh, yes, sir?"

"Acquaint yourself with Lieutenant Shinya and discover if he has useful talents or abilities. One way or the other, find something for him to do. Everybody pulls their weight." He looked at Tamatsu. "Is that understood, Lieutenant? Those are my terms."

Shinya bowed his head slightly and replied. "I understand perfectly,

Captain Reddy." There were murmurs of surprise when he spoke English. Most still wore set, closed expressions, but a few looked thoughtful.

Matt plowed right on to divert attention from their visitor. "First, as I'm sure you're aware, we've turned around. We should have found *Mahan*, but we didn't, so either we passed her somehow or . . ." He cast a hard glance down both sides of the table. "Or she's lost. We'll search as we retrace our steps, but we don't have enough fuel to go all the way to Australia and back to Surabaya. Besides, I don't really think Perth's there anymore."

"You've considered the probability that Surabaya isn't there either?" questioned Bradford.

"Yes. In fact, I don't imagine it is. But we must have fuel. Whatever's happened to the world, the geography's the same—at least around here. Can you think of any better place to find oil within our range? To be more specific, since you're our expert on this point, where around here would we most likely find oil? Oil that we can easily extract?"

Bradford steepled his fingers and looked thoughtful. The pipe between his teeth wasn't lit, but he sucked it speculatively. "I'll have to consider that. There's oil in this entire region, but I'm not sure where best to look. Surabaya, perhaps. There were significant deposits there, in our world. Deposits have been discovered recently under Flores as well. Allow me to consult my manuals. Perhaps they will tell me where it was first found, and how. That might have a bearing on where to look."

"Very well," Matt replied. "See what you can find and let me know as soon as you can." He shifted his gaze to Lieutenant McFarlane. "What else can we burn in the boilers? Can we burn wood?"

Spanky returned his gaze with horror. "Jesus, Skipper! You can't put *wood* in my boilers! It would screw everything up!"

Matt looked at him sharply. "I know it's not our first choice, but can it physically be done?"

"Yes, sir . . ." answered the engineer reluctantly, "but it would be terrible. All that ash—it would be hell gettin' it all out and it would screw up the boilers. Besides, we'd have to carry tons of the stuff. We've got nowhere to stow it and if we load it on deck, we'll be top-heavy as hell—beggin' your pardon, sir."

"But it would work in an emergency? To get us from one island to the next?"

"It would," he answered miserably.

"Very well. Come up with a plan to stow enough wood to take us, say, five hundred miles, if the need should arise."

"Aye, sir."

The captain turned to Sandra Tucker, and involuntarily his expression softened. "Lieutenant Tucker. How are things in your department?"

Sandra smiled at the mention of "her department," which consisted of herself, Karen Theimer—the only other nurse who'd remained with *Walker*—and Jamie Miller, the pharmacist's mate. There was no question it was her department, though, and a critical one. "Improving, sir. I think Rodriguez might return to limited duty in a week or so. His leg is healing nicely." She looked down the table past Tamatsu and glowered at Sergeant Alden. "Speaking of legs, though, there are some people running around on them that shouldn't be." Alden pretended interest in something under the table. "The others should survive, but it'll take time. There're plenty of 'walking wounded' still on duty, but even if I tried to keep them in their bunks, I don't think I could." She looked straight into Matt's eyes and continued. "Right now, everyone's keyed up, with so much work just to keep the ship going. When the crisis is past, I expect a lot of casualties from exhaustion. The crew's burning itself up. Wearing out." Matt nodded back at her, realizing she was talking about him as much as anybody. She continued. "Actually, the only one I'm really worried about is Davis. He has a persistent fever, and no matter what I do, it just won't break."

"He was bitten by the lizard?"

Sandra nodded. "Mr. Bradford says they're septic but not poisonous. That may be, even though they weren't the same lizards he's familiar with. It looks like a really nasty bacterial infection, but there might be some kind of toxic venom as well." She shrugged.

"Keep me informed," Matt said solemnly, and she nodded. "Mr. Garrett. How about guns? Small arms too." Garrett frowned. "Is there a problem?" asked Matt. Garrett's cheeks turned red, and he shook his head quickly.

"No, sir, no problem. I—I was just surprised by the question about small arms. I don't have the exact numbers off the top of my head. No excuse, sir."

The captain allowed a genuine smile. "A general idea would suffice, Mr. Garrett. I understand you've been busy with the number three gun?"

"Yes, sir," Garrett replied, visibly relieved. "We got it working. The main problem was in the wiring, but there's damage to the traverse gear. I'd like to get it in the machine shop as soon as I can. It binds."

Matt looked at him thoughtfully, but shook his head. "Not right now. I don't want any of our weapons out of action. Besides"—he looked at Ensign Sandison—"the condemned torpedoes have priority in the machine shop, except for essential repairs. Until we know more about those people on the big ship, I'd like to be able to put holes in it if we have to."

Garrett glanced at Bernie and saw him write notes on a pad. He looked back at the captain. "Well, sir, other than that, the main battery's okay. Gunner's Mate Silva's overhauled the machine guns, as well as the three-incher on the fantail. The magazines could be better. We depleted over a third of our four-inch fifty, and three-inch twenty-three point five—for all the good it did!" The uselessness of the three-inch gun at the stern would have been a running joke—if it were funny. "We picked up a lot of machine gun ammo in Surabaya, but those trigger-happy goons burned through nearly all the extra. We still have a little more than our full allotment, but . . ." He took a deep breath. "As for small arms, I don't have exact numbers," he repeated apologetically, "but we're in fairly good shape. It's not unusual for Asiatic Fleet sailors to act as Marines—particularly in China, and the armory's got sixty Springfields, and probably two dozen 1911 pistols. We also have four Browning automatic rifles and half a dozen Thompsons. The ammunition headstamps are pretty old—1918—but the stuff looks okay. There's even a few thousand rounds of the old thirty U.S., which is good, because there're several crates, down under everything, that say they have Krag rifles in them. Maybe somebody picked them up in the Philippines?"

Gray grunted. "I doubt it. *Walker* was commissioned in 1919, and a lot of Krags were still in the Navy. I bet they came with the ship. Probably never been out of their crates."

Matt nodded. "Look into it. Anything else?"

"Aye, aye, sir. No, sir."

"Very well. Sparks? Does the communications division have anything new?" Matt knew it didn't. He'd asked Riggs several times that day and left standing orders that if they received anything at all, he was to be informed at once.

Riggs shook his head. "Nothing, Skipper. The equipment's operating perfectly. Everything checks out. There just isn't anything to hear." Everyone already knew it, but to hear him say it again only deepened the gloom.

Matt sensed the darkening mood and pushed quickly on. As he often did, he turned to the Chief to boost morale. "Any major holes left, Boats?"

"Nothing you'd call *major*," he replied with a hesitant grin. "The old gal's always leaked like a sieve. No matter how many holes we patch, she was riveted together, and there's probably not a seam in her bottom that doesn't seep, but damage control's done a hell of a job." He glanced at McFarlane and grinned even bigger. "Apes and snipes been working together so well, it ain't natural. We haven't patched holes in the funnels and such, but everything that'll let water in has something welded over it."

McFarlane nodded. "She'll float, Skipper, and as long as we have power to the pumps I'll keep her pretty dry." He looked around the table. "She needs a yard, though." There were grim nods.

"We know, Spanky," said the captain quietly. "Anything else on your end?"

McFarlane shook his head, conscious that he'd lowered everyone's spirits again. "Uh . . . no, sir, not really. I was thinkin', though. As long as we're trying to conserve, we might want to figure out more ways to do it. Like, we might have the apes leave off chippin' and paintin' until we figure out what to use for paint when we're out. That sort of stuff."

Gray started to protest that if his holy deck wasn't maintained in these tropical waters, there'd soon be no deck to maintain. But you couldn't use what you didn't have. "Spanky's right," he admitted grudgingly. "I know how the apes'll moan if they can't perform their favorite pastime." He grinned encouragingly and there were scattered chuckles. "But we have only so much paint. I have to paint the welds, but maybe we can let the cosmetic stuff slide."

"That's a good point," said Matt. He turned at last to the supply officer, Alan Letts. Letts was a skinny kid from North Dakota with red hair and extremely fair skin, complete with freckles. He hated the sun, and even brief exposure left him resembling a radish. He was rarely seen above deck, and then only in the shadows, as if direct sunlight would melt him down to a puddle of wax. His sincere antics to avoid sunlight were vastly amusing to the crew, and he was very popular. He was a good sport too, and no matter how sensitive, his skin was also thick. Sometimes, in a spirit of fun, he allowed sailors to escort him around the ship with a Chinese parasol. Despite his efforts, even as he sat in the wardroom, great patches of chalky skin dangled from his face and arms and small specks had settled to the table. He was a good supply officer and knew all the bureaucratic angles, but those no longer applied. His greatest flaw, from Matt's perspective, was a complacent laziness. He suffered from the endemic Asiatic Fleet disease of "go with the flow." Matt hoped he could make the transition to the new imperative.

"How does it look for supplies?" the captain asked.

"We'll be okay for a while. We loaded up before we left Surabaya. Nobody wanted to leave anything for the Japs." Letts's eyes flicked toward their guest. "At present consumption, meaning normal, we've got three weeks, easy, before we feel any pinch on perishables. The refrigerator's stocked up. After that, we have canned stuff for about that long." He grimaced. "I'm not counting Vienna sausages. We better find something else before we're down to that, or there'll be mutiny in the chow line." He brightened. "Even if we don't cut back, we're in good shape food-wise for a month, month and a half."

"We can't cut rations," pronounced Matt decisively, "not as hard as the men are working. Besides, that'd really wreck morale. We'll just have to find food." He looked at Courtney Bradford, and his eyes twinkled. "I wonder what dinosaur steak tastes like?" There was general laughter at Bradford's incredulous expression.

"Eat dinosaurs? My God. The man's talking about eating dinosaurs!" the Australian muttered to himself.

Matt returned to Letts. "Fresh water?"

Walker's boilers were an open feed-water design, so they used seawater for steam, but the crew needed fresh water for cooking and drinking. The storage tanks were small and, even in normal times, bathing was a luxury. The men often lined up naked by the rail for a good spray-down with the fire hose. The salt water drove them nuts when it dried and caused rashes and other discomforts, but it was refreshing.

"Water's a problem," admitted Letts. "With the condensers in the shape they are, we have about a month's worth, at current usage."

"Okay. So we need fuel, ammo, food, water." The captain arched an eyebrow at Gray. "And paint." There were more chuckles despite the fact that no one knew where to find any of those things. "What else?"

"About a million things, Skipper," Letts replied, "but those are the most immediate. I'm sure Lieutenant McFarlane could add quite a list of spares, but—"

"Right. Make a list of everything we need, but more importantly, figure out how we're going to get it. Use anybody you need, but find answers." Matt swiveled in his chair to look at Courtney Bradford. "Would you mind being conscripted?"

The Australian took his pipe from his mouth and his eyes widened with pleasure. "Delighted, Captain! Delighted. How can I assist?"

"Work with Letts to sort this out. You'll be his special assistant. I know this isn't the same world you were such a student of, but you must have a better idea where we can find supplies than any of us do. Agreed?"

"Absolutely, Captain Reddy. I'll do my best!"

"Of course you will."

Matt glanced at Sandra when he said it, and saw the twinkle of amusement in her eyes. He smiled at her. He was pleased. All in all, the discussion had gone fairly well. His people were engaged, and actively working to solve problems. Morale was better than he would have expected, and the crushing terror of their situation was kept at bay—for now—by a veneer of normalcy. The tasks were unusual, but the familiarity of doing them within the extended family that was the crew of USS *Walker* was reassuring.

Throughout the conversation, Lieutenant Shinya was silent. After the initial hostility, he seemed to have been forgotten, and he just listened. He was amazed by the familiarity with which the Americans talked and worked together. No one was afraid to speak, not even the most junior person present. It seemed chaotic compared to his more-regimented experience, but it also appeared effective. There was no hiding the fact that they were in a predicament, but there was no hesitation to mention failings that might reflect poorly on any department. That made it easier for the captain to assess the situation. He doubted a similar meeting aboard his own ship would have progressed as well, and he felt strangely refreshed.

Just then, Juan entered the compartment with his carafe and began filling cups. He paused by Tamatsu. His face bore a look of anguished loathing, and Shinya was reminded that, no matter what, he was still considered an enemy. Juan took a deep breath and started to tilt the carafe. It began to shake. Suddenly he slammed it on the table as if the handle was too hot to hold. He looked at Matt in horror.

"I—I am sorry, Cap-tan Reddy," he whispered. "I cannot." He then drew himself up and strode through the curtain into the passageway. Everyone watched him go, except Tamatsu, who continued to stare straight ahead, but his gaze seemed somewhat lower. Matt sighed. Nothing was going to be easy.

Walker steamed leisurely in a west-northwesterly direction for the remainder of the day, back across the Flores Sea into the Java Sea once more. The sea picked up toward evening, and a gloomy overcast obscured the growing moon. Matt ordered the running lights lit—unthinkable just days before—and stationed men on the two searchlights. They were to sweep the horizon at ten-minute intervals, both to show the lights and to see what they could. The ship began to roll as the swell increased just enough to remind everyone that regardless of war, dinosaurs, sea monsters, or even strange beings on giant ships, ultimately, *Walker*'s greatest adversary was the very element for which she was made.

By 2200 that night, halfway through the first watch, she began to pitch as the sea ran higher. Matt was dead to the world, on the bunk in his small stateroom. *Walker*'s antics didn't disturb him in the least; he was used to them, and after everything else, the normal, unpleasant motion of the ship was even soothing in a way. When he finally surrendered completely to sleep, in his cabin for the first time in days, he found a depth of untroubled slumber that even the ghosts couldn't sound. So when they hit the fish and he was nearly thrown to the deck, it almost didn't wake him.

The small light over his desk was still vibrating when he looked at it, confused. The speaker above his pillow squawked in Lieutenant Garrett's urgent voice. "Captain! Captain to the bridge, sir. Please." He coughed and cleared his throat, then pushed the comm button. "On my way." He slung his legs over the side of the rack and yanked on his trousers and shoes. Pulling on his shirt and plopping his hat on his head, he hurried down the short corridor to the companionway and scrambled up the ladder. In the shelter by the radio shack, he finished buttoning his shirt and mounted the stairway to the pilothouse. The blowers had abated, and the way the ship rolled even more sickeningly told him the engines had stopped.

"Report!" he demanded. Garrett stood on the starboard bridgewing staring down at the water. The wind had picked up and he'd been drenched by spray. He turned. "Sorry to wake you, sir, but we hit a whale, or fish—or something. It looks like the one that ate the Japs. Down here, sir." He pointed and Matt peered over the rail. The searchlight above them couldn't depress far enough to directly illuminate the creature, but the diffused light was sufficient for him to see it clearly.

Walker broached to in the moderate swell when the engines stopped, and the giant "fish" wallowed and bumped against the hull in her lee. Garrett was right. It looked like the one they'd seen previously, although not as large. Every now and then, the waves caused its great head to rise, and the long, slack jaws were frighteningly clear. A large black eye the size of a trash-can lid stared sightlessly up at them. The cause of death was a huge gash behind its head, and the water was tinged black with blood as it washed from the wound. Sandra Tucker, her hair disheveled, appeared beside him, rubbing her eyes.

"It's horrible," she said. Excited voices came from the main deck below as destroyermen gathered to gawk. Bradford joined them and his voice rose above the others.

"Amazing! We simply must keep it! You there! Find something to tie onto it!" Matt heard one of his crew shout, "Bugger off, mate!" in a fair copy of the Australian's accent.

"Damage?" he asked.

"A lot of broken coffee cups," Garrett answered nervously. "That's all I know so far. The exec took Bosun's Mate Bashear to have a look. Lieutenant McFarlane and the Bosun said they'd meet them there."

The comm on the bulkhead whistled and Matt picked it up himself. "Bridge," he said. "Captain speaking."

"McFarlane here, Skipper. There's a little water coming in on the starboard side around frame number six. Nothing serious . . . just another seam." Spanky's voice was thick. He too had finally been asleep.

"Good. Can the current watch handle it?"

There was a pause before Spanky's voice returned. "Yes, sir. I think so."

"Then you and Boats hit the rack. That's an order."

"Aye, aye, Skipper," came the tired reply. Matt stepped to the rail with a soft sigh of relief. Sandra was still there. She'd overheard.

"Thank God," she murmured. "It may sound strange, but every time this ship gets the slightest scratch, I feel it in my own skin."

Matt grinned. "I know how you feel. When I first assumed command,

I honestly didn't think much of her. But now, after all she's been through . . ." He shrugged, and gestured at the dead fish. It had floated off a dozen yards or so. "Of course, her thin old skin's the only thing between us and those things. That tends to focus your appreciation amazingly." He chuckled, and after a brief hesitation, she joined him. They felt a faint, shuddering vibration under their feet, and another huge fish, probably two-thirds as long as *Walker*, rose beside the ship. It must have scraped her bottom as it passed. Without hesitation, it lunged at its dead cousin and snatched an enormous swath of flesh. Bright bone and white blubber lay exposed and more blood clouded the water. Silvery flashes began to reflect the searchlight's beam. With a startled cry, Sandra clutched his arm.

"Mr. Garrett! Let's leave our dinner guest to his meal before he samples the side dish, if you please!"

The blower wound up. A flying packet of spray struck Matt and Sandra and soaked them both. The water had an unusual taste and Matt realized it must be blood. He spat, then looked at Sandra apologetically and cleared his throat.

"Excuse me, ma'am," he said in a wry tone. "Got a bad taste in my mouth."

He glanced down at the main deck, where Bradford was watching the huge fish devour the smaller one with rapt fascination. He seemed oblivious to the spray that inundated him and swirled around his feet. Another form stood near him at a respectful distance, and the captain recognized Shinya in the gloom. He was watching as well, but his expression was entirely different. Matt wondered vaguely where Sergeant Alden was, but decided it didn't matter. Any mischief the Jap could cause was dwarfed by the perils all around them, and judging by his expression, the last thing Shinya wanted was to wind up in the water again.

Matt looked at the woman at his side. Her teeth were beginning to chatter from the wind on her damp clothes. Her long brownish hair hung down in wet tangles, but her eyes were wide and bright. He couldn't decide if it was fear he saw or fascination akin to Bradford's. He felt a chill himself and shuddered involuntarily. "Why don't we go down to the wardroom and dry off?" he suggested.

Gunner's Mate Dennis Silva sat on one of the "seats of ease" in the aft crew's head smoking a cigarette. He still didn't like the damn things, but he had only so much chewing tobacco and a man had to have his nicotine. The seats were little more than boards across a trough through which sea water flowed. The compartment stank of waste and sweat, and with the sea getting up, dark, nasty water sloshed back and forth on deck. Every time the brackish wave threatened him, Dennis raised his feet until it passed.

The aft crew's head was generally considered snipe country, and that was the main reason he went there to relieve himself. Just to aggravate the snipes. No one made a real issue of it because, for one thing, it didn't *exactly* belong to the engineering division and, for another, Silva was a big, powerful man who in spite of an easygoing nature had a dangerous reputation. Proprietary claims to the heads were even more ridiculous, at least to the outside observer, because only a single bulkhead separated them and both were located in the aft deckhouse, behind the laundry and torpedo workshop. That didn't make trespass less serious in the eyes of the crew, however. So naturally, Dennis Silva sat and smoked while men came and went and attended to their business on the other seats nearby. No one spoke to him, but they gave him many dark looks indeed.

Stites, Felts, and a torpedoman named Brian Aubrey found him there. They clustered around the hatchway as if reluctant to cross the threshold and braced themselves against the motion of the ship. "There you are!" exclaimed Stites. "You missed it. We ran smack into one of them big dinosaur fish, like ate the Japs, and killed it deader'n hell!"

"Good," muttered Silva. "It's time we killed somethin'."

"Yeah," added Tom, "and then a even bigger one took to eating the first one just like that!" He snapped his fingers. "It was something to see, and here you was all the time, in the snipes' crapper!"

Silva glanced disdainfully at the two snipes sharing the compartment. "This ain't the snipes' crapper," he said very slowly and distinctly. "It's Dennis Silva's crapper when Dennis Silva's takin' a crap!"

One of the "snipes" was Machinist's Mate Dean Laney, two seats down from Silva. He was nearly as tall as the big gunner's mate, and just as powerfully built. "You better watch your mouth," he growled. "You damn deck-apes don't belong here."

Silva sucked his cigarette and looked at him. "What are you gonna do, go whinin' to Spanky or Chief Donaghey and tell 'em I'm using your crapper?" He raised his voice to a high-pitched falsetto. "Lieutenant Spanky! Dennis Silva's in our crapper! And—he's takin' a crap! Do somethin'! Make him stop!"

Laney lunged to his feet with a curse and Dennis rose to meet him, both with their trousers around their ankles. Just then, the ship heaved unexpectedly and the combatants lost their balance and fell to the deck in a tangled, punching heap. They slid against the bulkhead in the disgusting ooze and just as quickly as the fight had begun, it ended as the men considered their battlefield. Dennis began to laugh. Laney didn't. He put his right hand on the seat nearest him and started to rise, but realized the seat was the red one—reserved for men with venereal disease. He snatched his hand away and splashed to the deck with a cry just as the ship pitched upward and the tide of muck flowed around him. Dennis laughed even harder and rose to his feet, pulling up his ruined trousers. He reached down to give Laney a hand, but suddenly stepped back.

"The hell with you, Laney! You want me catch it too?" He wiped his hands on his soiled trousers and, on second thought, rinsed them in the long sink across the compartment. He posed for a moment in front of the mirror, powerful muscles bulging across his chest and biceps. Then he relaxed and looked at his clothes. "Damn. Snipe shit all over me. I'll have to burn these duds and who knows when I'll get more?" He looked back at Laney, who was at least as filthy as he. The other snipe was still seated and had ignored the whole thing. "C'mon, Laney. Why don't you have a cup of coffee with some real live destroyermen? Someday you'll tell your grand-kids."

"Go to hell," Laney said, but he rinsed himself as best he could and followed through the laundry where they replaced their T-shirts. They exited on the deck behind the number three torpedo mount. The sea was heavier now, and the deck twisted beneath their feet like a live thing as they lurched forward, leaning into the spray. Above their heads, on the searchlight tower, the beam swept slowly back and forth, a beacon for their absent sister. Finally, they reached the protection of the gun platform that served as a roof for the galley. There were several men standing in line with cups and the galley hatch was up. They were waiting while the cook and his mess attendant filled the big coffee urn with a new batch. They grabbed cups and took their place in line.

"Hey, Earl," Dennis said to the cook, shouting over the churning sea, "you got anything besides peanut butter sammiches and scum weenies?"

Earl Lanier shook his head mournfully. "Sorry, fellas. Can't cook with the sea kickin' up. Hard enough just to make coffee. Got some cold beans, though."

"Scum weenies in 'em?"

"Yep."

Silva grimaced. "No thanks. Say, you got any of them apples left?" Again Earl shook his head.

"Juan says the rest of them apples are for the officers," said Ray Mertz, the mess attendant.

"Well, who's in charge here, Earl? You or Juan?" demanded Dennis as it came his turn and he filled his cup.

"I am, damn you. But Juan got them apples hisself for the officers' mess. You're just lucky he shared some out."

"Officers," grunted Stites, as if the word was a self-explanatory curse. Silva nodded, as he was expected to, but without much conviction. He normally didn't have much use for officers either, but he figured they could've done worse under the circumstances. Their officers sure had their work cut out for them. All their lives were in the officers' hands and he didn't envy them the responsibility.

"Still got some pickles left," offered Mertz. Dennis started to refuse, but then reconsidered. If things were as bad as he suspected, there was no telling when he'd taste a pickle again. Much less an apple. There might come a day when he'd dream about that last pickle he'd turned down.

"Sure, Ray. Gimme one."

Felts jabbed Laney with his elbow and motioned around the corner of the galley at a figure by the starboard rail, staring at the heaving sea. "Hey, snipe, lookie there," he said in a grim tone. "That's that Nip officer! What the hell's he doin' on the loose?" Laney's eyes widened.

"I'll be damned! You 'apes sure ain't particular about the company you keep!" Angry faces turned to the machinist's mate, but they looked guiltily uncertain that he might be right.

"Yeah, what's up, Silva?" demanded Stites. "You're tight with the Chief. What's he think about lettin' Nips run all over the ship? I think we ought'a pitch the bastard over the side."

Silva munched his pickle and looked from one to the other. "Gray don't like it, and I don't either, but leave him be. Captain's orders. He's on parole, or somethin'." He shook his head. "Whatever the hell that means. I don't reckon them Jap bastards paroled them boys on Wake." They were silent a moment, watching the shape as it left the rail and disappeared down the companionway. "'Sides," Silva added gruffly, "he's prob'ly the only fella in the whole wide world lonesomer than we are right now."

Spanky sat hunched in his favorite chair near the throttle-control station, his second-favorite mug clutched tightly in both hands between his knees. It was a big ceramic mug that held twice as much coffee as was generally considered right. On one side was a stylized view of Oahu from the air, and on the other was a raised-relief sculpture of a virtually nude hula girl reclined provocatively on a Chevrolet emblem. His very favorite mug with the totally nude *pair* of hula girls had been destroyed, and he wasn't going to let anything happen to this one. He raised it carefully to his lips and took a sip as he listened to the sounds of the ship laboring in the moderate seas.

Over the years, he'd grown used to the noises she made and prided himself on his ability to diagnose problems just by sound or "feel." After all the damage and repairs she'd undergone, *Walker* moaned with all sorts of new sounds and resonated with many feels he wasn't accustomed to, and he felt disoriented as he tried to identify and categorize them all. He shuddered to think of the stopgaps and jury-rigged repairs he'd performed, and he was secretly amazed that the ship was still afloat, much less under way. He grimaced at the thought of how they might have to stay that way. Wood in the boilers! That would finish them off. The thing was, if they were down to burning wood, that meant they had nothing else, so with a bleak but philosophical grunt, he resigned himself to the possibility.

He was supposed to sleep. The captain had actually ordered him to, but he couldn't escape the premonition that something would come disastrously unwrapped as soon as he did. Besides, while he worked he didn't have to think about the dark, looming scope of their situation. It was finally starting to hit the crew. There were several guys hanging out near the throttle station now, talking about just that. He listened only halfway, but for the first time really, he noticed an edge of fear.

He rubbed his tired eyes and looked up to see two pale faces peering at him from the gloom. He was a little startled, since he hadn't known the Mice were there. As usual, they ignored the conversation flowing around them. He sighed.

"What are you doing up? This ain't your watch. Get some sleep."

Gilbert blinked at him and looked around the compartment. The other men were arguing about the creatures on the big ship again. His gaze returned to Spanky.

"We seen a dinosaur before," he said in a conspiratorial voice. "Me and Isak. We seen one in New York, in a big museum, on liberty a few years back."

McFarlane's eyebrows rose at the non sequitur. "That so?" he managed.

Isak nodded grimly. "God's truth. Course they was all bones. There was more than one, but one looked sorta like those we saw on Bali the other day, only the one in New York was bigger." They paused and looked at him expectantly, as if waiting for him to comment. He just stared, baffled by their train of thought. Gilbert got impatient and spoke again. "Oil's made out of dinosaurs, they say. A long time ago a bunch of dinosaurs died and took to festerin', just like a dead cow, and all that old black ooze seeped into the ground and turned into oil. 'Least, that's what they say."

"Stands to reason," said Isak. "If oil ain't made out'a dinosaurs, why would Sinclair have one on their sign?" He paused thoughtfully. "Which them little dinosaurs on Bali looked a lot like the one on the Sinclair sign, 'cept they weren't green."

McFarlane's eyebrows had risen as far as they could go. He was way too tired for this. "Boys," he began, but Gilbert actually interrupted him.

"Beggin' your pardon, sir, but that got us thinkin'. We was both wild-catters when we was kids. Oklahoma, Texas, Colorado, Wyoming . . . We brought in a lot of wells before we got in the Navy."

"We didn't like it, though, neither of us. Too much damn sun and dust—and heat too, but heat ain't all that bad. That's why we got in the Navy, though," put in Isak, and what passed for a tentative smile crossed his face. "We know a thing or two about heavy machinery, but we like burnin' oil better'n findin' it."

Gilbert looked at his partner with an air of bitter resignation, but nodded agreement. "We got to thinkin'. If things is like they say, then if we're gonna keep our boilers fed with oil, I guess we'll have to drill for it." Gilbert took a breath. "We know how, and if that's what it takes, well . . . we know how."

Spanky looked at them with surprise and then slowly nodded. "Thanks, boys. I'll remember that."

Matt and Sandra dried their hair with towels from the officers' head. Matt's hair took only an instant, short as it was, and he watched Sandra, drying and brushing her long, almost-brass-colored strands. He'd known she was attractive, but at that moment, arms over her head, wet blouse tout against her bosom, she was the prettiest woman he'd ever seen and he resisted an electric urge to take the brush himself. Suddenly he realized she'd caught him staring and his ears burned. The expression on her face was . . . what? Fortunately, just then Bradford swept into the wardroom. He was still excited about what they'd seen.

"Amazing! Such jaws! I'm certain you're thankful we didn't hit the larger one, Captain Reddy! Of course you are!"

"I think we should all be thankful for that, Mr. Bradford," Matt replied, both grateful and resentful of the intrusion.

Bradford looked quizzically from one to the other, for the first time sensing tension between them, and attempted to quell his enthusiasm. "Quite so. Forgive me. I do get carried away. I've not forgotten the seriousness of the situation. In fact, it's been foremost on my mind. I've done a bit of preliminary research—oh, for my office library!—and I may have a few helpful suggestions for your Mr. Letts tomorrow."

"I'm glad to hear it."

"Yes. Bear in mind, however, anything I suggest is qualified by the assumption that we are, well, where we were, for lack of any better way to phrase it."

"I think you may safely assume that, Mr. Bradford," said Matt. "Our charts of this area are pathetic. Some actually date from the eighteenth century. Depths were all wrong even before . . . Anyway, I don't think there's ever been a proper survey unless the Dutch did one. That being said, there's enough agreement over landmarks and positions that we know to be accurate that I don't think there's any question we are, as you put it, where we were."

Sandra set the brush on the table and ran her fingers through her still-damp hair. She spoke for the first time and her lip quivered slightly. "That still leaves the question we've all been avoiding." There was a trace of bitterness in her voice. "What happened? I wish someone would think of something, even if it's wrong. It's driving me nuts, and I'm coping well compared to some. Ensign Theimer won't even come out of the cabin. Nobody wants to talk about it! I know everyone's afraid"—she looked at Matt with eyes reflecting a strange mix of accusation, respect . . . and something else—"even you, Captain. But everyone just keeps going as if nothing unusual's happened at all."

Matt smiled a sad, gentle smile. "Thank God they do, Lieutenant Tucker. You're right. We are scared. And between the three of us in this room," he confessed woodenly, "I'm more scared than anybody. But we'll continue to do our duty because we *have* to. It's all we've got to hang on to and it's our only hope to survive."

Bradford shifted uncomfortably and Sandra covered her face with her hands for a moment, but nodded. "Of course, Captain. I'm sorry. I'm just . . . tired." She looked up and her eyes were rimmed with red. "This crew—everyone—is exhausted, but I've just about emptied the dispensary of sleeping pills."

Matt's eyes narrowed, but she quickly dispelled his concern with a flick of her wrist, and the corner of her mouth quirked upward. "Oh, don't worry. There weren't many on board to start with and it's not an epidemic. I made it sound worse than it is. If the truth were known, half these guys would conk out if you gave them a chair to sit on in front of a firing squad." She shook her head with genuine admiration. "It beats me how most stay so calm." She frowned. "Not all have, though, and some you'd think have dealt with it really haven't." She sighed. "Like me, I guess. It's like a nightmare, or some H. G. Wells or Sir Arthur Conan Doyle novel."

"Well," said Matt, "since the charts are correct, that eliminates *The Time Machine*, according to you, Mr. Bradford. Also, there's the matter of furry people with tails on ships bigger than the *Hornet*. That leaves *The Lost World* our most likely scenario." Sandra looked at him, surprised that he'd read those works.

"Actually," said Courtney Bradford, "I think you're both wrong."

"So what do you think?" asked Matt with a half smile.

Bradford looked solemn. "I don't know yet. I expect an epiphany once we've done more than just sail about. The water looks quite the same as before, you know." There was a hint of accusation in his tone.

"Quite the same except for the fish," said Sandra dryly.

Bradford bowed his head to her, conceding the point. "Indeed." He paused and looked down at the table, then glanced at them both. "Have you ever considered how your life might have been if you'd done something different? What a monumental impact some choice or deed can have on the rest of your life? Captain, what if you hadn't joined the Navy? What would you be like today? Would you even be the same person? Some people think, if they think about it at all, that they'd be the same, just doing something different. I disagree. I believe it's our actions, as well as the context and environment in which those actions take place, that make us what we are. But what if? What if your mother had never met your father? Your grandmother, your grandfather? What if the United States had lost its revolutionary war? What if the Roman Empire had never fallen—or never existed? What would the world be like today? Would it be much the same, except for that one small thing?"

Neither Matt nor Sandra answered. Matt just looked at him with a tired, speculative expression. Sandra's face wore no expression at all, but the clenching muscles in her jaw betrayed a growing tension.

"I think the world would be entirely different," Bradford continued quietly, "and the more distance between the moment of change and the present, the more profound the differences would be."

"I've . . . studied history a little," Matt said self-consciously. "I've often wondered 'what if' about a lot of things. I suppose every historian does, whether they admit it or not. What if the South had won the Battle of Gettysburg, for example, or that Serb hadn't shot the archduke of Austria? Things might've been different. Maybe a lot different." He looked at the Australian. "What's that got to do with anything?"

"Maybe nothing," said Courtney Bradford in a cryptic, falsely cheerful tone. "Maybe everything."

The sun rose sharp and fierce in a cloudless sky. The storm, if it could be called that, was over, leaving only a slight chop as *Walker* eased back into the gap between Bali and Menjangan Island. All through the night they'd searched but found no sign of *Mahan,* and everyone harbored a forlorn hope they'd find her where they left her. Matt considered it possible, even likely, that if Jim couldn't nurse his ship all the way to their rendezvous, he'd bring her back here, thinking it the first place Matt would look. Unfortunately, when they cleared the shoals and nosed into their previous anchorage, they were disappointed.

Bali remained a clear reminder that they were lost to the world they knew, its shores still teeming with unlikely creatures and its unterraced coastline a vast, panoramic plain broken by copses of unfamiliar palmlike trees. Again the crew lined the rails to stare. Unlike the sea—normally a destroyerman's natural element, but now one that inspired dread—the land seemed populated by comparatively pastoral creatures. They all remembered

the lizard that bit Leo Davis and made him so sick, but that was on Menjangan Island. Maybe they weren't on Bali. The pygmy "brontosauruses"
and other apparent herbivores browsed, cowlike, in full view and in broad
daylight, seemingly content and unafraid of predators.

They crept closer. The outdated charts showed plenty of water, but
Matt figured two hundred yards was close enough, and they dropped the
hook once more. He peered at the shore and Courtney Bradford already
had his "own" binoculars up. Matt wasn't sure whose they'd originally been,
but possession being what it was, he doubted the owner would get them
back. He shook his head with a little grin.

"Lieutenant Dowden, you have the deck. We'll remain here for the
day and hopefully *Mahan*'ll show up. Double lookouts at all times. I'm not
really worried about Japs anymore, but anchored, we can't maneuver. I
think we've had enough surprises for a while. In the meantime, you'll plot
a course for Surabaya. If *Mahan* doesn't show by dusk, we'll proceed there."
He looked at Bradford and saw the desolate expression. His grin returned.
"Mr. Bradford, Mr. Letts, and a small party will accompany me ashore.
Have Campeti break out Springfields, sidearms, and ammunition for a
party of eight. Hmm, better make that ten pistols, and throw in a tommy
gun and one of the BARs. We'll leave two men and the Thompson with
the boat."

He studied the contrast between Bradford's excited happiness and
Lieutenant Dowden's horror. He chuckled. "Don't worry, Larry, we won't
wander off. In fact, I don't intend to leave sight of the ship. It's time we saw
face-to-face what we're up against. But if we get in over our heads, be
ready to blow the hell out of anything we can't handle. Understood?"

Dowden swallowed. "Yes, sir. Aye, aye, sir."

Silva hefted a BAR and a bandolier of ammunition. He flashed his friends
a toothy grin. "I'm goin' a'huntin'!" he said as he took his place with the other
members of the shore party, climbing down into the whaleboat. They were
Carl Bashear, Mack Marvaney, Glen Carter, and Alfred Vernon. Tony Scott
and Fred Reynolds would remain with the boat on the beach. They were in
it now, waiting for the others. Silva watched Marvaney climb down ahead
of him. His expression was wooden, almost vacant. "Cheer up, Mack!" he
said. "It'll be a hoot!" Marvaney glanced up at him and smiled, but the
expression never reached his eyes.

Reynolds stood in the bow with his Springfield at the ready, and Scott
fiddled with the throttle, a Thompson slung on his shoulder. Blue smoke
rose from the idling motor as one by one the party descended the rungs
welded to the side of the ship. The captain went last and he paused before

he did, looking briefly at the faces nearby. Lieutenant Garrett wore an anxious expression, and Matt winked.

"You and Larry take care of my ship, hear?" His eyes flicked toward number three. It was manned, and already trained to port. Stites was its captain and he met Matt's gaze with a confident nod. He nodded back and looked at Garrett. "Carry on, Lieutenant," he said and disappeared over the side. As soon as he stepped into the boat and found a seat, Scott advanced the throttle. With a gurgling rumble they left *Walker*'s comforting side and steered for the mysterious shore.

Immediately, they felt the bumping, and several men exchanged nervous glances. Even Silva gave a start when something hit the hull under his foot. They knew it must be the vicious silvery fish—or something like them—but fortunately nothing bigger saw fit to taste the boat. In spite of the heat, gooseflesh crept along Matt's arms at the very thought of falling overboard. The memory of the feeding frenzy for the shipwrecked Japanese was vivid.

There was a breeze out of the south-southwest and the sea was still choppy. Little packets of spray misted them as they neared land. The sky was almost painfully bright and clear, and its contrast with the shoaling water became less and less distinct. The greens of vegetation were more or less as they should have been and the sun was as bright and hot as always. Letts tried to keep his lotion-smeared skin under the shade of a wide straw hat. The normalcy of the scene only accentuated the striking abnormality of their situation and the impossible creatures grazing along on the coastal plain ahead.

There were no breakers, only a gentle surf washing onto a beach of gray-black volcanic gravel. The bumping subsided and then stopped completely a few dozen yards from shore. All the same, no one was anxious to step into the water, regardless how shallow. Scott skillfully nosed the whaleboat through the surf until they felt a crunchy resistance as it slid to a stop. For a moment everyone looked at the few yards of water between them and land. They could actually see the bottom, but there was nervous hesitation all the same. With a short bark of a laugh, Silva hitched up his gun belt and hopped over the side. The other men sheepishly did the same and Matt stepped up through the empty seats, jumped out into the shallow surf, and waded ashore with outward unconcern. Letts and Marvaney brought up the rear. Reynolds and Scott carried a line and began looking for something to tie it to.

"You men stay here," said the captain. "Keep a sharp lookout and don't goof around. We won't be far and if we hear you shoot, we'll come running. If you have to, cut your cable and clear off the beach, but hang close enough to come back for us. If you hear us shoot, stay here and prepare to shove off. Understood?"

"Aye, aye, sir," they answered in unison.

Bradford was already hurrying excitedly away from the beach with a couple of hesitant men behind. Matt sighed and raised his voice. "We'll all stick together, if you please!"

They marched inland in a loose column of twos, watching their flanks with care. Matt had grown up around weapons and had hunted all his life, so the Springfield he carried was a familiar and welcome companion. Especially now. He and Bradford walked side by side at the front of the column, looking at their surroundings. The grass was deep, waist high in places, and the broad, spiny leaves reminded Matt of johnsongrass. There were no brambles or thorns or such, but the grass was distinctly uncomfortable to walk through. *Maybe more like South Texas cordgrass*, he thought. Ahead was the first herd of the animals that looked like brontosauruses. They fed on the leaves of strange-looking palms that stood in a large clump. The way they moved and the sounds they made seemed entirely appropriate and very elephantlike. Any similarity ended there. Their necks were as long as their bodies, and they stood stripping vegetation much higher than any elephant ever could have.

There were about a dozen of the animals of all sizes in the group, and as the men drew nearer, they paid them no heed. The shore party slowed their pace as they approached, but made no effort to conceal themselves. At seventy-five yards they were finally noticed, but only in passing, and without alarm. A few animals momentarily stopped their contented feeding to look in their direction. With slow, stupid, cowlike expressions, they regarded the invaders, then resumed their ceaseless meal.

"Not real concerned, are they?" Matt observed quietly.

"Perhaps they're unaccustomed to predators large enough to be a threat," theorized Bradford, "or they consider the size and strength of their herd sufficient to ward off danger. May we get still closer?" Matt looked around. There was nothing on their flanks, just knee-deep grass stretching for a distance in either direction. He could see the boat and the men they'd left with it, less than a quarter mile away. Beyond was *Walker*, framed by an achingly beautiful panorama, Menjangan in the background.

"A little closer, I suppose."

They crept slowly forward. Instinctively, nearly everyone stooped into a semi-crouch as they walked, their subconscious minds insisting that nothing as comparatively small as they should ever stalk anything as big as the creatures before them without making *some* effort to conceal themselves. All except Courtney Bradford. He remained entirely erect, with his binoculars glued to his face. "Oh, my," he repeated over and over.

At fifty yards Matt was about to call a halt when suddenly every animal in the herd stopped eating and their small heads pivoted on giraffe-like necks simultaneously. The motion reminded him absurdly of antelopes and the way whole herds often changed direction as if by preplanned command.

"Uh-oh," said Letts from just behind. One of the biggest animals in the group appeared to gather itself and stretched its neck to full extension. Its sides heaved and a tremendous shrill bugling sound erupted. Other necks extended, and within seconds all the creatures were bugling and bellowing together.

"Okay, people, let's ease back a little."

Everywhere across the plain, groups of animals stared, and sounded off as well. Other creatures, the shape of rhinos, but with bony, spike-studded crests behind their heads, also began trumpeting, and one group tossed their heads and trotted to a more distant herd of brontosauruses and filled gaps in the defensive line they'd established. Together now, both groups raged thunderous defiance at the destroyermen. More interspecies alliances sprang up among the scattered herd groups. "Amazing!" Bradford gasped.

The big bull from the closest group stomped and pawed aggressively at the ground. A cloud of dust rose around him and saplings were cast aside.

"Back away," ordered the captain. He'd never seen anything like this, but whatever was going on, they were vastly outnumbered and ridiculously outmassed. *Walker*'s guns could break up a charge if the distant creatures made one, but the nearest herd was too close for that, and he had no illusions about how effective their small arms would be. A .30-06 could kill an Asian elephant if the shot was placed just right, but where do you "place" a shot in a brontosaurus? "Mr. Bradford, let's go."

Reluctantly, the Australian turned to face him. His gaze froze, however, on something beyond Matt's shoulder and his face drained of color. Matt spun, and there, not twenty yards away, eight large lizards rose from the grass, poised as if to attack. They looked vaguely like the Menjangan lizards except they wore dun-colored fur, or possibly downy feathers, and standing upright was clearly their natural posture. They were formed in a loose semicircle that effectively blocked the men's retreat. Behind him, the bull still rioted and one of the "lizards"—the leader perhaps—opened its mouth in a silent snarl, baring a horrifying array of razor-sharp teeth. Wicked talons lengthened the four long fingers of each outstretched "hand." The creature shifted its weight like a cat about to pounce. At that instant, from the beach came the distinctive *bra-ba-ba-ba-ba-bap!* of a Thompson and the deeper *crack* of a Springfield. Matt discovered he had plenty of adrenaline left, after all.

"At the lizards, open fire!"

Just as he gave the command, the creatures struck with a piercing shriek. Three fell in the initial volley, but the things were *fast* and as big as a man. Silva waded forward with the BAR and Matt was deafened by the metronomic *bam-bam-bam* of the weapon. His rifle was too cumbersome for close quarters and he fumbled for the .45. He yanked it from the holster and flipped the safety off just as one of the nightmare creatures hurtled past a madly dodging Carl Bashear and sprang toward him. He fired four times and then leaped aside as the thing crashed to the ground right where he'd been standing. It gathered its feet and tried to lunge, even with blood pouring from its chest and its left eye blown out. He shot it twice more before it collapsed. He fired once at another as it ran past him, fixated on Glen Carter, and cursed when the slide locked back. Carter was chambering another round in his Springfield, and he glanced up in horror at the death rushing toward him. Alan Letts, hat lost in the grass, turned and fired twice into the creature, shattering its leg, and it sprawled on the ground at Carter's feet. With a quick glance of gratitude at the supply officer, Carter slammed his bolt forward and shot the lizard where it lay, still scrabbling to reach him.

A wrenching scream arose to his left and Matt spun with a fresh magazine in hand, poised in the well of his pistol. One of the monsters was hunched over in the tall grass, struggling with someone on the ground. Bashear, Silva, and Vernon poured in a fusillade of pistol fire until it finally lay still. Another was on the ground struggling to rise, bright-pink froth spraying from its nostrils with each gasping breath. Bradford stood just yards away, rifle still pointed in its general direction, staring with eager fascination. Bashear strode up, shouldered him aside, and shot it in the head. There was an incredulous snarl on his lips as he regarded the Australian.

Matt turned, scanning all directions. The herd of brontosauruses, alarmed by the battle, had ceased bugling and drawn off, leaving only the big bull standing his ground. One of the attackers was still alive, running away with a long-legged, upright lope, faster than any man could match. Not much like the Menjangan lizards at all, he reflected. With a strangled curse, Silva snatched the BAR from the ground and loaded another magazine. He racked the bolt and brought the weapon to his shoulder. A sustained burst spat at the fleeing creature and clouds of dirt, rocks and shredded vegetation erupted around it. Suddenly it jerked and fell. Legs and tail flailed above the grass as Silva calmly replaced the magazine again and hosed the area until all movement ceased.

With another glance at the brontosaurus, Matt hurried to where the other men were looking at the ground. Lying half under one of the dead monsters was Gunner's Mate Mack Marvaney, his head torn nearly completely off.

"Goddamn lizards, or whatever the hell they are!" bellowed Silva, savagely kicking the carcass even after it rolled off his friend. Matt was shocked and somewhat embarrassed to see tears streaking the dust on the big man's face. He looked down at Marvaney and felt a spinning maelstrom of rage and anguish. His pulse thundered in his ears. What in the hell were they going to do? What was *he* going to do? They'd been ashore less than an hour and already lost a man. What kind of world had they wound up in where everything in the water and on the land was trying to eat them? How in the *hell* could they cope with that?

He looked at the men standing nearby. They all wore mixed expressions of rage, shock, and fear. He knew they'd rather face ten *Amagi*s than spend another hour ashore. Well, that was fine, because they were leaving and he knew just how they felt. But they'd have to go ashore again—if not here, then somewhere—if they were going to survive.

"Bring Marvaney," he croaked savagely, then pointed at one of the dead creatures. He cleared his throat and tried to speak more normally. "Bring that too."

The shooting by the boat had stopped, but two men still stood on the beach beside it. Thank God. The herds were bugling and trumpeting again and the big bull was growing bolder. It was time to leave.

There was sadness and angry murmuring when they carried Marvaney on deck. He'd been a fun-loving, friendly sort before depression over leaving his wife had set in, and he had no enemies aboard. Many sympathized and even identified with his unhappiness, although he'd taken it harder than most. But besides the fact that he was well liked, his death seemed somehow more tragic than those in battle. He was the first to die since they came through the Squall, and they couldn't even blame the Japs. All he'd done was go ashore. It showed them how vulnerable they were. The Japanese Navy had been a juggernaut, seemingly dedicated to their personal destruction, a task it nearly accomplished. But at least that was a threat they could understand. The things happening now, ever since the Squall, were beyond their comprehension. If Mack had been killed by the Japanese, it would have been tough, but that was the breaks. That came with being a destroyerman. Being killed by a giant furry lizard wasn't part of the deal.

The murmuring dwindled into shocked silence when they hoisted the creature aboard. The shore party, including the captain, watched while others did the work. Tony Scott and Fred Reynolds had easily killed the two creatures that attacked them, and nobody but Marvaney got so much as a scratch, but Matt figured they'd been through enough. All were pensive and subdued, except the Australian, who hovered like an expectant father as they lowered the lizard beside the number two torpedo mount. Matt was repulsed by the creature and found Bradford's solicitude mildly offensive, but he couldn't really blame him. That was just the way he was; besides, it was important that they learn as much from it as they could and he was the best qualified to do that.

The carcass already stank and the heat would soon make it worse. On its feet the lizard was tall as a man, but it was considerably heavier, so they shifted it onto a torpedo dolly and Matt followed as they rolled it into the shade of the amidships deckhouse. Part of its weight advantage came from the massively muscled legs, which looked more like those of an ostrich or emu than those of the Komodo-like lizards on Menjangan. The feet had three ostrichlike toes with vicious, hawkish claws. Slightly offset on the inside of each foot was a large scimitar-shaped claw, twice as long as the others. More of the weight came from a stubby, powerful tail, tapered sharply from the hips but flared into a thick, almost birdlike plumage of darker, striated "feathers"—for lack of anything else to call them. The "fur" covering the rest of the animal was dun overall, but the striations were faintly evident over the length of the beast. The arms looked very human, with distinct forearms and biceps, even though the shoulders were more like those of birds, where wings would mount. Four clawed fingers were on each hand, and one was very much like a thumb. The longish neck supported a toothy head straight out of a horror movie. The gray eyes were glazed in death, but retained a measure of reptilian malevolence.

Courtney Bradford was happily lecturing the spectators like a group of medical students with a cadaver. "And look!" he said excitedly. "The eyes are quite far forward and unobstructed! There's no question about stereoscopic vision! A formidable predator, believe you me! And those jaws! Terrifying!"

They were. The head tapered to a sharp point and the lower jaw seemed almost delicate, but powerful muscles bulged where it attached to the head. Matt had never seen anything with so many densely packed, razor-sharp teeth. It was almost cartoonish, like a piranha, but there was nothing humorous about it. Those teeth were clearly designed to tear flesh and crunch large bones. They reminded him vaguely of a cross between a shark's teeth and a cat's canines, only there was virtually no gap between them.

He was surprised to see how the crowd had swelled. Half the crew was present. He also noted that the gloom and dread that had been so pervasive had begun to lift somewhat. Many of the men most affected by Marvaney's death now listened with careful attention. *Of course!* he thought, and wondered if the Australian did it on purpose. Show them the enemy, especially a dead one, and it might still be scary as hell, but it also became clear that it could be killed. He looked at Courtney Bradford with new respect as the man jabbered happily on about how fearsome the obviously vanquished creature was.

He felt a hand on his arm and turned to see Lieutenant Tucker's concerned face, her eyes locked searchingly on his. He forced a smile. "How long have you been here?" he asked.

"Ever since you came aboard. Are you all right?"

He stepped slightly back. "Swell. We had some excitement, but we're all okay except—" He stopped and shook his head. "Why?"

She just patted his arm with a fragile smile. She couldn't tell him that the expression he'd worn when he came aboard had frightened her with the intensity of its rage, and devastated her with the depth of its hopelessness. She doubted anyone else had really noticed—men could be so stupid about such things—and he now seemed himself again. But that quick peek beneath his so carefully controlled veneer of confident self-assurance wrenched her heart, not only with fear for her own survival but also with compassion for this man who carried such a heavy burden for them all.

"Nothing," she said, and smiled a little brighter. She heard Bradford's voice rise above his dissertation.

"Ah! Lieutenant Tucker! There you are, my dear! You're quite the surgeon, I understand. Would you be so good as to assist me"—he grinned—"while I slice this bugger up and show these lads where to aim next time?" There were growls of approval and a predatory jockeying for the best view. Bradford wiped his brow and smiled wryly. "I'm afraid if we wait too long, it will be a nasty task indeed."

Matt sat on his bunk, his face in his hands. His sweat-soaked hair and clothes felt clammy under the fan. He sighed and spoke into the comm. "Bridge, this is the captain."

"Bridge, aye."

"Inform Mr. Dowden I'm in my quarters. I'll be up shortly."

"Aye, aye, sir."

Matt paused awkwardly for a moment. "Thanks," he said at last, and dropped back on the rack to stare at the overhead.

Another one, he thought grimly. All those men lost in the running fight, then *Mahan* and now Marvaney. What next? There had to be something he could have done to stop all this. Marvaney was a good kid. Unlike Silva, or pretty much the entire ordnance division, he'd never been a discipline problem aboard or ashore. He just did his job. He raised a little hell, like the rest, but he never pushed it too far. Maybe the pretty Filipino girl had something to do with that. Matt only saw her twice, both times when they docked in Cavite after some maneuver. She was always waiting on the quay, to snatch Marvaney up before he could escape with his hooligan friends. He always went willingly, too, without the false bravado and showing off of others under similar circumstances. It was clear he loved her very much. He was distraught when they left Cavite after the Japanese bombed it to splinters. After the Squall, he just sort of . . . went away. Matt shouldn't have let him go ashore. He hadn't even thought about it. Now Mack was dead, and it was his fault.

Finally he grunted and sat up. Sulking wouldn't do anyone any good, least of all Marvaney. He'd just have to do better, somehow. It was his duty, and he'd never shrunk from responsibility, but this was . . . different, and so very, very hard. He wasn't just a junior destroyer captain anymore, who only had to follow orders. His job had changed profoundly. For a moment he envied men like Silva, men who did their jobs but were free to leave the care and responsibility to others at the end of the watch. Matt's watch never ended. He *was* the job. He only hoped no one else would have to die before he figured out what, exactly, it had become.

He replaced his shirt with a dry one, ran a comb through his greasy hair, and put his hat back on. He searched the mirror above his little desk for signs of the anxiety that threatened to overwhelm him, and with a wary snort, he shouldered through the curtain to become captain of DD-163 again.

Dennis Silva leaned against the vegetable locker between the number three and number four funnels while Stites, Campeti, and Jamie Miller worked. They were sewing Marvaney into his mattress cover, and blood glistened black against the white cloth where it soaked through from his gruesome wound and dried in the afternoon sun. Silva felt . . . depressed, he guessed, and that was an emotion he'd never experienced before. He always said he had only four "feelings"—horny, hungry, happy, and mad—and he was less than half joking. Now he knew a fifth. Mad was part of it, sure. But it was deeper and less focused and had already lasted longer than the others ever did. He'd felt it since Marvaney was killed, and that had been what? Almost three hours ago? *Must be depression,* he told himself with a sigh. *No tellin' what I'll be pinin' over next.*

He would miss Marvaney. They'd been shipmates for four years and raised hell from Cavite to Singapore—until the dummy got married and reformed. But they had a lot of laughs and busted a lot of heads, and he'd always been a good man at your back. Now he was dead and Silva realized he'd lost one of the few people that his loose definition of "true friend" applied to. He wished he had a drink.

"Don't forget 'the object,'" he grumped, referring to the item that he'd chosen to carry his friend to the depths.

Campeti glared at him. "Can't you think of nothin' else? Christ, it ain't hardly fittin'! And besides, what are we gonna listen to?"

"The object" was a bundle of about fifty records, part of a large collection Marvaney had aboard and often played on a portable wind-up turntable. The 78s were plenty heavy, more than sufficient to carry him down.

"Relax, Sonny. I only picked the old stuff nobody else likes. He liked 'em, though, and he ought'a keep 'em."

Campeti shook his head. "All right, Dennis, but when they're gone, they're gone. We might never hear them songs again."

"Suits me. I like dancin' to livelier tunes. Them waltzes and shit is for grandmas."

"Dancin'!" snorted Campeti, a general, growing concern on his mind. "Who with?"

They were silent while "the object" was solemnly placed at Marvaney's feet and the last stitches finished. Finally, the young pharmacist's mate spoke tentatively. "Chief Bashear said he killed six lizards. How many did you get, Silva?"

Dennis snorted. "Six, huh? Where I was standin', I didn't see him kill any. Well, one, maybe. Give him an assist."

"How about you?" Miller prodded. Silva shrugged. "Two or three, I guess. Hell, everybody was shootin'. Who knows?"

Stites glanced at Campeti and then looked at Silva again. "How about the Skipper? Boy, he sure looked mad!"

Silva nodded. "Yeah, he got one or two. With his pistol. He just stood there and let one run right up to him and *bam*!" He clapped his hands. "Right in the eye! The Skipper's got guts, I'll say that." He looked thoughtful. "He was mad, though. I never seen him that mad. I don't know if he was madder that they got Mack or that we ran out'a lizards to kill. He wasn't even that mad that time in Subic when me and—" He stopped, and a huge grin slowly spread across his face. "Well, never mind, boys. I got that rocker back later anyway." The others laughed as they finished preparations to send their friend to his watery grave.

That evening, as the sun touched the horizon, there was a small, forlorn splash alongside the lonely, rust-streaked ship. For a while, it remained still as the gloom deepened and the running lights snapped on. It must have been a strange, alien image to any creature watching from shore. Puffs of smoke rose from the aft funnels and hung motionless in the calm evening air. Then, slowly, it began to move. Most of the creatures paid it no heed; their interests were wholly devoted to packing vegetation into their large, multiple stomachs. If they'd witnessed the strange events of the day, they'd already forgotten.

Not all had forgotten, however. Some watched intently and continued to stare at the lights as they moved through the slot and into the strait beyond, long after the shape of the ship itself was lost to view.

Keje-Fris-Ar sat on a stool beside his breakfast table in the ornately decorated chamber that was the foundation for the central tower of Home. It was the largest chamber on the entire ship that wasn't given over to livestock or cargo, and it was tastefully adorned with colorful tapestries and finely carved figures. Puffy pillows clustered in the various discussion areas, and in the center of all towered a nearly mature Galla tree, growing from a basin of earth that extended down to the very keel. Ample sunlight for it to thrive flowed through colorfully decorated hatches that were usually, as now, flung wide. A gentle breeze circulated to rustle the long, green-gold leaves. The only thing marring the dignity and splendor of the chamber was the small, plain table, set to one side, where Keje-Fris-Ar, High Chief of all the clans of *Salissa* Home, and his companion, High Sky Priest Adar, enjoyed their morning meal. The splendid hall was Keje's personal office, throne room, and council chamber rolled into one, where matters of great importance to all the clans were discussed. On such occasions, the ceremony and dignity were solemn indeed. But for everyday use, when there were no great matters to attend in proper form, Keje preferred his little table. Besides, he knew it amused Adar to dine with him thus.

The High Chief was the absolute monarch of Home, but the three towers supporting the great wings were controlled by their various chiefs, who enjoyed a degree of autonomy. An autonomy that could grow tiresome. Sometimes, the Sky Priests acted as intermediaries between the clans, because they were of no clan and all must serve the Heavens. Because of this trust, and because the Sky Priests—at least on *Salissa*—weren't oppressively spiritual, they enjoyed a position of esteem and a reputation for impartiality when dealing with the everyday squabbles among the several chiefs. But their efforts in this regard were subordinate to their primary duty. Their charge was to read the Heavens and ponder the stars and interpret them to others, who saw only points of light. The Sky Priests told them where they were, where they were going, and how to get there. They relayed the truths of the Heavens, which were above all things.

It was the High Chief who had to cajole, inspire, or force the clan chiefs to cooperate to do what the Heavens decreed if the Sky Priests couldn't help them agree, with him or each other. That was one of the reasons he generally declined the pomp of his exalted office, at least in everyday life.

He didn't demand the near deification some High Chiefs of other Homes enjoyed, through constant ritual and an untouchable attitude, but he enjoyed a higher, more genuine status than many of his peers through respect for his abilities and wisdom. There was always contention, but his Home suffered less from the incessant squabbling that sometimes plagued other Homes because he led by example and was followed by the willing.

That didn't mean he didn't enjoy his status. He believed he was a good High Chief, and the People of *Salissa* Home prospered under his rule. What it did mean was he felt more comfortable eating at a small table, with his Sky Priest, whenever important rituals didn't interfere.

"So tell me, my lord," spoke Adar, delicately dabbing at his whiskers with an intricately woven kerchief, "have you given more thought to our visitors on the quick, smoky vessel?"

"No," grunted Keje around a mouthful of baked akka egg. "None at all since we last discussed them before we parted last night, to sleep." He was mildly annoyed with his friend's preoccupation with the strange tail-less beings. Deep down, he was just as curious as Adar, but he had other things to concern him, and their meeting had been so brief that it was pointless to speculate and rehash questions for which they'd likely never have answers.

Adar blinked rapidly with constrained amusement. "Surely, lord, you have thought of them a little." He paused and grew more serious. "I certainly have." His lips moved into a full grin. "As you know." Keje's eyelids fluttered questioningly.

"My lord, consider again how momentous it was. We encountered an entirely different species, which, at the very least, possess knowledge of sea vessels far surpassing our own—or the Grik." Adar looked intently into Keje's eyes. "And I repeat: they did not attack us! When has that ever been? Only once before, by the Prophet, and they were tail-less beings as well! The Grik are our Ancient Enemy. That much is clear from the Scrolls. They drove us from our ancestral home—on *land!*—so long ago that the Scrolls cannot even tell us what that life was like. But it was the Grik who forced our people to build the great Homes to travel the world in safety, across the hostile sea. But the Grik have learned to travel the sea as well. Not as well, or as safely, thank the Heavens, but nothing has changed in all that time. Yet again they seek to drive us, whenever we meet. The war that began so many ages ago is not over for them." He stopped, and looking down, he shuddered. "I believe they are truly evil, just as it is written, and I fear for our people. Our race."

Keje blinked agreement, although he still couldn't divine the Sky Priest's point. What did the Tail-less Ones have to do with any of that—or was that his point?

"My lord, you know the sea and what manner of vessel best swims upon it, but something is changing. The Grik have found us, their ancient prey, but until recently they could do little about it." He held up a dark, furless palm. "They do invariably attack, and People are sometimes slain, but their vessels are as nothing compared to the walls of Home. Yet in our lifetimes we've seen the size of their vessels increase, as well as the number of attacks. When last I spoke to other High Sky Priests, at the Gathering of Homes, I heard the same from them. Their frail vessels cannot protect them all, and many are probably lost, yet they keep coming, senselessly. From what I can tell, there is no motive other than to attack us, and the Western Ocean is no longer the barrier it was."

Keje was silent as he contemplated the words. Beneath the stool, his tail swished. One of the youngling servants carried away their platters. When she was gone, Keje spoke.

"I know what you are saying. The Grik make advances and we do nothing but repel them when they strike. What else can we do?"

"They advance and we repel them," agreed Adar, "but what if they strike colonies, or trade lands, where people don't have the walls of Home to defend them? What if they attack in some new way that cannot be defended against? They already use fire, and that's bad enough. What will become of us? It would be like the exodus in the Scrolls once more, only this time with nowhere to flee."

"Well, but what *does* this have to do with the Tail-less Ones? We've discussed all this before!" questioned Keje. He was exasperated, but he felt a gnawing agreement with Adar's words. "Do you believe these new Tail-less Ones are somehow related to the old? Is that what you're saying?" Keje huffed. "It is coincidence, nothing more. Their ways are as different from the others as ours are from theirs."

"We cannot know, my lord, if they're the same or not. It may not even matter. I say only this: they did not attack us."

"Yes, yes, you've said that before!"

"They did not attack us, and they're clearly unafraid of the Grik. With such a speedy vessel, they would have no reason to fear."

With dawning comprehension, Keje regarded the Sky Priest. "You believe we have squandered an opportunity," he stated flatly.

"Yes, my lord, I do."

As if on cue, the sound of running feet and a rising tide of alarmed voices reached them through the open windows of the hall. The coincidence wasn't lost on either of them, and they stared at one another. Keje's personal Guard detachment raced in and stood before him. Some were adjusting their armor. Kas-Ra-Ar, Keje's cousin and captain of the Guard, bowed his dark-furred head. "My lord," he said simply, "the Grik come."

Keje blinked acknowledgment, and turning, he bellowed for his armor. "From which direction, cousin?" he asked.

"West-southwest, and south, my lord." Neither Kas's expression nor the tone of his voice changed when Keje's eyes pierced his. "Yes, lord, there are six. All larger than we've ever seen."

Keje paced the battlement spanning the great floating island that was Home. It was an open deck extending beam to beam and formed the ceiling to the forward part of the Great Hall. Since the hall was so large, Keje's vantage point was several dozen tails above the main deck. On the other two towers, the level wasn't as prominent, and merely served as the foundation for the towers of apartments between the wing tripods. The platform on the central tower was larger so the High Chief could direct his people in storms—and battle.

The turnout of the Guard was more disciplined than just a few days before. Every male, female, and youngling on *Salissa* Home that was old enough, fit enough, or large enough to bear arms was technically a member of the Guard, but the "active" Guard consisted of the strongest and most fit from each clan. Its members spent time each week engaged in martial exercises. These consisted of athletic training and practice with weapons, but since they were so rarely called to fight, the training was geared more toward preparation for the frequent competitions between the various clans.

Rivalry was fierce and provided entertainment for the People. But the rivalries sometimes became bitter, so the active Guards of the various clans, even while preparing for the common defense, almost never practiced together. The combined active Guard of *Salissa* numbered nearly four hundred and, when the reserves swelled their ranks, Home could boast almost sixteen hundred defenders. But many had never fought, and fewer had fought together. Standing together clan by clan, they didn't even know how. And none of them—none of Keje's people in all the world—had ever faced more than one Grik ship at a time.

As he paced, Keje stared aft and to the left, toward the distant haze of land. He confirmed with his own eyes no fewer than six ships of the Ancient Enemy stalking his people. His insides twisted. He wasn't afraid to fight, and he didn't think he was afraid to die, but he'd fought the Grik before. One-sided and seemingly senseless as those fights had been, he'd seen a glimpse of what they were capable of. Their appalling savagery and apparent disdain for their own lives was so utterly alien that he'd always harbored a secret terror of what might happen if they ever attacked in sufficient force to gain the decks of Home. Now it seemed that the nightmare was upon them. He would see what it was like at last.

The Grik were closing fast, and their speed made it seem that *Salissa* really was an island, incapable of independent movement, even though the great wings were taut and straining against the freshening breeze. He watched as weapons were issued to females and younglings who'd never held them in their lives, other than to prepare food. His eyes blinked furiously in impotent realization. It was all his fault. He'd lived with the nightmare for many years and he should have prepared his people better.

The festive tarpaulins and awnings came down. Perhaps the most evil and insidious thing about the Grik was they seemed to delight in using fire as a weapon. The Homes of the People were built to last virtually forever, and his Home was barely a generation old. But it was made of wood, and the woods that served best were hardwoods steeped in resin. Resin that took fire with an obdurate flame. Barrels of sea water were always kept at hand, but now more barrels and buckets of water were hauled up by ropes as quickly as possible while they prepared for the unprecedented deluge of fire that they knew would come. Water droplets misted down as the fabric wings were doused. More water sloshed on the decks, making them slippery, but it couldn't be helped. He hoped they wouldn't soon be slick with blood.

He looked around. Adar was there, surrounded by his acolytes. All were armed, but they blinked nervously, since none had ever trained for war. The Sky Priests trained only in the mysteries of the Heavens. It never occurred to them to study the mysteries of one race intent on destroying another. They couldn't be risked on the walls, but if the enemy reached this place there would be no noncombatants. There would be only fight or die.

Keje's immediate family was with him on the battlement as well, but that was ancient tradition, not favoritism. In battle, the High Chief had enough to worry about without adding concern for his family. That family held no official power simply by familial association. In theory, their status was no higher than that of any fish cleaner or wing runner of the People. They often held status of their own, through merit, but the idea of a fixed aristocracy—at least for the High Chief—was repellent to the fiercely, if inconsistently, egalitarian People. In practice, it was more complicated. The office that Keje held was hereditary—subject to ratification by the Clan Assembly, of course—but no one remembered when a succession had been blocked. Therefore, a certain "royal family" atmosphere and collective protectiveness existed toward the heirs of any High Chief.

Unlike the wings, whose chiefs passed their position to the elder heirs, the elder, or "senior," of the High Chief's heirs were expected to move on in Homes of their own when the time came. When the final heirs came of age and the High Chief died or stepped down, they would succeed him.

All could have Homes, if they chose, peopled by the younger heirs of the "parent" Home. This ensured continuity on the parent Home through the experience of the wing clans, as well as the Homes newly founded and led by the High Chief's elder heirs. "Wars of succession" did not occur, populations were controlled, and all the Homes of the People were distantly related to some degree. That more and more of the "elder heirs" were choosing to establish "Land Colonies" with the resources granted them concerned some, who feared dissolution of the old, traditional ways, but practically, the burgeoning Land Colonies provided support for the still-growing number of Homes. In any event, because of this arrangement, there really was no "crown prince."

In theory at least. In Keje's case, his only mate died young, leaving him a single heir, Selass. Keje wasn't old and would certainly mate again, perhaps many times, but for now, Selass was it. She therefore constituted the only "immediate" family to stand with him on the battlement that day.

Her new mate, Saak-Fas, was another matter. Keje didn't like him and his daughter knew it, but he couldn't describe his dislike beyond a general discomfort over a supremely self-centered attitude. His dislike intensified considerably today when Saak-Fas appeared on the battlement with Selass instead of on the wall where he belonged. The only fighters posted to the battlement were the High Chief's personal armsmen, and just a few of those. Everyone else, besides the Sky Priests, were bearers of commands, or runners, who would race down the catwalks and carry his orders where directed. Keje decided he would send Saak-Fas on such an errand when the time came, and he had no regard for what his daughter would think of that. He did notice that Selass appeared uncomfortable, and he wondered if it was shame, or simply the fact that death was so near.

He studied the Grik ships as they approached in three pairs. They looked identical to others he'd seen, but they did seem somewhat larger. Possibly sixty or eighty tails long. Even at a distance, he saw their decks teeming with the loathsome creatures, their mail and weapons glittering in the bright sunlight of the otherwise perfect day. Keje summoned the first of many runners he expected to send before the battle was done. One way or another.

"Instruct the lance throwers not to shoot beyond one hundred tails, and to shoot only where their hulls meet the water." The runner blinked acknowledgment and raced away. The lance throwers had the only stand-off weapons *Salissa* Home possessed. They were like the crossbows of the Guard except they were much, much larger. Intended for defense against mountain fish, or to slay their smaller cousins, four of the lance throwers were mounted on pivots along each side. It took six people considerable effort to crank the wrist-thick bowstring into the firing position, but they could hurl a spade-headed lance three tails long and a hand-span in diameter a distance of three hundred tails with accuracy enough to hit a mountain fish in the eye. That was a target only slightly larger than Keje's breakfast table. Such accuracy was essential because the eye was the creature's only vulnerable spot.

That was Keje's only preparatory command. Maneuver was pointless; the far more agile Grik could easily counter anything he tried. All that remained was to wait and see how the blow would fall.

Chack nervously clutched one of the massive shrouds supporting the forward tripod and watched the enemy approach. His stomach was knotted with fear, and the reason his hands were clamped so firmly on the shroud was so none would see how badly they shook. He and half his clan were on the forward platform, near enough to the fighters below to act as a reserve but also free to race aloft and adjust or repair the wing. His weapon, a large, long-bladed axe, leaned against the railing nearby and he devoutly hoped he wouldn't have to wield it. He was strong and athletic, but his fighting skills were poor.

He'd never done well in the frequent competitions. His form was good, but his timing was sloppy. Risa was much better with weapons than he, and she often tried to coach him, but it did little good. He knew no amount of practice could force martial competence upon his fundamentally unaggressive character. He'd been in fights—everyone had. No matter that *Salissa* was very large—it was still too small to avoid conflict. He never won those fights, but he was rarely injured. He was very good at avoiding blows, through speed and deft responses, but he'd always had an abiding reluctance to deliver them. His fights ended inconclusively when his adversary tired of trying to hit him. It was clear that he was no coward, because he was willing to stand and take it if they could dish it out. He just didn't dish it out in return. Chack considered that a victory in itself, even if it never settled anything. The problem today, however, was that if he raised that axe, it meant all was lost unless the last wing runners fought. Simply avoiding blows wasn't an option. The only way to stop the Grik was to kill them.

In all previous encounters, the Grik had never attempted to talk. Whenever they sighted the People, there was only one response. Attack. No matter how small the ship or how ridiculous the odds, they *always* attacked. And when they fought, if they ever actually came to personal blows, there was only mindless, berserk savagery without any concept of giving or receiving quarter. They fought until they were killed, even if they'd lost limbs or been disarmed. Always. It was madness.

It wouldn't be long now, Chack thought. They were close. A pair of ships closed within two hundred tails on the left, abreast of the forewing tower. Another pair ranged up on the right. The final pair was closing aft, as if they meant to strike three, or perhaps six, places at once. It was strange, Chack thought absently, that they should attack thus. But then, they'd never seen more than one Grik ship at a time, and the way they fought—Chack shuddered—they seemed incapable of cooperation. Yet this attack would be coordinated.

The ships themselves were huge by Grik standards, half again larger than any ever seen. Every detail seemed the same, only on a larger scale. Probably to hold more warriors, he thought. Each had three of the ridiculously puny masts that the Grik favored, with three billowing sails instead of wings on the first two and a triangular sail on the aft. Another stubby mast protruded from the front of their ships, but there was no sail upon it. It seemed to serve more as a countersupport for the stays that held the others.

The hulls were low and sleek, except for separate elevated decks at the front and back. The sides were painted a uniform red, the bulwarks black— what could be seen of them. From front to back, over the bulwarks, were hundreds of garishly painted oval shields. Some were one color, others were many, and most bore some design, but each belonged to a Grik warrior, and those masses of warriors packed the decks and stared at the People with an unnatural, cold-blooded quiet. Wisps of smoke swirled from their midst and vanished to leeward, and Chack swallowed hard when he realized their fire weapons were ready for use.

There was almost no sound from those around him either, only low murmurs of soft conversation. Risa had been spinning a ribald tale, but now even she was silent. They were as ready as they'd ever be, and yet there was no way to be ready to face the death—and the kind of death!—that they all, deep down, knew had come. Risa was at his side and she put a hand on his arm and looked deeply into his eyes. She bared her teeth in a feral grin.

"I know you will fight well, my Brother," she said, guessing his concern. "It's not as if they are People, after all." Then her grin faded and she looked away from him, toward the approaching ships. Very calculatingly, she spoke again. "I do not want you to die, but this time if you won't fight, you won't be the only one they kill." He looked at her and blinked a quick flash of betrayal, but then just as quickly, he knew she was right. A vague sense of shame and a fierce determination welled within him and, leaning over, he picked up his axe and laid it heavily on the rail before them. She saw it and recognized the promise it represented, but said nothing. Together, they watched and waited.

Rising voices reached them and they turned to face the battlement.

There, in the distance, Adar stood, arms outstretched, his long robe flowing around him. It was the stance of supplication. Quickly, most within Chack's view imitated the gesture and, almost as one, they turned to face the Sun. Risa poked him savagely in the ribs and he joined her in the pose. The warm rays swept across his face and he could see the mighty orb even through his closed eyelids. With the rest of his people he spoke the words: "Maker of All Things, I beg your protection, but if it is my time, light my Spirit's path to its Home in the Heavens!" He crossed his arms on his chest and knelt to the deck. There was an audible rumble of knees on wood as hundreds did the same. Clearly, not all participated because someone cried out in alarm and Chack looked up.

A crimson, snakelike pennant unfurled from the masthead of one of the ships, and even as it snapped taut and streamed over the sea, a great, harsh, hissing cry arose from all the ships at once. It came as a wave of sound like the wind and sea in a gale, but there was an unnatural malevolence that the sea had never meant. Shields were plucked from bulwarks and weapons clashed against them, adding a monstrous throbbing, metallic heartbeat to the sound. It was the loudest, most terrifying thing Chack had ever heard, as thousands of throats and weapons clamored at him across the water. Then, as the terrible din reached its peak, six Grik ships turned as one to destroy his Home, his family, his world.

The afternoon watch came on duty, and the normalcy of tradition-bound procedure left Matt heartened. For a moment the terrible, unreal events of the previous days seemed remote. The sea was mild, the sky was clear, and a firm, cool breeze washed across him from the open bridgewing. It seemed to cleanse him of the depression and trepidation that had settled upon him. It was one of those days that made destroyermen glory in the seemingly effortless speed and grace of their sharp-hulled ships instead of cursing them for their inconsiderate tendency to pitch and roll in heavier seas. It was a heaven-sent respite for him, as well as the rest of the crew, and whether they took their mood from their captain or not, he saw more smiles and normal, ordinary goofing around than he had in many days.

He sat in his chair and leafed through the pages of the report. Davis's leg was still not improving, but more of the invalids were ready for light duty. Spanky, Letts, and, of all people, the Mice were designing a drilling rig and had convinced Bernie Sandison to endorse their scheme to use the torpedo tubes on the inoperable number three mount for a condensation tower to refine the oil once they found it. He looked out at the fo'c'sle. Gray had the first deck division repairing topside damage, although Matt knew how the Bosun suffered over the dingy, reddening deck and the long streaks of rust that had begun to take hold. One man with a quart can of paint followed behind the welders as they refitted and straightened twisted stanchions and worked to repair the shell damage to the starboard hawse. The anchor on that side was gone forever, but they were winching the spare into place while he watched. He was surprised to see the Japanese officer helping, under the supervision of a certain Marine, who sat on the capstan bollard and watched like a chain gang overseer. The men working with Shinya kept their distance and cast many resentful looks, but they were letting him help. It was a start, Matt supposed. All in all, it was a pretty good day.

The only things darkening his mood were the subconscious fuel gauge, creeping ever downward in his mind, and the continuing dull ache over what might have happened to *Mahan*.

He heard voices behind him and turned to see Courtney Bradford and Sandra Tucker asking permission to come on the bridge. Matt smiled broadly, waved them over beside him, and stood up. "Good afternoon, Lieutenant Tucker, Mr. Bradford. A fine day, is it not?"

"Indeed it is, Captain," replied the Australian, and Sandra smiled back at him. "I thought you'd like to know that we've finished our 'science experiment' at last, and can manage without its, uh, services any longer."

"Thank God," said Matt, and chuckled. "I take it . . . I *hope* you mean you pitched the stinking thing over the side?" Sandra and Bradford had worked through the night and into the morning dissecting the dead creature from Bali. Some of the crew watched throughout, duties permitting, and Bradford kept up a running lecture the entire time. The rest of the crew, however, were increasingly vocal about the overpowering stench. Now they both stood, tired but with satisfied smiles on their faces.

"Yes, um, it has gone on to the reward it so richly deserved," answered Bradford in a dry tone. Matt chuckled again, but was secretly amazed that Bradford had given up so easily. He'd half expected him to ask to keep it in the refrigerator—or his cabin, if necessary. But Matt saw now that Courtney Bradford had undergone a transformation. It may have been subtle, and possibly fleeting, but he'd been there when they were attacked and he saw what happened to Marvaney. Besides, fascinating as the creatures were, they had also, at the very least, kept him from studying anything else. The furry lizards of Bali had become his enemies as surely as the Japanese.

"Well, what did you find out?"

"Quite a lot, actually. We don't believe they were lizards at all. At least I don't," he said. "Miss Tucker is not quite so fully convinced of that." He nodded at her respectfully. "But I believe they are somewhat more like birds in many ways."

"Birds? With teeth like that? You must be joking."

"No, sir, he's not," said Sandra. "I know a good bit about human anatomy, and anatomy in general, I suppose, but I'm obviously no expert on these creatures. Nobody is. Mr. Bradford has more experience studying . . . similar things than I do, and I can see his point. They're built like birds—or emus and ostriches, to be more precise—except for the upper arms, and their bones are hollow, but incredibly strong like a bird's. Our opinions diverge because of those upper arms, their tails, and well, their heads too, I guess. Their tails have feathers, but they're muscular like an alligator's. And their upper arms show no sign of being vestigial wings, but seem to have evolved as arms to *be* arms. And of course their heads." She shuddered slightly. "Or more specifically, their jaws. There's nothing birdlike about them at all."

"But my dear lieutenant," countered Bradford, evidently continuing an argument. "You're basing your opinions more upon what they *look* like and less on what they *are* like—"

Matt held up his hand, smiling still, to stop him. "Enough. While this is all very fascinating, my most pressing question involves their intelligence. Are they as smart as they seemed? I mean, there were ten of us and ten of them, and they displayed what to my mind could only be described as the *tactic* of hitting us and the men at the boat simultaneously—in a way that would keep us apart. As well armed as they are with teeth and claws, one on one, they had every reason to expect the advantage."

Sandra was silent, and Bradford shifted uncomfortably. "We don't really know, I'm afraid," he said at last. "Theoretically, yes. They certainly have the brain capacity, and in proportion to their body size, their brains are similar to our own. Then again . . ."

Matt nodded. The very idea of something that ferocious being smart was daunting indeed. There was no question that they would have to go ashore again. Maybe not on Bali, but the first time they had set a foot on land, something had tried to bite it off. They had to presume that other places wouldn't be any different. Somehow, they had to figure out how to go ashore—and work there—without being eaten.

The crow's nest comm whistled. "Bridge, lookout," came the tinny voice of Elden.

"Bridge, Riggs here," replied the petty officer.

"PO, I've got smoke on the horizon, bearing zero one five. A hell of a lot of smoke. There's so much I thought it was a cloud at first. It's pretty much the same color—not black like an oil fire. Whatever's burning is pretty big, though, and it's in the water. Not—repeat, *not*—on land."

"Excuse me, please," said Matt to his visitors, raising his binoculars.

"Can you see what it is yet?" Riggs asked the lookout. "Is it a ship, or what?"

"Negative, PO. All I see is smoke. Whatever it is, it's still . . . Wait!

Damn! I'd about swear it was that big monkey-cat ship!" Matt lowered his binoculars with a strange mix of disappointment, relief, and curious concern. Disappointment that it wasn't *Mahan*, but relief that it wasn't *Mahan* on fire. The curious concern was for the monkey-cats, as Elden called them, if that's who it was. *Well,* he thought, *if it is, maybe it's time we met.* Besides, they appeared to be in trouble.

"All ahead full," he ordered. "Come right, fifteen degrees."

Walker's head came around and she quickly gathered speed. Water peeled back from her bow as she charged, the feather nearly reaching the fo'c'sle. The men on the foredeck stopped what they were doing and stood with fluttering clothes, their faces turned toward the rushing breeze and the towering column of smoke in the distance. Five minutes passed, then ten.

"Bridge?" came Elden's voice. The normally unflappable shipfitter sounded unusually strained.

"Bridge, aye."

"It's the monkey-cats all right, and there are several large three-masted ships around 'em. Most are lashed to her, and it looks like they're fighting! The monkey-cats are definitely burning—and maybe one of the other ships as well." There was a moment's pause. "I think there's a hell of a fight going on."

Matt turned to Reynolds. "Get the range from Mr. Barry," he ordered.

"Aye, aye, Captain," said Reynolds, wide-eyed. It was his first stint as talker, and it was just his luck something serious would happen. He spoke briefly into the microphone and listened for the response. His voice squeaked slightly when he reported. "Sir, Ensign Barry estimates the range at about fifteen thousand yards."

"Very well. Sound general quarters, if you please."

The deep gonging sound that was part horn, part buzzer resonated through the ship, and surprised men snatched helmets and life vests as they raced to their stations. Some rolled from their racks, disoriented for a moment, and hesitated like they would never have done before the Squall. Feet clanked metallically on the ladder as Lieutenant Garrett and the rest of the fire-control team gained the bridge and scampered to the platform above. Bernard Sandison appeared, tucking in his shirt, along with torpedomen Hale, Carter, and Aubrey, who took their places at the torpedo directors.

Reynolds recited a litany of readiness reports, and after much longer than Matt approved, he made the announcement: "All stations manned and ready, Captain. Mr. Dowden has the auxiliary conn and reports . . . um . . . the chaos he viewed from his perspective looked like a shore-patrol raid on an Olongapo . . . whorehouse." His face turned pink.

Matt grunted and glanced at his watch. "Pathetic," he announced. "A Jap car salesman with a rowboat and a stick of dynamite could have sent us to the bottom by now. Sparks, inform the Bosun that the deck division was the last to report." Everyone cringed to think how the Chief would exact his vengeance for that humiliation, and he was heard even now, bellowing at the crew of the number one gun.

Much of the confusion was caused by the need to stow the "peacetime" awnings that now covered the deck spaces, but Matt knew most of the blame was his. He'd grown lax about daily drills since they no longer faced imminent annihilation by the Japanese. That didn't mean all threat of annihilation had passed, and despite their trauma—or maybe because of it—drill was now more important, not less. He resolved to make sure his destroyermen were never caught flat-footed again.

He sat back in his chair, Sandra and Bradford not entirely forgotten but relegated to that portion of his mind not preparing to fight his ship if need be. "Mr. Sandison. What's the current status of our torpedoes?"

"One, three and five are loaded, prepped, and ready in all respects."

"No news on the condemned torps?"

"No, sir. I still have them apart in the shop. One didn't even have a repair tag, so we're checking it out, piece by piece. The other's propulsion machinery works fine; it just needs recharging. But it's clearly a dud. The warhead housing is all crumpled in. The tag said one of our subs fired it into a Dutch freighter by mistake and it didn't go off, but it punched a hole in her side and got stuck. Yard-apes fished it out of the freighter when she got into port." Sandison smirked ironically. "Everyone was lucky on that deal."

There'd been far too many "duds" of every sort. In this one case it was fortunate, but Matt hated to think how many American ships and submarines might have been lost, and enemies spared, simply because of faulty ordnance. A lot of the antiaircraft shells on *Houston* had been duds, and they'd never even suspected it because they hadn't been allowed enough live-fire practice. The same was true for the torpedoes. The suspected causes ranged anywhere from faulty detonators to a tendency to run too deep. He knew they hadn't performed well at all during the night action at Balikpapan, and most of the success there was due to gunnery. Whatever the case, he prayed they weren't carrying around, carefully husbanding, and relying on useless weapons. "Keep working on it, Mr. Sandison," was all he said.

Facing forward, he peered through his binoculars again and focused at the base of the column of smoke. He now saw for himself that there was indeed a battle under way. But compared to anything he'd ever expected, the word "battle" was wholly insufficient to describe it.

"My God . . ."

The excellent optics and seven-power magnification of the MK1 M2 Bausch and Lomb binoculars transformed the distant, blurry shapes into a high-relief scene of unprecedented horror and desperation. The . . . medieval nature of the combat wasn't what shocked him, however. What left him speechless was the obvious total involvement of the defenders and the utter lack of regard for casualties and noncombatants by the attackers. And then there were the attackers themselves.

Courtney Bradford had his own binoculars in front of his eyes, and his hands began to shake. "My God," he finally echoed.

Snarling, Chack swung the axe with all his strength and entirely severed the tail of a Grik warrior, poised to finish Risa, who lay unconscious and bleeding on the catwalk. The Grik shrieked and toppled forward, robbed of its counterbalance, but it fell on Risa and the snout opened wide, revealing razor-sharp, densely packed teeth prepared to savage her throat. He swung again and buried the axe in the Grik's back, halfway to the breastbone. It collapsed instantly in a spray of hot blood and Chack heaved it aside. He grabbed his sister by the arm and slung her off the catwalk to a pair of ancient garden tenders below.

The garden tenders were the oldest and most frail people of Home and, so far, the only ones not actively committed to the fight. Their task was to help clear the wounded and try to tend their injuries. Chack feared his sister was dying. He hadn't seen the wound, or the blow that struck her down, but her fine fur was matted with blood and she felt lifeless in his arms. His own fur was matted with blood as well, some wet and some half dry. He didn't think any was his, however. He'd fought like a demon, like he'd never imagined he could, ever since the pompous Saak-Fas had arrived and imperiously sent their last reserves into the faltering defense. The last wing runners had seen the need already, but waited for Keje's command. Released at last, they charged down the shrouds, and Chack looked to see if Saak-Fas accompanied them, but he was nowhere in sight. Nor had he seen him in the long hours since.

Surely, the People had never known such a battle! In the beginning, the Grik used their fire weapons to disperse the defenders. Flaming spheres, twice the size of a person's head, arced across the water to explode against the side of Home. Fire ran like water into the sea, but some made it onto the catwalk and the flames rapidly spread. Some spread onto people too, and Chack raged at the memory of their screams and the stench of burning fur. While they fought the flames, the Grik closed. Lance hurlers fired with a crash, and the Grik ships were festooned with their shafts, but still they came. Finally they were alongside, directly below, and their hulls ground together. Crossbow bolts rained down and thumped into bodies, shields, and the enemy decks, but then the ladders came. Hundreds of grappling hooks and dozens of ladders from each ship rose and locked the combatants together. The Grik swarmed up. The Guard slashed ropes and pushed at the ladders, and attackers rained into the sea, to be crushed between the hulls or shredded by the incredible seething multitude of flasher-fish that churned the water into a glittering, silver-red cauldron of death. But still they came, as they always did, and there were so many.

Very quickly, the fighting became hand to hand when first a few, then many Grik gained the decks of Home. Scotas and axes rose and fell, as did the strange, curved short-swords and spears of the Grik. Spreading flames went unfought as defenders were forced to grapple with the attackers. Chack had stood with his sister, transfixed with horror as they watched the awful slaughter. A triumphant cheer began somewhere aft, and they turned to see a column of smoke and flames spew skyward from one of the Grik ships. Apparently their entire store of fire weapons was ignited on deck, and a keening, whistling, collective shriek rose from the burning warriors. Some, deliberately or in mindless panic, leaped into the sea and were torn apart. Gri-kakka had risen as well, and several cruised sedately through the turmoil, snapping at struggling figures. The Grik ship was rapidly consumed. Burning sails flapped, and crackling flames licked up the spindly masts until they withered and fell amid a huge cloud of steam and sparks. The hulk drifted slowly away, a roiling, lifeless inferno. But there were more.

Unaffected, the other Grik continued the attack. That was when the wing runners went into the fight and Chack became a warrior at last.

The first Grik he killed was an accident. He'd practically landed on it when he slid down the shrouds. Striking out instinctively with his axe, he clove through the leather helmet it wore and split its skull in two. He expected to be nauseated, to feel some remorse, but there was nothing. Nothing at first. Then a quickening surge of . . . exhilaration flowed through his heart and limbs. With a bellow, he waded forward, swinging the axe two-handed in the precise reaping motion he'd been taught. An astonishing, wondrous, visceral glee filled his soul as the murderers of his people fell before him. Through the long hours he hacked and slew, Risa by his side, shouting encouragement, and the pride in her voice was clear, even over the din of battle. Then she fell.

Now the sun was halfway to the horizon, above the mountainous shore to the west. He didn't know how many Grik he'd killed, satisfying as it was. He did know it wasn't enough. Their losses were terrible, but regardless how many were slain, still more waited on their ships to crowd onto the battlefield that *Salissa* had become. And those that still fought did so with a fresh abandon as shocking as their savagery. One ship had sunk alongside, pierced by lance-hurler shafts. So many lines held it fast that it hung, just below the surface, its masts crawling with Grik. The weight of the hulk caused *Salissa* to heel a few degrees.

Another Grik ship went up in flames, but only after it was lashed to *Salissa*. Its funeral pyre provided the fuel to ignite a fire on Home itself that threatened to consume it. Flames raged out of control on the right side of the first tower, and the forewing—the very symbol of Chack's clan—burned above. Flames roared hundreds of tails into the sky, while charred and smoldering pieces of fabric snowed down upon them. Ironically, the only thing saving the weary, dwindling defenders was that the heat on that side was too intense even for the Grik to bear. That left a front only fifteen tails wide to defend on the left side of the tower. Once, the Grik broke through into the very body of Home, and the slaughter among the garden tenders was terrible. A counterattack by Keje and his personal Guard managed to repulse the thrust. Keje had abandoned his position on the battlement and along with his personal Guard—and even Selass, Chack saw with surprise—he was everywhere. Whenever the enemy began to break through, he and his diminishing followers somehow stemmed the tide.

The battle aft was going well, but only one ship grappled there. Chack and his fellows were fighting the better part of three Grik crews, and one ship was still unengaged. It hadn't lashed on with the others when the one before it caught fire. For most of the day, it sailed around, looking for a good place to strike. The lance hurlers still in action flailed at it mercilessly, however, and it looked a little low in the water. At present, it actually seemed to be moving away, although Chack could barely see through the smoke, which stung his eyes and made each breath an effort. If he hadn't known better, he'd almost have thought it was leaving! That was absurd, of course. The Grik never ran. Always, they were either destroyed or left wallowing helpless in their intended victim's wake. It was probably positioning itself to take advantage of the wind so it could attack some uninvolved point. When it did, it would surely turn the tide. Of course, it made small difference. The fire that preserved them for the moment would destroy them in the end. If it wasn't extinguished soon, all of *Salissa* Home would burn.

Chack fell out of the battle line to catch his breath. Only so many fighters would fit in that limited space, and mercifully, it allowed them to rotate out briefly every now and then. He was panting with exhaustion, and his tongue lolled, but miraculously, his only wound was a shallow slash across his left shoulder. He trotted to a freshwater barrel and drank greedily. The water had a reddish tinge from bloody hands that had reached for the cup, but he didn't care. All that mattered was the soothing liquid wetting his parched throat. Dropping the cup back in the barrel, he looked about for a moment.

Younglings, garden tenders, and other old ones raced or crept back and forth, depending on their ability, carrying water to the fire. Their efforts, while noble, were in vain. Chack felt a growing dread that no matter how the battle went they were all going to burn. The entire forewing was gone, and the flaming debris had fallen on the tower, adding to the conflagration. It would all be for nothing. He hoped with a surge of grief that his sister was already dead—at least then she wouldn't die in the flames. In bitter resignation, he hefted his bloody axe with aching arms and turned back toward the fight—just in time to glimpse two large columns of water straddle the lurking Grik ship, and a mighty explosion of fire and smoke at its waterline that sent it rolling onto its side.

"My God, sir! How can we not take sides! Just *look* over there!" cried Bradford incredulously.

Matt stared at him, his face granite. "I didn't say we wouldn't help. I said I wish we didn't have to—because when we do, we take sides. We know nothing about what's going on. For all we know, those . . . attackers are the good guys! Just because they look like the lizards on Bali doesn't mean they are the same. What if somebody judged our actions simply because we look like Germans? Also—and I'll only tell you this once, Mr. Bradford— you're on my bridge at my sufferance. One more outburst and I'll have you removed. Is that clear?"

"Will you remove me too?" demanded Sandra, her eyes flashing like pistol muzzles.

Matt sighed angrily. "Lieutenant, I wish you weren't here *now*. We may be about to go into battle. In case you've forgotten, you have a battle station!"

She stared at him, unrepentant and smoldering. The rest of the men in the pilothouse very studiously observed anything but the confrontation with their captain. Even so, it was plain that their sympathies rested with Bradford and Lieutenant Tucker.

"Look," said Matt, as reasonably as he could, "this isn't our fight . . ." He immediately raised a hand to ward off interruption. "Yet. I feel inclined to help the—what did you call them? Lemurians?" Bradford nodded determinedly. Personally, he had had quite enough of this monkey-cat or cat-monkey business. "I feel inclined to help them too," Matt repeated, "but *we are all alone out here*. If we do, we might get involved in an all-out war, and we have no idea what resources the enemy has. *We* damn sure don't have any. Besides, look at those ships! Unlike the . . . Lemurians . . . those lizard people have ships right out of the eighteenth century. *Our* eighteenth century! The similarity in design is too perfect to be coincidence! They must've had contact with other humans! Maybe other people came through a squall—or something like we did—before. Don't you see? If that's the case, maybe these lizards can tell us about them! Maybe they're still here!" He was silent for a moment as he let his point drift home. "If we shoot at them, I doubt they'll give us answers."

He swiveled in his chair, gazing through the windows at the battle, closer by the moment. "On the other hand . . ." he murmured darkly, and said no more. The Lemurians were certainly outnumbered, and given the obvious disparity in the ships' speeds, there was no question who started the fight. So far, none of the creatures seemed to have noticed their approach. With the smoke so thick and the fighting so intense, that was understandable. But sooner or later, they would be noticed. Maybe the sight of the destroyer would have the same effect as before, and everybody would just stop what they were doing and stare. That might provide an opening. It wasn't much of a plan, but it was all he could think of short of going in with guns blazing.

In spite of his argument, he knew, deep down, that was what he wanted to do. Marvaney's death was still fresh, and the creatures battling the Lemurians certainly resembled the ones that had killed him. Besides, from what he saw, they weren't any more civilized than their apparent cousins on Bali. He might lose the chance to gain vital information, but sometimes you had to do something just because it was right. "Let's see what happens," he said at last.

"Captain, Mr. Garrett says they must've seen us," said Reynolds. "One of the lizards is coming about. Range is now twenty-one double zero."

Matt saw the change in aspect as the ship tacked, headsails filling and pulling it around. He'd walked the decks of the USS *Constitution* as a kid and was struck by her uncanny resemblance to the ship that was turning to meet them. The color was different—this ship was painted entirely red—and there were no gunports, but otherwise it looked just like an earlier version of the old frigate, even down to the number of masts and the sail plan. "Slow to two-thirds," he commanded as the range diminished.

"Twelve double zero," said Reynolds behind him, parroting Garrett's estimate as the range wound down. The lizard ship was wearing a lot of canvas and Matt estimated its speed at eight to ten knots. Respectable, but troubling. This bold, all-out approach was more like the behavior of the Bali creatures than he quite liked. They didn't seem overawed by the destroyer at all, or even carefully curious like the Lemurians had been. They acted more like they were trying to come to grips.

"Nine hundred yards, sir."

"Slow to one-third. Come left thirty degrees. Guns one, three, and four will track the target."

"Bridge," came the voice of Elden. "A lot of those lizard critters are gathering in the target's bows . . . They have swords and shields." The final words were incredulous.

"Pass the word for Chief Campeti. Have him issue rifles and sidearms to any deck personnel not part of the gun crews. Prepare to repel boarders." Matt was struck by the strangeness of the order even as he gave it. Probably not since the War of 1812 had the captain of a U.S. warship given the order to repel boarders on the high seas. He allowed himself an ironic smile. "At three hundred yards, the number three gun will put a shot across her bow if she doesn't ease off."

He glanced at Sandra and Courtney Bradford. They watched with mixed expressions, but at least Bradford's ire had faded. Matt raised an eyebrow with a look that seemed to say, "What were we arguing about?" and lifted his binoculars again. The sight that greeted him sent a chill down his spine. Elden was right. A large group of lizards stood in the bow of the oncoming ship, brandishing swords, spears, and garish shields. Their toothy mouths were open wide in an unheard shout or chant. Many clashed their weapons against their shields and seemed quite exercised. Even more ominous, many were holding what appeared to be grappling hooks, and as he watched, more and more joined those already poised on the fo'c'sle. There were hundreds of them, just on that one ship.

"Three hundred yards!" came Reynolds's breathless report.

In a calm voice, devoid of inflection, Captain Reddy uttered a single word. "Fire."

He never lowered his binoculars, but watched as the number three gun crashed and, a bare instant later, a geyser erupted between *Walker* and the approaching ship. A sheet of water cascaded down on the lizards and sent a few of them scrambling. But far from having the desired effect, the shot seemed to make those remaining in the bow redouble their clamoring and yelling. A moment passed, then another, and the ship showed no sign of turning or heaving to.

Suddenly, at two hundred yards, something roughly the size of a medicine ball arced lazily up, high in the air, from amid the gathered lizards. An instant later, a second object rose, and then a third. Everyone in the pilothouse saw them with unaided eyes. The objects reached apogee, tumbling end over end and trailing wisps of smoke. Down they came, closer and closer until two plummeted into the sea scarcely a dozen yards off *Walker*'s port beam. On impact with the water, they ruptured and a ball of fire rose skyward and burning fluid of some kind spread flames upon the waves. The third was closer, and when the projectile ruptured, burning fuel actually washed up *Walker*'s side, just below the number one gun.

Matt lowered his binoculars and looked at those standing nearby. When he spoke, his voice sounded vaguely surprised, but his eyes were suffused with fury.

"Did they just throw those balls of fire at *us*?"

For just the slightest moment, he reflected upon the consequences and ramifications of his next act, but the decision came without any apparent hesitation. He stepped briskly to Reynolds, took the headset from him, and spoke directly into the microphone. "Mr. Garrett, this is the captain. Commence firing."

Chack rubbed unbelieving eyes. Three more simultaneous explosions annihilated the stricken Grik ship. Debris and parts of bodies rained into the sea hundreds of tails in all directions. The shattered hulk was quickly awash. Shredded sails fluttered as the center mast teetered and crashed amid the struggling, dying Grik. The tumult of battle briefly ebbed as the People— and the Grik—tried in vain to pierce the haze and smoke with red, running eyes to see what had occurred. The ship sank quickly from sight, leaving only tangled flotsam and shrieking carrion for the insatiable fish. Beyond, Chack saw a strangely familiar shape.

The Tail-less Ones! he realized with a sense of wonder, then repeated his thought at the top of his lungs. "The Tail-less Ones! They have returned! The Tail-less Ones destroy the Grik!" With a gleeful bellow, echoed by many, and a surge of unexpected hope, he waded back into battle. The Grik fought just as fiercely as before and, if anything, with renewed frenzy. But the frenzy was different somehow. For the first time he sensed desperation and—could it be?—fear. Chack fed off that, real or imagined, as he swung his axe in great arcs that hewed heads and arms and chests. His own arms ached and the axe became difficult to grasp. Sometimes it slipped sideways and he struck a Grik or its shield with the flat of the blade and felt the blow jar his bones, but still he fought on. Others sensed the difference as well, and they pushed the Grik with renewed energy. The flames began to envelop the forward tower and, reluctantly, the Grik gave ground. It was that or burn.

Chack found a moment to cast a glance at their saviors. They approached closer, but after so decisively dealing with the unattached ship, they hesitated, as if unsure what to do. He understood. They'd clearly decided to help the People, but their magical weapons weren't selective enough to influence the battle for Home itself. At least he thought that at first.

"What now?" whispered Matt. They'd thrown away any hope of neutrality when they destroyed the lizard ship, and there was clearly no hope for survivors. That was a terrible aspect of naval war in this new world that he would have to bear in mind, he thought, watching the flashing shapes consume the last of the creatures in the water. They'd fired in self-defense, but he doubted the hundreds of lizards fighting the Lemurians would see it that way. Okay, so maybe two salvos were excessive, but they'd made him mad. Now, like it or not, he had chosen sides, and as precarious as the situation on the big ship looked, this wasn't the time for half measures. One side or the other would win this fight, and it didn't seem like a good idea to let it be the ones they'd shot at.

"Come left, to one three zero," he said coldly. "Gun crews stand by, but cease firing. Small arms will commence firing at one hundred yards. The targets are the lizards on the Lemurian ship. The machine guns may fire, but have them conserve ammunition and be careful of their targets. Concentrate where the enemy is massing, away from the 'friendlies.' Rig all fire hoses and have handlers standing by." He clasped his hands behind his back, listening to the responses, and stared straight ahead at the battle.

Sandra moved beside him, also looking at what they were getting themselves into. "I'm sorry, Captain," she said in a small, quiet voice.

He looked at her a moment, then nodded with a shrug. "Me too," he said. "I guess it's not in me to watch something like this without trying to help. But Lord above, we have enough problems without winding up in the middle of a war!" He spoke quietly, so she was the only one who knew, truly, what an agonizing decision it had been. They heard the crack of Springfields as riflemen on deck chose their targets, and the starboard .30-cal opened with short bursts of its own.

"These . . . Lemurians better be worth it," he said grimly. "Because every bullet we fire for them is one less we'll have to save our own asses with." With that, he stepped away from her and onto the starboard bridgewing to take *Walker* back to war.

"Hot damn!" growled Dennis Silva as he racked the bolt back on the starboard .50-cal. "We finally get to kill somebody!" Ordnance Striker Gil Olivera was beside him, poised to change the ammunition box when it was empty. He giggled nervously. Alfonso Reavis and Sandy Newman also stood nearby, Springfields over their shoulders, but their job was to gather spent shells before they rolled into the sea. Silva didn't know why; as far as he knew, they couldn't be reloaded. Even if they'd had more bullets— which they didn't—they didn't have powder or primers. Oh, well, he didn't care. He'd finally been ordered to kill the hell out of somebody, and he was ready. If Campeti wanted guys scurrying around picking up his empty brass, that wasn't his concern.

The sound of battle on the burning ship was awesome. The roaring flames could be heard over the blower, and the screams and shouts from alien throats lent the scene a surrealistic aspect. He couldn't see much through the smoke, though, and he squinted over his sights. There. There seemed to be a battle line of sorts formed just aft of the base of that big tower forward. It was burning like mad, and the heat and smoke must be hell. He pointed it out to Felts, who stood between him and the number three gun with one of the BARs. "Everything forward of there looks like nothin' but lizards!" he shouted. Felts squinted and nodded. If they got too much closer, they'd be shooting up. One of the lizard ships was sunk alongside, between them and the enemy horde, and men were shooting lizards from its rigging.

"I see it, Dennis. If we shoot in among that bunch, we ought to get half a dozen with each shot!"

"'Zactly!" said Silva, and grinned.

"Just be careful not to hit any of them monkey-cats!" warned Felts.

Silva rolled his eyes. "The hell you say, Tommy Felts! They're cat-monkeys, goddamn it! How many times have I got to tell you! Are you strikin' for snipe, or what?"

Before Felts could answer, Silva let out a whoop and pressed the butterfly trigger on the back of his gun. A stream of tracers arced across the short distance through the smoke and into the densely packed mass of lizard warriors.

"I'll teach you to kick *my* 'Cats, you unnatural sons-a-bitches!" Silva screamed.

Keje-Fris-Ar felt dazed as he sagged with his hands on his knees, panting. The world was upside down. He'd been wounded superficially in many places and was faint with fatigue and perhaps loss of blood. His tongue was swollen, his lips cracked and bleeding, and he'd lost his voice hours ago. He blinked thanks when Selass gave him a large copper mug, but his hands shook uncontrollably and he couldn't drink. From the gloom, Adar was beside him, helping to hold it still. Pridefully, he tried to shake off the Sky Priest's hands, but didn't have the strength even for that. Instead, he drank greedily with closed eyes as the tepid water soothed his throat. But even with eyes closed, his mind still saw the momentous things he'd witnessed.

He'd seen things that day that rivaled the epic power of the Scrolls themselves. Acts of courage and horror without compare—without precedence—as far as he knew. And he'd seen wonders beyond comprehension, such as the power of the Tail-less Ones who'd so unexpectedly come to their aid. Without whose aid they'd have surely perished. But beyond even that, he'd seen what that power did to the Grik. The People helped, of course, but it was the power of the Tail-less Ones that worked the miracle he could hardly believe, even now. The Grik had broken.

They hadn't been merely repulsed; he'd seen that before. They'd utterly and completely *broken* and fled in absolute terror from the combined assault of the Tail-less Ones' magic and the vengeful ferocity of the People. There'd been confusion on both sides at first, when suddenly there raged a hammering sound like nothing ever heard and the Grik—but only the Grik—began dying by the score. Hundreds fell, horribly mangled, in the space of a few short breaths, and they couldn't fight—couldn't even see—whatever was killing them! The panic began in their rear, behind the fighting, and Keje first noticed it as a lessening pressure in front of his fighters. Wary glances of alarm became shrieks of rage and terror, as the Grik saw their comrades dying and fleeing behind them. Keje saw it too, and despite his own shock, grasped the opportunity. He led the charge that swept the enemy entirely from the decks of Home.

The killing had been wanton and the victory complete. He couldn't count how many Grik were cut down from behind, or hacked and clawed one another to death as they fled back to the ships still lashed to *Salissa*. Hundreds simply leaped into the sea, so total had their panic been. One Grik ship got clear, so the victory wasn't entirely complete, but the other tried to flee in full view of the Tail-less Ones' amazing ship, and two thunderous booms from their strange tubes left it a sinking wreck. The ship then surged forward, apparently to chase the other, but almost immediately slowed and came about, back to the side of Home. The strange beings rushed to and fro, dragging heavy ropelike things around their deck, and then, to the further amazement of all, water surged upon the fires raging in the forward part of *Salissa*.

A gentle, refreshing mist still descended on Keje as dusk slowly ended this momentous day and his People gleefully rolled Grik corpses over the side. With an effort, he disengaged from the supporting hands of his oldest friend and daughter and crept painfully to the rail. There below, he saw the same figure looking up he'd seen just days before. Fighting pain and weariness with nothing but will, he raised his right arm and gave the Sign of the Empty Hand. He hoped, somehow, the gesture would convey a fraction of his gratitude.

In the glare of the dwindling flames, he was sure the creature raised its hand as well, and he slumped into the arms of his friend and his daughter—and others. As they carried him away he realized that tomorrow the sun would rise on a different world. One in which the Grik were more bold and more numerous than their worst nightmares could have foretold, but also a world in which the Grik had been broken, and his People had powerful friends.

The battle was over—at least the fighting part was. Like all battles, the aftermath looked as gruesome and painful as the strife. *Walker*'s searchlights illuminated the continuing toil on the deck of the huge ship that floated, still smoldering, less than a hundred yards away. The Lemurians tending their many wounded and throwing their enemies over the side appeared hesitant to enter the powerful beams at first, but they quickly recognized the friendly gesture, if not the power behind it. They now took full advantage of the unusual illumination. *Very practical creatures,* Matt observed. He'd hesitated to use the lights, concerned that they might perceive them as some sort of threat or an unwholesome act on *Walker*'s part. His concerns were quickly put to rest. Even if the Lemurians were uneasy, after what *Walker* had done for them, they were evidently prepared to accept her benevolence.

"Secure from general quarters," he said quietly, and joined Sandra, Bradford, and the torpedo-director crew on the bridgewing. The torpedo-men were unplugging their headsets and securing their equipment. He glanced up and behind to see Garrett and several others leaning on the rail of the fire-control platform, watching the labors of their "allies." A tiny meteor arced over the side as Chief Gray, on the foredeck below the splash-guard, guiltily flicked a cigarette away. "The smoking lamp's *lit,* Boats," Matt called down with amusement. The number one gun crew chuckled, and Gray turned on them in a vitriolic frenzy. Matt listened to the humorous tirade and shook his head.

"We should help them," said Sandra, referring to the scene on the wounded ship. She paused, remembering her meager resources. Their supplies were limited, and so were the personnel of her "division." Karen Theimer was increasingly withdrawn, and Jamie Miller was just a kid. Besides, they couldn't all go. Still . . .

"I should help them. I should go across immediately and offer assistance, Captain." She'd turned to face him, her words changing from an observation to a formal request.

He looked at her thoughtfully, but reluctantly shook his head. "That might be a good idea," he temporized. "It wouldn't hurt our résumé with our new friends either, as long as they recognize your efforts for what they are. But it's just not possible."

"I'm afraid I must insist, Captain. We had no casualties and I'm sure I can make my intentions known. Pain has no language. Even if I can't speak to them or know their physiology, I can help bandage. My God, they may not even know about germs!"

He nodded sympathetically and spoke very gently. "I admire your courage and compassion. But it really is impossible and you must not insist." He gestured over the side. The sea still churned with the silvery, tuna-sized fish. Whenever another lizard hit the water, it frothed and thrashed anew. Sandra followed his gaze and bit her lip. "There's no way I'm risking you or Nurse Theimer—not to mention a boat and crew—until things settle down. By morning the fish may have had their fill, and in daylight we might give it a try."

"There's no other way?" she asked, almost plaintively.

"No. In daylight, if those things are still down there, and we can get the Lemurians to understand, we might shoot a line across and rig a bosun's chair. But that'll take coordination and some very careful station-keeping. If one of those plesiosaurs shows up, we might have to maneuver . . ." He stopped. "That won't work either. Hopefully by then we can just use a boat."

He spoke no more and just stared across the water. His face was troubled, frowning. He was anxious to meet the Lemurians for a number of reasons. First, he certainly agreed with Sandra: if they could render medical assistance, they should offer it. More important, they'd just waded into a war in a big way, and he had no idea where they stood or how big a war it was. Possibly the lizards were simply raiders, the local equivalent of Malay pirates. Maybe the Lemurians represented the greater power, and even if there was a general war going on, they'd just ingratiated themselves to that power and all their problems were solved. But it was equally possible that the reverse was true. One of the lizard ships had escaped, and however powerful they might be, there was no doubt about the role *Walker* played in the battle. What's more, they might not be so easily discouraged by modern weapons again. He wanted answers. And there lurked another problem: how in the world would they communicate? Perhaps Bradford would have suggestions.

After a while Sandra tentatively put her hand on his in the darkness. "I'm sorry again," she said.

He looked at her, genuinely surprised—by the words and the touch. "What for?"

"For . . . a lot of things. For pressuring you. Doubting you. I know how hard it was, how much you wanted to avoid this. But you did the right thing."

He looked at her very frankly and sighed. "I think so too, or I wouldn't have done it. I hope we're both right." He smiled. "I guess we'll find out."

With the dawn, the sea regained its deceptively mild appearance and Captain Reddy ordered the larger motor launch prepared instead of the whaleboat. It was safer, and he wanted as many observers as possible. Sandra, Bradford, Gray, McFarlane, and Letts would go with him, along with two carpenter's mates and an armed security detachment consisting of Silva, Felts, Reavis, and Newman. Tony Scott was coxswain. On a whim, more than for any other reason, Matt accepted Lieutenant Shinya's request to go, although he would be the only one without a sidearm. He wasn't really worried that Shinya would do anything untoward, but he believed—and even took time to explain to him—that the crew wouldn't approve.

Again, he left Larry Dowden in command. "I don't expect any trouble," he told him, "but that's what I thought last time. Remain at general quarters while we're away. They've got to be expecting to say howdy in some fashion, but I'd rather do it on their ship first. If we wait around too long, they might decide to visit us, and I don't want them roaming around my ship until we know more about them."

"Understood, Captain, but I still ought to be the one to go," Dowden said with a frown.

Matt grinned. "May be, but I'm the captain, so I get to do what I want. Seriously, though, I agree in principle, but—well, we've already been through this. You can be the first to meet the strange alien creatures next time, Larry. I promise."

He climbed into the launch, which was already level with the deck. That was another good thing about the launch, he thought: it could be lowered with them in it. Slipping and falling into the water was no longer just an embarrassing gaffe; it was a death sentence. The keel smacked the waves and, with a burbling roar, they started across. The sun was up, but it was still early and Matt hoped they wouldn't catch the Lemurians in a crabby mood before their version of morning coffee. More important, he didn't want to surprise them. He needn't have been concerned. Evidently, they'd been watching his ship very closely because, as soon as they approached, many of the creatures stopped what they were doing and scampered to the rail. Strange, excited cries alerted others.

"Hail the conquering heroes," the Bosun growled.

As they drew nearer, the ship's sheer size was even more impressive from their lower perspective. The rail was easily a hundred feet over their heads, and there was no question that the thing was as large as one of the new fleet carriers. Maybe bigger. That made the damage it had sustained even more amazing. The forward superstructure was completely destroyed, and the foremast tripod stood naked and charred. The pagoda-like tower had collapsed upon itself to become a mere heap of smoldering rubble. Clouds of ash billowed to leeward like gouts of steam. The forward part of the hull was scorched as well, though there didn't seem to be serious damage to its structural integrity. It was massive, and while it was clearly made of wood, there was no telling how thick it was. Matt was surprised to discover that the bottom was copper-clad, much like *Walker's* sailing-navy ancestors. No doubt the copper extending several feet above the sea served the same purpose here—to protect the hull from wood-eating organisms.

They coasted alongside, approximately amidships, until the launch almost bumped. But Scott was an excellent coxswain even with the more unfamiliar launch, and he avoided actual contact by the thinnest margin. They saw no way up, however. There were no steps or ladders for them to climb, and for the moment they could only stare at the numerous heads, high above, peering back down at them. Suddenly, a very familiar-looking rope-and-rung arrangement unrolled down the side with a clatter and jerked to a stop almost upon them.

"Well," said Bradford, "not exactly a red carpet, after all, but certainly a warmer welcome than they gave their last visitors." There were several chuckles, and Matt took the ladder in his hands.

"Ordinarily, I always say 'ladies first,' but this time I'll break that rule." There were more chuckles and a few uneasy glances at Lieutenant Tucker. Her reputation and stature had reached an unprecedented level, for a non-destroyerman (and a woman). She possessed undoubted skill as a healer and was genuinely friendly to those in her care. But she'd flown signals of an equally unprecedented temper, and her sense of humor had yet to be tried. She didn't take offense at the captain's attempt to seem lighthearted about his protectiveness of her, however.

"Boats, you're next, then the security detail. Once they're up, everyone can follow as they see fit." He started up the ladder, but then stopped. "Everybody stay cool and friendly, and remember who you are and what you represent." With that, he resumed his climb. He tried to appear brisk and confident and hoped no one detected his nervousness. He wasn't afraid, exactly, but he had to admit to some anxious uncertainty. Never in his most bizarre dreams had he imagined that he would be doing what he was right now. Nothing he'd ever done had prepared him for this moment, and he didn't have the slightest idea what to do. The only thing he was sure of was that nobody else did either and he'd better not screw it up.

Finally, he reached the rail and paused for a moment before jumping to the deck. Many of the creatures had gathered around, and they drew back at the sight of him, their inscrutable faces staring with large, feline eyes. They were every conceivable color, like three generations of kittens from a wanton barn cat. Long, fluffy tails twitched behind them, seemingly independent of their owners' stoic immobility. And they were short. He hadn't realized it, watching them through binoculars, but they were much shorter than he'd expected. The tallest he saw came only to his chin, and it was considerably taller than the others. He? She? He assumed it was a he, though he had no basis, yet, to make that guess. The majority of the creatures were dressed haphazardly, in what appeared to be a mixture of daily garb and the occasional piece of leather and copper armor. All seemed weary and many were wounded, but most were still armed with an axe or a short scimitar-like sword. Significantly, none were brandishing those weapons at him.

What set the tall one apart, aside from his height, was that he was covered entirely in a dark purple robe with large stars sewn across the shoulders, and the long-tailed hood was pulled tight around his face so that only his piercing gray eyes could be seen. The creatures nearest him seemed more alert than the rest, more detached from the moment, and they had a protective, proprietary air about them. Because of this, and his dress, Matt took him for a leader, or at least an authority figure of some kind. Gray clambered over the rail to join him and as he did, he put his hand on one of the enormous backstays supporting the center tripod. He took it away and looked at it. The stay was coated with thick black tar. He arched an eyebrow at his captain and Matt nodded. He'd seen it too. He stepped forward and the two of them, the robed figure and the naval officer, quietly faced one another while the rest of the party boarded. All the while, there was silence. Matt couldn't even fall back on Navy custom and salute their flag, for there was none, at least at present, but maybe . . . maybe that didn't matter. Tradition was tradition, and he expected even if they didn't understand it, they would recognize it as such. Maybe they would appreciate the respect that went with it.

Abruptly, he pivoted to his right, facing aft, and snapped a sharp salute. Then he turned to the robed figure and saluted him as well.

"Lieutenant Commander Matthew Reddy, United States Navy. I request permission to come aboard, sir."

The Lemurian blinked rapidly with what might have been surprise, and his lips stretched into what looked for all the world like a grin. Matt held the salute a moment longer, and then on impulse slowly lowered his hand until he held it, palm outward, toward the creature in the purple robe. Very deliberately, it pulled the hood from its face. It was still "grinning" broadly, although the expression didn't extend beyond its mouth. Matt suspected that, like cats, their faces weren't made to display emotions as humans did. The "grin," if that's what it was, spoke volumes, however, and now others nearby grinned too. To the amazement of the humans, the one in the robe carefully imitated Matt's salute and held up his hand as well. Matt heard a gasp behind him, as well as Gray's gravelly chuckle.

"Permission granted, Skipper," he said quietly.

The Lemurian clasped both his hands to his chest and spoke: "Adar."

Bradford pushed his way next to the captain. "Upon my word! Do you suppose he means *he* is Adar, or that's the name for his people?"

Matt sighed. "I was about to . . . ask him that, Mr. Bradford. Please, let's have no more outbursts. It might confuse them and I'm confused enough for us all right now." He pointed at the creature. "Adar?" he asked.

The Lemurian blinked twice and, if anything, his grin grew broader. He spread his hands out from his sides and bowed.

Matt clasped his own hands to his chest and said, "Matthew Reddy."

The creature struggled to wrap his mouth around the unfamiliar sounds. Then he made an attempt.

"Maa-tyoo Riddy."

Matt grinned back at him. "Pretty good." He turned and proceeded to name those who accompanied him, and then pointed across the water where the destroyer kept station. She really was a sight, he reflected. Streaks of rust covered her sides and the patched battle damage was made conspicuous by the fresher paint. The lizard firebomb had scorched a large section of her hull just aft of her number, and the paint was bubbled and flaking. Most of the crew was on deck at the moment too, watching them. The tattered Stars and Stripes fluttered near the top of the short mast aft.

"USS *Walker*," he said.

A respectful silence ensued that lasted while all the Lemurians gazed at his battered ship. Adar's grin went away and he somehow radiated solemnity when he spoke again.

"Waa-kur."

He blinked rapidly and gestured toward an opening in the large deckhouse behind him. He hesitated uncertainly, looking back, then strode purposefully through it. The other creatures cleared a lane. Apparently, he expected them to follow. Matt looked at the Bosun, who shrugged, and he glanced at the others and caught Sandra's eye. He shrugged too, and strode after the purple-robed figure, followed closely by his companions. Silva made a half-strangled, incredulous sound. Matt looked back.

"What . . . ?" Then he saw it too. Suddenly, there was no doubt Adar was male. For the first time—driving home how distracted they were—they realized many of the Lemurians staring with open curiosity were also openly, glaringly—very humanly—female. Except for bits of armor, none wore much more than a kind of skirt, or kilt. Supremely practical, since their tails made other types of clothing inconvenient, but few tunics were worn by anyone. Furry breasts of a shape and proportion entirely, fondly, familiar (except for the fur, of course) unself-consciously jutted at them from all directions. Not surprisingly, Silva was the first to notice.

"Oh, my God!" squeaked Newman.

"Fascinating!" breathed Bradford.

"Not unusual," said Sandra, a little sharply, Matt thought, and he saw her cheeks were pink. "Even 'back home' it's not unusual at all for primitive people to go around like . . . this."

"Way too 'unusual,' far as I'm concerned," whispered Felts, and Sandra's cheeks went darker.

"Silence!" growled Gray with less than normal vehemence. Clearing his throat, he went on, "Quit gawkin' at their dames! You want 'em to eat us? Pick up yer eyeballs. They're *critters*, for God's sake!"

Matt coughed. "Not 'critters,' and not too 'primitive' to take offense, so keep your eyes"—he looked straight at Silva—"and your hands to yourselves. That's an order!"

They stooped to enter the doorway, but inside was a much larger chamber than expected. It spanned the entire "ground" floor of the tower and the ceiling was as high as a college gym. Tapestries of coarse but ornately woven fibers decorated the walls, and large overstuffed pillows lay about the room in groups. It was a scene of considerable opulence compared to the scorched and bloodstained exterior. But even here, the scent of burnt wood and charred flesh and fur was all-pervading. Matt wondered how long that dreadful smell would linger like a shroud. In the center of the hall, the ceiling opened up to allow a strange-looking tree to rise, far above their heads. The only trees he knew were live oaks, cedars, and mesquite, so he couldn't tell if it was more like a palm tree or a pine. But whichever, the thick, strangely barked trunk rose ten or fifteen feet before it branched into stubby limbs with delicate, greenish-gold palmated leaves. He looked at it curiously, but was more intrigued by the shape of another Lemurian seated on a stool at a small table nearby.

The creature sat completely still except for his tail, which swished slowly back and forth. Others stood around him, but it was clear that the short, powerfully muscled one with reddish-brown fur was who they attended.

Matt wasn't startled to recognize him as the one he'd waved to before. Without hesitation, he strode forward, closely followed by his companions, and held his hand up once again in what was evidently a universal sign of greeting, even here. Adar positioned himself next to the seated figure who, Matt saw upon closer inspection, had been wounded many times. Numerous cuts and slashes were evident across his powerful frame, and they hadn't been bandaged. Instead, a clear, but slightly yellowish viscous fluid had been smeared into them. Matt wondered what it was, and he could almost feel Sandra's anxious desire to go to him and help. He wasn't sure the Lemurian needed any assistance.

For one thing, the dark eyes that held his seemed clear and focused and devoid of any distraction that excessive pain or fever might cause. Very solemnly, the creature raised its own hand and held it up in greeting. It spoke a few gravelly syllables and its mouth spread into a grin. Again, the expression went no further, but Matt sensed sincerity reflected in the dark pools of the Lemurian's eyes. The one named Adar gestured with evident respect.

"Keje-Fris-Ar," he said and bowed his head slightly. All the other Lemurians did the same. "U-Amaki ay Mi-Anakka ay *Salissa*," Adar added, and the dignity with which he spoke implied a lofty title.

"I expect he's the big bull around here," whispered Gray, more to the others than to Matt. "Other one's probably a witch doctor or pope or somethin'."

In spite of himself and the situation, not to mention the tension he felt just then, Matt almost burst out laughing at the Bosun's inappropriate comparison. "Chief," he said through clenched teeth, "are you trying to get us killed? If you are, I bet one more comment like that will do the job." Matt hadn't looked at him when he spoke, but Gray's voice sounded sincerely flustered.

"Uh . . . sorry, Skipper. But, I mean, we could recite nursery rhymes and they wouldn't know the difference."

"No, but we would, and I doubt they'd react well if we all started laughing right when they're naming their gods or something. So put a lid on it!"

"Oh . . . *oh*!! Aye, aye, Skipper!"

"They are quite incredibly ugly," commented Jarrik-Fas, Keje's kinsman and head of *Salissa* Home's active Guard. He spoke quietly to Adar while the two groups regarded one another. "They have almost no fur and their skins look pale and sickly."

Adar replied from the corner of his mouth. "They looked beautiful enough yesterday when they helped drive off the Grik. Do you not agree?"

Jarrik grunted, but there was agreement in the sound. "The gri-kakka were welcome, too, while they devoured our enemies. But we'd not have wanted them to linger overlong."

"True, but had they remained, there's no question the gri-kakka would have done so in hopes of devouring us as well. Here there is that question. If the Tail-less Ones desired to devour us, they could have done so already with the power they possess. Yet they come peacefully before us."

"Not un-armed, though," observed Jarrik. "I don't know what those things are that some of them carry, but they must be weapons. And yet they give the Sign of the Empty Hand while their hands are not empty."

Adar was silent, thinking. He knew Keje was listening to the words of his two most trusted advisors, even as he watched their visitors. "That's true," Adar said, "but perhaps among their kind, the sign is more a figurative thing than a literal one. Perhaps it means their hands are empty toward us but not toward all."

"And perhaps the sign means something else to them entirely," grumbled Keje, speaking for the first time. "But the one who seems to be their leader has an empty hand, and it's with him I must find some way to speak. Besides, would you have gone unarmed with me to their ship, Jarrik?"

Jarrik looked at the back of his leader's head. "No, lord, I would not," he admitted. "Not that it would matter in the face of their magic."

The Tail-less Ones muttered among themselves as well, and Adar wondered if their conversation ran along similar lines. The long weapons some carried had been placed on their shoulders, suspended by straps. That was encouraging at least. Nearly all of them were talking now, and a large one, with less fur than the others, talked the most. Their faces moved in a manner he had to conclude displayed emotion in some way, since they had no tails and they rarely blinked. Their strange little ears couldn't possibly convey any meaning.

Another spoke quite a lot as well, one that was smaller than the others and had very long fur on its head. The proportions of its anatomy indicated it was female, but it was difficult to tell with all the cloth they wore.

"The Scrolls make no mention of these creatures?" Keje asked, and shifted uncomfortably.

"I'm not sure, lord," Adar temporized. "Not specifically. There is the reference by Siska-Ta to the tail-less race that departed into the East long ago," he said grudgingly, "but their vessels were utterly different. They had sails, much like the Grik." He tilted his head back, remembering, and quoted a line copied from the First Scrolls taught to him as a youngling, which he now taught his apprentices. It was in the forgotten language of the ancient Scrolls themselves, and none save the Sky Priests bothered to learn it. They had to, since it was the language of the ancients in which the secrets of the stars themselves had passed to them.

"And upon the longest of the long days, when the Sun Brother was large and close in the sky, they freed their great ship from the bottom of the sea and sailed into the East, into the emptiness of the Eastern Sea." Adar smiled slightly with pride in the power of his memory. He read the Scrolls often, but he rarely spoke the words. He glanced at the Tail-less Ones and was surprised that they'd stopped speaking. All were looking at him with what he surmised to be very intent expressions. The one with so little fur stared with his mouth open wide. The one with the black fur and the darkest skin stepped near their leader and spoke into his small, misshapen ear. The leader, eyes wide, looked at the speaker with even more apparent amazement, but nodded, and the black-furred one turned to Adar.

"This said . . . speech . . . yours?" asked the creature in the ancient language of the Scrolls.

Keje lurched to his feet in shock, just as Adar hit the floor in a dead faint.

Matt stood in *Walker's* pilothouse staring uneasily at the huge, wounded ship to starboard. They were creeping along in a generally north-northeasterly direction, at less than four knots. He reckoned that was as fast as the Lemurian ship could go in this wind, with all her damage. The Bosun stood beside him, as did McFarlane and Larry Dowden. The rest of the bridge watch went about their duties, but the usual banter was absent as the destroyermen strained to hear their words. He knew all the details would spread as fast as if he announced it on the shipwide circuit, but he felt no particular reason to keep the conversation secret. Everyone would know soon enough anyway.

"Latin," murmured Gray. "Who would've ever thought it?" Matt nodded.

"But how?" asked McFarlane wonderingly. "I mean, *how*?"

"How . . . any of this, Spanky?" Matt gestured vaguely around. "It should make it easier to communicate, though I doubt many of the men know more Latin than Lemurian. But I don't know how any more than you do. That's one of the things maybe Bradford or Lieutenant Shinya will find out."

Courtney Bradford, Lieutenant Shinya, Lieutenant Tucker, and the rest of the security detail had remained behind on the Lemurian ship and would stay for the rest of the day, with orders to learn as much as they could and render any possible aid. Once it was clear that his people had nothing to fear, Matt had decided to return to *Walker*. There was little he could add to the discussions, since he knew virtually no Latin, and with their now common enemy abroad in such unprecedented numbers—an enemy they now had a name for—he didn't want to be separated from his ship if the Grik returned.

"Finding out about the Grik was valuable, but frustrating. We still don't know very much. I don't think the Lemurians do either. They've never been attacked in such force before, though."

"They sure seemed appreciative for what we did for them," muttered Gray, and then he grinned. "Once that Adar fella came to, he jabbered up a storm."

"You understand some Latin, don't you, Bosun?" asked Dowden.

Gray smirked. "About enough to know that's what it is when I hear it. My mother was Catholic and she made me learn a little. Spanky should know more, though. Both his parents were Catholics." His eyes twinkled. "And he sure took up with enough good Catholic Filipino gals!"

"I'm Catholic," confirmed Spanky, narrowing his eyes at the Bosun, "but as far as understanding Latin, it might as well be Greek to me." He grinned sheepishly. "I never even tried to pick any up." He frowned. "Course, I never would have figured that little Jap could *speak* it!"

Gray turned to Matt. "Yeah, Skipper, what about that? I nearly joined Adar on the deck when he opened up. You think it's a good idea to leave him over there? I mean, he may have given his parole and all, but he's still a Jap. And how the hell does a Jap know Latin?" he grumped.

"Beats me," admitted Matt, "but Bradford knows it even better, and I guess he'll keep an eye on him. Besides, I think he's sincere about his parole," he added guardedly. "What possible advantage could he find in betraying us, anyway?"

"I don't know," said Gray darkly, "but he's a Jap. That's all the reason he needs to betray us."

Matt and the rest of his senior personnel were waiting for the launch when it drew alongside. He was anxious to hear what the rest of the boarding party had learned. As they came aboard, however, he quickly realized a few were missing. Bradford presented himself to the captain, although he didn't salute. He looked tired but excited.

"Where's Lieutenant Tucker?" Matt demanded immediately. "And Lieutenant Shinya and the two gunner's mates?"

Bradford made a shooing gesture. "They're perfectly fine, I assure you! Lieutenant Tucker has become engrossed in things medical and remained behind to assist with their wounded—as I'm sure you'll remember giving her permission to do." Bradford's face darkened. "They have quite a lot of wounded, I'm afraid. Perhaps half their people—and as many as a quarter killed—many of them children and the very old. The fighting must have been horrific, sir. Horrific!" He fumbled in his shirt pocket for a scribbled note. "Here's a list of supplies Miss Tucker would like sent over." Matt took the note and handed it wordlessly to Alan Letts. "In any event," continued Bradford, "the Jappo volunteered to remain and translate—extraordinary, that!" His eyes grew large. "Why ever in the world a young Jappo would want to learn Latin is quite beyond me, but I shall surely ask him! Yes, indeed! Oh, well, those two strapping lads—Silva, I believe, and . . . the other one—stayed behind to protect Miss Tucker, and the Jappo, I suppose, although they're in no danger, goodness, no! The United States Navy represented by USS *Walker* and all her people are quite popular and appreciated just now!"

Matt wasn't happy that Sandra had remained behind, but he had to admit she was in good hands if trouble arose. He was less sanguine about Dennis Silva's ability to refrain from starting trouble, however. "Very well," he said grudgingly.

"Were you actually able to talk with them? I mean conversationally?" Dowden asked.

"Well, yes, after a fashion. My Latin is slightly rusty—not many people speak it now, you know—but I've kept it up fairly well. It's virtually a necessity for my less professional pursuits. Did you know nearly every plant and creature has a Latin name? Of course you did." He gratefully accepted one of the precious Cokes and took a sip. "Ahem. Well, there are some differences, mostly in pronunciation. Frankly, the way their mouths are shaped, I'm astonished they can make human sounds at all. I did discover they learn their Latin from a written source—which makes sense. Otherwise, it would probably have become incomprehensible over time, passed down word of mouth."

Matt started to ask what written source, but Lieutenant McFarlane spoke first. "How long do you think they've been speaking it?"

"I don't think one could say they speak it, per se, as a language at any rate. Only a small percentage understand it at all, and those seem confined to a certain caste, or sect. Their society is segregated into several such groups, based on labor distribution, similar to the differentiation between your deck-apes and engine room snipes, but to a much higher degree.

"As best I can tell, there are three major castes, or 'clans,' among them, although it's a bit more complicated even than that because—" Matt held up his hand and made a winding motion as if to say "get on with it." Bradford looked sheepish and nodded. "Well, first you have the . . . I think 'wing runners' might be the most accurate translation. They're the ones controlling the masts and sails, much like 'topmen' would have done in our own sailing past. Then they have the 'Body of Home' clan—which is what they call their ship, by the way—*Salissa* Home. I've no idea what a '*Salissa*' is. Perhaps it means 'Home of our People,' or something like that. It may be their tribe." He blinked and rubbed his nose. "The Body of Home clan is the most numerous, and would be roughly parallel to 'waisters' in days of old. They're the ones who perform all the chores and duties required for everyday life: fishing, gardening, hull repair, et cetera. It's usually from this clan that their leaders arise, by the way. The third caste is the navigators or, to be more precise, 'Sky Priests.' There are very few of them, but they have a unique status. Their religion is all wrapped up in the semi-deification of the sun, the moon, and the heavens inclusively—which is not all that surprising, I suppose. I didn't have time to delve too deeply into their theology, of course, but I get the impression it's somewhat vague."

He looked at them and smiled. "The heavens are certainly important, not least because of their reliance upon the sky for navigation! There's much more to it than that, I'm sure, but you see? That's why their Sky Priests are taught Latin!"

Matt shook his head and wondered if he'd missed something. He was becoming used to Bradford's stream-of-consciousness way of communicating, but sometimes he missed the thread and it could be tiresome. He cleared his throat. "And why was that again?"

"Well, I don't know what they use as a general written language, or even if they have one at all. But one thing that chap Adar made perfectly clear was how surprised they were that we could speak the Ancient Tongue of the Sacred Scrolls themselves!"

"And what exactly are these Scrolls?"

"Why, I suppose they're much like our Bible! Complete with an exodus myth and admonitions to behave! I gathered from his few references that it is very Old Testament in nature."

"I take it, then," Matt said, trying not to let his impatience show, "that somehow these Scrolls are written in Latin?"

Bradford looked at him as he might a dull pupil in a classroom. "Of course they are! That's the whole point, don't you see? Not only are they a Bible, of sorts, they're also charts and navigation aids as well! That's why the priests must learn to speak a language that's even more dead here than it ever was back home."

"Prob'ly why there's so few of 'em," Gray put in with a snort. Bradford glared at him.

"It also raises an intriguing question," said Letts. "The Latin makes it clear they've had contact with humans at some time in their past. We already suspected the, ah . . . Grik had. Judging from their ships, it was within the last few hundred years. The question for the Lemurians is when did it happen? I'm not sure it matters in the grand scheme of things, but my impression was that none had ever seen or heard of human beings and we were as big a surprise to them as they were to us. Did they get Latin from a Latin—like Romans or something? Or was it some guy, like Mr. Bradford here, just passing through who taught it to them for a hoot?"

"That's an interesting point. I'd like to have the answer to that question myself," Matt said. He shrugged. "Partly, I admit, because it *is* a fascinating question, but mainly because it may make more difference than you realize, Mr. Letts. When they learned it, that is. I agree it probably wasn't in their living memory, but if it wasn't too long ago, maybe, somewhere, there are still other people like us to be found. If so, finding them is going to be increasingly important." He cleared his throat. "You may have noticed the men's reaction to the Lemurian females?" There were thoughtful nods. "As time passes, certain . . . frustrations are going to become more acute. If it's possible there're other people in this world, we're going to need to find them— and not just because of that. If the Lemurian/human contact was thousands of years ago, though, that possibility seems more remote. Besides, if that's the case, it might create complications beyond the obvious."

"Indeed?" replied Bradford. "How so?"

"Look at it like this. Hundreds of years ago, maybe more, somebody wrote these Scrolls, or taught one of them Latin so they could write them down. They've based their spiritual beliefs on those writings. Out of the blue, strangers show up, deliver them from their enemies, and speak the sacred tongue. All this may not have sunk in yet, and if only a few of them speak Latin, it might take a while. But when it does, we might be faced with a decision." He looked at the faces around him, all staring intently back. He sighed. "They might think we're *gods!*" he said quietly. "What are we going to do then?"

The items on Sandra's list had been brought over—needles and catgut for stitching, mostly. There were many, many wounded, and most had deep slashes, although there were a few arrow wounds as well. Those were the ones that concerned her most. She could handle stitching slashed flesh and binding superficial cuts, but she was very afraid to go fishing around inside the unfamiliar creatures trying to dig something out when she didn't know their anatomy.

She knew she would have to, though. The only treatment the Lemurians seemed to know for battle injuries was to apply the same viscous paste she'd seen on their leader. She had no idea what it was, but it apparently had certain analgesic and antibacterial properties. It might even be better than sulfanilamide. Whatever it was and however well it worked, it couldn't stanch blood loss or repair muscles and sinews hacked in two. Learning to deal with so many casualties at once had apparently never occurred to them—just as fighting such a battle hadn't. She hoped, however, that if the paste worked as well as they assured her through Lieutenant Shinya it did, very few amputations would be required.

It was slight consolation, looking at the sea of bodies stretched before her in neatly organized, blood-soaked rows. She was just a nurse. She was a very good nurse, but up until recently, she'd been a peacetime nurse who'd never faced anything like this. She'd taken it upon herself to learn more about her profession than required and she felt competent to assist in most surgical procedures, but until just a few days before, she'd never dealt with actual battle casualties. Now this.

The severity and variety of the wounds left her appalled. She knew that modern warfare often inflicted even more ghastly wounds, but usually at a distance. The idea that enemies could stand face-to-face and hack each other apart to produce wounds like those she saw made her skin crawl like the sight of a bullet wound would never have done. She was in so far over her head that she felt her composure and her previously unshakable confidence beginning to slip. With sudden clarity, she thought she knew precisely how Matt must feel, caught up in events far beyond what his training and experience had prepared him for. He'd done a pretty good job, she reflected, even if he didn't know what he was doing. Somehow he always managed to act as though he did. That might work well in matters of leadership, but it wasn't the best approach when it came to medicine, she thought wryly. Or was it?

Adar and several apprentices hovered nearby, talking with Lieutenant Shinya as she sewed. Many other Lemurians, young and old alike, watched her work intently. Besides her efforts, however, there was virtually no other treatment under way. She finished suturing a long gash in a young Lemurian's leg while it stared at her unflinchingly with large, liquid eyes. She stood and tried to wipe hair from her eyes with her forearm. It was covered with sweat and she only managed to paste the loose hair to her face. Without a word, an uncustomarily attentive Dennis Silva poured alcohol on a rag and handed it to her. She began wiping blood off her hands and trying to get it out from under her fingernails. The harder she tried to get it all, the madder she got.

"Lieutenant Shinya? Would you be kind enough to signal the ship and ask Captain Reddy to send Pharmacist's Mate Miller and Ensign Theimer over to help? My God, there must be two hundred or more I haven't even seen yet!" She paused, considering. "Also, please ask Adar why none of his people are helping. They may be unaccustomed to this kind of medicine, but all I'm doing is sewing them up." She gestured around. "And I know they can sew!"

"Of course, Lieutenant." Tamatsu turned and began to speak. Adar answered and Shinya relayed his message. "He said he didn't know you wanted help. It's customary among his people for those with specialized skills to guard their methods. He said their healers—many of whom are watching you work even now—would like to try the methods they have seen, but are afraid you will be offended."

She shook her head and almost screamed with frustration. "The only thing that offends me is they'd be willing to let their people suffer over something that silly!"

"Then I will tell him you will freely share your expertise. I will not relay your last statement, though," he said just a little primly. "To them, I am sure it's not silly at all."

"Then tell them to bring boiling water! And find out if they have any alcohol or anything I can use for an antiseptic! I'm just about out!"

Shinya nodded curtly and spoke to the Lemurian official again. Sandra wasn't sure how fluently the two communicated because the Japanese officer punctuated his statements with hand gestures and repeated phrases, but Adar seemed to grasp what was said and soon barked commands. To Sandra's surprise, within moments a cauldron of boiling water appeared, as well as a dark earthen cask, or jug, that had a pungent aroma. *They must have had the stuff nearby,* she thought. *They'd have been using it already if I hadn't been here.* Chagrin surged through her. She realized she'd just naturally assumed she knew more about medicine than these "primitives" and dived right in. They may have even been as angry with her as she was with them! *It says something for the regard they must hold us in,* she thought. *Otherwise, they might've just killed me!* She shook her head and pointed at the cask. "What's that?"

"It's a fermented spirit they make from fruit, Lieutenant Tucker," Tamatsu replied. "They call it seep."

Silva leaned forward, suddenly interested. "Hey, Jap, ask him if it can be drank!"

Tamatsu looked at the big destroyerman a moment before he replied. "Gunner's Mate Silva," he said in an icy tone, "I have given my parole to your captain, as well as my word of honor. But I'm still an officer in the Japanese Imperial Navy. If you do not address me with the respect due my rank, or at least that due one man of honor from another, I won't ask him that, or anything else for the remainder of our visit today. I do not think Captain Reddy would be pleased if our communications broke down entirely because one of his men was rude."

Silva bristled. The words "mighty uppity for a stinking Jap" actually formed in his mouth, but somehow he caught them and clenched his teeth. At his full height, he towered above the other man, but Tamatsu merely looked at him, unconcerned. Silva visibly uncoiled, and after a moment a grin spread across his weathered, stubbly face. "Well, I'll be damned, but you've got guts, Jap . . . I mean *Lieutenant* Jap." He held up a hand with a wider grin. "No offense, but I don't know your name."

Tamatsu bowed slightly. "Lieutenant Tamatsu Shinya," he said.

Silva nodded back, but his face darkened. "I ain't gonna call you sir, no way in hell. You *are* a Jap. But I'll call you Lieutenant Shinya, if that makes you happy."

"That will suffice, Gunner's Mate Silva," he said, and a slight grin formed on his face as well. "And, yes, the Lemurians do drink seep, although there's no telling what it would do to you."

Silva arched an eyebrow. "Well! In the interests of science, and prob'ly diplomacy too, I reckon it's my duty to find out!"

Sandra, who'd managed a grin of her own by now, cleared her throat. "Your duty, Mr. Silva, is to assist me and stay out of trouble. That duty most emphatically does not include testing the local booze. Do I make myself clear?"

Silva glanced at the cask and licked his lips. With a force of will, his expression changed to a beatific smile. "Aye, aye, sir!" He blinked. "Uh . . . ma'am—hell, that's a mouthful!" His face lost all expression whatsoever as Sandra looked at him sternly. "Perfectly clear!" he managed at last.

Sandra straightened her back. There was a pain high in her hips that had grown more intense from leaning over to tend the wounded. For the first time in a while, she looked around. Already, Lemurian healers had swept into the "hospital area" on the open deck between the center and the shattered forward tower. They treated the injured in their own way. Some examined the stitches she had made, and jabbered in their quick, excited tones. Obviously, body language added a great deal of meaning to their speech, and she was growing convinced that their blinking eyes conveyed much as well. She walked into the almost-shade under the catwalk above. She couldn't venture farther because that was where a sort of orchard of large pear-shaped fruit began. She'd heard it called polta fruit. The orchard ran entirely around the ship for a width of about fifteen feet. The wide catwalk was pierced at regular intervals by gratings that allowed light to the plants. The fruit itself, despite its familiar shape, had the color and shiny texture of purple grapes and grew in bunches as well, nestled in a mass of waxy, yellow-green leaves.

At the edge of the orchard was a Lemurian she knew was tall by the standards of his people, and his upper body was more muscular than most. He wore nothing but a bright red kilt stained dark by the blood matting his brindled fur and still seeping from a couple of cuts. He leaned on one knee over the still form of a female of similar color, raising her head so she could drink from a cup. One of the swords, like a cross between a machete and a scimitar, lay beside a blood-encrusted axe.

The female had clearly been in the fighting. Sandra had treated others as well. The first time she removed a bloody leather tunic from one of their "professional" warriors and discovered furry breasts beneath, she was shocked. Adar and his entourage were standing right there, though, and made no sign that the discovery of a female in the ranks was unusual. As she'd said earlier, the semi-nudity didn't surprise her—although she'd finally rounded savagely on Silva and his buddies when she overheard their comments about the "cat-monkey booby farm"—but she hadn't been prepared to find females not only fighting for their lives in a desperate situation but doing so as actual warriors.

After a time she grew inured—if not accustomed—to the apparent fact that among Lemurians there was total equality of the sexes. At least as far as warfare was concerned. But in this instance there seemed a contrast between that and the tender, very human concern she saw of a male for an injured female. She moved toward them unobserved. Adar was busy discussing something with Shinya and another Lemurian who'd approached. Silva, "distracted" again, suddenly noticed she'd wandered off and hurried after her, lugging his BAR. The big Lemurian straightened and regarded them as they neared. The female tried to rise, but Sandra made a lay-back motion with her hands and crouched beside her. The male and Silva remained standing, facing each other.

A quick survey showed Sandra no obvious life-threatening wounds, but there was a nasty cut above the left eye, slick with the healing lotion that Lemurians seemed to use as liberally as Mercurochrome. A possible concussion, then, but the eyes were alert. She smiled and crossed her hands over her chest. "Sandra," she said. The female's eyes fluttered rapidly and she glanced at the male who was now staring intently at Sandra as well.

With a wince, the female raised her left arm and patted herself. "Risa." Then she pointed at the male and said, "Chack."

Shinya and Adar joined them. "Lieutenant Tucker, Adar tells me their leader, Keje-Fris-Ar, desires we attend him once more."

Sandra nodded, but reached out and gently patted Risa's hand before she stood. "Very well, but please ask him to tell this one I hope she feels better soon." She turned to Silva. "Stay here, and when Ensign Theimer and Pharmacist's Mate Miller arrive, tell them whatever they do, don't act like they're taking over—just assist any way they can. Understand?"

"Yes, Miss . . . Lieutenant Tucker. I'll tell Reavis and Newman that very thing, but me and Felts'll tag along with you."

"Really, Mr. Silva, that's not necessary."

He grinned. "Maybe not, ma'am, but I think we will anyway. Skipper'd have us thrown to the fishes if we let you out of our sight."

Sandra sighed. "Very well. If you feel you must loom menacingly in the background wherever I go, I'll not upset you by protesting further, but promise you'll do so as peacefully as possible?"

"Absolutely, ma'am," Silva said with an expression of purest innocence. "Everybody'll tell you I'm as peaceable a critter as there is."

Near dusk, the launch bumped into *Walker*'s side for the final time that day, and the passengers carefully climbed the metal rungs to the deck above. The nurses went first. The one named Theimer seemed almost catatonic, and Lieutenant Tucker had to help her up. Tony Scott had noticed she wasn't quite with it when he took her across, but she looked even worse coming back, and she hadn't said a word either time—not that he paid much attention, or even really cared. He just wanted out of the boat. He'd been in the launch most of the day, with the terrible silvery fish—and occasionally larger things—bumping against it. He'd controlled the urge to fire the Thompson over the side in mounting terror, but he hadn't set it down all day. Now all he could think about was getting something more substantial than the wooden hull of a twenty-six-foot boat between him and whatever lurked below the surface of the water he'd always loved. He scrambled up last, urging Silva ahead of him.

"Calm down, Tony. What's your rush?" jibed Silva as he neared the top, over Scott's labored breathing below.

"Goddamn you, Silva! If you don't hurry, I guess you'll find out in a minute when I throw you in the water!"

Silva laughed as he clambered onto the deck and turned to offer the coxswain his hand. "Hell, they's just fish, Tony, just like sharks. Sharks ain't never spooked you before."

As soon as he gained the deck, Scott moved quickly to the center, as far from the water as possible. Silva and Felts followed. Miller, Reavis, Newman, and the two nurses went below while others hoisted the launch aboard. Scott took a cigarette from Felts and lit it with trembling hands. He took several deep drags, eyes flitting nervously from point to point but carefully avoiding faces. "I been on the water all my life," he said at last. "I grew up in Fort Lauderdale and had a sailboat, a fourteen-footer I'd take on the open ocean in the Gulf before my daddy figured I was old enough to drive." He drew in another lungful of smoke. "Had some scrapes, too. Bad weather. Sharks . . ." He glanced at Silva, searching the big man's face for ridicule. He shrugged. "From then to now, I ain't *ever* been afraid of the water." He shuddered. "Until today. It started creepin' up on me when I went across to *Mahan* right after the Squall, but I guess it finally got the better of me. Even those critters that got Marvaney didn't spook me like that constant bumpin' all day long. Knowin' . . ." He shook his head and looked back at Silva. "They ain't just fish, Dennis, and this ain't the Java Sea. Not anymore. I've known it from the start, but with everything going on, it just never sank in till today. I finally realized the water ain't even just the water anymore. The water's death, fellas, and if I had my druthers, I'd never go near it again."

He'd been speaking in quiet tones, but evidently louder than he thought. They heard a gruff laugh and turned to see Dean Laney by the rail, leaning on the safety chain by the number one torpedo mount. The big machinist's mate wore a sadistic grin.

"Don't that beat all? The *coxswain's* afraid of the water! Har! I bet you'll be strikin' for snipe now, so you don't have to look at it no more! Course, when I tell ever-body what a chickenshit deck-ape you are, Spanky won't even take you as a bilge coolie!"

Scott bristled, but Silva held him back. Then he grinned and sauntered over to the stanchion next to Laney. He peered over the side.

"Woo, Laney, you're so brave! I ain't never seen a snipe this close to the water before! I hope you're holdin' that safety chain tight. I wouldn't want you to fall!"

"Hell with you, Silva! Least I ain't scared of the wa . . . Aaah!"

He shrieked when Dennis pulled the pin on the stanchion that held the chain in place. He went over the side and the chain went taut with a clanking thud heard over Laney's high-pitched scream. Silva looked down and saw the machinist's mate bouncing against the hull, mere feet above the deadly sea, hands clenched tight on the chain, his upturned face contorted by a grimace of terror.

"SHIT! Help! *Help!* Goddamn you to *hell*, Silva! HELP ME!"

"But you ain't scared of the water, Dean," Silva called down mildly.

"I . . . I *am* scared, damn you! HELP ME!"

Silva heard running feet, and Felts and Scott grabbed the chain and started pulling.

"*Shit!*" exploded Scott. "You could'a killed him!" Other men arrived and between them they soon had Laney on deck, gasping and shaking, tears in his eyes.

"You could'a killed him!" Felts accused under his breath. Silva shrugged, then squatted and looked Laney in the eye.

"Damned ol' rusty pin must'a gave," he said. "No tellin' what might happen if a fella ain't careful what he does—or says." He stood and laughed. "Whoo-ee! Lucky you was holdin' that chain, Laney! Gives me the willies. The very idea of fallin' in the water scares the shit out'a me!"

Sandra scrubbed her hands in the tiny basin in the compartment that once belonged to Lieutenants Ellis and Rogers but that she now shared with Ensign Theimer. Karen sat expressionlessly on a small chair, knees together, staring at her hands on her lap. They were caked with dried blood, and black rings encircled her fingernails. There was more on her clothes and face, and it even streaked her hair where she'd been squirted by a pulsing artery.

"You did well today, Karen," Sandra complimented her. Which was true—to a point. She'd followed orders and done her job, stitching wounds in her professional, economical way. She'd done exactly what she was told to do—but no more. All the while her face was slack, her eyes dead, as if her body ran on autopilot but she wasn't really there. Sandra saw that the expression was still the same. She sighed.

"Get cleaned up and go to the forward berthing space with Jamie Miller to check on Seaman Davis. I have an idea I'd like to try." Ensign Theimer didn't respond. She didn't move. "Karen?" Worried, Sandra dried her hands and looked in the other nurse's eyes. For a moment she saw no recognition, no spark of human consciousness. "Karen!" she shouted and shook her roughly by the shoulders. "Karen, speak to me!"

Huge, shiny tears welled up in the empty eyes and when she blinked, they gushed down her face—and somehow she'd returned from wherever she'd been hiding. Her large, glistening, haunted eyes desperately searched Sandra's, but didn't see what they'd hoped. She closed them again, and a piteous moan escaped her lips.

"I want to go home!"

Sandra went to her knees, embracing the younger woman as tight as she could.

"Oh, God, me too, me too!"

The tears came then, like rivers, from both of them. For a long moment, Sandra held her while Karen sobbed and sobbed. Finally, when it seemed she'd exhausted herself, Sandra drew back and put her palm on Karen's face. "Me too," she whispered again, "but I don't think we can. For some reason, here we are and we've got to deal with that. I need you, girl. God, I can't do this alone! The ship needs you, and so do these men. We both have to be strong—to hold up."

"But it's so hard!"

"I know. Believe me, I know! I nearly lost it myself today. But don't you see? We can't! We don't have that . . . luxury. Too many people are counting on us, and we're all they've got. We can't let them down—we can't let ourselves down." She wiped the bloody hair from Karen's eyes with a gentle, tearful smile. "You okay?" Miserably, Karen nodded, and Sandra squeezed her filthy hands. "I'm glad you're back—don't leave me again. I'm the first woman chief surgeon on a United States warship. I'll mark you AWOL!"

Karen snorted a wet, almost hysterical laugh, but nodded.

"Good. Now get cleaned up and check on Seaman Davis. We don't want these goons to think we're weak sisters." She watched while Karen, still sniffling, washed her hands and then left the compartment. As soon as she was gone, Sandra felt the tension flow out of her and she put her face in her hands. "I want to go home too," she repeated, whispering, almost surrendering to sobs herself.

She still had to talk to Matt. It would probably be a long talk, and all she really wanted was to curl up in her bunk and fall into a dreamless sleep. She shook her head, wet one of the dingy washrags, and wiped the grime and tears from her face. Standing in front of the noisy little fan with her eyes closed, she let the tepid breeze dry her and tried to pretend it was refreshing. After a moment, she ruefully realized that she was fooling herself. She ran a brush through her sweat-tangled hair and stepped through the curtain.

Seated in the wardroom talking in quiet tones were the captain, Bradford, Gray, Dowden, Shinya, and Sergeant Alden, who seemed relieved that his charge had returned to his custody. The Marine was getting around better every day, but the idea of his climbing up and down ships, given the consequences of a fall, was ridiculous. He took his "escort" duty seriously, though, and he'd been disappointed when his request to accompany them to the Lemurian ship was denied.

They stood and greeted her with strained smiles, and Lieutenant Shinya nodded politely. They couldn't have avoided overhearing Karen's sobs, or indeed much of the women's conversation. Sandra realized with a start that Matt's "smile" seemed even more troubled than the others'. As soon as they resumed their seats, Juan appeared at her elbow and poured a cup of weak coffee (he'd begun to conserve) that she'd have mistaken for tea if not for the smell. Ordinarily, in meetings like these, Juan would have excused himself, but ever since the Squall, he often lingered, and Matt didn't send him away. He figured it was easier to inform the crew through the grapevine than make announcements every day. Besides, Juan would be careful what he passed on.

"I trust you're well?" asked Bradford. "Mr. Shinya told us your efforts were tireless."

Sandra smiled wanly. "Not tireless," she said. "It's been a tough"—she paused and looked reflective—"but interesting day. I think we were a help, once I figured out when to leave well enough alone, and we learned a lot."

The others nodded solemnly.

"True," said Matt, "but I wish you hadn't stayed behind."

"I wasn't alone. Lieutenant Shinya was there."

Matt glanced at the Japanese officer speculatively but nodded.

"As were several armed men," Tamatsu said. "She was in no danger. Your gunner's mate . . . Silva? He is a formidable man. If the lieutenant had been threatened in any way, I believe he would have contrived to destroy their ship around us, by himself."

Gray grunted. "Silva!" he muttered. "He's part of what I was worried about." Everyone, including Tamatsu, laughed at that.

"Well," said Matt, "you must be starving. Juan? Pass the word for sandwiches, if you please." The Filipino bowed his head and whispered through the wardroom curtain. There was no telling who was on the other side, but he returned to his place against the hull with the expression of one who fully expected the task to be performed.

"While we're waiting, tell us what happened when you went to see this Keje again," Matt suggested. "Lieutenant Shinya said you should be the one to speak, but I'd like to hear what you both have to say."

Sandra nodded. "He was weak from his wounds, but not debilitated, I think. Their medicine's not nearly as primitive as I expected. They have no concept of germ theory, but their infection rate is low. They clean wounds with hot water for no other reason I could see than that it just makes sense to do so. They hold cleanliness in high regard." She glanced down at her uniform blouse and wrinkled her nose to the sound of sympathetic chuckles. "They also apply a kind of salve to wounds that must be antibacterial in some way, in addition to being a local analgesic. I asked for a sample and they gave me a whole jar. There's no telling if it'll be helpful to humans, and I don't know what it's made of yet, but I want to try some on Seaman Davis, with your permission. His fever just won't go away. He's still in danger of losing his leg, at least."

Bradford nodded enthusiastically, but Matt regarded her thoughtfully. Gray looked downright dubious. "I know they believe in the stuff—nearly everybody over there had some smeared on 'em, but do we know it actually works?"

Sandra held out her hands palm up. "The only evidence I have after so short a time is their absolute faith and certainty. Many of their wounds were bites, you know, and some who were bitten far worse than Davis were treated with the stuff and considered lightly injured."

Matt scratched his ear. "Does it have the same effect on the Grik? I mean, have they used any on the Grik wounded and if so, do they think it'll work?"

Sandra glanced down at her hands, clasped on the table. When she looked back up, her expression was hooded. "There were no Grik wounded, Captain."

"But . . . that's impossible!" interrupted the Australian. "They can't all have died! It's imperative I see one alive!"

"There were no Grik survivors on the Lemurian ship, Mr. Bradford," Sandra restated. "Many committed suicide after they were abandoned, mostly by jumping into the sea. The rest were . . . helped over the side by the Lemurians."

"No prisoners, then," Captain Reddy observed quietly.

"No, sir." Sandra shook her head. "Like everything else we've observed in this world, there's no compromise between total victory and total defeat. You win or you die. Warfare among the Lemurians themselves—at least 'Home against Home'—is so rare there's no memory of it. They have their problems, sure, but evidently they don't kill each other over them, beyond the rare duel. The Grik, however, are the 'Ancient Enemy'—that's how they're referred to. Their conflict literally extends beyond their history, although pitched battles like the one we intervened in are rare, if not unheard of. Mostly, they've only had to contend with what amount to harassing attacks or raids. But the frequency is increasing, and no one's ever heard of attacks by six Grik ships at once."

"Any idea why they do it?" Matt probed.

"Not really. In spite of the Grik being the Ancient Enemy, the Lemurians don't know a lot about them. They just know that when the Grik come, the Grik attack. It's the way of things. They fight like maniacs and they don't take prisoners, so neither do the Lemurians." She rubbed her tired eyes. "I'm not sure they even understand the concept of surrender." She glanced at Lieutenant Shinya and was struck by how similar to his culture, in that respect at least, the Lemurians had been forced to become. However, unlike Imperial Japan, the Lemurians were anything but militaristic and expansionist. She noticed the others looking speculatively at the Japanese officer as well, but Tamatsu endured their stares with stoic indifference. If he was troubled by their scrutiny, he didn't let it show.

"Well," said Matt, and sighed with slight relief. "Maybe we're not stuck in such a big war after all—just a really long one." There were chuckles. "The Lemurians fought well against a really scary enemy, but if they thought the Grik were a major problem, I think they'd be better prepared. Be more warlike themselves. With a few simple expedients, I don't think a dozen Grik ships could board something as big as their ship." There were nods, but Sandra wasn't sure. America hadn't been very prepared for Pearl Harbor.

"Anyway," said Matt, "we were talking about the salve." He let out a long breath. "Try it, if Davis is willing. I won't force him to take some alien cure." Sandra nodded acceptance. She knew Matt must have hoped she could experiment on a wounded Grik first, but if the stuff worked as advertised, it would save Davis's leg. She'd done all she could, but the bite had left an incredibly persistent infection. His immune system was fighting it, but she didn't expect it could do so indefinitely or totally. She was sure she could get him to try it.

Bradford leaned forward in his chair. "Did you get any indication why our first meeting with their leader was so short?" he asked. "He seemed alert, eager, and energetic at first, particularly after we established communications. Then, suddenly, he spoke a few words, and we were ushered out. Was that normal protocol?"

"I don't think so," answered Sandra. "Maybe we did take them by surprise. He was probably under medication of some sort, something to make him sleep—they also put great store in the healing power of sleep, by the way—but . . ." She lowered her voice and looked pointedly at the curtain.

Matt noticed the direction of her glance. "Sergeant Alden, clear the passageway. I'm sure if there's anybody in it they have duties elsewhere."

"I will go check the sandwiches," said Juan. "Do not stir, Sergeant. I will shoo them off."

When the steward left, they all looked back at Sandra expectantly.

"Thank you, Captain. All I really wanted to say, though, is that quite a lot of Lemurian medicine is evidently intoxicating. They brought out some stuff that nearly got me drunk just smelling it. Even the salve seems to make them a little dopey. I think when we arrived, their captain, or whatever he is, had just taken a dose of something, and when it started to hit him he sent us away." She grinned. "I don't think he wanted to be tipsy in front of the powerful strangers."

"Indeed?" Bradford said appreciatively. "I wish more of our statesmen would refrain from conducting business in such condition."

There was a knock on the bulkhead beyond the curtain.

"Sandwiches, Cap-tan."

"Thanks, Juan. Come in, please." Juan stepped through the curtain and held it for Ray Mertz, the mess attendant, who carried a platter piled high with ham sandwiches. He set it on the table, then he and the steward ducked quickly back down the passageway. Everyone dug in immediately, and Sandra closed her eyes when she bit into the thick slice of ham nestled between two pieces of fresh-baked bread. With just a little mustard, it tasted heavenly. She was even hungrier than she'd thought. The Lemurians had offered them food, but it smelled strange and she wasn't ready to trust the local fare. Silva had eaten some of the purple fruit, and she wondered absently how he was feeling about now.

"So, what else did you talk about during your second meeting?" Matt asked.

Sandra sped her chewing and swallowed at last. "Well, pretty much the main point was that their leader, Keje-Fris-Ar, wants to come aboard us here. Tomorrow."

"Here they come!" Dowden said unnecessarily when the boat cast off and moved in their direction. Almost an hour earlier, they'd been surprised to see a large section of the Lemurian's hull, about twenty feet wide, open and swing outward, releasing a low, wide-beamed barge. The compartment, or whatever it was, had water in it, and the boat just floated out. There it stayed for a time, already crewed, until the more important passengers were lowered into it by means of a large platform that descended from the deck above.

"That's some trick," murmured McFarlane, scratching the young beard on his chin. He glanced apologetically at the captain. "Structurally, I mean. It's like they go around with a fully enclosed harbor. Makes sense, as far as they'd have to lower a boat, but the engineering problems and stresses involved must've been something else."

"The structural engineering capabilities of the Lemurians are quite formidable," said Bradford. "To construct such a colossal ship to begin with . . . well." He shrugged.

Captain Reddy, carefully groomed and resplendent in his whites—as were all his officers—glanced around the ship. They'd done their best to make her presentable, but the ravages she'd undergone were evident everywhere. Even a visiting admiral would understand, but he wanted to make a big impression. It would have to do. The crew was dressed as sharply as possible, but most had dyed their whites in coffee—as ordered—at the start of the war, and the result was an unsavory mottled khaki. Now, with the passage of time, most of the coffee had leached out in the wash and they only looked dirty. He grunted. The order had come down from somebody who thought the ships would be more difficult to spot from the air without a bunch of white uniforms running around on deck. It was one of the sillier of the panicky and often contradictory orders they'd been issued right after the attacks on Pearl Harbor and Cavite. There was nothing he could do about it other than group the men who still had whites separately from those who didn't, as if there were some great reason for it. It was all entirely symbolic, but he didn't know how important a part symbolism might ultimately play. He spoke to the Bosun.

"Assemble your side party, Chief. I'll join you shortly." He absently hitched the Sam Browne to distribute the unaccustomed weight of the holstered pistol and the other . . . object suspended from it. He grimaced. While running an inventory of their small-arms ammunition, Campeti discovered a crate of heavy long-bladed cutlasses, pattern of 1918, that had probably been commissioned with the ship. There were four dozen of the things in heavy blue-gray canvas-wrapped scabbards, and they looked absolutely new. Gray suggested that the officers wear them so the Lemurians would see weapons they recognized. He didn't intend it as a threatening gesture, or so he said, but to show the 'cats—even while they were surrounded by all sorts of incomprehensible things—that they shared some basic similarities.

Matt resisted the idea as ridiculous. If they had to fight with swords, a dozen of the Lemurians could slaughter them all, judging by their skill against the Grik. But Courtney Bradford weighed in on Gray's side, surprisingly, with the comment that it might be wise to remind their visitors that they were, after all, warriors. Matt grudgingly relented and ordered all the officers, POs—and especially the Bosun—to wear one of the damn things. He had it easier. Instead of the heavy cutlass, he had his ornate Naval Academy dress sword, which he'd worn precisely twice—once at graduation and once at a friend's wedding. He knew it was a fine blade, and it had certainly cost him enough, but even now he couldn't imagine any eventuality that would force him to draw it in anger. He looked down at the fat barge, pitching on the choppy swell as it came alongside. Hitching his belt up again, he stepped quickly down the pilothouse steps to the deck.

Heaved to, *Walker* wallowed sickeningly even in these light swells, her low freeboard giving them periodic glimpses of the approaching party as the ship rolled. It was going to be tricky—and a little undignified—gaining the deck of the destroyer after the genteel fashion in which the Lemurian leaders were lowered into their barge, but there was no help for it. Besides, the creatures looked better equipped to climb the treacherous rungs than humans were. Gray took his place with the side party, Carl Bashear with him, and raised the pipe to his lips.

"You want me to do it?" Bashear whispered as the first Lemurian hopped onto the rungs and quickly neared the top.

"No, damn it. If anybody's gonna pipe aliens aboard *Walker*, it's gonna be me."

The piercing wail of the Bosun's pipe startled the burly Lemurian with the reddish-brown coat, but then he cocked his head at the Chief with interested recognition. He seemed even more startled when all those present saluted. He wore the same copper-scaled tunic as the day before, but the bloodstains had been cleaned and the scales had been polished to a flashing glory. Beneath the armor, he wore a long blue shirt, finely embroidered with fanciful fishes and adorned with shimmering scales like sequins around the cuffs. A long mane covered his head and extended to the sides of his face like huge muttonchops and was gathered and tied at the nape of his neck with a bright ribbon. His very ape-like feet were bound in sandals with a crisscrossing mesh of copper-studded straps extending to his knees. From a baldric across his chest hung a short, fat-bladed sword, securely tied into its scabbard with another bright ribbon formed into an elaborate bow. He looked around for a moment, as if taking everything in—the aft funnels with their wisps of smoke, the four-inch gun above, the torpedo tubes.

And, of course, the people. He looked from face to face until he recognized Matt. Then he grinned a very human grin and faced aft and saluted the flag that stood out from the short mast. He turned to Matt, still grinning, and saluted again. With evident difficulty, his mouth formed the unfamiliar words: "Meeshin ta caamaa-burd, zur?"

There were incredulous murmurs, and Matt realized his jaw had gone slack. Sandra, standing behind him, leaned forward and whispered in his ear. "We spent about an hour on that yesterday. He wanted to do it. He said he owed it to our people."

Soon the entire Lemurian party, numbering almost a dozen, was aboard. To the surprise and delight of the assembled destroyermen, all saluted the flag and the captain. It was an important and very moving moment, and the Lemurians couldn't have done anything that would have more thoroughly ingratiated themselves with *Walker*'s crew. Grimaces and glances of suspicion disappeared, and a mood of camaraderie prevailed as Matt led the delegation under the amidships deckhouse, where refreshments were laid out. It wasn't much, but Juan, Earl Lanier, and Ray Mertz had done their best with what they had. On the stainless-steel counter running the length of the galley, a variety of light dishes were arrayed, along with carafes of iced tea.

After a brief hesitation, Keje himself tasted the tea and a grin of delight crossed his face. Whether it was the tea, the sugar, or just the novelty of ice that did the trick, it was extremely well received. Soon all the Lemurians were standing in the shade, drinking tea and exclaiming loudly in their chittering, yowelly voices, much to everyone's delight. Gray grudgingly offered Adar a Coke. After a trusting gulp, the dignified Sky Priest spewed foam from his mouth and nose, and the crew roared with laughter. Gray patted him hesitantly as he coughed, and then took a quick gulp from the same bottle to show their visitors he hadn't meant to poison their priest.

Ignoring the spectacle, Keje stood with the captain, eying a Vienna sausage rolled up in a slice of cheese with a toothpick stabbed through it. Bradford stood nearby, as did Shinya, ready to interpret. The Japanese officer still wore the dark blue uniform he'd had on when he was rescued, although it had been cleaned and mended as much as possible. He was the only one dressed in blue, and he stood out. Matt had contemplated having more men wear blues, in spite of the heat, to avoid drawing too much attention to the fact that Shinya was different, but he decided the men might resent it and he didn't want to add any fuel to that fire.

"Mr. Bradford," Matt said, "why don't you remain here as interpreter for the crew to the Lemurian party while Lieutenant Shinya accompanies me?" They'd already decided the crew would have Mr. Bradford. "Perhaps Captain . . . uh . . . His Excellency . . ." Matt stopped, at a loss.

"He is correctly referred to as U-Amaki," Tamatsu supplied.

"Yes. Well. Perhaps Captain U-Amaki and some of his officers would like to see more of the ship?"

Shinya spoke to Adar, but Keje blinked assent even before the translation was complete. He couldn't speak the Ancient Tongue, but through his lifelong association with Adar, he'd learned to understand it well enough.

"He would be delighted," Shinya said. "But his name is Keje-Fris-Ar. U-Amaki is his title—like 'Captain.'"

"Oh."

Keje, Adar, Jarrik, and Chack followed the leader of the Tail-less Ones. They were accompanied by the fat one, the female, and the dark-skinned one—who seemed different, besides just the color of his clothes. The rest of the group was left carousing and drinking the wonderful cold drink in the shade with many other Tail-less Ones.

Chack was enjoying himself, and was happy that the strange beings seemed so friendly, but he was unsure why he was there. He was proud to be chosen, of course, but he didn't know why. He still ached from his many small wounds, just as the High Chief did, but he knew he'd fought well in the battle. Perhaps Keje honored him for that? If so, it was an honor indeed, for he'd done no more than many others. At least it was a sign that Keje harbored no ill will toward him over Selass. At the moment Selass was a subject he didn't care to dwell on.

As the Fat One raised a heavy lid of some kind on the deck and gestured inside, Adar translated: "The Fat One—Gray is his name—says the fires that move the ship burn in that hole."

Keje bent over and peered within, but he saw nothing except darkness. When they'd all looked, Gray fastened the lid with a spinning wheel, and they moved toward steps leading to the deck above.

Chack was conscious of constant motion as the small ship moved on the water. Up and down and side to side. It was enough to make him queasy, despite living on the water all his life. He wondered how the Tailless Ones stood it all the time. He was unaccustomed to anything this small and cramped. He was a wing runner, and he rarely ventured forth on the barges or other small vessels, so it was disconcerting. He suppressed a shudder and tried to think of something else.

Inevitably then, his thoughts returned to Selass as they mounted the steps. Evidently she was again without a mate. Saak-Fas had disappeared in the fighting, and no one had seen him since he delivered the message sending Chack into battle. He wasn't among the slain, or anywhere else on Home. He must have gone over the side. Chack wouldn't mourn him, but his loss left Selass available. Strangely, he wasn't sure how that made him feel. He wasn't the same person she'd toyed with and rejected so short a time ago. Everything was changed. His home in the forward tower was gone. Risa, always the strong one, was weak with injury. His mother was well, but without a home for her clan. The Grik had come, but been destroyed and put to flight, and of course, they'd met these strange . . . what was the word? Amer-i-caans. So much that he had known and expected to remain constant was suddenly different or gone—and he'd changed perhaps most of all.

Preoccupied, tramping up the noisy steps, he nearly bumped Jarrik-Fas, who'd inexplicably halted. Shaking off his reverie, he peered around the guardsman at Keje, who'd paused at the top of the steps. Everyone else stopped, including the Amer-i-caans, to watch him. With one of his finger claws, he scraped at a reddish streak on the rail and raised it to his tongue. His eyes widened with astonishment.

"It is metal, as I suspected," he murmured to his companions, "but what it tastes like . . . cannot be."

"It is, my lord," confirmed Adar quietly. "Iron."

Chack's mind reeled and he looked around in shock. "But surely, lord," he stammered, "it cannot all be iron?"

Adar blinked sharp displeasure at Chack's outburst. "It's iron. All of it. It must be, for the red streaks are everywhere. Now speak no more unless you are given leave." He sniffed. "They will think us rude."

Keje muttered something that Chack didn't catch and joined the Amer-i-caans waiting above.

Gray was scandalized by the Lemurians' preoccupation with the rust. He took it as a personal affront that they should be so obvious about noticing the lack of maintenance. Shinya had spent more time among them, and he thought he understood. He spoke aside to Matt.

"Captain Reddy, they've just realized your ship is made of steel."

"I think you're right. Must be a shock too. They have iron weapons, so they know what it is, but the idea of making something this size . . ." He paused. "They had to know *Walker* was metal, ever since they set foot on her. I wonder what they thought it was?"

"Copper, most likely, Skipper," said Gray, simmering down. "Who knows? I sure as hell don't know how they made something the size of their ship out of wood!"

"Point." The captain stepped into the wheelhouse and beckoned their guests to follow. Once inside, with the self-conscious bridge watch going about their duties, Keje looked through the windows, at the wheel, at all the strange and mysterious devices and the maze of conduits overhead. His eyes swept everything, recognizing the utility, if not the function, of what was clearly the control area for the American ship. He was puzzled that the utilitarianism was so extreme as to preclude decoration of any kind, but everything seemed laid out with profound practicality. To his seaman's eye there was an aesthetic quality in that.

His gaze fell upon the chart table, and with quickening heart and mounting incredulity he recognized immediately what he saw. Adar saw it at the same instant and was staggered by the implications. With a cry, he rushed to the table and leaned protectively over the chart, his eyes sweeping back and forth, taking in the strangers' reactions. They showed no concern except perhaps for his inexplicable behavior. He tried to grasp the chart, but something was there—something clear—between his claws and the paper he sought. *What is this magic?* he thought desperately. *Why would they do this? Do they mock us with their power that even the Sacred Scrolls themselves are nothing but curiosities for all to gape upon without the training to understand?* He looked at Keje's stricken blinking, and the Amer-i-caans behind him, staring. They seemed bewildered. Adar sensed no hint of gloating or malice, only curiosity and concern. Even after his sudden outburst, none seized a weapon. Perhaps there was no mockery here. Perhaps there was something else? Perhaps they understood. Could it be?

Keje edged closer and peered at the chart Adar hovered over. "Their Scrolls are better than your Scrolls, Adar," he said dryly. "Really, you must control yourself. We are their guests. They will think us rude," he quoted.

"You go too far, Keje-Fris-Ar!" Adar retorted sharply. He glanced at the chart again. The detail was amazing! "The value is in the thing, not what is on it! You flirt with apostasy!"

"Wrong. I'm no Sky Priest, but wisdom is wisdom, regardless of the source. Is it apostasy to recognize the value of this Scroll, as they obviously do, and put it in an honored place where all may gain its wisdom? Or is it apostasy to suspect, like you do, that they might be as those Tail-less Ones of old who passed us this wisdom before?"

Matt and the others had gathered round and were watching the exchange. Clearly, the Malay Barrier chart had created a crisis of some sort, but they were at a loss to understand what it was. The 'cats plainly knew what the chart represented, but why should Adar throw such a fit?

"But to have them here, where all can see . . ." sputtered Adar. "It's not right!"

"Where is it written only the Priests of the Sky may know the mysteries of the Heavens?" Keje softly asked. "Among our people, only Sky Priests can interpret the drawings in the Scrolls because they alone have the Ancient Tongue, but anyone may strive to become a Sky Priest, not so? I've looked upon the Scrolls myself—you showed them to me! I can even read some of what is written. Does that make me a Sky Priest—or an apostate?"

Adar was quiet for a moment while he thought. Of course Keje was right; it just didn't *seem* right. He sighed.

"I apologize, my lord. It's just . . ." He'd been gazing at the chart while he spoke, his eyes taking in the shapes of the islands he knew so well, when he felt he'd been physically struck. "The words!" he managed to gasp. "The words are not in the Ancient Tongue!"

Keje saw it was true. Some of the island names were the same, but there was much more writing than he remembered and it was totally unfamiliar. "Their own language?" he speculated. Adar could only nod. It must be. The Amer-i-caans still watched them, and he suspected they were becoming impatient. He would have been. "Ask them where they come from. Maybe they will even tell us."

Adar cleared his throat and spoke the ancient words. As soon as Shinya translated, Captain Reddy peered at the chart himself. Adar knew their home couldn't be anywhere on the scroll he saw. The Scrolls of the People were more comprehensive. Less than a third of the known world was laid out before him, and he had at least passing acquaintance with all the places shown. The meaning of his question was clear, however, because Matt put his finger on what Adar recognized as their current position and then paced away, far across the wheelhouse, to stand on the opposite side. He pointed at the deck, looking intently at Adar with his small green eyes.

"They are from the East! Beyond the world, beyond even the Great Empty Water, perhaps! The way no vessel can go!"

"In case you haven't noticed, Brother," Keje said with heavy sarcasm, "this vessel goes wherever it wants!"

The humans were intrigued but not overly concerned by Adar's behavior. They assumed that he'd recognized the chart, and an example of commonality had been found.

"Ask them where they're from," Matt instructed. There was muttered conversation in their own language, and finally Adar pointed over the water at their ship. Matt nodded. "Of course, we suspected as much. It certainly seems self-sufficient enough for long stretches away from land. But your people must have some place, on land, where such things are built?" He spoke directly to them, even though Lieutenant Shinya was obliged to translate everything he said. "Wood only grows on land and other things—copper, cordage, things like that—can only be found ashore. Your people must have settlements where you can make repairs?" All four

Lemurians looked at him for a long time after Shinya finished speaking. They seemed hesitant to answer.

Matt understood that they might not want just anyone to know where their settlements were, but he and his crew had saved them from the Grik. If they wished them ill, that was not the simplest way to show it. This logic was apparently not lost on the Lemurians, because finally Keje leaned back over the chart. Adar said something, but the Lemurian leader shook his head and placed one of his clawed fingers on the map.

"Jesus Christ!" blurted Gray. "Borneo!"

Several crewmen on the bridge muttered in surprise. Matt looked over the shorter Lemurian, where his claw touched the chart. "Well," he said, "I believe we've been there once before." He straightened and looked meaningfully at the Bosun. "Balikpapan."

He turned back to Keje. "You have damage," he said, and then gestured around him. "We have damage too, and need supplies. Besides, the Grik may return. We'll help you get there, if you have no objection."

Matt led the Lemurians on a quick tour of the rest of the ship. The only attractions he avoided were the engines and the main armaments. They passed the guns and torpedo tubes several times and, plainly, the Lemurians were interested, but despite Bradford's advice, Matt thought they shouldn't focus too intently on the fact that *Walker* was a warship. And besides, what they didn't know about her capabilities, they couldn't tell to others. The same was true regarding the engines. It seemed to him that the Lemurians were sophisticated enough not to attribute everything they didn't understand to magic. But it wouldn't hurt to let some things remain mysterious. Particularly when that mystery protected the only two advantages *Walker* had in this strange, screwed-up world: her speed and her weapons.

Inevitably, not all the Lemurians were content to let *Walker*'s secrets unfold with time and trust.

Jarrik-Fas insisted that they ask the Amer-i-caans about their amazing weapons that could destroy the Grik from afar with such speed and efficiency. Keje was reluctant, since he could tell their hosts were less than willing to discuss it now. Ever since he'd seen the chart, however, Adar had assumed Keje's pragmatic skepticism. The reverse was true for Keje. That the Amer-i-caans had Scrolls of their own meant they almost certainly had some understanding of the Heavens. To him, that was reassuring. As different as they were, it was a sign that they were perhaps not all that different after all. Adar was in a mood to find fault, though, it seemed.

"I dislike secrets. If they would avoid speaking of their weapons, what else might they conceal?" he asked as they neared the amidships deckhouse again, with its squat four-inch guns, trained fore and aft.

Keje blinked exasperation. "A short time ago you were displeased that they display their Scrolls for all to see, and now you accuse them of being overly secretive? Brother, you contradict yourself."

Adar grunted and showed his teeth with a youngling's chastened grin. "I suppose you're right, my lord. Perhaps I was dismayed by the way they display their Scrolls as if just anyone can understand them. What struck me hardest, in all honesty, was that perhaps among them anyone can. Particularly if they're written in their own tongue. No one likes to think their life's work is un-needed, even by another species."

"Perhaps not all understand their Scrolls. Any one of them may be your counterpart, for all we know," Keje speculated. "But your knowledge and value are not limited to the Scrolls. You're a Sky Priest, after all. I doubt they could all be as conversant with the Heavens as you. It's one thing to read a Scroll. It's another to *know* the meaning. Yet another fascinating thing to learn about these creatures, in time. Besides, if they are as the ones who came before . . . of course they have Scrolls of their own!"

"Does that mean they are . . . gods?" Chack almost squeaked.

"Of course not!" snapped Adar. "There is but one God, silly creature! Even the 'others' were merely beings, as ourselves, who brought the wisdom of Heaven. They are to be exalted, but not worshiped. They admonished as much themselves. These creatures are wise as well. As wise as the others? Who is to say, but still merely beings."

"Whatever they are, I'm glad they like us." Keje grinned.

"I still want to know more about their weapons," Jarrik insisted.

"Oh, very well." Keje relented. "Ask if you must, Adar, but be discreet. I am usually the worrier, but after yesterday I'm inclined to trust these 'Amer-i-caans.' For now, I'm content to let them keep their weapons' secrets, as long as they use them on our behalf." His warning spoken, he had to admit he was as anxious to learn about the amazing weapons as they. He listened intently while the translations took place.

"They've asked about the guns, Captain Reddy. They want to know how they work. How they destroy things far away with only a puff of smoke and loud noise."

Matt sighed. "They were bound to ask. I'm surprised they waited this long. Hmm. Tell them the purpose is much like their big crossbow batteries—to throw a large bolt very far. Only we propel the bolt with an explosion, uh, expanding gas—smoke, instead of spring tension. The smoke throws the bolt very far, faster than the eye can see." He didn't want to get into a ballistics lecture then and there, so he temporized. "A lot of the destructive force of the bolt is caused by the speed alone. Tell them it's very involved and I'll be happy to tell them more when we can converse more easily. Oh, also tell them how fascinated we are with their weapons, and look forward to learning more ourselves." The creatures stared at the number two gun as they stopped almost beneath it. The four-inch hole with its spiraling lands and grooves gaped wide at the muzzle.

They rejoined the rest of the Lemurian party, who were still being fed and studied by the crew. The fraternization remained good-natured, and Matt was relieved to see everyone getting along so well. The camaraderie of their shared victory probably helped, but he suspected his destroyermen were happy to find anyone who wasn't hostile after all they'd been through.

"If you need any assistance, we have carpenters and shipfitters aboard," said Captain Reddy. He looked at Sandra before continuing. "Our medical division also remains at your disposal." Sandra nodded in agreement.

Keje blinked assent when Shinya told Adar what the captain had said, and he replied, "I would like to leave one with you so we can better learn your speech. I believe, with better understanding, the friendship between us will grow and become . . ." He grinned. "Less inconvenient." He gestured Chack forward, and the young Lemurian stepped up with some hesitation. "This one I will leave. Chack-Sab-At. He is not only a worthy person, but I've just recently discovered he's a brave and skillful warrior."

The statement was made without irony, and Chack couldn't decide if he was more surprised by the honor or the words of praise. Or was it just an excuse to get him away from Selass? For some reason, as likely as he'd have considered that a few days before, he was no longer sure. He was uncertain about too many things lately. "I won't fail you, my lord," he murmured.

"He'll be welcome," Matt said through Tamatsu.

"Excellent. Now, noble as young Chack is, he is small recompense for your generosity. Is there nothing we can do for you? You mentioned supplies? And repairs?"

"Our supplies are fine for now, although if you can spare some of your fruit, we'd like to try it." Matt gestured around and shrugged. "As you can see, we don't have space for gardens. The only other thing that might ease my mind is if you can tell me where to find the black substance you use to coat your stays and shrouds and seal your seams. Is it available where we're going? At your settlement?"

Keje was silent as Tamatsu interpreted, but then looked about with surprise. "You have leaks? I was not aware you had a use for gish. Of course. We carry much, just for that purpose. And yes, it is abundant where we go." He made a chittering sound that Matt now recognized as a chuckle. "At the trading land, it bubbles from the ground!"

When Tamatsu finally interpreted Keje's words, via Adar, for the first time he could remember, he saw the captain's lips spread into a genuine grin.

"Well! In that case, why don't we all have another glass of tea?"

The next week involved backbreaking activity for some, as work parties constantly plied between *Walker* and the Lemurian ship, and abject boredom for others, as the destroyer described slow, fuel-efficient circles around the plodding behemoth. Only the number four boiler was lit, but it provided more than enough steam for the monotonous six-knot circuits. With only two wings *Salissa*—or *Big Sal*, as almost everyone called her now—could average only three or four knots herself. If *Walker* went that slow, in the long swells of the Java Sea, she'd barely have steerageway and would roll her guts out.

To Matt, it seemed that Chack was constantly nearby, always out of the way but always there. Watching. In reality, he spent more time with Sandra, Garrett, and Sergeant Alden. Matt had no time to teach him English, and certainly none to learn Lemurian, but Chack was learning fast from his other acquaintances, and Matt understood him better each day.

Some of the men spent a lot of time on the 'Cat ship as well. Bradford practically lived there, and the English lessons were well under way. A lot of the men came back using Lemurian words for things—which drove the Bosun nuts. He never complained about Chinese or Filipino words, but for some reason he took offense to the "jabbering away like a damn cat-monkey." Only after Matt quietly explained that he wanted the men to learn the language did he relent.

Chack slept in the forward berthing compartment with the crew and ate what they ate and generally got along quite well. They'd adopted him, like a pet or mascot at first, but as he learned to speak English they began to realize he wasn't a pet, and that although he was small, he was probably as strong as Silva. His status was blurred. Not a pet and not a destroyerman—but he was becoming a shipmate.

In contrast to Chack's treatment, Shinya still faced open hostility, although his presence—and continued existence—had gained a meager level of acceptance. Strangely, that probably had as much to do with Silva and Alden as anyone. The two men didn't like the Jap, but a growing respect was evident. Matt hoped the men would lighten up eventually. Lieutenant Shinya was proving valuable, and not only as a translator. When not engaged as such, he often toiled with Sandison in the workshop on the condemned torpedoes. He wasn't a torpedoman, but he loved machines. Bernie actually *did* seem to like him. He certainly appreciated his help. If anyone could ever crack the ice between Shinya and the crew, the engaging torpedo officer from Idaho would be the one.

On the bridge, Matt glanced at his watch and looked at Lieutenant Garrett. "Sound general quarters, if you please."

"Aye, aye, sir. General quarters! General quarters!" the gunnery officer repeated in a raised voice. Electrician's Mate 3rd Class Mike Raymond activated the alarm and put on the headset at the talker's station, plunking a helmet on his head while the alarm reverberated through the ship. Chack, standing nearby, snatched a helmet and put it on as well. He looked slightly comical since it was much too large and covered his catlike ears. He grinned happily and blinked in excitement. Matt learned in one of his evening sessions with Bradford that Lemurians conveyed much the same meanings by blinking that humans did with eyebrow/facial expressions. It was like emotional Morse code. He wondered if they were born with the ability or had to learn it. At least it made more sense than Gray's theory that they all had a nervous tick, but he had no idea what the blinks meant, and except for their grins, Lemurian faces remained opaque and stony to his perception.

Chack cinched the chin strap and exuberantly scampered up the ladder to the fire-control platform and his "reserve lookout" post. There was no mistaking his body language—he was clearly enjoying himself. Seconds later, reports filtered in while Matt gazed at his watch. Finally, the last department reported and he smiled to himself. *Better*, he thought. *Not great, but shorthanded as they were* . . . He shrugged. Ever since the battle with the Grik he'd run twice-daily drills. Not only did it break the monotony and keep the crew on their toes, but it reminded them that USS *Walker* was still a United States Navy ship—wherever the rest of that Navy happened to be.

"Well done, Mr. Garrett. Pass the word; all departments have improved over their last time. You may secure from general quarters."

Spanky tapped a pressure gauge on number four and grunted noncommittally. Chief Harvey Donaghey, the assistant engineer, had reported for the division while he inspected the cantankerous boiler during the exercise. So far, it was operating perfectly. Number two was in reserve, and number three was cold for the first time since they'd made their dash from Surabaya. When he peeked inside, he wasn't at all happy about the condition of the firebricks. A near miss must've shaken stuff loose, he decided. He glanced up and saw that, as usual, the Mice were watching from the gloom. He sighed.

"Nothin' wrong with number four," Isak said. "Don't know why you don't like her. We gonna be somewhere we can tear down number three anytime soon?"

"We could do it now, but it wouldn't be easy." Gilbert glowered. "Would've been nice to put into Surabaya."

"Surabaya ain't there, boys," Spanky said—again. The Mice blinked at him.

"All he said was it would have been nice," Isak muttered.

They nearly had put in, the day after their first visit from the 'Cats. Not because they expected it to be there, but just to *see*. Captain Reddy finally decided against it, for several reasons. First, of course, was fuel. There was no use wasting it for a sightseeing trip. Second, Surabaya was inhabited, according to what Bradford had learned, but the people there weren't "of the sea," whatever that meant, and weren't necessarily friendly. It was strongly implied that if *Walker* steamed into the harbor unannounced, the consequences might be awkward. After all, even *Big Sal*'s people had thought *Walker* was some new Grik ship at first. Finally, there was the potential damage to morale to consider. Seeing someplace like Surabaya—or someplace where Surabaya should be—was yet another trauma that the captain would sooner put off.

Java was over there, though. Spanky had seen it receding on the horizon to the south. But even at a distance, he could tell it wasn't the Java he'd known. There were no picket ships or minelayers, no freighters loaded with weapons and supplies. No cranes and docks and filthy, oily water. No PBYs occasionally flying patrol and no haze from the industry—or smoke from fires caused by Japanese bombs. Of course, there weren't any Japs either.

As always, the Mice flustered him by jumping from one subject to another. For once, it was just as well.

"How come we ain't got a monkey-cat? Damn deck-apes have one. Why can't we?" Isak complained.

"'Apes don't have one either. They're not pets. They're allies."

"What? Like Limeys?"

"Yeah, sort of like that. Besides, it's too hot. I expect if one came down here, he'd die. They have fur, you know."

The Mice looked at each other. "Fur?"

Spanky eyed them more closely. "Haven't you seen one? Haven't you even seen the one that lives aboard?" The two firemen shook their heads. "Damn, boys! You've *got* to get out of here once in a while!"

At dusk, Keje stood with Adar, Jarrik, and Kas-Ra-Ar on the battlement, now cleaned of all evidence of battle. They couldn't forget the fighting, however, because of the charred, gaping wound that had once been the forward tower, tripod, and wing. There was also the constant smoke from the furnaces that carried the souls of their lost ones to the Heavens.

Ordinarily, there would have been a single pyre for all, and the funeral would have been somber but festive. The dead had gone to a better place, after all. But there were so many, and their loss was so keenly felt, that Adar could speak the words, but none could summon the customary gladness. Also, since only the furnaces could be used, the "Rising" went on and on, and the smoke was a constant reminder of all they'd lost. Even so, repairs continued, and the sounds of mauls, saws, and axes reached them over the breeze from aft. Some Amer-i-caans still worked too, even though their last boat of the day had left hours ago. The Tail-less Ones didn't seem to do anything by half measures, even when it came to friendship.

Keje was thankful. So many of *Salissa*'s strong young people had been taken that without the Amer-i-caan methods for moving heavy objects and debris, he doubted they'd have managed so well. He watched with admiration while cranes made from the charred lower portions of the tripod easily lifted huge pieces from where they'd fallen when the tower collapsed into the lower parts of the ship. The tower's survivors now lived with the other wing clans, but so great were their losses in battle that the other two wings were still understrength. He'd hoped this would be the season for the people of *Salissa* to branch out—for the Home to have a daughter—but that wouldn't happen now. They didn't have the people, and they'd be lucky to find the resources to repair *Salissa*—much less build a new Home.

He noticed a figure leaning against the rail, staring at the iron ship. It was Selass. She'd spoken little since her mate disappeared, and he wondered if she mourned him. Saak-Fas had been disagreeable, but he was young and powerful and possibly even attractive. He could see how his daughter might grieve even though their joining was so brief. He shrugged. She would recover and, in time, mate again. Perhaps even to the young wing runner of the Sab-At clan? There was much more to Chack than Keje had once thought. He'd been misguided to discourage that match.

"My lord?"

Keje realized that Jarrik had been speaking. "I'm sorry, cousin. My mind roamed. Forgive my rudeness and repeat yourself." Adar blinked mild reproof.

"We were discussing the Amer-i-caan ship, lord."

"Ah. It does dominate most of our conversations of late. By all means, continue."

Jarrik shrugged aside his chagrin. "But if their ship, this 'Waa-kur,' is indeed iron, how could it possibly float? Our swords and those of the Grik do not float, nor does anything else made of iron that I know."

"Copper can be made to float, and it's even heavier than iron," Adar said smugly. "Cast a drinking cup into a barrel. Does it not float? Home is sheathed in copper, yet we float as well. I do not marvel at the possibility of an iron ship, but the fact of it. That is perhaps their greatest mystery and their most significant advantage. The skill to work so much iron!"

"What about their weapons?" challenged Jarrik bluntly. "Their weapons are iron too. From the big weapons on their ship to the small ones they carry. The principle is the same for all, I think, and the pertinent parts are all of iron."

"I marvel at their weapons, but I confess greater envy for their speed," Keje said.

"What need we of speed?" Jarrik asked. "We live on the sea and by the sea. If we flew to and fro with such speed as theirs, we couldn't hunt the gri-kakka or even launch the boats."

"They do not always fly, and they slow to launch their smaller craft—which also move without wings or oars," Keje pointed out. "But if we had such speed, we would never have lost so many people. The Grik could not have caught us."

"True," agreed Adar, "but I've been wondering something, and Jarrik's thoughts about the fish hunt reinforce my—I hesitate to call them concerns, but . . ."

Keje frowned at him and blinked impatience. Since the incident with the Scrolls, Adar had become the skeptic. "What troubles you about our new friends now, besides their impious treatment of Scrolls?"

Adar looked uncertain. "I'm not sure, and I'm less concerned about the Scroll issue than I was, although other Sky Priests may be less understanding. I've yet to form an opinion regarding their piety, but it's clear that they have more Scrolls than we. I greedily learn their tongue so I can make sense of them. Bradford has explained much, and although it's impossible, I'm sure he actually believes they have Scrolls mapping the entire world! Even the bottom!" Adar chuckled. "For such a learned creature, he harbors some unusual notions!"

Keje looked at his friend, amused. "What, do Amer-i-caans believe the world is flat?"

Adar blinked a negative, but couldn't conceal a gentle grin. "No, lord, but he—and perhaps others—does not understand the most basic Laws of Things. That sweet water falls from the sky as a gift from the Heavens but, as it sours and turns to salt, it gets heavier and slowly slides off to the side of the world until it falls off." He grinned wider and quoted an old cliché. "No one can stand on the bottom of the world." The others laughed.

"Do their silly notions concern you, Brother?" Keje asked.

Adar's grin quickly faded. "No, lord. Two things brought the question to mind, and before you ask me what question, let me proceed. First, as far as we know, the Amer-i-caans do not hunt gri-kakka, or any fish at all. Nor do they grow crops. As amazing as their ship is, it's very small—which I must say became quite evident after a very short time—and dependent upon gish for fuel. That's the smoke from their pipes. Surely you recognize the stink? It's burning gish. I don't know how it works, but they must have gish, and quite a lot of it."

Keje blinked. "So? That's no problem. We know where there is much gish and they are welcome to it for helping us."

"Of course, but my point is, the Amer-i-caans are tied to the land by necessity. They eat only things of the land, as does their ship. They cannot be a true, self-sufficient, seafaring race such as we. I also know they don't spring from any land I've seen, and together we've seen it all." He held up his hand. "Second, and perhaps most striking, they have only two females. Not only is that obviously far too few, but they are not even mated."

"Most unusual," agreed Keje, "and perhaps unnatural. But I had the impression that the first healer—their 'high' healer, I suppose—was mated to their leader. The times we have seen them together, she seems to argue with him enough! Perhaps among them, only leaders may mate?"

"Not so, lord. She and the other female healer are not mated."

They were all silent a moment, pondering.

"Well. I can certainly understand your perplexity, but what about this is sinister?"

"I never suggested it was sinister, lord. Merely strange—and in keeping with my question. When their healer came to help our wounded, she was obviously shocked to learn that many of our warriors are female, that we make no distinction regarding them when it comes to fighting. I asked Bradford about this, and he confirmed that among them, females do not fight."

"Go on," Keje prompted.

"Their ship bristles with weapons and has no obvious means of support. There are no females aboard, except two healers who do not fight because they're not supposed to." Adar looked at the others and paused to convey significance. The sun had almost vanished, but they still saw the destroyer cruising lazily, effortlessly, ahead. The reflected glare from the last rays of light hid her rust streaks and other imperfections. A single wisp of smoke floated from the aftermost pipe, and heat shimmered at the top. The curious piece of cloth they called a "flag" flapped tautly from the small mast that could have little other purpose than to fly it. "With this evidence, the only conclusion I can draw is that the Amer-i-caan ship has only one purpose: it's a ship meant entirely for war." He sighed. "What manner of people, besides the Grik, would build such a ship, and why so formidable? Did you see that many of the holes they patched were larger than the holes in their weapons? It strikes me that they have been shot at by something with bigger 'guns' than theirs. The Grik have nothing that would do that, or they would have used it on us. Besides, they claim to know even less about the Grik than we." Adar frowned and his eyes rested speculatively on the dark shape as the sun sank from view.

"So what is this question of yours, after all?" Keje asked.

"Only this: have we befriended a flasher-fish, only to find a gri-kakka on its tail?"

Reveille blared in the forward berthing space at 0400 to signal the morning watch. Sleepy men groused and cursed, rolling from their three-tiered racks. Chack, however, practically vaulted from his—one of the uppermost—and quickly donned the white T-shirt that Alan Letts had given him to make him look more Navy-like than the red kilt alone—his only other garment. "Good morning, good morning!" he chanted cheerfully, weaving through the dressing men and scampering up the companionway.

"Ain't natural," grumped Rodriguez, who'd finally been restored to full duty. "Even monkey-cats can't be that happy to wake up every day. He's settin' a bad example. It'll ruin morale, I tell you."

Elden grinned. "Sleep on deck and you won't have to watch him in the morning."

"Hell, I would! But every time, I get woke up drenched by a squall."

"You'd rather get woke up drenched by sweat?"

Rodriguez shrugged. "This close to the equator, don't much matter where you sleep, you're gonna do that. Sometimes I actually pity those damn snipes. I bet it hits a hundred and forty in the fireroom today."

"Hey, man, God didn't make 'em snipes. If we were in the North Atlantic they'd be toasty warm and wouldn't feel sorry for us, out on the icy deck."

"Icy deck!" moaned Leo Davis dreamily from his rack. Ever since Lieutenant Tucker had applied the Lemurian salve to his leg, he'd rapidly improved. So much, in fact, that some began to suspect him of malingering. He stretched and smiled. "Is it morning already? Which one of you fellas'll bring me breakfast in bed?"

Elden pitched a rancid sock on his chest, and Davis yelped and squirmed, trying to get out from under it without touching it. "Damn you! I'm an invalid!"

Chief Gray poked his head down the companionway. "Move it, you apes! Skipper's lookin' at his watch! If you ain't at your GQ stations in one minute he's gonna throw a fit!"

"I wonder why we're still doin' that?" Elden pondered aloud after Gray disappeared. Every morning watch, *Walker*'s crew manned their general quarters posts until two hours after dawn so they'd be prepared while the ship was most vulnerable—when an enemy might see her silhouette before her lookouts saw the enemy. After that, she steamed under condition III alert, with half her weapons manned all day. "Ain't no Jap subs out there," Elden continued. "Ain't no Jap ships or planes. Ain't no Jap Navy. Hell, there ain't no Japs, 'cept ours!"

"I don't know why, but the Skipper does, and he's the only one that has to," Rodriguez said, tying his shoe and hurrying for the ladder. "C'mon, or the snipes'll clean out the galley!"

Chack happily munched the strange yellowish-white substance rolled in a slice of bread. He'd heard them call it "eggs," but Mertz made it from powder, so they must have been joking. He liked the way Amer-i-caans joked, and they did it all the time. Sometimes he wasn't sure if they were joking or not, however. After it was cooked, the stuff did taste a little like eggs, and he particularly liked it with salt and "caatch-up."

Finished eating, he climbed to the fire-control platform, then up the little ladder to his new battle station on the searchlight platform above it. It was still dark, but just a trace of red tinged the eastern sky. A stiff breeze cooled him, and he felt a sense of exhilaration and speed, even at only six knots. That was still about as fast as he'd ever gone before, and *Walker*'s relatively small size magnified the sensation wonderfully. He knew it was only a fraction of what she was capable of, and he yearned to be aboard when she "stretched her legs," as his Amer-i-caan friends described it.

Lieutenant Garrett appeared on the platform below and smiled up at Chack.

"Good morning, Loo-ten-aant Gaar-ret! Morning-day good!"

"Indeed it is. Good morning to you as well. Why don't you light along to the crow's nest and take the first watch? Sing out if those keen eyes of yours spot anything. Understand?" Chack blinked with pleasure and looked at the tiny bucket far above. He'd spent most of his life much higher, but it was the highest point on the ship and he was thrilled by the novelty and—in his mind—the prestige of the post.

"Crow's nest? Me?"

"That's right, Chack. Crow's nest. You. Up you go."

"You want I go higher? I go top of pole?"

Garrett chuckled. "No, the crow's nest is high enough." He pantomimed putting on the headset. "You have to be able to talk and hear. But don't talk unless you see something!"

"Ay, ay!" Chack said, and shot up the ladder. Garrett shook his head, still smiling, as he watched the Lemurian climb. The long, swishing tail did make him look like a cat, or for that matter, a monkey. Whatever he looked like, he was becoming a pretty good hand, and nobody came close to matching his enthusiasm or agility. He was wondering with amusement if they could recruit more like him, when all weapons reported "manned and ready" and he reported for his division.

The sky went from red to yellow-gray and visibility began to improve. The other lookouts scanned for any menace with their binoculars, and a quarter mile off their port quarter, *Big Sal* began to take shape. The gray became suffused with gold that flared against the bottoms of fleecy clouds and cast a new coastline into stark relief off the port bow. Ahead lay the Makassar Strait and, beyond that, Celebes. But right now all eyes were glued to the landfall. Matt paced onto the port bridgewing and joined the lookout there.

"Borneo, Skipper," said the man in a tone of mixed excitement and apprehension. They had almost exactly the same view as when they'd last seen it, astern, after the Battle of Makassar Strait—just a few months before. Then they were running as fast as they could, with the enemy nipping at their heels. They'd been scared to death but flushed with elation after the only real "victory" the Asiatic Fleet had achieved: against the Japanese invasion force at Balikpapan. They sank several transports and a destroyer—just *Walker* and four other four-stackers—but it hadn't been nearly enough, and they were lucky to escape with their skins. They should have had a larger haul, but a lot of their torpedoes either never hit their targets or failed to explode when they did hit. That was when they first suspected something was wrong with them. Now they were returning, but not like they'd imagined they would.

"It looks the same," said the lookout, then added with a grin, "only there's no smoke from burning Nips."

"There was plenty of smoke," Matt agreed, "but we wouldn't have seen it from here. Balikpapan's still a hundred and fifty miles away."

They heard a whoop over the crow's nest comm. "Surfuss taagit! Surfuss taagit!"

After a shocked delay, the frustrated talker responded. "Where? Where?! What bearing? Who the hell's up there foolin' around? Maintain proper procedures!" There was no response. Matt looked up at the crow's nest, and there was Chack, not in it but on top of it, standing as high as he could and waving both arms over his head. He uttered a low-pitched, but astonishingly loud ululating cry. He was signaling something or someone ahead, and Matt turned and stared as hard as he could, scanning back and forth. It was that tough time of morning when submarines were so dangerous. The sky was growing brighter, but the sea was almost black. Unless something was silhouetted, it was practically invisible.

"There, sir!" cried the lookout. "Not three hundred yards away, dead ahead! A boat!"

Matt shifted his gaze and sure enough, a boat appeared in his binoculars. It was about forty feet long, with two tripod masts and junklike sails. It was also ridiculously close. There was no silhouette since the masts were short and Borneo provided a backdrop. He was amazed that even Chack had seen it. "Helm, right ten degrees. All engines stop!"

"Right ten degrees, all stop, aye," came the reply. Matt studied the boat and saw figures now, scampering excitedly about.

"More 'Cats," he said. "I'll be damned."

"Skipper," said Rick Tolson, "look a little to the left." Matt did so, and to his surprise he saw another boat. And another! "They're fishermen!" Tolson exclaimed with complete certainty. "Coastal fishermen! Look!" Each small ship had one end of a net hooked to its side, while the other was supported by a long boom. As they watched, the boom on the farthest boat began to rise. The end of the net drew closed as the boom rose higher, and a multitude of flopping, thumping, silvery shapes poured onto the deck. Nimble Lemurians waded among them with clubs that rose and fell. At a shouted warning, a few club wielders stopped and looked in shock at the destroyer coasting toward them. Chack silenced his booming cry, but jabbered excitedly at the fishermen as they drew near.

"Mr. Tolson, relieve the crow's nest lookout and send him to the fo'c'sle to talk more easily with the fishing boats. Use the engines to maintain position to windward of them, if you please."

Moments later, Chack was on the fo'c'sle, leaning forward and conversing with the nearest boat. Its crew hadn't raised their net and they all stood, amazed, looking up at him.

"He sure got there quick enough," Tolsen observed. "My God, I think he slid down the forestay!"

Matt chuckled. "Well, thanks to his keen eyes, we didn't ram anybody. But do have a word with him about procedures. The last thing we need is other guys trying a stunt like that—which they will—just to prove that if he can do it, they can too." He looked back at the fishing boats, their crews now shouting excitedly back at Chack. Beyond them in the distance, clearer now, was Borneo. Lush and green and familiar. And yet . . . It was almost like seeing a photograph of a place he'd been. It looked like it, but it wasn't *it*. He remembered what Bradford had said about the "wild" Grik they'd dissected: judge it by what it *is* like, not what it *looks* like. There was a profound difference. He wondered how different Borneo would be.

They saw many more boats that day. Most were fishermen, like the first they met, and Chack explained that land People fished only mornings and evenings when the smaller fish came to the shallows where the gri-kakka felt confined. The big plesiosaurs could go shallow, but were usually content to linger in deeper water and wait for food to come to them. Most of the boats they saw weren't designed or equipped to hunt the brutes, although their fat was a valuable commodity. That was a job for a Home. Like all Homes, *Big Sal*'s People did hunt the big fish, and the result was her primary trade asset—gri-kakka oil. Much of her store was lost in the fire, but hopefully enough remained to finance her repairs.

Some boats ran away as soon as they sighted them, and some went on ahead after a short conference with Chack. A few stayed and took station on *Big Sal* as they made their way north-northeast. Occasionally, curious crews ventured to gawk at *Walker* and her outlandish folk, but generally they avoided the destroyer.

Late the next afternoon, as the sun neared the horizon and set the low clouds aglow, they entered Balikpapan Bay. For the first time since they'd seen her, *Big Sal*'s massive sails descended and scores of great sweeps extended from her sides like the legs of a giant centipede and she propelled herself against the ebbing tide right into the mouth of the bay. Matt wasn't sure what he'd expected. A small settlement perhaps. Chack and the others often referred to Balikpapan as the "land colony," and he guessed that made him think in diminutive terms. But the civilization they beheld was a virtual metropolis. Two more Homes, similar to *Big Sal*, were moored in the broad harbor, and hundreds of smaller vessels plied back and forth. A long pier jutted from a point of land almost exactly where they'd last seen Japanese troopships burning. The sensation was surreal. Lemurian fishing boats were tied to it now, and beyond the pier was a city.

That was the only word to describe it, even if the architecture was . . . unusual. Wooden warehouses lined the waterfront, but beyond were high pagoda-like structures much like *Big Sal*'s towers. Most were just a few stories tall, though broader than those on the ship, but a few reached quite stunning heights. These were multitiered, and each "story" was slightly smaller than that directly beneath it, which gave them the appearance of extremely tall and skinny Aztec temples. Otherwise, the pervasive "pagodas" continued to make a generally Eastern impression.

The most unusual architectural feature, however, was that every building in view—except the warehouses—was built on massive stilts, or pilings, that supported the structures at least a dozen feet above the ground. In the open space beneath them was an enormous market, or bazaar, that had no apparent organization at all. As far as they could see from *Walker*'s bridge, it occupied and constituted the entire "lower level" of the city. The market was teeming with thousands of Lemurians, coming and going, engaging in commerce, and deporting themselves more like the denizens of Shanghai than the 'Cats they'd come to know. Color was everywhere. Most of the buildings were painted, and large tapestries and awnings were hung beneath and, in many cases, stretched between them. The dominant colors were reds and blues, but gold was prevalent as well, and the whole thing starkly contrasted with the dark green jungle beyond and the dirty, gray-blue bay.

"Looks like Chefoo," Gray murmured, mirroring Matt's thoughts.

The arrival of the destroyer and the battle-damaged Home hadn't gone unnoticed. Hundreds of spectators lined the quay and watched as the two ships approached. Small boats sailed back and forth, jockeying for a view, and twice Matt ordered full astern to avoid running over the more intrepid or foolhardy sightseers. The smell of the city reached them on the gentle breeze, and although it wasn't unpleasant, it too was somewhat alien. Riotous, unknown spices on cooking meat and fish predominated, although there was a hint of exotic flowers and strange vegetation. All competed with the normal harbor smells of salt water, dead fish, and rotting wood. There was even a tantalizing undertone of creosote.

Big Sal continued past the wharf, the long sweeps dipping, until she reached a point opposite a large, empty dock with more warehouses and a tall wooden crane. There she backed water and ever so slowly began to inch her massive bulk closer to the dock. Lemurians scampered about in a very recognizable way, and huge mooring lines were passed to the ship.

"We'll anchor two hundred yards outboard of *Big Sal*, Boats," Matt said. "Let's keep a little water between us and shore until we find out what's what."

"Aye, aye, Skipper," Gray responded and clattered down the ladder. Dowden conned the ship to the point Matt instructed, and with a great booming rattle, the new starboard anchor dropped to the silty bottom of Balikpapan Bay.

"Maintain condition three, Mr. Dowden," Matt ordered as he turned to leave the bridge. "I'm heading over to *Big Sal*. Mr. Garrett, Chack, Lieutenant Tucker, and two armed men will accompany me. Pass the word, if you please: dress whites and crackerjacks."

They motored across to *Big Sal* and made the long climb to its deck. Matt had been aboard several times now, but he was only just becoming accustomed to the sheer size of the ship. Courtney Bradford and the destroyermen who'd been helping aboard greeted them. Matt sent Bradford back to *Walker* to make himself presentable and told him to return in thirty minutes.

As usual, they went through the boarding ritual, but as soon as they had, the Lemurian who'd given permission raced off. When he returned, he was accompanied by Adar and High Chief Keje himself. Both were dressed in garments representative of their status. Adar wore the same cape or "Sky Priest suit" he'd worn every time Matt had seen him. Keje wore his polished copper armor over an even finer tunic than the one he'd first worn aboard *Walker*. Gold-wire embroidery graced every cuff, and his polished and engraved copper helmet now boasted the striated plumage from the tail of a Grik warrior. A sweeping red and gold cape was clasped at his throat by a chain of polished Grik hind claws. *He won't let anyone forget that* Big Sal *broke the Grik for the first time,* Matt thought.

Matt and the rest of his party, including Chack, saluted him. Matt still thought it appropriate, since Keje wasn't just the captain of a ship, but was, in effect, a head of state. Bradford was trying to sort out all the nuances of Lemurian society, but so far it seemed rather confusing. The closest analogy he'd come up with was that of the ancient Greek city-states, or possibly even the United States under the Articles of Confederation. Each Lemurian ship was considered a country unto itself, with its own laws and sometimes very distinctive culture. The Trade Lands or Land Colonies had the same status, but as they grew in size, they also grew in economic influence. So, although still theoretically equal, some of the more tradition-minded Homes resented the upstart "mud-treaders."

"Greetings, U-Amaki, Keje-Fris-Ar," he said, and Keje grinned widely, returning the salute.

"Greeting you, Cap-i-taan Riddy. Bad-furd teech I speak you words. Good, eh?"

Matt grinned back. "Very good, Your Excellency. I regret I haven't done nearly as well learning your language." Keje was still grinning, but clearly he hadn't caught everything Matt said. Chack elaborated in his own language.

"Ah. Good! Chack speak for we! He learn good!" Matt nodded at Keje's understatement. Chack really had made remarkable progress. He'd seen people pick up enough of a new language to get by with in a week, through total immersion, but he'd never seen anyone learn one as well as Chack in so short a time.

"He has indeed."

They waited companionably until Bradford returned. All the while, locals came aboard and talked excitedly with Keje's people. Many were shipwrights, looking at damage they expected to be commissioned to repair. But most were just visitors who wanted to hear the story of how it happened, and wanted most of all to stare at the strange people with no tails who came from the ship without wings. The decks of Home had taken on a decidedly festive, holiday-like atmosphere.

"What'll happen now?" Matt asked when their party was complete. The answer ultimately translated that they would soon pay their respects to "U-Amaki Ay Baalkpan," Nakja-Mur, where they would eat and drink and tell their tale. In addition to the fact that they had a wondrous tale to tell, it had been more than two years since they'd been here, and the local potentate was somehow related to Keje. There would be much to celebrate.

At the mention of "drink" and "celebrate" Matt considered sending the ratings back to the ship, but finally decided against it. They didn't seem the least inclined to go haring off on their own, and at least Silva wasn't among them. He doubted Lemurian society was quite prepared for the likes of Dennis Silva on the loose. God knew his men deserved liberty after their ordeal, but he wanted to learn a bit more about this place before he granted it.

A procession was forming in the waist and nearly every 'Cat on *Big Sal* was part of it. Bright kilts and garish costumes were the uniform of the day, and the tumult and chaos of the happy, grinning throng was almost as loud as the battle against the Grik. There'd be liberty for them, at least, and they were prepared to make the most of it.

"All Amer-i-caans not come land?" Keje asked in his stilted English.

"No, Your Excellency, not yet. My ship is very tired and has many needs. This is the first time she has stopped among friends where it's safe to make repairs. There's much to do."

"Work tomorrow! Tonight is glory-party. Friends meet friends!"

"Perhaps later," Matt demurred. With a polite but brittle smile he excused himself and stepped to the rail, where he looked out to his anchored ship in the dwindling light. Even to his prejudiced eye she looked physically exhausted. When he had first assumed command of DD-163, she'd seemed old-fashioned and undergunned, but in spite of that she'd given the impression that she tugged at her leash like a nostalgic thoroughbred— past her prime but not yet out to pasture. Now she just looked worn-out. Rust streaked her sides from stem to stern, and the hasty repairs stood out like running sores. A continuous jet of water gushed from her bilge as the overworked pumps labored to keep her leaky hull afloat. The anchor chain hung slack, and instead of straining against it she looked burdened by the weight. He was surprised by a stabbing sense of sadness and concern.

Sandra had joined him, unnoticed in the hubbub. "A coat of paint and she'll be good as new," she said brightly, guessing his thoughts. He looked at her pretty, cheerful face, but saw the concern in her eyes. His brittle smile shattered like an egg dropped on the deck, and he saw her expression turn to anguish. For an instant her compassion was more than he could bear. He forced a grin that was probably closer to a grimace, but as she continued to look at him, her hand suddenly on his arm, his face slowly softened into a wistful smile. How did she do that? In a single, sharp, wrenching moment, she'd stripped his veneer and bared his inner torment, but with only the slightest touch, she'd buried it again. Deeper than before.

"It'll take more than a coat of paint, I'm afraid," he whispered. He saw Keje beyond her, motioning at the spot beside him. "Looks like they're ready to go." Unwilling to break the contact, he crooked his elbow and held his arm out for her. "Care to join me?"

Keje and Adar, along with Matt and Sandra, threaded their way through the throng and took places at the head of the procession. Bradford was several paces back, behind the wing clan chiefs and Keje's other officers. Chack and Garrett were with him, as were the two other destroyermen. They weren't carrying rifles, but they had sidearms and the ridiculous cutlasses. Bradford wasn't wearing one, even though they were as much his idea as Gray's. The one time he did, he'd somehow managed to cut himself without even drawing it completely from its scabbard. He wasn't wearing a pistol either, but only because he'd forgotten it when he changed his clothes. Captain Reddy wore his Academy sword. With many hoots and jubilant cries from the ship as well as the dock, the procession began to move and they marched down the gangway, into the teeming city.

The festivities were heard across the water, beyond *Big Sal*, where *Walker* rested at last. Spanky McFarlane wiped greasy hands on a rag tucked into his pocket. His sooty face was streaked with sweat. "Sounds like a hell of a party," he said, staring at the shore.

"Yup," said Silva, and he spat a stream of tobacco juice over the side. Stites leaned on the rail by the number two gun, a cigarette between his lips. Spanky fished a battered pack out of his shirt pocket and shook one out. Silva handed him a Zippo. "Think we're gonna get fuel here?" he asked.

"Dunno. Hope so. We're down to seven thousand gallons, so we ain't looking for it anywhere else."

"Not without burning wood, I hear," Stites put in. Spanky glowered at him. "I reckon if anybody can squeeze oil out of the monkey-cats, the Skipper will. He's done okay."

"No arguments there," Silva grunted. "I just wish I knew what we're gonna have to do to get it—and what we're gonna do then."

Spanky looked at him curiously. "What difference would it make if you did?"

Silva grinned. "None, I guess." He walked to the rail and leaned on it beside Stites. "Might be fun to go ashore. Kick up my heels." His face darkened. "Ain't no women, though. That's gonna get tough, fast."

"All them other nurses gone on *Mahan*," Stites grumped, "and the only two dames in the whole wide world is officers. Where's the justice in that?"

"Maybe there're women somewhere," encouraged Spanky. "The Skipper thinks so. Those lizard ships were human enough, and the monkey-cats speak Latin, of all things. We can't be the only people who ever wound up here."

"Then we better find fuel quick so we can start lookin' for 'em," Stites muttered emphatically.

"Oh, I don't know," Silva reflected. "Some of them cat-monkey gals are kinda cute, if you don't mind that furry, European style."

Stites looked at him with wide eyes. "Shit, Dennis, you're one sick bastard!" After a moment, though, he scratched his cheek. "Course, after a while, who knows?"

Spanky cleared his throat. He knew—well, suspected—the men were joking and that was fine. But the joke was barbed and reflected a very real concern. Best keep it a joke for now. "I wouldn't worry about it. Strikes me they have higher standards, and I doubt you'd measure up. A goat wouldn't be satisfied with a deck-ape."

Silva affected offense. "Now, sir, that's no way for an officer to talk. Downright uncharitable. Keepin' all the goats to yourselves might dee-stroy the perfect harmony between the apes and snipes!"

Spanky laughed out loud. "I'll bear that in mind."

Of course, if the rumors he'd overheard about Silva trying to "murder" Laney were true, there was little harmony left to destroy. Officially, a rusted pin broke. With nobody, even Laney, saying otherwise, that's all there was to it. But tensions were high. So far, everyone was too busy working together to keep the ship afloat for things to get out of hand—except the "joke" on Laney. Spanky was sure that was all it was. Silva played rough and maybe Laney had it coming. He could be a real jerk. It was even kind of funny—since nobody died—and Laney sure wasn't as puffed up as usual. But once the ship was out of danger, they better find one of two things pretty quick: dames or a fight. If they ever added boredom to their fear and frustration, the "jokes" would stop being funny at all.

The procession wound through the heart of the open-air market that was the city of "Baalkpan." It was somehow reassuring that the name of the place was derived from the ancient charts the Lemurians considered sacred. If nothing else, it proved that whoever transcribed or inspired the Scrolls didn't speak Latin as a first language. Matt wasn't positive; his historical interests were focused elsewhere, but he was pretty sure the place-names in the region had been given or recorded by the Dutch within the last two or three hundred years. That also meant that whatever religious importance the Lemurians placed on the Scrolls was a relatively new addition to their dogma. Not its sole foundation. Other than that fleeting thought, however, at the moment he and his companions were far more interested in their surroundings.

They were again struck by the vivid colors all around. Nothing went unpainted, and the tapestries and awnings were remarkably fine. Printing technology was apparently unknown, because the delicate and elaborate designs decorating virtually everything they saw were woven right into the cloth. Accomplished as they were at weaving, however, the Lemurians wore very little—enough for the sake of modesty, but only just. Kilts were the norm, although some, like Adar—and Keje tonight—might don a cape as well. Other than kilts, clothing seemed to be worn only for occupational protection. Occasionally they saw someone dressed in armor of sorts, but even then it appeared more decorative than practical. Matt knew Keje's armor was real—even though it was carefully cleaned and polished, it was scarred with many dents and cuts that proved it wasn't just for show. The people of Baalkpan seemed happy and prosperous, if just a bit garish. But unlike Keje and the crew of *Big Sal*, they didn't look like fighters.

What they lacked in martial manner, they made up for with their enthusiastic greeting of Keje's people and the destroyermen. Matt saw plenty of naked curiosity, but no hostility at all. Little apparent surprise either, and it dawned on him suddenly that of course they'd known *Walker* was coming. They'd dawdled along with *Big Sal* for days after being seen, and word could have reached Balikpapan on the slowest fishing boat. There'd also been plenty of time for them to learn what happened with the Grik. Indeed, that seemed to have a lot to do with the enthusiastic greeting. They were "hailing the heroes home from the war." They saw the battle as a great victory and were rejoicing.

"It's just amazing!" Sandra shouted in his ear, over the tumult. He nodded. Large feline eyes of all colors gazed intently at them from the crowd. Here and there, Lemurian children scampered on all fours, their tails in the air, dodging between the legs of their elders. Others openly suckled their mothers. Ahead, a smallish brontosaurus was hitched to a cart loaded with something pungent. It balked at a command from its driver, apparently startled by the commotion, and bellowed in protest. The procession paused while the driver regained control of the beast and then continued on.

"Amazing!" shouted Courtney Bradford, suddenly just behind them, oblivious to protocol. "They use dinosaurs like oxen, or mules! I wouldn't have thought they were intelligent enough to domesticate! The dinosaurs, I mean."

"You'd be surprised," Matt replied. "I knew a guy who rode a Longhorn steer around like a horse, and a Longhorn can't be any smarter than a dinosaur."

"Indeed?"

They passed fishmongers hawking their wares who stopped to gawk at the procession. Mostly, they sold the familiar "flasher-fish" they'd all seen quite enough of, but Matt was surprised to see other types of fish as well. He'd almost imagined that the flasher-fish, vicious and prolific as they were, must have virtually wiped out every other species in the sea. Now he saw that wasn't the case, although the other fishes, by their size and formidable appearance, didn't look any more pleasant to meet. There was a large crustacean resembling a giant armored scorpion with a lobster tail that looked able to propel it forward as well as back. He was intrigued by a small version of the plesiosaur they'd rammed, and a very ordinary-looking shark. He'd thought sharks wouldn't stand a chance in these far more lethal waters, and he suspected they weren't the dominant predators he'd always known them to be.

He glanced behind and saw that the procession was growing more boisterous, but it wasn't as large anymore. Many of *Big Sal*'s crew had been tempted away by diversions or acquaintances. There was still quite a throng, and city dwellers caroused along with them as they made their way toward a massive edifice, squat in comparison to others but much broader and more imposing. It rested on considerably higher stilts than the buildings nearby, and growing up through the center and out through the top was a truly stupendous tree.

At its base, the procession finally halted and the crowd noises diminished. Keje stepped forward and raised his hands, palms forward. When he spoke, Chack quietly translated as best he could.

"Greetings, Nakja-Mur, High Chief of Baalkpan!" Keje's voice seemed unnaturally loud now that everyone nearby was silent. "I am Keje-Fris-Ar, High Chief of *Salissa* Home, come from the Southern Sea with mighty friends, trade, and tales to tell. May we come aboard for counsel?"

There was a moment of silence, then a powerful voice from an unseen source boomed at them from above.

"Come aboard, and welcome, Brother. It is long since *Salissa* Home visited these waters, and some of your tale has arrived before you. Come, eat and drink and tell me your tale. Bring these mighty friends of yours. I would meet them!"

Adar glanced back at them and suddenly spoke urgently to Keje. Keje looked at them and seemed to hesitate, but then clapped Adar on the back and scampered up the rope ladder that was, apparently, the only way up. Adar looked at them again with what might have been uncertainty, but then followed his leader. Matt motioned for Sandra to make the twenty-foot climb and with a smile she grasped the ropes and started up. Matt would have sworn he hadn't consciously considered it when he suggested she go first, but he caught himself watching the shapely nurse ascending the ladder above and for a moment he was almost mesmerized. The white stockings didn't hide her athletic legs, and the way her hips swished from side to side at the bottom of her wasp-thin waist . . . He shook his head and looked away, vaguely ashamed, and saw all the other men watching as well. He coughed loudly and meaningfully and gestured Chack closer.

"How come these people build everything so high off the ground?"

Chack looked at him blankly, then his eyelids fluttered with amusement and he grinned. "Is, ah, tradition? Yes. Remind us of old ways. Also, keep dry when high water. Bad land lizards not climb good, too."

Matt grinned back at him. "Makes sense to me!" With that, he made his own way up.

Large as it was, Captain Reddy never imagined that the enormous hall he entered would possibly hold all who came along, but it did—as well as an equal number of locals. The size and shape reminded him of an oversized basketball court, dimly lit by oil lamps that exuded a pleasant, if somewhat fishy smell. Huge beams supported the vaulted ceiling and great gaudy tapestries lined the walls, stirring gently with the soft breeze from banks of open shutters. Dominating the center of the hall, the trunk of the massive Galla tree disappeared into the gloom above. Except for the size of the tree and the height of the ceiling, it looked like the Great Hall on *Big Sal*. Matt guessed there were close to five hundred occupants, talking animatedly, and for the moment, no one paid them any heed.

Along one wall, a long bar was laid with colorful dishes heaped with food. Every ten feet or so was a cluster of copper pitchers containing a dark amber liquid that smelled like honey and bread. Matt saw others grab pitchers and begin to drink, so he seized one each for himself and Sandra. Bradford took one too, but when the other destroyermen moved in that direction, Lieutenant Garrett scowled and shook his head. Matt peered into his pitcher and sipped experimentally. He looked at Bradford, surprised.

"Tastes . . . sort of like beer," he said. "Not bad, either." Sandra took a tentative sip and Bradford raised his mug. A moment later, he lowered it and smacked his lips.

"Ahhh! Beer! We've more in common with these Lemurians than we ever dreamed! I'd think the alcohol content is rather high as well."

Matt glanced at Garrett and the security detachment and felt a pang of remorse. They looked at him like dogs watching him eat. "Go ahead, men, but just one mug apiece. Mr. Garrett? See to it. All we need now is drunken sailors!" He and Sandra politely moved along the bar with the crowd, sampling small dishes here and there. The spices were different and some were quite brutal. Many of *Big Sal*'s 'Cats proudly pointed out this or that and made suggestions, but most of the locals just watched, wide-eyed.

"Cap-i-taan Riddy!"

Matt turned toward the somewhat familiar voice and faced Kas-Ra-Ar, Keje's cousin, and captain of his personal guard.

"Com plees."

Bradford had obviously been as busy teaching English on *Big Sal* as Chack had been learning it on *Walker.*

"By all means," Matt replied. "Mr. Garrett? Please supervise our protectors. Lieutenant Tucker, Mr. Bradford, would you accompany me?"

They followed Kas through the boisterous throng, threading their way down the far side, away from the buffet. At the other end of the hall, they came to a less-packed space, where Keje and Adar stood near a seated figure dressed in flowing robes of red and gold. The figure was easily the fattest Lemurian they'd seen, but he gave no impression of sedentary weakness. His dark fur was sleek and shiny with just a hint of silver, and he radiated an aura of strength and power despite the massive stomach his hands laid upon. He regarded them with keen, intelligent eyes as they approached and raised his hand palm outward and thundered a greeting in his own tongue.

Matt returned the gesture, and the Lemurian's eyes flicked to the sword at his side. Keje spoke quickly in Nakja-Mur's ear. While the Lemurian chief watched them, unblinking, Adar translated to Courtney Bradford.

"Never has he seen someone make the Sign of the Empty Hand when that person's hand wasn't empty. I believe he's referring to your sword, old boy."

Matt glanced with surprise at the sheathed ceremonial weapon. They'd worn the swords—as before—to seem less exotic. It hadn't occurred to him that it might cause trouble. Keje would have warned them if they were committing some terrible breach of convention. Wouldn't he? He thought quickly. "Tell him my hand *is* empty. Among our people, only the unsheathed weapon is a threat because it shows intent. The sign is given as a token of friendship and reflects more the intent than the actual fact."

"It is a lie, then?" came the question. Keje seemed uncomfortable and Adar radiated an air of vindication. Matt felt a surge of anger and wondered if they'd been set up. Sandra unobtrusively squeezed his arm.

"Tell him it's not a lie. We came here as friends, as we came to the aid of *Salissa* Home. We'd like to be the friends of all the People. Since our intentions are friendly, *not* making the sign would have been a lie. Among our people, friends may go among one another armed and still remain friends. Is that not the case among his?"

After the translation, Nakja-Mur just stared for a moment, but then slowly, his lips parted into a grin. Matt looked at Keje and saw he was already smiling. "I tell Nakja-Mur you people always armed because you always . . . warriors. Always. You ship made for fighting only. Not so?"

Finally, they'd come to the point. He'd never lied about it, but he had downplayed it. Now, Matt knew, there was only one possible answer. The truth.

"USS *Walker* is a ship of war," he admitted quietly.

"Who you fight?" Adar asked. "Who you fight all the time to need ship only for war?"

Matt realized it was the first time he'd heard the Sky Priest speak English. "We fight the enemies of our people . . . and the enemies of our friends."

"You fight Grik?" Adar translated for Nakja-Mur.

"We've already fought the Grik."

"You fight again?"

Matt glanced at Sandra and Bradford. They were both looking at him, realizing that what he said in the next few moments might have grave consequences for them all.

"If the Grik come and you can't fight them alone, we'll help. That's what friends do. But friends don't ask friends to do all their fighting for them."

Nakja-Mur spoke to Adar, all the while watching Matt's face as if curious how to interpret human expressions. Adar repeated his words as carefully as he could. "After battle tale of U-Amaki Ay *Salissa*"—he paused and looked at Matt—"Keje tell fight. Grik fight bad, but hard. Fight new way, bigger ship. More Grik than see before." He took a quick gulp from his tankard. "New thing," he said. "Different thing. Maybe Grik come . . . bigger, like long ago."

Matt was concerned about the Grik, of course, but he wasn't too worried about *Walker*'s ability to handle several of their ships at once, if need be. They were the "Ancient Enemy," that much he understood, and he knew the 'Cats held them in almost superstitious dread—with good reason. But he guessed he'd begun to think of them more along the lines of his "Malay pirate" model than as an actual expansionist menace. They'd been "out there" for thousands of years, after all. His assessment was based on his limited conversations, as well as the lack of any evident preparations to meet a serious threat. Especially here. He'd shifted his primary concern to establishing good enough relations with the Lemurians that they would help with fuel and repairs. If a limited alliance, in which *Walker* chased off a few Grik now and then, was the only way to meet those needs, then he was prepared to agree to one, but he wanted to avoid an "entangling" alliance that left either too dependent on the other.

Now, though, it seemed they were actually afraid the Grik might attack here. That didn't fit the "pirate" model. He was dismayed how vulnerable the people of Baalkpan were, even compared to their seagoing cousins. They'd always referred to it as an "outpost" or "colony," and he supposed that description had left him thinking Baalkpan was small and possibly even transient. Certainly easily evacuated. Now, of course, he knew that the land colony of Baalkpan would be about as easy to evacuate as . . . Surabaya. But even against six Grik ships, Baalkpan had enough people—complacent as they were—to repel an assault with ease. Something had been lost in translation—or had they been "downplaying" too?

Adar continued. "If Grik come bigger, like long ago, there be . . . plenty? Plenty fight for all." Matt looked at Nakja-Mur and then at Keje who stood by his side, watching him. Then he glanced at Sandra and sighed.

"Tell me more about the Grik."

The party proceeded around them, loud with happy cries and chittering laughter. A troupe of dancers found enough space near the trunk of the great tree to perform feats of astonishing agility and admirable grace. They were accompanied by haunting but festive music produced by drums and a woodwind/horn that sounded like a muted trumpet. All the while, a space was left surrounding the thronelike chair of Nakja-Mur and his guests while they discussed the peril they faced.

Nakja-Mur touched a chime. At the signal, a truly ancient Lemurian emerged—as if he'd been waiting—from a chamber behind his chief, dressed in the robes and stars of the Sky Priests. Around his neck was a simple brass pendant, tarnished with age but suspended by an ornate chain of gold. He clutched it when he suddenly spoke the same, but more polished, Latin that Adar had first used to communicate with them.

"You understand the Ancient Tongue," he grated.

"Yes! I mean, uh, that's true, Your . . . Eminence."

The old Lemurian gave a start when Bradford replied, but continued in his raspy voice. "I'm disquieted by that, but it's clearly true. I would learn how this can be. But that will wait." He seemed contemplative for a moment, but then visibly gathered himself to speak again.

"I'm Naga, High Sky Priest of Baalkpan. I will tell you of the Grik and of the People. The Scrolls are our ancient history, our guide, our way, our very life, but they are incomplete and there are gaps—great gaps—between their beginning and the now. Hundreds of generations passed between the beginning times and when we learned the Ancient Tongue. The Truth was passed by word of mouth all that time before it was recorded." He blinked several times in a sequence that Bradford thought signified regret. "Perhaps, much was lost," he continued, "but the Scrolls clearly tell of a time when all the people lived together in happiness and peace on a land in the west. A land vast and beautiful, safe from the capricious sea. A land lush and green and covered with trees and protected by water. And the Maker of All Things, the Greatest of all the Stars above, filled the waters around the Ancient Home with wicked fishes that kept our people safe from the monsters across the water on the western land.

"And thus it was, for age upon age. The People lived and died, but were prosperous and happy and needed only the trees for their homes." He shook his head in lament and blinked again, rapidly. "But for some, it wasn't enough. The fragile perfection of the People's existence was somehow lacking, it seemed. Some built boats, to range upon the sea and take fishes there. They wandered and explored, and finally it came to be that one of the boats was cast upon the western land of monsters. The Grik," he added darkly. "The Grik slew them and ate them, but then wondered from where did they come, this new prey?"

Bradford translated as quickly as he could, but began to fall behind. The old priest waited while he caught up, and then continued.

"The Grik built boats for themselves. They copied the very boats delivered unto them. They were poor sailors, and many perished and the flasher-fish and gri-kakka grew fat on their bodies, but there were always more. Finally, they reached the ancient paradise of our People. Only a few came at first, like now." He stopped and looked at Nakja-Mur. "And they were killed and cast into the sea. The People were not warriors and many died, but they were able, for a time, to slay all that came." He paused for effect. "But there were always more."

The party went on, unabated, but a circle of silent listeners had formed around them. The old Sky Priest lifted a copper mug to his shriveled lips and drank.

Bradford turned to Matt. "My God, Captain! Do you know what this means? Madagascar! This 'ancient paradise' simply must be Madagascar! These people are quite clearly related to lemurs—as I've believed from the start! I admit the relation has become somewhat distant . . ."

"Distant!" snorted Sandra. "Most lemurs are no bigger than a cat. None I know of are bigger than a chimp!"

"That's where you're mistaken, my dear. A species of giant lemur once dwelt on Madagascar, a species almost as large as our friends. I've seen their very bones!" His brow furrowed. "But they were not nearly so . . . humanlike in form. Nevertheless! This gives me almost enough information to advance my theory regarding—" He was unable to finish because the wizened priest spoke once more.

"The war for paradise must have lasted generations. We know not, because the Scrolls do not say. But during that time, the People learned to build great ships—the Homes of the Sea—and so were prepared when the

Grik became too many and the People were finally cast out, forced to wander the vast oceans, never to return to our sacred home." Naga paused to catch his breath and allow Bradford time to translate. While he waited, he looked wistfully at the great tree in the center of the hall. "At first, we wandered blindly. We had not yet learned the Heavens—to follow the paths they laid before us. We knew the Great Star, the Maker of All Things who lights the world and brings brightness to the void of night, and we knew his little brother, who washes the night with a cool, sleepy light, but we did not know that the smaller stars yearned to show us things. Many perished when their Homes were cast on unknown shores, and it's said the bones of those ancient wrecks bleach there even still. But enough survived to carry on. Lost and scattered by storm and darkness, our people did survive. Over time, they saw the light in the darkness and learned the wisdom of the Heavens. It was then that they knew the stars for what they are—the bright essence of those who have gone before and watch over us from the sky."

He looked at the humans for a moment and Bradford could have sworn that he blinked in speculation. He continued. "Some settled in the northlands, and others in the south. Some eked out an existence on tiny islands in the middle of the Western Sea, but always, where there was land, eventually there were Grik. The only ones to gain a shadow of freedom from war and fear were those who lived on the sea. Only the sea was safe, for the Grik do not love it and did not know how to build the great floating Homes. With the deep waters between us, where the mountain fish dwell, for a time there was peace and it seemed the Grik had forgotten the prey that escaped them. We found these lands where the Grik did not thrive and those that did were weak and primitive and we made colonies, or land Homes, for the first time in age upon age. A hundred generations passed. More. The people lived well and in peace. Baalkpan and other colonies rose to thrive and prosper and the great Homes of the sea plied the oceans and slew the gri-kakka for his sweet oil and restored contact between the scattered ones so we could become one People again. Different, diverse, and far-flung, but still one People even if languages and beliefs had changed.

"The Grik became no more than a myth, a terrible legend to frighten younglings into doing their chores, but no longer did they haunt our dreams. The terrible enemy that stole our home and nearly destroyed us had become less than a fable. The backward Grik here were hunted and slain, and those on the islands nearby did not know tools and weapons. On a few islands, some live still and no one ever goes there to stay."

"Bali," Matt said aloud, and the old priest blinked a curious affirmative.

"Then, like a gift from the Heavens themselves, the first Tail-less Ones came in three ships, suffering from storm and loss. They were tired and weak and poor in food, but friendly and rich in wisdom of the Heavens. We fed them and nursed them and helped them repair their ships and, in return, they taught us that the stars did indeed show the way, but one could *see* the way only through the Sun, since the Sun alone was the child, and as one with the Maker of All Things. From the Sun we take direction, and with direction, the stars in the Heavens would show us the way from place to place. They told us the names of the stars and the names of places as well, like Baalkpan and Borno and Baali. But the greatest gift they bestowed upon us was the Ancient Tongue by which the Scrolls were drawn and written at long last, and in which we now converse."

"My God," whispered Matt. "The stars are 'ancestor spirits,' the son of the sun is the sun . . . Father, Son, and Holy Ghost."

Sandra nodded. "Whoever came before left behind more than they thought."

"Yeah, I'd hoped the 'Scrolls' weren't so deeply incorporated—"

Naga interrupted. He'd watched their varied reactions, but he didn't pause for long. "At last there was a way for all the People to understand one another again, and to go from place to place without ever having been there, and in safety!"

"What happened to them? What did they look like?" Bradford asked quietly. His face remained impassive, but when he glanced at Captain Reddy, his eyes were intent.

"As far as what they looked like, all that is recorded is they had no tails, as you do not, which is strange and disturbing enough. The circumstance of their arrival is also somewhat similar . . ." He hesitated. "As far as where they went, that's a tragic story in itself, and one that, I fear, has finally returned to task us. A learned one among them, a scholar of great wisdom with the name Salig-Maa-Stir, taught our fathers the Ancient Tongue and drew the lands and waters and placed names upon them. It's said his leaders did not approve, and when they found out he'd done this thing, they forbade him to teach us their everyday tongue or the magic they guarded. Nevertheless, he loved the People and told us what he could through a tongue ancient even among his kind. Eventually, even this wasn't allowed, and Salig-Maa-Stir was kept away except to barter for goods. His greatest pupil, however, a female named Siska-Ta, picked up the narrative of the visitors. It was she who told the tale of the leaving of the Tail-less Ones.

"They claimed their home was far to the west, beyond even the Land of the Grik. But in spite of their wisdom, their Scrolls, and their tools, they were lost and alone and all their people were gone. Salig-Maa-Stir claimed that their land had ceased to be. Siska-Ta and our fathers assumed their people were slain by the Grik, and the horrors of old legends resurfaced. But before he was taken away, Salig-Maa-Stir said his people were not conquered, they had simply ceased to be."

Matt and Sandra looked at one another.

"This was a horror even worse than the Grik, but they never gave explanation. However, it came to pass that one of the ships wanted to go to their home and see what had become of it. Our fathers told them the legends, and warned them of the danger, but they knew. They *knew*! They'd met the Grik already! This was terrible news for the People, for it confirmed the legends and meant that the Grik truly did exist, as the priests had been saying all along. But what worried them most was that if the Tail-less Ones returned to that evil land, the Grik might learn their ways and soon find us as well! The leaders of the other ships shared this concern, but they had not the will or right to stop the one from trying.

"Finally, it was decided the one would go west, bearing only those who desired to go, with only the most rudimentary weapons and the scantiest of Scrolls. It was hoped that if they were taken, the Grik would learn nothing about where they'd been, where they were going, and most important to the other two ships, where we were and where they would go. On a blustery spring day, the one sailed west—we expect now to its doom—and the other two sailed east, and disappeared into the vast, empty Eastern Sea, beyond the known world. That was almost three hundred seasons ago."

The old priest took another long swallow from his tankard and smacked his lips over eroded, yellow teeth. It was evidently a story he'd often told and now that it was done, the somber theater of the telling passed and his mood once more reflected that of the party that continued to thrive.

"Did this Siska-Ta ever write any more?" Bradford asked.

"Oh, yes indeed! She became the first true Sky Priest and not only finished the early Scrolls but traveled the world and taught the Scrolls and the Ancient Tongue to all the People. It is from her we know the shape of the world, from this side of the great Western Sea all the way to the Eastern Ocean, where the waters fall away and the world ends. She also compiled histories of the many people she met and went among. She was a Prophet. A great Prophet."

"Do the Scrolls show where the Ancient Home of your People lies?" Bradford questioned eagerly, certain that he'd solved his riddle.

The old priest closed his eyes in a long, mournful blink. "Alas, they do not. We know it is beyond the Western Sea, where none dare go. The waters are without bottom, as are those of the Eastern Ocean, and great monsters dwell there. And of course, beyond the Western Sea are the Grik."

"Did the Tail-less Ones leave nothing of themselves at all? Nothing you could point to and say, 'This was theirs'?" Sandra asked.

"Some ornaments and cloth, some of which still exist," the priest said dismissively. Then he glanced at Nakja-Mur before speaking again. "Other than that, only this."

He raised the pendant resting against his chest and held it forth. Matt, Sandra, and Bradford all leaned forward and peered at the tarnished brass disk. It was about the size and shape of a hockey puck, or a can of snuff. Reverently, the priest undid a clasp and raised the lid of the device.

"Is it not wondrous?" he asked.

Before them was a very old pocket compass. A tiny folding sundial lay retracted to one side, and beneath the crystallized, almost opaque glass, a small needle quivered and slowly swung to point dutifully in a northerly direction.

"My God," murmured Captain Reddy. The compass itself was a fascinating discovery, but what caught his attention, and took Sandra's breath, was the inscription under the lid.

Jas. S. McClain
Sailing Master
H.E I.C. SHIP
HERMIONE

"My God," Matt said again.

"What's it mean? H.E.I.C.?" Sandra asked, almost a whisper.

"It means we were right, my dear," Courtney Bradford said. "We're not the first ones here. H.E.I.C. stands for the Honorable East India Company."

"As in the *British* East India Company?" she asked, astonished.

"So it would seem," Matt answered dryly. "I think we know now where the Grik got the design for their ships."

"You believe the Grik captured the ship that went west?"

"They must have. Indiamen at the time were built like warships, and the Grik ships we fought sure looked like seventeenth- or eighteenth-century warships—or Indiamen, I guess, come to think of it. I mentioned it at the time, and I also mentioned I didn't think it was a coincidence. Somehow I doubt the crew of that westbound Indiaman survived the technology exchange with the Grik. I wonder what happened to the other two?"

"But if they were British," interrupted Sandra, "why teach the Lemurians Latin?"

"They'd probably already figured out how messed up everything was, just like we did. According to Naga, they'd already run into the Grik too. They didn't want anybody knowing too much about them and, ultimately, where they went. But they had to communicate, just like us, and it probably seemed safe to teach the Lemurians a language no one knew. That would still leave them, or anyone else, unable to read their charts or get much information from the crew at large."

"That makes sense, I suppose," said Bradford, nodding. He glanced at Keje, who looked a little annoyed they were talking so long among themselves, but the other Lemurians just stared. "Thank God they didn't take cannon with them," he said fervently.

"That seems clear," Matt confirmed, "just like their Scrolls say. No weapons, or at least no extraordinary weapons, are mentioned to have been encountered since. I think it's safe to assume they must've removed the guns from the westbound ship. If they hadn't, the Grik would be using them and the Lemurians would damn sure know about them. Ask their old priest how long they've been fighting the Grik this round, and how long the Grik have been using this type of ship."

"The Grik have pushed us this time for only the last generation," Naga answered. "Until then, they were content to remain upon the land to the west. They'd still been mostly creatures of legend. But now they come again. It's just like the ancient times. The Grik come slowly at first, just a few at a time—but there are always more."

Keje spoke and Adar translated, since his English still wasn't up to the task. "During fight you help us, was first time we see such ships. Before, they look same, but . . . smaller."

"It seems a stretch that their naval architecture hasn't changed in three hundred years, except to enlarge an existing design."

"The Grik are not innovators," Keje said savagely. "They only take. If they've taken nothing better since they learned the three-masted ships, they would see no reason to change. Now they know where we are, though, they will keep coming. We will fight, and we will kill them, but they will keep coming until we are all dead or forced to flee these waters just as we fled our Ancient Home."

So much for the "Malay pirate" model. They'd need another one. The "slow creep" that Naga described left too much to chance—like "when." They *must* get more information about the enemy. A familiar feeling crept into his chest. It was like the days after Pearl Harbor all over again, when he knew they stood almost alone, in the face of . . . what? Something Big was all they knew, and they didn't know when or where. They'd been expendable then, an insignificant cog, and he was just following orders. He remembered how helpless and frustrated he felt that their fate was so arbitrarily sealed by unknown policies and strategic plans that seemed to make no sense. Now he was the one who had to make policies that might kill all his men—or save them. The crash transition from the tactical to the strategic left him overwhelmed. Sandra must have seen the inner desperation reflected on his face, because he again felt her reassuring hand on his arm. Finally, he looked at Keje.

"If they come, we'll help. I said that already. But we can help you now, better, before they come. Baalkpan's vulnerable, and no one seems ready to fight. If you prepare to fight now, you'll be better able when the time comes. Believe me"—he forced a half smile—"my people learned the hard way about being unprepared. Maybe this time it'll be different."

"I have not seen your amazing ship up close," said Nakja-Mur, "but Keje and Adar tell me of its wonders. Still, what can one ship do in the face of the Grik multitudes?" The word "multitudes" sounded bad, Matt thought with a sinking feeling.

"Not enough probably, by herself," he said flatly, "but a lot. The main thing *Walker* and her crew can do right now is help *you* prepare. And the first thing we need for that is fuel."

Walker swung at her anchor as the tide dragged her around until the busy, festive city of Baalkpan was off the port beam. It was totally dark and the lights cast an eerie, almost Oriental glow that reflected off the restless wave tops. Occasionally, sounds from shore reached Alan Letts as he leaned against the rail beside the number three gun. A party of men quietly worked on it, preparing to dismount it if they were allowed, so they could get at the balky traverse gear. Larry Dowden stopped by and spoke to Campeti, who supervised. ". . . in the morning . . ." was all Alan heard.

Screeching metal on metal and a string of obscenities came from the torpedo workshop. Letts was surprised to hear a hoarse Japanese shout respond to Sandison's tirade, followed by a crash of tools on the deck. When there was no further sound or cry of alarm, he chuckled. "That Jap's either going to make the best torpedoman Bernie has, or get fed to the fish." It still struck him strange having a Jap help with any sort of weapon, but Jap torpedoes worked just fine. Maybe Shinya knew something about them. He knew about machines; that was why Letts had suggested the appointment in the first place. If he had to work—and everybody did—that was as good a place as any. He stretched. It was nice to be on deck, breathing real air without the sun blasting the skin right off him. He scratched his forearm, rolling a ball of parched skin under his fingernails. *I'm starting to get just like the Mice*, he thought. *I can only come out after dark. God, I wish I was home.*

Off to the west, lightning rippled through dark clouds. *It'll probably rain*, he thought dejectedly, *and then I'll start to rot.* There'd been several days of uninterrupted sunshine—hot, as usual—but it normally rained once or twice a day. He didn't know which he hated worse, the hot sun that burned his skin or the hot, miserable rain that caused his skin and everything else to rot and mildew. All things considered, he'd *really* rather be in Idaho.

He lit a cigarette and let it dangle between his lips like he'd seen others do. It was an affectation he imagined they got from movies, but it looked cool, so he did it. Wouldn't be long before there weren't any smokes, he reflected. That wouldn't bother him as much as others. But some of the things they were running low on were important to their very survival, and he didn't have the slightest idea where to get more. He was the officer in charge of supply, but unless the lemur monkeys, or whatever they were, came through, there was no supply for supplies. He was a whiz at organizing and allocating and sending requisition forms through proper channels. In the past, if the stuff came, it came. But if it didn't, they always managed to make do or get by because there was always something to make do with. If the snipes needed a new feed-water pump, he would pick one up at the yard in Cavite or from one of the destroyer tenders like *Black Hawk*. If it was "the only one left" and they were saving it for *Peary* or *Stewart* because their supply officers did them a favor, then he could roll up his sleeves and swap and bid with the best. But when it came to getting something that wasn't there and never had been, and the only choice was to produce it themselves, he didn't have a clue what to do. He hoped the captain did.

He glanced to his left when someone leaned against the rail a few feet away. It was that nurse, the other one, with the auburn hair, the one that never said much. Karen something. Karen Theimer.

"Hi," he said. She glanced at him, but then looked back at shore. She put a cigarette to her lips and drew in a lungful.

"What do you think's going on?" She gestured at the city.

Alan shrugged. "Big Chief Powwow," he answered with a grin. "How should I know? I'm a meager lieutenant jay gee. Mine's not to reason why. I hope they come up with some supplies, though. Me being the supply officer, I always like to have supplies to be in charge of and, right now, there ain't much." She didn't grin or laugh, or say anything at all. She just took another puff. Standing so close, with the moon overhead and the flashes of lightning in the western sky, Alan was struck for the first time that she was really kind of cute. Of course, she and Lieutenant Tucker might be the only human females in the world—talk about a supply problem! He guessed it wouldn't be long before she started to look good if she had a face like a moose.

"I haven't been much help," she said matter-of-factly. "I've been having . . . a tough time adjusting to what's happened. I always led a sheltered life and thought becoming a Navy nurse would be a huge adventure."

She looked at him for the first time, and her lips formed a small, desolate smile. "I guess I was right. I have to try harder, though. Lieutenant Tucker's right. If any of us are going to survive we're all going to have to pitch in, and in ways we might not expect. Everything's changed, and I have to figure out a different way of looking at things. Going across to the Lemurian ship scared me to death." She shuddered. "I mean, they're like . . . aliens from another planet! Like Martians. Add in all the carnage of the aftermath of battle and I guess I didn't handle it very well. But I did learn that being a Navy nurse doesn't mean just being a Navy nurse anymore. Do you know what I mean?" She suddenly pulled her hair. "God, why am I even telling you this? You're just some guy."

He looked at her and sighed, chagrined. "Yeah. I'm just 'some guy.' Maybe that's been *my* problem all along. I think I do know what you mean, and I'm ashamed of myself. I've been wallowing in my 'meager supply officer' status so long it never occurred to me that might mean something different now too. It took me longer than you to figure that out, though. Thanks."

She smiled at him, and this time he saw her dimples in the light of the city. "My name's Karen Theimer. What's yours, Lieutenant?"

*L*ieutenant Benjamin Mallory and Lieutenant (j.g.) Perry Brister sat on chairs in Jim Ellis's cramped quarters on USS *Mahan* waiting for him to wake. Ellis's fever had finally broken the night before, and Pam Cross assured them he'd be fine—he just had to sleep it off. And so they waited, playing hand after hand of acey-deucey on the tiny table between them. Eventually, a groggy groan escaped the patient and he slowly came awake. His eyes seemed confused when he saw them, but he smacked his lips and croaked: "Thirsty."

In seconds the nurse appeared with a cup of water. "Here," she said in her brusque Brooklyn way. "Drink." Jim drank. When he spoke again, his voice was more normal.

"How long?" he asked simply.

"Almost two weeks since the fever hit. How much do you remember?" Brister asked.

"Not much," Jim admitted and tried to rise, but his expression contorted with pain and he settled back. "But I do remember that crazy bastard Kaufman shot me!"

It all came flooding back: the dinosaurs on Bali, the mysterious contact in the strait, the urgent signal for him to take *Mahan* east—which he did, but not for long. What was the point? There were *dinosaurs* on Bali! He didn't know what was going on, but there'd been no Japanese ships or planes since they came through the Squall, and he had a hunch there wouldn't be. He decided to turn around, to go back and rejoin *Walker*.

Kaufman argued with him, right there on the bridge. At first he remained reasonable, advocating that they continue to the rendezvous point off Alor. But when Jim gave the order to come about, Kaufman began to insist. He said Jim was risking all their lives and they'd die if they turned around. Jim ordered him off the bridge and that's when he just . . . lost it. He had a pistol and he took it out. Immediately, Jim and a couple of others jumped him and in the ensuing struggle, the gun went off. It probably wasn't even deliberate. Regardless, the bullet entered Jim's left leg, just below the knee, and exited the other side of his calf, right above the ankle. The men would have thrown Kaufman over the side right then, but he had the gun and time to talk. He said turning back was suicide; they'd done everything they could. The ship was a wreck and the men were exhausted. They deserved to live. Then Mr. Monroe, the only other officer besides Brister—in engineering at the time—took his side. He said they should listen to Kaufman, who was a captain, after all, and it was nuts to go back after all they'd been through. The crew began to go for it. They were angry about Jim being shot, but it wasn't like he was their captain or anything. He was just a strange officer who'd been put in charge. Kaufman only wanted to do what they'd been *told* to do, so that's how it was. Before Brister or Mallory even knew what happened, Captain Kaufman had the ship.

What he did next was inexplicable. Instead of heading for Alor, which had been his original purpose, he didn't make for Perth at all. He was convinced that there were carriers between them and Australia, so that left only Ceylon. They steamed east for the day, hugging the coast, and that night they shot the Lombok Strait. They'd still seen no sign of the enemy, but that made no difference to Kaufman. He'd become obsessed with reaching Ceylon and—Jim guessed—terrified of meeting *Walker*. He wasn't about to go anywhere the other ship might be. Jim was in the wardroom the entire time, undergoing treatment. Not under arrest, but more or less in exile. He kept up with events as best he could, mostly through Mallory and Brister. Much of the rest of the crew seemed hesitant to look him in the eye. There were exceptions, like Bosun's Mate Frankie Steele and Torpedoman Russ Chapelle, but not nearly enough to recapture the ship. Then, in spite of the best the surgeon and nurses could do, he lapsed into a fever. His last conscious recollection was they were nearing Tjilatjap, hoping to find some fuel. He cleared his throat.

"What happened at Tjilatjap?" His voice grew soft. "Was it even there?"

Brister and Mallory looked at each other, and finally Ben shook his head.

"No, sir. You don't remember any of that? We told you about it after we came aboard."

Jim just shook his head. "Pretend I wasn't there," he said, attempting to grin. "Start over. What did you find?"

"Nothing, sir. At least nothing that looked like Tjilatjap," said Brister. Like others who'd been there before, he pronounced it "Chilachap."

"What did you see?"

"Some strange, huge village—almost a city. I don't really know how to describe it. It was pretty big. Multistory structures, built on some kind of bamboo pilings. It was deserted, and most had been burned to the ground."

"Deserted?"

"Yes, sir. Well, sort of deserted. It wasn't abandoned willingly; it looked like there'd been a fight. Bones, sir. Bones everywhere, and a few mostly scavenged bodies off in the jungle. They were furry and had tails and . . . they weren't human."

"Sir," said Mallory stiffly, "there was nothing left alive out of a city of hundreds, easily, and it looked like whatever got them ate them. Not just scavengers either. Most of the bones were . . . piled up."

Pam Cross had left and reentered with a thermometer during the conversation. Her face was hard.

"Did you see it too?" Ellis asked.

"I did," she said simply and poked the device in his mouth.

Brister cleared his throat. "Well, sir, we got the hell out. Kaufman became even more unhinged. He insisted our only hope was Ceylon and had us pour it on. He wouldn't listen to reason. By then, almost everyone wanted to look for *Walker*, in spite of the consequences, but he said the next man who suggested it would be left in the whaleboat to look on his own." He wiped at the sweat beading his brow, and the nurse removed the thermometer from Jim's lips. She made a noncommittal sound. "Anyway, a storm kicked up and we shipped a lot of water. It wasn't much of a storm, but shot up like we are, we were lucky to survive. Things settled down by morning, but we had to pump out and make repairs, so we ducked into this little bay on Panaitan Island—"

"That's how we found the plane!" interrupted Mallory, a grin splitting his face.

"Plane?"

"Yes, sir. A PBY Catalina! If you can look out that porthole beside you, you might be able to see her!" Ellis struggled to rise, but he was very weak. Mallory immediately regretted the suggestion, but with a heavy sigh and rolling eyes, Nurse Cross helped him up. His head swam and his vision was blurred, but through the porthole, sure as the world, a familiar, battered seaplane was half beached on the island.

"You weren't kidding!" he exclaimed. "Where'd it come from?"

The two men shrugged. "Same place we did, I guess," said Mallory. "We steamed into the bay and there it was on the beach, its crew nowhere in sight. The place is crawling with lizards like bit your man on Menjan-gan . . ." He didn't need to speculate on the air crew's likely fate. "There were bullet holes all in it and it was full of water, but otherwise it seemed in pretty good shape—just out of gas. The radio's crapped out—we checked that right off. Salt water corroded all the connections was Signalman Palm-er's guess. He's been working with us. Anyway, we figure the same thing happened to it that happened to us, and it made it as far as the Sunda Strait before it ran out of fuel."

"Maybe it was one of the PBYs that broke up the air attack on our ships when *Houston* took that bomb hit," speculated Jim. "Bravest thing I ever saw, three flying boats diving among fighters and bombers, trying to throw 'em off their aim." He shook his head. "Crazy."

"Could be," said Brister, "but that was a while before whatever happened to us . . . happened. Anyway, the good news is *Mahan* has high-octane gas in drums, aft, just like *Walker*—ironically, in case they ever need to refuel a seaplane. We put some in her and ran up the engines; no problem there, at least. The three of us've been working on her while everyone else works on the ship. My place is really here, I guess, but I don't think Kaufman trusts me."

"How long have we been here, and how long have you been working on it? Will it fly?" Everyone saw the hope kindle in his eyes.

"A week or so, and"—he lowered his voice—"another couple days'll have her in the air."

The general alarm sounded and they all jumped. "Battle stations, battle stations! Make all preparations for getting under way!" They looked at each other, perplexed by the commands. Suddenly Frankie Steele skid-ded to a stop outside the compartment.

"There're ships in the strait!"

"Ships?" demanded Jim.

"Aye, sir . . . Glad to see you better! But big sailing ships, like in the movies—only these are real—and they're headed this way!"

Jim looked at Brister and Mallory. "Go!" he said. "Save that plane! Don't let Kaufman leave it!" Without another word, the men charged out of the compartment. On the weather deck they met Ed Palmer, rushing down to meet them.

"Go!" said Brister. "Get what you can. Food, water, whatever you can think of, and meet us at the whaleboat!"

"What are you going to do?"

"Make a deal with the devil!" he snarled and mounted the steps to the bridge. Kaufman was staring at the distant ships through binoculars, and his hands were shaking. "Captain Kaufman! What about the plane? We can't just leave it here! Hell, we can have it flying by the end of the day!

What are we running from?" Kaufman looked at him, and his bloodshot eyes were wide and glassy. He hadn't shaved or even combed his hair in days. There was nothing left of the cocky aviator Brister had first met when he came aboard off Menjangan. His face had the look of a hunted, panicked animal, and his condition had infected much of the crew.

"Here!" Kaufman said, handing him the binoculars. His voice was shrill. In the distance, three red-hulled sailing ships struggled to beat up toward them. He focused a little more, and a chill swept down his back. "Those aren't people," he said lamely. They were monsters.

"Now you see why we have to go?" Kaufman insisted with manic sarcasm. "Hoist that boat aboard!"

"Wait," said Brister, licking his lips. "The current and wind are both against them. It'll be hours before they reach us. Let us try to finish the plane." He paused and tried a different tack. "If we do, we'll fly to Ceylon. Get help! Maybe they'll send an escort." That got through.

"Will you stake your life you can take off before they get here?"

Brister nodded.

"Good, because we won't wait. Mr. Monroe!" he said, raising his voice. "Take Mr. Brister and his assistants ashore, then return as quick as you can!"

"You won't even leave us a boat?" Brister asked, incredulous.

"No. You can go ashore, destroy the plane, and come back with Mr. Monroe, or you can try to fly it out. The choice is yours."

Perry shook his head. "Captain Kaufman, you are a coward, sir."

Without another word, he turned and dashed down the ladder. On the way to shore, he told the others what had happened.

"The hell with him. I'd rather take my chances with the plane," Mallory exclaimed. Palmer said nothing, but his face was grim.

"You didn't see what I saw," Brister said. "I think our visitors are the same ones that wiped out . . . whatever they were at Chilachap. It's either fly or die."

The coxswain with Monroe giggled.

They reached the shore and tossed their gear on the beach beside the plane. "At least give us a hand bailing!" shouted Perry as the whaleboat pulled away.

"*Mahan*'s already pullin' the hook!" shouted Monroe. "I'm not going to be left behind." He threw a mocking salute. "It's your funeral!"

"Bastard!" Palmer was seething.

They turned to look at the plane. Brister hoped he could make good on his vow. He didn't know what was coming, but that one look had scared the hell out of him. "Well, what are we waiting for?"

They dove into their task with frantic abandon. They were too busy even to notice when *Mahan* steamed away, but when they did pause for a quick look, it seemed that one of the strange ships was trying to follow her. It was no use, of course, and it quickly turned back toward the bay. They'd seen the Catalina, and either the tide was making or the wind shifted just enough, because they were getting closer.

"Bail, damn it!" Brister yelled, and buckets of water flew from the observation blisters. The tide *was* making, because suddenly they were floating, but they were still too heavy to fly. Mallory leaned on his bucket, gasping, and watched the closing ships.

"No way," he said. "We have to get off this beach before they box us in."

"She's still too heavy!"

"Yeah, but not too heavy to move." He scrambled up to the flight deck. "Palmer, throw off the mooring line!"

Ed hesitated. "But the fish might get me!"

"Those things'll get us all if you don't! You can reach it through the nose turret! Can you operate the gun?" A .30-caliber machine gun was enclosed in a Plexiglas turret in the nose of the plane.

"Yeah . . ." he said, a little uncertainly, but he dodged his way forward. The plane was floating almost freely now. A few nerve-racking moments passed.

"Got it!" came Palmer's muffled shout, and the nose immediately swung away from the beach.

"C'mon, babies!" Mallory said, and then whooped when both engines coughed to life. With throttles and rudder, he pointed the nose at the bay. The ships were much closer, and now he could see the creatures upon them with unaided eyes. "Oh, boy!" he shouted. "Here they come! I'm gonna try to motor around them, so keep bailing till I tell you, but be ready to get on a gun as quick as you can!" There was also a .50-caliber machine gun in each observation blister, but that was the extent of the PBY's armaments.

"Jeez, they're scary-lookin'," breathed Palmer, glancing forward.

"Yeah," panted Brister. "Bail!" Mallory advanced the throttles, and the big plane began to move.

"They're almost making a lane for us, like they want at us from both sides!" he shouted. "I'll make for it. Be ready on those fifties, in case they try to close the gap!"

Closer and closer the roaring engines took them. Soon they edged between the two ships, and the details they beheld were nightmarish.

"Shit!" Palmer screamed when something "thunked" into the thick aluminum beside him. It was an arrow! As quick as that, the plane drummed with impacts. "Shit!" he repeated. "They're shootin' at us!"

"Let 'em have it!" Brister yelled, and they opened fire on both of the terrible ships. Clouds of splinters flew where the tracers pointed, and bodies fell from the rails. A keening shriek reached them even over the guns, the engines, and the clattering, heavy brass cases that fell around them. "Pour it in!" he shouted as the incoming barrage began to slack off. A big greasy ball of flame erupted right behind the starboard wing and actually singed his hair. "What the *hell* was that? Step on it, Ben!"

Mallory needed no encouragement. He'd watched the "bomb" all the way in. He pushed the throttles to their stops. Sluggishly, the waterlogged plane picked up speed. The roar of the engines and hammering guns made it too loud to think. Another explosion washed the sea, but it missed them safely aft. The faster target must have spoiled their aim. Then, as quickly as the battle had begun, they sped clear of the monsters' ships and Brister shouted to hold their fire. The other ship was closing still, but at their current heading, it would never reach them in time to cut them off. Water from the massive wake they made splashed in through the blisters and hissed on the barrels of the superheated guns.

Brister turned to Palmer, eyes wide. "Wow!"

There was still a lot of water in the plane, but they plowed upwind as far as they could before they powered down. Mallory left the motors idling, props feathered, and helped them bail some more.

"Talk about your floating freak shows!" he gasped, throwing water past the gun. "Damn plane looks like a pincushion! Goddamn *arrows*!"

"Just be glad they weren't muskets or cannons," said Brister. "We wouldn't have had a chance! Arrows and firebombs were bad enough!"

"I'll say! What now?" Palmer asked.

"Keep bailing," Ben replied. "A few hundred more pounds and we'll get her in the air. Then we can dump what's left." He grinned. "Once we do that, start looking for holes!"

Less than an hour later, the battered seaplane clawed into the air and followed after *Mahan*. Mallory didn't know if the monsters saw them or not, now they were stuck in the bay. If they did, he wondered what they thought. The plane quickly overtook *Mahan* and landed at her side. Brister seethed with rage at the man who'd left them to their fate, but to his surprise Kaufman met them himself in the whaleboat with smiles and waves.

"Keep hold of yourself," Mallory said. "Remember, we're going to fly to Ceylon and save the day. Stick to the plan!" Brister simmered down, but all he wanted to do was kill the Army captain with his bare hands.

"Let's just shoot him with the thirty in the nose," Palmer said through a clenched-teeth grin.

"Won't work. Like Mr. Ellis said before he got sick, he's got too many on his side. Even if we got him, there might be a bloodbath. Some of 'em are crazy as he is, and they have all the guns."

"Okay," said Mallory, adjusting the throttles so he wouldn't smack the boat as it came alongside. "I'll stay with the plane—I have to. Get all the fuel and anything else you can think of. Maps, more food, whatever. Maybe even more people, but don't be too obvious. We know he won't let Mr. Ellis come."

"Right." Together, Perry and Ed jumped in the whaleboat.

"You really did it!" Kaufman gushed. "Did you have much trouble?"

"No," lied Brister cheerfully. "Piece of cake. Let's hurry up and get the fuel on board. The quicker we're back in the air, the quicker we'll be in Ceylon!"

Kaufman refused to allow anyone to accompany them. Three was enough, he said, to risk on such a dangerous flight. Perry did manage to slip away to "get some gear," and he went to see Jim Ellis before he left the ship. Jim was trying to climb the companionway stairs when he found him, supported by crutches and Pam Cross and Kathy McCoy. Beth Grizzel wasn't there.

"You made it," he said. "Thank God."

"Yes, sir. Thank God. No thanks to that bastard Kaufman. He left us to die."

"I know. Listen, you *must* find *Walker*! Kaufman's nuts; half the crew's nuts. It's just a matter of time before he kills us all. You know as well as I do, Ceylon's not there. There's no telling what is. Find *Walker*, find Captain Reddy . . ." He gasped from the effort of his words and exertions.

"We will."

"Tell him I'm sorry I failed him. I'm sorry I let the men down."

"It's not your fault, sir!"

"Isn't it?" Jim sighed. "Maybe not, but it's my responsibility."

"He shot you!"

Jim laughed bitterly. "A good commander would have shot him first! Now get your ass out of here before Kaufman starts nosing around!"

Perry looked at the two nurses. He hated to leave them behind, but Kaufman wouldn't part with them. The surgeon was acting funny, and the nurses were it. There were still a lot of wounded on the ship. Besides, their errand might be doomed from the start. They had only so much fuel and they had no idea where *Walker* was.

"Aye, aye, sir," Perry Brister said, and shook Jim Ellis's hand. Pam stepped quickly forward and planted a kiss lightly on his cheek.

"For luck!" she said, then punched his shoulder. Hard. "Tell Lieutenant Tucker we're keeping the faith." She glanced at Kathy and grimaced. "Two out of three anyway. Beth's as crazy as Kaufman." She shrugged and kissed him again, on the mouth this time. "Double luck! Now git out'a heah!" Blushing, Perry saluted Lieutenant Ellis and raced for the boat.

Later, when they thundered into the darkening sky and circled the lonely, misguided ship for the last time, Brister thought he caught a glimpse of Lieutenant Ellis leaning on his crutches by the rail, a small group gathered around him.

The two and a half weeks since *Walker*'s arrival had been a whirlwind of frantic activity. Despite acknowledging the danger they faced, Matt suspected the 'Cats weren't quite prepared for the pace the destroyermen set. The trauma of getting their economy and society on a war footing was causing a stir, but Matt and his crew knew what had happened at Pearl Harbor and Clark Field. They'd *seen* what happened at Cavite. They'd learned a hard lesson in preparedness, and as long as their fortunes were tied to those of their new friends, they wouldn't let them waste time they might later regret. *Big Sal*'s crew was equally motivated, and repairs to the big ship moved apace. The very day after the "party," *Walker* was moved to the pier and as extensive an overhaul as possible began. The number three gun was repaired, and all the circuits coordinating the main battery were checked and spliced. Steaming on only the number four boiler to maintain electrical power, they checked the other boilers and repaired firebrick. There was nothing to be done for number one so it was stripped and prepared for disassembly and removal. Spanky wanted the space for more fuel bunkerage—once they got fuel.

The Baalkpan Lemurians were just as amazed as *Big Sal*'s that *Walker* was made of steel. Whenever the welders went to work, the pier lined with spectators watching the sparks and eye-burning torches with as much enthusiasm as if it had been a fireworks display. Iron wasn't unknown to the People, but it was so hard to smelt that it was little used. Dave Elden had spent two years in a steel mill in Pittsburgh. He'd already talked to the proprietors of the foundry on the northeast of town, where he'd gone to have brass fittings cast. He reported they used the sand-cast method almost exclusively but were very good at it and there would be almost nothing they couldn't cast with a larger furnace and a little guidance. He even figured he could get them started on iron if a source for ore could be found.

Half the snipes set out into the jungle with Courtney Bradford and about a hundred natives in search of oil. The procession had looked like a nineteenth-century safari. They hadn't searched long before they found a likely place. Bradford's charts and journals were helpful, and he had most of the Dutch surveys. As long as everything was the same geographically, there was every reason to believe that oil could be found in the same places it had been back "home." He hadn't yet shared his theory, but they'd all been very busy. Matt already suspected what the gist of it was and looked forward to the discussion, but for now there was too much to do.

Materials were rafted upriver to the site, where, under the direction of the Mice, the men were constructing something called a Fort Worth Spudder. Captain Reddy had heard of the device but never seen one. His interview with the strange firemen was . . . an experience. He'd seen them many times, of course, but he didn't remember ever speaking with them. Their conversation about the rig was what he imagined it would be like to talk to an opossum with a parrot on its shoulder. But they convinced him they knew what to do and how to do it. He just hoped they could explain it to others in a coherent fashion.

At the same time, men worked hard converting the tubes of the number three torpedo mount into a condensation tower. A place was being prepared near the drill site for their little refinery. A fueling pier with water deep enough for *Walker* to clear the silty riverbed was already under construction. The torpedo tubes were just a temporary expedient. Eventually they would build larger towers with greater capacity. But for now the empty tubes would have to do.

Lemurians scampered all over the ship, helping as best they could. Often they got in the way, but shorthanded as the crew was, the benefit of their curious, good-natured assistance outweighed the aggravation. Chack became like a Lemurian bosun's mate, and his coordination of the native labor was indispensable.

One morning, a large cart pulled by a "brontosarry" and driven by Alan Letts arrived, much to the delight of those aboard. The sight of the fair-skinned supply officer sitting on a seat under a colorful parasol—behind a dinosaur's rump—even brought a smile to the Chief's face. The crew's amusement quickly waned when they discovered what the cart was so heavily laden with. Somewhere the suddenly surprisingly resourceful supply officer had discovered keg after keg of white paint. Gray was guardedly ecstatic. He insisted on testing it, since nobody knew what was in it, or whether it would stick to steel. He wasn't about to let them smear a "bunch of whitewash" all over his topsides. When it proved satisfactory, he immediately began pestering Letts to find something they could mix it with to make a proper gray.

"Hell, Bosun," Letts replied, "this bucket's spent more of her life white than gray. It's not like we're hiding from airplanes anymore."

"Yah, but there's a war on, Mr. Letts. White's for peacetime."

The torpedo repairs were put aside. They still had the three that hadn't fired during their escape from Surabaya, but the others would have to wait. Under the supervision of Chief Donaghey and Bernard Sandison—who'd become quite a machinist in his own right—the machine shop was constantly in use making parts for the ship. They had little scrap steel, though, and wherever it would serve, they used copper or brass—both of which were readily available from local sources. Shinya had been reassigned as Alden's assistant—training the militia—but he still liked to help in the shop when he could.

It was in this maelstrom of apparent chaos, of flying sparks and paint chips, a fog of red rust dust, mazes of hoses and wires and a dozen different projects all over the ship, that they had their first visit by the High Chief of Baalkpan, Nakja-Mur.

Matt had seen him many times since their first meeting, and someone, usually Garrett or Dowden, went ashore to talk with him every day. But until now, the closest Nakja-Mur had come to *Walker* was to pace her length on the pier alongside, the morning after she tied up. He was fascinated by the ship, and Keje said he never tired of hearing about *Walker*'s role in the battle, but he'd never made an "official" visit and many were curious why. Now, with no warning whatsoever—a shocking impropriety among the People—the crowd of watchers and helpers on the dock parted and Nakja-Mur appeared at the gangway.

Keje and Adar, Naga, and a dozen guardsmen accompanied him. Despite the wonder that nearly forced a grin when he gained the deck, and the pleased curiosity he displayed when piped aboard by Gray's hastily assembled side party, Nakja-Mur wasn't happy.

"You are breaking me!" he growled when the captain met him with a salute. Matt blinked questioningly like Chack had taught him to do.

"Breaking you, my lord? I thought here, just as on the great sea Homes, the High Chief was the steward of the people's surplus—to be spent for the safety and benefit of all." Chack had quickly trotted up to join them and he translated the captain's words. Keje and Adar's subtle blinks of amusement indicated they no longer needed Chack's help.

"Of course you're breaking me! It's my duty to be a good steward, as you say, but it's also my duty to see the surplus wisely spent!" He looked about, speechless, and seized upon the sight of the paint kegs lining the pier. "There, do you see? Do you realize that's half a season's production of paint base? Do you have any idea what that costs?"

Matt shook his head. "You agreed that *Walker* should have anything Baalkpan could offer in the way of provisions and supplies if we would help you prepare for the Grik."

"Yes, but . . . paint?!" Adar leaned over and spoke into his ear. "Yes, of course I know iron rusts, but . . ." He stopped, and looking around again, he shook his head. "I apologize. They said your ship was iron, but I only now truly realized it. But, come, what difference does a little rust make?"

"My Brother," interrupted Keje, "once rust takes hold of iron it is not easily discouraged. That's one reason it's rarely used at sea. By us, at any rate."

"Well, but what of the scores of workers toiling northeast of the city, pounding a hole into the earth! What's the meaning of that?"

"Fuel, my lord. As we discussed. *Walker* must have . . . I believe you call it 'gish,' for fuel. Without it she can't move. She can't fight."

"But gish is plentiful in the north, in the coastal marshes. It bubbles from the ground, it pools, it reeks! It's of little use to any but seam sealers and makers of rope. New holes need not be made to take it up!"

"I'm afraid so. *Walker* needs more gish than can easily be imagined, and there must be a ready source close by."

"The People use wind to good effect," Nakja-Mur grumped.

"No doubt. So do the Grik. But *Walker*'s much faster than either— that's one reason she fights so well. To do that she needs gish, and lots of it. I told you all this," Matt said with some frustration.

"He doesn't know, my friend. He hasn't seen," soothed Keje. "He looks out for his people." He grinned. "And your ship is costing far more than the Grik yet have."

"He can pay now, with treasure, or later with blood," Matt snapped.

"He knows. He just doesn't like it. Believe me, on the whole, he's pleased. He's had many complaints, however, not least about the training your Marine person started. These land folk don't have strong bodies and are not used to the exertion required of warriors."

"Sergeant Alden knows the best warrior skills of our people, at least as far as land tactics are concerned. Lieutenant Shinya knows swordsmanship, and his methods are quicker and more lethal than yours." Gray suppressed a snort. He still thought Shinya belonged in the chain locker.

"True, but since Nakja-Mur decreed that all should learn rudimentary warrior skills, some ask why they must learn to fight when their treasure is paying you to do it for them."

Matt shook his head. "That wasn't the deal. I said we'd train them and help them fight. We won't fight the Grik alone."

"He knows."

Nakja-Mur spoke and Chack translated once again. "Two flasher-fishers arrived this morning with news of three Grik ships, nosing about in the strait. They didn't believe they were seen, but the Grik have never been so close. We're not ready to fight and I fear we will never be. All these preparations you make—the paint!—do not seem to make us more ready to fight!"

"We'll fight them first, if we must, until your people are ready. That was the plan from the start. But to fight, my ship must be ready!"

Off in the distance, they heard the low rumble of thunder.

"What will you do about the Grik in the strait?"

"If they enter the bay, we'll destroy them. If they linger nearby until we have fuel, we'll hunt them down and destroy them. You have my word. But you must talk sense to these complainers!"

Nakja-Mur looked steadily at him for a moment, then jerked his head downward in a Lemurian nod. The distant thunder continued to build, but it was drowned out by the number four boiler blowing tubes. They all looked aft and skyward as the soot settled on the deck and those working there.

"God*damn* snipes!" bellowed Gray, striding purposefully toward the aft fireroom hatch. "There's wet paint up here!" Captain Reddy stifled a grin. The thunderous drone rose a little higher in his consciousness.

"Maybe the High Chief of Baalkpan would like to tour the ship?" he said, but tilted his head, listening. With a start, his eyes widened in recognition and he glanced at the crow's nest. Empty, of course. Garrett was on the fire-control platform, however, and he'd heard it too. Their eyes met as realization dawned. The general alarm began to sound.

"General quarters! General quarters! This is no drill!" came Larry Dowden's voice over the speaker. "Captain to the bridge!"

Matt darted from the midst of the Lemurian delegation, ran through the chaos of the weather deck, and clattered up the ladder to the bridge. With no one to tell them different, the Lemurians followed after him. Men and 'Cats scampered everywhere, some purposefully, others less so, and Nakja-Mur was nearly sent sprawling by an ordnance striker carrying ammunition belts as he rocketed up from the companionway.

"What's happening?!" he angrily demanded.

"Something interesting, certainly," Adar replied.

Matt was gasping by the time he reached the fire-control platform. He snatched the binoculars someone offered and began scanning the sky.

"There, sir. Aft, bearing one two oh! Coming right up the bay from the strait! It's . . . it's an aircraft!"

"Agreed!" Matt snapped. "But what's it doing here and whose is it? Stand by all machine guns, Mr. Garrett, but hold your fire!"

They waited tensely, the men exchanging nervous glances while the clattery radial engine drone slowly grew more pronounced. Chack and Keje had joined them.

"What is that flying thing?" Keje's voice held an edge.

"Airplane," Matt murmured absently.

Keje glanced at the defensive preparations under way. "And I thought the Grik were a strange menace," he muttered. "You will fight this aar-plane?

It will attack?" Keje cast a quick glance at *Big Sal*, moored helplessly to the pier. He'd never heard of a flying creature large enough to threaten people, but he'd seen coast raptors snatch fish from the water, and he suspected how vulnerable they would be to something as big as what he saw now. Obviously, by their actions, the destroyermen believed it might be dangerous. "Will it attack?" he asked again, more insistently.

Matt lowered the binoculars and a small, wondering smile played across his features. "I don't think so," he said, and added as an aside to Lieutenant Garrett, "PBY."

The plane grew larger, and the sun glinted dully off the dingy blue paint as it banked over the bay. The wings waggled a little, as if the pilot was unfamiliar with the controls—or maybe not. Only one engine was running. The big seaplane thundered low over the water, just a little higher than the small boats' masts. Sheets went flying, and there were many near-collisions as the unearthly monstrosity lumbered by. Matt couldn't help but grin at the startled antics of the fishermen. All the Lemurians on the pier or the destroyer stopped what they were doing and clustered uncertainly together.

The pilot plainly saw them now; he banked the plane harder and then steadied up, aiming for a clear patch of water off *Walker*'s starboard side. The big rudder kicked rapidly back and forth to compensate for the uneven thrust of the single engine. Wing-tip floats came down and the bull-nose with the Plexiglas turret seemed to sniff tentatively at the water. The blue roundels with the white star and red dot stood out against the salt streaks and the stained, off-color paint. It was the most beautiful thing Matt had ever seen. With a great splashing *thump*, the flying boat struck the water, and its forward progress was almost immediately arrested by the unskilled or underpowered arrival. It wallowed to a stop as the pilot cut power, then increased it. The noise of the port engine was tremendous as the plane gathered speed in their direction.

Nakja-Mur had joined them. "What is that dreadful thing?" he demanded in a shrill voice.

"I suspect it's a friend of ours," Matt replied when Chack translated. The pilot cut the engine about fifty yards away, and the noise abruptly lessened as the propeller wound down. Matt felt the relief around him. "Prepare to fend off!" he shouted as the plane drifted closer. "Launch the whaleboat!" In less than a minute, the boat slid down the falls and slapped into the water. As they watched, a windscreen on the side of the pitching aircraft's cockpit slid back and a grinning, bearded face emerged.

"Another Amer-i-caan!" Nakja-Mur exclaimed. "One that flies! *Flies!*" He was silent for a moment of sheer amazement, then turned to Matt and grinned. "I suppose I will have to feed that thing as well?"

"How many more . . . unusual friends are you expecting, Cap-i-taan Reddy?" Keje quietly asked. *Big Sal's* "captain" was staring at the PBY with open wonder, but it was a serious question.

"I wasn't expecting this one. C'mon, let's meet our mystery aviator."

Lieutenant Benjamin Mallory's entire lower body felt numb and tingly from the long hours in the thinly padded metal seat of the shuddering aircraft. He had difficulty with his feet on the rungs as he ascended to the deck. He couldn't stop grinning, though. An hour before, he'd shut down the starboard engine and feathered its prop to stretch their fuel enough to reach this very bay. It was their final hope. They'd checked Menjangan, and pushed all the way to Alor before turning back. If *Walker* hadn't been at Balikpapan, he, Perry, and Ed would have been doomed, at best, to a lingering, miserable existence of solitude and privation without hope of rescue. More likely, some unfamiliar denizen would have quickly saved them the trouble. The sight of the old four-stacker nestled snugly against the pier amid the bustle of native people and shipping brought tears to Mallory's eyes. The smoke curling lazily from her aft funnel and the proud flag over her deck convinced him that, whatever the situation, *Walker* was here voluntarily and therefore they were safe.

He made it to the deck with the help of eager hands and threw a shaky salute at the flag, and another at Captain Reddy. He was startled by the sight of the . . . natives, but not like he would have been a few weeks before.

"Lieutenant Benjamin Mallory, United States Army Air Corps. I request permission to come aboard, sir." He took a wobbly step to make room for those behind him as they also gained the deck.

"Ed Palmer, Signalman, glad to be back aboard, sir," said the second man, his voice hoarse with emotion. The blond-headed signalman from Oklahoma had expected to remain on *Mahan* only until they reached Perth. His inclusion in the unlucky destroyer's odyssey had taken a toll.

The third was a dark-haired man in ragged khakis who looked vaguely familiar. "Lieutenant jay-gee Perry Brister, request perm—"

"Brister! You're engineering officer on *Mahan*—you all came from *Mahan*! Where is she?" Matt demanded.

"We don't know, sir," Mallory replied. "The last we saw, she was off the west coast of Sumatra."

"Sumatra? My God. What was Jim Ellis thinking?"

All three men shook their heads together. "Not Mr. Ellis, sir," Brister said.

"Right," confirmed Mallory. The aviator's grin was gone. "Captain Reddy, it's a long story and you need to hear it now." He gestured at himself and the others. "Could we have some cold water? Or . . . maybe even a Coke?"

"Certainly. Let's carry this conversation to the wardroom and you can tell me all about it after some refreshment." He turned to Dowden as the exec approached. "Is Mr. McFarlane back aboard? No? Then pass the word for Mr. Bradford—he returned from the well site this morning, did he not?" Dowden nodded. "Very well. Ask him, Mr. Letts, Mr. Tolsen, and Mr. Garrett to join us in the wardroom. Better ask Lieutenant Tucker and Lieutenant Shinya as well."

"Sir, Lieutenant Shinya and Sergeant Alden are drilling the militia."

Matt nodded. "Of course." He glanced at the Lemurians. He'd practically forgotten they were there. For a moment he contemplated excusing himself, but realized that if he did, they might suspect he was keeping secrets. That might not be best. They knew something important was going on; after all, it wasn't every day a PBY flew into Baalkpan and landed in the bay. "Our guests may accompany us, if they please, but space in the wardroom's limited. They'll have to leave their escorts behind." He spoke to Dowden, but his words were for Keje. They implied that this needed to remain an upper-level meeting. Keje understood, and spoke to Nakja-Mur.

Carafes of iced tea were on the wardroom table when they filed in. Like Keje and Adar had been, Nakja-Mur and Naga were unfamiliar with human chairs, but watching Keje's more experienced motions, they managed to make themselves relatively comfortable. Of more interest to them was the egalitarian way the Americans gathered around the same table and drank from the same carafes. Lemurians prided themselves on their social tolerance, and they knew the Americans operated within a system of strict official stratification. For the first time, Nakja-Mur and Naga saw that the American hierarchy had more to do with tradition and institutional discipline than with a concept that anyone, even their captain, was intrinsically superior. Somehow, in spite of their surprise, they were strangely comforted.

They sat for a long moment, drinking, while an oscillating fan stirred the tepid air. The Lemurians drained their tea with relish and then waited patiently while the haggard newcomers rehydrated themselves. Finally, Mallory wiped his mouth and cleared his throat.

"My God, sir, that was welcome. We only carried a little water, to save on weight. Enough to last a few more days, but . . . Anyway, thanks, sir. Your ship was a sight for sore eyes!"

"Thank you, Lieutenant. Seeing that plane was pretty exciting for us. But what about *Mahan*? Where the hell is she and what happened?"

The three men glanced at each other, then haltingly, together, told how Kaufman took over the ship. Matt and the other humans listened in stunned amazement. They just couldn't believe it. Not only was it blatant mutiny, but under the circumstances it was insane. Brister told how Jim tried to take Kaufman's gun away, and he saw the rage on Matt's face when he told him Jim had been shot.

"He didn't kill him, sir," he hastened to add. "In fact, I think it was more an accident than anything." He almost smiled. "I heard Mr. Ellis was beating the shit out of him, if you'll pardon the expression. But Kaufman did shoot him. In the leg." There was a pause while the lieutenant's words sank in around the table.

"Go on," Matt ordered harshly.

They told how the mutiny had proceeded, and of Kaufman's obsession with Ceylon. Jim Ellis lapsed into fever and they put into Tjilatjap for fuel—only Tjilatjap wasn't there, and they told of the horrors they saw.

Keje stiffened in his seat. "Chill-chaap? This Amer-i-caan speaks of Chill-chaap?" Larry Dowden had excused himself, and now he hurried back in with a chart that showed South Java and the waters nearby. Nakja-Mur and the Sky Priest fairly bristled at the way he spread the chart across the table, condensation rings and all, but Keje and Adar had prepared them somewhat, so they didn't cry out in protest. Brister was looking at Keje when he put his finger on the South Java port of Tjilatjap. "Here, sir," he said.

"Gone," muttered Keje. "Chill-chaap is gone." He spoke to the other Lemurians in his own tongue. Nakja-Mur rose to his feet and shouted something at Keje, then continued shouting at everyone in the compartment. "He is . . . excited," explained Keje in a subdued tone, barely audible over Nakja-Mur's rant.

"Well, tell . . . ask him to control himself! We must hear what else these men have to say!"

"I will try, Cap-i-taan. But forgive him . . . us. Chill-chaap is nearly as large as Baalkpan. It was one of the oldest colonies, and the only one on Jaava that remained friendly to us. Many thousands of people—our people—lived there." Keje turned to Nakja-Mur and spoke in soothing tones. Slowly, the High Chief of Baalkpan eased into his seat. But his rage had only been contained, not extinguished. A moody, uncomfortable silence filled the compartment, and the quiet, after Nakja-Mur's outburst, was particularly profound.

"Lieutenant Brister," Matt prompted.

"Sir," continued Brister after a last look at their guests. "Tjilatchap, or Chill-chaap, is gone. Nothing left alive. And it looked like the people there were eaten, and not just by scavengers."

"My God," gasped Sandra.

"Yes," Keje growled. "Did I not tell you? We are mere prey to them." He looked at the nurse. "You asked once why we threw them into the sea." He shook his head.

Brister cleared his throat and resumed his tale. With Mallory's help he brought them through the storm and the discovery of the plane. Then he spoke of the monsters.

"Grik," Keje snarled.

"How many ships?" Matt asked.

"Three, sir."

Matt looked at Keje. "They can't have been the same ones we tangled with. It was at least two weeks later and hundreds of miles apart!" He turned back to Mallory. "What happened then?"

Ben described the hair-raising effort to get the plane off the beach. Between the three of them again, they told how they ultimately fought clear of the "monsters" and finally flew back to *Mahan*.

"They just left you?" Bradford asked incredulously. "Without a boat?"

"Yeah. Even if we'd changed our minds, it wouldn't have done any good. We had plenty of motivation. Those creatures—I've never seen anything like 'em, sir. They were . . . pretty scary."

Matt nodded. "We've seen them too, and they *are* pretty scary. I congratulate you all on your escape."

"Thank you, sir," they chorused.

"Did the lizards see you fly?"

"Maybe," answered Mallory. "We could still see them when we took off. Why?"

Matt smiled at him. "Nothing, Lieutenant. Don't worry about it. It might've been a handy surprise for later, that's all."

Mallory looked at his hands. "Sorry, Captain. I didn't think of that. Not till later. We saw half a dozen more of their ships while we were looking for you, but we were pretty high and far. If they heard us, I doubt they saw us."

"My God," murmured Bradford. "As many as nine ships, then. Perhaps a dozen, if the ones seen in the strait are still others." He looked at Keje, who seemed stricken. "Your enemy *is* here at last, and in force. We've not a moment to lose!"

Matt held up his hand. "I'm afraid we must lose a few more moments, Mr. Bradford. Lieutenant Mallory? What happened next?"

"Kaufman wanted us to fly to Ceylon, and we didn't say squat, but 'Yes, sir, will do.' We took on all the fuel we could and then came looking for you."

"I saw Mr. Ellis before we left," Brister said. "The nurses were all fine and were taking good care of him." He looked at Sandra. "Nurse Cross said they were keeping the faith. We talked a couple of minutes, and Mr. Ellis said . . ." He turned to Matt. "He said to tell you he's sorry—but, Captain, it wasn't his fault!" Perry's gaze was emphatic. "Anyway, they probably all know we went looking for you by now. At least the ones that aren't crazy will have some hope."

Keje cleared his throat. "Excuse me," he said. "These flying men bring momentous news. We learn Chill-chaap has been sacked and the Grik are indeed rampant, worse than we'd even feared. The dark time we've dreaded seems at hand. Now is when we will learn if all we've worked for, for generations—our colonies, our culture, our very way of life—will survive, or be cast to the winds once more. This . . . is important to us." The irony of his understatement wasn't lost. "I would think it would be important to you, our allies, as well. Yet you seem more concerned with this ship, this *Mahan*. What is *Mahan*, and what, or where, is Say-lon?"

Matt took off his hat in the awkward silence. He wiped sweat from his forehead with a handkerchief and slicked back his greasy hair. "Forgive me, my friend. I am concerned, and this news means our preparations are even more urgent. The significance of *Mahan,* however, is this." He looked around at all of them, but rested his gaze on Keje and Nakja-Mur. "*Mahan* and *Walker* are the same. They're just alike, and she has the same capabilities we have. What's more, her people are my people, and I'm responsible for them. I'm obligated to help them any way I can, just as I'm obligated, now, to help your people to the best of my ability. The reason *Mahan* should concern you, however, besides—like you said, we're allies—is there's another ship just like this one, apparently steaming as fast as she can directly toward the Grik. What if they take her? You say they're mimics; they copy the works of others. How long to copy *Mahan*? A while, surely. Maybe a generation or two. But what of the meantime? How will they use her? At the very least, they might figure out ways to counteract our superiority." He stopped and looked around. "We've got to get her back." He paused. "Or destroy her."

Nakja-Mur rose to his feet and, after regarding them all with a steady gaze, he began to speak. Keje translated as he did so. "You Amer-i-caans, you know us now. You may not know us well, but we've kept no secrets from you and our desperation is clear. Yet we know almost nothing about you. At long last, tell us where you come from. If you have two smoking ships, why not summon more? The flying boat outside is clearly made of metal, and yet it floats! It flies! With but three Amer-i-caans on board, it is a match for three Grik ships! We've never seen such wonders! Surely you can do anything! You can save us from the Grik! Please, summon more of your people. Together, we could destroy the Grik menace completely, and our two peoples could live in peace for all time!"

Matt looked at Nakja-Mur when Keje completed the translation. Conflicting emotions swirled through him, but he knew, in spite of his desire to pass as little information as he could—the same desire he suspected the first "Tail-less Ones" had—the Lemurians who'd taken them in and now depended on them so heavily had a right to know. He glanced at Sandra and caught a nod of encouragement.

"We can't send for help," he said, "because there's no one to send to." He looked at Sandra and smiled resignedly. Then he held the gaze of each American for a moment before returning his attention to the Lemurians. "Remember how the first Tail-less Ones said their home was gone? Ours is too. Whether that makes us like them or not, I'll leave up to you to decide. But I think it's time you heard a story about a war that was bigger than anything you can possibly imagine. A war so big, the entire world was engulfed in fire and millions had already died . . . and it was only starting. This ship that seems so impressive and full of wonders to you was only the smallest, most insignificant part of that war, in the grand scheme of things." He took a deep breath. "And it was a war we were losing. Then something happened and somehow, we were . . . here."

Keje managed an expression of confusion. "But you've told us you come from near the Edge of the World, from a land so distant we've no . . . ah, charts that show its position."

"That's true. We do. But the war we fought—the part we were fighting, that is—was here. Right here."

There was no sound but the voices on deck and the paint chippers plying their tools on a scaffold rigged alongside.

Courtney Bradford leaned forward in his chair. "My dear friends, Mi-Anakka and Americans, there's no question we all spring from the same world. There's no other explanation." He laid his hand on the chart before him. "These are the same, for the most part, as the Scrolls the People revere. The land shapes are mostly the same, although we've noticed a few slight differences. But the water is water and the air is the air and the heavens are no different. But in the world Captain Reddy described, where all upon it were at war—the 'world,' if you will, we come from—all this"—he gestured at the charts—"was the same except for one thing: the people and creatures that inhabit it. Where we come from—evidently an entirely other 'here'—there are no Grik, no mountain fish, and . . . no People." He leaned back in his chair and it creaked beneath him.

"Personally, I don't come from 'the Edge of the World,' like my American friends. I come from . . ." He glanced at the chart and put his finger on the small piece of coastline southeast of the Sunda Islands, right on the edge of the paper. "I think your Scrolls call this place 'New Holland' or something like that, although I assure you there were few Dutchmen when I left."

Keje was looking at him like he'd just crawled out of a gri-kakka's mouth with its stomach in its teeth. "I've been to that land," he said quietly. "There are colonies there, and in the south, they build some sea homes as well. I've never seen an Amer-i-caan."

Bradford sighed. "I'm not a bloody American, but that's beside the point. By your charts, everything's the same, but there aren't any of *us*. By our charts, everything's the same, but there aren't any of *you*. The only explanation is that, somehow, there are two worlds . . . parallel worlds . . ." He stopped and looked around. "Two worlds side by side, perhaps even occupying the same space at the same time, only on which life has developed, for some reason, in two entirely different directions."

"But—but—" Keje stammered, "that cannot be."

Bradford sniffed and leaned back again. "Perhaps not, but it's all I've been able to come up with. Captain?"

"No, Mr. Bradford, that's a better explanation than I'd have managed, but the idea's essentially the same."

Nakja-Mur said something and Keje spoke for him. "If that is true, then how did you get here?"

Matt spread his hands. "We have no idea. All we know is *Mahan* and *Walker* were together, fighting a battle against a powerful enemy ship. We entered a strange squall, and the next thing we knew . . . No—" He looked thoughtful. "We didn't really know for a while. But somehow we were here. In your world." Abruptly, his expression hardened, and he leaned forward, placing his hands on the chart. "Which means, since we've no idea how we got here, we haven't got a clue how to get back. However it happened, we're stuck with each other. Unlike the old 'Tail-less Ones,' we're not going to run off and leave you. Even if we wanted to, we can't. Our fates are intertwined. The survival of our people, yours and mine, depends on defeating the Grik. So you better explain to your complainers, Nakja-Mur, U-Amaki Ay Baalkpan, they have not yet begun to be inconvenienced! After the information we've received today, we're going to have to kick into high gear."

"High Gear. It means, All Out? Sink or Swim? Same?" Keje asked.

"That's right."

Keje blinked solemn assent. "Your man, Silva? He told me these, and I agree. He also told me another." He looked around the table with quiet dignity and determination, then looked directly at Nakja-Mur. "However the Amer-i-caans came to us, it's clear only the Maker of All Things could have arranged it as they say. If that is so, then surely we must all either Shit, or Get Off the Pot."

For once, it was a beautiful day on Baalkpan Bay. The humidity was low and it couldn't have been much over eighty degrees. There was a cooling breeze out of the south-southwest, and the launch's motor droned pleasantly with the sound of good health and proper maintenance. The water had a slight chop, stirred by the wind, and the occasional packet of spray spritzed Matt, Letts, Bradford, and Shinya in the cockpit of the launch. To them, it was refreshing. But to Tony Scott, at the wheel, each drop that struck him made him shudder as if he'd been sprayed with caustic acid.

Matt knew something had come over his once fearless coxswain, who'd acquired a deep and abiding terror of the water. All he could do was hope he got over it. They were too shorthanded to put him on the beach, at least until their Lemurian "cadets" were fully trained, and the man stoically refused to be relieved from his primary duty. He clearly hated the water now and he constantly cast worried looks over the side as if expecting to see some huge, ravenous fish pacing the boat. But he was, after all, the coxswain, and he wouldn't shirk his duty.

For Matt's part, he was enjoying the outing. *Walker* had been laid up for more than a month, and he'd grown anxious and irritable over her immobility. Her refit had gone as well as conditions allowed, and he expected she was in better shape now than when they'd left Surabaya ahead of the Japanese. But his anxiety over *Mahan* and the growing Grik menace left him feeling frustrated and impotent. It was good to be moving over water again.

He looked back across the bay, toward his ship, but he couldn't see her. Seven of the huge Lemurian Homes lay at anchor off Baalkpan now, crowding the area near the shipyard. More were expected within the next few days. Nakja-Mur had sent word as far as his fishing fleet could reach, for a "Great Gathering," or in essence, a council of war, to be held. Many of the Homes were intercepted already on their way. The threat was apparent to all by now. There'd been other fights like *Big Sal*'s, although none against so many Grik, but at least one Home was overrun. Its smoldering, half-sunken carcass was seen aground on the northeast coast of Java, near where Batavia would have been. That news threw Keje into a frenzy, and he'd been willing, at last, to perform the modifications to *Big Sal* that Alan Letts had suggested. Even now, as the launch nosed into the estuary of the river the locals called the Sungaa, Alan was discussing his plan with Bradford. Captain Reddy was deeply interested in whatever scheme the recently hyper-motivated supply officer came up with, but for the moment he couldn't help but be overcome by the primordial landscape surrounding them.

The Sungaa wasn't long and was navigable for only a short distance before it choked into a narrow, swampy stream. But the waters that fled into the bay from the Lohr Mountains to the north provided a quicker, more convenient passage to the site where they'd sunk their first well. Except for his brief, tragic foray on Bali, Matt had stepped on land only for frequent trips into the city to see Nakja-Mur. Now, after passing the last hardy outposts of fishing huts and "frontier" hunters—only a few miles from town—he beheld Lemurian Borneo in all its savage beauty.

Amid raucous cries, dozens of species of colorful birdlike creatures whirled and darted with the erratic grace of flying insects. Their short, furry feathers covered streamlined and exotically lethal leathery bodies. They incessantly chased small fish, insects, and any "bird" smaller than they were. Vicious aerial combat flared when one of the creatures caught something another wanted or thought it could take. Unlike similar battles that Matt had seen among birds back home, the losers here rarely survived. The bodies of the slain never even made it to the water.

The deadly flasher-fish weren't nearly as numerous in the fresher water of the bay, and they didn't venture upriver at all. Matt's party passed a herd of large animals marching solemnly through the shallows near shore. They were the size of hippos, but looked like spiky armadillos with longer necks and forelegs. Here and there, ordinary crocodiles lounged on the muddy banks. For all Matt knew, the trees hanging over the water were quite normal as well, but he knew little about trees of any sort, so their wide, palmated leaves looked exotic to him regardless. Bradford said they were as unusual as the fauna and Matt took his word for it. The whole scene was simultaneously shockingly beautiful and horrifying in a deep, secret, instinctual way.

He tore himself from his reverie and saw that Shinya was equally absorbed by their surroundings, but Letts, and even Bradford, seemed unaffected. Of course, they'd both been to the wellhead several times. Letts must have asked him a question, because he and the Australian both looked at him expectantly. "I'm sorry, Mr. Letts. Could you repeat that, please?"

Alan grinned. "Sure, Skipper. What I asked is, should we concentrate all the guns on one side of *Big Sal*, like a floating battery, and just counterweight the other, or mount guns on both sides? We may not have time or materials to make enough for both."

Matt shook his head. "I'm not convinced there're going to be any guns." Letts assumed a wounded expression.

"Sure there will, Skipper, if we have enough time. I've been working with the guys at the foundry"—the "guys at the foundry" were two Lemurian brothers who owned and ran it—"and they say it's no problem. They cast anchors for ships like *Big Sal* all the time, so they're used to throwing lots of metal. You could cast five or six guns from the metal that goes into one of those babies. Labor's not an issue. The latest news has everybody fired up, and Nakja-Mur had kittens over the prospect of cannons of his very own. The only two stumbling blocks, well, three, really, were getting somebody to let us cut gunports in the side of their ship, finding enough metal to make the guns—a truly hellacious amount of copper and tin—and, of course, ammunition.

"Gunpowder's not a problem. All the components are readily available and sulfur's all over these volcanic islands. The real pain's building a powder mill. That's taking time. We can't use water power, since there're no swift rivers. Maybe we can try what the Mice came up with? Anyway, we'll get it sorted out. We can use copper for cannonballs—that's a cinch—but training gunners to hit something with them might be a little harder."

"What about boring true?" Matt asked, and Letts shrugged a little hesitantly.

"I have a few ideas along that line."

Matt shook his head. He didn't know what had cracked Alan Letts out of his amiable go-with-the-flow shell, but whatever it was, he'd become a dynamo. Maybe it was just that he, like the rest of them, had finally come to grips with the situation. "I bet Keje wasn't happy about chopping holes in the side of *Big Sal*," he mused. "How many guns are you planning to put on her, anyway?"

"I'm hoping on twenty per side, eventually. That may not seem like many, given her size, compared to the ships of the line back in the seventeen hundreds, but . . ." He shrugged.

Matt looked at him and blinked with surprise. It was a habit he'd picked up from their new friends. "Twenty! I thought you were ambitious thinking about two or three! How big are you planning to make them?"

"Well, that depends on what size we ultimately bore them out. I'm meeting with Mr. McFarlane and Bernie Sandison this evening and we'll kick that around."

Matt chuckled. "Very well, Mr. Letts. Keep me informed, but be sure you don't use anything the ship needs to make your tools!" A wry grin spread across Letts's face, as if he'd been about to ask permission to do that very thing. "As to what to do with them if you get the cannons made?" Matt paused. "Keje'll have to decide. It's his ship. A floating battery in the bay would be tough to get around, but if anything ever did, the whole defense might collapse. I've never been a big believer in static defenses, and I doubt Keje would be either."

Bradford nodded vigorously. "Yes! Yes! Look how much good the Maginot Line did the French! And I'm not even going to start on Singapore! As for Keje's opinion, I assure you you're right. With some quite obvious exceptions, the Lemurians are seagoing nomads. The very idea of being semi-permanently moored in any defensive position would be utterly alien, and perhaps hateful to them. I imagine they'd do it as an expedient during battle, but to actively prepare for such a thing? You might lose all credibility if you made the suggestion. So far, they're willing to take your advice on matters of defense, but that's all any of us really are. Advisors. We have no official status in the chain of command. I'm not sure there really is one. Nakja-Mur is the overall leader of the People of Balik—I mean Baalkpan—but Keje and any other ship captain who comes ashore, I suppose, all seem to be equals. They command their own People, but are subject to the laws and customs of the territory or ship they set foot on. It's all so very chaotic! It would be far more convenient if they had a king, and all the various ships and places were part of some grand commonwealth!"

"Like the British Empire?" Letts goaded.

"Well . . . yes! Precisely! This current arrangement is far too much like your own various states. Always squabbling, and never agreeing to work together toward a common goal!"

Matt smiled tolerantly at the Australian. "The United States usually manages to pull together over the important things."

"Yes, but it takes wars to make it happen, I might remind you!"

"That may be," Matt confessed, "but it looks like the Lemurians have their war too."

No one spoke for a while as the launch crept farther upriver. Once, Scott almost lost control when a crocodile bumped the boat and he flailed madly for the Thompson submachine gun he always carried slung over his shoulder. "Hold your fire, Mr. Scott," Matt said, just loud enough to be heard. The croc was swimming disinterestedly away, and Tony gave him a sheepish glance as he regained control of the boat.

"How are things going ashore, Lieutenant?" Matt asked Shinya. He'd been shaken from his trancelike study of the wildlife by the launch's capering.

"If you mean the preparation of the militia, Captain Reddy, I must report progress is poor, but improving." Nakja-Mur had decreed that all able-bodied People, male and female, should take training with Sergeant Alden and Lieutenant Shinya, as well as some of their own few warriors every other day. Attendance was mandatory, but from the beginning, participation was somewhat sparse. Many of the younger, more adventurous townsfolk turned out with a will, and some had achieved a level of training that let them perform as NCOs for the less-proficient attendees. Alden had even begun training an "elite" force of a hundred of the sharpest and toughest, which would, of course, become his "Marines."

The vast majority managed to avoid service at first, however, due to exemptions granted almost as a matter of course whenever they complained to the High Chief's secretaries that their occupations should be protected as "vital to the defense of the People." Some even had a point, and to be fair, many of the young, able-bodied Lemurians had been conscripted into the projects being undertaken for or by the Americans. All those were subject to military discipline, however, and put through a daily regimen of close-order drill and basic weapons training. As the Grik threat became more real, particularly over the last couple of weeks, Shinya had noticed an increasing number of faces at drill that he'd never seen before.

"What kind of numbers are we looking at?" Matt asked.

"It's difficult to say. Sergeant Alden and I drill them each day, but with a few exceptions, we only see them every other day." Drill took place on a large "common" at the foot of Nakja-Mur's Great Hall, and the High Chief often watched the proceedings. The place had once been, for lack of a better term, a "park" near the center of town. But the ground had now been so churned by marching feet and maneuvering troops that they'd taken to calling it the parade ground. It wasn't big enough for everybody, however, so roughly half the militia drilled one day, and the other half the next. It was dreadfully inefficient, but with the dearth of open ground in Baalkpan, it was the only answer. Shinya gazed thoughtfully at the water and turned back to the captain. "I think it's not impossible, right now, to field nearly fifteen hundred Baalkpan troops, reasonably well trained for the type of fighting we saw upon *Big Sal*. In two weeks, we can perhaps double that number. In six months, we could put ten thousand in the field, but that would include virtually the entire adult population of the city. To assemble such a force, however, will take an even greater sense of . . . urgency than they now have."

"You mean we'd have to be literally under attack, here, to expect that level of participation?" Matt muttered in resignation.

Shinya nodded. "I fear so. Of course, by then it would be much too late to organize them properly. A few of Sergeant Alden's 'Marines' have gone aboard the Lemurian ships to get them to learn our drill so coordination would be possible at need. They've received . . . a mixed welcome. As for the tactics we're teaching them, without the benefit of firearms, the only real options are those you suggested. A 'Roman' shield wall, backed by spearmen, backed in turn by archers." He shook his head. "One of the most difficult things was to get them to abandon their crossbows. These people are made for shooting bows, and a longbow has a greater range and rate of fire than a crossbow, but they didn't understand why we, a people with such technology, should advocate such simple weapons." He grinned. "Once they saw the superiority of longbows, it wasn't difficult to convince them." Shinya's expression became grim. "Of course, they want firearms."

Matt nodded. "I wish they had them, but without steel . . ." He sighed. "Once we drag them out of the Bronze Age, we can have a look at flintlock muskets or something, but for now?" He held his hands out at his sides. "I know Alden's training some of his 'Marines' to use our weapons. How's he doing?"

"Yes, he's training fifty of them, but they only get to fire a few rounds each. Mr. Sandison has solved the projectile problem—I think he called it swaging? But the difficulty remains making new cartridge cases if the empty ones are damaged or lost. And, of course, the primers. No one seems to think gunpowder will be a problem"—he bowed toward Letts—"but it won't be smokeless at first, so the automatic weapons won't function well." He shook his head. "Of course, all these logistics matters are not my concern, particularly since I know nothing about them. But I understand that one of Mr. Sandison's concerns is replacing *Walker's* depleted ammunition stores for her main battery. His experiments with the small arms are the 'test bed' for the four-inch guns."

"Lieutenant Shinya, I don't know how it worked in your navy, but logistics is the concern of any officer, infantry officers included—which is what you've become. I'm glad you're keeping up with it." Matt's gaze drifted forward, and he saw massive wooden pilings set in the riverbed some distance out from shore. As they neared, he saw that a framework connected them and a party of 'Cats was working to lay down a plank deck. They'd arrived at the fueling pier.

They secured the launch and trooped ashore. All were armed in spite of the small army of laborers nearby. Bradford had insisted, explaining that unlike in their own world, the large number of workers going about their business here wouldn't frighten predators away; they would only alert them to a smorgasbord. A fair percentage of the Lemurians present were, in fact, dedicated to security. They were armed primarily with oversized crossbows that threw a bolt two feet long and an inch in diameter. Matt remembered Bradford telling him there were some truly astonishing predators lurking in the jungles of this new Borneo, but he'd paid only passing attention at the time, preoccupied with the refit of his ship. Now he tried to remember some of the creatures Bradford had described. *They must be pretty big*, he mused, *if it took a handheld ballista to bring one down.*

At the edge of the clearing, three large cylinders stood atop adobe furnaces with a maze of heavy, local copper pipe twisting among them. Matt recognized the cylinders as the ill-fated torpedo tubes of the number three mount. He hoped they would prove more useful here than they had aboard the ship. Furry, kilted workers scampered around the apparatus that they hoped would become a functioning refinery—if they found anything to refine. Chief Donaghey and *Mahan's* Perry Brister were supervising the project, and by their filthy appearance, they'd done more than that. Matt waved at them to carry on as the party continued past the high tower set in the center of the clearing. In it was a now fully recovered Leo Davis and one of their precious BARs. He looked like a prison guard overseeing a chain gang, but the obvious distinction was that he was there to protect the workers, not to prevent escape. More Lemurians stood guard at intervals along the trail leading from the fueling pier into the dense jungle surrounding it.

The wellhead lay almost a mile inland. The trail was wide, and down the center was a pipeline constructed from the curious oversized bamboo that seemed, in every respect except for its massive size, just like bamboo "back home." They'd seen it used extensively in local construction and for masts, of course, and it was a natural choice for those applications, being generally the diameter and length of a telephone pole. Matt hadn't known they were going to use it to transport the crude. Bradford and Letts noticed him appraising the arrangement as they walked alongside.

"Bound to leak like a sieve, Skipper," said Letts resignedly. "The couplings are short pieces of tin pipe pounded into the ends and sealed with pitch. I guess we can build something better once we have the time."

"No, Mr. Letts. It's ingenious. I hadn't even thought how we'd move the oil from the well to the refinery. Well done."

Letts looked embarrassed. "Well, it was really Spanky's idea," he demurred.

"A good idea, no matter whose it was." Matt paused, looking at the pipeline with a thoughtful expression. "I can't help but wonder, though. A fueling pier, a pipeline, even a refinery—all situated where they are just because of the wellhead. Are you sure we're not taking one small detail a little too much for granted?"

Bradford blinked at him and wiped the ever-present sweat from his brow with a handkerchief that might once have been white. Then he grinned mischievously. "Never fear, my dear captain. As you Americans would so quaintly say, the fix is in." He stopped and glanced at the sky. It was visible above the quadruple-canopy jungle only because of the pipeline cut. As so often happened at this time of day, the bright blue they'd basked beneath much of the morning had been replaced by a sodden gray.

"Oh, dear."

Isak Reuben took a final, long drag off his cigarette, and it burned fiercely, almost to his lips. He flipped the tiny butt off the platform, where it hissed and drowned in a puddle. The deluge had become a gentle drizzle, but it fell long and hard enough to soak him completely. Not that it mattered. He was always soaked, with sweat, and his filthy T-shirt clung to his skinny torso like a slimy, splotched, translucent leech. His fireroom pallor was gone, as was Gilbert's, replaced by the harsh reddish brown he remembered so well from his life in the oil fields. It was a color he'd hoped never to see on his own body again.

"Goddamn," he exclaimed matter-of-factly, "ain't White Mice now." He grabbed the cable that dropped down from one end of the walking beam and disappeared into the hole at his feet. The slack felt about right. "Wind 'er up, Gilbert," he croaked at his companion, who made a rotating motion with his hand.

A short distance away, a pair of young 'Cats sat on a brontosarry's back, and one made a trilling sound and whacked its flank with a stout bamboo shoot. With a guttural groan of protest, the beast began to move. It was harnessed to a giant windlass, and as it trudged through a slurry of mud, round and round, a belt running from a large-diameter central shaft transferred its meager rotation to a smaller, faster wheel. Another belt ran to yet another wheel, between the two in diameter. This one turned a crank that raised and lowered a pitman, causing the walking beam to go up and down. As it did so, it raised the cable-tool bit far down in the hole and then dropped it with a resounding "thud." The bit drove a few inches deeper every time.

Isak looked at the sky, beyond the eighty-foot bamboo derrick that still struck him as just . . . wrong somehow, and saw patches of blue struggling to disperse the clouds. He shook his head unhappily. Every time a squall blew up, he hoped subconsciously that it, like the one that had brought them here, would take them home. Home to the real world, where he could bask in the honest warmth and isolation of his beloved boilers, where steam was magically made. Steam that turned honest turbines. He frowned. Anywhere but here, where steam rose from the ground because the sun cooked it out, and where stinkin' dinosaurs pretended to be motors! He groped for another cigarette and frowned even deeper, staring at the massive animal trudging slowly around. "RPMs ain't much, but the torque's pretty respectable."

Gilbert touched the cable himself at the bottom of its stroke, as he walked over to join him. "What?" he asked.

"Nothin'."

Gilbert nodded. "Quiet rig." Both were used to loud engines doing the work of the dinosaur.

"Too quiet," complained Isak. "Ain't natural."

Gilbert nodded again, in solemn agreement. "Gimme a smoke, will ya?" His customary monotone was as close to a wheedle as it ever got.

"No."

"Why not? I shared mine with you."

"Yeah, and now yer out, ain't ya? Stupid."

Gilbert stared down at the well as the cable went slack, pondering. No question about it, Isak was the smart one.

The other fireman sighed heavily, shook a soggy cigarette out of the pack, and handed it over. Then he peered inside. "Now I'm as dumb as you. Only one left."

The well was situated in another artificial clearing, and one of their Lemurian security guards trilled a call from his watchtower near the pipeline cut.

"What's he jabberin' about?" Isak asked, irritably reaching for one of the old Krag rifles they always kept nearby. "I hope it ain't another one of them Big Ones. We really need bigger guns for huntin' around here."

The "Big Ones" he referred to were forty-foot monsters Bradford insisted were allosaurs. Unlike most of the other dinosaur species they'd encountered, Bradford's modern allosaurs were not stunted. They'd hardly changed at all from those in the fossil record—the only difference he could see, if anything, was they were bigger than their prehistoric ancestors. There weren't many of them, though, and even if they looked built for speed, they preferred to lurk along well-used trails in the dense jungle and let their prey come to them. The destroyermen called them "super lizards" in spite of Bradford's protests. Isak only knew they were hard as hell to kill and they scared the shit out of him.

"Hold on, Isak," Gilbert said. "They all sound like monkeys to me, but that don't sound like a lawsey-me-there's-a-Big-One-a'comin' yell."

They both stared toward the cut for a few moments more, then relaxed a little when they saw humans emerge into the clearing.

"It was too," Isak said. "That's the Skipper."

Matt waved at the Lemurian peering down from the tower. It was one of Alden's Marines, armed with a Krag. This was arguably one of the most important parts of the "fuel project," but aside from the sentry, there were fewer than a dozen people, including the Mice, working the site. Most of the labor currently involved cleaning and stacking the "bamboo" pipes they were using to case the well. At this stage, few hands were really needed to operate the rig and most were needed only when it was time to bail, or pull the bits for sharpening.

A pair of bits lay across hefty sawhorses now, and two workers held them down while another vigorously worked them over with a file. The bits were Spanky's idea. He'd used a heavy I beam meant for shoring up buckled hull plates. He cut the twelve-foot beam into three segments and cast heavy copper slugs on the ends to give them more weight. By all accounts, they worked well, but they didn't hold an edge and had to be sharpened a lot.

Matt stared, fascinated, at the bamboo derrick and the ingenious contraption operating it. He'd seen oil wells, but he didn't know much about them. All he could say about this one was . . . it resembled an oil well. That the derrick was a strange greenish yellow did a lot to undermine the impression, however. His gaze swept to the platform and he saw the two firemen staring back. *That's probably another reason there's not more workers here,* he conceded. It took special people to voluntarily spend much time with the irascible Mice. Even if those people had tails. Together, he and his party slogged through the swampy ooze surrounding the rig until they reached the platform and clambered up.

"Good afternoon, men," Matt began amiably. "Thought I'd see for myself how things are going." Isak just shrugged and looked around as if to say, "Well, here it is."

Bradford stifled a cough. "Yes, well, I think you can see they've done a marvelous job. Marvelous!" He beamed at the two men. "How deep are we now?"

Gilbert had retreated a few feet and stood next to the sampson post that supported the walking beam. Neither he nor Isak had been spoken to by officers more than a dozen times in their lives—not counting Spanky—and it always unnerved them a little. For the most part, throughout their Navy careers they'd lived in the fireroom, and officers lived . . . someplace else.

"Three hundred and sixty-nine feet, when the cable goes tight this time," Isak said, and he glanced furtively between the visitors. He suddenly yanked the filthy hat off of his head. "If you please."

"Excellent, excellent!" Bradford exclaimed. "Can't be far now!" He turned to face Matt. "As I said, the fix is in! I happen to know oil was found on this very spot in 1938! A respectable deposit, too. Quite adequate for our needs!"

Matt smiled at him. "But what makes you so sure it's here . . . *here*?"

Bradford blinked. "Why, you did, of course! As you said, the geography is the same. As we've all discussed at some length now," he smiled patiently, "this is our very same earth. Only a few inhabitants have been changed about. The very same oil found here in 1938 should still be down there, since no one's ever drilled for it!"

"I sure hope you're right, Mr. Bradford. I'm not certain it's the same thing. Just because Borneo's here, does that mean the same oil's under it?" A trace of sadness touched Matt's smile. "I'm morally certain the North American continent exists . . . here. Its shores and distinctive landmarks are probably like those we remember. The Paluxy River may still run where my folks' ranch should be. Do the same catfish I used to catch still swim that river, Mr. Bradford? I doubt it. If they do, they'd probably eat you." He held up his hand before Bradford could protest. "I'm just saying if we don't find oil here, we need to keep an open mind about where to look next. Above all, we mustn't get everyone's hopes up that finding it here's a sure thing." Matt's smile twisted into a grin. "Always remember, gentlemen, oil is where you find it—but it may not be where you left it!"

Gilbert nodded solemn agreement with the captain's words. What was that damned Aussie trying to do? Jinx them? He reached over and felt the cable. "Tight," he announced. Isak nodded. He addressed the Lemurians on the draft beast.

"Hey, you monkeys!" he shouted. "Stop-o el dinosaur-o now-o! Time to bail! Chop, chop!" The two young 'cats gave very human nods and hopped down.

"Been picking up the local lingo, I see," Letts commented dryly.

Isak shrugged. "Yep. Got to, I guess."

In the launch, Captain Reddy was thoughtful. He was encouraged by how far along the "fuel project" seemed, and if Bradford was right, it was just a matter of finding the right depth at the rig before *Walker*'s bunkers were full to bursting. The thought felt good, even though he couldn't shake his nagging concern. Contrary to what everybody seemed to take for granted, there actually were subtle differences in geography. Nothing pronounced, but enough to make him worry. For example, the land around Baalkpan Bay was higher than he remembered "back home." Less erosion? Lower sea level? Or something else? If everything in the world was different now, why not oil deposits?

Bradford said it didn't work that way. He said the ground under the well was geologically predisposed to form a reservoir for crude. Matt hoped he was right. In any event, now that he'd been there, he was confident that if there was any oil, it would be found. The strange firemen had everything well in hand. He sighed. Of course, then the refinery had to work. It was one thing to find oil and something else to turn it into fuel they could burn.

He listened to the others chatting about the wildlife they'd seen as the launch left the river behind and reentered the bay. A few colorful flying reptiles paced the boat and shrieked and swooped at the small fish churned up in its wake. Matt tuned out the conversation and, as he often did of late, found himself thinking about Sandra Tucker as he stared at the feathery whitecaps. He couldn't deny that he was attracted to her. Who wouldn't be? For that matter, with so few women and a ship full of men, who, in fact, *wasn't* attracted to her? In spite of the situation, he really liked her a lot and believed he wasn't unduly influenced by the scarcity of females. He was sure that under normal circumstances he'd have already made a move. But these weren't normal circumstances.

So far, in spite of everything, the crew had stuck together. There was friction aboard—there always was—but not much more than normal . . . yet. He couldn't imagine how everything fell apart so fast on *Mahan*. Jim was a good leader and he should have sorted it out. Probably would have if he hadn't been shot. Brister thought the breakdown was due to Kaufman's hysteria and the stress of their ordeal. At all costs, he had to prevent that kind of stress from taking root here. Right now the biggest stress to *Walker*'s crew was a lack of "dames." He honestly believed they'd eventually find more humans, and the two Indiamen that had sailed east so long ago were a solid lead. But in the meantime it was hard to dispel the sense that they were all alone. All alone, with only two women. He'd always believed in leading by example, and regardless of his feelings, he thought it wouldn't be fair to the men if he pressed his suit now. How could he expect them to show restraint if he didn't set the example? At the very least, it would undermine his moral authority—and that was really the only authority he had left. The men sure weren't getting paid. The situation was far too tense to risk jealousy and resentment by chasing one of the only two eligible females.

He glanced at Alan Letts. Maybe the only eligible female. Letts and Karen Theimer were seeing a lot of each other. Maybe that was why he'd been so industrious of late. Letts had better watch out, though. Matt knew Bernie and Greg were both sweet on the young nurse too. That was probably why his young officers were so formal to each other lately. There'd be trouble down the line, and the more he thought about it, the more disquieted he became. The "dame famine," as the crew referred to the situation, was likely to be more explosive in the long term than any shortage of fuel or ammunition.

He wished, for the thousandth time, that he hadn't sent the other nurses off in *Mahan*. Not just because of the dame famine, of course, but their presence might have taken a little pressure off. What it boiled down to was that somehow they had to find more people, and the sooner the better. He owed it to his men. He took a deep breath. But that would have to wait, and in regard to Sandra, he would have to wait as well. And so would *Mahan*, wherever she'd gone—at least until they had fuel to search for her—or other humans. Right now they had a war to prepare for and to fight. That was a kind of stress his men were accustomed to and one he knew they could handle.

"Some kind of regatta or somethin' goin' on today?" shouted Tony Scott over the engine and the spray they were making. Captain Reddy grunted and looked where the coxswain indicated. Across the bay, fishing boats pelted toward town as fast as they could. The growing mass of boats seemed to gather in all they came across, and sheets flew as more fishermen came about or set a new tack toward the wharves. On instinct, Matt glanced at his ship. He saw her now; the off-white experimental gray that the Chief had mixed was clear against the riotous color of the city and jungle beyond. Perplexed, he looked back toward the mouth of the bay and the Makassar Strait.

Standing in toward them under a fair press of sail was one of the red-hulled Indiamen of the Grik. All over the bay, the large conch-like shells the People used to sound the alarm began to blow, and the men in the boat heard the dull bass hum even over the exhaust of the engine.

"Step on it, Scott! To the ship, as fast as you can!"

Sandra peered over the top of her book as her next patient entered the wardroom. She was reading a battered copy of Henry Thomas's *Wonder Book of History, Science, Nature, Literature, Art, Religion, Philosophy,* which was making the rounds. It reminded her a little of Courtney Bradford: engagingly pompous and full of a little information on quite a lot. The old book came from the large, eccentric library of the dead surgeon, Stevens. She closed it and regarded her visitor with raised eyebrows.

"Dennis Silva, as I live and breathe."

Silva merely stood, staring stoically straight ahead and she looked at him more closely. The refit had exacted a toll on the destroyermen and their Lemurian helpers, mostly minor injuries and torch burns, but there were occasional serious hurts—crushed fingers and lacerations requiring stitches, for example. The complaints constituted a steady enough stream that she and Karen stood alternating watches in the wardroom, tending the wounded as they presented themselves. They usually shooed them back to their duties. The big gunner's mate had no obvious injury, however.

"Well?" she demanded impatiently. "What's the matter with you?"

Silva's face reddened even beneath his short, dense beard and savage tan. "'M sick, ma'am."

She looked at him incredulously. "Sick! You?" Silva's constitution was legendary. His record showed his only previous appearances before the ship's surgeon had been of the type to be expected of a rambunctiously male Asiatic Fleet destroyerman. She doubted that was his problem today, although with Silva . . . There *had* been rumors some of the men were experimenting with local females. Both species were certainly adventurous enough to try. She shuddered involuntarily and shook her head to clear the thought.

"Sick how?" she asked. Then she felt a chill. So far they'd been lucky, but she lived in perpetual dread of some unidentifiable plague sweeping the ship, something they had no immunity to.

Silva actually looked at his feet. "Got the screamers," he muttered.

"The screamers?"

He nodded. "Been in the head since yesterday afternoon, and I . . . kinda need to go now." Her eyes flicked down the passageway behind her, and he looked at her as if she were nuts. That was the officers' head! "I, ah, can hold it."

"What seems to be the cause of your discomfort? Something you ate?"

"Well, you see, tobacco's worth its weight in gold, and that damn Chack—"

Sandra slapped her forehead and felt a smile of relief cross her face. Silva's expression became more wooden at her sudden lack of compassion. "Has had you running around chewing on every dead leaf he can convince you to stick in your mouth!" she finished for him and laughed out loud. "Oh, that's rich! I heard about that! You should watch out for that boy! He's not the 'simpleminded wog' some of you guys think he is!" She giggled, then looked thoughtful. "It seems our Mr. Chack has a wicked sense of humor!" She made a mental note to tell Chack that some things that didn't bother Lemurians at all might be poisonous to humans—and that he'd better grow eyes in the back of his head and expect retaliation.

"I'm sure you'll be all right eventually, Mr. Silva. I know your . . . experiments have been solely in the interests of science and the benefit of your fellow man, but why not take this opportunity to liberate yourself from your disgusting habit?"

Silva's expression could have been described as plaintive in a lesser mortal. "But what are we supposed to do? No tobacco, almost no coffee, no . . . um." He paused, but quickly recovered himself. "It was bad enough fightin' the Nips, and now this? It's more than a fella can stand without a chew!"

Sandra nodded slowly. He had a point. Almost everyone aboard used tobacco. She knew that wasn't the only . . . frustration, but she'd noticed tempers flaring more easily, and there'd even been some fights. Despite her feelings on the subject, there was morale to consider. She sighed. "Very well, Mr. Silva. I'll look into it. But I warn you, there may not be anything to replace tobacco."

He nodded gratefully. "Just as long as somebody's lookin'. Hell, these 'Cats don't even have betel nuts!"

Secretly, Sandra expected they probably did use some kind of stimulant besides the fermented polta fruit. Seep was already well known and much used when the men went ashore on the limited liberties Matt allowed, but it had some undesirable aftereffects. She still wasn't satisfied that it was even safe for humans, given the severity and duration of the hangovers, but Captain Reddy was right. Never give an order you know will be disobeyed. The only way to keep them from drinking the stuff was to confine everyone to the ship, which was unfair and would be worse for morale than the lack of tobacco.

As a replacement for the noxious weed . . . She again determined to speak to Chack. She was willing to bet that he, and many other young Lemurians, were enjoying their joke too much to share the knowledge if there was one. She would ask, she promised herself. And warn. If the rumors were true, Silva's pranks were not funny.

"Now, as to your complaint—" She held out her hands in resignation. "I don't even have anything left to relieve the symptoms. You'll just have to let it run its course. Be sure to stay properly hydrated, though."

"Hydrated? What's that?" he inquired darkly.

"Water. Drink plenty of water!" She paused. "But only ship's water. I don't even want to think about what the local water will do to you yet. Talk about the screamers!" She made another mental note to see McFarlane again. As long as they were burning the number four boiler, the condensers would manufacture fresh water in small quantities. Barely enough to drink, but nothing else. Everyone was constantly reminded not to drink anything that even *might* have local water in it. If they ever ran entirely out of fuel, they'd have to figure out something else. Boil local water, she supposed. At least there *was* local water and they could use it for cooking— and bathing—thank God!

Silva's expression became pinched. "I might, ah, better visit the officers' head after all, ma'am. Don't think I'll make it aft."

Sandra nodded and smiled. "By all means."

The general alarm began to sound.

The launch's occupants scurried onto the pier and raced for the gangway. They were nearly trampled by Lemurians scampering everywhere on the docks. The huge draft beasts bawled as their drivers whipped their flanks in panic. One of the elephantine brontosauruses bugled in fear at the commotion and reared up on its hind legs, upsetting the cart it was hitched to and then crushing it under its haunches. The driver barely jumped clear. Somehow, they managed to weave through the terrified crowd and run up the gangway. No side party waited and they hastily saluted the colors.

Chief Gray met them, puffing. "I have the deck, sir, I suppose," he said. "Mr. Dowden left about an hour ago with Spanky to talk to the yardapes. Should be back any time."

"Never mind. Single up all lines and make all preparations for getting under way."

Gray glanced about helplessly at the chaos around them for just an instant, then saluted. "Aye, aye, Captain."

Matt turned to Shinya. "Marines are on parade today?" Shinya nodded.

"How long to fetch Alden and a company of Marines?" Shinya scanned the mob choking the wharf and the pathways into the city. He shook his head. One Grik ship had appeared in the bay and the population acted like the enemy was loose among them.

"Sergeant Alden may already be trying to make his way here, but to go get him now? Impossible."

"I concur. Try to make it to *Big Sal*. Ask Keje for a hundred of his best warriors and get them here as fast as you can!" Matt didn't even ponder the irony of the Japanese officer's salute as he returned it and watched Shinya race back down the gangway. He turned and ran to the bridge.

"Captain on deck!" shouted Lieutenant Garrett. Matt nodded and stepped quickly on the bridgewing with his binoculars in hand. The Grik ship's dash toward the city had slowed, and it was practically hove to about four miles away. As if studying them. This ran contrary to everything he'd heard about their tactics. He'd expected them to charge right in.

"All stations report manned and ready, Captain," Garrett announced.

"Very well. Prepare to get under way."

Garrett seemed surprised. "But Captain . . . the fuel? We can sink him from here."

"I know, Mr. Garrett, but he's acting like he knows it too." He barked a dry laugh. "I think our reputation has preceded us. Besides, I don't think he's by himself." As he watched, brightly colored signal flags raced up the Grik's mast. "Yep," he said. "I bet there's at least one more hanging outside the mouth of the bay. Have engineering light number three and honk the horn. We'll give anyone close enough five more minutes to make it back on board."

"Light number three, sir?" Garrett cringed. Now he knew their fuel wouldn't outlast the day.

Matt sighed. "I'm afraid so. We also have to stop whoever that one signaled to. We can only make about ten knots on one boiler, but with this breeze picking up, maybe more out in the strait, I bet those Grik can make twelve." They'd taken on firewood for just such an emergency. He hoped they wouldn't have to use it.

"Aye, aye, Captain. Sound the horn, light number three, and cast off all lines in five minutes."

Two minutes later, Shinya and Keje asked permission to come on the bridge. Matt felt a surge of warmth at the sight of his Lemurian friend. Keje was dressed as Matt had first seen him, with his copper-scaled armor and a broad-bladed scota at his side. Shinya had found the time to buckle on his longer, thinner version that Sandison made from one of the cut-lasses. It wasn't exactly a katana, but he could use it like one now that the guard had been cut down and the handle extended. Shinya still mourned his own ceremonial sword—lost when his destroyer went down—and the cutlass was a crude replacement. But he'd been moved by Bernie's gift.

Larry Dowden raced onto the bridge, breathing hard. In the background Matt heard the commotion of Lemurian warriors thundering aboard amid bellowed commands from the Bosun. "Sorry, Skipper," Larry apologized. "We nearly didn't make it. Spanky's aboard too—headed for the fireroom. He said with his two best guys ashore, he better bat the burners himself."

"Very well. Cast off the stern line. Left full rudder! Port engine ahead one-third!"

With a vibrating moan, *Walker* came to life beneath his feet once more. Ever so slowly, amid a churning froth of dark, musty-smelling seawater that sloshed up around the port propeller guard, the destroyer's stern eased away from the dock. "All stop. Rudder amidships. Cast off bow line!" Matt paused until he saw his last command obeyed. "All back one-third!" With a distinct, juddering groan, *Walker* backed away from the pier and *Big Sal*, tied up just ahead. When they'd made a suitable gap, Matt spoke again. "Right full rudder, all ahead two-thirds."

Throughout the maneuver Keje was silent. Now he just shook his head. "Amazing," he said aloud. He turned his inscrutable gaze upon the captain. "I've brought you one hundred of my finest warriors, Cap-i-taan Reddy." He grinned. "All were anxious to fight, of course, but I had the most trouble limiting their numbers when they learned they would go to battle on your magnificent ship!"

Matt clapped him on the shoulder. "They may be less enthusiastic if we have to paddle home. We really don't have the fuel for this!"

"Ah!" Keje sniffed and blinked. "A nothing! Once again we'll kill Grik together!"

Greasy black smoke belched briefly from the number three funnel and *Walker* gathered way. Matt looked through his binoculars. "Oh, boy, that's done it! He's going about. Piling on more sail."

Keje stood beside him, binoculars raised to his eyes as well. Unobtrusively, Larry Dowden helped him fold them to fit his face and showed him how to focus. Keje exclaimed in delight but continued to stare at the enemy. "Yes. He's running. I see the signal flags myself." He looked at Matt. "Twice now I have seen the enemy flee, and both times because of your ship. The one that escaped after the great fight must have passed word to others, or perhaps that's the very ship that eluded us. Regardless, there's clearly another in the strait, and beyond that, perhaps another. They must all be destroyed! If they carry news of Baalkpan to the place where they assemble fleets, they will return in force. We are not ready for that." Keje's ears and tail twitched with annoyance. "I am sure you must agree after witnessing that disgraceful display on the waterfront."

"They'll be ready, Keje," Matt assured him. "What I saw on the dock was the natural reaction of people who've suddenly been confronted with their worst nightmare. Remember, for a lot of people in Baalkpan, the Grik weren't real until today. They were creatures of myth—boogeymen. They've never faced them. They've never seen with their own eyes the terrible way they make war. Now they know the enemy *is* real and we haven't been training them for hoots." Matt gestured out the windows at the distant Grik. "In a way, this might be just what we needed to make the land folk take things seriously."

"I hope you're right," Keje grumbled. "It looked to me that all it did was turn their bowels to water."

Matt arched an eyebrow. "You should've seen us when the Japs bombed Cavite."

Walker steadied on course and gradually increased speed. Spanky was fully aware of the state of their bunkers and there was no pell-mell acceleration. Matt glanced about, trying to find something to use as a gauge for wind direction and speed. He settled on one of the fishing feluccas that pelted by in the opposite direction. The small, beamy ship sailed admirably close to the wind. Keje saw him studying it.

"Yes. The enemy has a favorable wind with their . . . I think you call it 'square rig'? It's much the same principle as our 'wings,' and it serves best running with the wind on a quarter from behind, ah, quartering? Astern?" He shook his head. "I learn your language good, I think, but some words don't work yet."

Matt grinned at him. "They work fine, as far as I can tell."

Keje bowed in thanks. "Still, I think you could catch him before he makes it into the strait." Matt glanced at Garrett, who cast a quick look at the Lemurian. Matt nodded.

"He's in easy range, Skipper," Garrett confirmed. The Grik ship was less than two miles away, gaining speed. But the course reversal had cost him. Keje grunted as if to say, "I thought so."

"Very well. Let's let him get some more water under his keel, though. I don't want to sink him in the channel. Tell Spanky he can ease off the juice. Make him think he's keeping the distance." Matt smiled ruefully. "By the way, Mr. Garrett, my apologies. I have the deck. Please take your post on the fire-control platform. If there's another one, we might have some fancy shooting to do."

"Aye, aye, sir. Captain has the deck," he announced. After he was gone, Matt shook his head. *Got excited*, he chided himself. *Not too good for the image of the stoic, all-knowing captain.*

"What about me, sir?" asked Dowden. "You want me aft?"

"Not yet. This'll probably be as close to shooting fish in a barrel as we'll ever get. But I may have a chore for you. Helm," he said to Tolson, "keep us dead astern of the enemy, if you please. Adjust speed as needed."

"Dead astern and as needed, aye."

The Grik ship was leaning on her wide beam, the pyramid of white canvas contrasting sharply with the dark red hull and the blue, white-capped waves. A long, foaming trail spread astern. "You can say what you like about those damn lizards," he said, "but they make pretty ships."

The mouth of the bay widened. Beyond the Grik, the open ocean of the Makassar Strait looked vast and empty. A few high clouds moved with deliberation across the otherwise clear blue sky. A touch of gray brooded over Celebes, but the local visibility was near perfect. Where was the other ship?

"Lookout reports a sail beyond the headland, bearing two two five," proclaimed the talker. Matt shifted his glass, but saw nothing because of the dense jungle that grew right down to the shoreline off the starboard bow. The lookout had a better vantage point, and the high masts of the Grik allowed them to see and signal at an even greater distance.

"Well, two for sure," Matt said speculatively. "Question now is whether the one we're chasing will turn to join her consort or continue on, leading us away. It might tell us a lot about them."

"Will it make a difference?" Keje asked anxiously.

"It shouldn't, in the short term." Matt was silent for a moment. "Say you had two or three fast ships and had just found the home of the Grik. They pursue. There's no way you can win a fight, but it's vitally important that someone get away with the information. What would you do?"

Theoretical speculation wasn't always a Lemurian strong point, Matt had noticed, but now Keje stared at the stern of the Grik ship while his mind sorted possibilities.

"I'd flee in a direction different than my consorts and hope they might chase me or one of the others. Perhaps one might escape. Much like the original Leaving. If the herd splinters, the hunters cannot get them all."

Matt nodded. "Or the hunters might get them all one at a time. But what else might you try? If it looked like none would escape?"

"I might fight them, to delay them. Or ask one of the others to do so."

"Yeah." He paced to the helmsman and glanced at the compass pelorus in front of the wheel. Then he returned and looked at the sky, gauging the wind again. The Grik ship was in the strait. They also saw the other enemy ship, crowding more sail and hugging the coastline, sailing south-southwest. If the closer ship intended to follow, now was the time to turn. "The question is," Matt continued, "would you have ever thought the Grik might do such a thing?"

Keje was flabbergasted by the thought. He found it difficult enough to believe they were running away at all. The idea of any strategic or self-sacrificing thought entering a Grik head was so foreign and horrifying that it left him momentarily speechless. And yet he'd been watching the wind. Unlike the destroyerman, who relied so much on his engines, Keje was always conscious of the wind. He didn't need a compass to tell him the Grik should have already turned.

"If they think information about Baalkpan is more important than their lives, it would imply a more sophisticated enemy than the 'rear up and run at 'em' sort we thought we faced." Matt was watching the lizard ship as he spoke, and then he suddenly peered through the binoculars again. "Damn," he muttered as sails shivered and the enemy's hull changed aspect. "I sure hoped I was wrong. They can't get away, but they're not changing course to follow their friend—a heading that would give them more speed, by the way. Anyway"—he looked at Keje—"they want to fight. To 'delay' us." He shook his head. "Not happy about that at all." To the talker: "Have Mr. Garrett commence firing. Helm? Let's go after the other one. We don't have the fuel to screw around."

The salvo buzzer screeched. While *Walker* described a leisurely turn to starboard, three rounds from the number two gun left the large, once beautiful ship a shattered, smoking wreck, sinking in their wake. A four-inch projectile isn't very large in the grand scheme of naval riflery, but high-explosive against a wooden hull is no contest. Two rounds should have been enough, but Silva was pointer and his crewmates had noticed he wasn't quite himself. Good-natured ribbing followed his first inexplicable miss, but the 'Cats on board were suitably impressed by the effect of the second and third shells. Now *Walker* loped after the other red ship . . . and Silva glared at Chack. A moment later he grinned.

Keje stood beside Matt, sitting in his sacred chair on the starboard side of the pilothouse. Far ahead, but slowly growing, was their next quarry. Matt was impressed by its speed. There was a fine breeze and it must have been making close to thirteen knots. A short while before, they'd passed half-submerged casks and other objects and it was clear the Grik were lightening ship. He gauged the distance.

"Keje," he said, "I'd like to take that ship. They came snooping around to find out about us, and I want to return the favor. There's just too much about them we don't know, like where they come from, what they're doing and what they want. Do they really have a dozen ships in the Java Sea?

More? I'm *sick* of never knowing what my people have to face!" He paused. "After we take out her masts, I'll have the machine guns and rifles kill as many as they can. Then we'll board. My question to you is do you think we can do it with a minimal . . . loss of life? My guess is they'll mass in the open, to receive us, and we'll be able to whittle them down considerably. But I have to rely on your people to do the bulk of the fighting. I can't spare many men for the boarding party and still operate the ship. Besides"—he gestured at the scota at Keje's side—"few of us are skilled in this type of fighting. Most who are were at the parade ground when we left." He took a deep breath and saw the gleam of anticipation in Keje's eyes. No one had boarded a Grik ship! The glory for *Salissa* would be beyond compare. The deed would be recorded in the very Scrolls!

Matt held up a hand. "I said I'd *like* to take it. One thing I've got to check first." He got up, stepped to the aft bulkhead, and activated the engine room comm. "Engineering, this is the captain. Let me speak to Mr. Mc-Farlane."

"Aye, aye, sir." A moment later the engineer's gruff voice said, "Mc-Farlane here."

"Fuel, Spanky."

There was a momentary pause, then a sigh. "Captain, if we reduce speed, secure number three and turn back right now, we *might* make it in without a tow."

"What about the wood?"

There was silence on the other end.

"We can burn the wood, Spanky."

Lieutenant McFarlane responded resignedly. "Aye, sir, we can burn the wood, but then the boiler'll be down for however long it takes to clean out all the ash, and I can't answer for whether or not it'll screw anything up." His voice was almost pleading. "Captain, by some miracle we've managed to keep three boilers operational. But there're no major repair parts in the entire frigging *world*."

Matt's shoulders slumped and he nodded at the intercom as if Spanky was standing before him. "Very well. Prepare to secure number three." He turned to the expectant faces in the pilothouse, then glanced out the windows at the Grik ship little more than a mile ahead. "Damn." He saw disappointment on Keje's face, in spite of the feline lack of expression. "We'll get another chance. It's time we learned something about your 'Ancient Enemy.' We must!" He strode back to his chair and looked at the ship ahead.

"Sink it."

It was dusk when they crept back into the bay. The fuel bunkers were entirely empty and the steam pressure had dropped to the point that maneuvering alongside the dock was out of the question. They dropped anchor close to where they had when they first arrived, and Matt wearily rubbed his eyes. None of the locals came out to see what was happening in the strait in case they needed assistance, and he'd been afraid they'd have to burn the wood anyway. The PBY was floating in its usual spot by the pier and he wondered how much longer it would have been before Lieutenant Mallory squandered some of the precious fuel they'd topped it off with to come and look for them. He saw several figures standing on the wing in the gloom, staring at them even now.

"We'll start ferrying Keje's people ashore immediately," he said. "We'll warp the ship over in the morning."

"Do not be discouraged!" Keje admonished him. He'd gotten over his own disappointment and was now almost giddy with their easy success. "You've won a great victory, and for my own sake, I'm glad *Salissa* was with you!"

"He's right," said Sandra. She'd been with them on the bridge ever since it became clear that there'd be no battle casualties. She gestured at the city, the lights even now beginning to burn. The dock was again lined with a chaotic throng, only this time instead of panic there was jubilation. "Those people saw their enemy for the first time today, many of them, and now they know that enemy isn't invincible. It'll mean a lot."

"It would have meant more if we could've gotten some information, and we still don't know about that third ship." In the last moments before *Walker* destroyed it, the Grik hoisted the same signal the first one had. Nothing was seen by the lookout, so even if there had been another Grik nearby, it probably wasn't close enough to see the flags. Still . . .

"As you told me earlier," Keje reminded Matt, "there will be another time."

Matt turned to Bernie Sandison. "You have the watch. I'll escort Captain Keje ashore, or to his ship, if he pleases." He shifted his gaze to Sandra. "Would you care to accompany us, Lieutenant?"

Sandra smiled. "Of course, Captain. Just let me change." She took a step away from him and held her arms out. She was still dressed in the surgical smock she'd put on when the ship went to quarters.

"I don't think—" he began, but Keje put his clawed hand on his shoulder.

"Yes, she should. And so should you, my friend." Keje looked at him appraisingly. "Wear your fine sword and your finest hat. You . . ." He grinned. "*We* have just won a great victory! We must look the part!"

Isak Reuben and Gilbert Yager sat on the huge wooden cleat the Catalina was tied to and smoked. They were indifferent to the bustle as well as the repeated calls by Lieutenant Mallory out on the plane to put out their cigarettes. Occasionally, a reveling Lemurian coughed in surprise as it passed through the blue cloud surrounding them. The Mice paid no heed. Finally, Mallory squatted near the wingtip of the flying boat, almost at eye level and just a few yards away. He decided to try reason.

"Look, fellas," he said, almost shouting over the throng, "if you don't give a damn about yourselves, think of the plane. Nobody smokes around airplanes!"

Another boatload of *Big Sal*'s warriors arrived on the dock to be received with cheering calls and stamping feet. Isak took another puff and looked at him. "Don't care about your damn plane, Army Man," he said. "All it did was sit there and . . . float, while our *home* was out there by itself!"

"Typical," snorted Gilbert.

Mallory was in no mood to be harsh with the men—especially now. He did wonder where they'd gotten all the smokes, though. For the last hour, all they'd done was sit there and chain-smoke the damn things. Must've been Alden. The big Marine always had cigarettes. Some said when he came aboard in Surabaya, his duffel was stuffed with them. He must have loaded them down. And no wonder. Both the men were covered from head to foot with thick, sticky crude. It was matted in their hair and saturated their clothes. All that showed through the slimy black ooze was the whites of their eyes and, of course, the cherries on the ends of their cigarettes. He tried a different approach.

"But, fellas. This is a *Navy* plane!"

The next time the launch maneuvered to the pier it unloaded to a renewed crescendo of acclaim, which reached a furious peak when Matt, Sandra, and Keje climbed onto the dock. The triumphant crowd immediately mobbed them. Nobody really knew yet what had happened in the strait, but *Walker* was back and the enemy was gone. For now, that was enough. Sergeant Alden forced his way through the press and spoke briefly in the captain's ear. Matt stood at least a head taller than most of those around, and he looked about for a moment, his gaze finally settling on the Mice. Isak sucked down a last lungful of smoke.

"Crap. I bet he *makes* us put 'em out." Both men stood, leaving sticky blotches of tar on the cleat where they'd been. The captain was moving toward them. Finally, he stopped a few yards away, as if afraid to come any closer with his high-collar white uniform on. The contrast between them couldn't have been more profound. A strange, instinctual awareness blossomed in the back of Isak's mind, and his right hand moved upward in an unfamiliar, half-forgotten fashion, gluing his index finger to his forehead.

"We found oil, Skipper, if you please. Not an hour after you left this morning. Right where that Aussie said it'd be." He paused suddenly, at a loss. He didn't think he had ever spoken to an officer before he'd been spoken to. The smile that spread across the captain's face emboldened him, however. "Good thing you weren't there, sir. 'Specially dressed like that."

Gilbert nodded in solemn agreement. "Can we come home now?"

The din of celebration ashore had died down to some degree. Earl Lanier didn't know whether that meant the party was winding down or just moving farther away. He shrugged and wiped sweat from his eyebrows with his furry forearm. The small galley situated beneath the amidships gun platform was his private domain, but sometimes he wondered about the old saying that it was better to rule in hell than serve in heaven. Next to the boiler rooms, the galley was the hottest place on the ship. He might rule there, but he also served, and so as far as he was concerned, it was just hell without any perks at all. Groaning a little, because his stomach always made it inconvenient to stoop, he peered at the loaves baking in the big oven that traversed the aft bulkhead. They were ready. The smell of the bread made with what passed among the locals for flour was strange but not unpleasant, and the taste hinted of pumpkin. The crew complained, of course. Anything different was always the subject of complaint—which struck him as particularly ridiculous under the present circumstances. Lanier didn't care. As long as it made bread, of a sort, that filled the bellies of the men as they filed by, he was content. They'd have complained if it didn't taste weird. It was their duty to complain, he supposed, and it didn't bother him anymore. He knew they'd complain more if there wasn't anything to eat.

He opened the oven and removed the loaves and set them aside to cool. Then he went to his big copper cauldron and lifted the lid. A rush of wet steam flooded the galley and he grimaced. Inside the cauldron roiled a stew made from one of the local land creatures. He didn't know what it was, but it looked like a turkey with a tail. A short, stubby tail, to be sure, but a tail by any definition. It also didn't smell anything like a turkey. He plunged a ladle into the stew and stirred. Dark, unrecognizable chunks of meat pursued one another in the vortex. He raised the ladle to his lips, blew, and sampled the broth. His eyes went wide. "They won't complain about that," he muttered. "They won't even say a word. They'll just hang me."

He wiped his greasy hands on his apron and opened the spice cupboard. Not much left, he lamented. Plenty of salt, some curry, but almost no black pepper. Better save that, he judged. He pulled out a large tray heaped with little dried peppers he'd acquired in Java before the Squall and looked at them speculatively. He'd never tried one, but Juan said they were hot as hell. He picked one out and sniffed. Nothing. He touched it with the tip of his tongue. There was a little tingling sensation, but that was all. He grunted.

"What the hell?"

He grabbed a double handful of the peppers and pitched them in the stew. "Sure can't make it worse," he said to himself. He also shoveled in another cup of salt. "Fellas need salt," he muttered piously. "They sweat it out fast enough."

He stirred the cauldron's contents and replaced the lid with a metallic *clunk*. Then he wiped his hands on his apron again and checked the heat. Satisfied, he stepped to the other side of the galley and retrieved his fishing pole. It was a relatively short, stout rod made of a shoot from the curious Baalkpan bamboo. The line was rolled around it with about two feet of woven wire for a leader at the end. The hook was stuck in the handle. He took a stringy piece of the "turkey" innards and impaled it on the hook. The mess attendant, Ray Mertz, slept in a chair near the hatch. He was leaning against the bulkhead with the front legs off the deck. Lanier was tempted to knock the others out from under him, but settled for kicking his foot. The younger man nearly fell anyway when his eyes fluttered open.

"Watch the fires," said Earl. "Time to get *my* breakfast." Ignoring tradition, he whistled "The Krawdad Song" happily but quietly off-key as he strode from under the gun platform. "Bad enough I have to cook the shit," he told himself. "They can't expect me to eat it." Eat it he rarely did. He, almost alone among the crew, liked the silvery flasher-fish. Fried, mostly. The men were just squeamish, he decided. Sure, they'd eat anything that went over the side, from people to turds, but a catfish would too. Fried fish was his favorite food in the world and had been since he was a kid, near Pinedale, Wyoming. There the trout could be had with little effort, and they fulfilled their purpose in life only when they simmered in his skillet.

He stepped to the rail on the starboard side, next to the number one torpedo mount. Not far away, the lights of the city cast their ceaselessly shifting reflection on the small waves around the darkened ship. It was almost eerily quiet. The boilers were cold, and for the first time he could remember, the blowers were silent as well. The only sounds besides water lapping against *Walker's* plates were the snores. Most of the crew was ashore on liberty, celebrating the victory, and there was still an hour or more before the first wave of drunken revelers returned to the ship. Many who hadn't been so fortunate, or who simply decided to forgo the festivities—including some Lemurian "cadets"—were scattered about, sleeping on deck, away from the stifling confines of the berthing spaces. But they were exhausted, and Lanier's quiet whistling disturbed no one. He rotated the pole in his hand and the "turkey" innards began their slow descent to the water.

"Fishin'?" inquired a quiet voice from behind.

"No," Lanier sneered, "I'm rootin' up taters."

Tom Felts eased up beside him in the gloom. *The scrawny gunner's mate must have the watch*, Lanier thought.

"Did you hear them Mice found oil after all?" Felts asked.

The cook nodded. He felt genuine relief over that. "I wonder how long it'll be before we have any to burn?"

"Not too long, they say. Something about it being 'sweet,' or something. 'Cats already have storage tanks built. All they have to do is ship 'em over there and set 'em up. Few days, maybe." Felts sighed. "Sure hope so. I only thought I felt helpless before the fires went out."

Lanier nodded in the darkness. He cooked over charcoal, but with the lights out, it was hard to see in the galley. All he had were a couple of little lamps fired by the stinky oil of those big fish the 'cats hunted.

"Yup," he said, wishing Felts would go away. Suddenly, his pole jerked downward. There was no need to set the hook. Whatever had it, *had* it. He held on tight as the line whipped back and forth and the end of the pole jerked erratically. He didn't have a reel, so all he could do was keep tension while the fish tired and when it was spent, he'd drag it aboard. With the leader in the fish's jaws, the braided line would hold as long as the fish wasn't much over forty or fifty pounds. He grunted under the strain as it tried to go deep, under the hull.

"Whatcha got?" Felts whispered excitedly.

Lanier risked a quick, incredulous glance. "A fish, you idiot."

"No, I mean what kind?"

"Christ, Felts," the cook rasped, still trying to control his voice, "I don't know what *kind* any I've already caught are! It might be another one of them or it might not. Lay off!"

The fight went on a while longer, Lanier puffing with exertion and the gunner's mate peering expectantly over the side.

"I think he's runnin' out of steam," offered Felts encouragingly.

Lanier jerked a nod and blew sweat off his upper lip. He glanced behind to make sure the coast was clear. He didn't want to trample anybody. "Here we go," he wheezed. He turned and grasped the pole more firmly with his hands and under his arm and lumbered to port.

"Hey!" Felts exclaimed as something thrashed at the surface of the water and thumped and thudded up the side of the ship. Right next to him, less than a yard from his feet, some . . . *thing* right out of Felts's most fevered nightmare squirmed out of the darkness and onto the deck. It was six feet long, with the body of a flat snake except for a feathery "fin" that ran its length, top and bottom. Very much like an eel—except for the head. Its head looked sort of like a normal fish, but its eyes were huge and dark and full of malice and its mouth was stuffed with what seemed like hundreds of ridiculously long, needle-sharp teeth, flashing in jaws that opened impossibly wide. The lights from shore showed a rainbow color that shimmered as it flailed in spastic rage, snapping at the line, the deck . . . and Felts as it slithered past.

"Goddamn!" he squeaked and jerked back against the rail. Fumbling at his side for the pistol strapped there, he pulled it out, thumbing the safety off. An earsplitting roar shattered the night as he fired at the thing, again and again. Bullets spanged off the deck plates and whined over the water. Pieces of fish and flakes of paint rained down on the men who'd been sleeping nearby. The automatic's slide locked back, empty, and still Felts pointed it at the fish, jerking the trigger in convulsive panic.

Lanier flung down his pole. "You stupid son of a bitch!" he shrieked. Heads were coming up slowly off the deck as men raised them with understandable caution, and voices called out to one another. The sound of shoes running on steel approached and Chief Campeti arrived with a battle lantern in one hand and a pistol in the other. The Bosun wasn't far behind, dressed only in T-shirt and skivvies.

"What the hell's goin' on here?" Campeti bellowed. "Who fired a weapon?" He shined the lantern around. Eyes, human and Lemurian, squinted in the glare. Finally the beam fell on Felts's terrified face and the smoking pistol, still outstretched. Campeti redirected the light and involuntarily stepped back. Gray saw the fish too. It was shot to pieces, but its terrible jaws still snapped spasmodically. A hook gleamed brightly, piercing the lower lip, and the line trailed to port.

"Who brought that thing on my deck?" Gray demanded.

"I did!" Lanier snarled, stepping up. "I work my ass off feeding these goons and I try to catch a little fish for myself and what happens? One of 'em *destroys* it!" The cook had his filleting knife in his hand and Gray wondered if he meant to use it on Felts. Instead, he knelt beside the twitching fish as if by a dying loved one. The knife moved over the corpse in benediction. "Destroyed," he lamented. Quite a gathering of half-naked men and entirely naked Lemurians had assembled by now.

"Anybody hurt?" Campeti asked. There were murmured voices, but no replies.

"No eat!" came a voice from the group.

"What?"

"No eat!" One of the cadets edged forward and stared down at the fish. He looked up at Gray. "Bad fish. No eat. Make very . . . dead sick. Chops? Chopping? Chopper! Chopper fish not food. Eat . . . dead!"

Gray prodded Lanier with his foot. "You hear that? Felts just saved your worthless life."

Campeti shined his light at Felts, who'd finally lowered the gun. He was shaking. "You okay?"

Felts gulped. "Snakes, Chief. Ever since I was a kid. Then that thing came whoopin' up over the side . . ." He shook his head.

Campeti took the pistol from his hand and nodded. "Me too." He shook out one of his last cigarettes and handed it over, then lit it for him when the gunner's mate's hands shook too much to do it himself.

Lieutenant Garrett had arrived. He wasn't wearing any more than Gray, but he'd put on his hat. "What's up, Chief?" he asked, and Gray told him what had happened.

While he was talking, Lanier stood up. "I demand that man be put on report!" he growled. "Shooting a pistol while everyone's sleepin', hell, he could'a shot somebody! Not to mention wreckin' my fish! He's in your division, Mr. Garrett. What are you gonna do?"

Garrett sighed and looked at Felts. They'd had a tough day and nerves were raw enough. Discipline was essential, but looking at that fish, *he* probably would have shot at it. "Ahhh . . ."

"Yeah, and you're in *my* division, Lanier," said Alan Letts, stepping forward. He, like Campeti, was fully dressed, although he hadn't been on watch. "What am I going to do with you? Creeping around in the middle of the night, releasing dangerous, *poisonous* creatures to run loose on deck . . ." There were loud guffaws while Letts shook his head. "I hate to think what the captain would say about that." More laughter, and Lanier's chubby face blanched. Letts turned to Gray. "Bosun? Since the deck division seems most affected . . ." He paused until the laughter died down. "What with the damaged paintwork and the mess . . ." Even Felts was grinning now. "I suggest if Lieutenant Garrett agrees, you make the call."

Gray scratched his head and looked at Felts, whose grin immediately faded. Then he glared at Lanier, who wilted about as much as his abrasive personality allowed. When he spoke, his tone was very formal. "Mr. Lanier wouldn't knowingly allow anything more poisonous than the chow he feeds us aboard the ship"—hoots of glee—"so I hold him blameless so long as he cleans that nasty, slimy thing off my deck." His glare settled on Felts, who shriveled beneath its intensity. "On the other hand, I think the log should show Gunner's Mate Felts single-handedly defended the ship and her sleepin' crew from the sneak attack of a dangerous sea monster— provided I see him hard at work with a chippin' hammer and a can of paint first thing in the mornin', erasing all evidence of his heroic deed." He looked at Garrett. "Lieutenant?"

"If that suits you, Bosun, I guarantee he'll be here."

"Mr. Letts?"

"Fine by me. Chief Campeti has the deck, though."

Campeti shrugged. "Bravest thing I ever saw. Blood everywhere and every shot hit. Boy ought'a get a medal."

Gray called out to Lanier, shuffling away in disgust. "Let's see that thing over the side right now, Earl. I don't want to see it again on my plate."

As the drama ebbed and the snores resumed, Campeti stayed with Felts. He still had the duty, and he wanted to make sure he was all right.

"That was somethin'," Felts whispered. "Mr. Letts sure came through. I thought he was ashore. He's turnin' into a pretty good guy, for an officer."

"Yeah," Campeti muttered. "He was in a mighty good mood." Sonny Campeti was a man with many faults, and he was honest enough to know it. Spreading rumors wasn't one of them. Lieutenant Letts had stepped up to the plate beyond anyone's expectations. He'd gone from a comical, if popular, character to an essential member of the cadre that might get them through this alive. If the lipstick Campeti had seen smeared across his jaw in the light of the battle lantern was responsible for that, he wasn't going to make a peep. But damn!

Matt and Sandra remained at the celebration long enough to be polite, but the seep and other intoxicants flowed freely enough that they doubted their early departure was even noticed. It was the first time Matt had allowed the crew to really cut loose, and he was a little nervous about that. They'd been told to have a good time (they'd earned it), and there was much to celebrate. He just hoped they wouldn't celebrate too hard. They'd destroyed two Grik ships and they were beginning to hate the Grik almost as much as the Japanese. The Mice found oil right where Bradford said they would and the Australian's prestige soared. He was last seen sprawled, insensible, on a pillow with Nakja-Mur. The Mice had disappeared. Matt suspected they'd crept back aboard the ship, and he hated to tell them they were still needed at the well. Again he felt a thrill at the prospect of full bunkers. These long weeks he'd felt so helpless, unable to *do* anything, and he was haunted by the fact that, somewhere out there, was *Mahan*. With fuel, they might still save her. What haunted him more, however, was his battle with priorities, and his growing uncertainty over whether *Mahan* topped the list.

Intensely aware of each other's presence, Matt and Sandra strolled quietly and companionably in the direction of the pier. When they reached it, the dock was empty, but it hadn't been for long. A launch burbled slowly to the ship, filled with destroyermen in various states of animation. They were required to report aboard by 0100, and none were to remain ashore overnight. Dowden had gathered a few sober men and formed a "flying" shore patrol and was already sending those who'd become too rowdy back to the ship. He'd make sure they were all rounded up.

They stopped near the cleat where the Mice had been sitting, and Matt remembered to keep his distance. He still wore his sole surviving "dress" uniform. Some men in the launch began a song, and because of Sandra's presence, he cringed when he recognized it. The words carried over the water even above the boat's loud motor—it was plain the men were far more interested in volume than quality. The loudest voice sounded suspiciously like Lieutenant McFarlane:

> The boys out in the trenches
> Have got a lot to say
> Of the hardships and the sorrows
> That come the soldier's way.
> But we destroyer sailors
> Would like their company
> On a couple of trips in our skinny ships
> When we put out to sea!

"Nice night," Matt said, lamely trying to distract Sandra from the chorus, but it was no use. It was the men's favorite part and they always belted it out.

> Oh, it's roll and toss
> And pound and pitch
> And creak and groan, you son of a bitch!
> Oh, boy, it's a hell of a life on a destroyer!

Matt glanced at Sandra, expecting to see her cover her mouth with her hand in shock or something, but instead she grinned.

> Oh, Holy Mike, you ought to see
> How it feels to roll through each degree.
> The goddamn ships were never meant for sea!
> You carry guns, torpedoes, and ash-cans in a bunch,
> But the only time you're sure to fire
> *Is when you shoot your lunch!*
> Your food it is the Navy bean,
> You hunt the slimy submarine.
> It's a son-of-a-bitch of a life on a destroy—*er!*

Sandra did cover her mouth now, giggling. The boat was nearing the ship. There was no moon and in spite of her new, lighter shade, they only vaguely made out *Walker*'s form in the darkness. She seemed forlorn out there with no lights, and moored away from the dock like an outcast. The song's last verse reached them with less vigor, as if the singers sensed the mood of loneliness as they came alongside. Or maybe now, after all they'd been through with the old four-stacker, they were less inclined to hurt her feelings. The last verse was more somber anyway.

> We've heard of muddy dug-outs,
> Of shell holes filled with slime,
> Of cootie hunts and other things
> That fill a soldier's time.
> But believe me, boys, that's nothing,
> To what it's like at sea,
> When the barometer drops
> And the clinometer hops
> And the wind blows dismally.

"They're fine men, Captain Reddy. Your crew," Sandra said softly.

"Yes, they are." He sighed. "And that makes it even harder."

"What? Using them up?"

He looked at her, surprised, but nodded. "Yeah, and that's what I'm doing. I've gotten them into a war I know nothing about." He shook his head. "Oh, don't worry, I'm not feeling sorry for myself. I know there wasn't a choice. We haven't had a choice since we went through the Squall. I'm not even complaining about that. However inconvenient it's made our lives, it saved us. It's just . . ." He couldn't tell her how he felt. Especially couldn't tell her about the doubts and nightmares and guilt he felt over *Mahan*. He'd made so many mistakes! And he definitely couldn't tell her how he felt about her. He changed the subject.

"You came out on the old *Langley*, right?" She nodded. The *Langley* was America's first real aircraft carrier. She'd been built on a merchant's hull and had a goofy flight deck erected above the superstructure, earning her the nickname *Covered Wagon*. By modern standards, she looked very strange and was too small and slow to be considered a real carrier anymore, even before the war. She'd been transporting P-40s to Java when Japanese planes hammered her. She was helpless under the assault, and it was the most terrified Sandra had ever been—up to that time.

"We'd been on sweeps off Bawean Island, looking for the Jap invasion fleet for Java when we heard about *Langley*," he said. "We were heading to Surabaya to refuel when Doorman turned us around." Matt's voice became a quiet monotone as he stared across the water at *Walker*'s silhouette. "The Japs *were* off Bawean. We'd just missed them. We took off so fast, *Pope* couldn't catch us." He grimaced. "Not that it made any difference. As soon as we cleared the mines, we came under air attack again and there was nothing we could do but take it. We had a total of eight fighters left, and the Dutch were saving them to use against the invasion as it landed." He snorted. "Eight planes weren't going to stop the invasion force, but they might've helped us find it, and kept the Jap planes off our backs." He was silent for several moments before he continued. Sandra waited patiently, quietly.

"The Jap screen for the invasion convoy wasn't much heavier than us, for once, but we had no air cover at all. The Japs corrected their fire with spotting planes throughout the battle. It was a hell of a thing to see, though. Cruisers aren't battleships, but even cruisers look damned impressive steaming parallel, blasting away at each other. Of course all we could do was watch." He took a deep, bitter breath. "*Exeter* got hit, and a few minutes later, *Kortenaer* took one of those big Jap torpedoes. She just blew up. *Edwards* was right on her tail and had to swerve. By the time we went past, she was upside down, folded in half. We didn't see anybody in the water.

"*Electra*, one of the Brit destroyers, made a torpedo attack alone, to distract the Japs from finishing *Exeter*. She was flying the biggest flag I ever saw . . ." Taking off his hat, he passed his hand over his head and stared at the lights on the water, remembering. "I guess every Jap ship in the line concentrated on her. All we saw was waterspouts, then steam and smoke . . . then nothing." He shook his head with sad amazement. "It was getting dark and I guess Doorman'd had enough. We charged in and launched torpedoes while the cruisers turned away, but nobody got a single hit."

He shrugged. "We did break the Jap formation, though, and Doorman got away. You got to give him credit for guts. As soon as we gave them the slip, Doorman went looking for the transports again. We didn't. We were out of torpedoes and nearly out of fuel, and our engines were finished after running thirty knots all through the fight. Binford ordered us back to Surabaya."

The launch's engine could be heard again as it shoved off to return to the dock and await another load.

"Doorman wasn't an idiot. I didn't like the way they put him in charge, but his biggest problem was he never knew what he was up against, never knew what he was facing or even where the enemy was. Now I know how he must've felt. We don't *know* what we're facing either, and like I said when we first helped *Big Sal* . . ." He stopped and looked at her. "Don't get me wrong, I'm glad we did! These people, Keje, Adar, Chack, even Nakja-Mur, they're good people. They've helped us and deserve our help in return. I just didn't feel right getting the men involved in a war we know nothing about. The Grik are bad news, maybe even worse than the Japs. They need to be defeated and, however it happened, we're here now, and we'll never be safe until they are. We've had it pretty easy so far, but there has to be more to the Grik than these little two- or three-ship task forces. Somehow, we've got to find out!"

"How?"

He grinned at her. "I don't know, but I'm working on it. Any ideas?"

Sandra smiled. She suddenly knew he would never have shown such vulnerability with anyone else on the ship. He wouldn't have spoken of any of this. What did that mean? "What happened to Doorman?" she asked. Matt's grin vanished.

"He ran into the Japs again that night. *DeRuyter* and *Java* were sunk. *Exeter* and *Encounter* made it back to Surabaya—where you came on the stage. *Houston* and *Perth* got slaughtered trying to make it through the Sunda Strait."

"All because they didn't know what they were up against." She looked speculatively at the PBY floating nearby. "But now we have air cover and the enemy doesn't."

He followed her gaze. "Well, yeah, but unless we can make more fuel for it, it won't be much help. That's not out of the question, and we're going to try. Mallory says it'll burn gasoline, which we should be able to do, but it needs high-octane stuff. I don't know squat about that, but Bradford does and as soon as we have a decent reserve for the ship, he's going to try to sort it out." He shrugged and looked at the Catalina like one might a worn-out horse, wondering if it had the stamina for a few more miles or not. "Of course, parts to keep it in the air are even more impossible than the things we need for the ship."

"How much fuel does it have?" Sandra asked. "Enough to look for *Mahan*?"

When Matt answered, his voice was without inflection. It was a habit she'd noticed he used when he'd agonized over a decision and come to one he didn't like. "Maybe. But fuel's not really the issue. We tanked her up, and we have enough in drums on the ship to fill her again. But even if we had all the fuel in the world, I can't send anyone up in that thing unless *Walker*'s close behind. Not unless I have to. Riggs thinks he can fix its radio, and that might make a difference. Until then, I won't chance stranding somebody. It might also be different if we had some idea where *Mahan* is, but we don't. 'West of Sumatra' a few weeks ago is too damn vague to risk men's lives. For all we know, she's sunk . . . or the Grik have her already." He sighed. "My conscience tells me to chase her as soon as we have the fuel; she's my responsibility. But *Walker*'s my responsibility too, and I won't risk her on another wild-goose chase until we know the other team's lineup. *Mahan* and our friends'll have to wait—they'd understand."

"Do Mr. Mallory and Mr. Brister understand?" she asked. "I know they're pretty hot to look."

He set his jaw. "It doesn't matter if they understand. It's my responsibility."

"It does matter. They feel like they left them too. I think you should talk to them. Explain." She hesitated, and bit her lip before she spoke again. "Weren't you just criticizing the Dutch for being too timid with their planes?"

Matt smiled, acknowledging the hit, but shook his head. "It's not the same. That plane is precious, beat up as it is. But I *will* risk it if I have to, and I'm pretty sure I will. But only in coordination with the ship. If I learned anything from Admiral Doorman—or the whole experience of the Asiatic Fleet—it was to never ride a tricycle in front of a steamroller with your eyes closed. Are the Grik a steamroller?" He shrugged. "The 'cats make 'em sound scary enough—and they are scary—but if all they have in the Java Sea is a dozen ships—" He grinned. "Ten now—maybe they're the tricycle and we don't have anything to worry about." He held his fingers apart. "We were *that* close to maybe finding out today. Just a few gallons of fuel might have set our minds at ease. Now . . ." He paused. "Unlike Admiral Doorman, I don't intend to chase shadows or hang ourselves out in the breeze until—" He stopped, and a strange expression crossed his face. "Until they come to us . . ." He grinned. "Or maybe I will!"

"What?"

"Just an idea. I'll tell you later." He gestured at the arriving launch, and one of the men clambered onto the dock. He seemed surprised to see the captain. "Are you ready to go back to the ship, Skipper?"

Matt glanced at Sandra. She shook her head.

"Not just yet."

Another man climbed from the boat, cursing. It was Tony Scott, trying to get farther from the water—at least until the next load forced him to cross it again. The two destroyermen stayed discreetly out of earshot.

"You're not using them up," Sandra said in a quiet voice. "The men, I mean. The world—this world, the one we left—it doesn't matter. The world uses them up despite anything you do. If you're not careful, you *can* use yourself up. You love your men. They know it and so do I." She looked up at him and, for a moment, he saw the lights of the city shining in her eyes. "And we all love you for it. That and other things." He swallowed, trying to remain impassive. What did she mean by that?

"We love you because we know you'll do whatever you can to keep us safe. But we also know we're at war. No matter what else has changed, that hasn't, and sometimes you have to risk the thing you love to keep it safe." She nodded toward the ship. "They know that, and they know because you're the man you are, you'll risk them if you have to." She sighed. "When we have fuel, we could just leave. We could go to the Philippines, or Australia. Maybe find fuel there. Eventually get to Hawaii, or even the West Coast. Maybe there aren't any Grik there. Maybe there's something just as bad, but what if there's not? We'd be 'safe,' but what then? We *need* friends if we're going to survive, and we've been lucky and made some. They happen to be in a fight for their lives. Besides being the best way to keep us safe, in the long run, helping them is the right thing to do. Your men understand that, Captain Reddy, and I bet if you put it to a vote, most would choose to stay. They know they might die. Life on a destroyer's dangerous work. They could have died 'back home' any day of the week, a thousand different ways, before the war even started. So the best way you can ensure that most won't die is to continue doing your job the best you know how. And when the time comes, fight your ship! Don't worry about what you can't control—just fight to win!" She grinned then, her small teeth flashing. "And quit feeling guilty for getting us into this mess! It was an accomplishment, not a failure!"

"I, ah, how . . . ?"

Her grin became a gentle smile. "I live only two doors down, 'doors' being thin green curtains, and you talk in your sleep."

He cleared his throat and looked in the direction of the sailors near the launch.

"No, not bad," she assured him. "But I know you blame yourself for everything from Marvaney's death to losing *Mahan*." Her smile faded. "That has to stop. If you don't start getting some *rest* while you sleep, you will start making mistakes."

He nodded at her. "I'll try. And thanks, Lieutenant."

She gave him a stern look. "You call the other officers by their first names in informal situations, why not me?"

"Well, because . . ."

"Because I'm a woman? I'm also your friend. At least I hope so. I think Keje even still thinks I'm your *wife*! Don't you think we could use first names, at least when no one's watching?"

Matt felt his cheeks burn, but nodded. He wondered how slippery a slope that would prove to be. "Okay . . . Sandra. But only when nobody's watching." His voice was quite serious as he spoke. "I'm sure you must know why."

Of course she knew why, and as she suspected, it was duty that kept him distant. Duty to his men. She felt a thrill to realize he really was interested in her, but also a deep sadness that the situation prevented them from acknowledging it. She forced a smile.

"Yes, Matthew. I understand."

Right then, the look on her face, the tone of her voice—he might have kissed her in spite of everything, to hell with the consequences. If Silva hadn't intervened. More precisely, if the growing calamity of the spectacle that Silva was generating hadn't done so.

A rampaging super lizard would have seemed sedate compared to his arrival. He was literally *wearing* half of Dowden's "flying" shore patrol. Even as they watched, one of Dowden's men—Fred Reynolds—went "flying" dangerously close to the edge of the pier. On second glance, he wouldn't have fallen, since he was chained to Silva's wrist.

"Lemme go!" he roared. "Where'd you take my girl? I'm in the mood for luuuve!"

"Oh, my God."

Not to be outdone by his predecessors, Dennis began singing as the men wrestled him closer to the captain: "I joined the Nay-vee to see the world! And what did I see? I saw the *sea*! I'm not . . . I won't? . . . I *don't* get seasick, but I'm awful sick of *seeeaa*!" He vomited on Reynolds, who was lying at his feet. "Archg! Sorry, boy . . ." He looked wildly around. "Where's my girl? My lady love! I ain't through dancin' yet!" He proceeded into an astonishingly graceful waltz—for a drunk with two men hanging on him and another chained to his arm. He stopped suddenly, as though surprised at himself, and hooted: "I'm a Grammaw!" Then he saw the captain. He came to swaying, exaggerated attention and saluted, dragging poor Reynolds to his feet. "Eav-nin', Skipper! *Lootenit* Tucker!"

"Mr. Silva." Matt nodded. "You seem . . . true to form."

"Aye, aye, sir! Cheap seep! Hell, it's free!" He belched loudly.

"Are you ready to return to the ship? Peacefully?"

Silva blinked, looking around. "Hell, no! These bastards has . . . adducted . . . obstructed . . . *swiped* me from my wife!"

"What? *What?* Mr. Dowden, what's the meaning of this?" Before Larry could even begin to explain, there came a shriek from the darkness.

"Si-vaa!" Two brindled shapes ran toward them, one ahead of the other. The first, obviously female, leaped on the gunner's mate and, combined with his other passengers, nearly knocked him down at last. Matt thought she was attacking him until she wrapped her arms around his neck and started licking his face.

"There's my darlin' angel!" he cooed.

The other brindled shape caught up and slammed to attention, but even in the dark, it was clear that Chack-Sab-At was quivering with rage.

"What the hell's going on here!" Matt bellowed. "Silva, what have you *done?*"

"Cap-i-taan!" said Chack, "that's my sister, Risa. She is unwell. That giant . . . creature has intoxicated her and . . ."

"He mate? He *marry* me!" Risa squealed happily. "He Sab-At clan now!"

"*Never!*" seethed Chack. Sandra's hand now covered her mouth in earnest, but Matt couldn't tell if she was hiding shock or laughter.

"My God, Silva, I swear! If you've done anything to damage our relationship with these people, or if you forced . . . God! Are you *insane?* I'll *hang* you!"

"Skipper, I'll swear on a Bible or Marvaney's record stack—whatever you say—"

"You *lie!*" shouted Chack.

"He no lie!" Risa purred. "Nobody mad but silly Chack. People no mad. People no . . . embarrassed? By mate! Si-vaa *love* Risa!"

The shore party, those that could, eased away. Chack's ears were back and his tail swished like a cobra. He looked about to strike. Matt was preparing another volcanic response when Sandra tugged his sleeve and whispered in his ear. He looked sharply at her and was incredulous when he saw her nod.

"We'll get to the bottom of this," he promised darkly. "Mr. Chack, please escort your sister to her Home. At the very least, she seems . . . indisposed."

"But . . . Aye, aye, Cap-i-taan."

"What about my weddin' night?" Silva moaned, and Matt turned to him.

"My orders were that all personnel be back aboard by 0100. Since you had no special permission, you may not stay ashore to . . . consummate your 'marriage,' nor may you do so on my ship! USS *Walker* is not a honeymoon barge!" He paused. There was one way to find out if Sandra was right. "Tomorrow I'll speak to Keje and Nakja-Mur and discover what further process, if any, is required to finalize your and Risa's . . . nuptials. Perhaps a joint ceremony?"

He was rewarded by a marked widening of Silva's surprisingly sober eyes. Getting even with Chack was one thing, but he wouldn't enjoy the consequences of including his captain in the joke.

"Nighty night, sugar-lips!" Silva said, and gave Risa a kiss, which she returned with evident relish.

God, I hope it is a joke! Matt thought with a shudder.

After Chack stiffly led his sister away and a suddenly docile Silva was carried to the ship, Matt removed his hat and rubbed his eyes. "Jesus!"

Sandra laughed. "Is this the way it always was with these guys, back in the Philippines?"

"No! Well, yeah, but . . . yeah." He smiled.

"I told Chack to watch his back." Sandra chuckled. "I wonder when he'll figure it out?"

"I wonder if it's over!"

"You don't think he really . . . ?" Sandra gasped.

"If we're not surrounded by angry 'cats with torches in the morning, I'm going to pretend it never happened. But I guarantee Silva won't have the last laugh!" For a moment, the pier was empty again, but the electric tension between them was damped. Just as well.

Sandra cleared her throat. "Earlier, you said you had an idea. What was it?"

"What? Oh. Well, let me see if I can put my thoughts back together!"

What, then, would you have us do? How do we defeat them if the Ancient Ones could not?" The speaker was the High Chief of one of the great Homes. Seven of the huge vessels now floated in Baalkpan Bay, and all their chiefs, as well as a large number of senior "officers," were present in Nakja-Mur's Great Hall for this long-awaited council. There were even representatives from several smaller "land colonies." Gatherings on such a scale were rare, usually happening no more than once or twice a decade, and there was no official mechanism for summoning one. As far as Matt could tell, it might be as simple as shouted words from passing fishermen: "Big meeting at Baalkpan. Come if you want." Without better communications, that was probably exactly how it happened.

Great Gatherings were usually occasions for festivities, games, trade, and socialization. They were also times for crowded, prosperous Homes to branch off. To build new Homes and form new clans. It was a time that the People on their solitary wandering Homes looked forward to with pleasure and anticipation, wondering where and when the next would be held. But this one was different. All were aware of the seriousness of the growing threat, and those present, at least, seemed willing and even eager to discuss their next move. Few agreed what that move should be, however.

The Lemurian who'd spoken was Anai-Sa, High Chief of *Fristar*, one of the Homes that had been in Baalkpan Bay since before *Walker* arrived. He seemed young for his rank, with a jet-black pelt and a spray of white whiskers surrounding his face. His green eyes were intent. Besides his heavily embroidered kilt, he wore only a multitude of shimmering golden hoops around his neck and upper arms. His people were "far rangers" who rarely entered these waters. Their "territory" was most often the South China Sea, but Grik pressure had pushed them south. He was also the most outspoken of the "why don't we just sail off where there are no Grik" crowd.

Keje spoke in reply. "I would have you hear the words of Cap-i-taan Reddy of the Amer-i-caans, and High Chief of *Waa-kur*. He is High Chief of an independent clan and has as much right to speak as anyone here. More, to my thinking, since he saved my Home from the Grik. The Amer-i-caans have helped us prepare for this time with no concern for personal gain." Keje stood before the silent group, looking out among them. He said nothing about *Walker*'s brief sortie two weeks before that destroyed two more Grik ships. All were aware of it, even if they hadn't been there yet, and boasting sometimes detracts from self-evident truth. Besides, the last thing Matt wanted was everyone thinking *Walker* would save them all. As Keje suspected, there were murmurs of protest. Not because the humans weren't People, but because their ship was so small and sparsely populated. Would they grant "Home" status to fishing boats too?

Keje squared his shoulders and placed his hand upon the scota at his side. "I declare Cap-i-taan Reddy is my Brother as surely as any High Chief, and I offer combat to anyone saying he does not deserve to speak." These last words came in a growl.

There was some very unusual body language in response to this threat, and some glanced to see Nakja-Mur's reaction. He merely stared at Keje's back across steepled claws with his elbows on his knees.

"These Amer-i-caans come from far away, and know more about war than we. Before they came to help us, they were engaged in a struggle that defies belief. Their wondrous ship was just one of perhaps hundreds, and they modestly tell me theirs was but the smallest and least powerful Home to fight in that unimaginable conflict! Yet it prevailed!"

Matt winced at Chack's translation. Okay, so much for not bragging. Besides, they'd "prevailed" in the sense that they'd survived, but that was the only appropriate context for the word. Keje grinned at him ironically.

"Would you speak to them, my Brother? Perhaps you can sway them. I'll tell them your words."

Matt nodded. For his plan to work, they had to see the threat. But they also needed hope. How would he scare them into joining the fight without scaring them away? Particularly since the plan he was forming was risky, to say the least. The irony of the situation struck him like a slap. He remembered how unfathomable he'd thought admirals and politicians were. Particularly within ABDA. Why they made the decisions they did mattered only insofar as they affected his ship, his crew, and himself. Suddenly he was standing in similar shoes and found them most uncomfortable. He stepped to Keje's side and cleared his throat.

"I really don't know if *we* can defeat them," he said simply. Keje looked at him sharply, surprised by the dour opening, but Matt had stressed the word "we."

"I don't *know* much about them at all. Nobody does; not even where they come from, or what kind of society supports their warlike nature. We're probably outnumbered. Their ships aren't as large as yours, but they're much faster, and each carries nearly as many warriors as yours since their ships aren't Homes. They carry no families that we know of, and they grow no food. They're meant for one thing only: to transport warriors to battle." He paused. "That should be both an advantage and a disadvantage to them. They can pack a lot of warriors into their ships, but they have to keep supplied or they can't stay in our territory long. One thing we *do* know is they're a long way from home." He shrugged. "They raid for provisions—Chill-chaap proves that—but even that takes time from offensive operations, and the more there are, the bigger that problem becomes.

"That's about all we know about their strategic situation, though. We don't know what they want or why they're here, beyond an apparent hunger for conquest. We have no real idea what their 'grand strategy' is. Their efforts so far have not seemed well coordinated, although Keje tells me they're better now than in the past. The best I can figure, they have several independent task forces on the loose, looking for us, and they hope to eventually overwhelm us with numbers. That's also the historical model recorded in your Scrolls.

"We too have advantages and disadvantages." Matt looked at the faces staring impassively back.

"And what are our advantages, beside the ability to simply leave them behind again?" The black-furred Lemurian's voice dripped sarcasm.

Matt regarded him coldly. "Courage is one," he answered, returning the green-eyed glare. "Thoughtful courage, not the wild-ass, charge-tanks-with-horses kind." There was absolutely no context for the statement, but somehow they grasped his meaning. All present knew, at least by description, the abandon with which Grik fought. Their attack was like a school of flasher-fish. Maybe they employed tactics, but once they came to grips, it was individual mindless ferocity.

"We also have *Walker*," he said matter-of-factly, "and nothing they have can match her speed and the range of her weapons. We'll have more weapons soon. Cannons, sort of like *Walker*'s, that'll fit on your ships. But most of all—I hope—we're smarter than they are. Smart enough to use their strengths against them. And if their strengths become weaknesses . . ." He shrugged.

"Frankly, our biggest disadvantage is ignorance." There were hostile murmurs at that. The closest Lemurian word to "ignorance" was precariously similar to "stupidity." He continued hastily on. "That's a disadvantage I'm personally sick of . . . for a lot of reasons, and one I plan to correct. It's our biggest disadvantage because of how much bigger it makes our other problems." He counted on his fingers. "First, there might be five or ten of their ships in the Java Sea right now, but we don't *know*. We don't *know* if they're part of a probe or a real push. The Scrolls describe a slow escalation, but is it just starting, or has it reached its peak? We don't *know*. Our ignorance makes it impossible to formulate a strategy to totally defeat them." He motioned Benjamin Mallory forward. "Lieutenant, when you saw the aftermath at Tjilat—Chill-chaap, did you speculate on the nature of the Grik attack?"

"Yes, sir. It's hard to say, but I got the impression they made an amphibious assault, coordinated with an attack overland through the jungle."

"What makes you say that?"

"Well, it's just a guess. We didn't really study the battlefield, if you know what I mean, but the corpses in the jungle were in groups. Not really scattered around. Like the inhabitants were running away and ran into the Grik. Not like they were chased down and caught. It was just . . . the feeling I got."

Matt nodded. "That seems consistent—the multipronged attack. Like the tactic they used against *Big Sal*. Attack as many places as possible to split your defenses. That might even be an example of their overall strategy, writ small. If so, that shows us another one of our problems. We're way too scattered out. I know that's how you've always lived, but you've got to pull together. Believe me, we know about being all alone when the world is falling on us! The only way to defend against that sort of attack is to mass our forces. Keep them as united as possible and work together as best we can. But where do we mass? We can't do it everywhere—that defeats the purpose." He looked measuringly at Nakja-Mur. "We could mass at Baalkpan—fortify the city and build a wall around it, with fighting positions and maybe even cannons. We could clear the jungle around it and make a killing ground that even the Grik would fear. In fact, I think we should. But it'll take time, and that's a luxury we may not have. We don't know how much weight's behind them. It also surrenders all initiative to the enemy and sounds too much like what happened last time, if you ask me. Anyway, it all still boils down to: we just don't *know*!"

Nakja-Mur raised his bearded chin from his fingertips. "Could we defeat the Grik in such a manner?" he asked.

Matt hesitated. "No. We could prevent defeat for a time, but we couldn't win. While we sat behind our walls and fought them and killed them, and bled them white, we'd only grow weaker, while they would send more

Grik. Just as it's written in your Scrolls. Eventually, they'd wear us down. The only way to *win* is to attack!"

There were incredulous cries. "Attack them? Attack where? We do not even know where they come from!" shouted the black-furred High Chief. Others yelled questions and comments as well: "We could harry their ships, but will they fight if we bring a large enough force to defeat them?" cried one. "We certainly can't catch them if they run!" "What will happen to Baalkpan if we leave it undefended?!" another asked. "He was talking about mass. Mass where?" "What's 'mass'?"

Matt listened to the uproar for a few moments longer. Finally, he spoke loudly a single word.

"*Ignorance!*"

Keje repeated it in the same tone. The tumult abruptly stopped and all eyes turned to the captain of *Walker*.

"Ignorance," he said again. "I'm getting pretty tired of it myself. Let's see if we can enlighten ourselves."

Even Keje blinked surprise. "How do we do that, my Brother?"

"We mass."

Keje was confused. "But you just said . . . they are spread out, they are faster—we can't mass here and wait for them all to find us, and we certainly cannot mass together and chase them down!"

"No, but we can mass defensively and let a few come to us. I don't want *all* of them until we know how many they are. And we won't do it here."

"I thought you said we should attack," said Nakja-Mur.

"Think of it as a 'defensive' attack. It won't be easy and it sure as hell won't be safe, but if it works, we ought to learn a lot about our enemy at long last."

"My people will have nothing to do with such madness!" huffed *Fristar*'s High Chief.

Nakja-Mur stood, a little shakily, Matt thought. "You may leave whenever you wish, then," he said. "My people don't have that choice." He looked at Matt. "My people . . . I . . . have never known war, but I will support this plan of yours whatever it might be. I do not want the Grik coming here." He smiled sadly. "You may have all the paint or whatever else you want if you can prevent that."

"Thank you, my lord," Matt replied, glancing around the hall. "But what we both need most right now are more warriors. 'Mass' means numbers."

Sergeant Pete Alden, United States Marine Corps, stared at the "mass" of trainees flailing at one another with clumsy enthusiasm and padded-point practice spears. Some were really trying, and the "Marines" did their best to instruct them. But to most of the newer recruits, it was still mostly a game.

He cursed. Before now, the training had gone relatively well with the smaller groups he'd been dealing with. He'd applied a familiar regimen even if the exercises were different from his own experience. The rush of recruits since the Grik ship sailed right into Baalkpan Bay changed all that.

His carefully chosen, elite Marines were broken up to form a cadre of NCOs as the militia (now "Guard") swelled dramatically. Even warriors from some of the ships started to attend the drills. That was all well and good, but Parris Island had never seen a less likely draft, and he (who'd never been a drill instructor) now faced the impossible task of turning this collection of instinctively individualistic merchants, shopkeepers, fishers, and sailors into an army. And he had just a few weeks to do it. Right now, if he reconstituted his Marines, he could field two regiments of fairly well-trained, disciplined troops—and that's what he'd likely do for the captain's upcoming expedition. If they were successful, he would resume the training after they returned as veteran NCOs. Not just bright trainees who'd grasped the theory but couldn't yet teach from experience.

The warriors who came to train were accustomed to working together, but otherwise they were a pain in the neck. As "warriors" already, they had their own way of doing things. They understood that discipline was required in order to fight together—which the land folk didn't—but the close-order drill and concerted complexity of the captain's new/ancient tactics were too much trouble. Alden was having some trouble with them himself. He was a grunt, a fighting Marine, and he fully understood the concept of mass. But in *his* Marine Corps, standing shoulder to shoulder and hacking at enemies close enough to smell their breath was crazy. He had no problem with a little hand-to-hand; he was even pretty good at it. Like many Marines, he was an artist with a bayonet—when it was attached to his holy Springfield. The dogma pounded into him as a recruit was one of accurate, long-distance riflery, backed by a bayonet and the will to use it. Standing toe to toe and hacking away was for last-ditch defense or final assault. Not for the whole damn fight.

There weren't enough Springfields, however. Hell, there were barely enough for *Walker*'s crew. Some of the better Lemurian NCOs had Krags, but his army would fight with swords and spears. For those to work, you had to be right in your enemy's face. Only shield walls and deep, disciplined ranks might give them an edge over the Grik. The captain said the shield wall and discipline set the Romans apart from the barbarians. Alden understood, but it still struck his subconscious mind as nuts. He'd have to get a feel for the new tactics too.

No Springfields, but they did have archers. In fact, every soldier was an archer of sorts. The front-rank spearmen carried longbows over their shoulders to use until the enemy came to grips—which wouldn't take long on land, considering the close confines and thick vegetation hereabouts. The problem was it took a long time to get really good with a longbow. He'd just as soon have everyone stick with the crossbows they were used to, even if they weren't as fast and didn't shoot as far. It didn't take an expert to use one of those. But his front rank couldn't wield a sword or spear while swinging a heavy crossbow, so if he wanted standoff capability, longbows it had to be. Crossbows could still be employed by females or anyone too small or weak for the shield wall. Lemurian females weren't necessarily weak, but they had the same . . . encumbrances that sometimes made longbows difficult for their human counterparts. Many of Alden's best spearmen were poor archers, but he made them practice every day. Most were improving.

Right now, all were practicing their melee skills, learning to fight one-on-one in case the wall should ever break. That was also the type of fighting they expected for the upcoming operation. It was a fiasco. The parade ground looked like someone had kicked an anthill. A steady trickle of injured recruits walked or limped over to sit in the shade and be treated at Karen Theimer's "aid station." Some were really hurt, but most were goofing off.

Chack, Risa, and Lieutenant Shinya trotted up to join him. Risa was the training liaison for *Big Sal*, so she had a reason to be there, but Chack hadn't let her out of his sight since the "incident" on the pier. Alden couldn't believe she'd helped Silva with the scam. If it *was* a scam. Making Silva chew the leaves and get the screamers was a hoot, but the big gunner's mate's idea of "getting even" was . . . disproportionate. Chack needed a crash course in American joke rules. The question was, did Silva's jokes *have* rules? Were they "even"? Pete doubted it. He shook out one of the cigarettes he always seemed to have and lit up.

"God help us," he muttered when they were close enough to hear.

"They have learned to march fairly well," Shinya said to console him. "And form a wall. But if it ever comes to that"—he waved at the chaos—"we'll be destroyed."

Alden smirked, but nodded. It didn't help that they'd suddenly been told to train for a different type of battle. Until now, defense had been the priority. He turned his back to the practicing troops and took a small green book from his tunic. It was an old copy of *The Ship and Gun Drills, U.S. Navy,* from 1914. He'd found it in Doc Stevens's library while rooting for something to read. It was probably on the ship when she was commissioned. Much was obsolete (even for *Walker*), but it had a rather extensive section on physical exercises, including bayonet and sword drill. The pages were illustrated, too. The bayonet drill translated easily to a short spear, but there was, of course, no mention how to combine the sword work with a shield. It didn't really matter. The activities on the parade ground were not even slightly similar to the pictures in the book.

Shinya studied the pages over his shoulder as Alden held the book so he could see. For a moment he reflected how strange it was to be working with a Nip. Sometimes it seemed perfectly natural, but other times his skin practically crawled. A lot had happened in the last few months, but nothing could erase Pearl Harbor or Cavite or the Philippines or the Java Sea. But Shinya hadn't bombed Pearl Harbor and he couldn't help being a Jap. And every now and then, God help him, Pete Alden caught himself almost liking him. Not many felt the same. Bernie did, and maybe Garrett. The captain respected him, Pete thought. But the Chief still hated his guts. Gray was a good guy, steady as a rock, but something about Shinya gave him the heebie-jeebies. Alden wondered what it was.

"Damn," he said, and slapped the book shut. He handed it to Shinya. "Can you make heads or tails out of that sword shit in there?" he asked.

Shinya nodded. "I believe so. It seems straightforward. Believe it or not," he said, grinning, "I actually fenced in college."

Pete harrumphed and rolled his eyes. "Just don't teach 'em any of that Samurai bullshit. We want 'em to stay behind their shields, not run around flailing their swords in all directions. All that'll do is confuse 'em."

Shinya chuckled. "I'm a better fencer than I ever was a practitioner of Master Musashi's teachings. I learned enough not to shame my father. He was very insistent. But I doubt he was proud of my skill." His smile faded, and he looked at Alden, expressionless. "You see, the Way is very spiritual," he explained. "Regrettably, I am not."

"Yeah, well. Mmm. Closest thing I ever came to, looked like a sword, is this," Alden said, grasping the long bayonet at his side, next to the .45 holster. "Unless you count my granddaddy's Civil War sword over the fireplace." Teeth flashed in his bearded face. "I'm not much for this swords and shields shit, but bayonets I can do. And I think it's time to stir things up."

He retrieved one of the six-foot, bronze-bladed spears. "You do the swords. Teach 'em ways to use 'em in the open—we'll need that too, and maybe first. But also behind shields when they've got 'em locked. Ask the captain. He seems to know about that. C'mon, Chack." He gestured for the Lemurian to follow. "I need your mouth."

"What are you going to do?" Shinya asked.

"Pick a fight." He motioned toward the middle of the field, where a group of warriors from one of the ships gathered, taunting the recruits. "I'm going to show those Navy cat-monkey types they ain't as tough as they think they are. No offense, Chack."

Chack blinked amused approval. He'd experienced Alden's "bayonet drills" himself. Together, they waded through the play-fighting troops, and Alden knocked some aside as they went. That got their attention, and some followed in his wake to see what he would do. Eventually they reached the knot of warriors, a group from *Fristar*. Alden was surprised to see them, since all their High Chief talked about was taking off. They hadn't done it yet, but it was plain that all these showed up for was trouble.

They'd formed a rough circle and were pushing and shoving any land folk who came within reach. They were enjoying their game immensely and seemed to think it was at least as effective as the training going on around them. One reached for Alden as he came close, but pulled back when he saw he'd nearly grabbed one of the "Amer-i-caan Wizards."

"Go ahead," Pete said, grinning pleasantly. "I'm a Grik. Kill me." Chack translated. The *Fristar*, a wing runner, looked aside at his fellows. One, easily the largest Lemurian Pete had seen, dipped his head. The shorter 'cat gave a high-pitched cry. He leaped at Alden with arms outstretched. The sergeant's spear blurred. With a yelping, breathless grunt, the wing runner was on his back, looking cross-eyed at the spearpoint inches from his face.

"You're dead," Alden said. "Next?"

Another troublemaker stepped forward at a nod from the "leader." This one had a few white hairs lacing his amber coat. His tail twitched back and forth. He accepted a real spear from a companion and assumed a more cautious stance.

An experienced warrior this time, Alden thought to himself. *Good.*

The 'cat held the spearpoint forward, left hand grasping near the blade. His right arm was fully extended behind him, holding the shaft like a harpoon. He crouched and took a step to his right. Lightning-fast, he lunged with the spear. Pete stepped inside the thrust, knocking it aside as he turned and drove the butt of his own spear into his opponent's midriff. Somehow the Lemurian's face showed surprise as he doubled over with a "woof!" Pete reversed the spear and made a classic thrust, ending just short of the chest. Then he turned and looked at the gathering crowd. The point he'd made was obvious. One down, one gasping for air, and Pete Alden wasn't even breathing hard.

Some of the land folk cheered in their curious high-pitched, chittering way, but Pete knew it was more who he'd bested than how he'd done it. That wasn't what he wanted to get across. "Chack, speak for me," he said. He walked in a circle, scowling. Gradually, the cheering faded and he started to speak. Before he could, the big *Fristar* Lemurian stepped forward. He was tall enough to look Alden in the eye. He wasn't as heavily built as the Marine, but Pete had to concede that he was probably stronger. Muscle rippled under the dark fur as he drove his spear into the ground in formal challenge. There was a sudden hush.

"Why do you humiliate the *Fristar* clan in front of these mud-treaders,

Tail-less One? You who is a person of the Great Sea?" Chack translated as he spoke. Pete took a step closer to him and returned his glare.

"If you're humiliated it's not because of anything I've done. Your pride makes you believe you're a better warrior than you are. Besides, among my people, I'm a mud-treader too. *Walker* has clans, just like you, and we're all ruled by our High Chief. For us, that's Captain Reddy. I obey him, but I'm chief of my own clan. The Marines." He turned and looked at the gathering sea of faces. All training stopped as more recruits pressed forward to hear, and maybe see a fight.

"Among my people, Marines are *the* warrior clan. All they do is fight. Sometimes they fight at sea and sometimes on land." He grinned. "Sometimes they even fight in the sky. To Marines it makes no difference. We fight the enemies of our people wherever they are." He paused, considering. "We've made alliance with your people and we've seen the Grik for what they are. Your enemy is now the enemy of my people. That makes 'em *my* enemy and I'll fight 'em because that's what I do. In the meantime, it's my duty to train you to be better fighters. To fight like Marines. That means fighting them anytime, anywhere, at sea or on land. That's what it'll take to defeat them.

"They aren't coming to steal your things, just to loot and plunder. If the history of your Scrolls is true, they're coming to *wipe you out*! *Walker*'s people are your allies, and that puts them in danger as well. So anything less than your very best makes you my personal enemy! Do I make myself clear?" He turned, snatched the spear out of the ground, and flung it down, accepting the challenge—the formal challenge—that meant blood could be spilled.

"There! We can fight if you want, and I promise you'll be dead so fast you won't even know how it happened." He looked at Chack. "Or you can fight him, if you're afraid of me, but he'll kill you just as fast. Because I taught him how!" He looked at the tall leader of the *Fristar* group. "So what'll it be? You want to die? Or do you want to learn how to *really* kill?"

The Lemurian returned his stare. Around them, all were silent, expectant . . . afraid. The formal challenge was rarely made, and when it was, there was almost always only one outcome. All were nervous about the political ramifications. *Fristar*, at least, would leave the fragile alliance that had been forged at the council. No one really expected the American to lose, and there was always bad blood after a formal challenge was met. The big Lemurian looked down at the spear. He put his foot beside it and, with a grunt, kicked it away, withdrawing the challenge. There was an audible sigh of relief.

"Then show me, Maa-reen. Show me how to kill."

After securing Risa's laughing promise not to fly to join her "mate," Chack left her at the parade ground to continue her studies and headed back to

Walker. His Home. He didn't really know when it had occurred, but at some point all the ambitions of his previous life were supplanted by what he'd become. He was no longer a wing runner on *Salissa* Home. He was a bosun's mate, in charge of the Lemurian deck division on USS *Walker,* duly sworn into the Navy of the United States, just as all the accepted "cadets" had been. He had only a vague idea what the United States were, but that made no difference. He'd become a warrior and now he was a destroyer-man. He loved *Salissa* and always would, but he'd changed clans just as surely as if he'd become fas chief of another Home like he once aspired to do. That was an ambition for who he'd been before. He giggled at the irony of his outrage over Silva joining *his* clan. Now he'd joined Silva's. That didn't mean he wanted him for a brother.

He was encouraged despite Sergeant Alden's gloom. Unwarlike as he once was, the people of Baalkpan were even worse. Yet at least they were trying. It took actual combat to crack his pacifist shell and his dispassionate evaluation of the land folk as warriors didn't escape his sense of irony either. He believed they would fight. Some weren't so sure, but if he could do it, they could too. A lot was riding on it. Most of the Homes in the bay had joined the alliance, but had not committed themselves to offensive operations. They'd taken a wait-and-see approach. The expedition they planned was basically a raid, a reconnaissance in force. The objective was information, primarily, but depending on what they learned, they were prepared to follow up with more attacks. Perhaps, if the Grik were as yet no more numerous than some evidence suggested, they might even defeat them—and fairly quickly. Captain Reddy hoped they could at least cleanse them from the Java Sea and establish a "Malay Barrier" behind which they could further prepare. It was a giddy thought. The captain projected cautious optimism, and Chack envied how he did that. He'd learned a lot about the fantastic war in the other world, and he knew that the mistakes and uncertainty that plagued the Amer-i-caans there now drove Captain Reddy to avoid the same issues here. If they did, they must succeed. Terrible as they were, the Grik couldn't be as formidable as the Japanese had been.

In this happy frame of mind, he ambled along, the Krag muzzle down on his shoulder, picking his way through the fishmongers and handcarts that packed the wharf near the pier. He glanced up and saw *Walker,* snugged to the dock, smoke curling from her aft funnel once more.

"Chack."

He turned, and his heart flipped in his chest. Before him stood Selass, her silken silver fur radiating sunlight. The armor she wore, much like her father's, flashed with pink red fire. As always, she was magnificent. She was armed with a scota and was headed for the parade ground herself.

He'd seen her there several times, training. Sometimes she sparred with Risa. Chack's ears lay flat and he bowed low.

"I greet you, Selass-Fris-Ar. You are well?"

"I am well . . ." She paused and blinked sadness. Chack nodded.

"You still mourn Saak-Fas. I understand. I hope the pain will pass with time."

Her eyelids flashed impatiently. "I do *not* mourn him! If I ever did, the sadness is gone. But . . . I have another sadness."

He blinked concerned query. Her eyes flashed and she almost growled with frustration.

"You will make me say it, then, I see! Has your revenge not run its course?"

"Revenge?"

"Yes, revenge! For leading you on, toying with you, and making you a fool! Don't you think I've suffered enough? Saak-Fas was the fool! Now he's gone . . . and I am glad. I was wrong about you. I thought you weak. But I also thought you loved me. I hoped you would still want me. Was I wrong about that too? I see you often, yet beyond casual greeting you have not spoken. Will you make me beg?" She blinked furiously. "Very well! I was wrong about Saak-Fas and I was wrong about you. I do want you now!"

Stunned, Chack could only stare. For so long, his fondest wish was to hear her say such words. Now, though they stirred him, they didn't bring him joy. They only brought confusion and a trace of sadness. He gently replied.

"You did not make a fool of me. I did that myself. I *was* a fool. I was what you thought I was. But I'm no more that person now than a graw-fish is still a graw-fish after it sheds its tail and gills and flies out of the sea. I admire you in many ways, Selass, and am flattered that you desire me. But I do not pine for you. I suppose I do still love you, but it does not consume me as before. I've had much else on my mind of late. Your admission and . . . declaration have come as a surprise. May I consider it? I assure you my aim is not 'revenge' or to hurt you in any way. Let us speak again, after the expedition. After we know what sort of war we face. If my answer is still important to you, I will give it then."

Shame, sadness, and consternation flashed across her eyelids, but she finally bowed and with a quick nuzzle under his chin that almost crushed his resolve, she flashed away toward the parade ground. For a very long time, he watched her weave through the throng until she was lost to view. With a stab of guilt and astonishment, he realized he'd not even thought about her in weeks. He would have to do that now.

———

Matt stood on the bridgewing with a cup of . . . something in his hand. He grimaced at the foamy brew. He couldn't remember what Juan called it, but it was the local equivalent of coffee, evidently. It might even *be* a kind of coffee; it came from crushed, roasted beans. Not many Lemurians drank it. They used it as medicine, as a treatment for lethargy. Matt hadn't had any before, but it had earned a following among the crew. Some just called it "java" or "joe," as they always had. A few of the die-hard factionalists called it "cat-monkey joe" or "monkey-cat joe," but just as "'Cats" was becoming the general compromise term for the Lemurians, "monkey joe" was gaining steam for the brew. It seemed to follow somehow. Whatever they called it, the stuff sure didn't look like any coffee Matt had ever seen, although the aroma wasn't entirely dissimilar. Maybe it was the yellow-green foam.

The foam slowly dissipated and the liquid beneath was reassuringly black, but there remained a bile-colored ring around the edge. He willed himself to take a sip and tentatively explored it with his tongue. *Not bad*, he decided, surprised. There was a kind of chalky aftertaste, but that wasn't unusual for any coffee Juan made. And it did taste like coffee. Not *good* coffee, but the similarity was enough to fill a dreadful void he hadn't really recognized. He smiled.

Walker was tied to the new fueling pier and the special sea and anchor detail was withdrawing the hose from one brimming bunker and preparing to fill another. Chief Gray watched their progress like a hawk, lest they spill any of the thick black fuel oil on his somewhat pale deck. Under the circumstances, Matt doubted that he'd really mind if they did. This transfusion of *Walker*'s lifeblood had raised everyone's spirits to such a degree that it would be difficult for even Gray to summon much genuine ire over a splotch on the deck.

The benevolent thunder of the main blower behind the pilothouse was almost enough to mask Matt's uneasiness about the expedition they were about to begin. An expedition that they'd planned and prepared for weeks, awaiting only this final detail. Fuel. When enough had finally been pumped, transferred, and refined, some was brought to *Walker* so she could fire up a boiler to run her pumps and get ready for the short trip upriver. All the while, the massive copper storage tanks on the shore continued to fill, awaiting her at the pier. Now, all was in readiness.

The rest of the expedition consisted only of *Big Sal* and half a dozen of the larger fishing feluccas. Together they waited, moored in the inner channel. Two other Homes had actually volunteered as well, but for this operation they would be too many. As soon as *Walker* completed her fueling she would join the task force and they'd enter the Makassar Strait. From there, *Walker* would range ahead, screening her slower consorts.

Matt looked forward to being unleashed on the open ocean, where his ship could stretch her legs, but he felt trepidation as well.

It was a bold plan that he and Keje had designed and there was a lot of risk involved. But if they were successful they stood a chance of learning—at long last—quite a lot about the enemy. The lessons Matt had learned on the short end of the intelligence stick had been pounded well and truly home, and he'd managed to instill in Keje, at least, a similar obsession for information. So much was riding on this! Initially, success might accomplish little more than their destruction of the Grik ships in the strait—or the Asiatic Fleet's little victory in almost the same place against the Japanese. But he'd hoped that, in the long term, the strategic dividend would be all out of proportion to the effort, particularly if it led to sufficient information to roll up the Grik. If they knew the enemy dispositions better, *Walker* alone still had enough ammunition to wreck a *lot* of Grik ships. With victory, or even a breathing space, they could continue to strengthen their friends, look for *Mahan*, and maybe begin their search for other humans too. Those were Matt's ultimate goals. With bunkers full of fuel, they even seemed attainable.

Larry Dowden entered the pilothouse. "Skipper," he said, saluting as Matt turned.

"Exec."

Dowden glanced furtively at the other men on the bridge and lowered his voice. "Sir, I have it on good authority . . . the Mice have sneaked on board. I didn't see 'em, but I'm pretty sure they did."

Matt frowned. "Didn't they get the word when I ordered all fuel project personnel to remain behind?" Many of *Walker's* crew would miss the expedition. None was happy about it, but aside from having necessary assignments, Matt didn't want all his eggs in one basket anymore. Letts would remain and continue coordinating industrialization efforts, aided by Perry Brister, who was also in charge of supervising the construction of defensive works. Letts had worked himself out of a job on the ship. He was too valuable in his new, expanded role. Besides, Matt didn't want a repeat of whatever had caused the mysterious shiny black eye that he wore. Officially, he'd tripped. Karen Theimer would stay and teach their growing medical corps. Matt knew that leaving the two together would only intensify the resentment of his other officers, but it couldn't be helped. One of the nurses had to remain, and Sandra simply refused. He was glad he hadn't given the order when others were around to see him back down. He was furious with her . . . and glad she was coming. As far as Letts and Theimer were concerned, maybe "out of sight, out of mind" was the best course to pursue.

"I didn't tell 'em personally, but shoot, Skipper, I never see 'em even when they're aboard. Everybody knew it, though; the order's been posted for a week. They just ignored it."

Matt shook his head. "And they can claim they never saw it and so they didn't, in fact, violate a direct order." He sighed. "No sense throwing them off. Besides, they'd just hide." He thought for a moment. "Nobody else 'deserted' back to the ship? Bradford? Lieutenant Brister?"

Dowden shook his head, grinning wryly. "Bradford almost did. He's supposed to be helping Brister with the fortifications. He is an engineer, after all, but he didn't want to miss the show. Nakja-Mur finally bribed him with a safari to hunt down a 'super lizard.' Nothing short of that would have worked, I bet."

Matt chuckled, and then his expression became serious again. "I owe him. But as far as the Mice are concerned . . . Well, I'm not going to bring them up on charges. They're too damn valuable—I can't believe I just said that!—and that's exactly what I'll have to do if I make a big deal about it. Their rig's going fine with just a caretaker now. They're no longer indispensable, just . . . valuable."

He looked at the men working on the fo'c'sle. They were having difficulty with their usual chores since the cramped space was even further encumbered by a large apparatus that Matt hoped would soon prove useful. Some of the men stared curses at the thing as they maneuvered around it, and firing the number one gun to starboard would be tough while the thing was rigged for sea. But if that gun became essential to the operation, they'd failed anyway.

"Let them stay. They've earned it. But if they pull a stunt like this again, I won't care if they learn to piss oil. Make sure that information reaches them, if you please."

"Yes, sir."

Together, they walked across the pilothouse and Matt peered over the wing rail at the water. Even this far upriver, it was getting choppy. Above, the sky was like lead: a low, monochromatic overcast with none of the flighty characteristics of the usual daily squalls. The heavens seemed to exude a restrained, pregnant power.

"Looks like Adar's right," he mused aloud. "We may be in for a real blow." He turned and grinned at Dowden.

"Perfect."

Ben Mallory couldn't believe he was flying, particularly in such heavy weather. After the conversation in which Captain Reddy told him they'd have to wait to look for *Mahan*—and why—he'd been afraid the PBY would be treated like a museum relic. He'd been wrong. If the plane could let them know what was coming—and didn't fly too far—the captain was reluctantly willing to risk it. Especially now that the radio worked.

Mallory was battling through the driving wind and rain north of a cluster of tiny, rocky islands off the southwest coat of Celebes. The world was gray, and the sea below was a roiling, foamy white. The thundering, rattling, swooping turbulence was enough to make him sick, and he was enjoying every minute. He spared a quick glance at his copilot. The young sable-furred 'Cat was peering through a pair of binoculars through the open side window. His name was Jis-Tikkar, but he liked "Tikker" just fine. He was a good companion and a fast-learning "wrench." He worked as hard as anyone keeping the plane ready to fly. On this, his very first actual flight, he was enraptured by the wonder of soaring high above the world at a measly hundred and ten miles an hour. Oh, how Ben missed his P-40E!

Whatever Ben called him, Tikker wasn't ready to *be* a copilot yet. For one thing, he could barely see over the instrument panel. Mallory allowed him to take the controls for a little "straight-and-level" before they flew into the storm, but it would be a while before he did it again. As soon as the little devil got his hands on the oval-shaped wheel, he'd nearly put the big plane into a barrel roll. It was all very exciting, and the flying lessons abruptly ceased. Tikker's duties reverted to observation, and keeping Ben awake with his irreverent humor. Currently, the humor was absent as the 'Cat concentrated on the business at hand.

The rest of the flight crew consisted of Ed Palmer and two farsighted Lemurians in the observation blisters. Ed sat directly behind the flight deck, checking in with *Walker* and keeping track of their navigation. He wasn't a pro yet, but he was a quick study. In his short time aboard *Mahan* he had, for all intents and purposes, been the navigation officer, since Monroe couldn't plot his way out of a paper sack. As long as there were landmarks he could identify, he wouldn't lead them astray—and they were forbidden to fly at night.

"There is the felucca!" Tikker said.

Ben banked slightly and craned his neck. Far below, a dark shape slashed through the heavy sea. The Baalkpan feluccas were fore-and-aft rigged and surprisingly nimble, but heavy weather was rough on them. "He's headed southeast! He must have run into something!" Ben banked again and dropped the nose, peering through the windscreen. The wipers flailed as fast as they could, but they only smeared the water.

"There!" said Tikker, straining his eyes through the binoculars. He looked at Ben. "The third Grik ship! It is chasing the felucca!" Through the wipers, he caught brief glimpses of a distorted red-hulled shape.

"Should we get closer?" Ed asked behind him. "I'd just as soon not get closer. Besides, they'll hear us."

"Not a chance, with all the sea noise down there and the rain," Ben replied. "All the same . . ." He began turning south. "Get on the horn . . ."

"Wait!" said Tikker urgently. "There is another . . . ! And another! Two more Grik are in company with the first!"

"Shit!" said Palmer. "Any more?" For a long moment they stared.

"Nooo," Ben decided at last. The three ships were clustered close together, and no others were in sight. "No, I think that's all."

"That's enough!" Palmer cursed and headed for the radio. He picked up the mike. "You still there, Clance? Tell the Skipper we've got *three* hostiles inbound!" Palmer transmitted in the clear. Who else was going to listen?

"Roger," came Radioman Clancy's terse reply through the static. "What's the weather like up there?"

"Moderating," admitted Palmer. "It's gone from an eggbeater to a martini shaker. Adar was right. Those Sky Priests are way better than our weather weenies were!"

"I'll say," agreed Clancy. "Lots more to those guys than reading maps and wearing silly suits. Wait one." A moment later Clancy's voice crackled in Palmer's ear again. "Skipper says to double-double-check the enemy numbers, then get the hell out."

"But Ben . . . I mean, Lieutenant Mallory, thought we might fly cover. You know, shoot somebody up if you need us."

"Negative. Captain says to get your big blue butt back to Baalkpan! It's our show now. You've done what we needed you to. Hell, you can't even set down!"

"Wilco," Ed grumbled. He clipped the mike and lurched back to the flight deck.

"What's the scoop?" Ben demanded.

"We double-double-check, then beat feet for Baalkpan. Damn, we won't even know how it goes!"

"Yeah, there're a few more guests than expected. It'll make things more difficult, but not three times as difficult—I hope."

"Well . . . what are we gonna do?"

Ben looked at him. "We're going to follow orders, sailor. But he didn't say we couldn't come back in the morning!"

The storm had finally begun to subside. It had indeed been a real blow, more violent than even Adar anticipated. The wind still blew at thirty knots or more, and the whitecaps of the heavy sea disintegrated into foamy spray. Keje stood on the sandy, desolate beach and stared bleakly at his beloved Home. *Salissa* lay at an unnatural angle, decidedly low in the water, a few hundred yards offshore. She now rested, exposed for all to see, on the bottom of the gently shoaling sand of what Matt called the Gulf of Mandar. How they'd ever managed to get her there, through the maze of huge rocks and mountainous seas, he could barely remember. All he recalled at the moment, in his exhausted, sodden state, was that the effort had been *chi-kaash*—hell.

All around him, people erected shelters amid piles of vulnerable supplies and others tended smoky cook-fires for knots of soaked, bedraggled people who'd paused from their labors to warm themselves. As far as he could see, the beach was inhabited by the debris and pitiful, helpless survivors of a traumatic calamity. Some stood as he did, staring out to sea, and some just milled about. Others waded back and forth through the surf, bearing bundles on their shoulders from one of the feluccas driven onto the beach. Another felucca still stood offshore, beating impotently back and forth, unable to risk the rocks and surf to come to their aid. Behind him, the tufted fronds of the trees beat and cracked with the wind, and the tall, skinny trunks leaned forlornly against the gray afternoon sky. Keje looked back out to sea, straining his eyes against the stinging spray. *Walker* was nowhere in sight.

Even over the thunderous surf, he heard Adar's shout behind him. "They've seen something! They're running!"

Keje wiped his eyes and peered through the binoculars Bradford had given him. Sure enough, the distant felucca was piling on more sail and slanting rapidly northeast with a grace and speed he envied. Farther away, another was racing down to meet it. The feluccas could sail much closer to the wind than *Big Sal*. Closer than the Grik. Signals snapped to the tops of their masts, and he focused carefully on them. Keje grunted. "I must return to *Salissa*," he shouted back at his friend. He'd done all he could ashore.

It was a miserable trip in the barge, damp crew folk straining at oars against the marching waves, but soon they were alongside *Salissa*, sheltered in her lee. Keje scurried up a rope and hands pulled him aboard. He glanced quickly around. Other than those gathered near, his Home seemed deserted. The forward wing clan's pagoda that they'd so recently rebuilt was intact, but the great tripod lay athwartships, its huge wing trailing over the side. Frayed cables, shattered barrels, and other unrecognizable debris were strewn across the exposed deck area. With a surge of concern, he glanced shoreward where his helpless People raced around in panic as rumors began to fly. A few tried to rally a defense, but not many. Here was a prize, ripe for the taking. The enemy couldn't possibly refuse. An entire Home of the People, loaded with food and supplies. Riches beyond calculation to any Grik raider fortunate enough to stumble across her! And her

People! Their favored prey! Tired, traumatized, disorganized! There'd be no restraining them. He raced up the ladder to the battlement, and a memory of the last time he stood there, preparing thus, flashed through his mind. So much had changed since then. He raised the binoculars again.

Grik!

Three towering clouds of dingy canvas resolved themselves against the dirty-gray background, charging toward them as quickly as they dared. Already, the bloodred hulls were visible, and there was no question they'd sighted their prey. A stone seemed to churn in Keje's stomach. The Grik were as predictable as a school of flashers when a person fell into the sea, and just as remorseless.

"They've seen us," he muttered pointlessly.

For a long while he stood on the tilted platform with a handful of his officers. Jarrik-Fas was there, as was Adar's senior acolyte. Adar himself remained ashore at Keje's command, to take charge in his absence. His daughter, Selass, was aboard as well, somewhat to his surprise. They'd spoken little since Saak-Fas disappeared, but much of that was probably his fault. He'd been so busy. They didn't speak now, and she stood nearby but apart. That may also have been because Risa-Sab-At was present. She'd been recently promoted to commander of the Forewing Guard, and there was tension of some sort between the two females.

He knew Selass had expected Risa's brother to press his suit once more, but he hadn't. He just treated her like he did everyone else—with friendly familiarity. Just as if there were never anything between them. That would have been the hardest blow of all to his prideful, self-centered daughter, he mused. To think she was that easy to forget. It would . . . do just exactly what it had: leave her sullen and introspective and less sure of herself. He wondered with a burst of clarity if that was what the former wing runner intended. In spite of the situation, he felt a small grin spread across his face. He remembered that the big Amer-i-caan, Dennis Silva, had once called Chack a "scamp." A good word. If true, good for him.

But the war had changed Chack in many ways. Not only had he become a warrior of note, but he'd joined the Amer-i-caan clan. Keje had not foreseen that, although he didn't disapprove. It just highlighted how profound the change had been. He was more serious and much more mature—his feud with Silva notwithstanding. Keje grinned again. Unlike most, he was sure that Silva and Risa's "mating" was a farce, although along with Captain Reddy, he'd pretended it was real, hoping to make them uncomfortable enough to admit the truth and let it pass. But they hadn't. He didn't even want to contemplate whether an actual mating was possible, but he was convinced, personality wise, that Silva and Risa were made for each other. Life had become very interesting in many different ways. Much too interesting to end here, today.

The Grik ships grew. Antlike figures scampered among their sails, reefing and furling in a surprisingly orderly fashion, much like wing runners of the People would have done. Half a mile away, beyond the first of the rocks that stood like sentinels around the little island, the enemy hove to. Through the amazing binoculars he saw masses of armored warriors surging against the bulwarks, waiting for boats to go over the sides. Their garish shields and bright plumage seemed dingy and washed-out, but he still felt a chill as he watched them. They didn't descend to the boats with the same enthusiasm they had when they once boarded his ship, however. Perhaps the weather was affecting them? He felt vengeful satisfaction at the thought that Grik might be susceptible to the sickness that came to some if the sea was too lively. As he watched, at least two actually fell into the sea trying to gain the boats. He was appalled that no effort was expended to rescue them. "Fewer enemies to fight," he muttered, "but by the Stars, are they not loathsome beyond imagining!" There were also three times as many as they'd expected to find in the area. Little was going as expected. Oh, well. There was certainly nothing they could do about it now.

Before long, twelve Grik longboats set out from the sides of the ships. Each was twice the size of *Walker*'s launch, and the warriors were packed to overflowing. There must be eighty or more in each boat, and as the oars dipped, it was apparent that *Salissa* would be their first target. Once they secured it, he expected they would stage the rest of their fighters aboard his Home and prepare their assault against the people on the shore. The thought ignited the stone in his stomach. Over his shoulder, he saw that a semblance of order had been restored, and a larger number of his people now stood on the beach with swords and crossbows ready. He looked back at the Grik.

Terrifying banners of red and black unfurled above the boats, each festooned with some grim image or awful beast, and they rattled downwind in almost perfect profile. Long tufts of fur or feathers bordered each flag, and he assumed they were some sort of clan device. They'd crossed perhaps a third of the distance between them now.

Keje turned to the acolyte. "I believe now is the moment we've awaited," he said. The acolyte blinked wide-eyed acknowledgment. Reaching within the folds of his robe, he drew out a large brass-framed shape with a wooden grip on one end and a black pipe on the other. He pressed a button on the side, and the pipe tilted forward. Glancing in one end, he nodded to himself and closed it up again. With another glance at Keje, he wrenched the hammer spur back and pointed the thing at the sky, slightly into the wind.

There was a muffled *pop* and a bright reddish object rocketed skyward, trailing a plume of smoke that vanished as quickly as it was made. A moment later, high above, a harsh pulse of unnatural light blossomed, unheard but visible for miles around. It sputtered and glowed impossibly bright as the wind carried it away. After only a few seconds, it went out. Together, they turned back to the Grik. "Now we will see," Keje said.

For a moment the Grik hesitated, apparently startled, but when nothing happened they resumed their approach. Onward they rowed, steady and malevolent. Individual Grik, dressed gaudier than others, stood in the prows of the boats, exhorting the rest with brandished blades. It wouldn't be much longer before Keje would know if he and all his people would survive this day.

"There!" Jarrik-Fas cried out and pointed. From behind the concealing point of land about three miles to the north, a pale gray shape, barely discernible against the stormy sky, lanced into view. The tiniest wisps of smoke hazed the tops of three of her funnels and a cascade of white foam sluiced along her flanks from the knife-sharp bow. A sensation of exultant satisfaction erased Keje's dread. Their chore was bigger than expected, but they could handle that. They'd hoped for one, planned for two, but three should make scant difference. He turned and gauged the distance to the boats, now almost two-thirds to their objective. Sharp teeth were exposed as his grin became a snarl.

"They've risen to the bait. All that remains is to close the trap! Shall we reveal our surprise?" Jarrik-Fas strode to the new "jan-raal ay-laarm," a long bronze cylinder suspended in a gimbaled bracket. He struck it energetically with a heavy rod. The loud notes were clear, if somewhat flat, and experiments showed they carried well to all parts of the ship. Hundreds of Lemurian warriors erupted from belowdecks and raced to their posts along the seaward rail. In moments, *Big Sal*'s starboard side bristled with eager warriors—not all of whom called her home. Some represented other Homes that had come to Baalkpan, like *Nerracca*, *Aracca*, and *Humfra-Dar*, but most were Baalkpan land folk leavened by Alden's Marines. Below the catwalk, five large ports opened, their doors raised by a pair of ropes and half a dozen crew folk each.

The Grik slowed their advance momentarily when they realized they faced opposition. Keje hoped they wouldn't break from tradition and cancel the attack. He'd carefully held back more than half his troops so they would think they still had the advantage. A preponderance of numbers in their enemy's favor had never dissuaded the Grik before, but they'd been doing too many unexpected things of late. He needn't have worried. With a crescendo of snarling shouts, the Grik plowed on, waving weapons in fierce defiance. Closer and closer, gnashing their teeth and pounding weapons against their shields. Their large eyes were opaque with a frenzy of rage. It was terrifying, regardless of his confidence.

He spared a glance at the Grik ships, still hove to in the distance. Their remaining crews had not yet noticed *Walker* bearing down upon them. That was understandable, since the destroyer approached from directly downwind. There was no reason on earth to suspect trouble from that direction. He grunted. Finally some lookout must have seen, because sheets were loosed and sails began to shift. The thought of the pandemonium aboard the enemy when they first glimpsed *Walker* brought a predatory smile to his cleft lips. Slowly, chaotically, the Grik sails filled, and the first ship heaved far over onto its starboard side, quickly gathering way. The other two weren't as fortunate. One attempted the same maneuver, but its head came around too far and smashed directly into one of the mono-lithic rocks, shattering the starboard bow and bringing down the masts in a rush of thundering, crackling devastation. It rebounded from the rock as though kicked in the nose by some terrible god and swirled away in the maelstrom, rapidly settling low.

The third ship shaped a course that might bring it in collision with *Salissa*. *Very well*, Keje thought. *An even greater test, and one just as important.* He ground his teeth and waited. The first Grik ship was clear of the rocks, but there'd be no escape. *Walker* was *flying* down upon her prey, and pure joyful wonder at her speed flooded through him. Formal supplication had been made before they set out from Baalkpan, but he sent a quick prayer to the hidden Sun and those who had gone before to watch over his friends and brothers. Then he returned his attention to the role he had to play. The Grik in the boats had no inkling of anything taking place behind. They might if the ship overtook them, but for now they were entirely focused on closing with *Salissa*.

"At my command, Jarrik-Fas . . ."

"Commence firing with the main battery, but at masts and rigging only, Mr. Garrett!" Even before the salvo buzzer sounded, Matt felt, as well as heard, a deep, muffled *whuddump!* from the direction of *Big Sal*. He looked, but at this distance all he saw was a massive fogbank of smoke dissipating to leeward. *So far, so good*, he thought, in spite of the heavier odds. *Big Sal* would face more warriors than expected and maybe a ship as well, but *Walker*'s part remained essentially the same. He'd never really believed Letts could pull it off. The supply officer's ambitious plan to arm *Big Sal* with forty cannon had been reduced to five per side, but they were enormous thirty-two pounders—and long guns to boot. They were crudely shaped and probably heavier than necessary, but their bores were straight and true. He could only imagine what five hundred three-quarter-inch copper balls per gun had done to the Grik boats. For an instant, he even pondered later ramifications. History often showed that arming primitive people with artillery could be a very bad thing, but at this moment, under these conditions, he had no regrets. Besides, he had more-pressing matters at hand. The salvo buzzer shrieked.

Three guns fired as one. Only one round struck the target, but it was a perfect hit, exactly where Matt had hoped. A single high-explosive four-inch-fifty struck dead center beneath the maintop and detonated with devastating effect. Huge splinters and pieces of metal scythed through sails and rigging, and down upon the fo'c'sle. The mast and top above the impact were entirely severed, and the whole thing fell—canvas flailing and yards disintegrating in a mad carnival of destruction. Surviving stays stretched impossibly tight and parted like a volley of rifle fire. The foretopmast snapped and added itself and everything above to the mass of debris that fell in an impenetrable heap amidships. A forestaysail billowed to leeward and fell into the sea. That, and the sails still set on the mizzen, caused the Grik to heave rapidly around to starboard and broach to, a wallowing, helpless wreck. As a final calamity resulting from that single salvo, the un-stayed mizzen sails were taken aback, and the entire mast snapped off at the deck and plummeted into the sea astern.

"Holy cow!" breathed Rick Tolson at the helm. *Walker* had closed to less than three hundred yards.

"Reduce speed!" commanded Matt. "All ahead slow. Helm, ease us in to one hundred yards and come left ten degrees on my mark." He turned to the talker. "Boarders to remain undercover, but . . ." He paused and cast a glance at Chack, standing nearby. "I don't suppose they'll surrender?" The Lemurian just looked at him, uncomprehending. The Grik never gave quarter, or asked for it. They probably didn't understand the concept. Matt doubted that Chack did, even now, after he'd so carefully stressed the need to secure live prisoners. He rubbed his nose and gave the young warrior a grim smile. "Of course not. Never mind." To the talker: "Machine gunners may commence firing if they have a target, but don't waste ammunition!"

They'd left one of the .30s at the refinery as security against predators, but both .50s and the remaining .30 were all now on the starboard side. Almost immediately, the .30 overhead began hammering. The two amidships .50s quickly joined it, shredding the dazed Grik as they emerged from beneath the wreckage. Splinters, shattered bone, and gobbets of flesh erupted along the bulwark amid a chorus of wailing shrieks. In the pilothouse there was silence. They were well within range of the Grik firebombs, but the attack came so swiftly and unexpectedly, either they hadn't prepared the weapons or they'd been buried by debris.

Walker edged closer to the rolling derelict, and the stutter of machine guns became less frequent as fewer targets presented themselves.

"Well," Matt said crisply, hoping his voice betrayed none of his nervousness. He tugged absently at the sword belt buckled around his tunic. "Mr. Dowden, you have the deck. As we discussed, lay her alongside and try to keep station as best you can." He grinned. "Mind the Chief's paintwork, though! If you have to break off, by all means, do so. But don't waste time getting back in contact." Tolson tossed a worried look over his shoulder at the captain.

"Yes, sir, I have the deck," responded Dowden grudgingly. "Should I have the whaleboat made ready to launch in case, well . . ."

Matt cast an appraising eye at the sea and quickly shook his head. "Too dangerous. If anybody falls in, try to fish 'em out real fast, but there's no sense risking people in a boat. Not in this sea." He looked at the concerned faces on the bridge, meeting each eye. He prayed that if anything happened to him, they'd be all right. But he *had* to go. "Very well, carry on. You all know what to do." He removed his hat and handed it to Reynolds, exchanging it for one of the platter-shaped helmets. He buckled the chin strap and turned to Chack. "Let's go."

Together, they clomped down the ladder to join the boarding party sheltering beneath the bridge and the gun platform amidships. The party was as large as *Walker* could carry in such seas, numbering just over a hundred. Most were the cream of Alden's Lemurian Marines, armed with swords and spears. A few destroyermen would go as well, but only those who'd shown Shinya some proficiency with a blade. They were armed mostly with pistols and cutlasses, but Silva had one of the BARs and Tony Scott carried his personal Thompson. Matt shouldered his way forward to the hatch that led onto the fo'c'sle. There he ran into Chief Gray and Lieutenant Garrett.

"Boats," he said, nodding at the men. "Mr. Garrett. I don't remember mentioning either of your names when I put this boarding party together." Gray hitched his web belt, but it stayed right where it was. It couldn't ride any higher without being let out. He met Matt's gaze with an expression of determination.

"Well, Skipper," said Garrett, "you didn't exactly un-mention us either."

Matt frowned. "Be careful, then. We can't spare either of you."

"Like we *can* spare our captain?" questioned Alden as he squeezed his way to the front of the line. The crowd parted as best it could in the cramped space. There was an overwhelming sour odor of wet fur and sweat. "Captains don't lead boarding parties. As head of *Walker*'s Marine contingent"— Alden grinned, but with a hint of reproach—"that's my job."

Matt grinned back, remembering when he'd made the appointment.

At the time, Alden was the only Marine in the world. "Nevertheless, I'm going. We've been over this before." He gestured at those around, destroyermen, as well as their shorter allies. "Don't worry. These are your troops. You trained them. You'll retain tactical command if we run into organized resistance. Just don't forget the priorities."

"Right," Alden agreed. "Secure the ship, and don't let 'em scuttle. Take prisoners, but kill 'em all if we have to. Nobody speaks Grik and we'll probably learn more from the ship than we will from the crew."

Matt nodded agreement. "Don't risk anybody's life to save any of theirs. While you're doing that, ten 'Cats'"—he paused, looking at Garrett and Gray—"them too, I suppose, will accompany me into officers' country. We'll try to find any papers, maps, or other documents. Maybe we'll even catch their captain!"

Alden glanced through the small rectangular window near the hatchway to the foredeck and squinted through the spray that left it almost opaque. It was nearly time. "Maybe so, Skipper. But if he was on deck, he's a goner for sure." He whistled at the nightmare tangle of heaving debris. The machine guns had stopped firing and there wasn't a living thing in sight. "What a train wreck!"

"Hell," said Gray, "they might keep him in a bucket down in the hold, for all we know. Just because that thing has stern galleries like an Indiaman don't mean their leaders stay in 'em. They're as likely to hold Hin-doo revivals there."

The men laughed, and many of the Lemurians grinned too. None, not even Chack, understood what he meant, but humor for any reason was good at moments like this. Alden moved to the hatch and turned.

"All right," he bellowed. "Listen up! We're goin' out there to activate Captain Reddy's contraption. When we do, I'll blow this whistle." He held up a chrome whistle in his left hand. "When you hear it, *go*! Single file, as fast as you can! No goofing around or gawking! It's gonna be tough for the ship to keep station in this sea, and we've got to get as many aboard as fast as we can. We could lose the bridge at any moment! If we do, those left behind will try again. There's bound to be lizards left and they're not gonna be happy to see us!" He waved at Lieutenant Shinya, about midway down the press of boarders. The Japanese officer waved back and repeated Alden's instructions to those behind. "Good luck!" Alden roared, and opening the hatch, he dashed onto the fo'c'sle. Matt and the others quickly followed.

Atomized seawater drenched them immediately as they ran to a pair of heavy cleats on the forward bridge plating. Matt looked over his shoulder at the wallowing derelict and then up at Dowden leaning over the wing rail. Dowden was gauging the distance. Suddenly he pointed at Matt with an exaggerated gesture and yelled, but the words were lost in the crashing waves. Garrett and Gray released the cables holding the "contraption" upright against the side of the bridge, and it plunged down to starboard. Matt watched it fall with a fist on his heart, hoping it wouldn't just disintegrate when it struck.

It was a corvus, a device inspired by his interest in history. Specifically, in this case, the first Punic War. A corvus was basically a long, rigid ramp that dropped upon the deck of an enemy ship so troops could sprint across. A sharp spike attached to the descending end was supposed to drive itself into the deck, holding the ships fast together and forming a temporary bridge. It *should* work. It hadn't worked well for the Romans, he reflected bleakly, but they'd never had a chance to try it.

As advertised, the weight and inertia of *Walker*'s corvus drove the spike into the enemy ship with a tremendous crash. The entire structure bowed alarmingly, but sprang back to its original shape. The frame, like almost everything else from Baalkpan, was made of the heavy bamboo. Alden blew a long, shrill blast on his whistle. Sword in one hand, pistol in the other, Matt followed the Marine across the bouncing bridge. The rest of his immediate party raced after him, followed by a closely packed line of yelling destroyermen and chittering Lemurian Marines. As soon as they gained the enemy deck, they deployed into a protective semicircle, which quickly expanded as more boarders joined them. Grik bodies were everywhere. Some were shot to pieces, while others had been crushed by falling debris. The foamy water coursing across the deck was dark with their blood.

Matt glanced back. The second wave, led by Shinya, was just starting across. The dismasted hulk wallowed horribly and the strain on the corvus was unbelievable. The spike was battering a growing hole in the deck and despite Dowden's best efforts, the bridge began to fail. "Quickly, quickly!" he shouted. They couldn't be quick enough. Ultimately, it was the attachment to *Walker* that parted, not the spike in the deck. Shinya had almost reached them when the corvus behind sagged under the reinforcements and then, with a deafening *crack!* fell into the sea.

"Grab the manropes!" Alden screamed as the spike jerked out of the hole and the whole thing tilted over. Dozens did so, and fortunately it was already so entangled in the debris of the rigging that it couldn't have fallen completely, but Matt dreaded what he would see when he looked over the rail. At least a dozen men and 'Cats dangled by the ropes. Some were actually in the water, holding on for dear life. A few disappeared astern, waving their arms in the air.

"Get them up!" Gray leaned over, snatched Shinya like a doll, and threw him on the deck. Others joined him, hauling the men and 'Cats up as fast as they could. Silva's BAR hammered. The Grik were coming up too.

Tony Scott stood by *Walker*'s rail, wide-eyed, watching the figures struggling in the water or clinging to the ropes. He'd been next to cross. His foot was *on* the corvus when it failed. For a moment, all he could do was stand there, clinging to the chain. He would have been in the *water*! So far, none of the terrible fish had arrived. Maybe the heavy seas kept them deep or disoriented, but he doubted they'd stay away long. And there were still people in the water. One wore a helmet, like most of the destroyermen did, but seemed too stunned or injured to do more than hold a rope. With quickening dread, he saw the long brownish blond hair unfurl and stream out from beneath it when a wave washed over the helmet. He gulped.

"God in heaven! That's Lieutenant Tucker!" He glanced wildly around. No one could have known she was there! What was she *doing* there? He screamed, trying to be heard on the Grik ship, but the waves and growing gunfire drowned him out. Laney heard him, though; he was right beside him.

"Tough break!" shouted the machinist's mate with genuine remorse. Tony looked at him, appalled. But he was right. There was nothing they could do. Nothing *he* could do. Just like that, everything was falling apart. Only a little more than half the boarding party made it across. The rest were stuck on this side, with nothing to do but watch, and now the skipper's dame was in the water. He couldn't stand it. Terrified as he was, he just couldn't stand it. He saw Dowden's worried face over the wing rail and he caught his eye. He made a whirling motion over his head and pointed at the other ship. Dowden seemed confused, but within seconds *Walker* briefly nudged back within twenty yards of the derelict. Scott wound up like the pitcher he was and slung his heavy Thompson across the gap. He hoped it didn't hit anybody in the head. The ammo belt followed the gun.

"What the hell are you doin'?" Laney demanded, incredulous. Scott just looked at him, slapped him in the gut with his helmet, and leaped over the side.

The water was warm and familiar, but the memories of a lifetime spent within its comforting embrace couldn't prevent his shriek of terror when he thrashed to the surface. There, just a few yards away, was Lieutenant Tucker, eyes shut tight, trying desperately to pull herself along the rope. He looked up at the ship and saw that nearly everyone else was safely aboard or climbing out of the water. Either they hadn't noticed her or the rope was fouled and they couldn't pull her up. Something slammed into the heel of his shoe. He lunged for the rope, right in front of her, and shouted over the crashing sea: "Put your arms around my neck, Lieutenant! I'll pull us up!" He never heard her reply, but she did as instructed and he hauled against the rope with maniacal strength. In moments, he crashed against the side of the ship. Nearly stunned, he just hung for a moment. Something that felt like oak bark dragged across his leg.

"Help!" he screamed. "Help, goddammit! I've got Lieutenant Tucker here!"

Almost immediately, the captain himself was hanging above him by the wrecked corvus. Garrett and Chack and a couple of others too. Garrett was hacking at something with his cutlass while the rest tried to heave them aboard. Suddenly the rope was free, and Tony and Sandra snaked up the side and sprawled on the deck.

Scott got to his hands and knees and vomited into the water swirling around him. Then he felt himself rising, and there was Silva's grinning mug in front of his face.

"Here," he said, pushing the Thompson into his hands. "You idiot!"

Before he could respond, Sandra had her arms around his neck again, kissing his cheek. Blood thundered in his ears.

"Thank you!" she said, and kissed him again. His legs felt like melted wax. For the moment, the shooting had stopped. They must have chased the lizards back below.

"Yes, thank you, Mr. Scott!" Matt said earnestly, squeezing his shoulder hard. He looked at Sandra. The mixture of profound relief and rage on his face was something to behold.

"What on *earth* were you thinking?"

Her wet chin came up. "I was thinking, Captain Reddy, that you might need medical help over here!"

"And because of that thinking, I . . . We almost lost you!"

"Captain," Alden interrupted, "we have to push 'em before they get their act together! We're a little shorthanded, and it looks like there's more of 'em crammed below than we figured."

"Of course, Sergeant. Carry on. I'll deal with Lieutenant Tucker!"

Alden nodded. "Mr. Shinya . . ." He hesitated only an instant. "Take A company. Work your way forward! Be sure and check under all this shit before you pass it by. Chack, take C company and follow 'em. Find a way below from the fo'c'sle! We'll get 'em stirred up amidships and you can hit 'em in the rear! B company, with me!"

They'd gathered near the wreck of the mainmast on the raised quarterdeck, with an open companionway gaping in front of them.

"Grenade!"

Silva slung the BAR and fished in a satchel at his side. Retrieving a grenade, he pulled the pin and lobbed it into the hole. There was a muffled *whump* and the deck shivered beneath their feet. A chorus of shrieks and snarls punctuated the blast.

"Guess somebody *is* home," Silva quipped.

"Another!" shouted Alden. "Scott, you okay? You and your Thompson follow the grenade with first squad. We'll be right behind you!"

Tony jerked a quick nod and poised himself near the ladder. After what he'd just been through, a battle was a cinch. In the water he'd been helpless. Now there was something he could shoot. Silva pitched a second grenade. More screams accompanied the explosion, and the coxswain bolted down the hatch with a dozen yowling Marines. *Bra-ba-bap! Bra-ba-bap!* roared the Thompson amid yells and screams and clashing weapons.

"Second squad, with me!" Alden cried, leading the second wave into the belly of the ship. He had a pistol on his belt, but he charged down the steps holding a spear like a bayonet-tipped Springfield. He would fight as he'd trained his Marines. Gray grabbed at Silva's satchel as he brought up the rear.

"Gimme some of those!" he ordered. Silva quickly opened the flap so Gray could snatch grenades, then he bolted down the ladder. A moment later, the heavier bark of the BAR was heard.

"More down there than we thought," Garrett mused worriedly. "It may be a while before we can get through that way!"

One of the Marines in Matt's guard detail "oofed" and crumpled to the deck with a crossbow-bolt high in his chest. Sandra rushed to him, opening her soggy bag.

"Aft!" cried Gray. "That skylight in front of the tiller!"

Matt grabbed one of the Marines by the arm. "Five of you stay with Lieutenant Tucker and the wounded!" Sandra started to protest. "That's why you said you came," he accused harshly, opening his holster and taking out his .45.

"But I don't need that many. You do!"

"Nevertheless—" He pushed the pistol into her hand. "Can you use that?" She nodded, terrified, but not of the gun.

"Of course! But you're *not* going to fight them with just that stupid sword!"

He quickly stooped and whispered in her ear. "I wouldn't *have* to if you'd stayed where you belong!" He took a deep breath. "I think I love you, Sandra Tucker, but you're an idiot!" He flashed a quick smile and stood. "The rest of you, with me!"

Together, they rushed the skylight, hoping to make it before another bolt flew. They didn't quite, but the next went wide and thunked into the bulwark. Gray flung a grenade into the opening and dropped down beside it. Smoke and splinters rocketed from the hole, mixed with red droplets and a fuzz of downy fur.

"In!" Captain Reddy yelled, and he dropped out of sight.

———

Keje-Fris-Ar stared in shock at the devastation they'd wrought. The big bronze guns that Letts worked so hard to produce—along with the foundry at Baalkpan and more than a hundred helpers—had been inexpertly used, to say the least. Despite the assistance of the destroyerman named Felts and another Amer-i-caan supervising each gun, more than half the destructive force of each shot was wasted, churning up the already maddened sea for hundreds of tails beyond the target. Even so, it was more than enough. A total of fifteen shots were fired at the boats, three from each cannon, sending thousands of copper balls scything through the flimsy vessels and enemy warriors. Parts of bodies and large chunks of the boats themselves scattered among marching plumes of violent splashes and horrible, unearthly shrieks. When the smoke and spray had cleared, nothing was left of the enemy but shattered flotsam and struggling forms. Flasher-fish weren't active when the sea ran high. They couldn't sense the splashing of their prey, and the turmoil of the water was dangerous for them in such a shallow place. It didn't matter. The Grik had no more reason or inclination to learn to swim than People did. Within moments, there was no movement but the relentless march of the churning swells.

That left the Grik ship bearing down upon them. It was downrange during the firing, and its sails and rigging were savaged. The enemy aboard saw what happened to the warriors in the boats, but true to form, on they came. Tom Felts called for "round shot." The Grik bored in, without maneuver, no finesse at all. It apparently wasn't going to lay alongside and send its remaining boarders across. It meant to crash headlong into *Salissa*'s side. That might cause significant damage. Keje waited tensely while the big guns were loaded. At two hundred tails, they spoke. Massive detonations trundled the heavy guns back against their restraints. The brief "swoosh" of heavy shot ended in multiple crashes that launched blizzards of splinters and large, spinning fragments of the Grik's bow into the sea. When the smoke cleared, the Grik still came, but slower and lower in the water. The approach ended at a hundred tails, as the vessel filled. Keje saw a wisp of smoke and remembered the Grik firebombs.

"Once more!" he commanded. This time, when the massive smoke cloud dissipated, all that remained was jutting masts, rapidly slipping lower. With a jolt, the hull struck bottom, and the masts tilted crazily, almost disappearing, before they came to rest.

Then began the cheering. It was like the times before, when he'd witnessed *Walker*'s devastating powers to lay waste the hated foe. Only this time it was he and *Salissa* who'd unleashed it! It was a heady moment. With power like she now possessed, *Salissa* need fear nothing on earth! Perhaps the time *had* come at last for the Ancient Enemy that had haunted their lives and dreams to be laid low. Perhaps even their Ancient Home, the very cradle of their race, might be restored! The name Keje-Fris-Ar would be spoken with reverence and honor as great as that of Siska-Ta, the prophet who wrote the Scrolls themselves!

Keje knew exultation beyond any he'd ever felt. He clasped Selass in a joyful embrace and capered with glee along with the others. In that brief moment, anything was possible! Most of the people on the shore couldn't see what had happened, but hearing the cheers even over the wind and surf, they began cheering too.

"Look, look!" Jarrik-Fas cried, pointing out to sea. Far away now, *Walker* grappled with the dismasted Grik. The distance was too great for detail, even through the binoculars that he hastily raised. Keje's happiness was tempered by the realization that *Walker*'s role was by far the most dangerous. He hadn't really known that when the plan was conceived, before the glory of artillery against open boats was made abundantly clear. None of *Salissa*'s numerous defenders had even had to raise a sword. Now he knew that for *Walker* to succeed, his friends—the very ones who made his victory possible—must come to direct blows with the enemy. He felt as if his own kin were at risk, and the possibility their ship might be damaged filled him with sudden dread. He chafed at the distance.

Matt landed on a shattered table and it collapsed beneath him with a crash. He rolled off the debris and scrambled to his feet, coughing from the smoke and dust. From the corner of his eye, he glimpsed movement, and he ducked as an axe whooshed through the space his head had just occupied and sank deep into the wall behind him. A Grik, snarling in frustration, tried to wrench it loose. Matt yanked his Academy sword from its sheath with a well-oiled, metallic *snink*.

Without thought, he drove it through the Grik's chest, twisted, and yanked it clear. With a terrible screech, the hideous creature slashed and lunged falteringly toward him. Matt stepped aside and thrust again, stabbing deep at the base of its throat. Blood sprayed explosively between its terrifying teeth and it crashed to the deck, its tail beating a spastic tattoo. Another rushed him from behind—already wounded, thank God—and he dodged its clumsy leap. He slashed as it passed, but the dull edge of the sword had no effect. It had never occurred to him to sharpen it. Luckily, the injured Grik stumbled or slipped on blood when it landed, and he was on it in an instant, driving the sharp point of his blade into its back. He must have pierced its spine, because it instantly crumpled to the deck, jaws gnashing, but incapable of further movement. He spun in place, sword outstretched, but there was no other threat at present.

His heart pounded with terror at his close call—and just at the sight of the things. He'd seen them from a distance, of course, and they were much like the Bali creatures, but up close like this . . . A swaying lantern hung on a bulkhead, slightly askew, its feeble glow piercing the gloom of the compartment. Blood was spattered everywhere and two more Grik lay on the deck. From the look of one, it actually caught the grenade before it exploded. Shattered bone and gray-red lengths of intestine made up its torso. There were no arms. He forced his breathing back to normal and concealed his shaking hands by sticking his sword point into the deck and resting them nonchalantly on the hilt. The remaining four Marines hopped lightly through the skylight, followed by Garrett, who helped Gray lower his more difficult bulk onto the wrecked table.

"Well done, Captain! You made short work of them!" Garrett exclaimed.

"Thanks, Mr. Garrett. Now let's check these doors. This compartment must've been their wardroom. The doors may lead to officers' quarters." He pointed with his bloody sword to another door aft. "That's the captain's cabin, I expect."

The heavy door on the forward bulkhead crashed inward and Grik surged inside, slashing with swords and ravening jaws. The Marines lunged forward with their spears and Gray and Garrett fired.

"God, this is fun!" bellowed Silva, swinging his cutlass like an axe. It caught a Grik right across the bridge of its snout and cleaved almost to its throat. Blood geysered.

"Speak for yourself!" screamed Scott, fumbling with another magazine. Silva hadn't even tried to reload; there'd been no time. He had no idea where the BAR was now. There were *many* more Grik belowdecks than they'd expected and they'd jumped into a hornet's nest. The Marines' shields were useless—there just wasn't room—so it degenerated into a melee, as Alden had feared it might. Fortunately, at least the Marines were trained in that to some degree. If they lived, some damn good NCOs would come out of this one. Scott finally locked the thirty-round stick and racked the bolt. Silva ducked. *Bra-ba-ba-ba-ba-bap!*

"I *am* speakin' for myself!" Silva replied, hacking down at a lizard trying to crawl in under the fire. He nearly severed its head and the senseless body leaped straight up and bounced against the overhead, bowling others over when it fell. He laughed. He'd killed a lot in his life, before the War even started. Bar fights and back alleys in China, mostly—although there'd been that pool shark down in Mobile too. Most had it coming, by his definition, though he might have been hasty a time or two. The Japs had it coming, and he guessed he'd killed some of them with his number one gun. But that was a team sport. He'd never killed anybody because he was "good" and they were "bad." They'd just been "badder" than he was.

And sometimes Dennis Silva could be a bad man. But now he *felt* good because the creatures he killed were indisputably bad. They'd killed Marvaney (he made no distinction) and a bunch of his cat-monkey friends. Mallory said they'd wiped out a place the size of Baalkpan at what ought to be Tjilatjap. Now they were trying to kill *him*! They were mean and ugly and needed killing by anyone's definition—and utterly righteous killing had a liberating effect on Dennis Silva. He felt like the big mean dragon in the story that everybody was scared of, who swooped down and ate the evil king. Sometimes it felt good to be "good."

He almost tripped. Several Grik made a lunge for him, but Marine spears and Alden's pistol probably saved his life. With a nod, Alden reholstered the pistol and went back to his spear. For an instant Silva watched in admiration as the Marine parried another Grik thrust as simply as swatting a fly and drove his spear into the creature's belly. It screamed and intestines uncoiled on the deck. *That's* one *Marine I'm never pickin' a fight with*, he swore to himself. He looked down at what had tripped him. "There's my gun! Gimme a minute, Tony!"

Bra-ba-ba-bap! Bra-bap!

Silva stabbed his cutlass into a dead Grik to keep it handy and seized the BAR. It was slick with blood and rough with chunks of other things. He slammed in a fresh magazine.

"I'm almost out'a ammo!" gasped Scott. "A and C comp-nees should'a been here by now! If that Nip doesn't get his ass here quick, even you will be ready to play somethin' else!"

"Don't worry, he'll get here!" Dennis assured him and wondered suddenly why he was so sure. "Stand aside!" *Bam-bam-bam!*

The Grik "wardroom" was an abattoir by the time they hacked and shot their way through the initial push and managed to secure the door. It had a convenient bar to prevent it from being opened from forward. Matt wondered what that said about Grik discipline? One of his Marines was dead and Garrett's left arm hung almost useless, blood pattering on the deck to join the deep pool there. Matt wasn't wounded, but he was splashed with gore and his "ceremonial" sword was notched and bloody. Gray was tying a tourniquet around Garrett's arm, and the three Marines were wedging pieces of the heavy broken table against the door, which rattled with incessant pounding.

"Quick, let's check these other rooms!" They looked in both compartments on either side. There were no enemies, but the collections decorating each were disconcerting. Skulls, mostly. Like trophies. One cabin held nothing but rows and rows of clay pots or jars, suspended from the bulkheads by netting. At a glance, they had no idea what was in them, but the stench was overpowering. Maybe they were firebombs and the compartment was a magazine? Gray and one of the Marines guarded the door leading forward. Heavy fighting raged on the other side. It was becoming more intense, and they heard a couple of grenades and more firing. They remained there, watching the rear while Matt, Garrett, and the other two Lemurians checked the final door aft. It was locked from within.

"Stand back," Matt ordered and nodded at Garrett, who fired two shots into the familiar-looking keyhole below the doorknob. The Marines kicked it open and dashed inside. One fell back immediately, a spear through his chest. A Grik waiting beside the door slashed at the other, missing by the thickness of her fur. Garrett bellowed the first obscenity Matt had ever heard him use and fired directly through the wall. Matt lunged through the doorway and spun, raising his sword. The Grik from beside the door grappled with the remaining Marine, trying to tear out her throat. The one that Garrett had shot slumped to the deck, leaving a red stain on the wall. It was dark in the room, but blurred movement caused him to rush forward, driving his blade through a gaudily dressed Grik. It slashed at him with its claws, but they skated across his steel helmet. He yelled and stabbed it again, driving it backward to sprawl into some chairs behind it. Garrett was suddenly beside him, firing at the Grik where it lay. Together, they turned to the one fighting the Marine, and when it glanced at them with toothy, gape-mouthed astonishment, the little female Marine drove her short-sword into its belly, clear to the hilt.

Matt spun back, looking at something he'd glimpsed as he dashed inside. Seated at a dark, highly polished desk and silhouetted against the gray sea through the windows behind it, a startlingly obese Grik glared at him with intense, unblinking eyes. It was lavishly attired in a shimmering red and black silk-like robe and its fur, or plumage—whatever—was shiny and well groomed. A window was open and the desk was littered with tablets. Perhaps it was throwing things out? It snarled at him and a string of saliva foamed on its yellowed teeth. Without hesitation, it grasped a curved blade from the cluttered desk. Matt raised his sword and prepared to spring forward before it could rise. With a defiant cry, the thing drove the knife into its own throat and slashed outward, severing muscle, trachea, and arteries. Blood spumed, and the head, no longer supported by muscle and sinew, flopped backward before rebounding forward and slamming down upon the desk.

Matt lowered his sword and stared. Gun smoke eddied in the breeze through the window, but the sharp stench of blood and voided bowels was overpowering in the confined space. The female Marine, her blood-streaked sword still in her hand, retched in a corner, overcome by nausea and relief.

Gray hurried into the cabin, glancing about, taking it all in. He strode to the corpse of the Grik captain and heaved it roughly aside. It slid to the deck like a sack of wet tapioca. "Bugger was bleedin' all over the books!" he growled.

Matt shook his head and quickly joined the Chief. His eyes moved rapidly over the haul. "May be something here." He glanced at the dead Lemurian Marines, one still lying in the doorway and the other just outside. "I hope it was worth it." He reeled slightly as the ship rolled drunkenly and unexpectedly in a swell. The sound of battle had diminished, unnoticed, and there came a heavy banging on the barricaded door through the wardroom. They heard muffled shouts.

"Captain! Captain Reddy! Are you in there?"

"Who wants to know?" Gray roared.

"Why, it's me, Silva, you damned tyrant!" came the relieved, muffled reply. "Let me in! We've got the ship, or at least this deck of her. Some of them stinkin' lizards has sneaked into the hold. We're fixin' to root 'em out."

Gray approached the door while Silva spoke and heaved the barricade aside. The smoke and stench that filled the cabin were nothing compared to what wafted in from the long deck beyond. Silva stepped inside, leading a small pack of Marines. All were exhausted and their fur was matted with blood. Silva had a long cut on his forearm extending from his rolled-up sleeve to his fist. When he saw the captain, his bearded face split into a huge grin.

"Ahh, Skipper! Glad to see you well! We've killed a swarm o' them devils. I bet there was two hundred left aboard! Most fun I *ever* had! I feel like a blamed pirate!" He leered at Gray and waved his cutlass. "Arrr!" Gray's face went almost purple.

"What about our people, Silva? Anybody hurt?" Matt asked.

Silva shook his head. "I don't know how many we lost on the contraption . . ." Matt blanched. Another big mistake! "But in the fightin'?" He looked at the two dead Marines between them. "A lot of 'cats bought it. Don't know about any of our guys, past a few cuts and scrapes. It was a near thing too, when we first come down the ladders. Lizards got us backed up a mite. Then that Jap and my buddy Chack took 'em in the rear from the fo'c'sle. After that it was just pure, sweet killin'! Most of these lizards weren't even warriors, I bet. Prob'ly just ship keepers, 'cause some weren't even armed—not that they need to be with all them teeth and claws! But you should'a seen that Jap, Skipper! He's a real terror with a sword!" There was genuine admiration in the gunner's mate's tone.

"You should'a seen the Skipper!" growled Gray. "All he *had* was a sword!" Silva looked down and saw the bloody thing in Matt's hand. He whistled. Matt knew that unlike Shinya's, his own success with the sword had come from terrified desperation, not skill. But from Silva's expression, he realized he would probably be "Captain Blood" within a few days. The ship heaved sickeningly once again and he turned to the Bosun. "We have to get this wreck under tow right away, or get off it—one or the other. There're too many little islands around here for us to run into. Take some people. Try to secure a towline. Have a detail cut away all that wreckage topside. I bet she'll ride easier without it trailing over the side."

"Aye, aye, Captain," Gray responded, and started to turn. Matt stopped him.

"And check on Lieutenant Tucker." Gray nodded, and summoning Silva's companions, he picked his way through the bodies and debris forward and lumbered up the companionway. Matt turned to Garrett, who'd quietly joined them, holding his arm. "Maybe you should see the nurse?"

"I'm fine, Skipper."

"Well, see what you can come up with. Sacks, sheets, anything, and wrap up whatever looks useful. Have it ready to send across to *Walker* in case we have to abandon this ship."

"Aye, sir," he answered distractedly. "Sir, there's something you ought to see."

"What?"

Garrett flicked a glance at Silva and lowered his voice, but the tone was still insistent. "Please, Captain, just . . . look for yourself."

"Very well," he said, curious. He followed into the dead commander's quarters, paying attention to the surroundings now. More tablets like the ones on the desk were scattered on the deck. Against one bulkhead were shelves with square partitions containing what looked tantalizingly like rolled-up charts! He stepped forward, eager to examine them. "Outstanding, Greg! This may be exactly what we're looking for!"

"Sir," insisted Garrett with uncharacteristic fragility. He gestured at the heavy overhead beams. Along both sides of each, like in the other cabins they'd inspected, were many, many skulls. They were of all manner of creatures, some he knew even Lemurians ate. Matt had tacked up a few sets of deer horns himself, growing up in Texas, so he felt no innate revulsion toward taking animal trophies, even if it was creepy and bizarre to take it to such an extreme as this. What made him seethe with anger was that, by far, most of the skulls hanging in the dreary shadows were Lemurian.

He'd never seen a Lemurian skull, but by their shape, that's clearly what they were. Many were dry and yellow and covered with dust. Some were much fresher. A few were even decorated with garish painted designs, whatever that might mean. He shook his head, revolted, but from what he knew of the Grik, he wasn't surprised. *'Cats are* people, *damn it!* He looked at Garrett. It was clear he was shaken by what he'd seen.

"Yes. Well, make sure they're taken down carefully and with respect. We'll turn them over to our allies and they can deal with them in their way."

"Captain!" Garrett hissed, pointing directly above his head. He stood in the very center of the cabin, right in front of the desk. The gimbaled lanterns cast a crazy kaleidoscope of sinister shadows in the recess. Matt followed his gaze, and suddenly the rush of blood in his ears surpassed the crashing sea that pounded the hull outside. There above him, leering down from sightless, empty sockets, was an unmistakably human skull.

Silva had followed them into the cabin and was leafing through a tablet he snatched from the deck. He stared as well. His happy mood and customary laconic expression were replaced by anguish and rage.

"Oh, those sorry, sick, buggerin' bastards!"

"Skipper!" called Sergeant Alden from the doorway. "All the hatches are sealed, and we're ready to go in the hold. It's not gonna be a picnic, though. There may be thirty or forty down there, and they're crazy as shithouse rats! When they knew they were whipped, it was like *Big Sal* when they jumped over the side—only these had nowhere to go but down. They're cornered, so I bet they fight like shit-house rats, too. I'd just as soon smoke 'em out, or smoke 'em period, but I'm afraid they might chop a hole in the damn hull! Besides, you said you want prisoners . . ."

Matt's face was wooden. He held up his sword and ran a finger distractedly down the notched blade. When he spoke, his voice was unnaturally calm, but his eyes flashed like chiseled ice.

"Mr. Garrett, follow my orders—and do get Lieutenant Tucker to look at that arm. Our mission is a success. We've learned as much as we need to know about the *nature* of our enemy. The documents we've captured and the ship itself will teach us much, much more. Sergeant Alden, you said you don't speak Grik? Neither do I." He turned to look at Silva. "I don't think we really need any prisoners after all." He motioned through the door with his sword. "Shall we?"

Walker had managed to maintain close station with the madly wallowing derelict, her gunners hovering protectively over their weapons, but it was clear in an instant when Gray thrust his head from the companionway that they would be on their own for a while.

"Get to work clearing that debris!" he bellowed over his shoulder at the Marines following him up. He ran to a cluster of Lemurians helping Sandra with the wounded. She saw him coming.

"Are you all right, Chief?" she shouted over the wind. He was covered with blood.

"Nary a scratch, thanks for askin'." He saw her tense expression. "Captain's fine, ma'am." She visibly relaxed, but Gray decided now was as good a time as any to get something off his chest. "No thanks to you." He gestured at the pistol thrust in the web belt around her waist. "He could've used that." Stung, she touched the pistol with her fingertips.

"I told him not to leave it!"

"Like that made a difference! I didn't think he should even come over here, but he did and he's the captain. He figures he got us in this mess and he can't just sit back and watch. That's the kind of guy he is. But your coming was just a stupid female stunt and you nearly wound up killed." She bristled, but he stared her down. "Sure, sure, you came for 'the wounded,' but what if you'd been killed? What do you think that would've done to him? To all of us?" He watched his words sink in. Finally, he continued in a softer tone. "Look, we gotta clear this shi . . . stuff and this ain't no fit place for you or the wounded. The main deck's secure. It's a bloody mess down there, but it's out of the weather." She began to nod.

"If we can get them down there, that would be best. And Chief . . . I'm sorry."

Gray started to say something else, but shook his head. "Right."

He struggled toward a couple of Lemurians near the bulwark, clutching the chaotic mass of shrouds. They were two of the ones left on deck as a security force, but they'd obviously decided their own security was paramount. A wave crashed over the deck, knocking Gray to his knees and washing him in among the terrified forms. He reemerged from the warm gray water and grabbed one of the 'cats. A grinding and bumping was felt alongside as the ship's masts and spars, twisted in an impossible nightmare of tangled rigging, pounded against the ship as it worked.

"You useless bastards! Help Lieutenant Tucker get the wounded below!" He beckoned those behind him. "The rest of you, cut everything away!" he yelled, hoping they understood. "With your swords!" He pulled his own cutlass and laid into the cables with a will. They quickly got the idea and chopped with mad abandon at his side. Other Marines, relieved from the fighting below, arrived to add their swords. Piece by piece, rope by rope, the debris threatening to drag the ship over was released, and the hulk began riding more easily. The roll increased, but at least it was a more buoyant roll.

Gray's arm felt like lead as he swung the cutlass, huffing and wheezing with every blow. *I'm close to sixty, and too fat for this shit*, he complained to himself, but no word of complaint escaped his lips. Nor would it ever. *The Bosun is all-powerful and indestructible. He has to be.* He glanced at the sky. It was early afternoon when the Grik were first seen, so they couldn't have much light left. Already, it was noticeably darker. If they couldn't get a towline secured before dark, they were probably screwed. He left clearing the remainder of the wreckage to fresh, willing hands and ran to fetch something to signal the other ship.

Five grenades went down the hatch into the gloom of the hold. Each time one detonated, there was a chorus of nightmarish wails. Silva and Scott pounded down the companionway together this time, followed closely by Matt, Alden, Chack, Shinya, and a score of Lemurian Marines. They advanced through the darkness, blasting or stabbing at anything that moved and, as Alden suspected, the confined space in the bottom of the ship was working with the vermin. Footing was treacherous on the slimy ballast stones, and there were other things, barely glimpsed in the guttering torchlight. Bones. Thousands of bones intermingled with the rocks. The stench was unreal. Then, even as they fought, and their eyes became accustomed to the gloom, they entered a waking nightmare they would never forget. With the searing clarity of a lightning strike, Matt realized he *hadn't* learned the true nature of their enemy. Not till now. The belly of the ship was a slaughterhouse, in more ways than one. The gnawed and shattered bones in the ballast were mostly Lemurian. Half-butchered Lemurian carcasses swayed from hooks and all the grisly paraphernalia of the butcher's trade dangled, obscenely well ordered, nearby. Chained along the sides of the ship, conveniently out of the way but well situated to witness the horror they were doomed to endure, cowered maybe a dozen filthy, mewling, near-starved Lemurian captives. Matt knew then, that even if he ordered it, no Grik prisoners were possible.

The Marines went amok. They fought with abandon and no regard for their own lives. So, to a degree, did the humans. Scott staggered back, blood on his face, and Shinya dragged him from the fighting. Matt took the Thompson himself, firing controlled bursts at maniacally charging Grik. He burned with a towering, righteous wrath. At last there was focus for all the rage and anxiety, grief and loss he'd suppressed for months. When the Thompson clicked empty, he drew his sword again.

"At 'em!" he screamed. Once, he'd never imagined drawing his sword in anger, but now it seemed an extension of his very soul: the instrument of purification. The Marines surged forward, bronze spearpoints gleaming red in the guttering light. With a ringing whoop, Silva drew his cutlass, and so did the others. Alden knew with sinking certainty that of all the people in the world, Captain Reddy had the least business in this fight, but it was pointless to try to stop him. They charged. Without even shields, they slammed into the final, teetering Grik line and slashed it apart with a manic savagery that must have shocked even the Grik. The survivors broke. Shrieking in mindless terror, they fled farther into the darkness, flinging themselves against the hull, the overhead—anything to escape. Most had dropped their weapons. For a moment, Matt paused, leaning on his knees and gasping for breath. He started forward again.

"Captain," Alden said gently, grasping his arm. "It's done. It's done!"

Matt started to shake him off, but then stopped, shocked by the intensity of his emotions. He nodded. The Marines, still in a blind frenzy, shouldered past and slaughtered the twenty or so Grik holdouts that had fled to the farthest reaches of the dank, half-flooded hold. They mercilessly hacked apart every last Grik they found, and the Americans stood, listening, until the final shriek ended.

Chack returned from the gloom, limping and leaning on Dennis Silva. Both were drenched in blood and Chack was clearly hurting, but Silva looked like some mythical god of war. Marines filtered back into the dim light, dazed.

"Sergeant Alden, get our wounded out of here, then form a detail to release these poor bastards." He gestured helplessly at the captives.

Most of the captives had begun a shrill, keening sound. In their tortured reality they probably thought their time had come to face the knives and saws. They seemed utterly mad. Matt remained for a while, watching while they were gently released a few at a time and taken on deck to the open air, as far from their prison as possible, by expressionless, furiously blinking Marines. Once there, they were wrapped in sailcloth against the wind and spray that came over the rail. They were fed and watered and carefully tended, but their chains weren't removed. In their current state they might harm themselves or others if freed.

Silva was helping Chack through the stones (he'd flatly refused to be carried) when the Lemurian suddenly halted before a captive still chained to the hull. The wretched creature recoiled from his stare and made small gurgling sounds. Its skeletal chest heaved with terrified gasps. Matt stepped closer and regarded the creature with pity. He had great respect for the Lemurian people. He'd come to know them as stout warriors and generally cheerful, free-spirited individualists—not unlike his own destroyermen—but the things the captives had seen and endured would have broken anyone.

"Leave him alone, Chackie," said Silva, uncharacteristically subdued. "Can't you see he's fixin' to vapor-lock?"

Chack shook his head and leaned closer still. "I greet you. Do not fear," he said in his own language.

"You *know* him?" Matt demanded.

Chack nodded, a strange smile on his face. "I know him."

"Does he know you?"

Chack spoke rapidly, repeating a few words many times. A slight sheen slowly returned to the captive's flat, dull eyes and, hesitantly, he spoke. After a moment, Chack turned. "He said these were mostly survivors of Chill-chaap, but there were some from other places. He himself was transferred from another ship—as was a Tail-less One like yourself."

Matt remembered the skull. "What happened to the Tail-less One?" he demanded. Chack gestured as if it was obvious, and Matt nodded sharply. "You said you know him. Who is he?"

Chack almost seemed to sigh. "His name is Saak-Fas. Daughter-Mate of Keje-Fris-Ar."

Tony Scott and Tamatsu Shinya found Gray resting in the gloom near the ship's wildly spinning wheel. He was breathing hard and futilely wiping at the salt that stung his eyes. The coxswain had a cut on his shoulder that left a bloody scrap of sleeve flapping in the wind, and his lower lip was split and swollen. He still had no helmet, but he'd tied a rag around his head to keep the hair out of his eyes. The Thompson was lovingly slung over his undamaged shoulder.

"Cambin's commimenpfs, Cheeb," Scott said, trying to talk around his busted lip. "How are eberations goin' 'or da tow?"

Gray groaned as he rose to his feet. "We're *under* tow, you nitwit. Have been for the last fifteen minutes. I was about to report to the captain myself when you interrupted me!"

Scott nodded. "'Innat cay, cambin wans you ter sounderwell."

Gray looked at him in the near-darkness. The ship rode much easier now that *Walker* was towing her and she no longer rolled beam-on to the swells.

"What the hell's a sounderwell?" he demanded.

"Sound-the-well!" Scott painfully repeated. "Vinally got da las o' dat verbin cleared out o' da hold an' da cambin wants to know if she'll f-f-vloat. I'll go vif you."

Gray nodded. "Right. I'll report to the captain first, though. What's he doin', anyway? I figgered he'd of been up here by now."

"Lookin' at fings. Charts an' stuvv . . . an' udder fings. There's . . . awful fings down dere."

Gray turned for the stairs.

"Chief Boatswain's Mate Gray," said Shinya. "May I have a brief word?"

Gray's face darkened, but he jerked a nod.

"I know you don't like me, but you saved my life today, when the corvus parted. I would like to thank you."

Gray shrugged. "There was guys behind you. I had to get your Nip ass out of the way." He turned to follow Scott, but stopped again. "You got any kids?" he asked. Tamatsu was taken aback.

"No."

"I did. A boy. Close to thirty, now. Took after his old man—'cept he was a snipe. Machinist's mate. I hadn't seen him in four years, but I was proud of him. He was my son, you know?"

"What happened to him?"

"They never found his body, so officially he was missing. But he was in *Oklahoma*'s fireroom when she rolled over. At Pearl Harbor. So don't you dare thank me for saving your worthless ass! It makes me sick! I was just pitching you out of the way." With that, he stormed down the ladder.

"Yes," Shinya said to himself, "but it would have been easier to 'pitch' me into the sea instead of on the deck."

"Well, we did what we set out to do," Matt said grimly. "We've learned about the enemy." He, Sandra, Garrett, Shinya, and Alden sat around the Grik captain's desk poring over the tablets and charts they'd found. *Walker* towed the derelict charnel house in a wide, lazy circle across the Makassar Strait, into the Java Sea. That would keep them off the islands and shoals through the long night and bring them to *Big Sal* and their friends by morning. The sea was moderating, and Gray reported they'd float as long as the rhythmic *clunk-thump* of the chain pumps was maintained.

His report was uncustomarily subdued after he returned from inspecting the hull. It sustained little battle damage, but seams had opened while she wallowed in the heavy seas and water was coming in. That wasn't what bothered him about his tour of the well, though. All of them would be haunted by the things they'd seen and survived that day, and by what they'd come to know about the nature of their enemy.

"They're worse than Japs, sir!" said Alden with conviction mixed with quiet horror. The exhausted Marine belatedly glanced at Shinya, who bristled at the slightest comparison. "I didn't mean that the way it sounded. Hell, they're worse than *anything*!"

Captain Reddy had in fact been idly searching his memory for any culture in human history to compare with the Grik. So far, his tired mind wouldn't oblige. He rubbed his eyes and watched Shinya visibly relax. "Anything," he repeated dully. "I think you're right."

It had been a long, bloody day. Eighteen Lemurian Marines were killed and almost that many wounded. Most of his destroyermen were lightly injured as well, although only Norman Kutas suffered a serious wound. That was when Scurrey dropped his cutlass down a companionway and nailed his foot to the deck. Miraculously, it missed the bones, but Kutas was off his feet for a while. Aside from the quartermaster's mate's pain, it might even have been funny under other circumstances—but nothing was funny now.

They had one of the Grik charts spread before them on the desk. Matt thought how horrified Adar would be to learn that the Grik had "Scrolls." They were looking at an overview of the western Indian Ocean, Madagascar, and East Africa up to the equator and south to latitude 30. The eastern boundary of the map was the 80th parallel. The quality of the representations was poor—about on a par with sixteenth-century maps he'd seen in history books, but they, along with the printed information, were more than adequate for rudimentary navigation. The most startling and terrible thing about the charts, however, was that he could read them.

Most of the writing, and anything added by hand, was incomprehensible and resembled a slashing form of Arabic. But many of the place-names and nautical references used recognizable letters forming English words. All the numbers were familiar too. Obviously, the Grik got much more out of their British teachers than the Lemurians did. From what they'd seen that day, Matt imagined the Grik had certainly been more persuasive.

"Madagascar," Matt said at last. "I bet old Bradford's right about that being the original home of the 'Cats." Sandra peered at the island.

"Probably. It's been well within the Grik empire for a long, long time. In fact, every landmass shown seems to be part of their territory." Garrett glanced at Matt with a worried frown.

"They've got a lot of weight behind them, that's for sure. Way more than us."

Matt looked at Alden. "Anything from the tablets yet?"

Pete shook his head. He'd been skimming the roughly twelve-by-twelve-inch booklets while the others studied the charts. They were filled, mostly, with pen-and-ink illustrations. "Captain Grik was a pretty good drawer, or his clerk was. Mostly animals, bugs, places, and such. Must've been a naturalist like Bradford, in a perverted, lizard sort of way." Matt nodded absently and motioned Shinya to bring another chart. He unrolled it carefully and placed his cutlass on one end and a couple of .45s on the other.

At a glance, this one seemed most pertinent, at least in the short term. Even cruder than the others, it was less like a navigational chart than a map of enemy territory. It extended from the mouth of the Ganges River southward to include the Cocos Islands. From there, west to Timor, then back to Formosa. All French Indochina and the Dutch East Indies showed varying detail. The farther east, the vaguer the shapes of landmasses became. The Philippines weren't shown at all.

Matt leaned over the desk, trying to see better by the light of the swaying lanterns. He was painfully reminded he'd discovered unknown muscles that day.

"Skipper, look at this!" exclaimed Alden. He held a tablet close to his face to see in the dim light. Reversing it, he displayed the page. Sandra cried out and sprang to her feet. Matt managed only a short bark of incredulous laughter. There, on the yellowish paper, was a highly stylized but clearly recognizable drawing of USS *Walker*, down to the "163" on her bow.

"Son of a *bitch*!" Alden breathed. "This must be the one that got away!"

"Maybe," murmured Matt, "but does that make it the same one in company with the other two we destroyed? Why was it with two more so fast—if it's the same? I wonder how many others it came in contact with."

"Quite a few," said Sandra, leaning back over the chart. Her voice was brittle. "Look. Many of these coastlines have been updated or redrawn periodically, like survey corrections. Also, see this dark splotch here?" She pointed at a spot on the map. "I'm no navigator, but that's almost the exact place we came to *Salissa*'s assistance."

Garrett squinted. "Looks like . . . blood, Captain. And look! Next to it there's a little drawing of us! Just a thick line with four small lines sticking up, but I bet that's supposed to be *Walker*."

Shinya nodded. "It does look like blood. Possibly representing a place of battle? If that's the case, you may note there are many such spots on this map."

"There's one at Tjilatjap," Sandra confirmed. "Mr. Shinya may be right. There's dozens of 'spots.' If they denote battles, and the picture of *Walker* seems to confirm that, this ship couldn't have engaged in them all, or surveyed all these coastlines alone."

"That means they communicate among themselves, even from one task force to the next." Garrett's brow was creased with concern. "That means . . ."

"Right." Matt finished for him. "This may not be the one that got away. They might *all* know about *Walker*."

There was a contemplative, nervous silence as they considered the implications.

"Okay," said Matt, pointing back at the chart. "Battle here, battle here, battle here—each battle mark is accompanied by this thing that looks like a tree. Maybe that's their symbol for the 'cats." His finger traced the coast of Borneo. "Nothing at Baalkpan, so maybe they don't know about Nakja-Mur's People yet."

"There *is* such a symbol at Surabaya," Shinya pointed out, "although no battle mark."

"I bet it won't be long," Alden growled. "I wonder what these little triangle symbols mean."

Matt felt a chill, despite the dank, oppressive warmth of the cabin. "I bet those are Grik ships. And the circles around them represent their areas of operation. See? There're three in the Makassar Strait."

"Not anymore," Alden quipped.

"They're everywhere, then," Sandra murmured, her voice quiet with despair. "There must be a dozen triangles in the Java Sea alone. And all those other charts we've looked at—there're *scores* of triangles on them!"

"My God," muttered Garrett.

Alden was idly tracing the procession of battle marks up the coast of Java and Sumatra. Suddenly he stiffened. "Look," he said, his finger beside a brownish stain near the Banjak Islands. There was another thick line, but with only three smaller lines sticking out. With a rush of realization, Matt remembered a funnel that fell across a davit.

"*Mahan*," he breathed.

The storm dwindled to nothing as the night wore on, and its only remnant in the boulder-strewn approaches to the refloated *Big Sal* was a disorganized chop. Otherwise, the sun rose bright above Celebes and the sky was blue and cloudless. All was back to normal aboard the huge ship, fake debris was cleared away and the stores that littered the beach returned. Water still coursed over the side, and it would for some time, since so much had been required to "sink" the great vessel. That was the part of the plan Matt had been most concerned about, but Keje himself suggested it as bait for the trap. He'd assured his friend that sinking and refloating *Big Sal* wasn't difficult, or even unusual. They did it all the time.

Once a year it was deliberately done to cleanse the lower decks and "sweeten" the air. A suitable, sandy bottom in sheltered shallows was all they needed, and water was let in until *Big Sal* gently settled to the bottom of the sea. After a few days passed, she was pumped out and all hatches were laid open, allowing the interior to dry. This routine cleared the ship of vermin and insects, and washed away the foul smell of gri-kakka oil that seeped from barrels and grew rancid in the bilge.

The periodic "sinkings" were times for festivities and merriment, and contests in which younglings captured and tallied vermin that escaped to the upper decks. They never got rid of them entirely, and the little ratlike creatures were fruitful if nothing else, but for a long time afterward their numbers were diminished and *Big Sal*'s cavernous hold smelled fresh and clean. None of her previous soakings were accompanied by as much merriment and jubilation as this one, however, particularly when *Walker* appeared early that morning towing the dismasted hulk over the horizon.

Big Sal's forward wing still wasn't erected, but otherwise she was good as new when the great sweeps propelled her through the obstacles and into the open water to rejoin her ally. Hundreds of People crowded the shrouds and lined the catwalk to welcome *Walker* with thunderous roars and cheers of greeting. The great guns were loaded and fired in salute as the destroyer bore down with her prize.

Walker responded with repeated whoops from her horn. Destroyermen, Marines, and Lemurian cadets lined her rail, as did the prize crew on the captured ship. A makeshift flagstaff had been rigged atop her shattered mainmast, and an American flag streamed to leeward above the red and black pennant of the enemy.

For the first time since he'd seen the curious cloth, the meaning of the destroyermen's flag, and what it could represent, was driven home to Keje. He felt a surge of pride at the sight of it, even if it wasn't a symbol of his own People. There was also a twinge of something close to envy, and he determined then and there that one day his own People must have a flag. They had symbols aplenty that represented their clans, on the tapestries that adorned their great halls, but nothing they could look to that represented all the People everywhere. In addition to his heady dreams of the day before, it was a legacy that he thought the great uniting prophet, Siska-Ta, would surely approve of. The Americans had their flag and so did the Grik. It was time the People had one.

To cap the magical excitement of the moment, the great flying-boat descended out of the northeastern sky, thunderous motors adding to the joyful tumult of happy people. Keje watched as it skimmed low over the waves and made a proper landing for the first time, and the grace and power of the huge, flying metal contrivance took his breath away. It was a great day!

Walker hove to, her people returning *Big Sal*'s cheers. The launch went over the side and a few moments later arrived in *Salissa*'s lee, crowded with passengers who immediately climbed the netting lowered for them. An honor guard of excited Marines met them when the party reached the main deck, and a twitter of bone whistles simulated bosun's pipes.

Captain Reddy saluted aft, as he'd always done, and again Keje wished there was something to salute. Regardless, he fervently returned the gesture Matt offered him and then enclosed him in a mighty embrace.

"We were worried about you, my Brother," he said.

"We were worried about us too," Matt replied. "I never doubted the outcome of your battle."

Keje barked a laugh. "So certain were you? I was not! Not until the great guns spoke! It was . . . glorious!"

Matt couldn't help but catch Keje's infectious grin, but he asked a serious question. "Was the price very high?" Keje only smiled and allowed Jarrik-Fas to answer.

"We had no losses, lord. None! We slew the enemy with contemptuous ease! Our warriors never even drew their blades!"

"I'm grateful for that," Matt said, his smile fading. "We sustained . . . serious losses, I'm sorry to say, but the Marines and cadets fought bravely and well."

Keje lowered his voice in condolence. "Of course you had losses. Yours was the more difficult task and the People who were slain will find honored places awaiting them in the presence of the Maker and their ancestors!"

"Of course."

"Now!" said Keje, practically rubbing his hands together in anticipation. "What have you learned?"

Matt forced a smile, and glancing at the throng encircling them, he lowered his voice. "We have much to discuss, Keje-Fris-Ar, and unless you want to destroy the celebration, we'd better do it alone."

"You were right to suggest privacy." Keje sighed, shaking his head. "The world has fallen upon me." He sat on his favorite stool beside his simple table in *Salissa*'s Great Hall. Upon that table lay a Grik chart. He was revolted that the vile thing was in physical contact with the dark, warm wood. Other stools were occupied by his personal advisors, as well as Captain Reddy, Lieutenant Tucker, Lieutenant Garrett, and Sergeant Alden.

Adar hovered over the chart, sputtering with rage and indignation. "Blasphemy!" he hissed. "Unrepentant, black blasphemy! They desecrate the Heavens by their very existence! These . . . counterfeit . . . things must be burned! Destroyed! To think they take the gift of Knowledge of the Path of Stars and do . . . what they do with that knowledge! It is a violation! A rape! I—" Adar was incapable of further speech.

Matt shifted uncomfortably. "Certainly you may destroy them, Adar," he temporized, "but first let's learn as much from them about the enemy as we can."

The Sky Priest looked sharply at him, and a terrible intensity burned in his eyes. "By all means, Cap-i-taan Reddy! Study them well! Do whatever you must to destroy the makers of this abomination and the doers of these evil deeds! When you have done, then I will burn these loathsome pages and I won't rest until I've helped you bring that day to pass."

Keje sighed. "You will lose much sleep." He looked at Matt, and his eyes almost pleaded for some reassurance that things weren't as bad as they appeared. Matt couldn't encourage him. "You say these three-pointed symbols represent their ships? Possibly *hundreds* more of their ships?"

"We think so. Their strategy seems clear, at long last. It's conquest, of course, but I always wondered why, if they were such a big deal, they were just trickling in." He sighed. "Your ancestors were right. They're scared of the water—at least the deep water." He pointed at the Indian Ocean on the chart. There were none of the small islands depicted. Just a large, scary-looking fish.

"Their version of 'here be monsters,' I bet," Garrett offered.

"The Western Sea is vast and deep," Adar said. "And there *are* monsters there. That is why the enemy hugs the coast and why they have taken this long to find us—to conquer their way to us—it would seem."

Matt nodded. "That's exactly right. They seem to have all the territory bordering the . . . Western Sea, all the way to Singapore, although that seems a relatively new addition. Ceylon's their closest major concentration. The tree symbols seem to indicate settlements of the People they know about. A few even have blood spots beside them. We think that shows where a battle took place."

Keje traced a claw slowly from one spot to the next. "A tree," he said bleakly. "They use a tree to represent us. How appropriate and how . . . wrong." He looked up. "You said you found a human skull as well?" Matt jerked a nod. "I'm sorry to hear it, but how can that be?"

"The same way it happened to your people, Keje," Matt replied woodenly. "He was eaten."

"Saak-Fas saw it?"

Matt nodded. "He described a human being brought aboard—'one like you,' he said—but he had no idea where it happened."

"But how did they . . . get this person?"

"We don't know." Matt gestured at the chart. "They know where *Mahan* is—or was. But judging by the position fixes the lizard captain noted on the chart, the ship we took was never anywhere near *Mahan*'s last position."

"You think they got this person from another ship?"

"That seems likely, as well as the information where *Mahan* was."

"Do they have her?" Keje asked.

Matt could only shrug. "They will look for her, if they have not found her already." It wasn't a question but a statement of fact.

"They must not have her!" Adar cried. "For *them* to have the power you possess . . ." He trailed off.

"They must not have her," Matt agreed.

"What will you do? What must we do?" For the first time since Matt had met Keje, the Lemurian looked afraid.

"Two things," Matt responded. "First, we need help. Baalkpan's in it—they can't leave. But we need more help from Homes like *Big Sal*." He shook his head. "I really don't know what to do about that. Talk about isolationists! Otherwise, I suggest you put aside your differences, whatever they are, with the Surabayans. It looks like they're next on the list anyway. The enemy doesn't know about Baalkpan, but that can't last. The ships they sent to chart those seas have gone missing, and sooner or later they'll send more. If we help the Surabayans, it'll add depth to our defense and might gain us an ally."

"And second?"

"Find *Mahan*," Matt said, grimly determined. "We have to get her before the enemy does—or destroy her if they have her."

Keje still seemed overwhelmed. Well, that was understandable. "I never guessed the Grik could be so numerous," he whispered and glanced at Adar. "This map shows lands we never even knew to exist and all are in the realm of this evil!" He looked sadly at their faces. "Yesterday was a great day. A great victory. Or so we thought. Now I see it was less than nothing compared to that arrayed against us. We've won nothing! The fight has not begun!" He gestured vaguely toward the unseen Grik prize floating nearby. "Together, we've destroyed ten of their ships only to learn that is *nothing* compared to the strength they have! They were mere scouts!" He slammed his hand down upon the chart, claws extended. "Mapmakers!"

"It doesn't look good," Matt agreed, "but we have won a victory. We've learned what we're up against, which is more than they know." He smirked. "More than I've ever known."

Keje snorted derisively. "Yes, they face a disorganized mob that numbers less than one to their ten. An unpleasant surprise that will be!"

"No!" said Matt sharply, standing. "They face soldiers! Brave and determined! We boarded their ship with half the numbers we'd hoped—my fault—and fought them one to four! Our losses were grim, but we killed ten for one—in their kind of fight, not ours. They also face cannon, which will be a *very* unpleasant surprise. And they face *Walker*. While she floats, she'll never abandon you! I've seen evil before—at least I thought I had—but nothing in my experience compares with what I saw in the bottom of that ship. We've been friends and allies since we met, but honestly, I've often regretted getting my people involved in your war. And that's how I thought of it: *your* war. I felt kind of like a mercenary, and my men didn't sign up for that. But after last night—and *not* just because of the human skull—this war against the Grik became just as much ours as yours." He sat, leaning back in his chair.

"Now, we can sit around and mope and whine 'woe is me' or we can get ourselves in gear, make the tough decisions, and figure out how to win!" He saw Adar's predatory grin and knew he'd finally won him over. The Sky Priest probably had more swing with the other Homes than Keje did anyway.

But Keje wasn't out. He leaned forward. "Were you not overwhelmed when first you learned the odds?" Matt was guiltily aware that he'd been "overwhelmed" for the last six months. But this time it was different. The steamroller was coming and his tricycle had a flat, but he'd thrown the blindfold off. Keje huffed. "You'll hear no whining from *me!*"

Matt stood with Sandra on *Big Sal*'s battlement, leaning on the rail and watching the setting sun. Below, the victory celebration was still under way. Time enough later for the full extent of the challenge to make itself known. For now, let them enjoy themselves. They'd earned it. Adar swore the weather would remain fine for several days at least, so Matt hadn't ordered the PBY back to Baalkpan. It floated now, bouncing a little on the choppy sea but safe and snug in the sheltering lee of the massive sides of Home. Bradford cut short his safari. For such large creatures, super lizards were surprisingly difficult to find—particularly since his guides had been instructed by Nakja-Mur not to lead him anywhere near one. He'd arrived with the plane and was, even now, examining the "prize" with Spanky, Chief Gray, and a group of Naga's and Adar's acolytes. In the middle distance steamed *Walker*, festively alight from stem to stern but still screening the revelers against any approaching threat. As it should be. As she'd always done.

Matt blinked and looked around. It struck him odd that he and Sandra would have the vast expanse of *Big Sal*'s battlement all to themselves. Others had been there—Keje, Garrett, Pete, Jarrik—but he hadn't noticed when they left. Weird. Neither had spoken for quite some time, enjoying the companionable solitude.

"It's so sad about Chack," Sandra said, breaking the silence.

"Yeah, Keje's daughter too. I think she was expecting wedding bells when she saw Chack come aboard."

"Her name's Selass," Sandra reminded him. "We spoke before we left Baalkpan, and she told me her hopes and the understanding she had with Chack. She wondered what I thought he'd decide." She shrugged. "I had no idea. Now . . . she's in for a rough road. She loves him, but they can't mate, no matter what he had decided."

"Why not? I thought 'cats got married and unmarried whenever they felt like it."

"Sometimes, but they seem to take 'sickness and health' pretty seriously. Selass can't 'divorce' Saak-Fas until he's well—which I doubt he'll ever be—or until he dies, of course."

It had been a heart-wrenching moment. Selass greeted Chack with a joyful embrace, but then they hoisted Saak-Fas aboard. She had her answer—the only one possible—and Chack limped into the crowd while Selass desperately called his name.

They were quiet for a long moment, and then Sandra suddenly giggled. "That Silva and Risa sure carried on—right in front of everybody—

when he came aboard! They'll have everybody thinking they *are* married if they don't cool it!" She looked thoughtful. "That's probably gone far enough. They'll run it into the ground. Besides, I never figured Silva for the type to ride a joke down in flames. He's already got Chack's goat. They're just doing if for attention now."

Matt groaned, remembering the embarrassing spectacle. "I don't want to hear that man's name! As far as I'm concerned, he's restricted to the ship for the rest of his life! We'll see how married he thinks he is then!"

There was another long silence between them, and when Sandra spoke again, her voice was softer, hesitant.

"I wonder what Chack was going to say? To Selass. I wonder if he'd made up his mind. Would he"—she looked at him, eyes questioning—"have said the same thing you told me yesterday?" Matt looked confused.

"What, that you're an idiot?"

She snorted with laughter, but tears filled her eyes. Without even looking to see if anyone was watching, he took her in his arms.

"I don't know what he would have said. None of my business. But I do love you, Sandra Tucker." He kissed her on the forehead. She shuddered against him.

"I love you too," she whispered into his chest. Her breath was warm through the tear-soaked cloth. "What will we do now?"

"What do you mean?" His voice was husky. "Will we win? Will we ever find other people? Will we even survive?" He raised her chin to look into her shimmering eyes. "Will this be all we ever have?" He kissed her lightly on the lips and she returned it—hard enough to electrify every nerve in his body. For a long while they just clung to one another, each drawing strength and courage to replenish the wells they'd gone to so often. Then he brushed the hair away from her face and wiped the tears from her cheek.

"Well," he sighed sadly, "that's a whole other story, isn't it?"

Far across the water, nearly a dozen men leaned against the safety chain beside the number three gun on the amidships deckhouse. There were only two pairs of binoculars among them and they were making the rounds.

"It's about damn time," Silva grumped.

"Yeah," agreed Felts. "Way to go, Skipper!"

Silva looked at Laney. "Fork 'em over, snipe." Grumbling, Laney handed him two wrinkled cigarettes—careful to keep his distance so close to the rail. Cigarettes were the closest thing to money anybody had, and nobody ever smoked them anymore. Till now. Silva handed one to Felts and lit them both with his Zippo. They took long drags and exhaled contentedly.

"What are you so damn happy about?" Laney snarled, watching his wager go up in smoke. "There's only two dames in the whole goddamn world, far's we know, and they're both took!"

Silva looked at Felts and rolled his eyes. "Snipes' brains are like weeds. Not enough sunlight belowdecks for 'em to grow." He looked at the machinist's mate. "And some are stupider than others. It's like this, see? The Skipper and Lieutenant Tucker are nuts about each other—which everybody knows, but nobody's supposed to. But they ain't gonna *do* anything about it until they find dames for the rest of us." He shook his head. "Couple'a dopes. Anyway, that's a mighty incentive for 'em to find us some, don't you think?" After a moment, Laney grinned and lit a smoke of his own.

Eventually, the binoculars found their way to the Mice. No one knew why they were there. It was actually kind of cool on deck and they'd likely catch their deaths. Regardless, they waited and took their turn peering through the binoculars, one after the other. Then they shuffled off.

"I wonder," Gilbert said at last. "Maybe we could marry us one of them monkey-cat gals like Silva did."

Isak shook his head. "Won't work. Silva said the Skipper had his weddin' annealed, 'er somethin'." Gilbert looked perplexed.

"I thought 'annealed' means to heat somethin' red-hot an' let it cool off on its own so you can bend it."

"Yep."

Gilbert looked at Silva and cocked his head. "Didn't work."

Every human naval vessel named in *Destroyermen* was real. On February 27, 1942, the old *Langley*—America's first aircraft carrier—was mortally wounded by Japanese planes while carrying P-40 fighters to Java. On the night of February 28–March 1, 1942, *Houston* and *Perth* stumbled upon three Japanese cruisers and nine destroyers protecting a swarm of transports. Both were finally sunk after an epic fight in the Battle of the Sunda Strait.

(The only ship in the Asiatic Fleet with radar was the cruiser *Boise*, which had long since been sent to the States for repairs after striking a reef. The Japanese had no radar either, but they did have control of the air.)

On March 1, 1942, *Pope*, *Exeter*, and *Encounter* were destroyed by a combined Japanese force, including four heavy cruisers, while attempting to escape Surabaya and reach Ceylon (now Sri Lanka). Barring any mistakes that I take full responsibility for, and a little dramatic license with the pace and sequence of events, everything that took place or was mentioned to have happened in *Destroyermen* up to that point is true. The only exception is that *Walker* and *Mahan* were not there. Neither was *Amagi*.

The addition of two "four-stackers" and yet another Japanese capital ship would have made absolutely no difference to the historical outcome of that lopsided struggle. *Pope*, *Exeter*, and *Encounter* would have been destroyed regardless; the odds against them were simply too great. The only change to the history books (minus the Squall, of course) would have been two more rusting hulks at the bottom of the Java Sea—even before *Amagi* came along. But they were real.

As designed, *Amagi* was a thing to behold. At 47,000 tons, 826 feet long, and 101 feet wide, she was larger and more powerful than most of the battleships of her time. She would have been about the same size as the much later American *Iowa*-class battleships. It's possible she would have been converted to an aircraft carrier like her sisters, but she was never completed. Badly damaged by an earthquake in 1922 while still under construction, she was scrapped.

The story of *Walker* and *Mahan* is a little more involved. More than 270 "four-stacker" destroyers were built for the United States Navy during and immediately after World War I. They were built quickly (some being launched in as few as fourteen days) and were never intended to last more than thirty years—which some of them actually did. Already outdated, they remained in service throughout the 1920s and 1930s and ultimately fought in every theater during World War II.

Many didn't last that long. Because of restrictions on the numbers and tonnage of warships agreed upon at the Washington Naval Conference, many "four-stackers" languished in mothballs for years. Over time, some reentered service when an active destroyer was lost or wore out. Some were used for parts. A lot were converted into damage-control hulks or just simply scrapped. A few were even sold into the merchant service. One literally became a banana boat. Fifty were given/sold/traded to the British at the outbreak of World War II. Most that survived to fight in World War II were modified to one degree or another into minesweepers, fast transports, convoy escorts, seaplane tenders, and so on.

The point is, by the time the Japanese bombed Pearl Harbor, even the conservative, arguably moribund United States Navy knew the old "four-stackers" were obsolete, yet they used them anyway. This is not meant as criticism of the Navy—far from it. They used what they had. It was Congress that refused to build "up" even to the restrictions imposed by the Washington Treaty. It was this policy that left antique—and, in the case of the Asiatic Fleet, WWI surplus that hadn't even been altered or updated—ships to stand against the very cream of the Japanese Imperial Navy, the most modern and powerful in the world.

Walker and *Mahan* are presented in *Destroyermen* as two of these unlucky stepchildren, but in reality—the reality of the universe in which we reside—they were two of the ones that didn't make it. After sixteen years on "red lead row," *Walker* was slated to become a damage-control hulk, but she was scuttled seventeen days after the Pearl Harbor attack. *Mahan* was scrapped in 1931. Interestingly, both ships were involved in at least one epic undertaking: They served as pickets during the Navy's historic NC-flying-boat transatlantic flights. In any event, neither ship had a wartime record, so I felt less constrained in giving them a fictional, representative one.

If there are any old destroyermen out there who served on DD-102 or

DD-163, you certainly have my respect and gratitude, and I mean no disrespect toward the honorable service of either ship. Instead, I hope you will join me in engaging in a little "what if?" As Captain Reddy said, "All historians do it, whether they admit it or not."

A NOTE ABOUT
"BRONTOSAURUS" ETC.

Obviously, *Destroyermen* is set, for the most part, within the context of an alternate universe. The fascinating possibility of one or many alternate/ parallel universes has long provided wonderful worlds for science-fiction/ fantasy writers to explore. Even more fascinating is the growing scientific speculation that they might actually exist. Unfortunately, none of these new theories, attitudes, or even popular culture perceptions could be referenced in *Destroyermen*. The characters' perceptions of the alternate/ parallel universe must be viewed from the perspective that *they* had: a perspective prevalent in the 1940s, particularly among Asiatic Fleet destroyermen. I hope I have managed to capture that.

Unlike many stories involving a similar premise, the universe the destroyermen cross to is not just slightly skewed; it is the result of a profoundly and fundamentally altered evolutionary path. The "dinosaurs" in the story are depicted somewhat from whim, but with at least a little more modern perspective than the characters are able to perceive them. We now know so much more about dinosaurs than we did even when I was a kid—we have virtually started from scratch. Compared to those destroyerman in 1942, we live in an extremely enlightened age—at least as far as dinosaurs are concerned—so before you say, "What an idiot! Doesn't he know brontosauruses weren't real?" Yeah, *I* do. But the destroyermen don't.

My childhood books depicted dinosaurs as bloated, lizard-like beasts slouching along dragging their tails, or spending most of their days bobbing about in lakes or seas because they were too fat to stand. Tyrannosaurus was cool because he had lots of teeth, but his tail was just a third leg so he could stand upright like a man. And if anybody ever mentioned a dinosaur, the first thing that popped into your mind was the brontosaurus.

We now know the brontosaurus was a myth—a hoax—an extra head bone stuck on a decapitated apatosaurus skeleton. But in 1942, brontosaurus was real. It was the symbol by which any dinosaur would be judged and identified as such. *Anything* that looked remotely like a sauropod would immediately be called or compared to a "brontosaurus"—even by someone as learned as Courtney Bradford.

In our universe, dinosaurs have been extinct for around 65 million years. In *Destroyermen*, this is not the case. Those same prehistoric creatures have not remained stagnant. Everything has evolved beyond what the fossil record teaches us—the flora, fauna, the very ecology, and, because of that, even the geography to a certain extent. The "extinction event" is the obvious diversion point between the two realities, but there have still been ice ages, droughts, floods, and other cataclysmic events that would cause other extinctions and guide evolution for 65 million years. But "brontosaurus" remains. Stunted, perhaps, but physically similar to what the destroyermen expect to see.

Brontosaurus—or whatever it is the destroyermen *call* brontosaurus—is an amazingly well-adapted creature. Nature has been trying to replace him ever since he went away, but without too much success. Crossbreed a giraffe and an elephant and we would have him, I guess. Anyway, as long as there was green, leafy stuff to eat he wouldn't have to change. He would get smaller in the jungles of Indonesia, though, just like the elephants that live there today are smaller than their African counterparts. In fact, there's evidence that sauropods—and those that hunted them—were actually smaller in densely forested regions.

The Grik are descended from one of the many species of "raptors," as they're now inclusively known. They were relatively small, aggressive, possibly even cunning creatures that may have hunted in packs. If so, that would imply cooperative and therefore social behavior. Regardless of size, this gives them a leg up, in my estimation, on the ladder to the top of the evolutionary heap.

The seas are so hostile for a lot of reasons, but mainly because the creatures that lived there 65 million years ago sure scare *me* to death, and my imagination runs rampant with how terrifying they could become if they had a little more time. Also, if they're in the water you can't even shoot them—usually.

Almost alone among the creatures of this different earth that remained unchanged are sharks, crocodiles—and the mythical brontosaurus. Sharks and crocs are still here, even after the ancient unpleasantness that wiped out everything else. Compared to that, I imagine they would manage to cope with a little more persistent competition.

Considering that competition, one begins to wonder how mammals might have fared. Not too well, according to some scientists. In the tropical regions in which the Grik thrive, an isolated domain—thus Madagascar—would be needed for mammals to evolve to a sentient level. Let's face it, if humanity did spring from Africa, our ancestors wouldn't have lasted very long in constant contact with the Grik. Let us hope they were at least thought of as "worthy prey."

But what of the cooler climes? Remember, the destroyermen that came through the Squall have been able to sample only a very small part of this new world they find themselves in. A relatively isolated and environmentally homogeneous part. What amazing discoveries might they make once they are able to do more than "float about," as Courtney Bradford would say? But again, what if?

CRUSADE

As always, to my darling daughter, Rebecca Ruth. I know the time may come when Daddy's not your hero anymore, but I'll enjoy it while I can. I know you get tired of hearing the "honor speech," but it'll serve you well. It has me.

ACKNOWLEDGMENTS

The list of "usual suspects" is too long to repeat, but their assistance, encouragement, and friendship are no less appreciated. They know who they are. I hesitate to call them a "team" of helpers, even though most of them know one another and each has done something to contribute to the completion of this novel, even if it was just moral support. Maybe a better analogy is a crack gun crew. Each member has a specific task, sometimes performed independently of the others, and when all is going well, their endeavors often resemble a virtual ballet. In that sense, I guess they are a "team," because it requires all of them performing their tasks to perfection to send a single round downrange.

To my previous list, or "crew," I must add the following: Sheila Cox put my Web page together and never complained about all my stupid questions. My folks, Don and Jeanette Anderson, must be specifically recognized as my primary, initial proofreaders and sounding boards for crackpot ideas. My wife, Christine, continues to put up with my foolishness, and recognizes that I was Taylor long before she met me, and there's nothing she can do about it now.

Again, I want to recognize Ginjer Buchanan and all the people at Roc for their patience and support. Ginjer's the best editor anybody could have.

Finally, thanks again to Russell Galen. He's the best agent there is, and a true friend. If this crew has a "Master Gunner," he's the guy.

One last thing. I was *not* in the Asiatic Fleet. I've done my best to describe the situation, hardships, equipment, and conditions of operations it had to endure at the outbreak of WWII, but I'm sure I've made a bundle of mistakes. I want you to know those mistakes are all Jim's fault. (Just kidding—they're mine, of course, but I had to say that.) To all you Asiatic Fleet destroyermen out there, please accept in advance my most profound apologies for those mistakes, and I hope you'll enjoy the story anyway. It is, after all, ultimately—and most respectfully—dedicated to you.

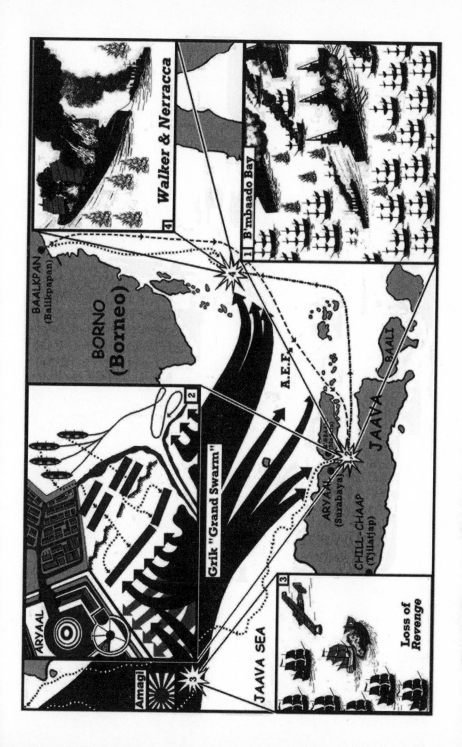

*T*salka, Imperial Regent-Consort and Sire of all India, lounged on his padded, saddlelike throne. The throne was raised upon a triangular platform in the center of a vast oval-shaped stone chamber. An arched ceiling left most of the chamber in shadow for much of the day, and flowering ivies transplanted from the dark jungle floor carpeted all. Only above the throne was there always sunlight. It beamed through a large, ingeniously mirrored opening in the center of the ceiling, and the warm, sensuous rays caressed and illuminated the regent with their favor.

Tsalka idly stroked a small, squirming miniature of himself as it chewed on his long finger-claw. Its sharp teeth were like little needles and its claws and flailing tail tickled his palm. A basket of its nest-mates wobbled near the throne. The tiny mewling growls of the occupants struggling with one another provided amusing distraction from thoughts of the disquieting interview he expected. Word had already reached him that a hunting-pack had been thwarted in some way and he awaited details. Details he might have to convey to the Celestial Mother herself. The first reports hinted that the pack had fallen prey and, deep down, a predatory quickening stirred.

He shouldn't have cared less, on a personal level. He was of the Hij, the elevated, and the primordial impulses no longer held sway. He was one of the few who, through birth and achievement, were allowed to advance beyond the Uul, or warrior/worker stage of life. Not many did, and he had few peers. It was from the Hij alone that the Celestial Mother and her sisters took their consorts and provided a gentle stream of hatchlings that might one day gain the awareness to aspire to elevation themselves. Some became engineers and shipwrights. Others became generals, planners, navigators, or scribes. Still others oversaw the making of arms. Some few, like him, became administrators and viceroys of conquered lands. All were ancient by the standards of the Grik. Tsalka was close to forty and a few Hij even labored to the impossible age of sixty or more.

That was the blessing—to continue to exist and achieve a level of awareness the Uul could never fathom. It was necessary that some should do so, and the responsibility for guiding the Uul and shaping a world for them to enjoy was immense. That was also the curse. The Hij could no longer surrender themselves to the joy of the hunt and the ecstasy of battle. Theirs was the role of organizer—gamekeeper, if you will—and they paid for their elevation by stepping aside to let their charges have all the fun. Sometimes, the burden of the curse was heavy indeed.

The philosophy of the Grik was simple: the Great Hunt was the justification for all existence—to chase prey and devour it, ultimately across the world. One is either predator or prey. Only the predator survives and thrives and it must always hunt. Other predators may join the Great Hunt, but if they refuse, they are prey. Worthy Prey perhaps, but still prey. There are no old Grik, besides the Hij. When they slow down, they become prey and are killed by their young. And so it had ever been.

Because of the blessed abundance of prey upon the world, there had also been an exciting variety of predators. Some were merely animals, but others were quite cunning. Grik history was a comforting series of slowly escalating, playful wars (or hunts) between them and other predators that refused to join them. Other predators—even other Grik—were by far the most satisfying prey. Over time, Worthy Prey became scarce and warfare among the frustrated Grik reached disastrous levels. In times such as those, non-Grik predators often became Worthy Prey whether they wanted to or not. Quite regrettable, of course, but family comes first.

And so, ages ago, a very wise Celestial Mother established the tradition of the "Patient Hunt." By this method, it took considerable time to hunt a species of Worthy Prey to extinction so the Grik wouldn't wipe them out too fast and turn on themselves again. When population and instinctual pressures finally grew too extreme, the Grand Swarm was created. Warriors from every region of the empire mobilized to mount a final campaign to eradicate the target Worthy Prey at last. This not only expanded the empire, but often brought them into contact with new Worthy Prey and the cycle recommenced.

For thousands of years, this custom worked extremely well. Wars still raged between the Celestial Mother's various possessions, but they were usually friendly affairs, often arranged by the regent-consorts so their Uul could enjoy themselves. No such entertainment was currently under way, however. Within the last Uul generation or so, the "Prey That Got Away" had been rediscovered. The histories referred to them simply as "the Tree Prey," because instead of fighting like Worthy Prey, they climbed trees to escape slaughter. They were cowards and not true predators, so they were viewed with the same derision as common grass-eating prey. They'd escaped, however, and that still ruffled Tsalka's tail plumage with the shame of those countless generations past who'd let it happen.

Now they were found—hiding again—across the bottomless sea. But instead of the stately dance of escalation, there was a mood of urgency to amass the Grand Swarm and finally finish this prey before it fled again. Tsalka was point for that effort. Ceylon was the gathering place for the preparing Swarm, and his task was monumental. Theoretically, his duty was primarily organization. The generals in their white ships would plan the hunt itself, but he was regent-consort and certain strategic decisions had been thrust upon him.

A horn thrummed, echoing dully in the chamber. A tall, scarred, massively muscled Hij general approached from the gloom and sprawled upon the triangular platform at his feet. Tsalka heard the scrape of armor and clatter of weapons and, for an instant, his pulse quickened. Sometimes he wished he'd been a general. They could still sometimes play. But they couldn't lose themselves in battle, and that took great discipline. He breathed. "Rise, General Esshk," he said, hissing a pleasant greeting.

Esshk stood and straightened his short cape. It was the bright red of the Celestial Mother's own house. "The Giver of Life sends her greetings to you, Regent Tsalka, her favorite and most noble consort."

Tsalka bowed, acknowledging the compliment. He didn't let it go to his head, though. Esshk probably said that to all the regents. Esshk was arguably the greatest living general. A nest-mate of the current Celestial Mother and probably royal consort as well, he had her ear and favor. He would command the Grand Swarm when it sailed and was subordinate only to the regents and the Celestial Mother herself. Tsalka didn't want Esshk to see him as a fool. "She is ever in my thoughts," he declared piously. "How was your journey?"

"Tedious, sire. Three ships were destroyed by the great monsters in the sea, but that is of little consequence. I brought many more. Still more will arrive when they are completed. You will victual them?"

"Of course."

Esshk paused and spoke again, in a different tone. "I saw . . . interesting things and heard tales from the Hij at the dock."

There it was. Esshk always came straight to the point. Tsalka sighed. "Indeed. There has been interesting news, and some also troubling. Where would you have me begin?"

"With the troubling, I think."

Tsalka's gaze drifted past the general and focused on another shape being escorted from the gloom. His expression hardened. "Very well, General Esshk. How convenient. The 'trouble' has arrived. Step forward, Ship Commander Righ. I would hear your words." Righ crept miserably closer. He'd been divested of his colors and armor and was entirely naked. He approached with his head down, tail between his legs, but did not abase himself before the regent, since such displays of respect were appropriate only from one worthy of it.

"My Uul fell prey. I couldn't stop them."

Tsalka bristled. "Of course you could! That's what the Hij are for—to protect and guide the Uul in their charge!"

"Nevertheless . . ."

Tsalka hissed menacingly but waved one of his long-fingered hands. "Nevertheless, it's done. Your crew will be destroyed—such a waste! What will you use for an excuse?"

Righ told of an attack by a six-ship hunting-pack upon a lone ship of the Tree Prey. All went well until a strange vessel appeared, moving magically fast. By no means he had seen, at an impossible distance, it destroyed the hunters on their own ships as well as those fighting the Tree Prey. His ship was severely damaged. In the face of this horror, all fell prey. All. Righ's crew fled without orders and knocked him senseless to the deck. When he recovered, it was night and they'd escaped. Only darkness saved them.

His crew was ruined, however, and could barely function. With no choice, he set course for Ceylon so at least he might report. On the way, he encountered the large hunting-pack that Tsalka had dispatched to raid the place called Java. He expected to be destroyed as prey but instead, after exchanging chart information, he learned that they too saw the terrible ship and fought it! Unlike Righ's, their ships did not fall prey but many were destroyed.

"What was the result of this fight?" Esshk demanded and Righ looked at him dejectedly.

"Victory, of course. They still lived and prey was taken. The strange ship fled, but under such a pall of smoke that it must have burned to the waterline. When the smoke cleared, the ship was gone. The prey they took was strange, without tails or fur or geydt. They offered and I ate."

"How did it taste?" Tsalka asked, genuinely curious.

"Bland, but tender, sire."

"Interesting. I should like to try one."

"You may, sire. The commander of the hunting-pack sent one with me to bring you as a gift. It's alive and fresh. All others were eaten and their skulls sent with the scouts so they might know them if they encounter more."

The infant in Tsalka's lap bit down on one of his fingers again—hard—and he suddenly remembered it was there. He popped it in his mouth and chewed distractedly. Its struggles tickled the roof of his mouth. He swallowed. "Very well, Righ." Tsalka sighed, still deep in thought. "Every hatchling knows defeat is no excuse to fall prey, and a good commander would never have allowed it. Conversely, you've done much to atone. Therefore, if you're certain you've withheld nothing, you have my permission to destroy yourself after you send this new prey to me."

"Thank you, sire." Righ breathed a sigh of relief. It could have been much, much worse. "Thank you!"

Tsalka waved his hand and Righ was dismissed. He cast an uneasy glance at Esshk. "A most unpleasant business," he observed.

The general hissed agreement. "I wonder about this strange ship and the tail-less creatures that drive it. Were they defending the Tree Prey? Perhaps they saw us as poachers?" He flicked his tail. "No matter. They were defeated, if Righ spoke truth. I see no reason to delay the Swarm. If anything, we might move forward more quickly. If there are more of these tail-less prey, numbers would seem the answer to their threat."

"I agree. I was going to suggest that very thing." Tsalka had a sudden insight. "Perhaps the New Hunters might offer suggestions. They may know of them."

Esshk bowed. "We must certainly ask. That brings us to the 'interesting,' does it not? The docks are abuzz—and I can certainly see why! Is it true they've joined the Great Hunt?"

"It is! And long has it been since that occurred!" Tsalka paused. "I ordered they be spared on my authority. If the Celestial Mother disagrees, I will, of course, destroy them."

"Do they hunt well?"

Tsalka snorted. "Very well indeed! As customary, three assaults were annihilated before the offer of joining was made. Only one ship of twenty returned. That is one reason I am glad you arrived with more! But come! Let us walk in the sun! We may view the New Hunters even as we discuss them." Tsalka rose and swept toward the hall adjoining the chamber. Through a vaulted passage they strolled, chatting amiably, until they reached a high balcony overlooking the vast bay below. It was an awesome spectacle. Hundreds of red-hulled ships dotted the purple water and in the midst of it all was something . . . stupendous.

"Is it not grand?"

Esshk bared his teeth and hissed appreciatively. "I would like to meet these New Hunters."

"And so you shall. They are quite amazing, really, if all I hear is true . . ."

Just then, the two guards that had escorted Righ into the regent's chamber appeared on the balcony. Between them was an emaciated, freakish creature with long, gangly arms and legs. It was naked and filthy and had only a stringy tuft of fur on the top of its head and a shorter growth on its face. The rest of its body was as pale and smooth as a just-hatched Uul. Only its eyes did not seem utterly wrong. They were small, but blazed with the universal expression of terrified hate. Both Hij had seen that before. They looked at the creature with revulsion.

To their surprise, it managed to stand up straight. Blinking in the light, it spoke a few scratchy words in its own tongue. It sounded like . . . something . . . "kaphmaan." Then, amazingly, it uttered a short series of numbers! Numbers they understood! Then it promptly closed its mouth and said nothing more.

"Remarkable!" Tsalka exclaimed. "Do you think it knew what it was saying? Or was that a trick Righ taught it on the long voyage home?"

"I cannot say," Esshk replied. "But it will be interesting to find out." He coughed a laugh. "It might provide conversation over dinner."

"Converse with food? What an appalling thought!"

"I agree. But if Righ may be believed, they are at least Worthy Prey, are they not?"

Tsalka snorted noncommittally. "Perhaps, but I have never spoken to any prey—regardless how worthy it might be."

Esshk replied with a hint of humor. "I beg to differ! Did you not just speak to Righ? Was he not made prey? Besides, what is the difference between Worthy Prey and our very pack-mates? One has joined the Hunt; one has not. That is all."

Tsalka regarded the general with keen speculation. "You're a philosopher, General Esshk. I have long thought it so. No wonder you're so popular at court. But that is . . . a dangerous thought. I urge you to keep it to yourself."

They were startled when the filthy, talking prey suddenly made a strangled cry and flailed madly against its restraints. In its weakened condition, it was quickly reduced to a sobbing, sagging shell; until then, it at least showed some courage. They realized it was the sight of the New Hunters that upset it.

"Well!" hissed Tsalka, pleased. "It must know the New Hunters after all! It reacted as prey to its natural enemy! Fascinating!" He paced to the edge of the balcony, clasping his hands behind his back, tail swishing speculatively. The Grik vessels looked tiny compared to the massive, dark gray ship the New Hunters called their home. It was nearly as large as one of the ridiculous Homes of the Tree Prey. Only *this* ship was iron, he was told, and bristled with huge, magic weapons. He wondered what its flag signified—the curious white flag with bloodred streaks radiating outward from the center.

"What do they call it?" asked the general.

"Hmm? Oh, the ship? I'm told it is called *Amagi* . . . whatever that means!" They both hissed amusement.

The morning general quarters alarm woke Lieutenant Commander Matthew Reddy, and he automatically reached for the little chain beside his sweat-soaked bunk and pulled it. The cramped stateroom was bathed in a harsh white light as he sat up, rubbing his eyes. Awareness came quickly, but not instantly. He always took a moment to get his bearings when he'd been having the Dream, and he'd been right in the middle of it. The same one. It came almost every night and he knew it at the time, almost consciously, but he could never remember it when he woke. He just knew he'd had it again. Even while he dreamed, his subconscious seemed to blot out each sequence of events as soon as they occurred so he was aware only of what was happening at that very moment and, of course, the crippling dread of . . . something he knew was yet to come. Sometimes, like now, if he was disturbed before the Dream reached its horrible, inevitable conclusion, he'd carry a sense of it with him for a while. But, as usual, details vanished as soon as he opened his eyes, like roaches when the lights came on. Even now, the last vestiges of . . . whatever the Dream was diminished like a wisp of smoke in a gale. All he really knew for sure was that the Squall was involved. The Squall that had somehow delivered them from destruction at the hands of the Japanese, but only by marooning them in this twisted, alternate . . . alien world. A world geographically little different from the one they knew, but utterly different in every other conceivable way.

For a while he sat there, struggling to classify the dark, lingering emotional perceptions and taking inventory of the things he knew. They were under way; he could feel the vibration of the warm, dank deck beneath his bare feet. The unusual strain he perceived in the fibers of the ship indicated the "prize" was still under tow. That meant all the terrifying events leading to its capture weren't remnant nightmare threads of the Dream, so everything else he suddenly recalled must have really happened. Damn. He didn't know why the Dream eluded him so. It couldn't be subconscious fear. Nothing could be as scary as the things they'd actually endured since the Squall.

Shaking his head, he stood and moistened a towel in his washbasin. They were already low on fresh water again so he couldn't indulge in a shower. He had to be content with a quick, unrefreshing wipe-down. Finished, he sparingly lathered his face with his last cake of soap and quickly scraped away the stubble. After wiping his face again, he ran a comb through greasy hair and briefly examined the results in his mirror.

"You look like hell," he muttered to himself, then shrugged. "But you've looked worse." There were puffy bags beneath his tired green eyes, and his once embarrassingly boyish face didn't look so boyish now, two months before his thirty-third birthday. A few silver strands had emerged in his light brown hair, certainly due to stress; neither of his parents began to turn gray until their late fifties. The stress was curiously lessened now, however, even if the danger wasn't. They'd fought a battle against a terrifying foe and learned their enemy was even more horrible than they'd imagined. Exponentially worse than the Japanese who had almost destroyed them. But the ship wasn't sinking and they had a steady source of fuel. They had good friends and allies in the Lemurians and if the Grik were a greater threat than they'd feared, the fact they'd finally learned *something* about them, even if it was bad, was a relief of sorts.

When Matt and his crew of Asiatic Fleet destroyermen aboard the old "four-stacker" USS *Walker* (DD-163) had been fighting the Japanese, they'd been outnumbered, outgunned, and on the run. Ridiculously outgunned at the end, when they and their sister ship, *Mahan,* slugged it out with the mighty Japanese battle cruiser *Amagi* right before they'd been swallowed by the Squall. During the two months between Pearl Harbor and their ultimate "escape," Matt's greatest frustration was the way the dwindling remnants of the Asiatic Fleet had been used merely to plug holes in the collapsing Dutch East Indies dike. Even outclassed as they were, the fight needn't have been so lopsided, but an utter lack of air cover, total ignorance of the enemy's strength, dispositions, and intentions, and inept, uncoordinated planning by ABDA's (American, British, Dutch, Australian) multinational leadership had meant they were doomed from the start. They knew they were threatened by an avalanche, but they never knew how big it was or where it would fall.

Until the recent battle, he'd felt much the same frustration about the

Grik. They were the Lemurians' "Ancient Enemy," but their allies didn't really know much about them. The incredibly hostile sea had kept them separated for countless generations. After they captured the Grik ship and the wealth of intelligence aboard it, they finally knew what they faced. It was horrible and it was huge, but at least now they *knew.* The Grik were savage monsters, as numberless as ants, and they were coming to wipe the Lemurians out. They were another looming avalanche that made the threat once posed by the Japanese seem almost insignificant. Since they'd lost track of *Mahan,* all that stood in their way was a single battered Great War–vintage destroyer and a flimsy alliance of disparate and often contentious Lemurian "sea folk" and "land folk" who were torn between fighting and running away. Perhaps unreasonably, however, for the first time since they came through the Squall, Matt actually felt guardedly optimistic.

His ship and her crew had a purpose again, other than simple survival, and the men were united in their determination to help their friends resist the Grik beyond even their earlier determination to resist the Japanese. After all, the Japanese—hated as they were—didn't eat those they conquered. With the discovery of a human skull on the Grik ship, a skull that could have come only from *Mahan,* the war against the Grik became an American war as much as a Lemurian one. That they were the only Americans around, besides those they hoped still survived aboard *Mahan,* was immaterial. *Walker* would lead the struggle. The weary iron ship and her tired iron crew would drag the Lemurians out of the Bronze Age and build an army and whatever else was needed to take the fight to the enemy. Some progress had already been made, but much more would be required before they were ready to begin the crusade Matt had in mind.

He dressed quickly and pushed aside the pea green curtain that separated his stateroom from the short passageway through "officers' country" between the wardroom and the companionway to the deck above. As he strode to the ladder, he almost collided with Nurse Lieutenant Sandra Tucker as she emerged from her quarters, headed for her battle station in the wardroom/surgery. They maneuvered around each other in the confined space, each aware of the electric response that proximity aroused between them. Sandra was short, barely coming to Matt's chin, but even with her sandy brown hair wrapped in a somewhat disheveled bun and her own eyes still puffy with sleep, she was the prettiest woman Matt had ever seen. Not beautiful, but pretty in a wholesome, practical, heart-melting way.

Sandra and five other Navy nurses had come aboard as refugees before *Walker, Mahan,* and three other ships abandoned Surabaya with the Japanese on their heels after the disastrous Battle of the Java Sea. In the running fight that followed, the British cruiser *Exeter* and the destroyers HMS *Encounter* and USS *Pope* were sunk by the remorselessly pursuing enemy, leaving *Walker* and *Mahan* to face *Amagi*—and the Squall—alone. In the frenzied action with the battle cruiser, the two destroyers were mauled, but they'd put at least two torpedoes into *Amagi* and when they came through the Squall, she was gone. They hoped they'd sunk her. Also gone, however, were half of *Mahan*'s crew and a quarter of *Walker*'s—including one of the nurses, killed in action.

Three of the surviving nurses went aboard *Mahan* to care for her many wounded and so, like the ship, they were lost to them. Only Sandra Tucker and Karen Theimer remained—on a ship full of rambunctiously male Asiatic Fleet destroyermen. So far, there'd been few problems, other than a mysterious altercation between some of Matt's junior officers over Nurse Theimer's affections, but Matt and Sandra had both early recognized a growing mutual attraction. They had, in fact, finally declared their love for each other just after the recent battle. But both knew, for the sake of morale, they had to remain aloof in front of the crew. The tension aboard caused by the "dame famine" would only be inflamed, they thought, if they openly acknowledged their affection. Matt was convinced there were other humans in this "new" world—there was too much evidence of previous contact—but he thought "taking" one of the only females known to exist for himself might erode the only real authority he had left: moral example. Matt and Sandra would have been surprised and chagrined to know how poorly kept their "secret" was—the men had eyes, after all—but they'd have been equally surprised by how much real authority Matt still possessed. In spite of the dame famine, his crew would follow him into hell. They already had. They'd done it because when they went, he always personally led them there.

As they turned sideway to pass each other, Sandra's breasts brushed against Matt, and he had to restrain a powerful urge to embrace her. Instead, he merely smiled.

"Morning, Lieutenant."

"Good morning, Captain," she replied, her face darkening slightly. As quick as that, the moment was past, but Matt had a springier step as he trotted up the companionway stairs to the exposed deck and climbed the ladder to the bridge above.

"Captain on the bridge!" cried Lieutenant Garrett, the tall gunnery officer. He had the deck.

"As you were. Status?"

"Reports are still coming in, but we're under time."

Matt nodded and went to his chair, bolted to the forward part of the starboard side of the pilothouse. Sitting, he stared out at the blackness of the lingering, moonless night.

"All stations report manned and ready," announced the bridge talker, Seaman Fred Reynolds. His voice cracked. The seaman was so young-looking that Matt suspected puberty was to blame. He glanced at his watch in the dim reddish light. 0422.

"Not the best time, Mr. Garrett, but not the worst by a long shot."

"No, sir." In spite of the fact the Japanese were no longer a threat, it had become clear that other threats were still very real. Because of that, Matt insisted they maintain all wartime procedures, including predawn battle stations. It was during that time when the sky began to gray but the sea remained black that ships were most vulnerable to submarines, because the ship was silhouetted but the sub's periscope was invisible. Matt wasn't afraid of submarines, but there were other, even more terrifying things in the sea and it was always best to be prepared. Besides, even as the men groused and complained, it was a comforting routine and a clear sign that discipline would be maintained, regardless of their circumstances.

Slowly, the gray light came and lookouts, mostly Lemurian "cadets" because of their keen eyesight, scanned the sea from each bridgewing and the iron bucket "crow's nest" halfway up the tall, skinny mast behind the bridge. As time passed, there were no cries of alarm. Ahead, on the horizon, like a jagged line of stubborn night, rose the coast of Borneo—called "Borno" by the natives—and at their present pace they should raise Balik-papan—"Baalkpan"—by early afternoon. Astern, at the end of the tow-cable, the Grik ship they'd captured began to take shape. She was dismasted, but the red-painted hull still clearly reflected the shape of the long-ago-captured British East Indiaman she was patterned after. Bluff bow, elevated quarterdeck, three masts, and a bowsprit that had all gone by the board in the fighting. Just looking at her, Matt felt his skin crawl.

The fight when they took her was bad enough: the darkness, the shooting, the screams, and the blood. He vividly remembered the resistance he felt when he thrust his Academy sword into the throat of a ravening Grik. The exultation and the terror. Exultation that he'd stabbed it before it could rip him to shreds with its terrible teeth and claws; terror that he had only the ridiculous sword to prevent it from doing so. The first Grik he killed on the ship had been disarmed, but certainly not without weapons. They were like nothing he'd ever seen. Fuzzy, bipedal . . . lizards, with short tails and humanlike arms. But their teeth! They had the jaws of nightmare and claws much like a grizzly's. So even though it lost its axe, he was lucky to survive. Then, and many times after. Of course, later it was different. When they chased the remnants of the Grik into the hold of the wallowing ship, they realized that the horror they'd felt before was nothing. Only then did the true nature of the Grik become clear to everyone, humans and Lemurians alike, and he *wanted* to use the sword. The hold was a slaughterhouse, where captives of every sort were butchered for food—while they were alive. Matt had wanted live Grik to study, but that became impossible. He couldn't restrain the Lemurian "Marines" under his command. He didn't even try to restrain himself.

The horrible nature of their enemy should have made their victory that much more satisfying, but when they studied the captured charts and learned the extent and population of the empire they faced, Matt, Keje-Fris-Ar, and ultimately Keje's Sky Priest, Adar, finally realized they must plan boldly or die.

It was light enough now that he could see the distant, hazy shape of Keje's great seagoing "Home." Even miles astern, it still looked massive—because it was. The incredibly thick wooden hull with its ingenious diagonal bracing was as large as one of America's new carriers, like the *Hornet,* and each of the three tripod masts rising around pagoda-like living areas supported immense junklike sails, or "wings," as tall as *Walker* was long. *Salissa*—"*Big Sal*" to the Americans—was typical of her breed of seagoing Homes, but she was now armed with ten 32-pounder cannons that had performed with murderous effect against another Grik ship and all the boarders from three. The cannons were the result of the efforts of the suddenly tireless supply officer, Alan Letts, whom Matt had left behind in Baalkpan to continue overseeing the production of more guns and other things. Also, to keep him away from his other officers, since he seemed to be the one Nurse Theimer had chosen. He hoped the period of "out of sight and out of mind" might help his officers reconcile when they met again.

He sighed and looked at his watch. Speaking of reconciliation and discipline . . . As soon as the men were released from morning GQ, the ship would continue steaming at condition III, as she always did now, with half the guns manned at all times. Some of the men would try to go back to sleep and others would remain to fulfill their morning watch duties. But the forenoon watch, at 0800, would begin with a session of "captain's mast," where he'd have to decide punishment for two of the most valuable members of the crew. For the sake of morale, he didn't want to break them—besides, he needed them too badly. But he couldn't be seen as just slapping their wrists either. He'd have to walk a fine line.

Eventually 0530 rolled around and visibility was sufficient to secure from general quarters. Lieutenant Garrett was replaced by Lieutenant Dowden, Matt's new exec. He'd been at his battle station on the auxiliary conn, aft, before arriving to relieve Mr. Garrett. The former officer to hold his position was James Ellis, but he'd been given *Mahan* after the Squall because most of her officers were killed when a ten-inch shell shattered her bridge. They'd learned from Lieutenant Ben Mallory, U.S. Army Air Corps, and Lieutenant Brister, *Mahan*'s engineering officer, that Mallory's superior, Captain Kaufman, had shot Jim Ellis and taken over the ship. That's why she hadn't been at the rally point after they split up. Mallory, Brister, and Signalman Ed Palmer had arrived in a "found" PBY Catalina after a harrowing escape from the Grik. That was the only reason they knew anything at all about what happened to the other ship. The last information had her off the west coast of Sumatra, heading for Ceylon, a place they now knew teemed with Grik. All they could do at present was hope Jim had survived and managed to retake the ship before the Grik wound up with her. The discovery of the human skull aboard the prize made that seem unlikely. So in addition to their other problems, they also had to either rescue *Mahan* or destroy her.

"May we come on the bridge?" came a hesitant voice from behind him. Matt turned and saw Courtney Bradford standing on the ladder with Sandra. Bradford seemed uncharacteristically subdued. Normally, the Australian engineer and self-proclaimed "naturalist" wouldn't have even asked. *Maybe Sandra made him,* Matt thought. He expected he might have seemed as though he was concentrating on something—which he was—but he was actually glad of the distraction. Bradford hadn't been there for the fighting, but he'd arrived on the PBY flying boat the following day. Since then, he'd spent most of his time inspecting the prize. That was enough to sober anyone.

Theoretically, no one was really in charge of Courtney Bradford. Since the Australian engineer was a civilian, his status was somewhat vague and had been allowed to remain that way because he worked well without constraint. Before the Japanese attacked, he'd been an upper-level engineering consultant for Royal Dutch Shell. That occupation allowed him to pursue his true passion: the study of the birds and animals of the Dutch East Indies. Also because of that occupation, however, stuffed in his briefcase when he evacuated Surabaya aboard *Walker* were maps that showed practically every major oil deposit Shell had ever found in the entire region. There'd been some skepticism that the same oil existed on this earth as the other, but after the success of their first well—exactly where Courtney told them to drill—they were all believers now.

"Of course. Good morning."

"Good morning to you, I'm sure," Bradford replied, stepping on the bridge. Sandra just smiled at him. Matt gestured through the windows at the landmass ahead, becoming more distinct.

"Almost home," he said, with only a trace of irony.

"Indeed," agreed Bradford, removing his battered straw hat and massaging his sweaty scalp. It was still early morning, but almost eighty degrees. Matt had noticed, however, that Courtney usually did that when he was upset or concerned. "I've been studying that map you gave me. The one that was apparently drawn by the Grik captain himself, not the navigational charts with all their incomprehensible references . . ." Matt nodded. Even though the Grik charts were disconcertingly easy for him to read, since much was, horrifyingly, written in English, Matt knew which map Courtney meant. It was just a drawing, really, that basically depicted the "Known World" as far as the Grik were concerned. It showed rough approximations of enemy cities and concentrations, and it also showed much of what the enemy knew of this part of the world—the part that should be the Dutch East Indies. It was much like what one would expect of a map showing "this we hold; this we want." The farther east it went, the vaguer it became, but Java, Sumatra, and Singapore were depressingly detailed and accurate. There were also tree symbols that represented known cities of the People, and many of those had been smeared with a blot that looked like blood, symbolizing, they believed, that a battle had been fought there. Currently, there was no tree symbol at Baalkpan, but there were two others that didn't have smears beside them. One was near Perth, Australia, and the other was at Surabaya, or "Aryaal," as the locals there called it. The map also depicted a massive force growing near Ceylon and Singapore too, which was believed to be their most forward and tenuous outpost.

"Captain, since only Perth and Surabaya appear on the enemy map, we can only assume the next blow will fall on one or both of those places. I'd bank on Surabaya myself. I'm no strategist, but it seems to me, judging by the dispositions on the map, the Grik are planning a major offensive against that place and it will probably commence within weeks, if it has not done so already."

"That's kind of the impression I got, too," agreed Matt.

"But what are we going to do about it?" Sandra asked, speaking for the first time. Matt shrugged.

"As you know, Keje and I have been kicking some options around and we've come up with some good ideas, I think. But we can't do it alone. A lot will depend on the other Homes in Baalkpan Bay, but most will depend on Nakja-Mur." He grimaced. "Not that I expect much trouble out of Nakja-Mur. He won't leave his city and unlike the seagoing Homes, he can't take it with him. I think he'll cooperate, but it'll be a tough sell." He sighed. "Lemurians are basically peaceful folks, at least the ones we've met. With a few exceptions, it's hard enough to turn them into warriors—soldiers that can defend themselves. To then send those soldiers far away to defend other people, Aryaalans, who they don't even like . . ." He looked at Bradford. "We need to find out what it is about those people that makes everyone dislike them so. Ever since we first came here, they've tried to steer us clear of Surabaya. Why?"

"I get the impression there are certain . . . frictions between them based primarily on substantially different cultures. There may even be a religious angle involved," Bradford replied. "I don't think it's insignificant that, unlike almost everywhere else in the region, only south-central Java ever had human-based names. Chill-chaap instead of Tjilatjap, for example. Other places are even more obvious. Borno for Borneo. Why do North Java's city names bear no resemblance to human names at all? The Lemurians we know base so much of their culture upon the 'Scrolls' or charts that were rendered from those British ships so long ago. Perhaps the Aryaalans and others like them never had contact with them, or the 'prophet' Siska-Ta who later spread the word?" He spread his hands. "I have no idea."

"We're going to have to find out. We might need them." Matt looked back at "Borno." Even at their crawling pace of five knots, towing the derelict and trying not to get too far from *Big Sal,* they should open Baalkpan Bay late that afternoon. It would be an . . . interesting homecoming. He wondered what the reaction of the people there would be. Joy at first, certainly, that they'd returned victorious. But he wondered what would happen when all they'd learned got out. Several of the huge seagoing "Homes" would probably withdraw from the alliance. Nakja-Mur, Baalkpan's High Chief, would be terrified, but he'd stand firm. He had no choice. Baalkpan couldn't go anywhere. Matt just hoped he'd understand the necessity to implement the plan he and Keje had begun to form. Even Keje had seen that a purely defensive war was hopeless. Static defenses in the face of the numbers the enemy had could not succeed. They could bleed them white and kill dozens to one, but as the Ancient Scrolls of the Lemurian "People" foretold, no matter how many Grik you killed, there were always more. In a defensive stance, sooner or later they'd be overwhelmed. If they wanted to win, they must take the fight to the Grik.

At the appointed hour, the two miscreants were brought forward to stand before the captain on the well deck behind the bridge. Sonny Campeti, master at arms, shouted for attention. One of the accused, Gunner's Mate 2nd Class Dennis Silva, was no stranger to the procedure and he snapped a sharp salute. If not quite an actual giant of a man, he was only the next size smaller, powerfully muscled and standing six foot three. His hair was still cropped nearly to his skull, but he'd allowed a thick brown beard to form on his face, which seemed perpetually parted in a gap-toothed grin. In addition to a black eye and a swollen nose, there seemed to be a bigger gap than before. Silva was *Walker*'s Hercules, utterly fearless in battle and an expert with any firearm. He'd also shown a surprising proficiency with a cutlass. But he was also, possibly, the most depraved individual Matt had ever known. He gloried in practical jokes, but his "jokes" often got out of hand. Sometimes dangerously so.

Matt turned his attention to the other accused. Chack-Sab-At was a Lemurian, or "'Cat," as the general consensus had compromised on. Some of the "snipes," or engineering division, still insisted on calling Lemurians "monkey-cats" while equally stubborn deck division "apes" remained adamant about "cat-monkeys." Simply "'Cat" had become universally accepted, however. Chack, a former "wing runner" aboard *Big Sal*, had been the first to join the "Amer-i-caan" Clan and learn the destroyermen's language. As *Walker's* Lemurian contingent grew, he'd been duly inducted into the United States Navy, given the rank of boatswain's mate 3rd class, and placed over the Lemurian—essentially second—deck division. He was tall for a Lemurian, topping five-six, and like any wing runner he was incredibly strong. He wore a bright red kilt over his lower body, and a white T-shirt covered the upper. Only his legs, arms, face, and carefully rigid tail exposed his dark, brindled fur. Wide amber eyes peered from an expressionless but highly feline face. His long ears twitched nervously. One eye was puffier than the other and his cleft lips were split and swollen. He'd once been a pacifist, Matt understood, but that was clearly no longer the case. He'd distinguished himself in several fights now, most recently with Dennis Silva.

Besides the wounds they'd inflicted on each other, both still bore wounds from the hellish battle with the Grik. Chack walked with a limp from a badly sprained ankle he got while fighting on the slippery bones and ballast stones in the belly of the Grik ship, and Silva's arm was bandaged from elbow to wrist from a wicked sword slash.

Matt was surprised how many of the crew had gathered to witness the proceedings. He knew all would be curious how it turned out and, because of that, he must not only be scrupulously fair, which he always strived to be, but he must be *perceived* as scrupulously fair. With so many men left in Baalkpan working on essential projects, almost half of *Walker's* crew were 'Cats. That was one reason he'd sort of rushed the "trial." He feared that if he waited until they reached port, word would spread and create a circus—possibly a highly partisan one—right when they all needed as much unity as possible. The situation had to be dealt with, but it was better to do it now, here, while they could handle it among themselves.

"Since you're both charged with essentially the same offenses and the offenses occurred simultaneously, we'll make this easy. Any objections?"

Chief Boatswain's Mate Fitzhugh Gray and Lieutenant Garrett stepped forward, representing their respective divisions.

"No, sir," they chorused. Matt looked at his exec, Lieutenant Dowden. "You're the reporting officer."

"Aye, aye, sir. The incident in question occurred aboard *Big Sal*, during the celebration after we joined her with the prize. *Walker* sent over several liberty parties during the course of the evening to participate in the festivities, but neither of the accused had specific permission to be aboard."

Matt looked at them. "How do the accused respond to the first charge: absent without leave?"

Chack began to speak, but Chief Gray stepped forward and interrupted him.

"Captain, Bosun's Mate Chack was escorting one of the 'prisoners' we rescued from the Grik . . . larder." Everyone, even Matt, flinched at the memory of that. The creatures had been emaciated and, for the most part, wildly insane. "One of the prisoners was known to him, and delivering him aboard *Big Sal* was a highly personal act and one that, had I known he was doing it, I certainly would have approved." He looked at Chack. "The accused pleads guilty, but under extenuating circumstances that include not only family but foreign relations." Matt had to smile at Gray's imaginative defense, but his own memory of the event was not amusing. The prisoner Chack escorted was none other than Saak-Fas, the mate of Keje-Fris-Ar's daughter, Selass. He'd disappeared in battle with the Grik many months before and was considered lost. In the meantime, Selass had developed a desperate love for Chack and had expected him to answer her proposal to mate, after the battle. The scene when he returned her mad, barely living mate to her, a mate she'd never really loved, was heartrending.

"In view of the 'extenuating circumstances,' the first charge against Bosun's Mate Chack-Sab-At is dismissed," Matt declared. "Mr. Garrett? Have you anything to say on Gunner's Mate Silva's behalf?"

Garrett looked at the big, grinning man and took an exasperated breath. "Guilty, sir. His only defense is that some other fellas did it too."

"Unacceptable. Mr. Dowden?"

"Uh, the next charge is that both the accused became involved in, well, a brawl, sir, and not only were they at the center of the brawl but they started it by striking one another."

Matt sighed. "I won't even ask who started it. I know I won't get a straight answer. Besides, I have a pretty good idea. If I'm not very much mistaken, I expect Chack threw the first punch—"

"He pulled my tail!" Chack interrupted, seething indignantly.

"Did not! I was just holdin' it. You did all the pullin'!"

"Silence!" Matt bellowed. "Trust me, you both would really rather keep your mouths shut and handle this my way! Silva, your unnatural and hopefully pretend 'relationship' with Chack's sister, Risa, was all very shocking and amusing . . . at first. It's now not only an embarrassment to this ship but a constant goad to Chack's self-control. I know Risa's as much to blame as you are. You're two peas in a pod, personality wise, if not . . ." He shuddered. "In any event, you'll cease tormenting Chack with the lurid details of your fictitious 'marriage' to his sister and you'll *definitely* refrain from any more . . . overt physical demonstrations when you are together. Is that understood?"

"But, Skipper . . ."

"IS THAT UNDERSTOOD?"

"Aye, aye, sir!"

"Very well. It's pointless to dock your pay, but you're both losing a stripe and you're both restricted to the ship for ten days—after we make port. Silva, you're losing another stripe for AWOL."

"But—"

"Shut up." Matt looked at Dowden, who cleared his throat.

"Attention to orders!" he said. Captain Reddy unfolded a piece of paper before him.

"For extreme heroism and gallantry in the face of the enemy, etc., etc."—he looked up—"I'm sorry to you other guys, but I'm still too damn mad to get flowery. Anyway, with my deepest gratitude, I'm proud to advance the following men one grade in rank: Coxswain Tony Scott, quartermaster's mate 3rd, Norman Kutas—" He stopped for a moment and sighed heavily. "Boatswain's Mate Chack-Sab-At and Gunner's Mate Dennis Silva. Most of you deserve it. Chack, you lose one, you gain one, so you're back where you started—except for the restriction. Silva . . ." Matt shook his head. "You're never going to get that first-class stripe if you don't settle down!" Dennis shrugged philosophically and Matt looked at Campeti, who concluded the proceedings. As they walked back to the pilothouse, Matt and Dowden were rejoined by Sandra and Bradford. Both wore broad smiles. "Cut it out," he said, almost smiling himself as he mounted the steps. At the top waited Lieutenant Tamatsu Shinya of the Japanese Imperial Navy.

"Mr. Shinya," Matt greeted him.

"Captain." Shinya was the sole survivor of a destroyer that took a torpedo meant for *Amagi*. Somehow, her survivors in the water had been swept through the Squall with the American ships, but before *Walker* could return to rescue them, they'd been eaten by what was evidently a plesiosaur of some sort, not to mention a ravening swarm of tuna-sized fish that acted like piranhas. They called the fish "flashies" and they were everywhere, at least in the relatively shallow equatorial seas within the Malay Barrier. Shinya alone was saved because he'd been unconscious atop an overturned lifeboat. It had been the first indication to the destroyermen that they were no longer in the world they knew—the first other than the bizarre effects of the Squall itself, of course.

Since then, Shinya, who had studied in the United States, had given his parole and had become a valued member of the crew. He was an excellent swordsman, if not in the traditional Japanese style, and he was a big help to Sergeant Alden, the Marine from the doomed cruiser *Houston,* whom they'd also carried from Surabaya. Together, they were building an army based on historical principles the captain had suggested. Matt had realized early on that the only way they could counter the overwhelming Grik numbers was with discipline—specifically, the Roman shield wall, backed by spears and archers. At least that's what they'd need in an open-field fight. Shinya also understood Latin, which was, amazingly, the language of the Ancient Scrolls of the 'Cats. Not because it was taught them by Romans, but because that's the language the sailing master of the HEIC (Honorable East India Company) ship *Hermione* chose to teach them and communicate in.

Matt suspected the earlier visitors did it to remain as enigmatic as possible, since there was evidence they'd already encountered the Grik, even before one of their ships was taken by them. The rest of the "Tail-less Ones" of that long ago visit had sailed into the "Eastern Sea" beyond the "edge of the world" and disappeared from Lemurian history. Matt suspected they were still out there, somewhere. British Indiamen often carried passengers and deportees, so there was reason to believe they'd survived. Anyway, that's how they first communicated with the 'Cats; Bradford and Tamatsu Shinya spoke the "Ancient Tongue" of the Lemurian Sky Priests.

Valuable as Shinya was, many of Matt's destroyermen still hated his guts simply because he was a "Jap." Matt respected him and trusted his honor, but even he couldn't put Pearl Harbor—and everything that had happened since—completely out of his mind. Chief Gray openly loathed him, despite saving his life in the recent battle. Tony Scott told him something he hadn't even known about the Bosun: his son had been on the *Oklahoma* when she capsized and sank to Pearl Harbor's muddy bottom.

"Where's Pete?" asked the captain, referring to the Marine.

"He'll be along," Shinya replied. Even as he spoke, Alden and Chief Gray arrived on the bridge. Matt noticed that Alden's limp was now totally gone and even the Bosun was in better shape. He was close to sixty, but the once chubby man wasn't even breathing hard after the stairs. After Ensign Bernard Sandison, the torpedo officer, and Brad "Spanky" McFarlane, the engineering officer, arrived, the entire group Matt had summoned for this little conference was present. Ahead, through the windows, Borno grew ever larger and more distinct as the clock on the bulkhead neared 0930. Baalkpan fishing boats began to gather around them, and Matt permitted a single celebratory toot from *Walker*'s whistle. Regardless of the news they bore, he didn't want too somber a homecoming. The people of Baalkpan would need a little happiness to balance the dread to come. Sheets flew on a few of the nimble fore-and-aft-rigged feluccas, and they surged ahead in a turmoil of spray taking the news of their arrival to the city. He motioned to the starboard bridgewing, and the others joined him there. Without further pleasantries, he began.

"When we make port, things are going to be a lot different and they're going to change really fast. We've been trying to ease these people out of the Bronze Age, and despite a lot of bitching and bickering we've made a lot of progress. Not enough. I've already spoken to Keje and Adar about this, as well as a few of you." His gaze lingered on Sandra. "When we dock at Baalkpan we all have to be on the same page with the same message: we're in a crummy spot, but we're going to *win,* and this is how we're going to do it." He smiled a little awkwardly. "I'll go into 'how' a little more in a minute. As for now, I'm not through giving out promotions. I'll have to run a few of these by Nakja-Mur, since they'll impact his people more than anyone's, but he's in over his head." Matt snorted ironically. No one felt that way more than he. "And he trusts us. The first thing we're going to have to do when we get back is call for another 'great gathering.' Way bigger than the last one. Try to get folks to come from everywhere. Right now, there's no real chain of command, so we'll have to get that sorted out. However it shakes out, I expect we'll be somewhere near the top. That means everybody's jobs are going to get bigger and harder." He looked at Pete. "Right now, the Marines are yours. We got that straight with Nakja-Mur from the start. That's close to a thousand well-trained troops," he said with a grimace, "with a fair sprinkling of seriously hard-core veterans. Some of them will get broken up again, to form a cadre of NCOs and even officers, because as soon as we get back, you'll continue to work to build the biggest, most modern army we can field without firearms. I'll talk to Letts about supplying some field artillery at least, but otherwise, keep training them like you already were. It's within my power, I think, to award you the brevet rank of captain under the circumstances."

Pete Alden gulped. "Sir, I'm just a sergeant. I ain't no officer!"

"You are now. Hell, I'd make you a general, but then you'd outrank me!"

"You could make yourself an admiral, Captain," Bradford suggested, but Matt shook his head.

"It's not right," he said softly. "I might take full captain because I bet all *Walker*'s officers would have jumped a grade or two if we'd made it to Perth, and that'll leave me a little room to raise some guys up that deserve it. For example, as of right now, there are no more ensigns aboard this ship. All are now jay-gees. The jay-gees are full lieutenants." He grinned at Dowden and Sandison. "That includes you two. Start looking for guys, human or 'Cat, that we can make ensigns out of." He looked back at Alden. "Who do you want as your second?" There was really only one choice, but Matt wouldn't force the Marine to make it.

Alden glanced almost reluctantly at Shinya. "You're the guy, if you want it," he said. "I got no reservations, but some of the fellas might. 'Course, you'll be commanding 'Cats for the most part and they don't give a hoot you're a Jap. But there's a few guys you might want to hold off giving orders to."

Shinya bowed. "I am honored to accept. There should be few occasions for me to command any American personnel. If the need arises and I cannot find you, I will try to be conscious of their"—he smiled—"sensitivity." Matt coughed.

"Fine. You'll stay a lieutenant, under Alden. Let's see, for chain-of-command purposes, since Marine captain equals general"—he grinned, much to Pete's discomfort—"first lieutenant means colonel, second is major . . . hell, that won't work!"

"As I was saying," Bradford insisted. "You could still be admiral and make things a lot simpler. No one back home would ever know or care!" Matt gave him a hard stare.

"Why don't I just declare myself king? What's the difference? Where does it stop?" He shook his head. "I don't know what we'll do, but we'll figure something out." He looked at Sandra. "You've made great strides, not only learning Lemurian medicine, which certainly has its virtues, but in teaching them our methods as well. I think both have complemented the other." That was certainly true. The Lemurians had an antibacterial, analgesic paste made, like many other things Sandra had discovered, from the fermented polta fruit that grew wild in the region and was cultivated aboard the massive seagoing Homes. A less arduous and more refined fermentation of the polta also produced the popular intoxicating beverage known as seep.

The 'Cats had learned from Sandra too. Being generally unwarlike, they'd never dealt with anything like the casualties they'd suffered during their recent battles, and her instructions in battlefield medical techniques had been invaluable. She'd already begun forming a hospital corps in Baalkpan. "I want you to keep up the good work, but be ready to really expand your operation. Concentrate on teaching teachers." Sandra nodded grimly. She knew what Captain Reddy planned. It scared her to death, but it seemed the only option.

"That leaves you, Mr. Bradford. Eventually, I want another well site.

We'll have to sort out where, but right now all our eggs are in one basket. What if there's an accident or some other stoppage at the site we have? What if, God forbid, the enemy overruns it? I want one that's essentially in a reserve position, building a reserve of fuel. Any ideas?"

Bradford looked thoughtful. "Again, let me consult my charts. I'll come up with some likely areas and you can tell me which is best for your strategic needs. Agreed?"

"Agreed."

Spanky snorted a laugh. "The Mice are gonna hate that!" The others chuckled in agreement.

No single word or phrase was adequate to describe the Mice. "Strange" came closest, but was still almost too specific. By their appearance, Isak Rueben and Gilbert Yager might have been brothers. Both were intense, wiry little men with narrow faces and sharp, pointed noses that contributed much to the rodentlike impression they made. They were irascible, unfriendly and annoying to just about everyone they came in contact with. They never socialized and had always shunned the ship's baseball team. They were quintessential "snipes"—firemen, to be precise—but they took it much further than that. Given a choice, they would never leave the sweltering heat of their beloved firerooms and the boilers they worshipped there. They were painfully insular and apparently just as unimaginative, but Spanky had recently learned there was more to them than met the eye.

Normally, their skins were pasty with a belowdecks pallor they worked very hard to maintain, but now their exposed skin still bore the angry red-brown tans they'd accumulated while operating the first oil rig outside of Baalkpan. A rig they designed based on a type they were intimately, if ruefully, familiar with from their years in the oil fields before they escaped that hated life and joined the Navy. Now they were back at it and not happy at all.

Matt looked back toward Borno. He thought he could just make out the mouth of Baalkpan Bay. "We're all going to have to do things we hate, I'm afraid, before this is over." He sighed. "It's going to be a hell of a homecoming," he added nervously.

As the day wore on and the crew went about their duties, *Walker* towed her prize ever closer to Baalkpan. The nearer they got, the more traders and fishing boats paced her advance. Opening the bay, the old destroyer steamed toward her customary berth near the shipyard and the fitting-out pier. They had been gone less than two weeks, most of that time laying their trap for the Grik scouts they engaged. The battle itself took only a day, and the return voyage took three. The people had known the outcome, however, since the very day after the fight. The radio in the precious PBY was working now, and there had been constant reports.

Then the big seaplane had flown out with passengers to examine the prize. Some, like Bradford, stayed with the returning ships, but those who returned on the plane were strangely tight-lipped. No matter. The dismasted hulk trailing in *Walker*'s wake was sufficient proof to the populace that the expedition had been a success.

As always, Matt was struck by the sight of the large, strange, but exotically beautiful city of Baalkpan. The unusual architecture of the multistoried buildings was strikingly similar to the pagoda-like structures that rose within the tripod masts of the great floating Homes. Some reached quite respectable heights and were highly decorated and painted with bright colors. Some were simple, one-story affairs, but all were elevated twenty or more feet above the ground by multitudes of stout pilings. Chack once told him that was done in order to protect against high water and "bad land lizards." It was also tradition, which Matt supposed was as good a reason as any. He'd never seen any creatures ashore that could threaten anyone twenty feet above the ground, but he was assured they did exist. He believed it. There was certainly plenty of bizarre fauna in this terrible, twisted world.

Among the pilings, under the massive structures, was what some would call the "real" Baalkpan. It was there, beneath the buildings themselves or colorful awnings stretched between them, that the city's lifeblood pulsed. It was a giant, chaotic bazaar that rivaled anything Matt had seen in China, or heard of anywhere else. Little organization was evident, beyond an apparent effort to congregate the various products or services in strands, or vaguely defined ranks. From experience, Matt knew there was no law or edict that required this; it was just practicality. This way, shoppers always knew where they had to go to find what they wanted. Along the waterfront, fishmongers hawked the daily catch with an incomprehensible staccato chatter. Beyond were food vendors, and the savory smells of Lemurian cooking wafted toward them, competing with the normal harbor smells of salt water, dead fish, and rotting wood. Still farther inland were the textile makers—weavers, cloth merchants, and clothiers. Closer to the center of the city, near the massive Galla tree and Great Hall of Nakja-Mur, one was more likely to find finer things, like ornamental clothing, exquisitely wrought jewelry, and even fine blades. The foulsmelling commerce in gri-kakka oil took place beyond the shipyard, as far from the center of Baalkpan as possible. The rendered oil was sweet, but only after separation from the often rancid tallow.

Matt took all this in: the vibrant, throbbing vitality of a city and people who'd never known threats other than natural ones. They had tails and fur, and if Bradford was right, they were actually descended from giant Madagascar lemurs, even if they looked more like a cross between cats and monkeys—with a little human thrown in, he reminded himself. But regardless, they were people. Many happily rushed down to the waterfront to cheer *Walker* and her crew and gape at the captured hulk of their dreaded enemy. Soon the dock was jammed with wildly celebrating multitudes, making it difficult for the line handlers to tie off. *Walker* remained singled up. Immediately, curious townsfolk tried to storm aboard the Grik ship, but Matt had foreseen this. Fifty hard-eyed "Marines" lined the ship's bulwarks and stood ready to repel them. Matt turned to look back at the mouth of the bay. Keje and his much slower *Big Sal* weren't even visible yet.

At least Nakja-Mur and Naga were aware of the situation, and a hundred guards, led by Lieutenant Alan Letts, arrived from the parade ground in front of the Great Hall. They immediately set up a protective cordon in front of not just the prize but *Walker* as well. The celebrating people didn't seem to mind. Good. If they'd managed to get aboard the Grik ship and have a look around, things might have turned ugly really fast. At the very least, they might have burned it—and he couldn't have that.

He noticed with slight reassurance that some effort had been made to begin fortifying the city since he left. A low earthen breastworks had been started here and there, and trees had been felled a short distance beyond it to make a killing ground. Inadequate as it was, at least it was something, but the People of Baalkpan were about to learn how pathetic their efforts to date truly were.

"The prize is secure and there seems a sufficient guard around it," reported Dowden from the auxiliary conn atop the aft deckhouse. The bridge talker repeated the message to the captain.

"Very well. Cast off the towline. Hoist a signal for Nakja-Mur. Tell him we're going upriver to the fueling pier. We'll fill our bunkers and I'll make a full report tonight, when Keje and *Big Sal* arrive."

"Aye, aye, Captain," replied Riggs. He went to supervise as one of the signalman strikers ran up the appropriate bunting. Matt still had the conn, and he directed the watch to use the engines and rudder to move them away from the pier once more. The rudder hard over, the port engine pushed the stern away from the dock. Then, after the special sea and anchor detail released the final forward line, *Walker* slowly backed clear. Matt looked at the crowd on the dock and smiled.

"Might as well give them a show," he said. With a quick glance to make sure they were clear, he continued, "Right standard rudder, all ahead full!" *Walker* gave a shuddering groan that seemed almost like a sigh of relief that she was no longer burdened with the deadweight of the prize, and her stern crouched down and churned a mighty, muddy froth above the fantail. Even over the rising roar of the blower, Matt heard the excited cries of the crowd's appreciation. Quickly, still on three boilers, the aged thoroughbred accelerated into a wide turn that took her deeper into the bay and, ultimately, upriver to the fueling pier. *We need another one of those down here,* Matt thought. He looked at Mr. Riggs. "Honk the horn!" he said with a grin.

The crowd still milling near the red-hulled ship cheered louder as a cloud of steam and a deep, resonant shriek jetted from the whistle and the amazing iron ship raced upstream, raising a feather halfway up her number, smoke streaming from three of her four funnels.

"Let 'em have a good time for a while," Matt said, his voice turning grim.

"Aryaalans!" snorted Nakja-Mur later that evening, standing on *Walker's* bridge where she was again tied to the Baalkpan docks. He hadn't waited for Matt to report. As soon as *Walker* returned from fueling, he and the just-arrived Keje tromped up the gangway. "You ask me to risk everything for those unfriendly land-bound . . . heretics?" Matt and Keje had been describing the details of the battle and the capture of the enemy vessel. The account turned to the discovery of the enemy charts, or "Evil Scrolls of Death," as Sky Priest Adar insisted they be called. That led to their theory of an impending Grik attack on the people of Surabaya: "Aryaalans," as they called themselves. Chack was present to interpret, but so far, between Keje, Nakja-Mur's rapid advancement in English, and Matt's slowly growing proficiency in Lemurian, he hadn't been needed.

Matt sighed. "With respect, my lord, it's essential we go to their aid if they're attacked."

"But why? Let them fend for themselves, as do we. They were invited to the last gathering and they chose—as always—not to dampen themselves with the company of sea folk!"

Matt was tempted to point out that Nakja-Mur was, however sensible, the very definition of a landsman. But to be fair, the People of Baalkpan were every bit as sea-oriented as the people of Old Nantucket ever were. They built and repaired ships and they dealt in the products of the sea's capricious bounty. Their livelihood was entirely centered around maritime toil and commerce. Whereas the Surabayans were . . .

"Just what the hell is it about them you don't like?" Matt asked in frustration.

"They . . . they are heretics!" Nakja-Mur proclaimed.

"Why?"

Nakja-Mur shifted uncomfortably and paced out on the port bridgewing. Matt and Keje followed him there, and Larry Dowden joined them. There was a reduced watch on the bridge since they weren't under way, but a torpedoman had been tinkering with the director connections. Matt motioned for him to leave them and the man quickly gathered his tools and departed.

"Why?" Matt asked again.

"Perhaps you should ask Adar."

"I can't. He and Bradford ran off to study together as soon as we rigged the gangway. Who knows where. Besides, I have to ask you because you're the one whose opinion really matters, in the long run, and we have decisions to make . . . *you* have decisions to make. I know, traditionally all 'High Chiefs' are equals here, but surely you know that in reality you're a little more 'equal' than the others? You have the largest force and Baalkpan's the most populous city this side of Manila—and it's on your industry we all depend."

Nakja-Mur grunted, but his tone wasn't unfriendly. "I have heard it said you're the most 'equal' among us, because of this ship." He patted the rail under his hand.

Matt shook his head. "Untrue. Without you and Baalkpan, this ship would most likely be a powerless, lifeless hulk on a beach somewhere and I and most of my people would be dead. I agree your people owe *Walker* much, but she owes you as well. It's pointless to keep score among friends. We're obligated, bound together, but as great as that combined strength might be, it's not enough and it'll be even less if Surabaya falls. We need those people on our side—not filling Grik bellies!"

Nakja-Mur recoiled as if slapped, but then nodded. "The Aryaalans are fierce warriors," he conceded, "but they do not revere the heavens. They may worship feces for all I know, but the sky is not sacred. When Siska-Ta went to them to teach the wisdom of the Scrolls, she was cast out and nearly slain." He made a very human shrug. "They are heathens, but their religion is unimportant to me. We are not intolerant of the beliefs of others. Many folk of other lands—even some upon the sea—do not believe as we do and yet we remain friends. Did we not befriend you and your people?" he asked.

Matt didn't point out the probability that they thought then—and probably still did—that the destroyermen had very similar beliefs to their own, and he remembered the scene Adar made in *Walker*'s pilothouse over the charts displayed there. He'd thought they mocked him with apostasy at the time, since the Ancient Scrolls or charts of the Sky Priests are not just maps but holy relics on which are woven the tapestry of Lemurian history in the words of the Ancient Tongue—Latin. Their religion is not based on the Scrolls, but they've become integral supplements—along with a few twisted Christian concepts that may have been passed inadvertently by the previous "Tail-less Ones" almost two centuries before. Matt had picked up a little Lemurian theology and, although it was fundamentally a form of Sun worship, he knew the heavens—and the stars in particular—represented far more than simple navigational aids. Since that first awkward moment, religion had not been much of an issue and he'd concentrated on other things. Maybe he needed to bone up. He would talk to Bradford.

"What confirms the depravity of the Aryaalans, however," Nakja-Mur continued, "is that they often war among themselves! They are constantly at war, one faction against another, and they often repel visitors with violence. I cannot help but wonder, even if we aid them, will they not simply turn on us as yet another enemy?"

"We have to try."

"Perhaps. But it will take another meeting, I suppose, and you will have to be very convincing."

"Sure," said Matt. "We'll have another meeting. We need one, bigger than before. But that's beside the point. Have you boarded the Grik ship yet? Spoken to any of the survivors?" Nakja-Mur shook his head. "You need to do that. Then you'll understand. This is a fight to the death. To the end. Total war and no more goofing around. Even if you could flee, like the sea Homes can, they'll catch you eventually because that's what they *do*." Matt paused. "You told me before we left on the last expedition to find out what we could, that you'd do anything to keep the Grik away. Did you mean that?"

"Of course!"

"Well, then, if we're not going to fight them here, we'll have to fight them somewhere else. Let's do it where we might have some help."

The gathering in Nakja-Mur's Great Hall was even larger than when they'd debated the previous expedition. This time the massive structure was nearly packed. Those present weren't just the High Chiefs of the Homes in the bay either, but their advisors, Sky Priests and senior war leaders as well. Alden, Shinya, along with their Marine and Guard officers and senior NCOs, represented Baalkpan's armed forces. As predicted, some sea Homes left, although *Fristar,* the most vocal advocate of simply running away, sullenly stayed. Others had arrived, as well as delegations from more land folk—one from as far as Maani-la, in the Fil-pin lands to the east. Some had arrived too late for the conference before the expedition; others came because of what they'd heard since. They came because the expedition had, after all, been a success: they'd learned much about the "Ancient Enemy" at long last, and they knew now what was at stake. Adar was determined to make the threat as clear as possible and had suggested opening the meeting to all, but there simply wasn't space. Matt countered that all would quickly know the situation through the many representatives.

A month before, the expedition had returned to Baalkpan with its malignant prize in tow. They were greeted with unparalleled euphoria, for it seemed that this, coupled with their other small successes, meant victory was on the march. Slowly, as the day of return progressed, the visitors and natives of Baalkpan began to learn the truth. Rumors of the horrors within the Grik ship spread like a typhoon wind and so did the scope of the threat. Few had actually seen the blasphemous charts that had been captured, and Matt and Keje tried to keep a lid on it, but somehow the unexaggerated fact that the enemy was numberless took hold of the populace.

The euphoria turned to panic first, but then the few wretched survivors of the Grik larder were carried ashore and, with them, the tale of what they'd endured. Deputations of merchants and townsfolk were allowed to tour the hulk and they came away in shock, but also with an appreciation—at long last—of the terrible choice they faced. They could run or they could fight. There was no other choice available. They might flee and hope to find some far-off land where they would be safe for a time, or they could defend their home against this evil. But if they chose to fight, the time for half measures and preparing only when the mood struck was over. Every waking effort of the entire population, those who stayed, must be devoted to a single-minded goal: fight the Grik and win. The released captives were a grim reminder that defeat did not bear contemplation.

As the days passed, some did leave. A steady trickle of feluccas, hired at exorbitant rates, carried the fearful to the Fil-pin lands. It became known that the enemy maps didn't show that place, and they thought they'd be safe. After the initial flurry, Nakja-Mur even chartered a few boats himself so certain treasures and relics might be carried away for safekeeping. These things were entrusted to the mates and younglings of some of the more talented artisans who were willing to stay as long as their loved ones were safe. Those who remained pitched in with a will—as if their lives depended on it.

The foundry fires glared night and day as every article of copper, tin, and zinc in Baalkpan was rounded up and sent into the crucible. The Bronze Age Lemurian industrial base went from accomplishing the impressive feat of casting one cannon every three to four weeks to the impossible rate of one every four days. McFarlane, Sandison, and a small army of helpers stayed busy at the crude boring machines and hones they'd made. Long lines of people, male, female, even younglings, escorted by Marines against the predators, carried their own weight in sulfur from the volcanic hills to the land home of Sular across the strait on Celebes, time after time. The cargoes were then transported to Baalkpan by ship. Open leaching pits were laid out to produce nitrates and a vast swath of timber was felled around the city for the charcoal, and to provide a better killing field for its defenders. Smoke hung everywhere and every eye streamed.

Oil continued to flow and the refinery ran around the clock. New storage tanks were constructed and a respectable reserve, at least for a single destroyer's needs, was beginning to accumulate. Alden, Shinya, Chack, and many of the now "veteran" Marines who'd participated in the bloody boarding action stayed busy drilling everyone on the new, larger parade ground that used to be jungle. There was no more complaining, and even the warriors from the Homes in the bay rotated ashore for drill. And in the harbor, the unpleasant, unwanted task of refitting the Grik ship progressed.

Matt wasn't entirely clear about Lemurian funeral conventions, but he knew they preferred to be burned so their life force, or soul, could be carried to the heavens with the rising smoke. There, they would rejoin in the firmament those who'd gone before. He wasn't sure if the People believed they became stars after death, or if the stars guided their journeys there much as they did below. Maybe a little of both. It was clear to him, however, that the 'Cats would *really* have preferred to just burn the thing that they believed still held the souls of Lemurians who'd been tortured and eaten by the enemy. He tried to explain that if all went well, the Grik ship would soon become the second-fastest gun platform in the world. Much as he'd have liked to defer to their cultural preferences, they didn't have time to build another ship of the type. They would start some, certainly, and incorporate many refinements, but for now he was going to need that ship.

The People were aware of the advantages. They knew how fast and maneuverable the enemy ships were, compared to their own lumbering Homes. The idea of arming such a ship with cannon appealed to them as well. They just didn't want to use *that* ship. It was the one instance where Captain Reddy's military plans were met with real resistance. He sympathized, but he wouldn't bend. The crisis was finally solved by Adar, who argued that the trapped souls would surely welcome the chance for revenge, and using the tool of their own murderers to help claim that vengeance would make achieving it all the more sweet. They would clean it out and give it a name. They would re-rig and repair the damage it had suffered, but unlike *Walker,* or *Big Sal,* or, hopefully, *Mahan,* it would never, *could* never truly be a live thing.

Matt was grateful for Adar's assistance. He hadn't been sure which side of the argument the Sky Priest would take. Nakja-Mur's aged Sky Priest, Naga, had begun to defer more and more to Adar in matters of "belligerent spiritual guidance." *Big Sal*'s "head witch doctor," as he was sometimes affectionately called by some Americans, had almost visibly swelled in importance and prestige. He didn't flaunt it, and he certainly didn't abuse the power, but he did have greater influence than ever before. His approval had been key. In word and deed, Adar had become the most outspoken advocate of this "total war" no matter what it took. He'd taken to heart his vow not to rest until the Grik were destroyed. At Adar's urging, in spite of their distaste, gangs of workers dutifully, if uncomfortably, toiled on the Grik ship, getting it ready for sea.

Light streamed through the Great Hall's open shutters and motes of dust drifted in the beams. Loud voices and shouted conversations carried on around Matt, Lieutenant Mallory, Courtney Bradford, Alan Letts, and Sandra Tucker, where they stood beside Nakja-Mur and his entourage, as well as Keje and Adar. Nakja-Mur stood, obese but powerful, dressed in his usual red kilt and gold-embroidered cloak that contrasted with his shiny dark fur. Fur with growing splashes of white. Matt thought of it as his "High Chief suit," since he'd always dressed thus when Matt saw him. Adar's purple robe with embroidered stars across the shoulders was an equally constant garment. The hood was thrown back, revealing his almost silver pelt and piercing gray eyes. Matt's friend Keje was dressed in a warlike manner, as Matt had first seen him after *Walker* saved his Home from six Grik ships and, by so doing, joined them in this terrible war. His armor consisted of engraved copper plates fastened to the tough hide of a plesiosaur they called "gri-kakka." At his side was a short, scimitar-shaped hacking sword called a skota, and cradled in his arm was a copper helmet, adorned with the striated tail plumage of a Grik. He also wore a red cloak fastened at his throat by interlocked Grik hind claws. Beneath the armor, as protection from chafing, he wore a blue tunic embroidered with fanciful designs. Other than the Americans, he wore the only "shirt" in the hall. All the 'Cats the destroyermen had met seemed to wear as little as they could manage, usually just a light kilt. Even the females went disconcertingly topless, and their very human, albeit furry, breasts were a constant distraction for the sex-starved destroyermen.

Large-scale addresses were rare among the People, and there was no way to speak directly to such a gathering from within its midst. Therefore, an elevated platform, or stage, had been constructed near the center of the hall where the Great Tree rose through the floor and soared high overhead to pass through the ceiling. Matt had seen the huge Galla tree many times now, but he was always amazed by its size and by the fact that he'd seen only one other like it. The one growing from the heart of *Big Sal*. He supposed other Homes had similar trees, and he wondered again if it was possible they were descendants of the trees the Lemurians had known in their ancient home.

The crowd was growing restless, anxious.

At a nod from Nakja-Mur, he stepped onto the stage. Immediately there was a respectful silence in the Great Hall—a much different reception than the last time he'd spoken to this assembly. Of course, he'd given them a "victory" since then—such as it was. He paced the small platform for a moment, staring at the upturned faces while Chack joined him to interpret. Many of those present had actually learned a smattering of English, but Matt hadn't yet acquired a conversational ability in their tongue and he was slightly embarrassed by that. He'd always thought he was pretty good with languages, but there was something about the strange, yowling words of the People that absolutely defeated him. Bradford, Letts, and even Sandra could jabber away like natives—at least as far as he could tell—but he was just as likely to insult somebody as to tell them it was a temperate day. Maybe it was a mental block, or his mind was too busy. Whatever the reason, he was glad Chack was there.

He gestured at Lieutenant Mallory. "My friends," he began, "as you know, the flying-boat has returned from its scout in the south." He paused. He'd hated sending the PBY and its crew off by themselves, but Bradford and the Mice had managed to refine a small amount of high-octane gasoline. They had done it somehow using salt water, of all things. Also, since Riggs had the plane's radio working, they'd never been out of contact. Ben flew under orders to avoid being seen at all costs, so he didn't have a firm count of the number of enemy ships that invested Surabaya. The only thing he could verify was that the lizards were definitely there. All the air crew could see from ten miles away and an altitude of 13,000 feet—a distance that should have muted the Catalina's loud engines—was "lots of ships." Unrealistically, Matt had hoped Mallory would spot *Mahan*—even though he had instructed him not to specifically look for her. Judging by how long he was gone and how much fuel he'd used, the Air Corps aviator must have covered as much ocean as he could anyway. There'd been no sign. "What Lieutenant Mallory and his companions have reported confirms our fears," Captain Reddy resumed. "Aryaal is under siege." He waited for a moment while the tumult died down. "I must propose that we lift that siege."

This time, many minutes passed before he was able to speak again. There were a few shouts of agreement, but many more cries of incredulous protest. The initial response degenerated into a general roar of discussion and debate. "We have no choice!" he shouted over the hubbub. "If the enemy establishes a permanent base as near as that, Baalkpan is doomed!"

He picked out a small gathering of High Chiefs and fixed them with his eyes. "Many of you can just leave. Your Homes aren't tied to the land. But if Baalkpan falls, what then? Where will you replenish stores? With whom will you trade? Who'll repair your Homes? I know there are other lands that will serve that purpose for a time, but how long will it be before they too are lost? If we don't stop them now, one day all that will remain of the People will be scattered clans, alone on the sea, without sanctuary and without hope."

"We have no hope now!" snarled Anai-Sa, *Fristar*'s High Chief. "We should flee. We've seen the charts you took, many of us, and the Grik are as many as the stars above."

"We must not flee!" Adar bellowed, joining Matt on the stage. The intensity of his glare caused many to flinch. "I was in the belly of the Grik ship not long after its capture. I have spoken to the 'survivors,' though such a word mocks them! I have seen the perverted way the Grik twist our faith and use it against us. Speak not of flight! Any who would flee in the face of this scourge is aiding it! They are not only cowards but traitors to their people!" There were shouts of dissent, but some loudly agreed. Anai-Sa brooded in silence.

"Much has happened since we last met like this," Matt continued when the uproar began to fade. "Since then we've accomplished much, in spite of the doubts of some. Most importantly, we've won our first real victory over the enemy. I don't speak of simply destroying their ships. That's been done before. Besides, I agree it's now plain that such small victories are pointless in the face of the numbers the enemy possesses. What we've won is priceless intelligence!" He smiled. "We're no longer as 'ignorant' as we were before, and so we can begin to plan for greater victories. Victories that will make a difference. The first such victory should be the relief of Aryaal."

"How can it benefit us to spill our blood for them?" asked Kas-Ra-Ar, Keje's cousin. The question wasn't confrontational, but genuinely curious. "The Aryaalans have never helped us before."

"If we save them from the fate that awaits them in the Grik hulls, I bet they will then," Matt answered simply. "Don't you see? The Grik are through 'probing.' This is for all the marbles—I mean . . . polta fruit!" He grimaced, wondering how well that would translate. "They've taken Singapore, destroyed Tjilatjap . . . possibly others. Now they threaten Surabaya—Aryaal. This is *it*! The conquest you've feared since you fled them the last time so very long ago!" He blinked appropriately to convey frustration and anger. "Well, I say this time we stop them! This time we throw their asses back!" He stopped and took a breath, wishing he had some water. He was sweating and he knew he was allowing his own frustration over the litany of events that had brought his ship and her people to this moment to color his argument.

Once again, the long retreat in the face of the Japanese was fresh upon him. The terrifying escape from the Philippines, the lopsided battle of the Java Sea, the doomed retreat from Surabaya and the death of *Exeter* and *Pope* and all the others haunted him anew. The fate of *Mahan,* and the horrors he'd seen in the Grik hold. Not to mention the enigmatic human skull. At that moment, emotionally, it all became one. The Grik had become an arguably far more terrible, but just as implacable, surrogate for the naval avalanche that had claimed the rest of the Asiatic Fleet and had begun *Walker's* nightmare odyssey in the first place. He was tired of running, and he just . . . couldn't do it anymore.

"We make alliance with the Aryaalans by destroying the Grik forces there," he continued with grim resolve. "Then we'll throw them out of Singapore. Once we've done that, we fortify. We build fast, dedicated warships that can blow the hell out of anything the Grik send against us and, in time, we'll kick their asses all the way back to where they came from!" There were enthusiastic shouts of support this time.

"And we'll do that only because we have secure internal lines—an area where the enemy dares not tread. The Malay Barrier will be our defensive wall—but we have to secure it. Java—Aryaal is an essential part of that." He looked out upon them and could see they wanted to believe. "This time we fight! And this time let *their* survivors frighten their children with tales of the fierce creatures that threw *them* out of paradise!"

Nakja-Mur strode onto the stage, holding his hands high to stifle the cheers and shouts and stomping feet. "I propose that Cap-i-taan Reddy, U-Amaki Ay *Walker,* be named War Leader of All the Clans for the duration of the campaign he described!" Matt was stunned with surprise in the face of the roar of acclamation that ensued. He looked at Nakja-Mur with an expression of betrayed . . . gratitude. He'd had no inkling that the High Chief of Baalkpan intended to make such a proposal. But it would certainly simplify things. The Lemurian grinned back at him.

"Aahd-mah-raal!" he said smugly.

The "Allied Expeditionary Force" crept slowly southward under a pale blue, cloudless August sky. Matt doubted the weather would last, however, because Keje had told them they were entering a "stormy" time of year. So far, he'd noticed a few differences between the weather "here" and "back home" and he imagined they had to do with the infinite ecological differences he was slowly growing accustomed to. These ranged from the understandable, such as undredged river fans that created unexpected shallows, to ash-belching volcanic islands that weren't even supposed to be there. Whatever had caused the life on this earth to take such a divergent evolutionary track was still hard at work doing the same with the planet. Therefore, he really had no idea what Keje meant by "stormy." By Matt's reckoning, they should be well into the wet monsoon season by now, when it could be expected to rain all day most days instead of just for a short time. But, for the last couple of weeks it had been drier than he'd have thought.

He reminded himself that "stormy" could mean anything to Keje. He hadn't been impressed by the tempest that raged during their most recent battle when they'd used a "grounded" *Big Sal* for bait. Several times he'd grumped that the plan would fail because no Grik would believe the storm was strong enough to drive *Salissa* onto the rocks. Of course, riding out a storm on *Big Sal* was probably exactly like doing so on one of the big new fleet carriers Matt had seen. *Walker* wasn't so fortunate. She rolled horribly and she was a very wet ship. Any storm seemed severe to those aboard her. The only consolation was that the colossal typhoons spawned in the deeper waters to the east shouldn't be much threat in the relatively shallow Java Sea. He'd never endured a typhoon, but he knew they could make the sometimes large hurricanes that occasionally struck his native Texas coast seem like a spring shower by comparison.

Today there was no storm, by anyone's definition. The sea was placid and the visibility infinite. To the east was the Gulf of Mandar, site of their most recent fight, and to the west he could barely see the tiny dark smudge of the Laurot Islands. The Kangean Islands still lay about a hundred and fifty miles to the south. They were far beyond the usual range of the fishing fleets and it still felt poignantly strange not to see the distant smoke of some wandering freighter or tanker plodding along in an everyday, workmanlike . . . reassuring way. The only ships they had reason to expect now were those of the enemy.

He stood on the signal bridge next to the fire-control platform and felt the firm, cooling breeze of *Walker's* twenty knots on his face. Beside him stood Greg Garrett, respectfully but companionably silent. Together they viewed the vast panorama of the "task force" arrayed to starboard. *Walker* was steaming a zigzag course several miles in advance of the fleet, screening against enemy ships that might detect their advance. Five miles ahead of *Walker,* the ex-Grik ship, *Revenge,* tacked lazily in the light airs, serving as *Walker's* advance picket. She was refitted to look just as she had for her former owners, and no Grik would flee from her. She would immediately signal *Walker* if she spotted anything in their path. If she somehow came to grips with the enemy before the four-stacker came to her aid, *Revenge* was well prepared to defend herself.

She sailed under the command of Ensign—now Lieutenant—Rick

Tolson, who'd been a yachtsman before he joined the Navy and had even worked on a steel-hulled topsail schooner for a year. He was the closest thing they had to a true sailor, and he had Kas-Ra-Ar, Keje's cousin, as sailing master and second in command. Kas had been hesitant about accepting the title "sailing master" since that's what the great tail-less prophet who had taught Siska-Ta had been called; "Sa-lig Maa-stir." When it was explained to him (and many others) that "sailing master" was a position, not a name, he finally accepted the post with reverence and more pride than if he'd been given command. Matt thought that was appropriate and he suspected they'd helped form the foundation of a proud and unique naval tradition. He just hoped they hadn't set the stage for a blood feud between sailing masters and Sky Priests, since their duties were quite similar. More to the point, however, from a defensive standpoint, Rick's ship was equipped with twenty brand-new shiny bronze guns. They were twelve-pounders, much like the ones they'd made for the Marine landing force, except for the carriages and the bore diameter. Right now the guns crouched, hidden and secure, behind gun port doors that had been cut in the side of the ship. Any Grik that tangled with *Revenge* would be in for a dramatic surprise.

Matt gazed at her in the distance with a strange mix of pleasure and pride, tempered with an underlying sense of revulsion. Her classic lines appealed to the historian in him and her sailing qualities inspired respect—and, of course, he was proud they'd taken her—but he couldn't forget what he'd seen aboard her and what she represented. Nakja-Mur had christened her *Revenge* and everyone considered that an appropriate name. Baalkpan's High Chief had been given the honor of naming her for the simple reason that she was the property of the Baalkpan People. There was no precedent for prize ownership among the People, and it was generally assumed that she belonged to *Walker* and *Big Sal,* even though a large number of Baalkpan warriors had assisted in her capture. Keje and Matt quickly decided among themselves to present the prize to Nakja-Mur as a gift. That action served a variety of purposes. First, it allowed for a much quicker refit, since Baalkpan had far greater resources to devote to the project. (This was mainly just an excuse—Nakja-Mur had long since ceased to stint on anything they asked of him that pertained to the war effort.) There was also the touchy religious angle, which they rightly figured the Baalkpan High Chief could smooth out more easily—with his own people anyway—than either of them could.

Mainly, though, Matt and Keje wanted Baalkpan to have a real piece of the naval war. Most of the landing force were Baalkpans, and most of their supplies came from there. Baalkpan truly was the "arsenal" of the alliance. Despite that, there was no great floating presence that represented

Baalkpan in the order of battle, and the way such things were reckoned by their quintessentially seagoing race, the greater share of honor fell to those whose very homes went in harm's way. *Revenge* more than satisfied that requirement of honor, since the plan called for her, the physical representative of Baalkpan, to be first in battle and perhaps even the key to the campaign's success.

Matt turned to stare back at the bulk of the fleet. Five of the "flat-top"-sized Homes lumbered slowly in their wake, screened by forty of the largest feluccas in Baalkpan's fishing fleet. Somehow, they'd managed to arm them all to some degree. The feluccas each carried at least one of the huge crossbow-type weapons that had usually been associated with the main armaments of Homes. In fact, most had come *from* the Homes. A few of the feluccas even carried small swivel guns that Letts thought to cast as antipersonnel weapons. The Homes—*Big Sal*, *Humfra-Dar*, *Aracca*, *Nerracca*, and sulky *Fristar*—were now each armed with ten of the larger guns like *Big Sal* had used to such effect off Celebes. Matt still couldn't believe Letts had pulled that off. He was proud of the former supply officer, who'd become the greatest logistics asset on the planet.

He smiled wryly at the argument Letts put up when he was told he'd worked himself out of a job and was too essential to the war effort to go on the expedition. He, along with a disconsolate Sergeant Alden, would command the Baalkpan defenses at Nakja-Mur's side and continue the good work. Together they would supervise the construction of fortifications and gun emplacements for the shore batteries and mortars that the foundry had turned to once the ships were armed.

The cannons had been an extraordinary achievement, but they had taken time, as had the other preparations necessary to mount the campaign. Two agonizing months had passed—had it been only six months since they passed through the Squall?—and Mallory's weekly reconnaissance flights showed that Aryaal still held, although the noose was tightening. He had also gotten a better idea of the forces involved. Thirty Grik ships, representing who knew how many thousands of invaders, were squeezing Aryaal now. A battle had been under way every time Ben flew.

Against that, the Allied Expeditionary Force carried six thousand warriors and Marines. That constituted almost half of Baalkpan's entire defensive force, male and female. Matt shook his head. He still couldn't get used to that. Instead of crying and waving good-bye from the pier, Lemurian females hitched up their sword belts and joined their "men" with their spear or crossbow on their shoulders. He had no doubt about their ability; he'd seen them fight. But it was possibly the most disconcerting thing he'd seen since he got here. He felt a rueful twinge. Sandra enthusiastically supported the idea of female warriors, once she got used to the concept, and it wasn't like she herself had exactly been sheltered from the dangers they all faced. But in her case, it wasn't as though that's the way things were *supposed* to be . . . He rubbed his chin and gave an exasperated sigh. It just didn't seem *right*. In any event, given the combination of artillery and disciplined tactics, he felt confident they could raise the siege and break through to the relief of the defenders. He just hoped it wouldn't be too late.

Garrett raised his hands and pressed the earphones more tightly to his head. He listened for a moment and then turned to Matt. "Lookout has the Catalina in sight, Skipper." Matt nodded calmly enough, but inside, he felt a supreme relaxation of tension. He hated it every time the plane flew out of sight for two reasons. First, it always carried a crew of bright, talented, and irreplaceable people whose chances of survival were poor at best if the plane was ever forced down. Also, dilapidated as it was, the PBY was the only airplane in this world, and it represented the greatest intelligence-gathering asset he had. It was an asset only if he used it, but that didn't mean he had to like it. The radio usually worked—and that helped a little—although it was strange to talk in the clear without fear of the enemy listening in! But radio or not, he couldn't shake his near-obsessive desire to preserve not just the crew but the plane itself. Important as this campaign was, he knew it was just a single campaign. Maybe it was a reflection of his still-smoldering bitterness over the lack of air cover for the Asiatic Fleet that reminded him you could take nothing for granted. But he couldn't throw off the premonition that if they used up the Catalina now, the day would come when they would really wish they hadn't.

In the meantime, he contented himself with a surge of relief over its safe return from this scout, at least, and he looked forward to hearing what Ben Mallory had seen. "Very well," he said. "Ask Lieutenant Dowden to close *Big Sal* and signal the fleet for all captains to repair aboard her for a conference. Please inform Captain Keje, with my respects; we'll come alongside as soon as they've hoisted the plane aboard. Ask him to rig hoses as well. I want to keep the bunkers topped off."

"Aye, aye, sir," Garrett replied and spoke into his mouthpiece.

Matt watched the PBY grow larger as it neared, its thundering engines loud and reassuringly smooth. Mallory waggled his wings as he roared by the destroyer and began a wide, banking descent that brought him down alongside *Big Sal*. Matt dropped down the ladder to the wooden strakes below and stepped into the pilothouse.

"Captain on the bridge!"

"As you were," replied Matt and smiled as the ship heeled into a tight turn toward the fleet. Juan, the diminutive but supremely dignified Filipino officer's steward, had just arrived with the midwatch coffee, and he was desperately attempting to stabilize the serving tray so the coffee wouldn't slide off onto the deck.

"Juan, Mr. Dowden and I will be crossing over to *Big Sal* at eighteen hundred. Would you present my compliments to Mr. Bradford and Lieutenant Tucker and ask them to accompany us?"

Juan finally got control of the carafe with an exasperated sigh as *Walker* steadied on her new heading. "Of course, Cap-tan Reddy. Might I recommend formal dress?"

Matt thought for a moment, then nodded, a grin stretching his face. "By all means, Juan. As formal as we can manage, at any rate. We must set an example." He glanced around at the quizzical expressions. "We *are* the flagship, after all!"

Lieutenant—now Lieutenant Commander—"Spanky" McFarlane stood in the aft fireroom with his hands on his skinny hips and his eyes closed. He was *feeling* the ship and her machinery around him. The Mice watched expressionlessly, but two of the new "monkey-cat" snipes stared at him with reverential awe, as if they were in the very presence of some diminutive but all-knowing God. He nodded with reserved satisfaction at what he sensed. The limited rehabilitation they'd managed to perform on *Walker*'s engineering plant had done wonders, sure enough. One of his biggest worries, gasket material for the ship's many leaky seals, seams, and steam lines had been laid to rest. A very satisfactory replacement had been found. They'd also replaced corroded fittings with newly cast brass ones, and all the working boilers had been rebricked. He worried about what they'd do when really serious stuff began to fail and their spares were exhausted—things like bearings, springs, etc.—but for now he figured his engines and boilers were in better shape than they'd been in years.

He opened his eyes and caught the big-eyed stares of the new "firemen" before they averted their gaze. He chuckled to himself. Damn, but he liked those little guys! With so many of the destroyer's under-strength American crew assigned to such a wide range of projects and responsibilities—from the oil program and the rapid industrialization of Baalkpan to serving as gunnery officers aboard the Homes of the fleet—almost half of *Walker*'s complement was made up of Lemurian recruits. All of whom were duly sworn into the United States Navy. Of course, they had no real idea what the United States was, but their oaths were real enough. They sure weren't like the coolies on the China Station. *Walker* was their Home now, and every one of them felt fortunate to be serving aboard the most amazing vessel in the world. Where McFarlane might see tired iron and dilapidated equipment, they saw only wonders, and they did their work with a zeal and enthusiasm that no engineering officer of a four-stacker had probably ever seen. Those that became snipes certainly suffered, though, confined below in the hellish temperatures with their furry coats. None ever complained, but God, how they shed!

Spanky had figured few of them could take it in the fire-room, even aside from the heat. Lemurians were accustomed to open spaces and freedom of movement, even on their ships. Accordingly, he thought those who'd be willing to toil in the steamy confines below *Walker*'s decks would be few, but he'd been wrong. Ultimately, he turned many away. They *loved* working with the machinery, and no matter how hot it got, the elite few he accepted never grumbled.

They often followed him, surreptitiously, staring with blank fascination at a gauge he'd tapped with a finger or a pipe he'd felt with his palm, trying to divine what magical significance the act had held. He found it difficult not to laugh out loud at some of their antics of childlike wonder, but he always contained himself and maintained an expression of stern forbearance. Partly because he liked them, but also because he *needed* them. They were quick learners and cheerful workers, and even if it felt really weird being the object of semi-deification, he wasn't about to discourage them.

Even the Mice had gained a following, despite their irascible mannerisms. One of the young monkey-cats, a soot-gray female who'd worked at the well site, had followed them into the fireroom. Her name was Tab-At. They had, of course, immediately dubbed her "Tabby" in spite of the obvious fact she was female. Whether it was ignorance on their part or a conscious effort to block her full, rounded breasts from their consciousness was unknown. She followed them around like a devoted pet—which was pretty much how they treated her. Spanky suspected there was more to it than that, at least from her perspective. Chack told him his cousin—for that's what she was—admired their competence and interpreted their inscrutable manner as guarded wisdom. He shrugged mentally. Maybe they were wise; they were good at their jobs, but he was afraid all she'd learn from them was how to be a pain in the ass.

He admitted his suspicion in that regard was mostly due to his prejudice against *any* female in his fireroom. Chack's cousin or not (*all* Lemurians seemed to be related in some way, so what difference that made he hadn't figured out), she was still a *she,* and he wasn't happy about it at all. She worked as hard as any of the monkey-cat snipes, and her size and agility probably made her the best burner batter out of the entire native draft, but there was no getting around the fact that she was, well, a she.

The captain, with some reservations of his own, Spanky suspected, decreed that strict equality of the sexes would be observed at all times with regard to the new personnel. The Lemurians themselves made no distinctions in tasks or duties between the sexes, the sole exception, of course, being maternity. The captain told him that unless they wanted to offend their allies in a very fundamental way, they would do the same. Fine. Half-nude female monkey-cats capering around on deck with the rest of the apes was no concern of his, but this was the goddamn boiler room! Tempers—and passions!—ran high down here in the heat, and the presence of any female of any species only served, in his view, to highlight the frustrations they all felt in that regard.

What made things even worse, if that was possible, was if you could get past the soot-gray fur and long catlike ears, the feline face and clawed paws and feet . . . yeah, well, and the tail too, Tab-At was kind of cute. As soon as that thought registered in Spanky's mind, he realized everyone else in engineering—with the possible curious exception of the Mice— had undoubtedly already thought it, particularly after the much-speculated-upon possible affair between Silva and Risa-Sab-At. He determined then that everyone in *his* division at least, regardless of the heat, would By God wear clothes. If Gray wanted to let them run around on deck with nothing but a skirt, that was his lookout. But not down here!

Spanky had hoped, with a guilty twinge, his decision would make Tab-At strike for a berth in the deck division; there was no question she'd be more uncomfortable. No such luck. The next time he saw her she was wearing a T-shirt that, to his horror, actually accentuated her breasts by concealing the fur, which made them appear even more human! Someone had even gone so far as to give her a pair of trousers with a hole in the seat for her tail. He'd never required that—since a 'Cat's tail made breeches impractical. He realized he was being mocked and finally gave up.

That didn't mean he had to like it, and as he looked at her now, standing with the Mice as they monitored the feed water and the fuel flow, he saw her watching him. She didn't look away like the others, and he didn't sense abashed worshipfulness either. Nor did he detect any hostility over his persecution of her. She wore . . . a look of amused triumph. He sighed, and then grinned at her. She at least knew he didn't know everything.

Matt sat on one of Keje's humble wooden stools in *Big Sal*'s Great Hall. With the exception of Keje, Lieutenant Tucker, and himself, everyone— including Courtney Bradford—lounged comfortably on the overstuffed pillows in a loose group around the ubiquitous table near the base of the great tree that dominated the ornate compartment. Larry Dowden, the only one not seated, stood near a hastily drawn map supported on the table so all could see. Matt shifted uncomfortably on the hard stool and wished, once again, he'd brought a chair of his own. He could've used one of the cushions, he supposed, but that would have made him feel even less at ease. He noted with arched-brow amusement that Lieutenant Mallory felt no similar reservations. The exhausted aviator was sprawled on a particularly deep and soft cushion and seemed to be having difficulty staying awake.

It had been a long day for Ben and his crew. They'd flown out of Baalkpan early that morning to make a final aerial observation of the objective. For the first time, Mallory was allowed to fly directly over the city—and the enemy forces. His observations weren't reassuring. Almost forty Grik ships were now in the bay before Surabaya and they'd dispatched a sizable landing force. Unlike Baalkpan, the defenders had a sturdy wall all around their city, with what appeared to be formidable defenses. But the Grik army was more than large enough to encircle most of the settlement. The only exception to complete investiture was a stretch of waterfront and a portion of the bay between the city and the island of Madura, about three miles from the mainland. A large assemblage of native small craft was concentrated in the passage, and another fortification, as yet unengaged, was constructed on the point of land on the island closest to Surabaya. A dense cloud of smoke from burning buildings—probably set alight by what everyone was calling Grik Fire—hung over everything, and Mallory couldn't see much detail. But this time there was no question whether the Grik saw the PBY.

Matt disliked allowing the plane to be seen by the enemy, but they had to know what they faced. Perhaps the unnatural thundering apparition that swooped low overhead had unnerved the Grik, Matt consoled himself. In order to avoid doing the same to the Aryaalans, Mallory's crew had dropped hundreds of "pamphlets" over the defenders' main position. These pamphlets consisted of light wooden shakes etched with a Lemurian phrase that said: "Your brothers to the north will aid you. We bring powerful friends. Do not fear." It was all they could do to assure the defenders help was on the way. With his mission complete, Mallory returned to join the task force. Tomorrow, he would fly back to Baalkpan, since they dared not risk the plane in the fight to come. Once there, he'd stay in radio contact with *Walker*.

Sandra Tucker sat primly at Matt's side, also on one of the stools, and showed no discomfort whatsoever. He wondered what she was thinking. He'd come to rely more and more on her intuition as time went by, but he had to admit he also just liked having her around. They'd evolved an unspoken understanding after they declared their love for one another. Aboard ship, a wall of strict propriety always stood between them in spite of their mutual attraction. They thought they hid it well. But sometimes when they were alone, a more . . . comfortable . . . familiarity existed between them. They both felt compelled to restrict any further exploration of their feelings, and Matt felt almost guilty that they shared as much as they did when the rest of the men had no prospects at all . . . unless you believed Silva and Risa really . . . He shook his head. Perhaps someday they'd find more people; even the Lemurian legends hinted at the possibility, but right now there was a war to fight. Terrible as it was, at least it had released some of the pressure-cooker tension caused by the "dame famine."

In the meantime, for the sake of the men, Matt and Sandra must control their passions. That didn't mean Matt intended to ignore her excellent insight. He leaned over and whispered in her ear: "What do you think of that Anai-Sa?" he asked, referring to the High Chief of the *Fristar* Home. The black-furred Lemurian had arrived at the conference late, as usual, and now sat hunched on a cushion in sulky disdain while the rest of the attendees finished the refreshments that were a prerequisite to any council.

"I think he only volunteered so he could get the cannons that were promised to the Homes that take part in the campaign," she whispered back. "I don't trust him. I hope you don't have to rely on him for a critical assignment."

Matt nodded. Anai-Sa had been the most outspoken proponent of just packing up and sailing off, but to possess the power of the guns was a mighty incentive to hypocrisy. "Do you have any less vague impressions about our other commanders?" he asked with heavy irony.

A quiet chuckle escaped her, but she nodded. "They seem pretty solid for the most part. You know you can count on Rick, on *Revenge*, and Keje, of course." She paused, considering. "I really like Ramic-Sa-Ar of *Aracca* and Tassat-Ay-Aracca of *Nerracca*."

"They're father and son, aren't they?" Matt asked, referring to the pair of Lemurians who sat close together talking animatedly among themselves. There was certainly a strong resemblance. The younger one seemed a virtual replica of the older.

"Yes," she confirmed, "and Tassat is actually younger than Anai, even though you could hardly tell by the way they act." She sniffed. "As far as Geran-Eras of *Humfra-Dar*, it's hard to say." She was referring to the only female High Chief present. "She's been a vocal supporter of the expedition from the start," Sandra continued. "You may even remember her showing rather . . . energetic approval of your plan?"

Matt did remember then, and cringed. Even Lemurian females had surprising upper body strength, and Geran-Eras had actually embraced him after he made his pitch for the relief of Surabaya. He was sure she'd almost cracked some ribs.

"I think, as your Mr. Silva would say, 'she has more than one dog in this hunt.' Adar told me her mate and one of her children were killed in a Grik attack right before they came to Baalkpan. Might've even been one of the ships we destroyed, so she *really* likes you. Also, I imagine she sees this expedition as a chance for revenge. You might need to keep an eye on her."

Matt nodded soberly and glanced around. The refreshments had been consumed and Keje was looking at him expectantly. "Better get started," he said to Sandra, and cleared his throat. "Ladies and gentlemen," he began aloud. "We have a battle to plan."

Standing on *Walker*'s bridge with his binoculars raised, Matt reflected that his return to Surabaya wasn't altogether unlike his departure so long ago. Once again, the clouds above the distant city glowed and flickered with the reflected light of fires caused by an enemy bombardment. This time, the spectacle was all the more surreal. *Walker*'s blowers roared at a pitch consistent with her ten knots, but in spite of that, even at this distance, the loud *whump* and overpressure of Japanese bombs would have been felt and heard. Instead, only an eerie silence accompanied the distant battle. They'd opened the bay from the east at 0120 and picked their way carefully through the Sapudi Islands, which were scattered haphazardly there. The last time Matt traversed these waters, *Walker* had had the services of a fat Dutch pilot, and Matt wondered suddenly where the man was now. Had he even survived? He banished the thought. All *Walker* had this time was a waning crescent moon. Of course, this time there was no minefield either.

As they drew closer, they could discern the stern lanterns of dozens of Grik ships moored in the bay, close to the city. All were ablaze with light and all rode secure at their anchors, never suspecting any threat might descend from the sea. A few, closer in, kept up a continuous desultory bombardment with their catapults, flinging "Grik Fire" bombs toward shore. Sputtering trails of fire arced high in the air and hung seemingly motionless for a moment, then plummeted down near or behind the walls of the defenders. Usually, a red gout of flame mushroomed upward into the sky. The festive, brightly lit ships in the bay provided a stark contrast to the suffering inside the city beyond.

Matt carefully refocused the binoculars dead ahead, watching one Grik ship in particular. Alone among its identical sisters, this one was under plain sail, creeping slowly among its brethren on a light southerly wind. Apparently accepted without fanfare as yet another reinforcement, the ship with the unusual blue glass in its lanterns moved deep into the enemy formation. Matt marked its progress by that blue light that identified it as *Revenge*.

He stepped onto the bridgewing and glanced aft. The Homes were hanging in there, totally darkened, as was *Walker*. He could see the occasional flash of white water alongside them as the hundred mighty sweeps propelled each huge ship forward at close to the ten knots *Walker* was making. He marveled yet again at the strength and determination that took. *Fristar* was lagging behind the others, leaving a small but growing gap between her and *Humfra-Dar,* but otherwise his "battle line" was holding together. The shoal of feluccas brought up the rear. He stepped back into the pilothouse and resumed his post beside his chair.

The bridge watch was silent other than an occasional whispered command, and he felt a tension that was different from any he'd sensed since the battle of the Makassar Strait. Like that night, there was fear and tension, but there was also a certain . . . predatory eagerness. A realization that they'd caught their overwhelming enemy with his britches down, coupled with a determination to make him pay. General quarters had been sounded long ago, and all stations were manned and ready except the torpedo director. Sandison's "torpedo project" to repair the two condemned torpedoes they'd filched from a warehouse in Surabaya was still on hold, and they wouldn't be using any of the three "definites" tonight. Sandison and his torpedomen had filled out the crews of the numbers one and four guns.

Matt turned to Lieutenant Shinya, who was in quiet conversation with Courtney Bradford. "Assemble your riflemen amidships and hold them as a reserve for any point of contact if the enemy try to board," Matt instructed. Virtually everyone topside had a rifle handy, but at their stations, the crew was too spread out to mass their small-arms fire. Shinya saluted him with a serious expression and turned to comply with the order. It would be the first time he'd commanded any of the destroyermen in action, and his self-consciousness was evident. He was directly in charge of close defense of the ship and had half a dozen Americans assigned to his reserve. Matt doubted there'd be any friction. Most of the destroyermen still didn't like him, but his abilities were evident. Some had even begun to consider him just another part of *Walker*'s increasingly diverse extended family. They never would forgive the Japanese, but Shinya wasn't just a Jap anymore. Besides, they were all on the same side now. It even seemed as though Dennis Silva kind of liked the former enemy lieutenant, and if Silva would put up with him, the rest of the crew certainly could.

"Be careful, Lieutenant," Matt cautioned as Shinya departed the bridge.

"Not long now, I should think," commented Bradford when they were alone. Matt nodded. He hadn't really wanted the Australian on the bridge during the action. He would have preferred that Bradford stay in the wardroom with Sandra, but the man had practically insisted. Chief Gray had just as "practically" offered to force him to go below, but the captain allowed him to remain. It was probably better this way. In spite of his peculiar manner, Bradford often made valuable observations, and Matt had to admit it was sometimes refreshing to have a sounding board close at hand who was apart from the official chain of command. It would have been unthinkable for him to ask one of his bridge watch for advice, but since Bradford was a civilian, no one would even raise an eyebrow if he did the same with him. Especially in matters of diplomacy or anthropology. Those were two subjects that, if they were lucky, they might need Bradford's expertise on that night.

They closed to within two hundred yards of the first Grik ship, and Matt couldn't believe they'd remained unnoticed, even as darker shapes against the starlit horizon. Of course, he knew nothing about Grik night vision, but their own lights were certainly enough to spoil a human's, if not a Lemurian's. *Revenge* was so far inside the enemy formation now that her distinctive light no longer distinguished her. Could it be that *everyone* from the ships had gone ashore? Or were they just that arrogant? Certainly *Revenge* would be challenged soon! Almost as if in answer to his unspoken question, a series of bright flashes erupted from within the enemy fleet, and a moment later the sound of a rolling broadside shattered the fragile quiet of the bay. According to the plan, *Revenge* was to sail as close as she could to the city, and very ostentatiously attack the enemy within clear view of the defenders. Failing that, she would open fire as soon as she was discovered. Matt had no idea which had occurred, but regardless, her fire was the signal for the rest of the allied force to attack.

"Signal the fleet!"

A bright red flare soared high above from the fire-control platform and exploded, leaving tendrils of fluttering sparks.

"Inform Mr. Garrett he may commence firing all guns under local control," Matt instructed the talker. "Pointers are to aim at the waterlines and disable as many ships as they can, but make every shot count!" The last was merely repeating what Garrett had already said to his gun crews, but it never hurt to remind them. Soon they'd be able to manufacture simple solid copper projectiles for the four-inch guns that ought to fire accurately enough on top of a charge of black powder, but they were still quite a ways from producing high-explosive rounds, and the war had just begun.

The searchlight above the fire-control platform sprang to life, its brilliant beam lashing the darkness, illuminating the targets ahead. Grotesque figures raced about on the enemy ships, or just stood, staring back at them in blinded shock. The number one gun on the fo'c'sle spoke first, with its door-slamming *crack,* and a large section amidships of the ship directly ahead of them disintegrated when the round exploded. Number two fired immediately after and the shot was rewarded by another explosion close aboard. In the distance, they heard *Revenge's* twelve-pounders pouring it on. Behind them, the battle line relentlessly advanced.

Walker's job was to blow a hole through the Grik anchorage through which the battle line would follow, pounding ships to either side with their massive guns. The primary objective was the "safe" zone between the city and Madura. There, they would land their troops. The secondary objective was to kill Grik and sink their ships. Since the secondary objective was essential to the success of the first, *Walker* set to with a will.

The night became a hellish maelstrom of explosions and muzzle flashes as *Walker* slashed through her unsuspecting prey. Tracers arced from machine-gun positions and deluged ships with splinters, lead, and shattered, jagged body parts. The enemy's very bones became projectiles as more and more shocked and groggy Grik surged from belowdecks, adding themselves to the packed targets. The three-inch gun on the fantail pumped star shells into the sky, casting a weird, ethereal light on the battle below, even further terrifying the enemy. Another Grik ship blew up, then another. One exploded violently, its store of Grik Fire probably going up, and furiously burning debris rained down on other ships anchored nearby, setting them alight as well. The gun crews performed their intricate ballet of death, the pointers and trainers madly spinning their wheels to keep each gun pointed at whatever target the gun captain had designated. Matt saw Dennis Silva, captain of number one, bellowing and capering with glee each time a shot went home. Lemurian shell men scampered back and forth keeping the breech fed while others with leather gloves snatched up the precious, still-hot shell casings and collected them in baskets before they rolled over the side. All the while, they whooped and hollered and shouted encouragement to one another in two different languages.

The panic created by the ferocity and total surprise of the attack was complete, at least on the nearest ships. A few cut their cables and tried to make sail, but most were too shocked even for that and they died under the bright glare of the stabbing searchlight or burned to death when their ships went up like piles of dried leaves. And then the battle line struck and the destruction took on a less frenzied but more methodical pace as the larger ships delivered broadside after broadside at point-blank range. *Walker* dashed on, zigzagging through the densely packed forest of masts and hammering anything her guns would bear upon.

"Ahead slow!" Matt yelled from the starboard wing. "Come right twenty degrees!" A Grik ship, sails flapping, had run afoul of its neighbor in its haste to escape, and now the two of them blocked the channel that led to *Revenge*. Beyond the snarl, Matt saw the ship with the blue lights pounding enemies on either side.

"Captain Reddy!" Bradford shouted, pointing. Another ship loomed in the darkness to starboard and *Walker*'s knife-sharp bow was swinging directly for it.

"All stop! Full astern. Left full rudder!"

The ship groaned in protest, the strakes vibrating violently beneath Matt's feet as the turbines were reversed and the screws bit deep to arrest the forward inertia. The gunners on the fo'c'sle stopped firing for a moment and watched as *Walker*'s bull nose swung ever so slowly away from the collision that had seemed imminent. Matt watched too, mesmerized, his knuckles turning white as he clutched the rail. Ponderously, his ship slowed to a stop less than a dozen feet from the enemy's head-rails. Grik stood watching, from a pistol shot's distance, equally horrified. But not for long. As soon as they saw the collision had been avoided, they sprang into action. Crossbow bolts thumped against *Walker*'s plates, gouging the paint and ricocheting into the dark. Red tracers from just overhead played across the enemy fo'c'sle as *Walker* backed away. A man went down on the foredeck, and another.

"Right full rudder!" Matt yelled to the helmsman. "Replacements to the number one gun!"

The number two gun fired into the Grik from a distance of less than fifty yards, and the shell detonated within the forward part of the ship. An instant later, a massive secondary explosion knocked Matt and Courtney Bradford against the chart house bulkhead, shattering the windows on the starboard side of the pilothouse. Large wooden fragments rained down on *Walker*'s deck, and the high-pitched, catlike wail of an injured Lemurian rose from forward. Matt shook his head to clear the ringing in his ears and blinked his eyes. Bradford was staring, stunned, at a foot-long splinter embedded in his left biceps. Jamie Miller, the pharmacist's mate, was below, shouting at a detail of Lemurian stretcher bearers to clear the wounded off the foredeck. Matt lurched to his feet and shouted down at him. "Miller, Mr. Bradford is wounded, but I think he can walk. Please escort him below." He turned and gently helped the disoriented Australian to his feet. "I'm afraid you'll have to go to the wardroom now, Courtney. I'll send for you if I need you."

Bradford's expression was wan and there was sweat on his forehead. He'd lost his hat. "Yes. Of course, Captain. Please do."

Matt looked back at the Grik ship that blew up in their face. *Must've been more of their bombs,* he thought. It was sinking now, quickly, by the bow. "All stop," he called into the pilothouse. "All ahead slow, rudder amidships."

For an instant, Matt was able to take quick stock. The way ahead was still blocked, but the number three gun had turned the tangled ships into so much sinking junk. Soon they could go *over* them, if the water was deep enough. Silva, his T-shirt torn and bloody, was directing replacement gunners into their positions. Aft, the battle line advance had slowed to a crawl as its ships couldn't resist pounding as many of the enemy as they could as they passed. Keje and *Big Sal,* in the lead, were no less guilty of the distraction than the others. Burning and sinking Grik Indiamen were everywhere and the dense smoke made his eyes water as he viewed the spectacle.

From his vantage point, however, he could also see that the enemy was recovering from the shock. Some ships had made sail and were attempting to escape, but others were trying to move in close, in typical Grik fashion, so they could grapple and board. Those that did would be in for a surprise when their under-strength crews went to face Lemurian Guards and Marines, but that wasn't the point. The first priority was to get those troops ashore. Matt spoke to his talker. "Signal *Big Sal* and tell her to step on it. If they fool around killing Grik too long, we're going to get cut off from each other and we'll have to shoot up the lane again. We don't have the ammunition to spare." *I bet it is hard for them, though,* he thought, *to quit killing their Ancient Enemy when it's this easy. They have met the boogeyman, and he is theirs,* he misquoted to himself.

"Aye, aye . . . Captain? The lookout says *Revenge* is in a little trouble."

Matt grabbed his binoculars and scanned ahead, past the quickly sinking "obstacle." *Revenge* was still engaged with ships on either side, both of which were little more than drifting hulks by now. But two other enemy ships had closed with her. As he watched, one threw a firebomb that barely missed. Other bombs were flying now too, and one struck the water off the port beam and whooshed into a wall of flame as it ruptured. An icy tendril of dread raced down Matt's spine.

"Expedite that signal!" he prompted. *If we give the lizards time to get their act together, they'll burn us all,* he thought grimly. Another bomb broke against *Revenge*'s side and a pool of flame spread across her deck. Her guns fell silent as their crews raced to extinguish the fire. "Have Mr. Garrett concentrate all guns that will bear upon those ships nearest to *Revenge!*" he shouted at the talker. The range was just under six hundred yards, and the guns were in local control. Even so, one of the four-inch-fifties hit just under the foremast of a Grik ship that was trying to cross *Revenge*'s stern and throw a bomb down her length. Much like the ship that had blown up beside them, it exploded with an unexpected violence, sending flaming debris and timbers in all directions. The masts slumped toward one another and then teetered into the sea. A plume of flame roared skyward and was quickly quenched as the ship abruptly sank from view. Its lightly damaged companion was trying to perform the same maneuver ahead of *Revenge,* but it fell away to leeward and then heeled hard over and came to a sudden stop as it ran aground.

A bomb landed close alongside *Walker,* and burning liquid washed across her deck plates forward of the aft deckhouse where the number three torpedo mount had been. Matt heard a high-pitched scream. Whipping his head around, he saw a figure, engulfed in flames, stagger to the railing and leap into the sea. "God almighty!" he breathed in horrified prayer. He had no idea if it was an American or a Lemurian, but it didn't really matter just then. Everyone aboard *Walker* was part of her crew. Smoke billowed from burning paint and whatever noxious substance the Grik used in their bombs as hoses played on the fire. The number two gun fired, its muzzle trained far out over the side.

Then, just as *Walker* broke into the clear and began to race through the open lane toward where *Revenge* continued pounding her helpless foes, Matt felt something under his feet that he knew was entirely wrong. It began as a violent bump that shook the ship from stem to stern and rapidly became a sickening vibration that grew with every instant. "All stop!" he shouted, and he raced to the comm, disdaining his talker. Even before he could press the TALK button for engineering, Spanky's voice, terse with stress, came to them over the speaker.

"Lieutenant Commander McFarlane here," he said. "I think we've thrown a blade on the port screw and I've secured the shaft. What happened? Did we hit something?"

Sure enough, the terrible vibration had ceased as quickly as it began, while *Walker*'s speed diminished. Matt hesitated a moment, pondering, before he replied. "I think we probably did. Probably a sunken ship. How soon can I have the starboard engine back?" he asked.

"Right now, Skipper, but just remember we only have one left!"

The captain's lips turned upward slightly in a small grin of relief. "Thanks, Spanky. I'll watch where I'm going from now on." He stepped back from the bulkhead and turned to the bridge watch, his face impassive once more. "Starboard engine, ahead two-thirds!" With an unbalanced, rattling groan, *Walker* resumed her course toward *Revenge.*

The crew of their captured ship greeted them with joyous cheering as they neared, the last of her adversaries still settling to the bottom nearby. They'd made it through the gauntlet. Together, *Walker* and *Revenge* positioned themselves so their broadsides could support the battle line as it emerged to join them. This disposition was doubly suitable to *Revenge,* because it allowed her to deliver murderous fire from her steaming-hot guns into the stern of the helplessly grounded Grik ship. For just an instant as he watched, a tiny fragment of pity toward the defenseless enemy crept into Matt's consciousness, but it was fleeting. The far more powerful and lingering sentiment of visceral loathing quickly banished it, prompted by a mental image of what he'd seen in *Revenge*'s hold the stormy evening they'd taken her. Not to mention the tense apprehension that still consumed him over the discovery of the human skull. To the Grik, there was no question of surrender, and it was horrifyingly clear how they treated *their* prisoners. Suddenly Matt felt vaguely ashamed he was even capable of pitying them.

Clusters of feluccas began to break through, their speed and maneuverability serving them well in their passage through the chaos. The entire bay was awash in flames, the scope of destruction awe-inspiring. A number of ships continued burning furiously, and many more Grik were so involved in preventing their own ships from catching fire, they were unable to contribute to the fight. Matt knew *Walker* had savaged them and he had no idea how many Grik she'd sunk. The number of burning ships was surprising even so, and he realized some of them must have set fire to each other, flinging their bombs haphazardly in the midst of battle.

The battle line was almost through to them now, their massive guns spitting hate at the Ancient Enemy, blasting great gaping holes in hulls and smashing masts and bodies on any vessel that dared draw near. Some still did, regardless of damage, in the predictable Grik style. The very waters of the bay burned with Grik Fire as bomb after bomb exploded against the stout, scorched sides of the Homes or spilled their burning contents onto the sea. Any fires that were started on the great wooden fortresses were quickly extinguished, and very little had been left exposed that would burn. The decks were soaked before the battle and the huge fabric wings had been stowed, leaving only the massive sweep-oars for propulsion. One by one, the blackened and smoldering but otherwise unscathed leviathans crashed through the final obstacles separating them from *Walker* and *Revenge* and slowly took up positions lengthening the line with their port batteries bearing on the bay.

Even then they continued to fire, without nearly as great an effect at the increased range, but with just as much determination. The surviving Grik that could began to flee. At least half the enemy's fleet of forty ships had been destroyed, and most of those remaining afloat were damaged to varying degrees. Matt was tempted to allow *Walker*'s main battery to continue firing, but he knew he had to conserve ammunition. This was but the opening stroke, and he inwardly cringed at his expectation of what they had expended.

"Cease firing," he said, but the guns had already fallen silent, probably at Garrett's command. After the noise and turmoil of battle, his voice sounded strange . . . disassociated. He glanced at his watch and experienced the usual sense of disorientation when he realized the seemingly hours-long battle had lasted less than forty minutes. The rest of the fleet's cannonade became more desultory as the remaining targets drew away, and a great tide of cheering voices from thousands of throats rose and washed over him.

Larry Dowden appeared at his side. He'd been at his battle station on the aft deckhouse and was black with soot and sweat from the fire that came too close. He stood with Matt and stared at the scene of destruction as the roar of exultation continued. "Even better than Balikpapan . . . in the old war," he finally managed. His voice held a trace of wonder. Matt nodded. The enormity of the victory was beginning to sink in. "This even *feels* better," Dowden continued. "God knows I hate the Japs . . . except Shinya, I guess, but he's the proof. At least Japs are *people.* This feels more like . . . killing snakes."

Matt looked at him and grinned, shaking his head. "Mr. Dowden, shame on you! To insult snakes in such a way!"

"Captain," interrupted the talker, "Mr. Garrett says . . . He says you should go to the starboard wing, sir." Exchanging puzzled glances, Matt and Dowden complied. Several of the watch were already there, staring over the water at the walled city that reflected the light of the burning ships in the bay. It was an impressive sight. Matt had become so accustomed to the strange Oriental-style bamboo architecture of Baalkpan that the far more conventional, even vaguely medieval European design of this world's Surabaya struck him as more exotic than it once would have. He looked at Garrett, who was leaning over the rail above.

"What is it, Mr. Garrett?"

"Listen, sir," he said, almost shouting, and pointed at the city. Matt turned back toward shore and strained his ears to hear over the cheering. He couldn't imagine what it was that Garrett wanted him to hear over— then it hit him. The cheering of the fleet wasn't just echoing off the walls of the city, it was being answered from within! Even at this distance, and in the dark, he saw hundreds of figures standing on the walls, waving banners and weapons in triumph and shouting their defiance to the massive Grik army encamped outside their walls. From that army there came only a shocked, sullen silence.

Matt clasped his hands behind his back and strained to keep his relief in check. Underlying all the concerns he'd felt over the meeting with the Grik had been not knowing how the people here would receive them. They'd still have to guard against friction, but for now . . . "It seems the Aryaalans are glad to see us after all, wouldn't you say, Mr. Dowden?" His statement was met with a few hopeful chuckles.

"Captain!" cried the talker, who'd come as close as his cord would allow. "Lookout says there's a small boat coming up to starboard!"

Matt heard the bolt rack back on the .30-cal above his head. "Hold your fire!" he shouted, looking up. "Mr. Garrett, inform all stations to hold fire!" He turned and peered into the darkness that lay between them and the shore. The blazing wrecks threw a lot of light on the fleet and the fortress, but the space between them was in shadow, cast by the battle line. Even so, he saw what looked like a barge approaching from landward. It was about thirty feet long and broad in the beam. There were six banks of oars on each side and they rose and dipped with admirable precision. "Get Chack up here, on the double," he said, glancing forward. In less than twenty seconds, Chack and Chief Gray were both beside him. Matt was looking through his binoculars and when he noticed their arrival, he handed the glasses to Chack. "What do you make of them?" Chack looked through the binoculars, mainly because he liked to. He didn't really need them to see who was approaching.

"Aryaalans, Captain," he said simply. Then he looked at Matt, inscrutable and expressionless as always, but he was blinking a sequence reserved for surprise. Intense surprise. "And others."

Matt had started to turn and issue an order, but stopped and looked back at Chack. "What do you . . . ? Just a moment." He did turn then. "Signal the fleet 'Well done' and compliments. Also, all battle line captains please report aboard *Walker*. They can send a representative if they have damage or other pressing concerns." His gaze returned to Chack. "What were you saying?"

Chack wordlessly handed the binoculars back. Slightly annoyed, Matt raised them once more. The boat was much closer now, and even as he looked, he heard several exclamations of surprise from some of those crowding with him on the bridgewing.

The first thing he noticed was the Aryaalans themselves. He was struck by how different they appeared from the Lemurians he was used to. Counting the rowers, there were sixteen or seventeen of them on the barge, and almost all of them had dark-colored pelts. It was impossible in the dim light to tell exactly what color they were, but he had an impression of sable. That was unusual enough, since no two Lemurians he'd met were precisely the same color. And yet the differences didn't end there. The People they'd grown accustomed to—Spanky's efforts notwithstanding— wore as little clothing as they could get away with—usually just a kilt. The people who approached were quite well-appointed. Even the rowers wore platter-like copper helmets—not unlike the steel ones Matt's own destroyermen wore at stations—as well as thick leather, knee-length smocks.

What appeared to be "officers" or dignitaries stood clustered on a platform near the back of the boat, resplendent in robes and highly pol-ished bronze armor. Feather plumes adorned their helmets, and unlike their seafaring cousins who generally kept their facial fur cropped short, these creatures sported long, flowing manes that outlined their aggressive features. All of these impressions became a whirlwind of peripheral detail when he noticed the two individuals on the platform with the four poten-tates.

"My God."

An hour later, they all sat in the hastily cleared wardroom. The casualties were mercifully few, but they'd encompassed the extremes, being mostly either slight or fatal. The victim of the fire had been a Lemurian whose name Matt didn't know, but they'd also lost Andy Powell, ordnance striker on the number one gun. Tom Felts and Gil Olivera were wounded, but so slightly that they'd already returned to duty. Two other Lemurian crew folk had been hurt, and after patching them up and applying the magical antiseptic paste, Sandra bundled them off to their racks. Bradford's wound was a little more serious and had actually required surgery to remove the jagged splinter from his arm. He sat with them now, however, the very pic-ture of the modest wounded hero, with his arm heavily bandaged and in a sling.

Also seated in the cramped compartment were two of the Surabayans, or more properly Aryaalans, which was their name for themselves. There had evidently been no assimilation of European chart names here. Whether there had been any early contact at all remained to be seen. The younger of the two was Prince Rasik-Alcas, only son of King Fet-Alcas and heir to the Aryaalan throne. It took a little while for Matt to understand that. He'd picked up a smattering of the 'Cat tongue, but even though Keje as-sured him the Aryaalans spoke the same basic language, the dialect was so different he couldn't follow it at all.

Prince Rasik spoke little, however, leaving most of the talking to the older visitor. His name was Lord Muln-Rolak, and he was obviously used to talking quite a lot. Of the two, he radiated a less arrogant air, although he certainly possessed one. To look at him, it had been earned. Unlike that of his young prince, Rolak's pelt was crisscrossed with fur of lighter shades, suggesting a great many battle scars beneath. He looked, spoke, and carried himself like a consummate feline predator. A preda-tor that was getting along in years, perhaps, but was deadly neverthe-less.

Keje, Geran, Ramic, Tassat, and Rick were all there, as commanders of the battle line. Anai-Sa had not deigned to come but had sent a cousin in his stead who seemed to have learned manners from his High Chief.

Right now, he merely sat apart from everyone else and peered out the porthole at the fires on the bay.

And then there were the others. Seated at the far end of the table, hands wrapped around two precious Cokes from the refrigerated machine beside the galley door, were Bosun's Mate Frankie Steele and Lieutenant James Ellis, captain of USS *Mahan*. Expressions of wonder were still fixed on their haggard faces.

Except for a few quick, incredulous words of greeting, Matt learned only that *Mahan* still floated and had been here only a short time. Not long enough to accomplish anything like what *Walker* had at Baalkpan. The two men had been joyous but cryptic, and Matt could hardly wait for the current meeting to end, important as it was, so he could learn more of *Mahan*'s tale. Judging by the appearance of Ellis and Steele, it had been a hard one. Both men's uniforms were badly stained and battered, and a dreadful experience of some sort seemed to haunt their eyes. Jim still limped too, and Matt remembered that Captain Kaufman had shot his friend. He returned his attention to Lord Rolak, who was speaking.

"They will certainly attack at dawn." Keje translated for him. "They attack most days, but after tonight . . ." He shrugged in a very human way. "They will certainly come and I doubt they will stop this time. I propose that your"—the Aryaalan lord actually sneered slightly—"warriors join ours in the defensive positions. They should take direction from our captains, of course."

Matt suddenly found all of his commanders' eyes on him as Keje told him what Lord Rolak had said. He answered their unspoken question with a single word.

"No."

For just a moment, after Keje relayed the response, there was an uncomfortable silence. Prince Rasik finally spoke up. "This . . . creature speaks for you all?"

Keje grunted and answered in an ominous tone. "He does. He not only speaks for us, he commands us for the duration of this campaign." He gestured angrily toward the porthole. "In case you did not notice, we swept your little bay clear for you this night. He was the architect of that."

Lord Rolak shifted, and visibly regrouped his argument. "Your victory tonight was impressive," he hedged, "but you are sea folk. Surely you see the wisdom of letting land folk lead when a fight is on land. Aryaalans are a warrior race. The warrior's way is bred into us and nurtured in us as younglings. You sea folk do not even fight unless you have to! We have the experience . . . !"

"It seems to me that you were about to experience defeat, Lord Rolak,"

Bradford interrupted quietly. "What is your estimate of the forces arrayed against you?"

Rolak was quiet for a moment as he looked around the table. Finally he sighed. "There are, perhaps, fifteen thousands of the enemy." Matt nodded when the translation came. That was consistent with Mallory's estimate of the enemy force.

"How many warriors do you have to face them?" Matt brutally cut to the heart of the matter. If the Grik truly were going to attack at dawn, there was no time for this foolishness. Rolak answered him in a slightly more subdued tone.

"King Alcas has twenty-four hundred warriors in the city, fit for battle. Queen Maraan from B'mbaado Island across the water has sent another six hundreds to our aid."

"She should have sent more!" seethed the young prince, speaking for the second time since his introduction.

Rolak looked at him. "We are lucky she sent anything at all! Do you forget we were at war with her before the Grik came?" Rolak shrugged again and glanced at the others around the table. "War is a . . . pastime . . . among my people. That is why we are so good at it." He paused and his tone subtly changed. "It is different this time. The Grik do not follow the rules. They do not *have* rules. No truce is accepted. There is no parley, no discussion of aims or demands, and . . . no respect for the dead." His tail swished and he blinked outrage. "They eat fallen warriors, you know, whenever we cannot recover them. Sometimes they even stop fighting long enough to feed . . ." Quickly controlling himself, he glanced at all of them, but Matt in particular. "I know it is difficult for sea folk to understand, but perhaps not so much for you, Cap-i-taan Reddy." He gestured toward the far end of the table, where the long-lost destroyermen sat. "We have learned more from your friends than they know. We know that their great iron vessel, so much like this one, is very powerful despite its wounds. We also know your people surely fight each other. How else could it have suffered such wounds but by battling against others like yourselves? To Aryaalans, war is . . ." He smiled slightly, searching for the proper word. "Play?" He tried it, and seemed satisfied with the fit. "I suppose you could say we fight as much for entertainment as anything else. We fight for trade concessions, to elevate our status, for honor. Loot. A contest between honored competitors. Perhaps your people fight for such things, Cap-i-taan?" He blinked rapidly as his mood turned to one of anger. "We do not," he continued harshly, "fight to exterminate one another!"

"We may not always fight for a noble cause, Lord Rolak," Matt replied coldly, "but war isn't play to us." He gestured at the other Lemurians present.

"As you yourself have pointed out, entertainment is even less a motivation for sea folk to fight, and yet we are here. Do you know why? Because this *is* a war of extermination! It's *us* or *them* and you're right: they don't have any rules. We, all of us, are nothing to them but prey. You, Lord Rolak, are their *prey*!"

Rolak bristled and stiffened in his chair. For the first time, the formidable fangs behind his lips revealed themselves, but he reasserted his urbane control, recognizing the truth. "Thirty hundreds," he said at last. "That is the total with which we can face them alone, but each is worth many of the enemy."

"I'm sure," Matt replied, nodding respectfully, "but not enough. We have about that many with us. Actually, more. We have artillery—big thunder weapons like those on these ships—and we can have all of it on the ground to help defend your city by the time the sun comes up *if*"—he looked directly at Rolak, unwaveringly—"you understand that any forces we land will be under *my* command, seconded by Lieutenant Shinya. Also, you will agree to join with us in alliance, because after we help save your city, we intend to destroy the Grik forever. We help you, and you help us. That's the deal."

Prince Rasik sputtered and began to speak, but Lord Rolak silenced him. He stared directly back at Matt. "Very well. To the first, I agree. I must speak to my king about the second. I will tell you this, however: if we beat them, you shall certainly have *me* as an ally."

There was a sharp knock in the passageway beyond the curtain. "Come," said Matt, and Sandra and Lieutenant Shinya entered the wardroom. Sandra sat in the empty chair beside the captain, and Shinya stood before him and came to attention.

"You sent for me, Captain?"

Matt forced himself once again not to smile at Shinya's formality. It wasn't an act on the Japanese officer's part, but Matt always thought such "proper" behavior was a little out of place in the wardroom. Right now, with their visitors present, the courtesy was probably appropriate, as much for Jim's and Frankie's sake as for the Aryaalans. The last time they'd seen the Japanese officer, he'd been in chains and guarded by Pete Alden. "Yes, Lieutenant," he said and pointed at the map before him on the table. It was little more than a crude sketch, having been drawn by Mallory from the air. The Air Corps lieutenant had assured him it was accurate in the pertinent details, however. "As soon as this meeting ends—almost immediately, I believe—I want you to begin coordinating our troop landings here, in the dockyard area north of the . . . castle." He supplied that word, lacking any better. He glanced at Keje. "How many of the feluccas did we lose?"

"Most are accounted for, but some are not. I fear we must assume they were lost breaking through the Grik."

Matt nodded somberly, looking at Rick Tolson. "*Revenge* will make a quick search after dawn to see if any are adrift, disabled."

"Aye, aye, Captain."

"Don't take too long, though. I want you back as soon as possible." Tolson nodded. "Mr. Shinya, you will land three-quarters of the Marines and Guards at the dockyard. I'll leave the choice of units to you, but I want you to reserve one-quarter of the force to demonstrate as if they're going to land here"—he pointed at the map—"across the river. Hopefully, we can keep the Grik reserves tied down, prepared to defend against a landing. The battle line will support that impression with a bombardment." He paused. "The main force will assemble at the breastworks that join the castle walls to the beach."

Most of those present were already familiar with the plan, but Lord Rolak leaned forward and peered at the map. "Why gather there?" he asked, puzzled. "It will take time to move your forces within the walls and through the city. Would it not be better to send them in as they arrive?"

"No, Lord Rolak," Matt explained. "The Allied Expeditionary Force won't be going inside."

Shortly, after escorting the dignitaries and the battle line commanders to their boats and watching them scurry to their various commands to begin preparations, they returned to the wardroom. They didn't have much time, but Matt was determined to know, at last, what had happened to *Mahan* and her people. Sandra and Bradford were present, as were Spanky, Gray, and Dowden. By now, the whole crew had heard the exciting news that the lost lambs had returned. As usual, Juan hovered in the passageway prepared to bring coffee, so Matt knew none of them would have to repeat the story to the men.

"So," he said, smiling reassuringly, "I guess it would be a gross understatement for me to say we've been a little worried about *Mahan*."

Jim looked at him and managed to return a ghost of a smile himself. "We've been worried about you too, Skipper." He stared down at a second Coke and rubbed at the beaded condensation on the cold bottle with his thumb. "We . . . we never thought we'd see you again. I don't really know where to begin."

"We know about what took place up until Kaufman tried to send Mallory and the PBY to Ceylon," Matt said gently. "They found us, by the way."

Ellis was nodding. "Yes, sir. We saw it fly over the day before yesterday and we knew it must have. That's how we knew you were coming.

'Powerful friends' is right! When we heard the four-inchers and saw the star shells, I can't tell you how we felt." He paused, controlling his emotions. "We still didn't really think you could make it through," he admitted. "There were *forty* of 'em, for crying out loud! Then we heard the other guns and Rolak came out to the ship to fetch us . . ." His face clouded with shame. "I just wish we could've helped you, but *Mahan*'s anchored around the north point, and the guns wouldn't bear. We've been positioned there as a sort of floating battery to keep the channel between Madura and Surabaya—I mean Aryaal—open." He paused. "By the way, in case you didn't know, unlike 'back home,' the northeast channel is impassable with anything but small boats. Too shallow. There's only one way in and out of the bay."

Matt nodded appreciatively at Nakja-Mur. "Our friends' 'Sacred Scrolls' showed us that. You may have noticed yourselves that our charts don't always entirely agree with the local geography and conditions. They're much more comprehensive than the Lemurians', but not as locally precise. The differences usually tend to be a generally lower water level." He chuckled. "Much as the local temperatures seem unchanged, Mr. Bradford"—Matt nodded at the Australian—"believes this earth might be caught in the throes of an ice age. Farther north and south might be considerably cooler than we're used to." He waved his hand. "Enough of that. I want to know what happened to you. Spotting you on that barge was the biggest surprise I've had since, well . . . since we got here in the first place."

Jim looked like he'd just realized something. "You didn't know we were here, did you? If the PBY saw us, you would've known we knew—" He grinned. It was fragile, but real. "Thank God!" he said with huge relief. "I was afraid all this risk you put *Walker* to was a rescue mission just for us! We didn't know if the plane saw us or not. We heard it, but didn't see it until it was over the island, moving away. The point must've blocked its view."

"Rest assured," Dowden said grimly, "if we'd known you were here, we would've come in spite of . . . all this. And sooner, too!"

"You bet," grumbled Gray. "And we didn't need any help getting through those damn lizards, neither."

"Getting out again might have been a bit trickier," observed Bradford judiciously. "Without the destruction the battle line wrought."

Matt nodded in agreement. "What happened after Mallory left? He said you knew he had no intention of going to Ceylon."

Jim looked at Steele as if he expected the bosun's mate to answer, but Steele merely stared at the table in front of him. Matt had the distinct impression that the putrid green linoleum wasn't what he saw just then, however. Jim cleared his throat. "I was . . . sort of out of it for a while,

Skipper. Fever. Thank God we had the nurses or I probably would have lost my leg, at least."

"But I thought *Mahan*'s surgeon survived?" Sandra spoke up. Jim looked at her and lowered his eyes. "He did. But he quickly figured out, like Frankie and I and a few others, that we . . . just weren't in Kansas anymore." He looked back up at Matt and a brief, sad smile crossed his face as he remembered the conversation he and the captain had that morning off the coast of Bali. "He took it harder than most, though. He sank into a depression that nobody could snap him out of. He . . . shot himself."

Sandra gasped, but Matt just shook his head. He hadn't known *Mahan*'s surgeon, but he imagined he knew how he had felt. Under the circumstances, it was probably a miracle they hadn't lost more of the men to suicide. If it had been any other destroyer squadron in the Navy other than that attached to the Asiatic Fleet, they probably would have. Once again, the unique temperament of his destroyermen had proved to be an asset.

"Anyway," Ellis continued, "the nurses pulled me through. In the meantime, *Mahan* creeped up the Sumatra coast, headed for Ceylon. The crew—those who didn't already know it—finally figured out Kaufman was nuts, but there wasn't anything I could do, laying in my bunk. I think what finally made him completely flip, though, was as soon as we made to cross the Bay of Bengal, the lookout spotted an island where there shouldn't have been one. I thought it was one of the Nicobars myself, at first. Frankie and some of the other fellas had taken me on deck so I could get some air."

"Kaufman let you loose?" Spanky asked.

"Yeah. I think he felt bad about shooting me," Ellis reflected. "He wasn't a murderer; he was just nuts. Crazy with fear, I think. Also, once it dawned on him the fix we were in, I think he wished he hadn't done what he did. But he couldn't take it back. Anyway, I saw the island." His face took on an expression of remembered amazement. "Only it *wasn't* an island, Skipper. It was a *fish*! It was *huge*! It looked like one of the ones like *Walker* shelled right after we came through the Squall, that nobody on *Mahan* got to see—'course, we've seen plenty of them since! It was like that, but a hundred times bigger. A thousand! It was bigger than any whale that ever was." Frankie Steele shivered despite the warm, humid air in the wardroom, and Matt realized *Mahan* must have encountered one of the monstrous "mountain fish" Keje had told him about. "I guess we got too close because, all of a sudden, it turned and made for us! I swear, it was big enough to *eat* the ship! Well, we came about and raced back for Sumatra as fast as we could, making eighteen knots or thereabouts, and even then it nearly got us." Jim shook his head, still astonished, and took a sip of his

Coke. "I doubt it could sustain a speed like that, but for a sprint—anyway, it finally gave up the chase when the water began to shoal."

"Astounding!" gasped Bradford. "Just imagine! A fish that large!" He turned to Matt. "Captain Reddy, as soon as this current . . . unpleasantness . . . is at an end, I must simply insist that you allow me to study one of these creatures!"

Matt couldn't resist the grin that sprang to his lips. "Sure, Mr. Bradford. You can take the whaleboat." Those around the table chuckled appreciatively and even Steele managed a smile. Ellis spoke again. "After that, Kaufman gave up on Ceylon. There was no way he was crossing any deep water. So there we were, just fooling around burning fuel, day after day in the islands off the west coast of Sumatra. He was scared to death of being spotted by more lizard ships, like nearly got the PBY, but he was just as afraid of heading back this way. Finally, we anchored off Nias. The condensers were screwed up and we needed fresh water so Kaufman led a party ashore to find a source. I think he just wanted off the ship."

His voice became a whisper. "It was a fiasco. I was on my feet again, sort of, and we'd determined to take back the ship. We didn't really even need a plan. With him and his stooges gone, we just armed ourselves and waited for him to return and be placed under arrest. He had twenty men with him, about a third of the crew, as security. They were all armed to the teeth, but we didn't think a shot would be fired when we made our move. They weren't going to actually get any water, just find it if they could and then we'd organize the best way to get it to *Mahan,* or get *Mahan* closer to it. At least that was the plan he told us. I think he was looking for a place to stop—to build shelter and stay." Ellis's expression became angry. "That would have been fine with me, and good riddance! If only he hadn't . . ." He shook his head. "Anyway, we waited and waited, and they . . . just didn't come back. The whole place was a jungle and we couldn't see a thing as soon as they left the beach. A few times, we thought we heard shots, but it might've been the surf. Night fell and we could still see the boats dragged up on the beach but no sign of anybody."

He looked around at the expressions of those listening and saw their horror. He looked down at the table. "We couldn't go ashore in the dark," he muttered quietly and glanced back up. The horror remained on their faces, but there was also sympathy for him, for the decision he'd been forced to make. A part of his soul might have even felt a surge of relief at the absence of condemnation, but it was far too small a part to provide him any solace. He condemned himself enough as it was. "I left twenty men on board the next day, about half of whom were fit for duty. There was no way I was able to go tromping through that jungle, so I stayed on the beach with Pam Cross—one of the nurses—and one other man. I—" He stopped and looked at the bosun's mate beside him. "Frankie led the party inland."

"Mr. Steele?" Matt prompted.

Frankie looked at the captain with tortured eyes. Sweat beaded on his forehead. He'd been twisting the hair of the beard on his chin—hard—for the last several minutes.

"Uh, we followed the trail they made about three miles into the jungle, kind of skirting along the southern slope of a big mountain or volcano that's right in the middle of the place, see? Hadn't seen a thing up till then but tracks. Then, all of a sudden . . ." He gulped from the cup of coffee that Juan had placed, unnoticed, by his elbow. "There was a clearing, kinda, and one of the guys picks up a canteen and there's blood on it, see?" He closed his eyes. "There was blood all over the place! A boot, a couple o' hats, a few shell casings . . . nothing else but a bigger trail leading toward the other side of the island, with blood on it too, in places." He covered his face with his hands, then ran his fingers up through his hair, knocking off his hat. He didn't even notice.

"But that wasn't the worst of it. I sent one of the guys back to the beach to tell Mr. Ellis what we found and the rest of us pushed on. The island's about eight or ten miles wide there and we never would'a made good time if it wasn't for the size of the trail they left. Close to noon, we heard the sound of surf and eased out to the edge of the jungle overlooking the beach on the southwest side of Nias and we seen . . . we seen them lizard ships! Dozens of them, beating down to southward! You could see they'd been ashore, lots of 'em, and their cook-fires were still smoking." He cleared his throat and licked his lips. When he spoke again, his voice was a whisper.

"I, uh, went out on the beach alone to take a look around and I looked into one o' them fire pits. There was bones in that pit, Captain. Human bones. They were all gnawed up like—" He couldn't continue. He just sat there, twisting his beard and staring at the tabletop. No one said a word, each alone with the mental image Frankie Steele had conjured in their minds.

Finally, the tough, Bronx-born bosun's mate met their stares and his eyes were red and tears threatened to spill. "Them lizard bastards ate my friends," he grated. "I transferred out'a *Walker* to help Mr. Ellis, Skipper, but them guys was still my shipmates." He shuddered. "I want to kill 'em all!"

Matt nodded. At that moment he knew with complete certainty that all the rhetoric he'd used to justify this expedition—this war—to his allies and his own people hadn't been merely rhetoric. It was clear, blinding truth. The things he'd seen in *Revenge*'s hold had been proof enough of that, but ghastly as it was and as much as he liked Lemurians, the war he'd committed *Walker* and her people to had still been mainly the Lemurians' war. There'd always been something of a disconnect, particularly among some members of the crew. Most of the men who felt that way, few as they were, kept their opinions to themselves. All knew they had a stake in the fight, but a few of the more mercurial hadn't been sure exactly what it was— aside from food and fuel for fighting.

Matt had recognized his own hypocrisy when the human skull had elicited a deeper response in him than all the other atrocities he'd seen, but a fair portion of that could be explained by his fear and uncertainty about what that skull implied. Now he knew. If *Revenge* herself hadn't been there that day, she had acquired the skull from a ship that had. As a trophy? A curiosity? Or as something to use as a guide to look for more? Whatever the reason, it was immaterial now. *Walker* was already in it and he'd have supported his allies to the hilt regardless. But now it had become profoundly personal. It was *Walker*'s war now, and *Mahan*'s too, just as much as anybody's. When the details of this conversation filtered through the ship, as he was sure they would, even the few who'd wondered why *Walker* had to get involved would have their answer.

"What happened then, Mr. Steele? Did it look like all of Kaufman's party had been . . . eaten?"

"I don't know, sir," Steele said, shaking his head. "We pulled out pretty quick. The lizards ambushed Kaufman closer to our side of the island, and I was afraid they knew where *Mahan* was, so we headed back in a hurry." A shadow crossed his face again as he spoke. "About halfway back, we came under attack ourselves. Leroy Bennet was bringing up the rear and some kind of lizards, kind of like Griks but different . . . like Grik . . . what's the word, Mr. Ellis?"

"Aborigines," Jim supplied somberly.

"Yeah, Grik aborigines got him. Just tore him apart!" He sighed bitterly. "Well, we got some of them too. I don't know how many, a couple dozen I guess, but they just kept comin'. Behind us, in front of us, through the jungle on the sides. It was a running fight all the way to the beach. We lost four more guys to the bastards before we made it to the boats!" The tears were streaming now and he wiped at them with a tattered sleeve.

"They were armed with bronze swords and hatchets," Ellis said. "I think they were the ones that originally captured Kaufman's party and they sold or traded them to the other . . ." He hesitated and curled his lip with hatred. "More *advanced* lizards.

"Anyway," he continued, "by the time we made it back to *Mahan* with the remainder of Mr. Steele's party, the ships he saw were rounding the point to the south." His eyes gleamed. "We didn't even try to run. We just went right at them! Fire control was still out, but we had the number two and number four guns operating fine in local control. Number one would fire, but the recoil cylinders were damaged and still leak like a sieve." He shrugged. "We also had the machine guns amidships and the three-inch. We probably shouldn't have fought them, but we *wanted* to. In the end, we destroyed five of their ships and crippled God knows how many—at least twice that number." He paused, reflecting, and they could see the satisfaction that that part of the story had given him. "I wanted to destroy them all, but we needed to conserve ammunition. So much of ours had been damaged by flooding." He shrugged again. "So we blew through them and headed south-southeast, making smoke. Finally wound up here and didn't have the fuel to keep on."

His brow furrowed. "The locals didn't receive us too kindly at first. The Surabayans were fighting the Madurans, and when they got over their initial shock both sides thought we were here to help the other. When they figured out that wasn't the case, both sides tried to *get* us to help them against the other and all we could do was sit there and try to stay afloat." He smiled wryly. "'Course, it was amazing how fast they made up after the lizards got here and they had somebody else to fight besides each other. Both sides started being pretty nice to us after that too, for what good we could do."

"What were they fighting over?" Gray asked.

"Close as I can tell, that snotty little prince that was in here with Rolak wanted to marry, or mate, or whatever they do, with the queen on Madura. They call the island B'mbaado, by the way. Anyway, she's a looker by their standards, I understand, and they call her the 'Orphan Queen' of the island." He grinned. It was a fragile grin, but it was real. "She also thinks Prince Rasik-Alcas is a walking turd."

Sandra shook her head. "The political situation here seems entirely different from what we've encountered elsewhere."

Ellis nodded and looked at Matt. "It's pretty different, from what little I could tell by meeting your 'commanders,' Captain—or should I call you Commodore?" The tentative grin grew. "Admiral? Congratulations on your promotion, by the way."

Matt grunted noncommittally.

"The setup here seems pretty feudal to me," Ellis said, "like Europe five hundred years ago. Lords and ladies and knights and such. Peasants too, of course. There are distinct social classes."

"We can sort all that out later when we have the time," Matt said. "I just hope our people and theirs can get along." He leaned forward. "What kind of shape is *Mahan* in, Jim?"

"Not good." Ellis's grin faded and he raised the Coke to his lips and took a sip. Matt saw that in spite of the conversation and the fact it had veered from the trauma they'd suffered on Nias, Jim's hand was shaking and the mouth of the bottle tinked against his teeth. "She's in no shape to fight, or even move, for that matter. We're real low on four-inch-fifty and ammo for the machine guns. No torpedoes, but you knew that. We still have a full load of depth charges." He shook his head and snorted. "Maybe we can use the explosives in them for something? Anyway, the condensers, refrigerator, radio . . ." He shrugged. "All shot. We've been burning wood in the number one boiler so we keep up enough steam pressure for electricity to run the pumps, but that's about it."

"We can fix that," Matt assured him. "Is the number two boiler still up?"

"Yes sir. I wouldn't let them burn wood in that one—boy, it sure fouls everything up"—Matt avoided Spanky's triumphant glare—"and I guess I kept hoping . . ." His voice trailed off and he paused, looking at Matt with shining eyes. "You mean you have fuel?" He caught himself and looked around. "Of course you do. You're here! But how?"

Matt smiled as he saw hope begin to reanimate his friend. "We have allies, Mr. Ellis, as well as friends. As do you now. *Mahan*'s bunkers will be full just as soon as we can arrange it. I suggest you douse the fires in number one and start cleaning it out as a first order of business, as soon as you can make steam with the other. I want *Mahan* shipshape and ready to move as soon as possible. You'll have all the help you need." He glanced quickly at his watch. "I wish I could come over and have a look at her myself. Battered as she is, she'd still be a sight for sore eyes. But I doubt I'll have time . . . today." He looked up and his eyes held a savage gleam. "Today, I have a battle to fight!"

The sky in the east had begun to take on a pinkish tinge, blurring the stars, when Matt stepped out of the launch onto the long, low dock. His eyes burned and felt sticky with fatigue, but he felt a sense of anxious excitement nevertheless. He'd been awake for more than twenty-four hours, fought a battle, and found *Walker*'s long-lost sister. Still, he felt as though some sort of postponed retribution was at hand. A part of him whispered he was out of his depth, that he had no business directing a land engagement. But he was a historian and he'd studied the great battles of the past. That was probably as good a qualification for this type of fight as any other. What's more, for the first time, he'd be going into a fight with a pretty good idea of what he faced. The Grik were fearsome warriors and if they were allowed to mass, they'd outnumber his force more than four to one. What made him able to feel, as well as radiate, a sense of calm confidence was the fact that the enemy couldn't mass too effectively here on their right flank. They occupied only a narrow strip of land between the Aryaa-lan fortress and the swampy-banked river. Also, fearsome as the enemy was, they fought as a mob. Today they would face well-drilled and disci-plined *soldiers* who were highly motivated to destroy them.

Chief Gray stepped across from the launch behind him and Matt gave the Bosun a wry, grateful smile, then looked around with a confused sense of déjà vu. He had never set foot on Aryaalan soil before, but he'd spent time in Surabaya. Of course, nothing except the longitude and latitude was the same. Even the geography was different. The great wharves and piers that had once altered this coastline into a major seaport didn't exist. The Aryaalans weren't seagoing folk, and there was only this one dock to ser-vice their small fishing fleet and the occasional ferry to Madura. The dock and the immediate vicinity were crowded with troops still off-loading from the ships of the battle line.

Feluccas, launches, and small boats of every description came and went as fast as they could, and Lemurian NCOs scurried about, pushing and shoving their charges into some semblance of order by squads and com-panies. The apparent chaos didn't dishearten him. New to all this as they were, the Lemurian force began to coalesce at least as quickly as he'd seen human troops do before. He glanced at the brightening sky. Now all they needed was a little more time. Behind him, he heard Sandra shouting at her orderlies as they transferred medical supplies and equipment ashore. Her first order of business would be to establish a hospital, or surgery, to tend to the wounded that would be arriving very shortly. She wasn't shouting in frustration or anger, but merely to be heard over the turmoil, and her calm voice helped, as usual, to bolster his self-confidence. Ahead through the throng, he caught sight of Lieutenant Shinya. Lord Rolak and Chack were beside him, and he was gesturing for a company commander to move his troops out of the assembly area toward the barricade that was lost in darkness.

Wide-eyed, furiously blinking Marines and Guards parted before Matt as he strode toward the Japanese officer. Shinya and Chack both braced to attention and saluted as he drew near, and he saw Rolak cast an ap-praising eye upon the gesture as he returned it. "Lieutenant Shinya, Bo-sun's Mate Sab-At," Matt said in amiable greeting.

"Captain," they chorused in return.

"How goes the deployment?"

Shinya glanced at Lord Rolak with a hint of exasperation before he spoke. "A little noisier than I would have liked," he grumbled, "but so far there's no sign the enemy has reacted to our arrival. The Second Marine Regiment relieved the locals at the barricade as soon as they arrived and threw out a picket force a couple of hundred yards. The Grik are moving, but they seem to be focused on preparing to assault the fortifications."

"As I said!" interrupted Rolak. "If you have truly come to help us, then I ask you . . . no, I beg you to come inside the walls and help us face this attack!" He gestured around. "With the forces you have brought, Aryaal would be secure and the enemy would pound himself to pieces against our defenses!"

"That may be," Matt said as quietly as he could over the tumult, "but that would only result in maintaining the status quo." He paused, realizing that Chack had stumbled on the term during his translation. "The current situation. We didn't come here merely to help you hold your city, Lord Rolak. We came to destroy the Grik. We can't do that by assuming a defensive posture." He waved toward the blackness of the bay. "How long do you think it'll be before another fleet arrives? Some did escape. They'll return with larger and larger forces until, even with our help, Aryaal will fall. We must not allow that to happen. Not only for your sake, but for our own."

He looked around them at the army as it took shape. A barge had arrived next to the pier loaded with four light artillery pieces—six-pounders—mounted on "galloper" carriages with big wheels and two long shafts instead of a heavy trail so they could be either pulled by draft animals or easily maneuvered by hand. Marines worked feverishly to place ramps so they could bring the guns ashore. Another barge with a similar cargo waited to unload behind that one. Matt had every confidence the training and tactics that Alden and Shinya had hammered into the Marines and the Baalkpan Guard would make the difference against the Grik horde, but eight guns broken up into four two-gun sections advancing behind the shield wall would certainly help.

"You must trust us, Lord Rolak," Shinya said. "This army has been trained to fight in the open. Baalkpan does not have fine walls such as yours to shield her people and so we've not learned to rely on such things. I mean no disrespect," he added hastily, "but by necessity, we carry our wall with us when we fight. For this reason, we can also carry the fight to the enemy."

"But—" Rolak stopped and blinked in consternation. "If that truly is the case, and you're so sure of victory, then what are *we* to do? Aryaalans must be part of this fight! Were you not listening to me before? Battle is not a sport for spectators to enjoy! Even the contingent of B'mbaadans would rail against merely watching you fight the battle we've earned with our suffering these last months!"

Matt grinned at him. "Don't worry, Lord Rolak. There'll be plenty of fighting for all, but you'll have to come out to do it." Rolak blinked at him, a mixture of question and intrigue. Matt summoned a mental image of the map of the city Lieutenant Mallory had drawn. He should have asked Rolak for one with more detail, but he believed the one in his head would suffice for their current purposes. "Garrison your walls as lightly as you can. The initial Grik onslaught will probably fall on you—in fact, I'm counting on it. Gather a reserve force, as large as you can spare, near the main south gate. Did you see the bright red ball of fire that flew high in the air and burst just as the battle began on the bay last night?"

Rolak nodded. "Everyone saw it. It was like when a star falls from the sky, only that one fell upward!"

"It's called a 'flare.' When you see one today, that's when you must come out. You'll know why when it happens, because the opportunity should be clear. You must wait for it, though! Don't come out before you see it, but when you do, don't hesitate or all may be lost."

Lord Rolak looked steadily into Matt's unblinking eyes and he saw the light from the nearby torches reflected there. "I tell you now," he said, "upon my honor and my life, it will be as you say."

By the time the first rays of the sun fell upon the smoking remains of the Grik fleet in the bay, the Allied Expeditionary Force had fully deployed behind the barricaded breastworks that extended from the walls of the city to the harbor. Glistening bronze spearpoints rippled and swayed above the heads of the troops, shining bloodred already in the light of the morning sun. An eerie silence had settled upon the host, almost twenty-six hundred strong, as they gazed over the barrier and across the coastal plain. Matt and the Chief walked behind them, their shoes squelching in the ooze that had been churned in the damp sandy soil by the milling and marching of so many feet. Matt wished he had a horse to ride that would give him an elevated perspective not only of the events that were about to unfold but of the mood of "his" troops as well. It was hard to judge their feelings at that moment, with their inscrutably feline faces. But he'd learned to read Lemurian body language fairly well, and he'd learned to read much of the blinking they used instead of facial expressions.

Most were nervous, of course. Hell, *he* was nervous. But some few were blinking uncontrollably in abject terror. Most of those were surrounded and supported by steadier hearts, however, in a Lemurian way that Matt admired. But the vast majority of the troops poised for battle showed every sign of grim determination, if not outright eagerness. He nodded to himself. They would need all the eagerness, determination, and courage they could muster because across the marshy field before them lay the right flank of the Ancient Enemy.

The only sound was the flapping of the banners in the early-morning breeze. Each of the six regiments of infantry had its own new flag and most were emblazoned with some symbol that was important to the clan that dominated the regiment. The flags were Keje's idea, and at his insistence each also bore the symbol of a tree. It was a sacred sign to all Lemurians and it gave them a unifying identity. It was also the symbol that the Grik themselves used to identify them and to Keje that made it even more appropriate. In the center of the line flowed a great, stainless white banner adorned with only a single stylized green and gold tree. Beside it, also borne by a Lemurian color guard, flew the Stars and Stripes. Keje told him that it was the first flag the People ever fought under, and beneath it they'd tasted victory. It was also the flag of their honored friends and allies, so of course it should be there. Matt felt a surge of pride at the sight of it and he wondered yet again at the irony that had placed it on the field that day.

Across the expanse, the Grik had finally noticed the force assembled on their flank and had begun to react. The mob of warriors facing them swelled, as more were shifted from other parts of the line and others came slowly from across the river on barges. There was no help for it. They had known it would happen before they were ready to strike. Sneak attacks are all but impossible when armies have to assemble and move everywhere they go on foot, not to mention within plain sight of each other. Perhaps their tactics would be surprise enough. Whatever the Grik thought, though, it didn't look like they intended to let this "diversion" take their attention from what they saw as their main objective: the city beyond the wall.

Horns sounded a deep, harsh, vibratory hum and thousands of voices took up an eerie, hissing chant that sounded like some creature being fried alive in a skillet. Accompanying the chant, thousands of swords and spears clashed against their small round shields and the staccato beat built to a deafening crescendo.

"It's even more terrifying on land than sea," admitted a voice beside him. Matt turned to see Keje standing there, resplendent in his polished copper mail. His helmet visor was low over his eyes. "At sea, the noise is muted by wind and distance."

"What are you doing here?" Matt demanded.

Keje grinned. "What a question to ask! I would ask the same of you if I thought I would get a different answer. Adar commands the battle line in my stead," Keje assured him. "He knows what to do and he will be obeyed."

With a great seething roar, the Grik horde surged toward Aryaal, waving their weapons over their heads and jostling one another to be in the vanguard. The beginning of the attack must have been plainly visible to the lookouts high above the decks of the Homes in the bay. Most of the Grik directly across the quarter mile of soft ground from the AEF didn't join in the charge, but continued to face them, securing the flank. Even at the distance, it was clear they were unhappy with the task and a steady trickle was bleeding away to join the assault.

"Now would be about right for him to give the order," Matt said of Adar. As if somehow the Sky Priest heard his quiet words, a bright flash and a white cloud of smoke erupted from *Big Sal*'s side, followed immediately by four more. The heavy, booming report of the big guns reached them a moment later, and by then the sides of all the ships of the battle line were enveloped in fire and smoke. The canvas-tearing shriek of the heavy shot reached their ears, and seconds later huge geysers of mud and debris rocketed upward from the midst of the Grik reserve across the river. Matt watched through his binoculars as troops swarmed over the bulwarks of the big ships and crowded into boats alongside. The guns continued to hammer away, each one sending a thirty-two-pound solid copper ball into the enemy camp. The balls shredded the densely packed bodies and destroyed the tents and makeshift dwellings as they struck and bounded and skated through, unstoppable, to kill again and again.

One of Lord Rolak's aides, left as a liaison, vaulted to the top of one of the brontosaurus-like creatures that had been on the waterfront when they arrived. This particular specimen had bronze greaves on its legs and wore polished bronze plates over its vitals. Besides being beasts of burden, the ridiculous brutes apparently served as Aryaalan warhorses. Matt had noticed the thing when he came ashore, but it never even occurred to him that anyone would try to ride one of the amazingly stupid animals into battle. Now he self-consciously reached up and grabbed the aide's outstretched hand and allowed the powerful Aryaalan to help him swing onto the dinosaur's back. He took a moment to secure himself to the rock-steady platform and then quickly raised the binoculars again.

The camp across the river looked like an ant bed stirred with a stick. Shot gouged through them, but the Grik had begun to assemble on the beach, preparing to attack what seemed to be an imminent amphibious assault. He turned to look at the river. The barges carrying reinforcements into the assault had stopped halfway across and were beginning to return to the far bank with their teeming cargoes. The assault itself had reached the obstacles and entanglements at the base of the wall, and rocks, arrows, and other projectiles rained down upon the enemy. Ladders rose out of the mass and fell against the wall, only to be pushed back upon the attackers. For now. The attack had weight behind it, however, and regardless of the terrible losses they were inflicting, the defenders were too thin on the walls to hold for long. Matt leaned over and looked down at Shinya, Gray, and Keje, who were staring up at him expectantly.

"The army will advance!" he said in a loud, firm voice. He smiled briefly at the irony. It wasn't an order he, a naval officer, had ever expected to give.

The barricade parted before them, and at the shouted commands of their officers, the Marines and Guards from Baalkpan and *Big Sal* and all the other Homes and places that had come to Aryaal's aid stepped through the gaps with a precision that would have warmed Tacitus's heart. For several minutes, they passed through the breastworks until the final ranks had joined the others on the exposed side, with nothing between them and the enemy but a gently swaying sea of marsh grass and flowers. There the army paused for a moment, flags fluttering overhead, as it dressed ranks and waited for the guns to make their more difficult way through the obstacles. Matt patted the Aryaalan aide on the arm and motioned for him to follow. The dinosaur bellowed a complaint when the aide pushed forward on a pair of levers that caused two sharpened stakes at the back of the platform-saddle they rode to jab down hard into the animal's hips. With a sickening pitching motion, the beast began to move and the aide released the pressure on the stakes. Two long cables, like reins, snaked back along the beast's serpentine neck and the aide pulled savagely on one of them, physically pointing the creature's head in the direction he wanted it to go. Slowly, they trudged through the barricade and joined the army on the other side.

"God a'mighty, Skipper! I wish I had a camera!" came a voice from below and behind. Matt looked down. Dennis Silva and half a dozen other destroyermen were falling in on the animal's flanks.

"What the hell are you doing here?" Matt called hotly. "We already have more men ashore than I'd like. You're supposed to be assisting Lieutenant Ellis!"

Silva assumed a wounded expression. "I am, Skipper! But he's a captain now too, you know. What with his own ship and all. He plumb *ordered* us off of it!" He gestured at the other men. "Said he couldn't stand the very thought of us deck-apes foulin' his engineerin' spaces! I think he must'a been a snipe himself once upon a time," he added darkly. "Put us ashore, and made us take these guns"—he brandished the Browning Automatic Rifle, or BAR, in his hand—"to keep 'em out of the workers' way!" Silva shook his head. "No way back to *Walker* now, so we figgered we'd come along over here and keep you comp'ny watchin' this fight."

Matt tried to maintain a stern expression, but an unstoppable grin broke through. "My God, Silva, you missed your calling. Hollywood or Congress, that's where you should be. I've never seen anyone tell such a ridiculous lie with such conviction." He looked at Gray, glowering at Silva. "Chief, put these men on report. They can stay, but they're in your custody and control. They will *not* fire their weapons without my orders. Is that understood?" Matt gestured at the backs of the Lemurian troops as they prepared to move forward again. "The last thing we need is for these people to start relying on our modern weapons to fight their battles. We just don't have enough to make a difference." He smiled sadly. "We could probably do it once, but that would be even worse." He looked squarely at Gray. "Emergencies only. That's an order."

"But, Skipper, beggin' your pardon, haven't we been doing that already? With the ship?" Silva asked, genuinely confused.

Matt nodded. "Yes, we have, but there's a difference. The ship is who we are. She's *what* we are, as far as these people are concerned. She's what's given us the credentials to advise them and help them technologically and be believed. Of course we fight with the ship. That's what's allowed us to give them the confidence they'll need to win this fight—and it'll be their fight for the most part. It has to be."

"But . . . even some of the cat-monkeys have guns—"

Matt's voice took on an edge. "I'm not in the habit of explaining myself to gunner's mates, Silva, but you may have noticed that Sergeant Alden's Marine rifle company isn't here. They're in reserve in Baalkpan." Matt's face softened slightly. "Don't worry. I'm sure you'll get a chance to shoot somebody before the day is out. Maybe you can snipe a general or two, but the victory, if there is one, must be theirs." He waved at the army again. "Won with their arms. Do you understand? That's the only way they'll ever win not just this battle but the war."

Matt was convinced he was right. He just hoped it would turn out that way. Being right in theory wasn't always the same as being right in practice.

"Does that mean we have to sling our rifles and just use these crummy cutlasses, Skipper?" asked Tom Felts from the other side of the dinosaur.

Matt grinned. "No, just don't shoot unless I say so. Damn, I thought I said that."

"Just shut up, you stupid apes," growled the Bosun. "Can't you see the cap'n's got a battle to think about? One more word out of you and I'll drag your asses back to the dock and you'll miss the whole thing!"

Lieutenant Shinya's voice rose above the silence of the waiting army. "Soldiers of the Allied Expeditionary Force! People of the Sacred Tree and sons and daughters of the Heavens!" Others answered his shrill voice, up and down the line. Many didn't hear him over the stiffening breeze, but they heard the voices of those closer to them.

"First Guard Regiment!"

"Second Guard Regiment!"

"Second Marines!"

And on and on, followed by the shouts of company commanders and squad leaders.

"At the quick time, *march*!"

As a single entity, the entire army stepped off with their left feet just as they'd been taught and began to move forward with long, purposeful strides that ate up ground at a surprising rate. The guns went with them, and two dozen artillerymen per piece manhandled the weapons and ammunition right along with the infantry. It was amazing. To Matt's knowledge, the army had never been able to train together on such a scale before, either on the parade ground or in the newly cleared zones around Baalkpan City. But for the most part, the formation held together with almost total precision. Here and there, NCOs called a cadence or shouted instructions for their squads to keep up or slow down, but the overall impression of discipline was impressive. Pete Alden, the man who, more than anyone, had built this army, would be proud. Matt was proud. Despite his inner anxiety, he felt a sudden thrill. He knew then what it must have felt like to be Caesar, or Alexander, watching his well-trained army march into battle against disorganized barbarians. The historian within him continued to whisper insidiously that the barbarians often won, but for the moment, he didn't—wouldn't—listen. The die was cast and the time for strategy was past.

There would be little maneuver; there was no point. When they engaged the enemy, the army would extend from the walls of the city almost to the banks of the river and he was reminded of one of his favorite Nelson quotes: "Never mind about maneuvers. Just go straight at 'em." That was about all they could do in this confined space. When the two forces came together, there'd just be fighting and hacking and killing. His great hope then was that the training his people had received would make the difference. Of course, they did have a few surprises for the Grik even before that happened.

The battle raged with more intensity at the base of the distant walls, and more and more ladders fell against them. Occasionally, firebombs arced up in high trajectories and fell among the defenders beyond his view. Matt surmised the enemy must have some sort of portable machine or catapult that could hurl the apparently smaller bombs than those used aboard their ships. It was difficult to tell through his binoculars how well the Aryaalans were holding because of the odd, jouncing gait of his mount. He heard a different note from the horns of the Grik in front of them, one with a kind of strident edge. He thought, incongruously, that they really needed to come up with some means like that for the Lemurians to signal one another. Their mouths were shaped all wrong to blow on a bugle. They had some woodwind-type horns, but they just weren't loud enough. Maybe the conch-like shells they blew as a warning? Even simple whistles would be better than nothing. He should have thought of that sooner. He wondered how the Grik managed it. The way their mouths were shaped, he couldn't see how they could do anything with them other than tear flesh.

At three hundred yards, a single command echoed up and down the line.

"Shields!"

The tall, rectangular shields made from bronze plate backed with wood that the first two ranks carried clashed together as they were locked, side to side, overlapping one another to form a mobile wall. Spears came down in unison and rested on the top edges of the shields as the army advanced. It was an impressive display and Matt wondered what the enemy thought. He knew the sight had horrified the enemies of Rome, but he had no idea how the Grik would react. A smattering of crossbow bolts fluttered toward them. Most landed short, but a few thunked into the shield wall. A single piercing scream reached his ears from far to the left. His unlikely mount lumbered mindlessly along with a kind of quartering, rolling motion, following behind the trotting ranks but easily keeping up with its plodding, long-legged pace.

"Halt!" came the cry at two hundred yards, and the advance ground to a stop. For a moment there was a little confusion as the ranks realigned themselves. A runner dashed up from where Shinya had stopped with his staff a short distance away. He spoke in carefully enunciated English. "Lieutenant Shinya sends his respects, sir, and asks if he may commence firing?"

"By all means," Matt answered. With a salute, the young runner scampered away. Matt glanced down and saw Keje standing with Chief Gray. The Chief was practically supporting him as the Lemurian wheezed and Matt felt a pang of shame. The advance from the barricade had to have been tough on his portly friend. Keje was strong as a bull, but Matt doubted he'd had many occasions to trot as far as he had. "Keje," he called, "why don't you join me up here? You can sure see better. There's plenty of room."

Keje eyed the beast with suspicion, but gratefully nodded his head. He climbed swiftly onto the platform and settled next to Matt and Lord Rolak's aide. He was still puffing a little. "I grow too old," he said, "and my legs are too short for this fighting on land." He shook his head. "It is unnatural."

Matt glanced behind them and smiled. "But you didn't come much farther than the length of *Big Sal*. Hell, I doubt it was as far."

"Perhaps, but *Salissa* does not clutch at your feet as you run, and her decks are flat and you do not sink into them."

"Batteries, forward!" came the command. "Archers, prepare!" Gaps opened in the shield wall to allow the guns to be pushed through. Their crews immediately raced to load them with fixed charges consisting of thin tin canisters filled with two hundred three-quarter-inch balls on top of a wooden sabot to which was attached a fabric bag of powder. In carefully choreographed, highly rehearsed drills, rammers whirled and shoved the charges down the barrels. Pricks pierced the powder bags through the vents and priming powder was pooled atop them. Other members of the gun's crews stood nearby, blowing on lengths of smoldering slow match in their linstocks.

Around them, bows came off shoulders and arrows were nocked and poised at the ready. Crossbows were cocked and bolts placed in grooves. Before them, the Grik horns had fallen silent. They were close enough to hear the fighting for the walls, but from the Grik that stood refusing the enemy flank, there was no sound at all for the moment. Perhaps it was fear that quieted them? There was no way to know. More likely, it was simple curiosity as to why the machine-like formation that had been coming on so quickly had stopped. They were about to find out.

"Fire!"

Roughly two thousand arrows and crossbow bolts soared into the sky with a whickering crash of bowstrings. An instant later, the deafening, almost simultaneous thundering crack of eight light guns snapped out, belching fire and choking white smoke that entirely obscured the enemy until the wind dissipated the cloud. Sixteen hundred one-ounce balls scythed downrange. Many struck the ground far in front of the enemy, and some of those were absorbed by the damp earth. Many more flew high, missing the target completely and eventually falling, mostly harmless, among the enemy forces hundreds of yards away. Hundreds more went screaming right in among the densely packed, unsuspecting foe and struck like a cyclone of death. Grik were shredded and hurled bleeding to the ground, felled by one or a score of projectiles. Many were hit by shattered pieces of others who were hit. In an instant, fully one-quarter of the blocking force lay still or writhing on the ground. Then, before even their initial shock could begin to register, the arrows that had been fired at a high trajectory began to fall upon them. A high-pitched, wrenching wail built across the field as the plunging arrows pierced armor and flesh.

Already, the second flight of arrows was in the air and Matt saw dozens of shapes collapse to the ground as the deadly rain descended. Fully half the enemy flank was down and some that remained simply fled. Most did not. They charged. With wild, whooping screams, they bolted from their positions and sprinted across the marshy plain, trying to come to grips with this unusual and deadly threat. With staccato thunderclaps, the guns fired again, independently, and were quickly drawn back behind the shield wall, which re-formed where the guns had been. There, the first ranks waited expectantly for the charge to drive home. Less than a hundred wounded, disoriented Grik ran or staggered out of the smoke and slammed against the shields. Their deaths were almost anticlimactic.

As the smoke drifted away, the full impact of the blow they'd dealt began to settle in. The Allied Expeditionary Force had utterly annihilated a force almost as large as its own and had lost less than a dozen to do it. A cheer began to build and soon it became a roar. Flags waved jubilantly back and forth and Matt could see that discipline had begun to fail.

"Silence!" he bellowed at the top of his lungs. Keje joined his shout in his own tongue. Matt beckoned to one of his runners that stood nearby. "Tell Lieutenant Shinya we must push on! We've got to keep up the pressure! This has only just begun." Shinya was already giving those very directions. Runners and NCOs paced the line, outward from the center, yelling for silence and telling the troops to prepare to advance. Matt scanned the wall ahead to see how the defenders fared. It was difficult to be sure, but it seemed like fewer ladders were going up. Either the steam was going out of the attack or a new, more pressing threat had been recognized. The thrumming horns were sounding again, and the notes were clearly different than before.

"A glorious beginning!" said Keje with a tone of satisfaction and clapped him on the shoulder. Matt nodded absently, still staring through the binoculars. He was certain now. The attack on the city was withdrawing as he watched, and a redeployment had begun. There was no order to it, no organization, just a general surge as the Grik army reevaluated its priority objective and moved in that direction. Toward him. "Sure was," he said, confirming Keje's enthusiastic evaluation. "But it's about to get a little tougher."

Lord Rolak impatiently paced the open bastion above the wall near the southeast corner. Risking a bolt from below, he leaned far out over the wall and stared to the north. Past the southeast bastion of the old castle to which this wall was added, great clouds of smoke arose on the right flank of the enemy. He'd known that the sea folk and their Amer-i-caan allies had small . . . gonnes—he thought they called them—like those upon their ships, that they could bring with them to battle on the land. Even so, he'd still been stunned by the sound and effect those weapons had wrought. He had stripped the defenses as much as he dared, just like the green-eyed Amer-i-caan had asked, and then gathered the resultant force in the open marketplace near the south gate. There they waited, nearly sixteen hundreds of them, for him to give the command to sally. He had begun to feel concern when the Grik attack came, and wondered if perhaps he had thinned his defenses too far.

The Grik attacked like the night demons they were—enraged by the defeat they'd suffered the night before and slathering to wreak vengeance upon his city. As the fight raged, he even began to fear the sea folk wouldn't come. They would seize a moment of treachery and allow Aryaal—a city they couldn't love—to fall. All they would have to do then would be to file back upon their great ships and sail away, having accomplished effortlessly what they would never have been able to achieve by arms. He shook his head. But that was pointless. What possible motive would they have for that? Would they really have broken the siege simply to rescue their damaged iron ship? Possibly. He believed the Amer-i-caan, Reddy, would have. But he was sure they'd been surprised by the ship's presence here. He knew nothing of the strange face-moving of the Amer-i-caans, but the sea folk weren't so different that he could miss the genuine shock they betrayed at the sight of the other Amer-i-caans he carried out to them.

Besides, there was just . . . something about them, and the Amer-i-caan leader in particular, that convinced him they were here to help. He cherished no illusion that was the only reason they came, and in fact they'd told him as much. They needed Aryaal's help as much as Aryaal needed theirs. To them, this wasn't just a battle. It was a war. A war of a scope beyond any Rolak had ever heard of. A war in which victory wasn't determined by how much territory or tribute was gained, or by how many trade concessions were wrung from the enemy, or even simply by how entertaining it had been. The sea folk, who almost never fought, had come to save Aryaal so his people could join them in a war to annihilate their enemy. It was unreal. But these Grik . . . they did not fight the old way. They came to destroy his people, not just drive them to their knees. And the things they did to those they took alive . . . He shuddered. No, the sea folk and their strange friends were sincere, and so was he when he gave his own word to help. He had just hoped the Amer-i-caan leader's plan would begin to unfold before it was too late.

Then he had begun to sense a stirring on the far left and had seen the strange banners, which the sea folk had never used before, begin to advance. The fighting for the walls continued unabated, and he began to fear their "allies'" force was too puny to gather the enemy's attention as Reddy's plan hoped. Then he had heard the thunder. Not just the thunder from the ships, which he'd begun to hear already, but the thunder that came from the sea folk land force. That was when he had known it wouldn't be long before they called him, and he stood ready to dash down to the south gate as soon as he saw the flare.

"The wait is . . . distracting," came a soft voice beside him. Lord Rolak turned and looked at Safir Maraan, Queen Protector of B'mbaado. She was dressed all in black, from the leather that backed her armor to the long, flowing cape that fell from her shoulders and fluttered fitfully in the breeze. Her fur was black as well—entirely, without the slightest hint of a past mixture that would attest to any dilution of the royal blood. Her bright gray eyes shone like silver in her ebon face and artistically justified her only concession to the dark raiment, which was a form-fitted breastplate made of silver-washed bronze.

She is perfect, Lord Rolak admitted frankly to himself. He was almost three times her age, but he hadn't grown so ancient he couldn't recognize fact. It's no wonder that young fool of a prince would have them fight a war to have her. That war had ended inconclusively, of course, when the Grik had come. As much as she hated Rasik-Alcas, she'd brought six hundred of her finest warriors, her personal guard, to help defend against them. Lord Rolak rather doubted if Fet or Rasik-Alcas would have done the same.

One of those warriors was a massive B'mbaadan, scarred and old as he, who shadowed Queen Maraan's every move. His name was Haakar-Faask, and Rolak respected him greatly. They had battled often and inflicted their share of scars on one another. After Safir became the Orphan Queen, it was Faask who became her mentor, chief guard, general, and, in some ways, surrogate father. Right now, Rolak wished he would exercise a little more protectiveness. He looked at the warrior and blinked with exasperation, but Faask remained inscrutable. With a growl, Rolak stepped quickly back from the bastion wall, hoping to draw the queen with him. Dressed like that, she had to be a tempting target for the enemy crossbows. Unconcerned, she continued to peer over the side at the roiling enemy below. To her left, some distance away, a great cauldron of boiling water poured down upon the enemy and agonized shrieks rose to their ears. Rolak saw a slight smile of satisfaction expose a few of her perfect white teeth. She turned and stepped from the edge just as a flurry of crossbow bolts whipped over the wall where she'd been. Rolak sighed exasperatedly, blinking accusation at Haakar-Faask. "My dear Queen Protector, you must not take such chances. You must be more careful!"

"Like your own king?" she asked with a mocking smile. Rolak didn't respond. "Unlike the great Fet-Alcas, I am not only the leader of my people in peace, but in war. That is why I am also called 'Protector.' I take that duty seriously. I won't shirk any danger I ask my warriors to face."

"I have not seen you ask your warriors to flaunt themselves pointlessly in full view of the enemy, my dear," Rolak observed with a wry smile as he blinked with gentle humor.

"Have you not? What then do you think they are doing here?" As before, Lord Rolak had no reply.

Shouted voices registered and he looked to the north. To his admitted surprise, the tide of Grik began to ebb, the closer to the harbor it was. The fight below them had not abated, but to the north there was a growing hesitancy. Confusion. The enemy horns brayed insistently, and he ventured nearer the parapet.

"It is working," he breathed. Below him, the Grik were slowly, even reluctantly, backing away from the wall. Some continued to try to raise ladders in their single-minded, berserker sort of way, but the vast majority responded to whatever call the horns had made and began to move, en masse, toward the sea. Rolak turned to face the young queen with shining eyes. "Come! Quickly! If you must protect your people with your life, they will need you very soon!" He motioned to one of his staff. "Stand here!" he commanded. "If we do not see the flying fire, you must tell us when it comes!" He turned for the stairs and, together with their staffs and guards, Lord Rolak and Queen Maraan took them two at a time as they raced toward the southern gate.

Down they went until they reached the cobbled street that threaded through the homes and shops of merchants. The open market area wasn't far and they burst upon a scene of impatiently milling warriors who had been listening to the sound of battle outside and were anxious to join it. Aryaalan warriors fought with each other to get out of Rolak's way and he and his entourage moved through the gap forming in his path with ease. Nearer the gate stood B'mbaado's Six Hundred in their black leather tunics and their shields with the single silver sun device of the Orphan Queen. They also parted so their leader and her chief guard could pass. Before them loomed the great gate, its huge wooden timbers hung upon hinges as thick as an Aryaalan's leg.

Rolak glanced over his shoulder, high over the wall, and waited for the fiery signal. When it came, soaring high above the city, its amber-red trail so different from the firebombs of the Grik, he felt as though a great weight had been lifted from him. All his fears, his paranoia, had been misplaced, and now that those who had come to their aid had done their part—just as they had promised—he felt a surge of eagerness to spring forward and do his. "Open the gate!" he shouted. "All together!"

With a roar, the warriors surged forward, ready to push through the opening as quickly as they could. Lemurians in the gate towers prepared to heave on the windlasses that would cause the gate to swing wide.

"Lord Rolak, you *will not* open that gate!"

Even over the thunderous din, the bellowed command was heard by all. A terrible hush fell over the crowd as all eyes turned to a raised sedan, or shoulder carriage, borne by a dozen muscular guardsmen in immaculate white jerkins that forced its way nearer the gate. Atop the carriage was an ornate golden seat covered with crimson cushions and upon it lounged

Fet-Alcas, king of Aryaal. Seated beside him, on the litter itself, was his son, Rasik, and his eyes gleamed with triumph as he stared at Safir Maraan.

"You will not open that gate," Fet-Alcas repeated in a quieter, raspy tone, gesturing angrily with his brown-and-silver-furred hand. The flab that had once been muscle swayed beneath the bone of his upper arm, and the exertion the movement took made his bloated body quiver. Outside the gate, they could hear the turmoil as even the forces arrayed there rushed past, on their way to join the fighting to the north.

Lord Rolak was struck dumb. His first impression was that there had been some mistake. "What did you say, Lord King?" he asked, uncertain if age and his many wounds had finally deprived him of his mind.

Fet-Alcas blinked in consternation as if he was speaking to a stone. "I commanded you not to open that gate, Lord Rolak," he wheezed. His earlier, unaccustomed roar had left him nearly spent. "You will obey me. We will not engage the enemy from beyond these walls."

"But why?" Rolak asked. It was all he could manage for the moment.

"Because I command it!" coughed the king. "I need not explain my reasons to you!"

Rolak's eyes narrowed. "Yes, Lord King, you must. I am Protector of Aryaal and it is my duty to protect this city. I explained to you the plan this morning. You had no objection then."

"You are Protector, appointed by the king!" sneered Prince Rasik. "You will do as he says."

In a calm, patient voice like one would use with a youngling that had just found a sharp sword and was preparing to examine its sibling's eyes more carefully, Rolak spoke. "Great King, I have made alliance—which is my right—with the sea folk and the Amer-i-caans to defeat the enemy who threatens us. Even now they are fighting at our side as they promised. They have drawn the enemy away from our walls and upon themselves so we can attack from behind. We are moments away from victory, or days from total defeat!"

"It is your right to make alliance, Lord Rolak, but it is my right not to support that alliance if I do not think, in the interests of the people, you have acted wisely." King Fet-Alcas could no longer bellow, but his tone was imperious. "You have not."

"In what way have I not acted wisely, that you did not recognize before our allies committed themselves?" Rolak felt a tension building within him, a tension bordering on rage. He had given his word to the Amer-i-caan leader and even now the sea folk were fighting and dying outside these walls based upon his word. Soon the moment to strike would pass and whatever they did would be too late. Queen Maraan stirred beside him, a small growl deep in her throat. She hadn't been party to the agreement, but she too recognized the opportunity that was being squandered.

The king waved his hand again and glanced at his son. "That is not your concern."

"It is my concern if my honor is at stake, Lord King. I beg you to satisfy my honor and that of your people by telling us what your plan might be."

"That is simple. The strangers refused your offer of honor to join us within these walls and fight at our side. They chose instead to fight alone. It is my order that we let them! They came here unasked for and without my permission—"

"To save us!" Rolak interrupted.

"—with fanciful plans to continue this war far from here. They did not come here to save us, and if they did, what is their price? That we should fight for them as their slaves? No! We will let them fight the Grik and bleed them, and when they are properly and courteously dead and their unnatural smoking ships have gone, then we will destroy the Grik they have left us!"

"No!" Lord Rolak shouted. "Don't you see? The Grik are like the sand on the beach, the water in the sea! The Amer-i-caans showed me a map they took from them. They have conquered the entire world! If we do not stop them now, and push them back, they will return with twice, three times the numbers we now face!"

Fet-Alcas glanced once more at his son. There was fear there, Rolak knew. But what was the greatest source? "You have heard my words!"

"I have heard the words of a coward!" shouted Safir Maraan in a high, clear voice. "And as an 'ally'"—she bared her teeth in contempt—"who came here unasked for and without permission, I choose to go to the aid of another who was foolish enough to do the same!" She turned toward the wide-eyed Aryaalans in the gate towers.

"Open!"

"Do not!" screeched Prince Rasik. "I will have you impaled!" The windlass crews, torn between what they wanted to do and their terror, fled.

Queen Maraan turned and made a follow-me gesture to her guard. "We will go out the north gate, then," she said to her warriors and stared at the royalty of Aryaal with feral hatred. "Perhaps we will only arrive in time to help them retreat, but it would be better to die with honorable strangers than continue to breathe the same air that has been corrupted by such cowardice." Queen Maraan and her Six Hundred began to push through the Aryaalan troops.

"Stop her!" Rasik-Alcas screamed and leaped down from the litter, drawing his sword. In that instant, with hundreds of swords beginning to slide from their sheaths, Lord Rolak knew what he must do. He also knew that, whatever happened, they were probably doomed. He drew his own sword and stepped between Rasik and the queen. The prince stared at him in shock. Then, with a wild snarl, he lunged at Rolak with his sword. The old warrior batted it away with contemptuous ease and then laid the edge of his blade lightly against his prince's throat. He looked over at Safir for just a moment, and nodded.

Another flare soared insistently into the heavens. He watched it rise, pop, and dissipate downwind. Physical shame coursed through his veins as he looked at the now cowering prince. With a growl, he lifted his head to shout. "I, Lord Rolak, Protector of Aryaal, am going to continue as before!"

"Any who follow him will die, as traitors to their king!" screeched Fet-Alcas.

"Who is with me?" Rolak insisted. Hesitantly at first, but then with greater enthusiasm, roughly a third of the Aryaalan warriors gathered around Rolak, shouting their support. Rolak estimated the force, but grimly shook his head. Not enough. They would never be able to break through from the south with so few. With sudden determination, he strode to the Orphan Queen. "My dear Queen Protector, it looks as though we will have to follow your plan after all, if you will have us." He looked around at the troops who had stayed loyal to the king. Many were blinking in shame. "Together, we may still not have the numbers to relieve the sea folk from the south, as we hoped, but we have more than the king can stop with warriors who fear him more than the loss of their honor. With your permission?"

She smiled and nodded graciously and Lord Rolak raised his voice.

"To the north gate, as quickly as you can!"

"Go and die, Lord Rolak!" shrilled the king as he pounded the elaborate arms of his seat. "*Die!* The gates of Aryaal are closed to you forever! All of you! And when the Grik turn their might toward B'mbaado, we will not come! *We will not come!*"

The king's rant echoed behind them as they ran through the deserted inner city. Word of what had happened spread as fast as they ran, and they gathered almost two hundred more warriors who wanted to join them. Some of these came from the east wall, where they could see the battle between the Grik and the strangers who had come to help them. "Hurry!" was all they said.

"They're not coming," Matt muttered to himself, and lowered his binoculars. He was standing on top of the dead brontosaurus to get one last look, to assure himself of the unbelievable. Keje held shields for both of them that were festooned with dozens of crossbow bolts, but so far neither of them had been hit. It wasn't from lack of trying. Rolak's aide had been killed, and the brontosaurus had finally taken what must have been the critical number of wounds to trigger a pain reaction reflex and it had gone amok. Silva emptied a BAR magazine into the thing—without orders, thank God—before it could stampede through the army and decimate a regiment with its death throes. Among other things, that would have immediately lost them the battle. The shield wall was the only thing that had kept them alive this long. Together, Matt and Keje slithered down from the dead beast and the thrumming bolts immediately diminished. Only when they were elevated did they present a real target for the enemy.

"They're not coming," Matt repeated with a tone of wonder in his voice. "My God, how could they be so *stupid*?"

"I told you about them," Keje said grimly.

Matt smiled sadly. "I hate to say I told you so, huh?"

Keje looked at him and blinked. "No, I *did* tell you so."

Matt shook his head.

"Buggers said they liked to fight!" groused Chief Gray.

"Yeah, so did them Eye-talian Marines that time in Shanghai," Silva accused the Bosun. "I still can't believe you put me on report for that!"

"You were pickin' on 'em, damn it! One nearly died!"

Matt almost smiled despite the situation. He and his irrepressible destroyermen, two of whom had taken minor wounds, walked slowly along behind the battle line, shouting encouragement as they went. So far, the fighting at the shield wall had been remarkably one-sided. The Grik just didn't know how to cope with it. They slammed themselves against it, battering with their bodies while the first rank leaned into the onslaught, doing little but holding the enemy back with their interlocking shields. The ranks behind did most of the killing, stabbing, and slashing with swords and spears through gaps and over the tops of their comrades. And how they killed! The ground in front of the shields was piled high with the dead, making the footing difficult for those that came behind. But still they came. Fresh Grik arrived every minute, and the shield wall was beginning to tire.

Occasionally the Grik eased back for a moment and tried to gall them with bolts. Whenever the pressure slacked, the muzzles of the six-pounders poked through and a double load of canister scythed into them, killing hundreds with each blast, so densely packed was their formation. But still, more came. It was insane.

Lieutenant Shinya trotted up with a reduced staff. Matt wondered how many had been killed and how many had been used to fill gaps in the line. Shinya himself was bleeding from a cut under his left eye. "We're getting thin on the left, Captain." He shouted to be heard. "They keep pushing there, trying to roll us back and force a way through by the river."

Matt nodded. "It's the same on the right, but probably not as bad. At least those bastards on the walls will still shoot arrows at them if they get close enough." He paused. "They're not coming, Tamatsu. We're going to have to start pulling back."

Shinya nodded. "It's going to be difficult, Captain. Holding the line together is one thing. Holding the line together and advancing is another. Doing it while pulling back is . . . something else."

"We have that one spot about fifty, seventy-five yards back where the front will be wider," Matt reminded him. "We'll have to extend the line to cover it. After that, particularly as we get closer to the barricade, the land narrows back down and we can thicken things up, I hope. Pass the word; at the next flare, we start to pull back. We've *got* to keep it together." Shinya saluted again and trotted off. Matt looked at the destroyermen around him, cradling their weapons as they watched the battle. All were armed with Thompsons or BARs—probably half the weapons of the type that they had. No choice. "Forget the 'no shooting' order. I want one of you to each regiment, ready to pour fire into any breakthroughs if they occur. We've got to keep this line together at all costs. If it breaks, we're dead. Conserve your ammunition and don't get trigger-happy, but use it if you have to. Now go!"

They all hurried off except Silva, who stood rooted with a worried expression on his face. "But what about you, Skipper?"

"Never fear, Mr. Silva. I have my pistol. If that fails, the Bosun will protect me."

Silva arched an eyebrow and a grin crept across his face. "But who's gonna protect him?"

Gray's face turned purple with rage. "Buzz off, you goddamn weed-chewin' ape! Or I'll let that crazy cook use you for fish bait!"

"Just worried about you, is all," shouted Silva as he loped off down the line. Gray shook his head and stifled a grin. They were standing right behind the rear rank of the Second Marine Regiment. The Second was near the center of the line and it was spear-heavy, all of its members being large and strong enough to stand in the front rank. Those at the rear were methodically shooting arrows over the heads of those in front, and periodically they'd move forward and take the place of an exhausted comrade. It was a good drill and Matt wished the Guard regiments had learned to do the same. Many of those who came to the rear were wounded, some badly, and an increasing number of them were pushed or dragged out of the ranks as the fighting continued. A growing number of bodies, some moving, others not, were gathering behind the lines, waiting to be carried back to the barricade on stretchers to be tended in the field hospital.

"There ain't enough stretcher bearers," Gray observed grimly. "When we start to pull back, things could go bad in a hurry."

Matt recognized one of the wounded Lemurians as he was tossed roughly on a litter. It was that runner of Shinya's he'd spoken to before. He had a terrible slash across his chest and blood-soaked bandages were heaped high upon him. Matt hurried to his side. "Do you understand me?" he asked urgently. The young Lemurian nodded, his teeth clenched with pain. "The hospital must evacuate! Get the wounded to safety." He grasped the runner's hand in his. "Tell Lieutenant Tucker . . ." He paused. He didn't know what to say. "Tell her to pull out now. That's an order." He squeezed the hand.

"I will tell her, Cap-i-taan," the runner replied with a strained voice. Matt nodded and the stretcher bearers raced to the rear with their burden.

Chack-Sab-At gasped with pain as a Grik spearpoint skated off his shield and laid open the top of his shoulder. The thrust had overextended his enemy, however, and Chack drove his own spearpoint into the Grik's throat with a triumphant snarl. An explosive spray of blood and spittle flecked his face as the enemy warrior went down. If it screamed, Chack didn't hear it over the constant roar of battle.

For just an instant, his thoughts turned to his sister, Risa, and he wondered what she would think if she saw him now. It seemed so long ago that she'd virtually shamed him into taking the warrior's tack. How little he'd known at the time; beneath his nervousness and protestation a warrior was what he *was*. Or perhaps, deep down, he knew it all along. Maybe that was why he allowed himself to be bullied and never tried to win the frequent bouts of his youth. Or maybe he was afraid of what he'd become. Afraid he would like it. That day upon the decks of *Salissa*, fighting to save his sister and his people and ultimately his very soul, he'd discovered he had been right to be afraid. He had *loved* it, and much to his great surprise, he had been *good* at it as well.

His warrior-minded sister had seen the change in him when she recovered from her wounds, but she'd believed it was just a sign that he'd grown up at last. She hadn't realized the more fundamental nature of the change. Once, his greatest ambition had been to one day become a wing clan chief. That goal no longer even entered his thoughts. He no longer cared about running *Salissa*'s great wings, or those of any other Home. He still loved *Salissa*, but *Walker* was his Home now and he was a destroyerman through and through. He knew most people believed he was playing a game with Selass, rubbing her nose in her rejection of him for Saak-Fas. But as far as he was concerned, she could remain mated to the mad, broken shell that Saak-Fas had become. The only thing he really felt for her now was pity. He didn't care about anything that once seemed so important—other than his sister, of course, despite her bothersome behavior, and the safety of his people and their strange tail-less friends. All that mattered now was the joy he felt when he was destroying their enemies. A joy he felt even now, in spite of the pain and thirst and exhaustion.

He'd spent most of the fight in the second rank, where his height gave him an advantage, stabbing and thrusting powerfully with his spear. Then the one in front of him, another wing runner from *Salissa,* fell. Chack immediately took his place. He couldn't kill as many of the enemy from the wall, fighting and straining to hold back the weight of thousands, it seemed, but the wall had to hold. Another Grik took the place of the one he had slain, battering furiously at his shield with its sickle-shaped sword. Chack dug his feet into the slurry of sandy, bloody mud and leaned hard into his attacker. He let his spear fall toward the warrior at his back—quite certain it would be put to good use—and drew the cutlass that the destroyermen had given him. He slashed at the Grik's feet under the bottom edge of his shield and was rewarded with a jarring contact of blade on bone.

The pressure eased, but as he stood up straight, a blow from an axe right on top of his head drove him down again. He was stunned for a moment and he'd bitten his tongue. His comrades to the right and left helped support him while his senses returned. Thank the stars for the strange, platter-shaped helmet, he thought. He spat blood between gasps for air. There was frenzied shouting from behind him and he risked a quick glimpse. The muzzle of one of the cannons was inching through the press. He and the others near him shielded its progress until it was right behind them and then, at a shout, they gave back on either side.

Instantly, there was a deafening thunderclap, seemingly inside his head. The pressure turned his bones to jelly and the fur on the right side of his body felt like it had been driven into his skin. A choking cloud of smoke engulfed him and a high-pitched ringing sound replaced the noise of battle. He didn't care. For just a moment, all that remained of the enemy in front of him was a vast semicircle of churned, shattered gobbets of flesh. He barked an almost hysterical laugh and was surprised he couldn't even hear himself. Recoil had driven the gun backward, and the wall closed up tight where it had been. Something caught his eye and he looked up. High in the air, beginning to descend, was yet another flare.

"It's fallin' apart, Skipper," Gray wheezed, his hands on his knees. He had lost his hat and his hair was matted with blood. To their left, they heard the rattle of a Thompson on full auto. None of the guys could have much ammo left, thought Matt as he inserted his last magazine into the butt of the Colt. He glanced at the barricade behind them just a little over a hundred yards away now. They would never make it.

The withdrawal had begun well enough. They'd even made it past the wide spot he feared without too much difficulty. But the enemy had attacked with renewed frenzy as soon as they realized the army was retreating. There was only so much anyone could take, human or Lemurian, and as fresh enemy warriors arrived from across the river, the exhausted troops of the Allied Expeditionary Force had finally begun to break. It started on the left, as he'd expected it would. As the Grik lapped around their flank, the ever-shortening line tried to fold back on itself like it had been trained. But a maneuver like that was difficult even for troops that weren't already almost too tired to stand. The line finally cracked and most of the Fourth Guard had been cut off. They bought the rest of the line enough time to complete a similar maneuver, but there was no way they could break through the enemy and rejoin. The dwindling survivors of the Fourth still fought, surrounded by a seething swarm of triumphant warriors from hell. Determined to sell their lives dearly, they coalesced into a rough square, their proud flag still waving in its midst, but they were doomed.

The rest of the line had no choice but to continue the retreat. There were other breakthroughs, at every point, and many died sealing the breaches. Matt, Keje, and the Chief had gone into the line themselves several times, fighting with swords and pistols until the enemy was beaten back. Matt's expensive academy sword was now notched and encrusted with drying blood. He remembered doubting that he would ever draw it in anger. More irony. With salty sweat burning his eyes, he looked at the sky, at the soft, fluffy clouds and the bright, hot sun that glared down from directly overhead. To the south, twenty-five or thirty miles away, a continuous line of massive mountainous volcanoes loomed indifferently above what transpired on the coastal plain. They stood out, sharp and clear in the distance, their towering peaks lost in wispy clouds. Or was it steam? Could be. The long string of volcanoes that made up the spine of Java were all active as far as he knew. Or they were, anyway, back . . . Well. No matter. The view was so very similar to the one he remembered and yet also so alien. Besides the terror of battle that raged all around and the unfamiliar, embattled city, the very fact that he could see the mountains clearly without the smoke and haze of bombed-out Surabaya seemed strange.

He glanced back toward the bay, beyond the barricade. The battle line continued pouring fire into the enemy across the river, but *Big Sal* had her sweeps out, trying to maneuver into position to shell the barges as they crossed. He glimpsed rapid movement and saw *Walker* sprinting across the bay toward *Big Sal.* She'd been around the point, transferring men and equipment to *Mahan.* That was a sight he'd seen before, he realized sadly. *Walker,* confined in this same bay while events around her swirled out of control. *Less than three hours for it to come to this,* he thought. It had all begun so well. He stared at the walls of the city, forgotten now by the enemy, and wiped sweat from his brow. "Damn you to hell."

Chief Gray fumbled at his side for his canteen and took a long gulp, then handed it to his captain. Nodding his thanks, Matt raised the canteen to his lips and felt the warm water soothe his chalk-dry throat. He'd been shouting for so long, mostly orders but at times with an animalistic rage when he waded into the fight, that he doubted his voice would be audible in a quiet room now. It didn't matter. There was nothing left, really, for him to say. Beyond the diminished line he saw the mass of enemy warriors surging forward, heaving with an elemental energy. Grotesque standards waved above them as densely, it seemed, as the grass that had covered this plain.

A tremendous roar went up from the Grik, a predatory roar of triumph as the shield wall broke yet again. This time, it was as if some critical point had been reached beyond all endurance. One moment, a few Grik were racing through a small gap, hacking and slashing as they came, and in the next, like a pane of glass in a hailstorm, the entire wall around the gap shattered and fell away. Lieutenant Shinya raced by, aiming for the breakthrough, but Matt caught his arm. The Japanese officer whirled toward him, an insane light in his eyes that dimmed just slightly when he recognized the captain.

"Save the guns, if you can," Matt croaked. "Try to form a square around them. If we can make it to the breastworks, we might be able to hold them there." Shinya nodded reluctantly, deterred from his suicidal charge. He ran off shouting for runners. They both knew it was hopeless. Too many had already started to run. But it was all they had left and they had to try.

Maybe not hopeless after all, Matt amended as he wiped his eyes and struggled to see through the developing chaos. The Second Marines and most of the First Guards had already formed a square of sorts. It was a maneuver the Marines practiced often and the Guards had simply retreated into the formation with the Marines. They'd managed to save at least a couple of guns too—suddenly a pair of bronze snouts pushed through and barked spitefully at the Grik that had begun to curve around and try to get between the square and the barricade. Scores fell beneath the billowing smoke and the banshee wail of canister. To the right, the line still miraculously held. But its severed end had curled back toward the wall to form a semicircle at its base.

Separate from either force, however, Matt, Gray, and Keje stood alone as the shield wall in front of them melted away, oblivious to anything but the need to escape. Behind them raged the thundering horde. Matt gauged the distance to the Marine square. Many within it were shouting his name, or Keje's, and waving, urging them toward it. There was no way.

A lone Lemurian gunner, abandoned with her dead crew, stood waiting while the Grik swept down upon her. Crouching behind the axle as bolts whizzed by or spanged off the barrel of her gun, she looked small and frail compared to the monsters coming for her. There was no doubting the determination of her stance, however, and her tail flicked back and forth as if she was preparing to pounce. At the last moment, she touched the linstock to the vent and the gun blew itself apart with a tremendous blast. Grik bodies were hurled into the air or mowed down by fragments of the tube or pieces of the carriage. She must have loaded it to the muzzle, Matt thought, stricken by the act. Of the lone Lemurian gunner, nothing remained.

"Come, my friends!" Keje bellowed, pointing at the Marine square. "We must try!" With a final glance through the smoke at the momentarily stunned Grik advance, Matt and Gray joined Keje, racing toward the square as it resumed a slow, shuffling retreat.

Gray uttered a sudden, startled grunt of surprise and fell to the ground as if he'd tripped. Matt and Keje both stopped and turned toward him. He was lying on his side with a black vaned crossbow bolt protruding from his hip. Irritably, he waved them on. Keje disemboweled a Grik warrior with his scota as it ran toward them out of the lingering cloud and Matt took careful aim and shot another with his pistol. More were coming. Soon it would be a flood. "Go on, damn it! I'll be along!" Gray yelled.

"Shut up," Matt grated as he and Keje helped him to his feet. Stifling a groan, the Chief managed to trot painfully between them as they continued toward the square. Matt shot another Grik and then another as they struggled closer to the Marines, whose formation had started to expand toward them as it moved, hoping to take them into its embrace. Keje deflected a blow from a Grik sword with his small shield and Matt shot the creature as it snapped at Gray with its terrible jaws. His pistol slide locked back. Empty. He tucked the gun into his belt and parried a spear thrust with his sword. He wasn't much of a swordsman, but holding the Chief and fighting with his left hand, he was almost helpless. He managed to deflect the spear just enough that instead of driving through his chest, the sharp blade rasped along his ribs. He gasped with pain but clamped down with his arm so the Grik couldn't pull the spear back for another thrust and Gray drove the point of his cutlass into its eye. It shrieked and fell back, but then Keje went down, pulling them down on top of him.

Matt rolled onto his stomach to rise. All around him he saw running feet, Grik feet with long curved claws that slashed at the earth as they ran. He felt a searing blow of agony in his left shoulder blade that drove him to the ground, out of breath. He raised his head once more. There, just ahead, was the Marine square. He could see the tired, bloody faces of the people he had brought to this, staring expressionlessly back at him, but with their eyes blinking in frustration. He could feel Chief Gray, trapped beneath him and struggling to rise, and he tried to roll aside. *Got to let him up,* he thought. Then something struck him on the side of the head, and bright sparks swirled behind his eyes, quickly scattering into darkness.

"Through! Charge through! Do not stop at the barricade!" bellowed Lord Rolak, waving his sword above his head. He was nearly spent and his old legs ached from unaccustomed exertion. He stopped, gasping for a moment as his warriors flowed past, shouldering their way through the debris of a shocked and splintered army. He stared at the survivors of the sea folk as they stumbled, slack-jawed and empty-eyed toward the dock as if they knew, instinctively, safety for them could only be found at sea. He couldn't believe it. They'd broken, yes, but they had fought against impossible odds for longer than he'd ever expected, and his shame warred with his pride for their accomplishment. Never again could it be said with honesty that sea folk would not fight.

Some fought still. A solid block of sea folk warriors with several flags held high in their midst was churning its way through a mass of enemies back toward the relative safety of the barricade. The block was dwindling even as he watched, but the path they hewed through the foe was out of all proportion to their losses. His sense of failure and shame was only slightly assuaged by the fact that he wasn't entirely too late. It had taken his and the Orphan Queen's forces almost two hours to work their way through the streets of Aryaal, streets that became ever more congested as they neared the north gate. The fighting had caused a general exodus of townsfolk to gather there seeking refuge from the firebombs and hoping that if the city fell they might yet escape to B'mbaado. It was an empty hope, of course, but it was the only hope they had. Then, when they finally forced their way to the gate itself, they found it closed and fortified from the inside as well as out. The king, or his brat, must have foreseen something like what Rolak was attempting and ordered his personal guard to prevent anyone from trying to leave. It was then that Rolak's defiance of his king had sparked a civil war in the city of Aryaal.

He stormed the gate with Queen Maraan at his side. The fight for the towers that housed the gate windlasses was difficult and costly—he himself had overseen their construction years before with that very purpose in mind—but they finally hacked their way to the machinery that opened the massive doors, leaving scores of white-clad bodies behind them. When the gate swung wide, Queen Maraan's Six Hundred and a slightly larger number of Aryaalan warriors—rebels now—swarmed down into the waterfront shantytown where fisherfolk and boat people dwelt. Through the squalid alleys filled with muck they raced, until finally they emerged behind the breastworks to see the disaster their king's treachery had wrought. Tears of guilt and humiliation stung Rolak's eyes as he beheld, at last, the extent of Aryaal's dishonor. The fact that any of those they had betrayed still lived—let alone fought—was proof that if only they'd followed the plan, a great victory could have been achieved. Now all that remained was to save what he could of this valiant army as well as his own people's soul.

"Straight through the barricade!" he urged hoarsely once more as another cluster of soldiers passed. He noticed a group of warriors standing nearby, leaning on their spears and watching the battle beyond the breastworks as the last of his own troops clawed through the gap and slashed into the milling Grik. "What are you doing?" he demanded. One of them looked at him and blinked confusion.

"We are the guard here. This is our station. We have no orders but to defend this position."

Furious, Lord Rolak struck the hapless Aryaalan with the flat of his sword. "You do now!" he bellowed. "Through, now, the lot of you! Or I'll have your tails for baldrics!" More terrified of the raging Protector than of the Grik, the entire barricade garrison hurried to obey. Rolak stood waiting, catching his breath and cursing his age and frailty until the absolute last of the defensive force hurried through to join the battle. He felt a hand on his arm.

"Rest here a moment," spoke the queen of B'mbaado. Her eyelids flickered with concern.

"Never," he said, "will I rest again until the honor that was stolen from me is restored."

She turned her gaze to the battle that raged a short distance away. B'mbaadans and Aryaalans didn't fight in the strange, ordered way she'd seen the sea folk begin the battle, but their tightly massed attack of screaming and slashing reinforcements led by an almost berserk Haakar-Faask had taken the Grik unawares. In moments they had battered a deep wedge through the enemy and were on the verge of linking with the exhausted Marines.

"In that case, Lord Rolak, let us salvage what we may of it while we can!" She flashed him a predatory grin and drew her sword. He nodded and smiled back at her. Aryaalan females never became warriors; it was forbidden. B'mbaadans almost never did, but there were a few exceptions—a noted one stood before him now. Sea folk females fought right alongside the males, and hundreds of them had died that day defending all the people of Aryaal, including its proud male warriors who had done nothing. He knew it was no use trying to make Queen Maraan stay out of the fight. She'd already been in the thick of it at the gate.

"Of course, dear queen, just promise not to outrun me. What little honor I have left would not survive." She clasped his arm tightly this time, and together they charged into battle.

Matt's eyes focused slowly on the battle lantern swaying above him. He didn't know how long he'd been staring at it, but it seemed like quite a while. It was only now, however, that he realized what it was. He blinked and it felt like sandpaper rasping across his eyes.

"Unnh," he said. It was all he could manage. His lips were cracked and stuck together and his tongue felt swollen and dry. He was lying on his back on what seemed to be a cot. Dingy canvas rippled in a stiff salt-smelling breeze just beyond the lantern and he knew he was beneath some sort of tent or awning. Around him he heard murmured voices, whimpering, and an occasional sob. A sudden sharp, short scream sent a chill down the back of his neck, and the movement was enough to awaken a terrible pain that existed somewhere in his shoulder. "Unnh!" he said again, and was distressed to hear his own voice sound so much like those around him.

Almost immediately, Sandra Tucker's blurry face hovered inches from his own. Her light brown hair had fallen down from where she usually kept it tied behind her head and she wore an expression of grim concern. A cool hand gently caressed the side of his face. Someone else sponged water on his lips and, when they parted, let some trickle in his mouth. The sensation of refreshment it gave him was so intense that he felt utterly wretched. He reached up with his right hand and grasped Sandra's wrist as he stared into her eyes. She smiled at him, raised his hand to her lips for just an instant, and then laid it at his side. "You just lie still for now, Captain Reddy," she said huskily.

"Can't," he managed to croak, and he tried to rise. A searing wave of agony swept over him and he fell back onto the cot with a groan. "Unnh!" he said again.

"If you pull those stitches out, you're liable to bleed to death!" Sandra scolded. "Just lie still! Everything's being taken care of. There are others who can manage quite well for a while without you. You're not indispensable, you know!" She forced another smile while inwardly she railed. *Of course he's indispensable, you idiot girl! To you as much as to this whole messed-up world!*

Matt managed a sheepish, lopsided grin, but then drank greedily when someone held a canteen to his lips. Long before he was satisfied, it was taken away. "Aye, aye, Lieutenant," he said, his voice more normal now. "I'll try to behave." He looked around for the first time, as best he could. Many more cots surrounded him and figures moved among them with lanterns or candles in their hands. The flames of the candles flickered with the same breeze that stirred the canvas overhead, and for the first time he recognized it as the fo'c'sle awning from the ship. It was rigged on poles driven into the sand to create an open-sided shelter like . . .

"We're still on shore, right near the dock!" he exclaimed. Beyond the poles it was dark, but other lights moved about on the ground between the jury-rigged hospital tent and the breastworks. "But . . . the line broke! I saw it . . ." He paused and grimaced. "Hell, I was *in* it." He looked at Sandra. "I ordered you to evacuate. Didn't you get the word?"

She nodded. "Yes, but by the time I did, there was no reason to." She didn't mention that she would never have followed the order in the first place—something he'd suspected when he gave it. His mind did a sudden double take.

"What do you mean, no reason to?" he asked carefully. "The battle was lost! A disaster!" He closed his eyes. "My fault."

"No! No!" she said in alarm and sat beside him on the cot. In an instant she knew the torment he must feel after the horror he'd seen—that she knew he'd feel responsible for. She'd forgotten he didn't know what had happened at the end. He'd been unconscious and there was no way for him to know. She took his hand in hers again and, when he opened his eyes, he saw tears running down her face, leaving tracks in the grime. "Captain Reddy," she said, her voice rising slightly so others nearby could hear her speak his name. An excited murmur began to build. "The battle was not lost!" All he could do was look at her in wonder and confusion. "The only ones to know defeat today were the Grik!"

A ragged cheer broke out and quickly spread to the area beyond the tent. It didn't last long, because the voices that made it were exhausted and hurt, but it was real and it was sincere and he knew somehow that her words were true. He closed his eyes in confusion and saw it all again, those last terrible moments when he knew all was lost. He couldn't imagine how they'd escaped disaster, but they must have. Sandra said so. He was alive, so it must be true.

Victory, he thought. "My God." He squeezed her fingers gently.

Long after she felt his hand relax in hers, Sandra sat beside Matt on the cot, looking down at him, wiping away her tears of relief while he slept.

It had been like a terrible nightmare. They'd all been so confident, God knows why. Maybe the string of small victories Matt led them to had made them think they could accomplish anything. After the battle in the bay, that confidence was reinforced. Sandra had watched with the rest as the proud army marched across the field, banners flying, and opened the battle with a terrible, one-sided blow. Even from her vantage point, where she had a better perspective of the horde they faced, she'd still been confident. The battle was unfolding precisely as planned. The Grik reserve was distracted on the far side of the river and the entire force attacking the city had been diverted down upon the Allied Expeditionary Force. And then, like a puff of smoke in a high wind, the grand plan that would have led them to victory, perhaps even with relatively light casualties, was just . . . gone.

The whole thing depended on the Aryaalans coming out and striking hard into the enemy rear, which might not only have sent the Grik into a panic, but would also have cut them off from reinforcements at the ferry landing. She ran her fingers through her hair, scooping the loose locks out of her eyes, and glanced around at the countless wounded around her.

They'd been so stupid! Even in their own world people so rarely did the things they ought to do—had to do!—when the need was so clear! Look at how long Europe had appeased Hitler. How long the United States had tried to accommodate Japan's unspeakably brutal expansionism in Asia. Treachery wasn't a unique and alien Aryaalan trait. Nakja-Mur had warned them, and Keje had too, not to count too heavily on the people of Surabaya. But under the circumstances, surely they *had* to see the logic? She snorted quietly. They'd applied their own concept of self-interest to others, she realized, and that was always a dangerous thing to do. It had been the greatest flaw in their plan.

She'd known something was wrong when the second flare went up. The battle line held and held for what seemed an eternity—surely longer than they'd expected to feel the full crush of the enemy assault. All the while, the booming of guns and the drifting white smoke made it impossible to see much detail. The first steady stream of wounded began to arrive, however. Up to that point there'd been a trickle, a few at a time, and most of those had made it to the rear under their own power or assisted by a comrade. Those that came as the battle raged on were carried, and their wounds were almost always desperate. She flew into the fray of spurting blood and severed limbs and directed the surgery with an energy and steady detachment that helped instill calm and confidence into the overworked staff of healers under her command. She was overjoyed when Kathy McCoy and Pam Cross arrived from *Mahan,* but there was no time for a proper reunion. Most of Sandra's medical staff had learned to converse in English, so the two nurses could at least make themselves understood. But they hadn't been part of the "team" Sandra had trained for just this situation. It took a while for Pam and Kathy to integrate themselves and find their most effective roles.

And still the battle raged. The wounded that returned from the fighting were no longer excited and boastful. An atmosphere of exhausted desperation began to prevail. They were fighting like fiends and the field was choked with Grik dead, but something was wrong. The Aryaalans hadn't come. Then came Shinya's runner, horribly wounded but able to tell her the order Captain Reddy sent. By then she half expected it, but it still struck her like a slap. She quickly instructed her orderlies to prepare to move the wounded and raced to the barricade to see for herself. The horror was beyond anything she'd ever expected, or could possibly have imagined.

The battle was much closer now, close enough to see individuals, and she quickly picked out the white and coffee-khaki dress of the captain and the Bosun near the center of the line. Occasionally, she caught a glimpse of other destroyermen here and there and she heard the sound of their weapons when they fired. Beyond the diminishing, wavering line was an endless sea of menacing shapes surging forward with a single-minded, palpable ferocity. She still heard the thunderclap of cannon, but the surf-like roar of the Grik and the clash of weapons absorbed the sound of all else except thought.

Abstractly, the struggle before her brought to mind a scene from her childhood. A small green grasshopper had inadvertently landed upon an ant bed. Before it could recover and launch itself again, dozens of ants swarmed upon it, biting and stinging as fast as they could. Within moments, the insect had been completely obscured by a writhing mass of attackers as they continued to sting and sting and slash at their victim with their cruel jaws. Occasionally, she saw one of the grasshopper's legs twitch feebly, hopelessly, but it was doomed. As she watched the battle, to her horror, that mental image was re-created before her very eyes. Like a plank stretched across two points, bowing ever lower beneath a remorselessly increasing burden of stones heaped upon it beyond all sense or reason, the shield wall broke completely with the suddenness of a lightning bolt. She knew she had to leave, to get the wounded out, but she couldn't move—so deep was her shock and terror, not only for herself but for the trio of distant forms that suddenly stood entirely alone in the face of the relentless onslaught. A trio that included the tall, white-uniformed figure of Captain Matthew Reddy. Her heart leaped into her throat and she cried out in anguish—just as a gun exploded and a blanket of smoke billowed outward and mercifully obscured the last moments from her view. She could only stand, stunned and lost, with tears streaming down her face and her soul locked in a maelstrom of grief. All around her, battered, blood-matted troops streamed through the barricade and ran to the rear as fast as they could, but she could think only of what lay within that dissipating cloud of smoke.

Someone bumped against her and she almost fell, catching herself by grabbing the barricade and drawing to the side. It had been a warrior who bumped her, accidentally, of course, but she suddenly realized that this warrior, unlike the others, was racing through the barricade toward the enemy. And then another passed, and another. Within seconds, the trickle became a flood and she watched, amazed, as hundreds more went surging past to join the fight.

The Aryaalans had come at last. She knew it was true when she saw Lord Rolak trot up behind them, bellowing furiously. She could see that he was winded and breathing hard, and he rested for a moment nearby. She wanted to shout at him, to curse him for his tardiness, but all she could do was stare. Then she saw another join him. A dark, exotic beauty she hadn't seen before. They didn't notice her, she thought, although the black-furred female's eyes strayed across her. Their focus was solely on the battle. After a moment more, they hurried past her through the barricade and disappeared into the swirling chaos beyond.

Courtney Bradford found her there, sitting in the mud and weeping like a lost soul while just a few dozen yards away the greatest battle ever fought by the Lemurian people raged. All she knew was that with Matt Reddy lost, all the suppressed loss and grief she'd felt ever since they came through the Squall had suddenly shattered her own fragile veneer of self-control. All the while, as she had tried to be his rock, he had been hers. Now she felt totally bereft. She'd lost her whole world at last.

Bradford gently escorted her back to the hospital tent, where she was met by the shocked expressions of the other nurses and questioning blinks from the Lemurian healers. Wiping her face and forcing herself to concentrate on the grisly business at hand, she dove back into her work, stitching and cleaning the horrible wounds. Forgotten in her misery was Captain Reddy's last command to evacuate the hospital. At some point, Courtney Bradford left her. He'd still been aboard *Walker* when the battle began and she never even wondered why he was here.

She didn't leave the hospital again. She just continued to struggle against the impossible flood of blood and death. Therefore, she hadn't personally seen how the battle came to an end. Despite her concentration on her duty, she could still hear, and she developed a fairly clear picture of what transpired. The Aryaalan and B'mbaadan reinforcements finally managed to batter a corridor through the Grik and link up with the surrounded Marines. Even so, the situation remained grim, and the result would probably have been little more than a postponement of the inevitable had it not been for the timely arrival of the diversionary force that had been menacing the Grik reserve all day. The reserve had long since come across the ferry, and when Adar saw what was happening, he ordered all available transports to take his landing force to the Aryaalan dock. With it came the warrior crews of the battle line as well. Most of the destroyermen, led by Jim Ellis, joined them. They were armed with rifles and pistols and all the working .30-caliber machine guns from both destroyers.

Big Sal's sweeps came out and Adar maneuvered the huge ship as close as he could and began plying her guns upon the densely packed Grik rear. *Mahan* was still helpless, but Larry Dowden carefully conned *Walker*—on one engine!—right up the river until she virtually ran aground on the silty bottom. There, the destroyer unleashed a barrage of high-explosive shells into the raging horde onshore. It was a massacre. Ellis positioned all three .30-cals on the far left flank where the barricade met the sea, and together with the two .50-cals on *Walker,* they poured a solid stream of lead into the enemy flank.

The panicking Grik fought back with renewed ferocity, but they were caught between the heavy reinforcements pouring through the barricade and the wall at the base of the city, where, miraculously, a small group of holdouts from the shattered right flank still held. Added to this was the catastrophic fire from the ships and the machine guns. The increasingly terrified Grik army began to melt away like an ice cube on *Walker*'s midday deck. Once again, just as in the battle for *Big Sal* when *Walker* had first truly met the Lemurians, the Grik broke. It was as though whatever cause, motivation, or collective madness made them capable of fighting with such heedless ferocity and abandon suddenly gave way to a crystal-clear understanding of the danger they faced. At the same instant, whatever it was that drove them, be it blind instinct, courage, or a combination of the two, spontaneously evaporated. Within moments, what remained of the entire Grik horde had transformed from a juggernaut of destruction into a panic-stricken mob of mindless animals consumed by an instinctual, unthinking impetus to escape.

Once again, they trampled or slaughtered one another in their effort to flee, and whatever ability they had for cooperative effort dissolved into blind self-preservation. And once again, through their own surprise and relief, the weary and battle-worn Aryaalans, B'mbaadans, Marines, and shattered Guard regiments, Home clan Guards and destroyermen as well, all sensed the opportunity and pressed their advantage home. It was believed that as many as a thousand Grik might have escaped the butchery that followed.

And Sandra Tucker heard it all. The crash of *Walker*'s guns and the deep-throated roar of *Big Sal*'s. The staccato yammering of the .50-cals on the water and the sharp but almost puny by comparison report of the .30-cals on the left. The triumphant roar when the Grik broke and then the screams and the shooting and the muffled throbbing thud of blades striking flesh—and then, after what seemed like hours, a strange, awkward, almost-silence.

The wounded continued to stream in, however, and their cries broke the spell. She knew, somehow, that they'd won, but her battle wasn't over. Then, like some massive war demon straight out of hell, Dennis Silva swept into the tent. He'd lost his helmet and he was covered with black, drying blood from the top of his stubbly head to his oversized feet. The whites of his eyes and his intermittent teeth shone like beacons through the grime and gore on his face.

"Got a good'un here, ma'am," he said, referring to an equally grimy form slung almost effortlessly over his shoulder. Stunned, Sandra led him to a bloodstained cot and, with surprising tenderness, the big gunner's mate lowered Captain Reddy down upon it. Behind him, Chief Gray limped painfully through the press of wounded, supported by Earl Lanier, of all people. The fat, irascible cook still held a cutlass in his left hand and his expression was hard and deep. Finally, to make the miracle complete, Chack and an exhausted Marine carried Keje between them.

"But I saw . . ." she began weakly, then stooped to feel Matt's pulse and began tearing off his blood-sodden shirt.

"A hell of a thing, ma'am," Silva interrupted. "They was maniacs! The whole Grik army swoopin' down on 'em in a rush and it was flashin' swords and rollin' heads!" He turned to look at the Bosun, who still stood with Lanier. His face was a mask as he watched Sandra examine the captain's wounds. "Three rare killers, and I don't care if you hear me say it." He stuck his bloody hand out to Gray.

With an effort, Gray shifted and took Silva's hand in his. "You big idiot," he growled, but his scowl softened slightly when he saw Sandra's upturned face. "It was him and Chack that saved us, ma'am," he explained. "They ran out and fought them buggers off while some Marines dragged us into the square. Tom Felts and Shinya did too."

Sandra began to speak, but she saw Silva's eyes fill with tears that threatened so spill down his face.

"Old Tom's gone, ma'am," he said in a husky voice. "Cut down right when we was almost back in. He was a good'un too." Sandra briefly touched the big man's arm and gave him a sad, thankful smile. Then she returned all her attention to Matt.

Now she looked at his bruised and battered face. The light from the battle lantern cast strange and ghastly shadows upon it. *He's suffered so much for us all*, she thought, *ever since the very beginning*. Most of that suffering was inside, where no one else could see. But she had glimpsed the inner turmoil, even though he kept it hidden. He fought it alone because that's what he had to do. If he'd ever shown an inkling of his concern and doubt to the crew—or their Lemurian allies—they certainly wouldn't be here now, in the aftermath of a miraculous victory. More than likely they'd have been dead long ago, like Kaufman. With indecision, everything would have fallen apart.

She gently touched his lips, reassured by the warm breath she felt. He was getting old beyond his years, with the burden placed upon him, and she noticed for the first time that a few white whiskers had appeared in the stubble on his chin. Maybe he *had* been wrong to trust the Aryaalans, although she would never, ever, tell him so. Maybe even his whole grand strategy to roll back the Grik and create a world where all of them, destroyermen and Lemurians, could live in safety, was hopeless and doomed from the start. She slowly stood so as not to wake him, and stretched her painful muscles. *That may very well be,* she thought grimly, *but it's something that needs doing, and we have to try.* If *Walker* and *Mahan* had been saved from the Japanese only so they could linger in some sort of purgatory of endless strife, so be it. At least she would be there to support Matthew Reddy however he would let her, and patch him up when the need arose as well. And if he believed they could make a difference, then somehow she would believe it too.

P rince Rasik-Alcas sprawled on the heap of cushions opposite his father's massive throne in the Royal Chamber of the high, sprawling palace. Blood matted his fur—none of it his—and he idly reflected that the opulent pillows would be ruined, but he didn't care. He was exhausted by the fighting that had convulsed the city, even while the titanic struggle raged beyond the walls. He had, of course, never intended to get as caught up in it as he had, but when some of the palace guard, spurred by rage and shame, actually rose against the king, Rasik had been forced to fight. It was something he didn't much enjoy, strangely enough—at least the physical aspects of it. He was keenly interested in war and strategy and politics and all the heady matters a future king should be interested in, but the actual fighting was something he'd just as soon leave to others. That didn't mean he wasn't any good at it.

And a good thing too, he mused, watching his bloated father nervously stuffing food into his jowly face. The king certainly wasn't much good in a fight. He'd literally squeaked in surprised terror when the guard's sword flashed down from behind. It missed him by the very thickness of the royal cloak it slashed, and Rasik was still amazed that anyone could miss something so fat and awkward. *It just goes to show,* he thought philosophically, *if you're going to retain a palace guard, always choose them from the nobility. Then, if they are treacherous, they will probably be incompetent as well.*

He lifted an eyelid and glanced idly at the only guard currently in the chamber. *A loyal one,* he thought with a smirk. Rasik didn't know the guard's name and didn't care what it was, but he was a formidable warrior. He'd fought alongside Rasik, defending his king and prince from the very beginning of the attempt against them. He had, in fact, been the only one for a time. Now he stood, nervously vigilant, as the occasional sounds of renewed fighting wafted through the broad arched windows that led to the balcony ringing this level of the palace. The coup had failed, but it might be a while before they managed to root out all the traitors. And, of course, there was Rolak. Rasik seethed. He could still feel the cold metal of Rolak's blade against his neck. That one would surely die, he promised himself. And the Orphan Queen as well.

"I told you!" proclaimed Fet-Alcas in a frail attempt at a menacing growl. "We should have let Rolak out!"

Rasik sighed. "No, you didn't, sire."

Fet-Alcas blinked. "Well, he got out anyway," he grumped. "And then those ridiculous sea folk actually defeated the Grik!" His voice became shrill. "That . . . *that* you *did* tell me would not happen!" Rasik lazily blinked unconcern. "And then a rebellion!" wheezed the king, spewing food across the tiled chamber. "Never before in history has Aryaal rebelled against its rightful king!" Fet-Alcas's rheumy eyes smoldered. "And all because you counseled me to deprive our people of their place in the battle! A battle arranged by the rightful Protector himself." He stared out the windows at the darkness beyond. "No wonder they rebelled," he murmured. "The greatest battle ever fought—and a victory!" He glared back at his son. "You *did* that!" he accused darkly, draining a cup of seep. Rasik yawned and blinked irony. "I did not want Rolak to go," the king admitted, "but only because you said the sea folk would lose! We could fall upon the Grik remnants and have our great battle to ourselves!"

Fet-Alcas belched then, and shifted uncomfortably on his throne. "But no!" he continued bitterly. "The miserable sea folk and their friends with the iron ships did *not* lose! It is we who lost!" He stared back into the darkness with a grimace. "The greatest battle ever fought!" he repeated and took a gulp from another cup of seep.

"Do not complain, sire," Rasik sneered. "Our people had their battle after all!"

Fet-Alcas turned to him and began a furious shout, but all that emerged was a gout of blood. It splashed down on his white robe and pooled like vomit at his feet. Both Rasik and the guard rushed to his side and stared at the king as he looked at them in shock.

"The king is ill!" cried the guard in alarm.

"No," said Rasik, as he drove his own sword into the distracted retainer's throat. Blood spurted down the sword onto Rasik's hand and splattered on the king's white robe. The guard fell to the floor and thrashed, describing great crimson arcs upon the tile as his mouth opened and closed spasmodically. His tail whipped back and forth for a few seconds more, smearing the blood still further, and then he lay still.

Fet-Alcas, stunned, looked at the corpse that had fallen almost at his feet. He tried to speak, but yet another gush of blood poured forth and he was wracked with spasms of agony. Silently, for the most part, he continued to retch, but by now the blood had slowed to a trickle. The poison in the seep from the cup he still held was of a type that deadened all pain and sensation while it corrosively ate any flesh that it touched. At least it deadened it for a while. Fet-Alcas looked at the cup in his paw and then dropped it in horror.

Rasik slowly sheathed his own sword and drew the one worn by the dead guard. His eyes were wide with excitement and his tail twitched nervously back and forth. "No," he repeated with a hiss, drawing his thin lips hard across his teeth. "You are not ill, sire. You are dead. Killed by another traitorous guard!"

With that, he slashed down repeatedly across the king's neck and upper chest, grunting with effort as the blade bit deep. Finally, with a gurgling exhalation, Fet-Alcas slid from the throne and joined the guard on the tile abattoir. Rasik stood motionless, listening, while his breathing returned to normal. Laying the bloody sword on the floor, he drew his own again and looked at it wonderingly. Then he dipped the tip into the pool of blood rapidly spreading beneath his father's corpse.

"A king's blood on a king's sword," he whispered, and stepping toward the hallway that led to the chamber door, he began to run. "Murderers!" he screamed at the top of his lungs, flinging the door wide. "They have murdered the king!"

Courtney Bradford stood at the barricade staring through his "borrowed" binoculars at the scene of the previous day's battle. The first rays of the sun were creeping above the horizon, but so far all he could see was a seemingly endless sea of indistinct shapes, alone or massed in piles, across the marshy plain. Occasionally he saw movement. Either a wounded Grik that the searchers hadn't dispatched the night before, or possibly some scavenger darting furtively through the unprecedented smorgasbord.

It was the scavengers he hoped to see. Queen Maraan—a delightful creature, he thought—had told him about skuggiks, which she described as vile little predators about the size of a turkey. They invariably appeared to feast upon the carrion after a battle. They walked on two legs and actually looked a lot like Grik, she said, except they were considerably smaller and had no upper limbs at all. They were walking mouths, for all intents and purposes, with quick, powerful legs and a long, whiplike tail. Bradford couldn't wait to see one.

Perhaps there? he thought, as something seemed to move. He was having trouble holding the binoculars with one hand since his other arm was still in a sling. "Blast!" he exclaimed, lowering his good arm to rest for a moment. He would just have to wait until there was enough light to see. He glanced to his right and was surprised to find a number of Lemurian warriors, on guard against a renewed Grik assault, staring at him with open curiosity. He looked to the left, saw much the same, and felt a twinge of unaccustomed self-consciousness. "I'm a scientist, not a ghoul!" he announced harshly, brandishing the binoculars. They continued to regard him with their inscrutable stares. He sighed and stepped away from the barricade. Most of these wouldn't understand English, he realized, since the majority were Rolak's or Maraan's people. They had made every effort to retrieve all of their own few wounded and many dead throughout the night, but some would undoubtedly remain. The idea of him watching in fascination while some scavenger chewed upon anyone besides Grik—and maybe them too—might be a less than popular morning activity.

With as much dignity as he could muster, he stuffed the binoculars into his sling and strode away from the breastworks toward the guttering torches that surrounded the hospital tent. Marine guards ringed the area, nearly dead on their feet. After the treachery of the day before, they'd been reluctant to allow the Aryaalans and B'mbaadans to take their place on the barricade, but they were exhausted and Adar ordered them to rest. They weren't about to trust undependable allies with the security of their wounded comrades and leaders, however. Battle-weary Marines rotated the duty throughout the night. Bradford knew now what had happened, and he personally felt nothing but gratitude for the warriors that came to their aid, but he could sympathize with how the Marines felt.

There were many, many wounded lying on the ground in the vicinity and he carefully picked his way through the sleeping forms. Many, he suspected, would never awake. Most would, however, and that was largely due to the efforts of Lieutenant Tucker, who he now saw step tiredly from under the awning into the gray morning light. He realized she'd probably brought little in the way of medical science to the Lemurian people. In many ways their medicines were more effective than those she knew—the strange antiseptic paste for one—but she had introduced the idea of battlefield triage and the associated patch-and-splice that went with it. That was something the local healers had never considered. The sea folk didn't need it because they so rarely fought anything like a major battle, and the locals, who fought all the time, had just never thought of it. Perhaps it was because even they had never fought a battle such as this, in which the sheer numbers of casualties were so high. Unlike anyone they'd met so far, the B'mbaadans and Aryaalans understood the concept of surrender, at least among themselves. Maybe they had never let things go this far before one side or the other just quit. Whatever the case, the exhausted young nurse had done heroic work that night. He picked his way toward her.

"You should rest, my dear. You are destroyed." He spoke quietly so as not to disturb those nearby whose sleep was only temporary. She nodded at him and smiled weakly. "But you know that, of course."

"Yes." She sighed. "The healers we brought are a wonder. I couldn't have managed without them." Her face brightened somewhat. "Pam Cross and Kathy McCoy came from *Mahan* to lend a hand. God, I'm so glad they're safe!" She gestured under the tent and shook her head. "They're in there now. Last night was bad, but they sure had a rough time on *Mahan*. Everything from constant fear for their lives to attempted rape. With Kaufman in charge"—she snorted—"pretending to be in charge—there was chaos. They told me things . . ." She didn't finish, but instead looked in the direction of the barricade and what lay beyond. "Beth Grizzel went ashore with Kaufman. Did you know that?"

Bradford nodded and gently patted her arm. "Mr. Ellis told me last night."

Sandra shivered, but continued to glare at the barricade. "Damn Kaufman!" she muttered fiercely. "So much misery because of him. I hope he roasts in hell!"

Bradford felt his eyebrow arch, but decided now wasn't an appropriate time for the response that leaped to mind. Pity. "I'm quite certain he did, my dear." He guided her to a bench and hovered near her as she sat down at last. "And how then are the captain and his extremely lucky companions? I still can hardly believe they survived, from what I hear."

She stared bleakly at her hands on her lap. "As you say. Lucky to be alive. Keje has a concussion, I think, but other than that he didn't get a scratch. The Chief had an arrow in his hip, but it struck the very edge of his pelvis and went down instead of up. Lucky. If it went up, it would have perforated his bowel. God knows if that Lemurian paste would have any effect on peritonitis. It'll hurt when he walks for a while, but he should be fine. Matt?" She closed her eyes tightly and tried to control the relief in her voice. "His cheekbone is cracked, at least, and he has a deep gash in his side, down to the ribs. Besides that, he was stabbed in the back, through his shoulder blade and out his chest with a spear." She laughed bitterly. "At least it was a 'clean' wound. Not many bone fragments or other debris. Those Grik spears are sharp!" The tears came then, in spite of all she could do.

Bradford sat beside her and put his good arm around her shoulders. "You care a lot for him, don't you, my dear?" He spoke in a kindly voice.

"Of course I do," Sandra whispered, answering his question before he could himself, for once.

"Of course you do," Bradford repeated, oblivious to her response. "As do we all."

The sun finally rose and showed for all to see the results of the Battle of Aryaal. By late morning, the skuggiks had arrived in force, and soon there were so many even Bradford couldn't watch them anymore, so sickened did he become. Beyond the barricade and across the plain, all the way up to the base of the wall that surrounded Aryaal, a seething mass of raucous scavengers feasted on the thousands of Grik corpses underneath the brilliant sun and cloudless sky. The ground itself came to look like one huge corpse, working with maggots as the light gray skuggiks capered and hopped among the bodies, gorging themselves on the remains. The smell was overpowering, but the sounds the creatures made while they ate were even worse.

Jim Ellis walked, still limping a little from the wound Kaufman had given him, up to the awning that served as a hospital tent. There he found Rolak, pacing anxiously back and forth while Chack stood in one place and spoke quietly to him. Jim had met the Lemurian bosun's mate only the night before, but he didn't feel the least bit ridiculous returning the sharp salute Chack gave him when he joined them.

"Good morning, sir," Chack said. There was a blood-soaked bandage on his shoulder, and he wore his battered doughboy helmet with a jaunty air. Over his other shoulder was slung a long-barreled Krag-Jorgensen and a Navy cutlass was belted around his blood-spattered kilt.

"Good morning, ah, Mr. Chack." Ellis gestured at Rolak, who had stopped his pacing and was now looking at him. "What's with him?"

"He is anxious to see the captain."

"Me too," Jim said with feeling. He glanced at his watch. "I guess we'll get to in about fifteen minutes. I got word there's an officers' call at twelve hundred hours."

Chack nodded. "Yes, sir, but not in the tent. It's down at the left flank of the breastworks, close to the water. I'm directing everyone there as they arrive."

Jim Ellis looked at him in surprise. "You mean they carried the captain over there in the shape he's in?" he demanded.

Chack blinked. "He walked."

Matt was seated stiffly on a stool near where Ellis had placed the .30-cals the day before. His left arm was bound tightly to his side so he couldn't move it, even accidentally, and risk opening his wounds. His sunken eyes and the purplish-yellow bruise that covered the left side of his face made his pain clearly evident in spite of the clean uniform and fresh shave. Behind him stood Lieutenant Tucker, wearing a disapproving frown, and Chief

Gray, supporting himself with a pair of crutches from *Walker*'s medical locker. His hat was back on his head. Someone had found it while retrieving the wounded and dead and had returned it to him. Lieutenant Shinya stood beside him, wearing a slightly bewildered expression. Somehow, throughout the battle, he'd received only a few superficial wounds, even though he'd been in the thick of it from the start. Often his gaze drifted to the field beyond the barricade, where the scavengers now reigned, and his hand strayed to the hilt of the modified cutlass at his belt as if he wanted to reassure himself it was still there.

The gathering, or "officers' call," was quite large. All the battle line "captains" were there, including Rick Tolson from *Revenge*. Matt had already praised him and his brave crew, and he and Kas were about to burst with pride. So were some of the *"Revenges"* that accompanied them. Chack was now the de facto commander of the Second Marines, since the CO of that regiment had been killed the day before. In fact, almost all of the original regimental commanders had fallen and been replaced by their second or third in line. The Fifth Guards had a sergeant in command. There was no representative present for the Fourth, since it no longer existed.

Keje was there, also on a stool, with his head bound in a bandage that resembled a turban. Nearby stood his daughter, who stared at the striking, black-furred queen of B'mbaado with expressionless eyes. If Safir Maraan noticed the scrutiny, she gave no sign. She was immaculately groomed, which alone was enough to set her apart from most of those present. Her black cape and brilliant armor had been just as muddy and bloodstained as anyone's the day before, but since then it had been either cleaned or replaced. Now she cut a most imposing figure as she stood, slightly aside, with Haakar-Faask and four of her elite personal guards in attendance. They were not quite as resplendent as she, but they had groomed themselves. Adar was speaking softly to Keje, who nodded without thinking and winced at the pain from the sudden movement.

Larry Dowden and Lieutenant Garrett were the only officers from *Walker* that weren't there and Matt watched nervously as they slowly, carefully, backed his ship from the mouth of the river just a few hundred yards away. Slow maneuvers in any kind of current were difficult for the old four-stacker, but going backward on one engine in a confined space . . . It was positively nerve-racking for him to watch. Jim Ellis shouldered through the crowd to stand next to him and Matt glanced at his watch. It was on his right wrist for now.

"I guess everybody's here that's coming," he said.

"Sorry I'm late, Captain," Ellis apologized, although it was only just now 1200. "I went over to check how repairs to my shi—" He grimaced guiltily.

"I mean *Mahan*—are progressing. I was only told the meeting had moved when I came ashore."

Matt made a dismissive gesture with his good hand. "You're not late, Jim, and *Mahan is* your ship. No apology necessary."

"Thanks, Skipper," Jim said in a tone of relief. He wouldn't have been surprised to be relieved. After all, he deserved it. He cocked his head toward *Walker* and made a wry face. "She's still my ship too. You don't think maybe I . . . ?"

Matt shook his head with an assurance he didn't feel. "Nonsense. Lieutenant Dowden's a fine officer. He'll have no trouble. Now then . . ." He turned his attention to the gathered officers, who had silently watched the short exchange. There was a sudden commotion in the ring of onlookers and Matt vaguely recognized Lord Rolak as he pushed his way through to stand before him. His fine helmet was dented and the feather plume was gone. Unlike Queen Maraan, he hadn't refreshed himself in any way since the battle the day before. He stood squarely before Captain Reddy and his eyes blazed with inner torment. He drew his battered sword.

In an instant Gray had his pistol pointed at the Protector's face. In the shocked silence, there were several metallic rasps of bolts slamming home as other destroyermen reacted to the threat. Matt raised his hand. Slowly, never taking his eyes from Matt's, Lord Rolak went to his knees and laid his sword on the ground at Matt's feet.

"My sword, my life, my honor—which is all that I am—is yours," he said in a keening monotone.

Astonished, Adar hurried to him and knelt at his side. "I am Adar, Sky Priest to *Salissa* Home and councillor to Keje-Fris-Ar," he whispered urgently. "I know little of your customs, but of this I have heard. Must you do this? I know the Amer-i-caans well and I assure you this gesture is not required."

"It is not a gesture, Priest!" Rolak growled harshly. "If you know what I have done, then tell him. I gave my word and it was broken."

"It was not your doing. We all know that!" Adar hissed.

"Nevertheless. The word of Muln-Rolak will have meaning!"

Adar stood, blinking in consternation. He turned to Matt, who was looking at him with a puzzled expression. "I am sorry, Cap-i-taan Reddy," he said. "But if I am not mistaken, Lord Rolak wishes to make a"—he quickly sought a word besides "gesture"—"representation, regarding his remorse over yesterday's, ah, change of plans."

"Unnecessary," Matt promptly replied. "We're indebted to Lord Rolak and all who fought with him for coming in spite of his leader's orders to the contrary." He shrugged with one shoulder. "He saved my life and many, many others by doing so."

If it was possible, Adar looked bemused. "I told him you would react this way, but it's already too late."

Without thinking, Matt used the Lemurian blink of surprise in response. "Too late for what?"

"He has already done it. He has proclaimed a debt of honor and has given himself to you, as a slave if you wish. Do not be angered. He does not know your ways! But regardless, his life now belongs to you."

"But . . . !" Matt was speechless and he looked at the elderly, kneeling Lemurian before him. "Tell him no! He can't be my slave! Tell him thanks, but *no*!"

Adar sadly shook his head. "I knew you would say that too. In that case, you must kill him. It is the only way his honor can be restored." Adar held his hands out helplessly at his sides.

"What? *Damn it!* I don't need this today! I'm not going to do that!" Matt clenched his eyes shut in pain from his own outburst.

"Very well. I will tell him," Adar said. "But if I do, it's my understanding he will immediately kill himself as being so without honor that he is not even worthy of being a slave." Adar shrugged again. "Strange folk, as I have said." He started to turn to Rolak.

"Wait!" Matt said sharply. "Don't tell him that! Tell him okay!" He sighed. "Tell him to pick up his sword and stand ready to answer some questions. We'll sort this out later!" Adar complied, and with supreme dignity Rolak retrieved his weapon and stood. He looked around at those assembled. Not really knowing what to do next himself, he stepped back.

Matt stood, and his face paled when his slashed muscles tensed. Sandra was caught by surprise and seemed unable to decide whether to support him or try to force him back down. Ignoring her, Matt spoke to the faces that watched in silence. "I guess we won."

A spontaneous cheer erupted from those who understood his words, and the others joined in when they were told what he said. The roar of approval and relief continued for several minutes, startling the skuggiks on the other side of the barricade and echoing off the walls of Aryaal. At the tops of those walls, grim-faced defenders watched in silence. Matt waited for the cheering to subside.

"We won the battle and I've heard how each of you distinguished yourselves. I'm proud of you all, and I give thanks to my God for your bravery and mourn your sacrifices as well as those of all who fell." His face became grim.

"It was a costly victory and you have my apology for that." There were shouted protests. He knew none of them expected him to assume responsibility for their losses—but they were his fault regardless of what had happened. It had been his plan and he was in command. In the face of that surprise and disagreement, he remorselessly tallied the casualties. "Almost four in ten of the brave soldiers, sailors, warriors, and Marines who began the battle were killed or seriously wounded. Seriously enough that most of them are out of this campaign, at least." He looked at Safir Maraan. "Her Gracious Highness, Queen Protector Maraan of B'mbaado told me her losses were similar. I imagine the same is true for those who followed Lord Rolak. Let no one here doubt for a moment their courage and honor. It wasn't they who betrayed us, but King Fet-Alcas, who still sits safe behind the walls we preserved for him." There were angry growls. "But let's put that aside for now. I think Her Highness has an announcement to make." He nodded at Adar, who whispered something to the queen. She stepped briskly forward, her cape flowing behind her. When she was in the middle of the circle, she looked around and began to speak in her husky, self-assured voice.

"B'mbaado is proud, grateful, to have fought beside such warriors as yourselves. Never has there been such a battle, and never have warriors achieved so much against such odds." She listened to the appreciative murmurs. "B'mbaado is a warlike nation," she continued matter-of-factly. "We war often. With Aryaal, or the other nations up the coast, so fighting is not strange to us. But this war is unlike anything we've faced. The Grik are Evil. They are not even People. They do not fight for, or with, honor but only for death. Beyond that? Territory perhaps. We do not even know. We do know what happens to those they vanquish." She took a breath. "For the first time, when the Grik came here, B'mbaado faced a war it did not want, was not prepared to fight, and knew it couldn't win. We even tried to join forces with our most bitter rival, Aryaal, because we knew that only together might we have a chance." She paused. "But it was to no avail. They were too many. We knew it was just a matter of time until Aryaal fell, and then B'mbaado would be next. I brought the Six Hundred, my personal guard, to help delay that day as long as possible, but in reality all hope was lost." She turned to look directly at Matt.

"Then you came. Not for loot or conquest, or for anything from us at all. You came to *help!*" She shook her head and blinked with remembered surprise. "Sea folk!" She glanced quickly at Jim Ellis. "The other iron ship had been here for a time and we knew it had great power, but in our shortsighted, uncurious way, neither Aryaal nor B'mbaado had any use for it or its people once we knew it would not help either of us against the other." She blinked apology at Jim. "Besides," she said, "it was badly damaged. Every day I expected to look out and see that it had sunk. When the Grik came, it tried to help us against them, but it couldn't move. All it could do was use its power to keep a passage clear between Aryaal and my home." She bowed to Jim Ellis. "For that, I thank you."

She looked back at Matt, and again at the surrounding officers. "But then you came, with yet another iron ship, and the great Homes of the sea folk. You *erased* the Grik from the bay! It was the greatest thing I ever saw. I am sure that were it not for Fet-Alcas's treachery the battle for Aryaal would have been just as one-sided, and just as complete."

She paused and blinked significant resolve. "I have come to realize that this war you fight to destroy the Grik forever is not just a war for honor, as we've so often fought, but an honorable war—and one we must be part of." She looked around. "Until the end," she added grimly. Then she straightened her back with an air of solemn dignity and spoke once more.

"I, Safir Maraan, Queen Protector of the People of B'mbaado, beg you will accept my nation and my warriors into your Grand Alliance to destroy the Grik menace once and forever."

There were appreciative howls and stamping feet, and the humans that could clapped their hands together. Matt stood and watched while the queen bowed formally, acknowledging the praise, and he managed a smile. Behind it, however, as he so often did, he was considering ramifications. The B'mbaadans were considerable warriors. Much like the people of Madura were reckoned in the world he came from. The question was how best to integrate them into the shield wall. They would have their own ideas how to fight, and he hoped they wouldn't prove too difficult to teach the new way of fighting, as they'd done with the others. If the battle had taught them anything at all, it was that the tactics Matt had suggested and Shinya and Alden had drilled into their troops worked. The last thing they needed was a gaggle forming part of the line.

Surprisingly, Queen Maraan immediately answered the question for him.

"I was, of course, impressed by the skill and courage with which you fought," she said. "As an ally, might I presume you will teach us these skills of war?"

Matt stirred with relief when Adar told him what she had asked, and he cleared his throat. "Certainly, Your Highness. I'm sure something can be arranged." He waited until Adar began telling the queen what he'd said. "Lieutenant Shinya?" he whispered quietly.

Shinya stepped up beside him. "Sir?"

"See to it, if you please. Set up an abbreviated drill for our new allies. Or if they're willing, maybe we can integrate the B'mbaadan troops directly into our existing regiments, at least for now. Sort of a 'jump right in' form of basic training. God knows, we need the replacements after yesterday." While he spoke, he noticed the queen of B'mbaado staring at Chack with as close to an expression of interested speculation as her face was capable of. Perhaps Adar had mentioned him? Maybe she'd asked about the powerful young Lemurian who stared brazenly back at her from beneath the jaunty angle of his dented helmet. "I know you've learned to speak 'Cat pretty good, Lieutenant," Matt said in a thoughtful tone, "but use Chack as your liaison. If you want him to keep the Second Marines that's fine with me—hell, he helped train them—and that'd be a good outfit to put their officers in to work them up."

Lieutenant Shinya nodded. "That was my thinking exactly, Captain."

Matt looked at the battle line commanders for a moment before addressing them. "All of you are not just captains but also heads of state. You have an equal say in this matter. Do any of you object to this alliance?" There was only a respectful silence from the Home high chiefs, although Anai-Sa of *Fristar* seemed oblivious. "Good." He turned to Safir Maraan. "Your Highness, as commander of the Allied Expeditionary Force, it's my honor to accept your nation into our alliance on behalf of its other members, with my gratitude." There was another short cheer, and Queen Maraan bowed graciously once more. Matt took a breath and regarded Lord Rolak, who stood watching what transpired with a tired, wistful posture. "Lord Rolak."

The Aryaalan seemed to clear his thoughts as he quickly knelt before the captain. "Yes, Lord?"

Matt understood that much of the People's speech, and he rubbed his eyes with his good hand and peered down at the Lemurian, cursing the fact that he'd never found the time to become fluent in the tongue. No time, he asked himself then, or just too lazy? Maybe too arrogant? He honestly didn't think so, but it was high time he learned to speak without an interpreter. "Adar," he said, "please try to explain to Lord Rolak that he's not a slave. I know what he did—what he risked and what he lost—in order to keep his word. I don't doubt his honor or his courage, and no one else should either. I admire it. Tell him that. Then tell him I'd be grateful for his service, and the service of all those who followed him and fought so well at our side. Not as slaves or vassals, but as friends."

Matt carefully lowered himself until he was kneeling on the ground. As Adar spoke, Rolak lifted his gaze until it rested heavily and searchingly upon Matt's face. With an encouraging smile, Matt extended his hand. Rolak looked at it, unsure, until Adar quickly explained the human custom. Then Rolak slowly, almost tentatively, extended his own hand. Matt grasped it between them and pumped it up and down.

Seeing Matt's difficulty in rising, Shinya and Sandra helped the captain back onto the stool, where he sat, puffing slightly and watching the Aryaalan.

Rolak stood and brushed sand from his knees. "We are friends then, yes," he said, talking to Adar. "But that in no way absolves me of my honor debt. If anything, it makes it a greater burden. Sometimes friendship can be the cruelest slavery of all, but in this case I accept it gladly. Tell Cap-i-taan

Reddy he is my lord, as Fet-Alcas once was, and my sword, my life, and my honor are still his, but they are freely given as a friend and not as a slave."

Matt listened to Adar's translation and sighed. It was probably the best compromise he would manage for now, given the dire nature of Rolak's original pledge, and he was grateful that, however it happened, the alliance had grown still more.

"Now," he said, holding himself as still as possible while the pain of his exertions subsided, "that's over with. I've heard your reports, but this meeting is to get everyone on the same page regarding our current situation. Mr. Shinya, would you describe the disposition of the enemy?"

"Yes, sir." Shinya shifted and spoke so his voice would carry to all those present. "As far as we can tell, they're gone. Our original estimate of their embarked force seems to have been . . . a little off, and several hundred of them, at least, escaped at the end of the battle. There is no indication that they retreated in any semblance of order, though. They just fled. I would recommend that when the Catalina flies in from Baalkpan this afternoon, Lieutenant Mallory be requested to fly a quick search pattern, fuel permitting, to ensure that the enemy has not reconstituted himself nearby."

"Do you think that is likely?" Keje asked. He spoke very carefully because he, like Matt, was trying to remain as still as he could.

"It's possible. I do not think it likely, however." Shinya paused and his brow furrowed in thought as he tried to decide how best to explain himself. Before he could, Courtney Bradford spoke up.

"If I may, Lieutenant?" Shinya nodded and the Australian cleared his throat. "Well. First of all, when the Grik finally broke, it was quite spectacular. Quite spectacular indeed! They just ran in all directions, like bees! As if they'd entirely lost their minds. Although I wasn't, um, actually in the very thickest of the fight, I saw the end from what might have been a better vantage point than most. Their demeanor couldn't have been more different from one moment to the next. It was as though one just pulled a cord and flipped a light." He looked owlishly at Keje. "It was like the deck of *Big Sal* all over again, the day we first really met. Many hundreds—I couldn't possibly count them—were slaughtered without attempting to defend themselves at all. It was as though the solitary thought in all their heads was escape. Quite spectacular indeed. Even if they did at some point recover themselves, I doubt they'd have the slightest notion how to reassemble into anything like a threatening force. Besides"—he grinned with what could only be described as anticipatory glee—"I am reliably informed that Java is populated with quite a variety of fascinating predators. Perhaps not as terrifying as some inhabiting the inner reaches of Borneo, but . . ." He looked around and arched an eyebrow. "Well. Certainly we should mount an expedition to go and see?"

Sandra leaned forward and whispered in Matt's ear. "Sometimes I wonder if everything that's happened since we came through the Squall has been God's attempt to overwhelm Courtney's curiosity."

"Never happen," Matt whispered back, then raised his voice. "Perhaps at some point, Mr. Bradford, but first let's win the war. Speaking of which, could you tell, from your 'vantage point,' what broke the Grik? What caused their extraordinary behavior? They still had us pretty badly outnumbered, as I recall. Mr. Shinya? You were speculating on the remaining enemy force. We should have a better idea now how many lizards there were to start with?"

Shinya looked grim, but that same expression of bewilderment returned as well. He opened his mouth, closed it, and finally waved at the plain beyond the barricade, black with skuggiks and enemy dead. "It's impossible to say for sure, Captain, but our best estimate is almost nineteen thousand enemy dead. More than we thought they even had." His face became a stony mask and there was a sharp intake of breath by some of those nearby. "No prisoners, of course. No wounded."

"Of course." Matt already knew their own losses had been more than seven hundred killed, with almost twice that number seriously wounded. Five more of his precious destroyermen had died as well, and a knot appeared in his throat when he remembered their names. Tom Felts, Glen Carter, Gil Olivera—the ordnance division had certainly had a bad day. Loris Scurrey and Andy Simms had made it almost as tough on the first deck division. He could see their faces in his mind—all of them—and he felt he'd failed them too, just like Marvaney, the first man they lost after coming through the Squall. He would have to try to forget for now, to push them away. There'd be plenty of time later, in the darkness of his quarters, for them to demand his full attention.

"Ten to one, Skipper," said Gray, sensing his mood. "Them Romans knew a thing or two, I guess."

"Not all Roman," Matt replied absently, then blinked and shook his head. "Very well. I'll ask you again, Mr. Bradford. Why?"

Courtney tucked the hand of his unwounded arm in his belt and stood on the balls of his feet. "Captain Reddy, you cannot possibly appreciate the position you have placed me in! To speculate upon such behavior based upon so little—"

Adar interrupted. "You already have a theory, one we have discussed. Otherwise, instead of bouncing on your toes, you would have removed your ridiculous hat and wiped your hairless scalp." Adar had sensed the need to lighten the mood. He may be a Lemurian Sky Priest and no type of real preacher, parson, or holy man, in any of the destroyermen's eyes at least, but he'd gained tremendous respect for his wisdom—hell, he could talk English as good as Chack! He could predict the weather better than anyone alive, and he definitely had a sense of humor the men could appreciate. A lot of worse fellows calling themselves priests came aboard back before the War.

"Grik Rout," Bradford confirmed. "We saw it once aboard *Big Sal* and again, well, yesterday. I don't think it's a phenomenon we can feel certain enough of to base any strategy upon."

"What *do* you think it is?" growled Chief Gray.

Bradford shrugged. "Some kind of massive, instinctual panic attack that renders them totally incapable of concerted efforts—such as war. Be lovely to turn it on and off again at will, but so far the only things I've seen do the trick are massive doses of automatic weapons, heavy artillery, and having their assault stopped cold by what were, at least briefly and locally, superior numbers that attacked *them* with mindless ferocity." He beamed at Lord Rolak.

Matt frowned. "So, in other words, pretty much the same thing that has stopped every other attack in history."

"Indeed. But the *effect* was still significant, don't you think?"

"It was certainly significant," Shinya confirmed. "And if we could learn how to create it at will, even strategic perhaps." He turned to Matt. "But Mr. Bradford is right. We cannot 'plan' for it. We have fought the Grik enough now to know that it does not always happen. In fact, sometimes their 'rout' can make them even more dangerous." He was remembering the losses they'd taken in the hold of *Revenge* when they scoured the last of the Grik from below. Slowly he brightened, his hand still resting on the pommel of the cut-down katana/cutlass Sandison had given him. "But they are gone from here now!"

"Good," said Matt with a genuine smile. "At least the 'land' lizards no longer seem a threat." There were a couple of chuckles from the destroyermen nearby. "What's the condition of the task force?"

"All is well, Cap-i-taan Reddy," Keje said, but then he put a hand to his forehead and closed his eyes. Adar continued for him. "No serious damage yesterday, or in the fighting with the Grik ships. Ammunition is depleted. We expended more than half of what we brought. As you know, weight and storage is not a problem, only production. We brought what we had. As more is made in Baalkpan, it will be sent."

Matt nodded. "What about those feluccas we couldn't account for?"

Rick Tolson spoke up. "We found one, Skipper. Hard aground in the shoals around those crummy little islands off the southeast coast of Madura. Everybody got off okay, but the ship was a total loss." He shook his head. "Lucky we didn't lose a dozen of 'em in there. No sign of the others. Lizards must've got 'em."

"Poor bastards," muttered Gray. Matt glanced at him, then looked at the bay where *Walker* had finally backed clear of the river. Even as he watched, her horn tooted exultantly, and Matt grinned in spite of himself. Dowden must have known he'd be as nervous as a cat. He had every confidence in his exec's seamanship, but he still felt tremendous relief.

"Well, now that it's clear our exuberant Mr. Dowden has saved my ship from further exposure to freshwater, I guess I'll report that she came through the fighting with no damage except for some scorched paint, some busted glass, and the loss of one of her propeller blades."

The Lemurian sea folk all nodded seriously at the news. They'd never seen *Walker*'s propellers, of course, but they'd seen drawings of the magical things that moved the iron ship so swiftly. Also, they'd seen the propellers on the PBY and knew the principle was the same. Matt had been taken aback that an airplane's propellers weren't harder for them to understand. If a PBY had shown up among his own ancestors two thousand years ago, he figured they'd have thrown spears at it or started a new religion. They certainly wouldn't have acted like "Oh, yeah. Pretty neat. *We* can't make one, but it makes perfect sense."

The fact that their culture—at least that of the sea folk—revolved around the reality of moving air, or wind, must have given them a pretty good grasp of the idea that air had substance whether you could see it or not. There were enough creatures that flew to prove flight was possible too. So from there, the notion that people might fly in a machine of some sort wasn't as big a stretch to them as it probably would have been among Bronze Age humans. Anyway, it was just another example of how sophisticated Lemurians could sometimes be. He didn't know why it surprised him anymore.

"That brings up another matter," he said, addressing Jim Ellis. "I want *Mahan* to make for Baalkpan as soon as possible. We don't have a dry dock, of course, but there are facilities there. Whatever we decide to do next, *Mahan*'s in no shape to fight. If we can get her to Baalkpan, at least we can start to change that." He paused and grimaced. "Before she leaves, though, I want one of her propellers if we can manage it."

Jim whistled. "That's a tall order, Skipper. How are we going to get at them? Hell, we can't even go in the water."

Matt was relieved that Jim didn't show more resentment at the prospect of crippling his ship further. He hated to ask it of him, but he didn't see any choice. If *Walker* couldn't run on two engines, it would seriously hamper any plans they made for further offensive operations.

"I don't know, Jim, but we'll think of something. I'll get with you after the meeting and we can hash it out. We'll work out a schedule to get *Mahan* as seaworthy as possible too. Now"—he looked back at Rolak—"what's going on in the city? I see guards on the walls, but no one's answering the door."

"Civil war," growled Rolak through Adar. "Warriors came out during the night, warriors loyal to me. They told of fighting throughout the city and . . . horrible deeds." He cast down his eyes. "It seems that by trying to save my city's honor, I may have caused its destruction. None have come out since morning, though, and I don't know what's happening now. My best guess is that the king's loyalists have retaken control of the main gate."

"What happened?" Matt asked gently.

Lord Rolak sighed. "As you know, when Fet-Alcas refused to allow us to strike the enemy rear, as we agreed, my forces and those of Queen Maraan swept north through the city and came out through the north gate. We had to fight to get out even there. Apparently, word spread of the specifics of the disagreement and many were appalled not only by the king's treachery but also by the fact that they had been deprived of participating in such a great battle. I know it may be hard for some of you to understand, but to watch such a fight from behind stout walls and do nothing, regardless of the honor at stake, would be difficult for Aryaalans to bear. Fet-Alcas has never been a popular king. He assumed the throne upon the death of his brother, who *was* popular and widely respected. Even, I think, in B'mbaado."

Safir Maraan nodded. "Tac-Alcas was a worthy opponent," she agreed without reluctance. "We warred with him often and he was difficult, difficult, but my father respected his courage, as well as his honor. As did I. Tac-Alcas would never have betrayed us as his brother did."

"In any event," Rolak continued, "there were already factions, political ones, long before the Grik came." He spoke the word "political" with a sneer. "I suspect most of those who actually supported me and my decision to come to your aid managed to make it out during the night. Any fighting still under way is probably between the king and other factions within the nobility that, like skuggiks drawn to carrion, have seen an opportunity. I imagine my return would be as unwelcome to any of them as it would be to the king."

"We must talk to them, nevertheless. Whoever's in charge," Matt observed.

"Indeed. Many of my warriors who would wish to join you still have families within those walls. None of them are bound by my friendship with you, although most will consider themselves so. I will storm the city myself, if necessary, to get their families out."

"Hopefully that won't be necessary," Sandra said in a fervent tone.

Heads nodded in unison and Matt cleared his throat. "Well. That's pretty much how things sit, I believe. The way I see it, we have, almost in spite of ourselves, won a major victory here. It was costlier than it should have been and we're not in as good a shape as we'd hoped to be at this point. But that doesn't change the ultimate strategy of our campaign.

We've got to keep up the pressure and move against Singapore as quickly as possible. The intelligence we gained from the captured charts suggests the enemy has only an outpost there so far. While we can presume that the force we destroyed here probably at least stopped off at Singapore, there's no indication in the charts that they dropped off any sizable force. That being said, I expect that's probably where the ships that escaped the battle in the bay retreated to, but they left their troops behind. With the addition of Queen Maraan's troops, and those of Lord Rolak, we should have sufficient forces to evict them—if we act before they reinforce." He looked at the gathered faces and wished again that he had some inkling of their thoughts. "Therefore, our priorities are these: first, bring the B'mbaadan and Aryaalan troops up to speed as quickly as possible." Matt let his gaze rest on Queen Maraan and Lord Rolak in turn. "That's going to take considerable cooperation from both of you. Your people are proud warriors and they may resist training in the new tactics, particularly since their instructors will be 'mere' sea folk."

"They won't resist," Queen Maraan assured him. "Not after yesterday."

Matt hoped she was right and he tried to hide his skepticism. He knew how difficult it had been for Europe to accept the lessons of modern war that Americans learned during their own Civil War. "Second, I want every felucca in the fleet either transporting supplies from Baalkpan or scouting the coastlines for any further incursions by the enemy. If they've established other outposts—at Tjilatjap, for example—we must know about it immediately. We'll also reconnoiter toward Singapore. Rick Tolson and Kas-Ra-Ar will assemble a small squadron of the fastest craft around *Revenge* for that purpose." He looked at Rick. "Don't push too hard. They have to expect us to check them out, but I don't want them to expect an attack."

"Understood, Captain."

"I also want the wounded out." He looked speculatively at his battle line commanders. "We should move them aboard a Home. Decide among yourselves which one it'll be." Matt had no doubt they would choose *Fristar*. Even now it was clear that the High Chiefs of the other Homes were avoiding Anai-Sa. His Home had lagged throughout the Battle of the Bay and had shown no initiative with her fire the following day. Adar told him that he doubted she'd fired a dozen times—as if Anai-Sa was hoarding his ammunition. "Whoever it is," Matt continued, "must deliver the wounded and return here as quickly as possible with as many more warriors as Baalkpan can spare." He took a deep breath. "Finally, we have to resolve the situation in Aryaal. I hope we can do that peacefully, but when we move on Singapore, I expect we'll be taking as many B'mbaadan warriors as Her Highness can spare from her island's defenses." He looked at Queen Maraan and blinked a question. She nodded slowly in reply. He had no idea if she was reluctant or merely contemplative. "Since we can't afford to leave a sizable force here to secure our lines of supply and communication—or to protect B'mbaado from an opportunistic Fet-Alcas trying to reunite his people against a common enemy—we must ensure that we aren't leaving a hostile presence in our rear."

There was considerable murmuring over that, as he'd expected. The sea folk harbored absolutely no moral qualms over battling the hated Grik to extinction, but the idea of fighting other Lemurians—no matter who they were—was anathema. It was what had always set them apart, in their view, from the people of Surabaya. He let them continue to talk among themselves a few moments more, but then silenced them. "Mr. Shinya, the Second Marines and half the remaining artillery will deploy in front of the north gate, and the rest of our forces will guard the barricade in case old Fet-Alcas starts feeling adventurous." He looked at the others.

"If there's nothing else, we all have a lot to do over the next couple of weeks. That's all the time we can spare, so make the most of it. If any of you have questions, I'll be back ashore tonight"—he stopped, and his eyes became hooded and his voice grew quiet—"for the funeral. Right now, I'm going back to my ship."

The meeting broke up and the attendees drifted off, some talking excitedly among themselves, others silent. Matt summoned his reserves and stood up from the stool once more, casting an impatient glance at Sandra when she tried to help. She shook her head and stayed back, but the displeasure was clear on her face.

"I want you out of here as quickly as possible, Jim. How soon can you get under way?"

Ellis visibly calculated how long it would take to accomplish the necessary preparations. "A week or two, Captain . . . I think." He assumed a troubled expression. "But I'm not sure how we're going to manage the propeller trade. That might slow things down."

Matt nodded. "I know, and I'm sorry to do this to you, but it can't be helped. *Mahan* can't steam any faster on two engines than she can on one. We'll fix that as soon as we can, but right now we need at least one of our ships to be fast." He grinned. "At least by local standards."

They began walking slowly toward the dock at a pace set unobtrusively by Sandra to minimize any chance of the captain stressing his wounds. Chief Gray hobbled along on his crutches, joined by Chack and Lord Rolak, a respectful distance behind. With so much to do, Matt flatly refused to return to his hospital bed, but no one was about to let him run around on his own. They reached the dock and waited for *Walker* to complete a wide, easy turn out in the bay that would eventually bring her alongside the pier. After a long silence in which each of them stared at the slender, light-gray ship with different and sometimes conflicting thoughts and emotions, Jim Ellis cleared his throat.

"Captain?" he said. "Matt?"

Matt arched an eyebrow and looked at his former executive officer. Jim was his friend, but even so, the number of times he'd addressed him by his first name could be counted on the fingers of one hand. In the past, he'd done it only when he wanted to speak to him *as* a friend and not as a subordinate officer. "There's something I've got to say. I wanted to, night before last, after the battle in the bay, but everything moved so quickly and besides"—he shrugged and gestured at the destroyer, which had completed her turn and was slowly approaching the dock—"I was just so glad to see you and that old 'can, the last thing I wanted to do was argue." He frowned. "But that was before yesterday." He glanced at Sandra for support and then looked to see if anyone else was in earshot. There was a general commotion and bustle all around, but the only ones close enough to hear were Gray, Rolak, and Chack. Currently, however, the Bosun and Matt's new . . . whatever he was . . . were deep in discussion, with Chack translating for them. He sighed.

"Skipper, I really don't think you should let yourself get caught up in any more desperate land battles, and I'd take it as a personal favor if you'd refrain."

Both of Matt's eyebrows rose then, but he managed a chuckle. "I had to be there, Jim. Nakja-Mur and all the High Chiefs put me in overall command. It would have looked pretty lousy if I wasn't willing to face the same danger as those I was supposed to be leading. Hell, Keje was there."

"Keje was there because *you* were there, and he almost got killed too," Sandra pointed out.

"Well, you're the one who so forcefully assured me I'm not indispensable," Matt reminded her with a gentle smile.

"I lied," she retorted. She wasn't smiling. Matt's grin faded and he looked at her intently for a moment. Jim seemed to be considering his words. When he spoke, at first it appeared he was changing the subject.

"When's the last time the men got paid?" he asked. Matt blinked at the apparent non sequitur.

"Before we left the Philippines," he answered guardedly.

"What do you suppose would have happened, before the War, if they'd gone that long without pay?"

Matt made a "what next" gesture, wondering when Jim would get to the point. But instead of Jim, Sandra spoke up. "What he's trying to say is you *are* indispensable! After everything that's happened; the War, the Squall, making an alliance with the Lemurians, and now this battle, *Walker* and her crew have continued to carry on and follow orders and do what you asked of them regardless of the fact that, besides her, and now *Mahan* thankfully, the

United States Navy doesn't exist anymore. Not to them. Even the country they fought for is gone. The only thing that's kept everything together up to now is you. The possibility that the crew might not continue to follow orders never became an issue because you didn't let it. You just continued ruthlessly on, as you always had, and made it clear you expected everyone else to do the same. The United States is gone, but *Walker's* their center, their core, their cause to cling to, and you're the one who made that happen." She rubbed her tired eyes. "Do you have any idea how fragile that is?"

"She's right, Skipper," Jim said solemnly. "If anything happened to you, it would probably all fall apart. I'm only beginning to learn what all you've managed to accomplish in Balikpapan. I mean, *fuel,* for Christ's sake!" He took a deep breath. "I might be able to carry on for a time—at least I hope I could. I kind of doubt it, though. My command experience so far has been less than stellar. Or maybe Dowden or Letts could swing it for a while, or Bradford could keep things going. But if you're lost, the unique relationship you've forged between *Walker* and the people here would be lost too. What effect would that have on this war against the Grik? Do you think it would even continue?" He waved around, a gesture that encompassed those close by as well as the walls of the city. "Hell, most of these people wouldn't even talk to each other before you made them. Do you think they still would if you were gone? They see you as an honest, impartial broker. One who's not caught up in their petty disputes. The way I see it, you're the glue that's holding this alliance together, and even adding to it." Jim grunted in frustration. "Hell, when I got here with *Mahan,* I couldn't even get the locals to *talk* to me.

"Besides," he continued, "from a purely selfish perspective, think what it would do to the crew. You're the last visible vestige of supreme authority they have left to cling to. The last physical connection to the world they've lost—to normalcy, I guess, and duty. They still follow your orders because you're The Captain, and that's the way it's supposed to be. Even here." Jim looked down at his feet for a moment, and then met Matt's eyes again. "I like to think I could fill your shoes on the bridge someday, as far as seamanship is concerned. Believe me, I thought about that a lot over the last few months. Then I look at *Walker,* with her new paint job and fuel oil burning in her boilers and I see . . . guys . . . like Chack over there, filling out her crew. I see a ship that was *whipped* but has since become the most powerful ship in the world, more than likely." He sighed. "I compare that to *Mahan,* which hasn't done half of what you have since we split up, and she still looks whipped."

"We were lucky," Matt murmured.

"Maybe so, but that wasn't all." Jim stopped and rubbed his temples, but when he spoke again his expression was pained. "I don't know if I could've stopped Kaufman or not. It never dawned on me that he'd try to take over the ship. Then, when he did, I never thought anyone would obey him, but they did. After what *Mahan* went through, it was hard to blame them, I guess. He sounded like he knew what he was doing when nobody else did, even me. But I've seen what happens when chaos and fear set in and a ship loses all sense of purpose and hope. I don't want to see it again."

Spanky McFarlane stood on *Walker*'s fantail, hands on his skinny hips, peering down through the portside propeller-guard tubing at the water below. Occasionally, small waves lapped against it and disrupted the almost perfect, wine-bottle blue-green clarity of the bay. That itself would prove to somebody who just woke up that this wasn't the cloudy, oily, Surabaya/Madura Bay they remembered. Through the occasional ripples, the sandy bottom was visible about thirty feet below, and between it and the surface, the growth-encrusted propeller shaft and support protruded far out beyond the line of the deck on which McFarlane stood. The only thing glaringly wrong with the view was the decidedly queer appearance of the now two-bladed screw. That, and the malevolent silvery shapes that glided and darted hopefully about.

McFarlane was surrounded by half a dozen helpers, snipes and deck-apes together. All stared at the water as if it were fresh molten lava oozing from the ocean floor. The most persistent shark had never received as much attention as the smaller but infinitely more numerous "flashies" did. A short distance away, so close the 'guards almost touched, floated *Mahan*, with a similar assembly peering at the water between them with identical expressions. Noisy sounds of difficult labor and coarse shouts echoed from the other ship as repair parties worked to make her seaworthy, but on *Walker*—just a few yards away—men and Lemurians almost tiptoed around, ridiculously making as little noise as they possibly could. The Skipper was asleep and the titanic racket from the ship alongside had no bearing on their stealthy efforts. If somebody woke the captain, it wasn't going to be any of them.

Machinist's Mate Dean Laney looked from the water to Spanky's hard, solemn face with wide eyes. "I ain't goin' down there, boss!" he said, with just a trace of panic.

McFarlane never even took his eyes off the damaged propeller. "If I say you're goin', you're goin', Laney. Even if I have to throw your worthless ass in." Nobody even mentioned that Laney had fifty pounds on the engineering officer. If Spanky wanted Laney in the water, one way or another, Laney would wind up in the water. "You and Donaghey are the only ones qualified in the diving gear 'sides me, and I'm too important to go. If we can't figure out a better way to get this done, we won't have any choice."

Wisely making no comment on Spanky's perception of his own importance compared to how Laney rated his, the machinist's mate tried sweet reason instead. "Why can't we just flood her down forward? Then we can take it off from a raft."

Spanky shook his head. "Won't work. I already thought of that. We'd have to sink the whole forward part of the ship plumb to the bottom to get those screws out of the water." Laney looked at him with an expression that seemed to ask, "So?" Spanky sighed.

Dennis Silva had joined him at the rail. The big gunner's mate spat in the water and watched as the white bubbles dissipated.

"Why not see what a grenade'll do? A stick of dynamite works pretty good in a lake."

Spanky looked at him and opened his mouth. Then he closed it. "Go get one."

Silva grinned. "Campeti don't just leave 'em in baskets outside his door."

"Tell him I said you could have one." Silva's sheepish expression gave him pause. "Shit. How many times have you told Campeti somebody said you could have a grenade? Never mind, I don't want to know." He took out his notepad and scribbled something on it. Then he tore out the sheet and handed it to Silva, who glanced at what he'd written.

Sonny: Give Silva a grenade.
I swear to God it's for me.
You can ask me later, or bring it yourself.
To the fantail.
Spanky

"Looks like a po-eem," Silva said, admiringly.

"Just go get a goddamn grenade!" Spanky raged.

"Shhhh!" cautioned Laney. "You're gonna wake the Skipper!"

Spanky's angry expression changed to a worried frown. "Say, you know, a grenade'd probably do that too. Damn it. I better go talk to the exec. See what he thinks. If he says okay, I'll pick one up myself." He started forward, but then stopped in the narrow space between the rail and the aft deckhouse. He turned and looked at Silva. "Gimme that note back, you." With an expression of purest innocence, Silva passed him the small rectangle of paper and Spanky wadded it up and threw it over the side.

Twenty minutes later, he returned with two hand grenades hooked on his belt and a sour expression on his face. "Skipper wasn't asleep at all. He was on the bridge." He cast an accusatory glare at *Mahan*. "Bastards over there kept him awake, I'll bet, with all their damn noise." He plucked one of the grenades like a pear and held it in his hand. "He said to give it a try."

Without another word, or a warning of any sort to the men clustered near *Mahan*'s stern, he pulled the pin and dropped the grenade over the side. The spoon flipped away as soon as it left his hand, and with a sullen *ker-plunk!* the grenade was on its way to the bottom of the bay. Seconds later, there was a dull flash and the sea between the ships turned opaque white. Even as the surface heaved, they felt a jolt through the deck plates beneath their feet. A geyser of water erupted skyward and the prevailing wind carried the bulk of the spray down upon the men on *Mahan*'s fantail, who gestured and cursed.

Cheers and happy, good-natured jeering broke out on *Walker*, and even on *Mahan*, since the man most thoroughly inundated was Al "Jolson" Franklen. Franklen had once enjoyed a measure of celebrity throughout the squadron before the War. He did a really good Al Jolson impersonation and he wasn't shy about performing. But even before Pearl Harbor, his act had begun to sour—for a variety of reasons—and most of his fans became distant. Then, of course, he was one of the few *Mahan*s still alive who'd supported Kaufman's mutiny. He only agreed to resume his duties with a full pardon—which Jim Ellis had been obliged to give because of how shorthanded his ship was. In any event, he wasn't a celebrity anymore and the jeering continued long after he strode forward, stony-faced and soaked to the bone.

Ignoring the noise, Spanky, Laney, and Silva too were staring intently at the water. Dead flashies, belly-up, appeared at the surface. Many trailed bloody tendrils but most were unmarked. The other crewmen on both ships quickly forgot their momentary indignity or amusement and joined them in their scrutiny of the grenade's effect. A large flashy swirled and bumped gently against the side of the ship. It twitched. It twitched again. For an instant, they thought it had resuscitated itself, but then it jerked violently and a dark cloud spread around it. Within moments, the surface of the water around and between the two destroyers' propeller guards boiled and seethed with ravenous flashies as they gorged on the bodies of their schoolmates. Laney looked at Spanky, his face a pale, waxy green.

"Fire in the hole!" Spanky warned this time, and dropped the second grenade. The effect was similar to the first, with the exception that the *Mahan*s had time to scramble under the aft deckhouse overhang before they were drenched again. This time, there was only the briefest calm before the roiling frenzy redoubled.

"Oh, well," Spanky grumped, regarding Laney with deadpan remorselessness. "Back to plan A."

"Captain, Lieutenant Mallory's on the horn," reported the radioman, Clancy. "He's crossing Madura—I mean B'mbaado—now, sir."

"Very well," Matt acknowledged. "Tell him to watch out for wrecks in the bay when he sets down."

"Aye, sir," came the reply and Clancy disappeared back down the ladder.

"Too bad we can't just roll a depth charge over the side," Steve Riggs said, resuming the interrupted conversation. "We still have a full load of those."

Garrett shook his head. "A depth charge is not a hand grenade. If we did that, we'd blow the stern right off the ship." Matt nodded agreement. He was sitting in his chair on the bridge sipping "monkey joe," the local equivalent of coffee, which actually looked and tasted somewhat like coffee except for the greenish foam. He mostly just listened while his officers and senior NCOs brainstormed about the propeller problem.

"I can't send a man over the side," Spanky said. "He'd be torn to bits."

"Maybe we could beach *Mahan,* take off her screw, and then refloat her with the tide," Dowden suggested doubtfully. "Then do the same with *Walker.* If one ship gets stuck, we can pull her off with the other."

"That's something to consider," Jim mused. "How high do the tides run around here? The charts ought to say, but it's awful risky this close to the equator. I doubt they run more than a couple feet. Besides, more ships than I like to think about have been lost trying to pull stranded vessels off a bank in confined waters. What was that cruiser, twenty years ago or so, that tried to pull that sub off a shoal? The line parted and the cruiser went aground. Total loss. What was her name?"

"Milwaukee," answered Spanky.

Gray grunted. "That's all we need. Our own little Honda Point." He referred to the 1923 catastrophe when seven four-stackers ran hard aground on the California coast in a dense fog. "A fine stupid mess we'd be in then."

Matt shook his head. "I have to say, that's my least favorite option so far, gentlemen. Nobody wants to deliberately beach his ship."

"Maybe we could build a cage of some sort," Sandison speculated. "Lower it over the side next to the screw and let the divers take it off through the bars."

Spanky looked at the torpedo officer with surprise. "Hey! That might work. We've only got the one little crane aft for handling the depth charges and it won't lift a screw, but we could use it for the cage and then rig a boom off the main mast to raise the propeller, I bet."

"Keep working on it. I know you'll get it figured out," Matt said. Then he frowned and looked at his watch. "I'm afraid Mr. Ellis and I have to leave you now. We have . . . a couple of funerals to attend." He glanced at Garrett and Chief Gray. "You too. The men we lost were in your divisions. Have the burial party turned out as sharply as they can manage." He sighed and stood carefully from his chair, groaning slightly. "I'll meet you ashore at, say, sixteen hundred. The Lemurians have some sort of funeral planned for dusk, I believe. We may have to be flexible, but I want to bury our people as close to eighteen hundred as we can."

"You sure we shouldn't just bury them at sea?" Gray asked quietly.

Matt took a breath and grimly let it out. "I'm sure. I hated putting Marvaney over the side and I've never felt right about it. Not like I probably would . . . back home. Not like I *did* when we buried all the people we lost in the fight running away from this damn place. But that was different—at least we thought it was." He shook his head, but his frown remained. "Besides," he finally added, "these guys fought for this crummy place . . ." He didn't continue. There was no need. The following silence was broken by the lookout's report that the plane had been sighted.

"Sixteen hundred, Mr. Dowden," reminded Matt as Riggs replied to the lookout. "Carry on here. Show the flag at half-mast, if you please, and I'll want one to take ashore. I doubt we have enough to cover them all, so we'll just have to make do." Instead of departing as he'd intended, he remained a moment longer with a thoughtful expression. In the distance, the droning engines of the PBY could be faintly heard. "What happened to our flag they carried during the battle?"

"The Second Marines, Skipper. They have it," Gray answered.

Matt nodded with approval. "Good. We'll use that one instead."

"Aye, aye, sir," they choused.

Freshly shaved and dressed in his less than pristine whites, Matt appeared at the place he had specified for the burial services to commence. Sandra, Ellis, Bradford, and Shinya accompanied him. Together they waited amid a growing crowd of curious Lemurians and stared somberly at the Marines guarding the five small graves. There might have been six as far as Matt was concerned, had the 'Cat they lost during the Battle of the Bay not gone over the side. The location of the new cemetery caused considerable controversy. Matt insisted on the flat, high ground right beside the road from the waterfront and just a short distance in front of the hasty breastworks they'd thrown up facing—and in clear view of—Aryaal's main gate. From which, there had still been no word at all.

Lord Rolak joined them, as did Queen Maraan. Rolak had polished his armor and replaced his missing plume, but in spite of his expressionless eyes, his deep frown left no doubt he was troubled. He spoke to Captain Reddy through Courtney Bradford. "My lord," he began hesitantly, "I am yours, as you know, and will do as you command. But since you've placed the burden of friendship upon me, it is my duty to counsel against this act." Matt turned cold eyes upon him as he continued. "If we and the sea folk agree on one thing, it is that the souls of the dead belong in the heavens, where they are taken by the flames of the pyre. Not planted in the ground—from which they may never ascend." Rolak had little experience upon which to base his perception of human expressions, but Matt's darkening mood was clear enough. As a credit to his courage, he continued. "Please. Do not take offense. I understand you have different beliefs, as do we differ from the sea folk regarding where those souls ultimately reside. But to do this here, like this, can only breed resentment among those beyond the walls who wish us ill."

Matt nodded calmly enough, but when he spoke, his quiet words were iron. "On land, burial is the way of our people. We believe our God can find our souls wherever they are. The men we're going to bury here today died to save your city—the same as the sea folk and the people who followed you did. I'm going to bury them in the shadow of that city, so, from now on, people who live here will see their graves and remember the sacrifice they made for a people who—with a few noble exceptions—didn't lift a finger in their own defense and then betrayed those who did. Tomorrow, we'll talk to whoever rules behind those walls whether they want to or not, and you'll tell them what I said and why we're doing this. You'll also tell them that if I ever hear these graves have been desecrated in any way, or the memory of the men we bury here is ever given less than the respect it deserves, I'll steam here in *Walker* from wherever I am and reduce this city to dust. No offense."

Adar arrived beside Matt while he spoke, and he wore a different robe than the one in which they usually saw him. This one was black instead of purple, and golden stars covered it entirely instead of the usual silver ones upon the shoulders. "Not until this moment," Adar said, "did I truly realize how different your people are from mine, Cap-i-taan. I knew from the beginning that we worshiped differently, of course, but I always believed that, in the end, we only sailed a different wind to the same destination. Your 'charts,' as you call them—when I first saw them, I was angry. I believed you didn't treat them with proper respect, but I made that judgment from within the context of my own belief. When I came to know you, I lost my anger, particularly in light of the kind of people I now know you to be. I believed you were heretics, yes, and misguided, but certainly not nonbelievers." Adar sighed, looked at Matt, and blinked compassion. "But you are." He held up a placating hand. "Do not be angry! What I mean is, I now know you do not believe *at all* the same as we, and I suppose I am relieved." There was a rattling growl deep in his throat that was a kind of chuckle. "You're not warping the True Faith as I feared. Any similarity between your practices and mine are entirely coincidental. You do not disrespect my faith either intentionally or otherwise—you don't share it at all! This 'burying' of souls in the ground is proof enough of that!" He stopped and glanced at Rolak. "Although, if it must be done, I find it highly appropriate for you to do it here."

Matt looked at his friend with new respect. With a human Bronze Age priest, this would have been about when the torches would be lit.

"You're not angry that we don't share your beliefs?" Sandra asked.

"Of course not," Adar replied. "No one can be forced to accept the True Faith. It would not then be True, would it? I was only . . . uncomfortable . . . when I thought you mocked it." He looked darkly at Rolak. "As the Aryaalans do."

Rolak sniffed. "A lie," he said pedantically.

Matt was looking at the Marines and the graves they guarded. "You might be wrong, Adar. My people sail many winds to reach the same destination, but once there, I believe the place might yet still be the same. Perhaps the same as yours." A commotion grew behind them and they saw the approach of seven destroyermen dressed in whites. They had probably scrounged both ships to find so many bright, clean outfits. All of them carried Springfields on their shoulders and they marched in step well enough, despite being more than a little rusty. Matt swelled at the sight, as well as when he saw the battle-scarred American flag that had been rescued by the Second Marines leading the way. He was surprised to see who carried it. Walking slowly in front of the riflemen, also dressed in whites with gaiters laced on above his bare feet and with his battered helmet on his head, was Chack-Sab-At. His eyes were grimly set and focused before him and his tail was held erect as it swayed back and forth behind him as he walked.

The firing party halted beside the graves and the flag fluttered in the breeze between them and the walls of Aryaal. "I have to go now," Matt said quietly, and stepped quickly through the Marine guard to stand before the graves, facing the growing crowd with his back to the city. He reached into his coat pocket to retrieve his small Bible, but found himself faced with the difficulty of opening it with one hand. Sandra rushed to join him, opening the book to a page where he had inserted a small piece of paper. He looked at her and smiled.

"Please stay," he said. She returned his smile with a supportive one of her own and took her place beside him. A column of thirty destroyermen was moving toward them, swaying in step from side to side. Between each group of six was the body of one of their comrades, sewn in his mattress cover. Chief Gray led the procession, hobbling on his crutches. When they drew even with Ellis, Jim joined the Chief and the column followed the pair to the graves. Matt noticed that almost half of the party who bore the bodies of his crewmen were Lemurians, in spite of what might be a religious aversion toward what they were doing. He felt a surge of affection for them, mingled with a sadness that the original crews of the two destroyers had dwindled so far. When the bodies were deposited beside the graves, the bearers stepped back.

To Matt's further surprise, the final member of the procession was a stony-faced Dennis Silva. Before him in his hands he carefully carried Mack Marvaney's portable phonograph. He stepped into position beside Chief Gray where a bugler would have been if they'd had one, set the phonograph on the ground, and opened it. It had already been wound and he merely released the brake and positioned the needle on a record as the turntable began to spin.

"Atten-*shun*!" barked Gray.

Sounding tinny and forlorn, emanating from the open louver in the side of the small machine, "The Star-Spangled Banner" began to play. Instinctively, all the destroyermen, human and Lemurian, snapped a salute to the flag that floated over Chack's head. The recording was an upbeat, cheerful, even sort of jazzy rendition like Matt had heard played by a lot of dance bands before the War to start things off. For a poignant moment he could almost smell the perfume of a girl he'd danced with in San Diego when he was on his way to the Philippines to take command of *Walker*. Many of those in the gathered crowd gasped at the unexpected music, but Matt felt a sudden tightness in his throat and a strange pressure behind his eyes. He blinked.

Looking sidelong at Sandra, he saw a sad, wistful expression and as the anthem ended and Silva leaned down to turn off the machine, he saw tears streaming down the gunner's mate's face. Tears for Tom Felts, or Mack Marvaney, or any of the dozens they'd lost, there was no way to know. Or maybe he was just thinking about all they'd left behind.

"Pa-*RADE, REST!*"

Matt cleared his throat and looked at the book Sandra held open for him. Then he shook his head. "I never was one much for church," he apologized, "and I guess we've all missed a few services lately." Some of the men chuckled quietly, in spite of themselves. "It's not my way, or my place, I think, to preach a sermon here today. I do want to say a few words about these men we are burying, as well as all the rest of you destroyermen. Like all of us—except maybe Juan—Tom Felts and Glen Carter, Andy Simms, Loris Scurrey, and Gil Olivera were a long way from home even before the Japs bombed Pearl and Cavite. For some reason, all of us are even farther away now. Tom was from Arkansas. Glen and Andy were both from Ohio. Gil was from New York and Loris was from California." He paused for a moment, collecting his thoughts.

"Mr. Ellis is from Virginia and so is Lieutenant Tucker. Sonny Campeti is from New Jersey and Frankie Steele is from Brooklyn. Chief Gray and Dennis Silva are from Alabama. I miss Texas as much as any of you miss the places you're from . . ." He shrugged. "We might be stuck here, however it happened. My guess is we probably are. But no matter how far we've come from those places we yearn for, they'll always be with us—part of us—deep down. And no matter how far apart they were from each other, those places had one thing in common. They were part of the United States of America, and that made us all Americans." He looked out at the faces of the firing party and the bearers, and some of the others who had come ashore. He saw out into the bay where *Walker* and *Mahan* floated side by side in the distance and, for the moment, those who'd stayed aboard them lined the rails and the flags flew low. "We're all still part of that no matter how far we've come. We were still Americans in the Philippines, and by God, we're still Americans here."

He paused for a long moment before continuing. "A few of us have gone even farther than the others now, but it's my belief that, in so doing, they've gotten closer to home, not farther away. I believe there's one God, above all things, who made the world we came from and this one too. Has to be. Only God could've figured out anything as complicated as *this* situation. I think He can probably manage to sort things out and put us where we belong when we die. I believe the men we bury here today in this strange but familiar place are with their loved ones that went before them now just as surely as if they'd died at home in bed." He stopped again to let that sink in. He really believed it was the truth, too. At least he hoped it was. The idea of their very souls being banished to this strange world as well was more than he could bear.

"But they didn't die at home," he said, "or in bed. They did die fighting for the same principles they fought for back home. For Duty, Honor, and Country. For freedom and liberty and against aggression." He grimaced. "A more horrible aggression than we've ever known. Most importantly, though, in some ways, they fought for *you*. They fought for their ship and their shipmates. Old and new. They died in a fight we didn't want but we have to win if we or our friends are ever going to be able to live here in peace and freedom from the evil that sweeps this world." He glanced at Sandra and saw her looking at him with an expression of pained concentration. Then he looked out at the Lemurians, most of whom couldn't understand him, but were getting a quick translation.

"You know, it just came to me that maybe I *do* know why we're here after all. Back in our world, our two ships, *Walker* and *Mahan*, were expendable. Hell, they'd already been expended. Their loss or survival didn't make any difference at all to whether the United States won or lost the war. Here, they *do* make a difference. *We* make a difference." He looked at the graves that lay in the center of the gathering and when he spoke again, his voice was a husky whisper.

"*They* made a difference."

Quickly, he reached into the Bible in Sandra's hands and took out the piece of paper there.

"I am the resurrection and the life, saith the Lord," he resumed in a wooden voice. "He that believeth in me, though he were dead, yet shall he live: and whosoever liveth and believeth in me, shall never die . . ." He continued on in a dwindling voice until the passage was complete, but quite a few of the others echoed his words from memory.

"A-tten-*shun!*" bellowed the Chief's raspy voice.

"Firing party, *pre*-sent, *arms!*"

Most of the Lemurians had seen what was coming, but they flinched anyway when Gray commanded the riflemen to fire three volleys. Matt then stumbled through the committal, clumsily substituting "the earth" for "the deep" and ended with a harsher command than he'd intended for everyone to bow their heads. He was surprised and a little embarrassed to see quite a few of the Lemurian troops follow his order. Now that it was over, he thought it had been a hokey speech, right out of a B movie, but he couldn't help it. It was how he felt. Sandra took the piece of paper from him and squeezed his hand gently for a moment. Then she placed the page back in the Bible and closed it.

There was no one to play taps. Silva crouched down beside the phonograph and removed the platter that bore the national anthem. Beneath it was another record. They all stood still and listened while a very old and melodramatic choir performance of "Rock of Ages" oozed from the louver. There was no telling why Marvaney had it, or why Silva hadn't sent it with him when they buried him at sea. Toward the end, the spring began to wind down. Matt cleared his throat uncomfortably and Silva applied the brake.

"Mr. Ellis."

"Sir?"

"The flag will remain uncased. It'll fly here as long as we remain. Signal the ships to resume normal duties. The burial party will proceed with the interment. Afterward, those who wish to do so may remain to witness the Lemurian ceremony. The firing party will remain as well."

"Aye, aye, Captain." Ellis hesitated.

"Yes, what is it?" Matt replied distractedly, wiping sweat from his brow with the sleeve of his good arm.

"You did all right."

"Never was much good at public speaking," he demurred.

"You did all right, Skipper," Ellis repeated.

"Yes, you did," Sandra agreed. "And you know? Maybe you're right. About why we're here, I mean."

"Makes as much sense as anything," said Jim. "And if it's true, it proves God sure is an imaginative guy."

"What do you mean?"

"The way the war was going back home, and in the shape our ships were in, *only* God could've found a use for them. Even if we'd managed to get out of our fix without the Squall—which I doubt—they wouldn't have been any good to the Navy anymore."

"God works in mysterious ways, huh?" quoted Matt with a small smile of his own. "What an understatement."

The crowd dispersed, many to attend to their military duties but most to continue preparations for the Lemurian service later that evening. Labor parties resumed tearing down the wooden warehouses that lined the wharf to use them for fuel for the pyres. Others swarmed over one of the Grik hulks that had been driven ashore during the battle and were quickly reducing it to its skeletal framework. The ghetto housing, such as it was, was left untouched. The allied commanders were unhappy about the necessity of destroying the warehouses—or any property at all—but since there was no suitable timber nearby, they had no choice. They needed all the wood they could find to send this unprecedented number of souls to the sky. At least the warehouses were mostly empty, their contents having been moved into the city when the Grik arrived.

"An . . . unusual ceremony," remarked Keje to Adar and Rolak, referring to the Amer-i-caan funeral they'd just seen. Keje had arrived late and had been supported by his disapproving daughter. He was still dizzy from the blow on his head.

"Unusual," Adar agreed thoughtfully. "Short, too. And very somber. Their grief was quite clear."

"They see death more as an ending than we do, perhaps. As if they do not expect to meet their lost ones again," Keje speculated.

"I think not," countered Adar. "Cap-i-taan Reddy told me to hear his words and I might better understand their faith." He shook his head. "I listened, but my understanding is no less uncertain. I think he was right, however, that we may only sail a different wind to the same destination. They certainly *hope* to meet again those who go before them, as do we, but perhaps they are less certain their God will find them here, so far from their home."

"Even more reason not to hide their dead underground."

Adar looked at his lifelong friend but shook his head at Keje's obtuseness. "You know as well as any novice priest that the souls of those lost at sea will rise to the heavens as surely as those sent by the pyre. The smoke of the pyre is symbolic. The ashes of the dead that rise within it settle back to the land or sea, in time. No," he continued, "their customs may seem bizarre, even distasteful. But the meanings behind them are not so different as they may at first appear. I will have to speak more with them about this, but I think we must consider: they are willing to fight and die with us despite a fear that if they *do* die, they will be utterly lost. I believe our service for the dead would be considerably more somber if that concern lingered in our minds." He hesitated. "Although I must confess I feel less positive about this ascension than I have in times past." He held up a hand to forestall the shocked blinking of his companions. "No, I've no doubt the souls we free tonight will find their way, but I do grieve that there are so many. Their concerns are over, beyond those they may retain for us. I do not begrudge their contentment in the heavens . . . but we will regret their loss in the battles to come. Do not think I've forgotten my oath," he said.

The three Lemurians lingered in silence a short while longer, watching as the mixed human and Lemurian burial party proceeded with their chore. Shovelfuls of soil disappeared into the rectangular holes with soft thumping sounds.

"It was surely a ceremony for warriors," Rolak stated. "Except for the part when they are buried."

The Lemurian "service" was just as alien to the human destroyermen who witnessed it as theirs had been to the Lemurians. Matt watched the initial ceremony accompanied by Jim, Sandra, and Courtney. Except for the firing party, whom Matt had ordered to remain as a show of honor and respect, most of the other members of the funeral party had returned to the ship. He'd ordered Gray to go, ostensibly to help coordinate repairs but mainly to get him off his feet. To his surprise, all the Lemurian destroyermen returned to the ship as well. All except Chack, who had remained behind along with the equally surprising Dennis Silva. Silva sent the phonograph back with Stites but stayed ashore talking quietly with Chack, waiting for the Lemurian funeral to get under way. Matt doubted they had ended their feud, but they appeared to be observing a truce for the evening, at least. Matt joined them briefly, out of curiosity.

"Chack?" he said.

"Sir?"

"Why did the other people . . . your people, go back to the ship? I thought I made it clear they were welcome to stay."

Chack looked at him and then glanced out at the deepening gloom of the bay, beyond the pier, where the two ships lay. Nearby, and lower down, the dark silhouette of the PBY floated now as well. The Lemurian ceremony was about to take place on the west side of the point, nearest to Madura, where *Mahan* had been anchored almost since she arrived. A power cable had been rigged between the destroyers, and portable lights and lanterns glowed harshly on the decks, contrasting brightly against the dull glow in the western sky where the sun had slipped away.

"They grieve, Cap-i-taan," he said. "But they are Navy men, yes? They are destroyermen."

Matt nodded. "Yes. They are."

"*Walker* is their Home. You are High Chief for *Walker*. You are High Chief of all the Amer-i-caan Navy here, so *Mahan* is their Home too. Both Homes need us now, more than the dead, and so they want to work." He paused. "I am here because I do not know what you want me to do."

Matt was taken aback. "What do you mean, Chack?"

"When I came to *Walker*, Keje-Fris-Ar was my High Chief. *Big Sal* was my Home. When I joined the Amer-i-caan Navy, I thought *Walker* was my Home. I was Bosun's Mate," he added proudly. Then he sighed. "Lieutenant Shinya tells me now that I am to be Chief of the Second Marines. What does that mean? I have become a good warrior," he said matter-of-factly, "which is something I never expected, and I . . . *am* good at it. But is *Walker* no longer my Home? Do I not *have* a home?"

Matt was perplexed for a moment; then realization dawned. "No! I mean, yes, *Walker* is certainly your Home, Chack, and you're still a bosun's mate! Good grief, I'm sorry if I made you think otherwise!" Matt scratched his chin in thought. "The way things are, a lot of us—you included—have to do more than one job, though. Do you think Lieutenant Letts and Tony Scott—and all the others we left in Baalkpan doing other jobs—have lost their Home?" Grudgingly, Chack shook his head. "Then don't worry about it. I'm glad you're here, though. It's appropriate that you should be. The Second Marines fought well. Hell, the battle would have been lost without them, and a lot of the credit for that goes to you. You helped train them and you fought with them and they trust you to lead them well. We all do. And your being here now is one of the duties of command."

Later when the funeral finally got under way, Matt imagined as he watched that Chack probably was beginning to contemplate some of the consequences of command.

The great pyres, three of them, were erected in a triangular pattern between the city walls and the sea. In each case, a huge bed of timbers had been laid on the ground with the dead gently arranged upon them. Above them all, a carefully erected A-frame latticework of timbers was created that gave the pyres the appearance of three stranded Homes. The air was thick with the ripening reek of the dead and the fishy stench of rendered gri-kakka oil that the dreary structures had been painted with. No living Lemurian had ever seen such a large pyre before, let alone more than one. None had ever seen anything like the battle that forced the need for them. Chances were, Matt grimly reflected, this wouldn't be the last time the People would send so many souls to the sky.

At the base of the triangle, Adar stood alone in the twilight. Torches were arrayed nearby and the golden stars of his robe twinkled and shimmered, reflecting the light. In a new touch, he was flanked by the proud, hopeful flags of those who'd fought and died. In the center, behind him, flew the lone-tree flag that Keje had fashioned to represent them all. The only flag missing was the Aryaalan flag, even though Rolak had begged one from the city. There had been no reply. The American flag still flew over the American dead, but not very far away.

Rolak had also tried to acquire an Aryaalan priest, but again there was no response. Queen Maraan had been satisfied by Adar's assurance that his service wouldn't stress the differences between their religions. From what little Matt knew, the differences weren't extreme, but like any religion, he supposed, the devil was in the details. In a nutshell, Bradford softly explained while they waited, land folk and sea folk both believed that something like a soul was carried into a heavenly afterlife. The main friction stemmed from what the two peoples believed the souls did after they got there. The sea folk, Adar told him, carried on in a peaceful, idyllic existence as, or among, the stars (this was still unclear) where they helped guide the lives and seagoing paths of those on earth. Kind of like angels, Bradford explained. The sun, of course, was the benign, gentle creator and nurturer of all things. In other words, sun-god worship with a twist.

To the land folk, however, the heavens were like a utopian Valhalla. Full of willing servants and lovely females, food, drink, and great, glorious battles in which nobody ever died. The dead paid no heed to those who remained behind because they were having too much fun to notice. The sun was God, under whose judgmental gaze one had to perform the great deeds that earned a place above. Other than that, as an arbiter of who got to play forever and who didn't, the sun was just a big lightbulb—at most, a spectator. Most distressing of all to the sea folk, however, to the Aryaalans and B'mbaadans the stars were just "up there." Matt understood why the stars would have much greater importance to a people who used them for navigation, but he found it difficult to imagine anyone being incurious enough not to think of them at all. That was a tough difference to bridge and he knew major religious wars had been fought throughout human history over less profound differences. Matt had to admit that the sea folk's religion was probably closer to what he'd been brought up with—profoundly different, of course, but still closer than Rolak's or Queen Maraan's. Although, he admitted wryly to himself, he could understand the attraction of the land folk religion to its adherents. At least to the males.

He looked at Sandra and saw the torchlight reflecting off her gold-tinged, sandy hair and fresh-scrubbed face. Her nurse's uniform was immaculate and exotically feminine compared to the dungarees she wore day to day. He couldn't help it, but a deep sadness, unrelated to the day's events, swept over him and he looked away so fast that his throbbing shoulder made him wince.

She looked at him with concern. "Are you all right?" she asked anxiously. It had been a long day for him, emotionally and physically, and she'd not be surprised if he passed out at any moment. Triumphant maybe, considering the dark predictions she'd made all day about the consequences to be expected if he overtaxed himself, but not surprised. "Just a little sore," he whispered, forcing a smile. Most of the crowd had grown silent as Adar prepared to speak.

"Now what?" asked Jim Ellis irritably as they stared at Aryaal's petulantly silent north gate. Arrayed before it was the newly expanded Allied Expeditionary Force. Expanded by membership anyway, if not by actual numbers. An acrid haze from the funeral pyres that had burned throughout the night served as a constant reminder of why there had been no net increase in force levels. Another reminder of the long, strange "funeral" was the pounding headache that Matt's former exec was enduring at the moment. A mass celebratory drunk to rival Dennis Silva's wildest dreams had followed Adar's sermon and subsequent igniting of the pyres. Adar's requiem for the fallen had progressed from praise for their deeds to, ultimately, an almost envious bon voyage to the departing souls as they swept to the heavens atop the roaring flames. What followed then was an insane "wake."

The seep flowed from casks brought ashore from the ships of the battle line in such abundance that Matt was frankly stunned they even had an army in the morning. At one point he questioned Adar about the wisdom of prostrating half their force on the doorstep of a possibly hostile city and the by then already sozzled Sky Priest had assured him that even the most depraved Aryaalan would never attack them while they were in "mourning." Matt was fairly certain the Lemurian meaning of the word conveyed a few subtle differences. Adar then sternly pressed a cup of seep into his hand and solemnly asked him to celebrate the "rising" along with his friends—if he didn't think his own God would be too terribly put out.

Matt took a few sips of the bittersweet brew under the watchful stare of Sandra Tucker. He finally even allowed the rest of those present, with the exception of the firing party, to imbibe as well. The unfortunate firing party was retained as an impromptu shore patrol to make sure everyone got back to the ship. Besides, in spite of Adar's assurance, Matt felt compelled to maintain at least a small armed and sober force ashore. Letting them drink, with weapons at hand, didn't even bear thinking about. Silva became a vocal convert to the Lemurian faith, although the denomination he embraced was unclear. Courtney Bradford was carried to the ship.

Now Matt had to admit his worst fears had been for naught and at least the majority of the AEF had stood to when called. With the dawn also came a return of the army's positive nature, as if the smoke and flames of the night before had lifted much of their gloom. The smoke had eliminated the stench of the diminishing Grik carrion beyond the barricade and the seep had washed away their dread. He shook his head. A different wind, certainly, he thought. And maybe even a better one as far as warriors were concerned.

Jim Ellis pinched the bridge of his nose and clenched his eyes shut when the roar of the PBY reached them from the bay. Lieutenant Mallory was departing on a belated scout and Matt swiveled his head and watched the battered flying boat skip across the choppy morning wavelets and claw its way into the sky.

"You drank too much seep," he accused good-naturedly, turning back to look at the gate. Many figures were atop the wall above it, but there had been no response to their hails.

"No," Ellis denied, "but I guess I drank enough." He nodded toward the gate before them. "And I repeat, what now? If they won't even talk to us . . ."

Matt snorted. His wounds were healing, thanks to the mysterious paste, but the pain was pretty severe and he had to guard against a tendency to snap. On the slope before them, Lord Rolak continued to pace back and forth, haranguing the inhabitants of the city to send somebody out to talk. "I guess we're just going to have to make them." He turned to Lieutenant Shinya, who stood nearby with his hands behind his back. "Mr. Shinya, have Chack carry a message to Lord Rolak to deliver. Tell him to instruct them to clear an area around the gate if they don't want to be killed."

Shinya nodded. "Aye, aye, Captain. *Chack!*" The new commander of the Second Marines ran to join them and Shinya passed on Matt's instructions. With his dented helmet on his head and rifle slung muzzle down, Chack hurried to where Rolak stood, radiating impotent rage. Matt noted with interest that Queen Maraan's gaze never left the burly Lemurian bosun's mate.

"What are you going to do?" Keje asked, stepping closer. Unlike Jim Ellis's, his head seemed much better after last night.

"I'm going to blow the gate in," Matt answered stonily, gesturing at the two fieldpieces in the center of the line, directly opposite the entrance to the city.

"But if any inside are killed . . ." Keje began. Regardless of his own frustration, the idea of killing other Lemurians came hard to the High Chief of *Salissa*.

Matt turned to face him. "We can't leave Aryaal to threaten our rear, or our allies." He nodded toward Queen Maraan. "If we have to storm that city—and we will if they force us—there's no telling how many will die. My hope is if we knock down that gate it'll show them how vulnerable they are to our guns and maybe we can talk sense into them."

"But surely they saw the effect of the guns against the Grik?"

"Sure, but they're pointed at *them* now, and my guess is they don't think we'll do it."

"Cap-i-taan Reddy speaks truth," said the B'mbaadan queen through an interpreter they'd assigned her. "They know sea folk do not war among their own race." She grinned predatorily. "But we did not think you would fight the Grik either. If you 'knock down' that gate, they will wonder what else they were wrong about. In any event, they know I would have no qualms taking *my* army inside!"

When Rolak delivered his ultimatum there was, again, no response. The sentries atop the wall above the gate did surreptitiously ease away from it, however. Matt lowered his binoculars.

"Damn," he muttered after twenty minutes passed. "If we wait any longer, they'll start to go back. Mr. Shinya? Proceed." A moment later the two guns in the center of the line fired almost simultaneously. At a range of only a little over two hundred yards, it was impossible to miss. With a thunderclap roar and a billowing rush of white smoke, the guns leaped back and the brief, ripping-sheet sound of two solid shots was drowned by their impacts on the heavy wooden gate. The effect was spectacular. One shot struck near the center, blowing a large jagged hole and sending splinters in all directions. The second struck near the top hinge on the right-hand gate and it slowly toppled inward, tearing the bottom hinge as it fell. There was a muted scream from within.

"Again!" Matt commanded, his lips set in a hard line. The second two shots obliterated the left-hand gate. "Mr. Shinya! The Second Marines will advance!"

"Second Marines! Forward . . . march!"

As a solid rectangular block, the veteran unit stepped forward toward the gap made by the guns. Matt was suddenly struck by how eerie it was to see such a mass of troops move with such precision without even the beat of a drum to keep the cadence. The regiment had been whittled down to only three hundred now, but they weren't like any warriors that had ever approached those gates before. They were a battle-hardened killing machine. Matt also knew that none of the Marines now marching toward Aryaal wanted to fight fellow Lemurians. They would, though, if it came to that. He was certain. He just hoped his bluff wouldn't be called—because it wasn't one. Most of those present thought it was, probably even Keje, and he didn't know how they would react if fighting actually began. Just in case, he'd detailed Queen Maraan's Six Hundred as the follow-on force. Unlike the Marines, the Orphan Queen's guard had been reinforced from across the water and actually had six hundred members. Also unlike the Marines, they'd seen their dreams come true when the gates of Aryaal fell. There was no question that they would fight, and the Aryaalans had to know it.

Chack strode ahead of the Marine regiment as it approached the gate with his Krag at port arms. The long bayonet he had been given was fixed, and behind him the Marines formed their shield wall, with spears bristling from it. After what the Arylaans had seen that force do just a day before, this reorganized, grim, and fresh-looking block of warriors must have been a horrifying sight to the dazed and deafened defenders. Not quite halfway there, Chack called his troops to halt when a group of Aryaalans hurried out. They were waving a white flag—just as Rolak had been instructing them to do all morning if they wanted to talk.

Matt lowered his binoculars again with the beginnings of a relieved grin.

"Would you have let them go on?" Keje asked quietly.

Matt looked at him. "For what we have before us? Yes. The stakes are too high."

Keje nodded sadly. "That is what I thought."

"Would you have tried to stop me?"

"No. As you said, the stakes are too high. We must win. I just hope we do not destroy ourselves to accomplish the victory."

Matt nodded his understanding, and together they went forward to treat with the Aryaalans.

"So. Fet-Alcas is dead," noted Safir Maraan with some satisfaction. "Why is it only now they are telling us this?"

Bradford grunted. "Evidently there were . . . irregularities surrounding his demise. Prince Rasik has of course assumed the throne, and they would have us believe that everything, even the delay in speaking to us after the battle, was caused by confusion while they hunted the murderous conspirators."

Matt shook his head. "Sounds awfully Byzantine to me—or Soviet."

Courtney Bradford laughed out loud. "I don't believe we need look to Uncle Joe Stalin for examples of a dirty and complicated rise to power. Our own shared English history is replete enough with those, Captain."

Matt smiled. "I'm Irish American, with a fair measure of Scot. O'Roddy—Reddy—you know."

"Hmm."

They were aboard *Walker,* in the wardroom again, and it was full as usual. They were engaged in an informal discussion of the situation, but nearly every faction was represented, except the Aryaalans, so whatever they decided would have the effect of policy. Nearly two weeks had passed since they blew down the north gate of the city, and in that time Matt had spent precious little time on his ship. He was glad to be home. *Revenge* had sailed with a small squadron of feluccas to scout the enemy and Mallory flew every other day, either probing north toward Singapore or carrying news and people between Aryaal and Baalkpan. So far there was no sign that the Grik intended to renew their offensive. The ragtag remnants of their fleet had gone to ground at Singapore, but no other forces had joined them there. Given everyone's reluctance—the Grik included—to cross the menacingly deep water of the Indian Ocean, it seemed unlikely the enemy would use any other avenue of approach.

Sergeant Alden came to help Shinya integrate the B'mbaadan forces into the AEF. His envy of the Japanese officer regarding his role in the battle had been palpable. He managed to contain it, however, and the burgeoning friendship between the tough Marine and the former enemy lieutenant wasn't in danger. Alden was gone again, but the news from "home" was welcome, and good for the most part. The Baalkpan defenses were strengthening every day and the cottage arms industry was beginning to flourish. Matt knew *Walker* missed all the people they'd left in Baalkpan, Letts most of all, but he was glad the fair-skinned supply officer was there. Letts, Alden, and Brister, together with Karen Theimer, had been working miracles. Besides, with the dame famine still under way, keeping Letts's and Theimer's affair out of the local eye was certainly prudent—even now that they had two more nurses for the guys to ogle. It was one less latch on the pressure cooker. Some tension still existed regarding Silva and Risa's apparently ongoing transspecies relationship and there was little doubt now that they had one. But it now seemed more platonic than anything and few really took it seriously anymore. They were clearly great friends, and ever since captain's mast they hadn't been as blatant about "it" anymore either, whatever "it" was. Both were popular characters—not to mention dangerous—and as long as they maintained a semblance of dignity their "friendship" was ignored beyond the mild humor it inspired. Mostly. Occasionally there were still words.

One "relationship" Matt thoroughly approved of seemed to be flourishing as well. He looked at Queen Maraan with a puzzled expression. "Queen Protector, I just realized you spoke to us in English."

"Yes," she confirmed with a toothy grin and a series of blinks that indicated pleasure. "I spoke . . . Did well?"

"You sure did," Jim Ellis confirmed.

She looked across the table at the commander of the Second Marines. "Chack teach," she explained.

"Well. Yes." Matt arched an eyebrow at the young Lemurian. "He's a remarkable fellow."

"Re-maak-able," said the queen, testing the word.

"The question is," Jim said, returning to the subject, "how long are we going to let Rasik yank our chain? They stopped us from taking them down when they waved the white flag, but nothing's really changed."

"I'm not so sure about that," Matt disagreed. "I haven't really wanted to push things since we're not ready to move yet. But Rasik's announcement that he was king included assurances that Rolak's people were free to leave. He also swore undying loyalty to the cause we're fighting for—"

"Which we know is a lie," interrupted Chief Gray harshly. "Beggin' your pardon, Captain."

"No, you're right, Chief. I'm pretty sure it's a lie. But what can he do? Their little civil war about wiped out the last core of solid warriors in the city. He's in no shape to cause much trouble now even if we do leave him behind. I doubt he'd even be much of a threat to the 'old men and boys' militia Queen Maraan has proposed leaving to defend B'mbaado. Lord Rolak's troops are the only viable Aryaalan infantry left and they could probably retake the city on their own—especially with the new training they've had. Rasik doesn't *want* them back. They're solidly in our corner and they hate him as much as they did his dad. I'm pretty sure he'll make good on letting their families out. Right now he thinks he needs the security of being their 'Protector.'"

"That's not what I mean, Captain. He's been 'protecting' our friends long enough."

"I know, but I don't think we have much to worry about from him for the time being. I hope I'm not underestimating him, but I imagine he'll be too busy sewing up his power base for the foreseeable future to spend much time causing us trouble."

"So, when do we move, Skipper?" Garrett asked from the far end of the green table.

"Spanky says he'll be ready to pull our damaged screw in a couple of days. If it works, he hopes to get *Mahan*'s off by the end of the week and then *Mahan* will leave immediately." He turned to Jim Ellis again. "You ready for sea?"

"Just say the word, Skipper."

"Good. Then if all goes right, we should be ready to resume the offensive in three weeks. I'll want increased recon, of course, and that'll give us plenty of time to finish training up the troops as well. When we move on Singapore, I want to land on it like an avalanche."

"I sure hate to miss it," Ellis grumped. "Seems like *Walker*'s always doing the heavy lifting and *Mahan* gets a pass."

"You call what you went through a pass?" Matt asked derisively. "You were lucky to survive."

"Sure," Jim responded defensively, "but she hasn't been much help in *this* fight. I haven't either."

"Don't worry about it. Get her fixed up and she'll get her chance. Alden took a set of prints back with him and they're going to cast a new screw in Baalkpan." Matt grinned. "He also said there're more volunteers for the 'U.S. Navy' than he could shake a stick at. It won't take long to bring her complement up."

Ellis nodded with a strange expression on his face. He was still not used to that idea. The Asiatic Fleet had a long tradition of employing native auxiliaries to fill out its crews—mostly on the China Station—but "native" had meant something else entirely back then. From what he'd seen, *Walker*'s new destroyermen were more competent than the Chinese coolies he remembered, and a hell of a lot more loyal.

"We take this . . . Sin-Po-Ar . . . war end?" asked the Orphan Queen.

Matt sadly shook his head. "No, Queen Protector. It won't even be the beginning of the end," he said, quoting Churchill. "But it'll be the end of the beginning."

"My God!" exclaimed Bradford. "I wonder what dear Winston would think to hear his words used in this context?"

"I bet he'd find it appropriate," Matt responded thoughtfully. "And pretty familiar too—except I don't really believe the Krauts eat their prisoners."

"Ready to go!" announced Spanky over the intercom at the auxiliary conn on top of the aft deckhouse. His voice was more gruff than usual with repressed tension as he watched the slack go out of the cables that trailed past the propeller guards. A vicious squall had marched across the bay late that morning, threatening to delay the operation. It passed quickly enough, however, leaving the sky bright and clear and the water almost dead calm. Now the only thing marring the otherwise perfect Java day was the customary oppressive heat and humidity—and, of course, the critical nature of the task at hand. *Walker* and *Mahan* had maneuvered into the middle, deepest part of the bay. Now they were poised stern to stern with lines trailing down to *Walker*'s port side shaft support and across to *Mahan*, where they were carefully secured to the propeller they planned to pluck. The low angle was necessary so they would pull the screw straight off, without putting an upward bind on the shafts—not only so the screw would come off easier, but to avoid warping either of the shafts themselves. They needed the deep water so when the propeller came off, it wouldn't plunge down and damage itself on the bottom of the bay. The "practice run" had been a success. That was when they used a reverse arrangement to pull *Walker*'s useless propeller the day before.

Spanky spared an unusual sympathetic glance at Dean Laney, who stood beside the starboard depth-charge rack, shivering, in shock most likely. He was black and blue with bruises, and Silva, just as uncharacteristically, had draped him in a blanket as soon as he came out of the suit. They'd hoped to use a welded-steel cage to lower the machinist into the sea, but there was one problem they just couldn't solve. It had to be tight enough to keep out the smaller flashies, but still let Laney work through it to secure the cables and remove the huge nuts that held the screw in place. Ultimately, they resorted to the ancient technique of passing one of *Big Sal*'s coarse, heavy sails under the hull of the ship and securing it tightly wherever it came in contact. This created a flashy-free pocket for Laney to work. Captain Reddy told them sailing ships had often used the same strategy in shark-infested waters to make repairs, or just to have a place to swim or bathe in safety. It worked like a charm—until the swarming predators figured out something was inside the pocket.

It may have been noise or movement, but even though they sensed nothing edible, they began bumping aggressively against the bulging canvas with their hard, bony heads. Often, of necessity, Laney was right behind it and they very nearly beat him to death. Somehow he managed to finish the job in spite of the pain and terror. Spanky cringed to think what would have happened if any of the blows had broken the skin. Even through his suit, enough blood would have entered the water to drive the damn things nuts.

Now Spanky stood, watching intently as the lines Laney had secured grew taut. Captain Reddy himself stood at the auxiliary conning station, looking over his injured left shoulder with his right hand on the wheel. Now was the critical moment. If the maneuver wasn't performed or the current judged just right, the cables might foul the rudder or the other, turning, screw. Besides that, they had to pull *straight* back. Spanky squinted hard. The line looked good to him.

"Let her buck, Skipper."

Matt nodded, his face a mask of concentration. "Starboard ahead slow," he said to Dowden, who relayed the command to the engine-room throttle station. Almost imperceptibly at first, the distance between the ships began to grow and Matt carefully adjusted the wheel to counteract the thrust of the single screw. Then, in a rush, the cables went completely taut and began to strain against the anchored ship astern. *Walker*'s fantail rose high enough that the prop wash from the starboard screw flashed white on the surface and all forward motion came to a stop. A deep, tired groan emanated from the ship as she strained against her sister.

"Starboard ahead two-thirds!" The frothing wake reappeared at the surface and the vibration increased dramatically. A slight fishtail began to manifest itself and Matt compensated accordingly. Still the screw refused to budge. "Somebody wipe this sweat off my face!" he ordered tersely. It was beginning to run down and burn his eyes. He couldn't do it with his left sleeve since that arm was still immobilized against his chest and he didn't dare let go of the wheel with his right. With nothing else at hand, Dowden sopped at the sweat with his own sleeve.

"Starboard ahead, *flank*!" Matt grated. Dowden looked at him for an instant, but relayed the command. He glanced past the captain at Spanky, who was clearly concerned about the cables, but the engineer only shrugged. The prop wash from the starboard screw erupted into the air, inundating Laney, Silva, and the others who were poised on the fantail with axes, ready to cut the cables. A considerable spray even reached the auxiliary conn. The ship writhed in protest. The rattling groan was so loud now that it wasn't possible to be heard below a scream. For two whole minutes it seemed the ship would tear herself apart while the captain fought the wheel. Smoke from the overworked boilers piled straight up into the still air in spite of the violent expenditure of energy, creating a surreal effect. The crew, human and Lemurian, exchanged worried glances.

"Back her down!" Matt finally yelled. "Two-thirds!"

Slowly, so rudder control could be maintained, the commands came to throttle back. When the engine stopped and the deck grew still, it seemed as if the ship herself was panting with nervous exertion, along with the crew, as steam pressure vented from the stacks.

"That didn't work too good," Matt said with a tired, wry smile. Juan appeared with a carafe of ice water and cups for those on the aft conning station and he received grateful thanks.

"What now, Skipper?" asked Dowden, wiping his mouth and handing his cup back to Juan.

"Well," said Matt, "we tried pliers. Let's see if the old 'door and string' will work."

Slowly, *Walker* eased back until the cables went slack and dipped low into the depths of the bay. More slowly still, until the jackstaffs on the fantails of the two ships were nearly crossed.

"The cables will never bear it," Laney whispered nervously to Silva, standing beside him leaning on the rail. "And if they do, they'll tear the shafts right out of us both."

Silva looked at the machinist's mate and then slapped him on the back of the head.

"Hey . . . !"

"You idiot snipe! You tryin' to jinx us? I guess the Skipper knows what he's doin'! Here, gimme that blanket back!" A short Lemurian ordnance striker named Pak-Ras-Ar, hence of course, Pack Rat, stood behind the pair and Silva threw the blanket at him. "Here, Pack Rat. You have it. I ain't sleepin' under no damn snipe-sweaty blanket!"

Pack Rat held the blanket at arm's length and wrinkled his nose. "Smells mostly like Silva sweat to me," he said.

"Goddamn little hairball."

On the deckhouse, Dowden took off his hat and ran shaking fingers through his greasy hair. The captain's expression was like stone as he calculated the angle. How could he be so calm? What he didn't see was Matt's left hand shaking at his side and the typhoon of acid roiling in his stomach. His right hand was on the wheel, the only thing that kept it still.

"Signal to *Mahan*: Hold on." Matt waited a moment while the message was passed. A high, fluffy cloud passed overhead, dulling the glare of the sun on the water and he looked quickly forward to check the angle of his ship once more.

"Starboard ahead full," he said quietly.

Black smoke chuffed skyward from the aft stacks and *Walker*'s stern crouched down. Vibration quickly built as the old destroyer leaped from the block.

"She's comin' up!" Silva bellowed unnecessarily as the cables raced from the depths once more. Fifty, sixty, seventy yards—the distance quickly grew. There was a hundred yards of cable. Suddenly there came a tremendous, wrenching groan and it felt as if *Walker* had slammed into a wall of rock. Crewmen were thrown to the deck and the bow heaved to port, nearly spinning the wheel out of the captain's hand. Then, as quick as that, *Walker* lunged free and resumed her dash away from *Mahan*.

"All stop!" Matt cried.

Dowden passed the word and then ran to the rail. Below him, Silva and Laney were trying to heave on the line that trailed over the side. "Do we have it?" he shouted down.

"Aye, sir! And it's heavy enough! I hope we didn't yank *Mahan*'s shaft and turbine too!" A cheer built as men and 'Cats picked themselves up and word quickly spread forward.

Dowden pounded the rail in triumph. "Quit fooling around with that line, men. You'll never lift it without a winch!"

"Ain't tryin' to lift it, sir, just want to feel if it hits bottom. We got three hundred feet of line and three hundred twenty feet of water—we think."

Dowden's face grew troubled. "Well . . . let us know."

Walker's momentum bled off until she coasted to a stop about a quarter mile from her anchored sister. At rest, she had a slight list to port, caused by the weight of the screw. Silva was the last to let go of the cable. "Swingin' free and easy, Mr. Dowden," he announced.

Spanky sighed with relief and turned to relay the report from the engine room. "Seals are fine, Skipper. No more water coming in than usual."

"*Mahan* reports the same," Riggs said from behind them as he watched *Mahan*'s signal light with a pair of binoculars. He lowered them to his chest. "Thank God."

Matt nodded, keeping his hand on the wheel so it wouldn't betray him. "Thank Him indeed," he said. "Good work, Mr. McFarlane. Pass the word to all hands: Well done." He grinned. "My mother always used to say it's easier if you just yank it out! Works for teeth, sticker burs, and apparently destroyer screws." There was a round of appreciative chuckles and the crew had begun to cheer again now that they knew the precious propeller was safe.

Spanky gulped another cup of water and hitched his breeches up on his skinny hips. "Now, sir, with your permission, I'll see about landing this fish."

"By all means. Mr. Riggs? Send a message to *Mahan*. I'd be obliged if Captain Ellis would join us this evening." He turned to Juan. "Something special tonight, if you please. I think a celebration is in order."

As night fell, the two destroyers were moored side by side once more, but this time they were snug against the Aryaal dock. Men and Lemurians capered from deck to deck to shore and a party atmosphere reigned on land and sea. Many stopped to gawk at the dingy brown screw that floated aft of the ships, lashed securely to a large raft. Paul Stites was spinning records on Marvaney's phonograph and broadcasting the music on the shipwide comm. Silva had done it for a while, but Stites spelled him so his friend could "cut a rug." On deck, he glanced around for Risa, his usual dance partner, but she was nowhere in sight. He emitted a sonorous belch as though it was a mating call, but there was no response other than nearby laughter. Alcohol was still strictly prohibited on board, but kegs of seep had been tapped on the dock and there was a steady stream of destroyermen and Lemurians going ashore and tanking up before returning to party on the ship. His second (and by captain's decree, last) mug of seep now glowing in his stomach, Silva watched wildly gyrating Lemurian forms try to imitate the dances the Americans showed them. Most gave up and reverted to dances they knew, but it didn't matter. They had the beat.

Silva caught a glimpse of long blond hair leaning on the cowl vent by the engine-room access trunk. He realized with a jolt that it was one of those nurses from *Mahan*. Pam Cross. That was it. She was watching the dancing with an amused expression on her pretty oval face and keeping time to the music with her chin. He suddenly, desperately, wanted to talk to her—just to hear a dame's voice—but for the first time in his life Dennis Silva felt unable to throw a line. Any line. In fact, because of the dame famine, it'd been so long since he'd even *seen* a woman other than the captain's, he wasn't sure he could speak at all.

"What's the matter with you?" he growled at himself. "Just go talk to her. Damn." He sauntered through the dancers and found himself standing beside and slightly behind her. His mouth opened.

"Buzz off, sailor boy," she said over her shoulder. Obviously, she'd noticed his approach. The words came in a harsh Brooklyn accent and were intended to send him slinking away. Instead, a slow grin spread across his face. Everything would be fine now, he thought. If she'd been as sweet as she looked, he probably would have been stuck.

"Hey, doll, that's no way to talk," he said in his best wounded tone. "It's just, you standin' there, you reminded me so much of my girl back home." He feigned a sad, faraway look. "Gone forever, now."

She rolled her eyes and swiveled her head to stare up at him with a mocking expression. She barely came up to his chest. "In the Asiatic Fleet? I bet you haven't had a girl without black hair and dark skin since you came aboard this bucket."

He leered down at her. "My third-grade sweetheart had hair just like you."

She locked an iron-hard stare upon him for a full ten seconds before her stiff facade dissolved into an uncontrolled giggle. "Jeez," she said. "We must be twins."

"The spittin' image," he confirmed. "Wanna dance?"

She shook her head, still smiling. "Can't. You're cute, but I'm not supposed to."

"Cute?!" Silva demanded, puffing out his mighty chest. He stepped back and struck a pose that displayed his massive biceps to good effect. "The Great Dennis Silva is *not* cute!" he bellowed in mock outrage. Those nearby stopped for a moment at the outburst, but quickly recognized one of Silva's playful spectacles.

Pam Cross laughed out loud. "Okay! Okay! So you're a great big hulking stud! But you're still an enlisted stud, and I'm an officer!"

Silva flung himself on his knees at her feet—which still left the top of his head almost even with her chin.

"Aww, c'mon! You're an ensign, right? That's only barely an officer." He leered again. "I'm a gunner's mate . . ." He had to think for a moment. "Second class! That's an *awful lot* of enlisted man!"

She laughed again, and then peered around. "Oh, all right, you big goon! It's not like it matters anymore anyway. What are they gonna do? Throw me out? Come on!"

And Dennis Silva, for a while, was in heaven.

They started out with a rusty jitterbug that might have looked worse, but Dennis wasn't the rusty one; Pam was. It came out all right, though, because Dennis didn't so much as dance with her as pose her while he danced around her. There were hoots of glee for the first couple of dances, until they fell into a third dance—a waltz this time. Inevitably, it was "Ramona" and Stites never should have spun it because it always made the guys misty-eyed at best. At worst . . . a much bruised, sharpened, and put-upon Dean Laney tried to cut in between Silva and Cross.

"Ease up, ape!" he said. "Jeez, you two." He glanced a sidelong appraisal at Pam. "Come up for air! Why don't you spread it around, Ensign?"

This struck Silva *and* Cross as particularly uncalled-for, since they were only, in fact, dancing.

"Ease up yourself, Fatso," Pam snarled at Laney. "I don't belong to you or nobody and I'll dance with who I want."

Laney glared at Silva. "Let her go, Silva. She ain't yours." He smirked. "'Sides, you already got a dame. We all ought'a have a turn."

"What she does ain't up to you, you filthy, stinky, chickenshit snipe. You heard her just fine and if you don't get your rancid, slimy grabbers off her I'll put your greedy eyes in the bilge. You got me? 'Sides, dancin' with you'd be enough to put her off guys at all. The rest of the crew would hang you!"

It was then that Laney swung.

Inasmuch as their frequent bouts usually went to Silva, mostly because of ruthlessness and experience, the two men were physically fairly well matched and Laney's blow landed like a pile driver on Silva's cheekbone, staggering him for the merest instant. It might have even been enough for Laney to finish him on a better day, if Chief Gray's bearlike forearms hadn't descended around him like a tractor tire and held him helplessly immobilized while Silva shook it off.

"Lemme go, goddamn it!" Laney bellowed desperately, wriggling like a mackerel.

"Yeah." Silva smiled at the unexpected opportunity, rejected it, then began to consider it again as his cheek began to sting. "He's got one comin'."

"Break it up!" Gray snarled. He glared at Silva over Laney's madly ducking head, while the taller man took his time, aiming for a shot.

"He cold-cocked me, Bosun," Silva said conversationally. "We didn't even square off."

"Finish it later," Gray growled in a lower tone. "We got problems."

Silva's face went flat. The party continued unabated around them, tinny ragtime strains on the comm replacing the waltz. His eyes flicked to the couple of other faces who had arrived with the Chief and he noticed Chack, Donaghey, and Campeti from *Walker*. Steele and the new 'Cat bosun's mate from *Mahan* were there as well. He sensed a hell of a lot of body language from the humans and the 'Cats.

"I take it these ain't 'officer' problems?" He didn't point out that, as acting exec of *Mahan*, Steele was an officer now. That's not the way it worked.

"If we can keep it that way," Donaghey agreed. Silva looked at Pam Cross, who was watching, wide-eyed. Gray cursed.

"Don't worry, fellas." Pam poked Silva in the ribs with her elbow. "As this big dope just told me, I ain't much of an officer. I can keep a secret."

Gray exhaled. "Right. We need a nurse anyway." He looked around and glared at the few curious faces nearby until the party resumed full force and the small gathering was forgotten.

"Okay, a few at a time, without a word, we'll ease on shore. Meet up by the seep kegs—hell, get another cup, then walk on up to the cemetery."

"What's this all about?" Laney almost whined. Gray had been holding his arms so tight and so long, he was beginning to lose feeling in his hands. Gray let him go, but spun him around.

"I guess you'll find out a lot of things tonight, Machinist's Mate Laney, and you'll keep every goddamn thing to yourself, is that understood? We're trusting you to be a man, but you don't get to be a kid again. Hear?"

Laney was startled, but he didn't hesitate. He knew what he was being asked.

"I won't blow."

There was a fair-sized gathering near the cemetery. Human and Lemurian chiefs and senior NCOs, for the most part, all eerily silhouetted against the star-picked clouds that floated above the American graves. Two Lemurian Marines armed with Krags, sergeants both, glowed in the light of the small fire that burned to illuminate the tattered American flag. The flag would remain under the protection of the Second Marines for as long as it was uncased on this hallowed ground. The fire would also draw distant attention away from what transpired nearby. A few others were armed, too. Russ Chapelle was holding a BAR when he nodded the group through the small cordon to join the others. There were perhaps sixteen all told.

"Campeti'll make sure we're not noticed away from *Walker* for a while," Gray mumbled.

"*Mahan*'s taken care of," agreed Steele.

The two men led the newcomers over the small rise and down onto the beach where *Mahan* had been tied up for most of her stay in Aryaal. She might have never been there, for all the evidence remaining, except for the small shelter that had been erected for Ellis's meetings with the suspicious natives. Sealed now from outside view, the shelter served another purpose.

Gray paused before entering and addressed Pam Cross. "There's two patients in there for you, Ensign. One needs you pretty bad." He paused. "The other won't need you at all, directly, but you might make sure he's not going to bleed to death or pass out before we're through."

Wide-eyed, but less shocked than she expected, Cross nodded and stepped inside. Silva, Chack, and Laney followed.

In one corner of the "tent" was a young female Lemurian. She looked about the size and maturity of one of their "teenage" younglings, although she was dressed as a warrior in one of the Guard regiments. At least she wore the remnants of such garments. She was stripped almost entirely, only her shin greaves held where the lashings had survived the knife. Anywhere else her clothing or armor might have resisted, her fur was matted with blood.

Risa held her like her very own child, sobbing right along with her, stanching the blood that welled from her face and a nearly amputated upper lip. She gave Silva the slightest nod and then her eyes flashed daggers when she glared into the other corner.

Gagged, trussed in leg irons and even bloodier was *Mahan*'s quartermaster's mate second, Al "Jolson" Franklen, and Silva knew they were in a hell of a lot of trouble. Franklen was an ugly bastard, even when his face wasn't beaten nearly off, but he'd always enjoyed a degree of popularity because of his uncanny Al Jolson imitations. Sometimes when a bunch of the ships were in Cavite, he'd even put on blackface and stage a show. Do it up right. Some of the other fellas might throw in and it was better than a movie. Usually.

Sometimes it got ugly.

The thing was, in the Asiatic Fleet, the men were steeped in the diversity of centuries of empire and trade. It was not a real "melting pot" in the American sense of the word, but the men were in constant contact with Chinese, Filipinos, Malays, Arabs, Javanese, Indians . . . And that was just in the cities. Almost every island had its own distinctive culture. Regardless how they felt about them, eventually they at least got *used* to the locals. Even the most hard-core racist sometimes found his prejudices at least tempered to some degree, if not washed away entirely. Until the Japs came.

But Franklen wasn't like that. He was a Kard-Karrying Klansman from Michigan who thought the U.S. should have thrown in with the Nazis—at least until the Japanese bombed Pearl Harbor. As far as he was concerned, only white humans were even people. Now with the dame famine, the booze, the party—and the fact the *Mahans* hadn't had near the contact with Lemurians that the *Walkers* had—Al "Jolson" Franklen had gone and done something he was probably going to have to die for.

They should have been more on the lookout for something like this. Silva reflected guiltily that he might even have contributed to it, but it made no difference. The unthinkable had happened. Sexual assault had been perpetrated upon a Lemurian by a human, and somehow, tonight, they had to sort it out.

It was obvious to Silva what was going on. They couldn't report it. By morning, in the aftermath of the "great party," news of the atrocity would spread. The captain would come down like the end of the earth, but the damage would already be done. Lemurian females did not ordinarily give their favors indiscriminantly, Silva's real relationship with Risa notwithstanding. And that's what they were: *favors.* Jealously guarded and given with care. They would not be *taken,* any more than from a human female. That they had been—and so brutally—could breed resentment and hate. This one would have to stay with the chiefs—if they could keep it that way. Possibly nothing less than the alliance, and maybe even the war, was at stake. All because of one selfish, perverted, racist bastard.

A lot was up to the girl. They'd allowed Pam a few minutes to assemble a bag and without even a glance at Franklen she rushed to the young victim and began a quick, softly murmured examination. As she and Risa began to ask quiet questions, the grim-faced men turned to the prisoner. Chack crouched beside him in the sand, resting his chin on his cutlass guard, staring at him from inches away, his inscrutable eyes somehow radiating malice.

"Pull his gag," Gray instructed. He looked at Chack. "If he does anything but quietly answer questions, kill him." He peered hard into Franklen's eyes. "You got that? You answer questions and keep a civil tongue, you might just survive this night."

In spite of himself, Franklen snorted and blood bubbled from his shattered nose. The Bosun shrugged and nodded at Donaghey, who yanked out the nasty, bloody rag.

Franklen coughed and spat for several minutes before his spasm subsided enough that he might be understood. Finally he spoke.

"You gonna kill me any-ay, Chee. You ne'er 'iked me." Black blood and wrecked lips made him almost unintelligible.

"Not so. I thought you were funny as hell. When you're made-up, you're not near as ugly. You can act and talk as much like Al Jolson as anybody I ever seen, and you can tell the funny stories like he can. You just wouldn't leave well enough alone. Hell, a lot of the coolies and Filipino guys got treated like crap for days after one of your shows. Not to mention the mess attendants." He snorted. "Besides, I got news for you: you can't whistle and you can't sing . . . and your big Hollywood role model—who loaned you the only popularity you ever had—is a Jew!"

"Das a damn lie!"

Gray rolled his eyes.

"An for de others," Franklen went on, "they was just lyin' Tagalog Bastards. Flips. Like Nigras back home. Takin' jobs in de fact'ries from hardworkin' white men just 'cause they'd work for less." He looked around and sneered as best he could. "And now these goddamn 'Cats puttin' on airs like real destroyermen. Real soljers!"

Gray slapped him hard. He couldn't help himself.

"Like real people, you mean? You don't even think of 'em like that, do you? You figure you can just have your way with one like one of your farm animals back home. Is that about the size of it?"

Franklen stared at him defiantly. "You're one to talk." His tiny eyes squinted around. "All of you, I bet." They fell at last on Silva. "And you most of all, you 'Cat-lovin' traitor!"

Gray and Donaghey almost weren't quick enough to stop Silva from drawing the long bayonet at his side and ramming it into the top of Franklen's head. Chack stood up, though, and watched Silva's reaction with interest—as well as that of his sister, who came partly uncoiled from around the victim Pam was tending. With both a shudder and a sense of wonder, he realized their "carrying on" couldn't be quite entirely a joke after all. Whatever it was, he was certainly getting a major contrast lesson in Silva and Risa's relationship as opposed to others that were possible.

"We can't get anywhere with him." Donaghey sighed emotionlessly. "He just don't get it."

"I'll get through to him," Silva said softly, resheathing his bayonet and dropping to his knees in the sand. The two 'Cats who'd been holding Al fought his struggles, but were replaced by Laney on one arm and Chack on the other. For quite some time, Silva stared across the tent at the intensity of the eyes that glowed back at him from the females. One was filled with a murderous passion and the other . . . similar, but with a measure of devastation he'd seen only once before. In the belly of *Revenge* when they took the ship from the Grik and rescued the "provisions" there. He'd never been the sensitive sort and he'd used women like toys himself, but this . . . He almost felt ashamed to be a man. And to add a measure of icy mercury to his shame and his resolve, it suddenly dawned on him that this was the first time he'd ever seen a Lemurian teenage female seem just like a vulnerable, devastated, teenage girl. He was filled with a smoldering rage like he'd never known. Pam's frequent glances in his direction weren't much different from those of the Lemurians.

"I'll tell you something, Al. I like these 'Cats. A hell of a lot better than I like you. And I do think of 'em as 'people.' Hell, maybe even human. They're a lot more human than you are; that's a fact. I've fought with 'em and worked with 'em and spilled my blood alongside 'em. We've helped them and they've helped us." He pointed at the crumpled child. "I don't recognize her after what you done, but I bet I've fought alongside her!" He looked intently at Franklen. "The way I hear it, you never fought alongside anybody. Why don't you tell us what you've done for 'us humans' since we got here, Al, 'cause by all accounts, it ain't much. You supported Kaufman's mutiny against Mr. Ellis, and look how many died because of that . . ."

"Pardoned," Franklen gummed, but Silva went on.

"Let's see, how many battles *have* you fought against the Griks that are swoopin' down? You'll at least agree they're worse than 'Cats, won't you?" There was no response. Dennis started counting on his fingers.

"Well, let's see. I seen—helped—the 'Cats fight like hell to save *Big Sal* from a gob as big as the one Mr. Ellis fought through. Which you was in the brig waiting for Captain Kaufman to come back aboard if what I hear is true. Skipped that one, didn't you? Even stayed in the brig as 'insubordinate' the whole time the ship was laid up here and made no effort to give a hand."

"We were screwed, Silva, you dumb son of a bitch! Just look around yourself! The stupid 'Cats around here wouldn't talk to us. They didn't even care about the Griks until it was too late. All they cared about was fightin' each other." He spat a gobbet of blood. "Ellis weren't no officer. He couldn't get anything sorted out between 'em. And I did too agree to work on the ship."

"You agreed to work on the ship—for a pardon," Gray glowered, "because the ship was so shorthanded. Mr. Ellis should'a hung you. Instead, your skipper *forgave* you and let you loose. Figgers 'let bygones be bygones and we're all together now.' My God, after seeing that field in front of the city how could you *think* anything else? But you sat out the battle on shore. Again. Even when it started to fall apart and everybody went to fight."

Silva raised his eyebrows. "So on top of everything else, you really are a coward." He shook his head. "Except where little girls are concerned. All you could think of, the first time nobody's really watchin' you, was grabbin' up some . . . child and tearin' her up like that. What were you gonna do next? You couldn't have let her live."

There was a sharp intake of breath and suddenly everyone in the tent knew Silva was right.

"Nah, Silva," Franklen gushed. "It wasn't like that! I wouldn't'a really hurt her . . . I just wanted a piece—like you got!"

Risa practically leaped across the distance separating them and grabbed him by the hair in iron claws.

"Silva no have 'piece,' you piece of *shit*!" Her glare moved to encompass her brother as well. "He have *friend*. We make big joke, scare Chack. Scare Captain too, have big laugh . . . but we more than friends too." Now she was talking directly to her brother. "Okay with you, the Captain." She glanced at Pam. "Or anybody, that's fine. Not okay?" She blinked sublime unconcern. "Still okay with Risa."

"Now see," Franklen whined, "I got no problem with that! That's what—" He was almost dead before Silva and Chack could pull Risa off him and move her back across the tent.

Gray, Donaghey, Laney, and Steele were kneeling over the unconscious form as if deciding what to do with a dead snake, when Silva and Chack returned. Silva didn't come right out and say "Sorry about that," but his body language did. He did apologize for "using up all the air so far."

"Hell. You just said what everybody was thinking," said Gray. "Make no mistake. This is a trial. He's admitted what he done, and you pointed out it would have been a lot worse if he hadn't got caught."

"Who caught him, anyway?"

"Steele. Sheer luck. He was runnin' a final check before he went on deck for the party and heard her cries. Damn, he's got good ears! Franklen had her down in *Mahan*'s steering engine room to show her the 'machines.' Hell, they can't resist that. It's like offerin' 'em candy."

Silva felt another uncharacteristic twinge of guilt.

"How much of me and Risa 'Carrying on' mighta, you know, contributed?"

Several faces became unreadable.

"I don't reckon any," said Gray at last. "For one thing, nobody really knew *what* you were up to, and I guess we still don't. I'd just as soon keep it that way. 'More than just friends' can mean anything. Outside this tent, they still won't know that much." His eyes bored into Laney's. "Besides, whatever it was, it sure wasn't . . ." He spit on Franklen as the man groaned and began to come to. "Like this."

"So," Chack said at last, "what shall we do with this creature?" For the first time in a long time, he didn't appear to be thinking about Silva when he said the word "creature." Maybe he'd started to think over what his sister and friend had said—or maybe their "relationship" had finally been put in perspective for him. "We've already decided we can't make an example of him, which is actually a shame. There are more than a few of my people who don't think of humans as 'people' either."

"That's changing fast enough. We've spilled enough blood together. Besides, most of the ones who feel that way are on the other side of that wall, yonder, or they've run off." Franklen was fully conscious again when Gray finished. "And pretty soon, there'll be one less of ours who feels like that."

"Let's ask the girl," Laney suddenly blurted. They were the first words he spoke. Donaghey nodded.

"Yeah. Let's see what she wants to do with him." Franklen began to thrash and moan, but the bloody gag went back in his mouth and Chack and Laney held him again. Having made the suggestion, Laney was more than willing to let others carry it out. The last thing he wanted to do, in his heart of hearts, was speak to a teenage rape victim of any species.

She looked better as they approached her. She was covered now, by what must have been clean linens from the ship. The blood had been cleaned from her fur and in its place was the viscous healing paste. Pam was still gently applying stitches to her lip, but she didn't seem to notice any pain. Silva was uncomfortably aware that, like "Tabby," the 'Cat "snipe" the Mice had taken on as apprentice, or whatever, this one was young and, well . . . stacked. After so long without female companionship, it was easy to understand how passions could flare. But rape was rape.

"She speak English?" Gray asked. A small, dark-furred head briefly nodded.

"Surprisingly well," Pam said, glaring at the prisoner. "Most of the Baalkpan Lemurians I've met, and the ones from *Big Sal* too, are all pretty talkative. Kind of like they *want* to be *our* friends."

Franklen spit out his gag. "The nastiest cur-dog will lick your hand before it bites it off!" He began to scream before he was silenced again.

"Shut up, you!" Gray roared loud enough that Silva was half convinced they'd hear him on the ships. Gray turned back to face the Lemurian and when he spoke again, his voice was softer than butter. Dennis's mouth hung open, shocked by the Bosun's transformation into something so . . . unsuspected.

"What's your name, child?" he asked.

"Blas-Ma-Ar," she whispered. "*Nerracca*, Body of Home clan." She straightened slightly. "Striking for the Second Marines. I was in the square," she added proudly. Gray smiled.

"I happen to know the acting CO of the Second Marines and I'll have a word with him this very night."

The young female's facial fur stood out in a 'Cat blush when she looked over at Chack. Gray's voice became more serious. "Now, all that aside, a man's life is at stake. I've heard about all I want to hear out of him, but you have to tell me your side of the story."

Blas hesitated and Pam and Risa practically melded into her with their caresses and reassurances.

"It will be difficult," she said in a distant voice.

"I know, sweetie," Gray whispered back. "I know."

When she was finished, Gray nodded. It was about what he expected. It was also very detailed and disturbing. Since Lemurians had virtually no concept of modesty, no detail was left to his imagination and since, conversely, Blas-Ma-Ar (he'd taken to thinking of her as Blossom) had experienced the assault much like any teenage human girl might, with the same outrage, terror, and even guilt, Gray found himself controlling his killing rage with difficulty. He looked at Franklen and was surprised to see him dozing. Oh, well. He looked back at the "girl." No, "girl" wasn't right even before tonight. She was a proven warrior who'd fought for her people. More than Al Franklen ever really had.

"You understand why we have to keep this between ourselves for now?" he asked gently and she nodded. "People *will* know, and it won't happen again. But word will spread slowly and it will add power to the words. That's why we have to do things like this sometimes."

"Captain no have power for this?"

Gray shook his head. "No, sweetie. The captain has *too much* power for this right now. His anger would overcome everything else, and then others would get mad, and others, until everything was just about this. We might even forget to fight the Grik. You don't want that."

"No," she whispered softly. "I don't want anything like that. I want to be a Marine." She paused, looking at Franklen, who had awakened and was looking back. "And I want to eat his eyes."

Donaghey glanced at his watch. "Whatever we do, and whatever she eats, we better get on with it. Sooner or later *some* officer is going to figure out there's a hell of a lot of Indians running around without any chiefs to tell 'em what to do."

"Right," agreed Gray. "Call 'em in and we'll sort this out."

Except for Russ Chapelle and the Lemurian Marines, everyone else managed to squeeze in the tent. They made solicitous comments as they passed by "Blossom," but had only hard stares for their former shipmate.

"We ain't gonna have no jury," Gray said. "The 'accused' was caught in the act, admitted what he done, and invited Mr. Steele to 'get some' himself. No one has since heard him deny he raped and brutalized one of our young female allies. He *is* guilty, so I won't even call for a vote. The only thing we have left to decide is punishment."

Steele sighed. "We're kind of in the same boat there. There's only one punishment for what he did, and he probably would've done worse before he was finished."

"I never figured chiefs had so much power," Laney whispered. "This ain't in the book!"

"No, it ain't," Gray growled. "There're lots of things that ain't in the book. This world we've wound up in, for one. But chiefs have always 'handled' things." Gray looked at Donaghey. "And this ain't the first time we handled somethin' like this. Sometimes problems just have to go away and Franklen's turned himself into one of those problems tonight. With all that's at stake, we can't dump this on the captain."

"It will even look better from our point of view," confirmed Chack, speaking very close to Franklen's ear, "if news of this . . . event comes forward over time. It will show your people honor your leader and the alliance, but you also honor a youngling's virtue enough not to wait until the 'time is right' to sort things out." Blossom bristled at the "youngling," but Chack blinked reassuringly. "You are still a youngling—I am scarcely beyond that myself—but you are also a Marine."

"So, how are we gonna do it?" Silva asked, ever practical and to the point. "I'd kinda' like to get some more dancin' in before the party winds down."

"We can't shoot him, for obvious reasons," Donaghey mused.

"Easiest thing is to take him down to the water and just throw him in. Let the flashies have him," said Silva. "Where'd ol' Al Jolson go? Hell if I know. Musta' got drunk that night at the propeller party and fell in the water. Yeah, seen him swipin' everybody's half-empty seep cups when they was dancin'. Serves the bastard right."

Gray looked thoughtful. "Say, that's just how we'll work it. You're a fiend, Silva, but you're a pretty good acting chief so far."

Throughout this exchange, Franklen was unable to speak, but his eyes had begun to move rapidly back and forth. They were talking about killing him, right in front of him, matter-of-factly, like he wasn't even there.

"You— You can't do that!" protested Laney. Franklen leaned against him in relief and began to sob.

"What do you mean?" Gray asked menacingly. Laney gulped, but didn't look away.

"I mean, kill him, sure. The bastard deserves it." He shivered and held the quivering form farther away. "But don't throw him in the water alive. And"—he looked almost apologetically at Blossom—"don't let her eat his eyes."

"Don't worry. We won't throw him in the water alive, and that girl is sure not gonna eat his eyes. We've got rules during these illegal get-togethers, Laney. That's the thing that makes us different from the Grik and from guys like Al. We've got rules of decency, of honor to follow, even when we're breaking the rules of the Navy. And it's because we take those rules so seriously that we're breaking them in the first place. To protect the honor of our Navy, our ships and our people. See?"

"So how *are* we gonna kill him? We ain't gonna hang him—not in here," Silva persisted. "I don't mean to sound all insensitive, but the bastard's gotta die, and we prob'ly oughta' quit sankoin' along."

"He's right," said Steele. "Let's get on with it. Lots or volunteers?"

"Oh, for cryin' out loud," said Silva in an exasperated voice. "Somebody draws a short straw, or long straw, you gonna *make* 'em kill him, Frankie? What if he can't do it? Whoever kills him is gonna have to use their hands. What if they ain't strong enough? Might as well sell tickets for that." He turned to Laney.

"Would you like to kill him, Dean?"

Surprised, Laney looked around, then looked at the ground. Anywhere but at the prisoner or his victim. "No, Dennis, as a matter of fact I wouldn't. Not in cold blood. I'll do it, but I wouldn't like to." He looked up. "I guess I just ain't the killer you are."

"Few are," agreed Silva equably. "Thing is, I shouldn't have to kill him either, even though, for reasons of my own, I'd really kind of like to. But we all been told a chief's job is to lead. Well, we're all of us chiefs, or acting chiefs or petty officers now, but some are higher than others. I been here before, even if I never got The Hat, but I never could keep it because I didn't want the responsibility." He walked over and looked Gray in the eye. "A *lot* of responsibility comes with that chief's hat. You got time in grade on everybody. You're 'in charge.' Maybe Frankie outranks you now, but there ain't no officers here. Right here, right now, you're it. So lead, Bosun. You either got to pick somebody to do it or you have to do it yourself."

After a long moment, Gray nodded. "You would'a had The Hat a long time ago, Silva, if you weren't such a maniac. Come on, we'll do it together."

With Laney and Chack still each on an arm, Silva grabbed the burly quartermaster's mate around the chest. Wide-eyed, he struggled and moaned through his gag.

"I'll pull this gag and let you have some last words if you'll keep 'em quiet and decent," Gray offered. Franklen went slack. Taking this as a sign he agreed, Gray pulled the bloody rag. Instantly, Al began screaming at the top of his lungs. Gray grabbed his head and began to twist and the screams abruptly ceased.

"You hear that kind of weird crackin' sound, Al? Sounds like it's right under your skull? Just grunt if you do." Franklen made a noncommittal sound. In Fitzhugh Gray's very best Al Jolson voice (which wasn't half bad) he spoke the real Al Jolson's signature line: "You ain't heard *nothin'* yet!"

Rasik-Alcas, King and Protector of Aryaal, paced back and forth before the large arched window, his rich, supple gown flowing as he walked. Barely visible in the distance beyond the north wall, bonfires, lighted ships, and muffled sounds of merriment goaded him into a dangerous, seething rage.

"Yes, my Lord King Protector," confirmed Lord Koratin with a nervous glance, "the invaders revel."

"Why?" Rasik snapped.

Koratin bowed his head. "I am not sure, lord. Some needed repair, long delayed, is the word I hear. We have few spies among them yet." Rasik-Alcas began to scold his senior and currently only advisor for taking so long to build a network of informants, but he hesitated. Lord Koratin represented one of the oldest houses in Aryaal, and the creature was politically savvy. He was urbane, vain, and quick to take offense—but fear would prevent him from challenging his new king. For now. Rasik was fairly sure that Koratin harbored firm suspicions as to how Fet-Alcas had died, but for now the Aryaalan noble seemed willing to let the matter stand, and even to help. It made Rasik uncomfortable to rely on Koratin for anything, particularly anything critical to his consolidation of power, but he had no choice. "Perhaps when their repairs are complete, they will go away," Koratin speculated.

Rasik growled. "Of course they will—to fight the Grik."

Koratin blinked. "Then that is good! They will be gone from here and things will become as before." He paused. "We are weakened, true, but we can stand against B'mbaado. In time—"

"No!" shouted Rasik. "Don't you see? As long as they war against the Grik, they will have a presence here! They will never go away as long as the war continues!"

"Is that so terrible? What if the Grik return?"

"Return?" Rasik snorted. "With what?" He gestured eastward. "Have you not seen the carrion beyond our walls? Mere bones now, but the bones of *thousands*! It will be generations before those losses are made good." He shook his head. "No, the Grik menace is gone. They won't return in our grand-younglings' lifetimes."

Koratin was not so sure. He proceeded carefully. "I have heard it said they are not like us—in more ways than are obvious. They breed quickly and their kingdom is vast. Some say they are the Demons of Old, come to harry us again, and what they sent here is but a tithe against what they are capable of."

"Nonsense! You really should let your females tell stories to your young." Koratin's devotion to his younglings was no secret, and he often recited tales to them—and others—in open forum. He enjoyed perform-ing, and while he recognized his own failings, he secretly hoped he could atone to some degree by telling tales of real virtue and clear morals to the young. "You begin to believe your own fables," Rasik accused. Koratin remained silent. "As long as the sea folk war against the Grik, we won't be rid of them," Rasik repeated, returning to the subject at hand. He resumed pacing, deep in thought. Then he stopped. "But what if the war was over?"

"What do you mean, Lord King?"

Rasik's eyes had become predatory slits. "Tell me, Lord Koratin. Do you think those silly sea folk would have the courage to fight without the iron ships?"

"No, Lord King," Koratin answered honestly.

"Do you believe they'd even consider carrying on without them?" Koratin felt a chill.

"No, Lord King," he whispered.

Rasik barked a horrible laugh. "So simple!" he said and resumed his pacing, but for the rest of the evening, his mood was much improved.

Courtney Bradford was drunk again. His civilian status and eccentric behavior outside the chain of command were still tolerated, as long as he didn't push it. Sometimes he did, usually by covertly exceeding the strict limitation on alcohol intake. He sat in one of the chairs around the ward-room table idly fingering a freshly stripped Grik skull, retrieved from the battlefield, while Juan Marcos and Ray Mertz cleared the dishes left by the dinner party. It had been a fine meal, mostly Americanized local fare, but a few purely native dishes had been presented. Bradford wasn't accustomed to the unusual Lemurian spices and, for the most part, he just stuck to salt. At least salt hadn't changed, thank God. His morbid trophy hadn't elicited the excitement he expected when he flourished it at the beginning of the meal. He'd been politely but firmly asked to place it out of sight until everyone had eaten.

Now, most of the diners had returned to their duties or joined the party on deck, leaving only the captain, Sandra, Jim, Keje, and Bradford himself. Without fanfare, the grisly thing reappeared upon the table. "This is the face our own world would have taken if whatever killed the dinosaurs . . . hadn't," Bradford announced muzzily, interrupting the conversation at the other end of the table.

"Probably," Matt agreed. They'd had this talk before. He began to re-sume his conversation with Jim.

"But have you considered," Bradford plowed on, "that maybe this is the way it *should* have been? Just look at this thing!" he demanded. "Simi-lar brain capacity, large eyes, wicked, wicked teeth! Obviously a far better-adapted natural predator than we!" The rest of the group reluctantly turned their attention to the Australian. He was on a roll, and even drunk, whatever he said was bound to be interesting.

"Well, there's no doubt they're intelligent," agreed Ellis grudgingly, "and they're certainly better fighters on land than at sea. I don't see how that makes them 'better natural predators' than us. We beat them."

"Ah," said Bradford, controlling a belch, "but we beat them with our minds, not our bodies. Only superior technology won the day, in the end. Consider: as far as we know, humanity has not risen on this world. We may be its only poor representatives. Where we come from, man is the greatest predator, but here that's not the case. Here"—he tapped the skull—"this creature—or similar races—might predominate all over the globe." He shifted his bleary stare to Keje. "Even on the islands that the People control, there are Grik, are there not? You've said so yourself." He paused. "We've seen them," he remembered. "Primitive, aboriginal, but plainly related to the more sophisticated enemy we face." Keje nodded, peering intently at the man.

"What's your point, Mr. Bradford?" Sandra asked quietly. The Australian's fatalistic tone was giving her the creeps.

"It's quite simple, my dear. We all, myself included, have from the beginning considered the world we came from to be the 'normal' one—the 'right' one—and this world the aberration." He blinked. "No offense, my dear Captain Keje." The Lemurian blinked acknowledgment. "But if you compare just the sheer physical lethality, there's no way we humans would ever have evolved to become 'top dog,' as you Americans so aptly put it, if these creatures had anything to say about it—" His belch finally escaped. "Back home, that is. Here, we would have been an evolutionary impossibility . . . excuse me, please."

"But what about the 'Cats?" asked Matt. Bradford shrugged.

"They apparently evolved more recently, in an isolated environment—Madagascar, I am quite sure. Two sentient species rising independently, but necessarily separate or it could never have taken place." He stared at the skull. "At least I don't think so. I'm convinced that my poor, lost Fritzi—a standard poodle—was more intelligent than most people I've met." He shook his head. "In any event, the existence of Lemurians in no way alters my thesis. They are dodos."

"What is a Do-Do?" Keje asked.

"A large, flightless bird that looked quite a lot like a skuggik." Bradford beamed. Keje started to rise from his chair, his tail rigid with indignation.

Matt put a hand on his shoulder and whispered, "He's drunk, my friend, and he means no insult." Then he continued in a louder voice. "Dodos were birds, as he described. I can't remember where they lived—"

"Mauritius," Bradford supplied. "Not too dreadfully far from Madagascar, in fact." He blinked. "How odd!"

"Anyway," Matt resumed, "dodos lived on an island with no natural predators and they thrived despite being extremely vulnerable creatures. When humans discovered the island, several hundred years ago, they were killed for food. To make matters worse, some animals, livestock animals called hogs, escaped and went wild—destroying the eggs and nests of the dodos. Soon, they were extinct."

"I have heard this word, 'extinct.' It means 'rubbed out,' 'gone,' correct? That's what the Grik mean to do to us." Keje turned back to the Australian and fixed him with a hard, expressionless stare. "If that is the case, then what are you Amer-i-caans? Dodos too, you think? No. We are not this stupid bird that couldn't fly. We can fly. We *did*! We flew to safety when the Grik came to destroy us and we've not lost our wings! One day, we'll fly back to our nest, across the Western Sea, and it will be the Grik who are extinct. Not us!"

Tsalka stared at General Esshk in abject disbelief. "Impossible!" he gasped.

"Impossible indeed. But true." Esshk himself still seemed shaken by the news. They were standing on the quarterdeck of the *Giorsh,* flagship of the fleet. Above them a bright, loosely woven awning fluttered in the mild breeze. It reduced the glare but still allowed the warming rays of the sun to wash upon them. It was also the only thing on the entire ship that wasn't painted a bright, sparkling white. Tsalka often took his late-days beneath the awning on the quarterdeck even though it was inconvenient for the crew to rig. He had no command authority, having accompanied the fleet on a lark, but he was the highest-ranking Hij in the Eastern Empire and if his comforts caused annoyance, no one dared to say. A short time earlier, a dispatch vessel from the New Conquest had closed the flagship to report. A report that General Esshk had just related.

"All of them?"

Esshk hissed a negative. "Not all, Lord Regent . . . but most. A few made their escape to the New Conquest and not all fell prey. Some were not involved and managed to avoid the hunt—a simpler thing on a ship. Those that did fall prey have already been destroyed."

Tsalka paced the width of the quarterdeck, stunned. "An entire Pride-Pack of hunters made prey!" he whispered.

"Not all—" began Esshk.

Tsalka waved a clawed hand impatiently. "As near as makes no difference! It was bad enough when the hunting-pack fell prey, but *this*!"

"We often lose ships, Lord Regent."

"Lone hunters!" Tsalka snapped. "Scouts! Victims of the sea, as often as not. A Pride-Pack has not been lost to prey . . . ever!"

"We have lost that many and more to other hunters, sire, while we still considered them prey."

Tsalka glared at the general. "You have spoken thus before, I recall. Have a care." He hissed a sigh. "What is the world coming to when prey do not know their proper place?" He shook himself. "What caused the calamity this time? How did the Tree Prey resist?"

"The same as before, sire," Esshk replied. "They had the aid of the smoking ship."

Tsalka turned to face him. "I did not think to hear of it again. If Righ yet lived I would give him the liar's death!"

"Perhaps he did not know. It was the report of others that he passed."

"All the same," Tsalka mused, "I should probably destroy his mates when we return." He resumed his pacing, but stopped near the rail. Beyond it, the sea was covered with red-hulled ships as far as the eye could see. Here and there were the white hulls of generals. Far away to the east and west were the lands that bordered their path. The drawings of the world called it the Malacca Strait. The sight stirred him in spite of his elevation. He knew he shouldn't concern himself, but it was an inauspicious beginning, this latest tale of disaster. He consoled himself that in the end it would scarcely matter. Nothing could stand before the Grand Swarm.

What difference would it make if the contemptible Tree Prey had allied themselves with some Worthy Prey? It would only make the hunt more exciting. With an amused hiss, he glanced far astern, where the "new" hunters that had joined the Grand Swarm struggled to keep pace. He knew little about them; their language was unspeakable, but they were fearsome hunters. They were so like his tail-less pet—Kaufman—in form, and yet different enough that they could not be the same race regardless they both used iron ships. They were different enough that his pet was terrified of them, clearly natural enemies. That was the main reason he had given his pet to them as a gift, and he still remembered the shrieks as they carried it away.

He turned to face forward and rejoined General Esshk. What if the Tree Prey did have strange new friends? So did the Grik.

T he day after the party, just as the forenoon watch came on, Matt and Sandra stood on the starboard bridgewing alone. He wasn't sure exactly when the nurse had achieved unlimited bridge access, but by now it was a fait accompli. She never abused the privilege, but nobody ever questioned her when she arrived. Others lined the starboard side as well. From his vantage point, Matt saw Silva leaning against the rail next to the number two gun. On his face was an uncharacteristically thoughtful expression as he stared out to sea. Beside him, Paul Stites made some kind of crack about Silva's "dame running off" and the big gunner's mate didn't even respond. *Strange,* Matt thought, wondering what that was about.

He looked into the east and watched *Mahan*'s distant shape steaming down the bay toward the island gate that led to the Java Sea. To have searched for her so long, only to have her leave once they found her, left him with mixed emotions. It was different this time, though, wasn't it? She would return in a couple of months and rejoin her sister, wherever that might be. By then she'd be a different ship. Better, with a full and willing crew. She would finally become an asset instead of a liability, and together again, the two old destroyers would sweep the Grik from the sea. His optimism couldn't stop him from worrying, though. They'd made her as fit for sea as they could, under the circumstances, but she was still in sorry shape and she was still shorthanded. Even more so this morning, since Jim had actually reported a man missing. He was known as a malcontent malingerer and chances were he'd turn up in a day or so. Where could he go?

Matt suddenly realized that Sandra's small, soft hand had found its way into his own. Clearing his throat, he released her fingers so he could ostentatiously adjust his hat. He glanced around, but the bridge watch all seemed preoccupied with their duties.

"It's hard to watch them go," Sandra murmured beside him. He nodded. To the south and east, the sky was clear and the harsh glow of the morning sun touched the wave tops with fire. To the north, however, the sky seemed smeared with a muddy brush. He stepped away from Sandra, heading toward the opposite wing, glancing up through the windows as he walked, until he saw the sky beyond the city in the west-northwest. Across the horizon, a great black mass was forming, as dark as the blackness of night. Wispy stringers of gray and white crawled across it like snakes, or worms. In spite of the morning heat, he felt a chill as Sandra joined him.

"Keje said this was the stormy time of year," he whispered nervously.

"What's that?" she asked.

"Something bad."

Rick Tolson was having the time of his life. He'd always loved the sea—even as a kid, having run away aboard a fishing schooner when he was ten. He hadn't enjoyed that life, to be honest, but it taught him a lot about the sea and sails and how to be a man. When he returned as a prodigal son, his father arranged for him to spend the summers with the crew of a sixty-five-foot racing yacht named *Bee* that belonged to a wealthy Chesapeake-area business associate of his. All through high school, the summers found Rick converting the wind into raw speed. While other kids his age worked at gas stations and soda fountains, he got paid (a meager salary) to play, racing against the other sleek playthings of the rich.

He learned everything, and by the time he went to college he'd commanded *Bee* in several high-stakes races and won, always against newer and faster competitors. In college he didn't have much time for racing, since he took summer classes as well, but he always had a place aboard the *Bee* when he went home on weekends. He also joined the Naval Reserve Officer Training Corps—against his father's wishes—and that was how he'd wound up here. He was glad.

Not in his wildest boyhood fantasies had he imagined that a Navy life would put him in command of what was, for all intents and purposes, a square-rigged frigate. Like Stephen Decatur, Isaac Hull, or Porter before Valparaiso, he was living the life of his childhood heroes with the greatest assignment any frigate captain could ask for: independent command. It was a fantasy come true, and he was loving every minute of it. *Revenge* was fast—by Lemurian standards—and surprisingly well made considering her builders. The Grik had taken her draft directly from the lines of the stout, fast-sailing British East Indiamen, and it was obvious now that they'd captured one centuries before and used it as a pattern—scaled up or down—ever since. *Revenge* had one major difference, of course. She was armed with twenty guns. More a ship-sloop than a frigate, in the old scheme of things, where a ship's class was reckoned by how many guns she carried, but "frigate" sure sounded better.

Rick's crew was entirely Lemurian, with the exception of an ordnance striker named Gandy Bowles, fresh off of *Mahan*, who'd been jumped to "master gunner." The rest of the crew couldn't love their ship, remembering constantly what she represented. Despite everything they did to eliminate it, the cloying scent of her previous owners and what they'd done aboard still lingered, and that didn't help. They loved the *idea* of her, however, and they were ecstatic about what she could do. She was faster and more maneuverable than the stolid, plodding Homes—and faster than any other Grik ship they'd encountered. They'd encountered several. Rick remembered each action with a warm glow of excitement. All had been stragglers or scouts and showed no concern as *Revenge* drew near. She was one of theirs, wasn't she? All were destroyed.

Revenge's speed was due primarily to some innovative rig improvements that Rick and his crew came up with, and he liked to think his racing background helped. Also, in spite of her guns, she wasn't as heavy as other Grik ships. Her crew was smaller and she didn't carry a regiment of warriors and their supplies everywhere she went. That might be a problem if the enemy ever grappled, but so far, *Revenge* had destroyed her surprised victims from beyond the range of even the enemy's shipboard bomb throwers. Whatever the reasons for her success, *Revenge* had been a wolf on the prowl for the better part of three weeks now, earning her name in spades, and the enemy had no idea she was even there. Rick felt like Robert Louis Stevenson had written this part of his life and he couldn't wait to see what happened next.

"Good morning, Cap-i-taan," greeted Kas-Ra-Ar as the Lemurian joined him on the weather side of the quarterdeck.

"Morning, Kas." Rick smiled. "A brisk day and a stiff wind." He glanced aloft at the single-reefed topsails overhead.

"When should we expect the plane, do you think?" Kas asked. Every four days, the PBY flew out and rendezvoused with them so it could carry a report of their sightings back to Surabaya. The latitude wasn't prescribed for the meetings, but the longitude was. That way, the Catalina could just follow the line north until they met. In theory. *Revenge*'s consorts tried to stay in line of sight, and they would signal her with any sightings they made as well. Once, amazingly, they encountered a Lemurian Home headed north into the China Sea. They closed to speak to her and had nearly taken a fusillade of the giant crossbow bolts for their efforts. They finally managed to convince the Home they weren't Grik (an understandable mistake) and they passed them the news of the war. That news came as quite a shock, since these people hadn't even known there *was* a war. They told Kas they might go to Baalkpan, or they might not. They did turn around and head south.

"Sometime this afternoon, I think," Rick replied to his sailing master's question. "We're farther north than they probably expect us, but not close enough to Singapore for Mallory to worry about being seen."

"Will the plane try to find us if there is a storm?" Kas asked, nodding toward the horizon. Rick had been watching the growing clouds since dawn.

"You've got me there. If it gets bad, no." Rick snorted. "If it was me, I wouldn't let them fly the only bloody airplane in the world if the wind was over five miles an hour." He glanced at his second in command and then pointed at the sky. "Do you think it'll get bad?"

Kas cocked his head to one side and blinked. "It is difficult to say. Possibly. This *is* the stormy time of year."

"So everyone keeps saying," grumbled Rick.

A silence stretched between them, but it was broken by a high-pitched cry from the maintop. "Deck there! Sail!"

Rick snatched a speaking trumpet. "Where away?"

There was a short pause while the lookout pondered the best way to translate the bearing. "Two points the left . . . the *port* bow!"

Rick scrambled into the port main shrouds and secured himself as best he could. Then he raised his binoculars. Yes! There she was, running toward them under all plain sail. Probably trying to escape the storm building behind them, Rick mused. "Shake that reef out of the fore-tops'l!" he shouted. "We'll wait till they get closer. Act like we're turning to run, too. We'll rake him as we turn!"

He beamed down at Kas-Ra-Ar. "One way or another, it's going to be an interesting day!"

"Captain, the launch is alongside."

Matt nodded. "Single up all lines and prepare to cast off."

The rain was falling in sheets now, and he could barely see past the fo'c'sle. He was accustomed to the dense squalls of the region, but this was different. He could feel the power behind the thing. He wondered fleetingly if this would be the event that snatched them back where they belonged? For some reason, in spite of everything, he caught himself hoping it wasn't. Jim was right. Back home, *Walker* was just another over-age 'can. If they didn't break her up and scatter her crew through the fleet, she'd probably spend the war towing targets for newer, more capable ships to practice against. Here, she and her people could make a difference. They had already begun.

"The work detail is back aboard and the launch is hooking on," Dowden reported as he entered the pilothouse. Water coursed down his saturated clothes and drained away through the strakes at his feet. The work detail had been winching the screw onto shore, raft and all, so that working against the dock wouldn't damage it.

The talker spoke again. "Radio says Lieutenant Mallory's about to turn north, but it's getting pretty boogery up there—his words—and he wants to know if you still want him to rendezvous with *Revenge*."

"No sense. He can't set down even if he spots her. Tell him to make for Baalkpan. Fly around the storm if he can—he should have plenty of fuel."

The attention of the bridge watch was diverted by another figure entering the pilothouse. It was Keje. He must have come over on the launch that delivered Courtney Bradford, Sandra Tucker, and a few others to *Big Sal*. Matt sent them with the explanation that it wasn't wise to keep all their eggs in one basket. Also, since they weren't critical to the operation of the ship, it made no sense for them to endure a major storm aboard *Walker*—given her less than sedate performance in heavy seas. It would result only in unnecessary suffering. Bradford went with an appreciative smile, but Sandra had been reluctant. Matt finally traded heavily on her professional concern for the wounded that remained on *Big Sal*. Most had been shipped home on *Fristar,* but not all. As to her suspicious concern regarding his own injuries, he blithely reassured her that he'd take it easy.

"Good afternoon, Cap-i-taan Reddy."

"Hello, Keje. I'm glad to see you, but we're about to cast off. It looks like we're going to have some of that 'stormy' weather you talked about."

Keje nodded agreement as he wrung water from his fur. "Indeed. Quite stormy."

"Well." Matt paused, unsure how to continue. "Shouldn't you be with your ship?"

"Unnecessary. Both her feet are out," he said, referring to the giant copper anchors, "as are those of the other Homes. This is a wide, deep bay. They will ride comfortably. The feluccas have all run upriver and, as long as the surge is not too great, they will be fine. We usually moor when a Strakka comes, but it is my understanding you prefer to face them in the open sea. How exciting! I thought, with your permission, I might enjoy this one with you."

Matt looked at his friend for a moment, expressionless. "That's fine, Keje," he said at last. "Glad to have you. I don't think I've ever heard that word, though. What's a Strakka?"

Keje waved his hand. "I don't know if there is a proper word to describe Strakka in Amer-i-caan. The closest I can think of might be . . . typhoon? Is that it?"

"You know what a typhoon is?" Matt asked with surprise. "Those are storms we only used to get in deeper waters than the Java Sea."

"Yes. Mr. Bradford described the typhoon very well. It did sound like a Strakka, but on a different scale."

Matt smiled. "Yeah, a typhoon's as bad as they come. But you're in for a heck of a ride aboard *Walker* in any kind of storm!" There was knowing laughter in the pilothouse.

Keje looked at him and blinked. "No. You misunderstand. A typhoon is bad, but a Strakka . . ." He smiled tolerantly. "A Strakka can be much, *much* worse!"

The Mice had wedged themselves between the forward air lock of the aft fireroom and the access-hatch ladder. Nearby, clutching the grating as if the ship itself was trying to shake her loose, Tabby continued the dry retching that had wracked her small body since the storm began. Isak's and Gilbert's stoic expressions belied the real concern they felt for their furry companion. The monumental cacophony of sound was stunning even to them. The blowers howled as they sucked the sodden air, and the tired hull thundered and creaked as the relentless sea pounded against it. Condensed moisture rained from every surface to join the nauseating sewer that crashed and surged in the bilge as the ship heaved and pitched. The firemen on watch weren't doing much either, just holding on as best they could and trying to supervise the gauges and fires.

"Reckon she's gonna die?" Gilbert Yager asked, peering through the muck that streaked his face. As close as they were, he still had to shout for Isak Rueben to hear him. Even Tabby's soggy tail lay still—he'd never seen that before. Her ordinarily fluffy light-gray fur was almost black, and plastered to her body like it had been slicked down with grease.

"Nah," Isak Rueben reassured him after a judicious glance. "Poor critter's just a little seasick, is all. Must be sorta' embarrassin' for her to be seasick after spendin' her whole life at sea." He was thoughtful. "'Course, on them big ships o' theirs, I don't reckon it ever gets quite this frisky. Don't carry on so. You'll make her feel worse."

Gilbert looked at the exhausted, wretched, oblivious form.

"Okay. She wouldn't want us coddlin' her." He paused. "Damned if I ain't feelin' a little delicate myself," he admitted, glancing around the dark, dank, rectangular compartment. He could certainly *feel* the violent motion of the ship, but the only visual evidence was the sloshing bilge and the way the condensation sometimes fell sideways. "Now I know how those idiots who go over Niagara Falls in a barrel feel."

The air lock beside them opened, but the "whoosh" was lost in the overall din. Spanky McFarlane spilled out onto the grating, nearly landing atop the afflicted 'Cat. He crawled to his feet, holding on to the catwalk rail.

"What's the matter with her?" he shouted.

"Seasick, we figger," Isak told him.

"What's she doin' here? If she's that sick, she ought'a be in her rack." Spanky remembered then that he hadn't seen Tabby for a couple of days.

"She was," Gilbert confirmed. "She crawled down here today. The roll's just as bad, but there ain't so much pitch. Maybe she'll feel better."

Spanky hesitated. "Well, try to get her to drink something. She'll get dehydrated."

The Mice nodded in unison. "Say, how're things topside?" Isak asked, uncharacteristically interested in something besides the fireroom. Spanky blew his nose into his fingers and slung the ejecta into the bilge.

"It's a booger," he said. "It's startin' to taper off a little now, though. I just came from the bridge and, I'm telling you, that was a ride! It's a miracle we haven't lost anybody overboard. Even the lifelines have carried away!" Spanky was thoroughly soaked, but that alone wasn't proof he'd been on deck. The Mice were soaked too. "Skipper's been up there ever since the storm hit and he looks like hell. Lieutenant Tucker would give him a shot to put him out if she was here—and if she had one. The man needs rest, with his wounds and all. Other than that, the damage ain't as bad as you'd think. Antenna aerial's gone. Took the top of the resonance chamber with it so the radio's out." He saw their blank expressions. "You know that big pointy cylinder on the back bridge rail, right next to the main blower vent? Looks like a great big bullet?"

"You mean that's what makes the radio work?" Gilbert asked, amazed.

". . . Yeah. Anyway, the launch is wrecked too. Hell, it crashed on the deck right over your heads." The Mice looked at him and then up at the deck above. They hadn't heard a thing. "The life rafts are gone—not that I'd ever get on one of those things on *this* ocean—and we've lost just about everything else that wasn't bolted down." He patted the railing under his hand. "But the old girl's doin' okay—on one engine too. I think Skipper's more worried about *Mahan* than anything. As usual. If she got hit as hard as we did . . ." He grunted. "Anyway, that Keje's up there too." Spanky grinned. "He's havin' the time of his life."

"Where are we?" Gilbert asked and Spanky shrugged.

"If we run into something big and rocky, we'll know it was one of the thousands of pissant islands scattered around out there, but that's as close a guess as I'd care to make."

"You've been out in a 'can like this in the North Atlantic, ain't you?"

Isak asked and Spanky nodded, accustomed to the Mice's abrupt subject changes. "Is this as bad as that?"

Spanky just looked at him. "Son," he said, shouting above the turmoil, "I was on the old *Marblehead* in a typhoon in the Philippine Sea back in '36. That storm tore up a 'can like this and a fleet oiler too, like they were paper cups. It wasn't a patch to this one. We're doin' fine." With that, he shook his head and crept away, lurching hand over hand along the rail to resume his inspection of the engineering spaces.

"Well," Isak said, "didn't feel that bad to me. Maybe we ought to get out more, Gilbert."

"Well," said Captain Reddy as the bow buried itself under a roller, "now I know what a Strakka is." The entire ship shuddered with effort as it came out the other side. Gray-green water sluiced down the deck, submerging the number one gun and erupting upward against the pilothouse. After *Walker* spent two days running east-southeast before the wind while the nightmare storm hammered at the ship with a ferocity Matt had never seen, the raging vortex had climbed all over it and then, apparently, passed it by. The trailing edge of the storm was still quite lively, and the chaotic hash it had made of the Java Sea was rougher than any sea *Walker* had steamed through before. Not as big as it might have been in deeper water, but certainly rougher. Still, they'd been able to bring the ship about and begin the difficult—and even more nauseating—task of working back in the direction from which they'd come.

"How much longer before things quiet down?" he asked through set teeth as *Walker* dove under another, lesser, wall of water. In spite of Keje's fatigue—which had to be almost equal to Matt's—the Lemurian still radiated a vague exuberance. He had absolute faith in Matt's skill and *Walker*'s iron construction, so the whole thing had been just an exciting adventure to him.

"A day. Maybe more. Strakkas move swiftly, as you've seen, and they usually leave as quickly as they come."

"Thank God for that!" Dowden gasped. The youthful exec had the conn and was struggling mightily against the forces of the sea and the thrust of the single propeller. "I'd sure hate to see what a deepwater Strakka's like!"

"There are greater dangers in deep water than a Strakka," Keje reminded him darkly.

"So you say," Dowden wheezed. "Mountain fish and such. But that's a creature. Captain, I thought Mr. Bradford said creatures were the only things different here, but he's talking like storms like this are common in the Java Sea."

"Only at this time of year," Keje reminded them. "And I have to admit, this was an unusually intense Strakka. Of course, it might have just seemed so since we are on such a small ship." Matt grunted and Keje grinned. "No offense, Cap-i-taan, I assure you! Never have I been so exhilarated! It's very like the gri-kakka hunt, in a small boat, but even more exciting and prolonged—at least when the lance strikes true. Gri-kakka die quite quickly then." He peered at the captain with his large reddish-brown eyes. His tail twitched with mischief. "You must try it sometime."

The worst of the storm passed Baalkpan by as it roared down in a great semicircle of destruction from the South China Sea, across the Java Sea, and then pounded the Lesser Sunda Islands on its way toward Australia. Borneo had been struck a glancing blow, by comparison, but tornados, pounding rain, and lashing winds hadn't left Baalkpan unscathed. Lieutenant Mallory had brought the Catalina in just before the whitecaps on the bay would have made it suicide to set the plane down and, together with hundreds of guards and volunteers and the help of the engines, they heaved the big plane out of the water and up a steep, muddy ramp that wasn't yet complete. Once ashore, the plane had been lashed down securely. The PBY weathered the storm, but it had been a near thing. Now, all that remained of the storm in Baalkpan was an incessant deluge that drummed on the plane's sloping wings and ran off the trailing edge in sheets. Ben Mallory, Alan Letts, and Perry Brister were gathered under the port wing with Pete Alden and Tony Scott. Together, they watched the Strakka slowly die.

"I wish this would quit," said the coxswain in a loud voice so he could be heard above the rumbling aluminum overhead. His fear of water didn't encompass rain, but he was heartily sick of it nonetheless. Mallory nodded and glanced at the fuselage. Ed Palmer was in there, still trying to raise *Walker*. They'd heard nothing for two whole days and were beginning to worry. Both destroyers and *Revenge* had been in the path of the biggest storm they'd ever seen.

"Yeah," said Letts, whose thinking mirrored Mallory's. "How's the plane doing? Engines okay?" he asked.

The pilot hesitated. "Sure," he answered in a defensive tone. "The oil we're getting isn't quite up to spec, but we change it every time she flies. Other than that, she's better now than when we got her." He grinned and gestured at the rain. "Cleaner too." He pointedly didn't remind them that "when they got her," the PBY was full of holes and half sunk on a beach.

"Good," Letts murmured, looking carefully at the aviator. He turned to Brister. *Mahan*'s former engineering officer had become the general engineer for all of Baalkpan. Captain Reddy and Pete Alden had designed the city's fortifications with an eye toward successful historical port defenses. Alden added a few things based on local conditions. Also, with an infantryman's eye, he'd stressed additions based on the possibility that the enemy might make a landward approach. In addition to his other duties—which now included direct supervision of the massive (by local standards) foundry—Lieutenant Brister was responsible for making the dream come true. The result might very well be the most formidable defensive works this world had ever known.

Instead of the stone walls that Aryaal enjoyed, a huge defensive berm had been thrown up around the city, the approaches festooned with entanglements and sharpened stakes. Moving the vast amount of dirt had also created a wide, deep trench that had subsequently filled with water and become an impressive moat system. The jungle was pushed back at least five hundred yards on all sides, except where the ground sank into swamp. Some of the wood was stockpiled for later use—much of it was fine hardwood after all—and some was used to shore up the breastworks and put a roof over the heads of the defenders to protect them from plunging arrow fire.

The pièce de résistance was the twenty-four heavy guns that pierced the berm at regular intervals through stout embrasures, mostly facing the harbor. These were carefully concealed. The thinking was that, since the harbor was their most heavily defended point, they didn't want to scare the enemy away from it—now they'd had a taste of cannon. If the Grik ever did attack Baalkpan, the defenders wanted them to do it in the "same old way" because the waterfront was where they would smash the invaders' teeth. Still more guns were situated in a heavily constructed and reinforced stockade named Fort Atkinson, overlooking the mouth of the bay.

Again thanks to Alden, the landward approaches hadn't been neglected. One hundred crude mortars were interspersed among the defensive positions. Little more than heavy bronze tubes, they could hurl a ten-pound copper bomb as far as the extended tree line. A little farther if you were brave enough to put a dollop more powder beneath it. The poor fragmentation characteristics of copper had been improved by casting the things with deep lines that ran all around and up and down the spheres—just like a pineapple grenade. When all was said and done, there wasn't so much as a copper cup or brass earring in Nakja-Mur's entire city, or anywhere they could quickly trade with. But what they had, hopefully, was a slaughterhouse for the Grik.

"How have the defenses held up in the rain?" Letts asked.

Brister snorted. "A little rain won't hurt anything. Pack it all down a bit, is all. I may not be a combat engineer by trade, but when I put something together, it stays put together."

Letts grinned and looked at Ben. "All right. As soon as this lets up and you think it's safe, I want you back in the air. See if you can find our people."

"There's an awful lot of water out there," Mallory replied thoughtfully.

"True, but as the storm winds down, *Mahan* should head here and *Walker* ought to head back for Surabaya. I figure they were both carried a good ways east-southeast, so throw a horseshoe in your search. You can refuel at Tangalar," he said, referring to a small outpost they'd established for that purpose on the southern point of Celebes. "That is, if it hasn't been washed away. Then head for Surabaya."

"What about *Revenge*?"

Alan grimaced. "If she was northeast of Bangka, like you said, she could be anywhere by now, with just wind power." He shook his head. "If she didn't sink, or wind up scattered all over some beach, she might be in the middle of the Java Sea by now."

"If they're out there, I'll find 'em," Mallory promised.

Letts turned to Tony Scott. "If the rain slacks off later today, take the launch and check out the refinery. Make sure it came through the storm okay. Take some help. All we had out there was a couple of caretakers. If anything cracked, fix it if you can or come get Mr. Brister. Take a look at the wellhead while you're at it. It was shut down during the storm, but the Mice'll have a fit if a tree fell on that mechanical dinosaur of theirs."

Tony kept a straight face, but gulped at the thought of the boat trip. "Aye, sir," he said. He knew it was a necessary trip, but he sure didn't want to go.

Tony Scott was no coward—everyone was well aware of that. At the height of the Battle of the Stones, when they captured *Revenge*, he'd proven his courage beyond question by jumping *in* the sea to rescue Lieutenant Tucker. This was the ultimate proof, because he had become profoundly terrified of the water—and all the creatures that lurked there. Anyone who might have scoffed at his newfound fear was silent after that. But nothing changed. There was no revival of his old spirit, no catharsis. No feeling of being back on the horse. He was no longer worried that he might have become a coward in general, but he was still afraid of the water.

It was morning before the rain paused long enough for Scott and his half dozen 'Cat roughnecks to embark on their inspection jaunt upriver. It took a while to bail out the boat, and while they worked they watched those on shore maneuvering the heavy Catalina down to the water. Tony shuddered as a group of line handlers actually waded out up to their waists. He knew, philosophically, that they were relatively safe. There were fewer flashies in the bay than in open water. There were fewer still in the shallows, and after a storm there'd be almost none inshore. Still . . . The launch's motor started on the first try and for a while he concentrated on performing the tasks that once had made him happy. As the boat nosed away from the dock, the PBY floated clear and Tony waved his ever-present Thompson gun at the army pilot as the man climbed on top of the wing to supervise the final preparations. Mallory waved back.

A decent guy, Scott thought to himself as he spun the wheel and pointed the bow toward the distant river mouth. Sure wouldn't want *his* job. Flying around in that beat-up plane over miles of empty ocean. Nothing but water below, packed with millions and millions of voracious . . . He shook his head to keep from shuddering again. The captain had left him here as a mercy, and maybe even as thanks for saving his dame—although that probably didn't figure too consciously in the skipper's mind. *He's giving me a rest so I don't lose my nerve completely,* Scott decided. *He knows all it might take is one more trip across that deep, dark sea to send me absolutely ape.* It would wreck him. Even if he came back to his senses, it wouldn't matter. Everyone would *know.* Tony Scott, coxswain, was helplessly afraid of the water. The pity would be worse than jeers. He'd blow his brains out. Thank God he could still handle the bay.

Behind him he heard the clattering roar of engines as the PBY thundered across the bay and took to the sky. He looked over his shoulder as a fleeting ray of sunshine flickered on the rising plane. *All that water,* he thought. It was bad enough in the bay, where few of the monsters were present, but . . . out there, where the plane was headed and most of Tony's pals might even now be slipping down into the dreadful embrace of the sea, so far from land. The safe, dry land.

He fought the current upriver and dodged the dead trees and other debris that had washed down from the distant mountains. Crocodiles floated by, disoriented or dead, and he knew the river must've been something at the peak of the deluge. It was still out of its banks. The damp world had begun to reawaken, however, evidenced by the flocks of lizard birds that rose amid raucous cries and riotous colors to greet them as they churned upstream. Finally, after another hour of enduring the buckshot of bird shit that peppered them constantly from above, the fueling pier came into view around the bend.

The willing hands of the caretakers caught the rope, and Tony gratefully leaped up to the dock and onto the shore. His relief at feeling the motionless earth beneath his feet was palpable, and his mood brightened immediately despite another round of drizzle. "Everything all right?" he asked the first Lemurian caretaker/guardsman that joined him.

"No pro-bleemo," mimicked the 'Cat, proud of his English.

"Anything come apart?" Tony asked the other one, who he knew could speak much better.

"Don't think so. Everything fine here. Won't know for sure until the pump is back on."

"Okay," Tony said. "I'll go check it out. In the meantime, why don't you fellas try to get the fires lit? God knows it'll be a week before any local boats can make it up that river and bring the rest of the crew. I'll have to ferry 'em up in the launch." The idea of spending the better part of the next two days on the water didn't appeal to him, but at least for now he could bask in the safety of the shore. He stuck his hands in his pockets and, whistling, followed the pipeline cut into the jungle.

He didn't whistle for long. The ground was mucky and the grade was steep. Soon he was gasping, trying to suck a few molecules of oxygen past the moisture that hung in the air. There was absolute silence except for his breathing, and the humidity deadened the sound of that almost before it reached his ears. Halfway to the wellhead, he stopped, huffing, and contemplated sitting on one of the wet, mushy tree trunks that had been moved to the side of the cut.

"Out of shape," he scolded himself, still in a good mood in spite of his exertion. He began unbuttoning his trousers as he stepped to the side of the trail to relieve himself.

Over the sound of his rasping breath he thought he heard something. Something else . . . breathing. He peered into the misty jungle. There, directly before him amid the tangled tree trunks, two trunks didn't quite match the others. His eyes went wide and his hand flew to his shoulder for the sling of the Thompson—which at that moment lay behind the control station in the launch, ready to protect him from the horrors in the water.

"Shit," he whispered as the gaping jaws descended upon him.

Ben Mallory had coaxed the reluctant aircraft up to three thousand feet, all the while listening intently to the engines. So far, so good. The steady, throbbing drone of the Pratt & Whitney R-1830-92 Twin Wasps seemed healthy enough. Contrary to Lieutenant Letts's suspicions, Mallory really thought the engines were fine. Of course, it was hard to tell over the excessive rattling and violent vibrations the rest of the aircraft made. Everything except the engines on the hard-used plane was falling apart. He tried his best to take it easy on the old gal, but metal fatigue was beginning to take its toll. Sooner or later, good engines or not, the battered flying boat would fold up like a paper kite and fall out of the sky and the only airplane in the entire world would be no more. He shrugged mentally. When it happened, it happened. Until it did, he would fly.

He spared a quick glance at his "copilot." The young sable-furred 'Cat on his right was peering through a pair of precious binoculars through the open side window at the ocean below. His name was Jis-Tikkar, but he seemed to like "Tikker" just fine. He'd been a good companion on the long flights between Baalkpan and Surabaya and he was still fully enraptured by the wonder of flying high above the world at a measly 110 miles an hour—oh, how Ben missed the glorious P-40E! Whatever Ben called him, Tikker wasn't quite ready to assume all the duties of his position. For one thing, he could barely see over the instrument panel.

On a couple of occasions, Mallory had allowed him to take the controls for a little "straight and level," but it would be a while before he did it again. The second time the little devil had his hands on the oval-shaped wheel, he'd nearly put the big plane through a barrel roll. It was all very exciting and the flying lessons abruptly ceased. For now, the "copilot's" duties had reverted to observation and keeping Ben awake on the long flights with his irrepressible humor.

The rest of the flight crew consisted of Ed Palmer, and two more far-sighted Lemurians in the observation blisters. Ed sat in the compartment directly behind the flight deck, still trying to raise *Walker* when he wasn't keeping track of their navigation. The young signalman had been studying under Bob Flowers to raise his grade before the lieutenant was killed. In his short time aboard *Mahan* he had, for all intents and purposes, been the navigation officer. He wasn't a pro yet, but he was a quick study. As long as there were landmarks he could identify, he hadn't led them astray—and they were forbidden to fly at night. Besides, they'd made the trip often enough now that the Makassar Strait was pretty familiar. Ben liked having someone to bounce his reckoning off of, though.

They broke out of the dreary overcast at last and the sky ahead was bright and clear. The trailing edge of the storm was still visible far to the east beyond Celebes, and a few petulant squalls marched about at random. Below them, evidence of the storm was still apparent from the lingering whitecaps. Three hours of flying had them in the general vicinity where they'd captured *Revenge,* and nearing the way point where they would either turn southeast and prepare to set down and refuel or head due south on the next dogleg that would complete the bottom of their horseshoe search.

Ben glanced at the fuel gauges. More than enough. The flying boat had a theoretical range of over twenty-eight hundred miles, and the search pattern Letts had suggested would consume less than half of that. Mallory intended to cover more area than the plan called for, but there'd still be ample fuel. He decided to forgo a visit to their remote gas station on Celebes. Every time the plane touched down there provided potential for an accident, particularly on the still-rough sea. Besides, there were no pumps at the station and they would spend half the day hoisting and pouring the two-gallon jugs. He much preferred idling up alongside *Big Sal* and letting the fuel run *down* into the plane.

He called Palmer forward. "We're going to zigzag south across the Flores Sea on hundred-mile legs, west-east, west-east. But I want to check out those islands north of Sumbawa. Keep track of our turns so we don't miss the damn things. I'd rather catch them headed east so we can cross them twice. There must be a hundred of them."

"Most of those islands aren't much account," Palmer replied.

"No, but if somebody got driven east by the storm there's a good chance they might've wound up on one of them," Ben reasoned grimly.

As it turned out, they didn't have to go that far. Shortly after they made their first eastward turn, Tikker spotted a lonely wake below them. Ben immediately began a spiraling descent.

"*Mahan*, sure enough!" Tikker said excitedly. "Only three smokestacks, see?"

Mallory grunted when he banked the plane far enough to see for himself. "Unless the storm knocked one off *Walker*," he agreed doubtfully. "But mainly, she's headed north, toward Baalkpan. *Walker* would be headed west. Yeah, that's *Mahan*, all right. There's her number. Looks even worse than the last time I saw her, but she's under way."

"We're not going to set down, are we?" Ed asked nervously from between the two seats.

"No way. Look at those swells! Let's signal them with the navigation lights."

The sun was setting beyond Java's distant volcanic peaks when *Walker* steamed through the Pulau Sapudi and returned to Aryaal/B'mbaado Bay. The naked tripods of the battle line Homes were silhouetted against the evening sky and the lights of the city. Safe and sound, right where they'd left them. Captain Reddy was dozing in his chair and Keje had gone to the wardroom for a sandwich.

"Just like a bunch of battle wagons moored at Pearl," Garrett quipped, referring to the Homes. "Those guys never know what they're missing when the wind kicks up."

"Maybe so," Dowden agreed, "but small and fast beats slow and fat when bombs and torpedoes are falling out of the sky."

Garrett grinned sheepishly back at him. "Yeah, but we don't have to worry about bombs and torpedoes anymore. The next time we get caught in the middle of a Strakka, tell me again that small and fast beats fat and slow." He gestured at the huge ships in the bay as they drew closer. "Especially since they don't even look like they noticed it."

Appearances were deceiving. The full fury of the storm had passed right over the bay. *Humfra-Dar* had dragged one of its feet and nearly gone aground. Superficial damage had also been sustained by the pagoda structures on all the ships, but the Homes of the People were designed to withstand far worse. Onshore it was a different story. The waterfront ghetto had been knocked flat. Since the buildings there had provided most of the shelter for the AEF, there had been numerous injuries and even a couple of deaths. The rest of the troops had spent an extremely miserable couple of days, exposed to the full violence of the storm. Nevertheless, there were cries of happy greeting as the ship passed through the anchored fleet and neared the pier.

There had evidently been some concern that *Walker* might not fare well against a Strakka of such severity. The concern was better founded than most Lemurians would have believed. They knew she was small, but iron still enjoyed an almost mystical status among them. Surely, with her entire hull made of the mighty metal, *Walker* must be invincible? Some knew better, like Keje and Chack. Adar too. But for the most part, only the Lemurian crew aboard her fully grasped how close the old destroyer had come to disappearing forever. It was a testament to how ferocious the Strakka had been that disquiet over *Walker*'s fate existed at all.

Keje returned to the bridge munching a second sandwich and bearing a cup of "coffee" for the captain. Matt roused almost magically at the smell of the brew and sat, sipping, while Larry Dowden conned the ship alongside the dock. The outward calm he displayed during the maneuver was admirable. On deck, he could hear Gray bellowing at the special sea and anchor detail as they prepared to throw lines to those waiting on shore.

"All stop," said Dowden, with a nervous glance at the captain. "Finished with engines."

Matt spared him a nod. The approach had been fine—slow and careful. The ship's momentum would bleed off sooner than was ideal, leaving a larger gap between her and the dock than would normally be considered perfect, but there was plenty of line. Better to let the line handlers and the capstan heave her in than try to fend off if she came in too fast. That was a losing proposition.

"Lookout reports aircraft at one two zero degrees, Skipper. Range six miles."

Matt nodded, pleased again by the improved quality of the reports from the crow's nest. All of their lookouts were 'Cats now. With their amazing eyesight, they were naturals for the duty. At first, however, their reports had been . . . unusual, to say the least. With time, that changed. Matt glanced at his watch and then out at the darkening bay. Lieutenant Mallory had come very close to disobeying his order not to fly at night.

"He ought to be okay, Captain," said Garrett, sensing Matt's concern.

"I bet the bay's pretty clear now. The rough seas probably tore up any of the lizard ships that were still sticking up."

"Yeah," supplied Gray as he entered the pilothouse. He'd discarded his crutch and was getting around almost as well as before. "But now all that junk's out there floatin' around. That cocky flyboy's liable to torpedo himself with a mast or something." He turned to Captain Reddy. "All lines are doubled up and secured, Skipper."

"Very well." Matt upended his coffee cup and grinned wryly. "Mr. Dowden, you have the watch. I'm going ashore to see what we missed."

The makeshift hospital tent had been re-erected behind the entrenchments facing the north wall of the city. It had been used to shelter some of the injured after a desultory daylong drizzle replaced the worst of the storm. Now, the stars shone bright overhead and it was the scene of a relieved reunion of the officers of the AEF. Currently, as was his custom, Matt was receiving individual reports from all the commanders before he addressed the group. Around him, the other officers did the same, less formally. This way they could enjoy a somewhat laid-back visit—which was the preferred Lemurian custom—and everyone would be pretty much up to speed by the time the real meeting commenced.

"So, I'm to believe you made the flight only on Mr. Letts's orders?" Matt asked Lieutenant Mallory, who was next in line. "And you went into the air kicking and screaming with a written protest?"

Mallory shifted uncomfortably. "Not exactly, sir. Mr. Letts did order me to fly, but it's not his fault we got in late. We altered the flight plan a little to increase our search coverage, true, but I'd respectfully point out that we wouldn't have seen *Mahan* otherwise." He shrugged. "We ran into a headwind on the last westward leg."

Matt nodded. "I'm glad you found *Mahan*. Knowing she's safe takes a load off my mind. I just wish you wouldn't cut it so close. You're the only pilot we have."

"Yes, sir. Flying the only airplane. But when we couldn't raise you on the radio we got worried. The last we knew, everybody was at sea in the path of that god-awful storm. I guess we needed to know we weren't suddenly all alone."

Matt studied him in the torchlight. "What would you have done if you found one of us, *Walker* or *Mahan*, in a sinking condition?"

"I . . . don't understand, sir."

"Yes, you do. Say it was *Walker*. No power and low in the water. Just wallowing in the swell." Matt grimaced. "And nothing but the whaleboat, which is, incidentally, all we have left. This afternoon you might've been able to set down, but not this morning. What would you have done?"

The young aviator looked stricken. "I . . . I don't know. Maybe . . ."

Matt interrupted him. "No 'maybe,' Lieutenant. There's absolutely nothing you could've done." He put his hand on Mallory's shoulder. "Nothing. Not if you're a responsible officer. This isn't the world we knew, where you could whistle up some ship to come get us. We're on our own. That's why you and Letts should've waited another day before coming to look for us." He smiled and squeezed the shoulder. "By which time—tomorrow—the radio ought to be fixed. I'm glad you're here, don't get me wrong, and I'm glad you saw *Mahan,* but we can't spare you or that airplane." His smile became a grin. "It's going to have to last the whole damn war." He dropped his hand to his side and nodded toward the chart laid out on a table nearby. Together, they looked down at it. "Now, since you're in a rescuing mood, I want you to take off in the morning—weather permitting—and find *Revenge.* We're going to start on the propeller first thing, but we ought to have the radio repaired by morning. With Riggs gone to Baalkpan, Clancy is chief radio operator and he says with Palmer's help he can get it done. Clancy's already fixed the resonance chamber—used a coffee cup for an insulator!—and he says now that the ship's not pitching her guts out he can re-string the aerial." Matt looked up at Mallory. "By the way, if the radio's not working, you don't fly." He returned his gaze to the chart. "If you find *Revenge* and she needs assistance, with any luck, we'll be able to come and get them." Matt pointed at the chart. "Concentrate here first," he said grimly, indicating a large island surrounded by dozens of smaller ones about halfway between Sumatra and Borneo. "I have a feeling that's where she'll be."

Captain Reddy glanced at the group gathered around them. Many were engaged in animated discussions, while some were relaxing on cushions that had been placed under the awning for their convenience. "It looks like I'm going to be here for a while," he said. "Go get some sleep. You'll need it."

"So," Matt said at last, when the briefings were complete and the "meeting" had been officially under way for some time, "correct me if I'm wrong, but it seems the situation remains unchanged. The battle line is fit for sea, in spite of some slight damage. The B'mbaadan infantry and Rolak's volunteers have been thoroughly integrated into the AEF and are ready to embark. I have every reason to believe my ship will have the use of both engines after tomorrow. Fuel and provisions, as well as some minor repairs, might take a couple more days, but essentially, we're prepared to resume the offensive. Correct?"

"Correct," confirmed Adar. "Essentially."

"Except for Rasik," Rolak growled.

Matt nodded. "Except for Rasik."

"My host will follow you, Cap-i-taan Reddy," Queen Maraan told him, "whatever you decide. We've sworn to do so and that . . . skuggik who lurks behind his walls poses no threat to B'mbaado now. However, Lord Rolak and I have fought together. He is my sword brother—if a slightly elder one." She smiled, baring her perfect teeth. "But Rasik"—she spat the name—"has yet to release the families of Rolak's warriors from the city. He sends excuse after excuse, but it is clear they are his hostages!"

"I fear that is the case," Rolak agreed, still using Chack to interpret. "He believes we won't sack the city with our families inside."

"But we have no intention of sacking the city!" blurted Courtney Bradford. "My God! We have more important fish to fry!"

Rolak looked at him in the low light. "I don't think King Rasik believes that. He has a very narrow view of the world, and it all revolves around him and what he wants. To him, the greatest treasure in the world is the throne of Aryaal. He cannot imagine that anyone else would not want it too."

"But what about the Grik?" asked Ramic-Sa-Ar, High Chief of *Aracca* Home. "Doesn't he fear their return?"

Rolak shook his head. "My . . . spies say he does not. He believes that menace is ended, that they couldn't possibly raise another army like the one we destroyed before his walls."

"But when we showed him the chart—the map showing the extent of the enemy frontiers—he seemed to grasp the peril," Adar interjected sharply. He had acted as emissary in all their dealings with the Aryaalan king.

"Fabrications," Rolak growled. "He believes we make it up—which adds to his paranoia. He believes we intend to carry the war to the Grik, but he does not think they are a real threat. He fears us. Therefore, he keeps the families of my warriors as security against attack. Perhaps he even hopes to lure some of us back into his service. I do not know."

"What about you, Lord Rolak?" Bradford asked in a quiet tone. "Does he hope you will return?" Rolak's gaze rested on the Australian.

"No. He most certainly does not hope that."

"What will you do?" Matt asked after a lengthy silence.

"I will follow you to battle the Grik, lord, as I have sworn to do. But . . . my warriors must remain here. Perhaps to bolster B'mbaado's defense. I cannot ask them to abandon their families to Rasik's mercy. I am sorry."

"There's nothing to apologize for," Matt replied. "I understand completely, as I'm sure the others here do." He glanced down for a moment and then looked back at the Lemurian. "I wish I could offer you the AEF and we'd just storm the city and retrieve your folk, but as Mr. Bradford put it, we've bigger fish to fry." He looked around at the uncomfortable blinking of the gathered officers. "Besides, it might be difficult for many here to fight others of their kind, particularly measured against the greater threat we all face."

"It would be different if we were attacked," explained Keje in a quiet voice. "But we have not been. My warrior soul cries out to assist you, Lord Rolak, but my teaching and my sense of what we risk bids me refrain."

"I do understand," Rolak said. "You sea folk are different. You do not fight without great cause. That is why I believed you so readily when you told me of the greater threat. You're certainly the better choice to lead in that fight now."

"We'll miss your warriors, and you most of all, Lord Rolak," Matt said at last.

"You won't miss me, lord, for I at least will be at your side. I have made an oath."

Matt shook his head. "I release you from it. Stay here and lead your people."

"It's not your place to release me from my pledge, my lord. You cannot do it." Rolak spoke with quiet patience, but there was an edge to his voice. Chack relayed the refusal.

"Then I order it!" Matt retorted with an edge of his own. "As my friend or as my slave, you'll remain here and lead your people." There was a collective intake of breath and then a murmur of approval rippled quickly among those present. Rolak regarded him with wide, staring eyes, then bowed his head in assent.

"As you command, my lord. But now I am even deeper in your debt."

"Well. That's settled," Matt muttered hopefully, suppressing a huge yawn. "What else do we have to cover? I haven't had much sleep lately and it's past my bedtime."

Mank-Lar, soon to be Lord Mank-Lar and captain of the palace guard if all went well, squinted hard into the moonless darkness as he drew closer to the iron ship. There was a muffled *clunk* and a curse behind him. "Quietly, fools!" he hissed at the royal retainers plying the sweeps. It had taken hours to row the large, heavy boat from the river to where the invader was moored and they were almost ready to strike. Mank-Lar didn't know what the Amer-i-caans would do to them if they were discovered, but he knew how the king would react if they failed.

"Of course, Task Leader," came the whispered reply.

Mank-Lar peered back at the ship, still squinting to conceal his highly reflective eyes. A few muted lights would not reveal his ragged cape and dark-furred visage. If anything, they would make it harder for any guards to detect his approach. At the moment he didn't see anyone moving at all and he concentrated on the lights. They didn't flicker like a proper torch and he wondered how they did that. Sorcery, he assumed. It was clear they were not believers. He'd heard how they buried their dead in the ground before Aryaal's very gate.

"Carefully, now," he whispered as they came within a tail of the iron ship's side. He leaned far out over the water and felt along the cool plates until he found what he was looking for. It was a loop of metal protruding from the ship. He knew from looking at it in daylight that there were many others that led all the way to the deck. Quickly, he tied a rope to the loop. The two retainers carefully laid aside the tarp that covered the large object in the bottom of the boat and quietly climbed into the smaller boat they had towed behind them. Mank-Lar knelt and ran his hand along the surface of the object in the dark. *Such a wonderful machine,* he thought. And such a shame to use it so. He didn't know what the sea folk called it, but "fire spitter" seemed appropriate. He had watched from the safety of the walls while this one and others like it had wreaked such havoc on the Grik. It had been as though the Sun God himself spat upon them and swept them aside with his hand. A glorious, glorious machine!

This one had belonged to the sea folk who fought near the river and were overrun. Some Grik had seized the weapon as booty and tried to drag it to the ferry even while the battle raged. When the rout began, the fire-spitter rolled down the embankment, destroying its carriage, and splashed into the river. Mank-Lar had seen where it disappeared. When he told Prince Alcas—now king, of course—the prince commanded him and a small group to venture forth in that dreadful darkness across the sea of carrion and retrieve it at all costs. At the time, right after the battle, not all the carrion were dead and he feared that if he was killed, the Sun wouldn't see him fall and his soul would be doomed to linger there forever, upon that plain of bones. He persevered, however. The reward of Heaven is the Sun God's to grant. The rewards of earth would be granted by the prince.

Wounded Grik weren't his only concern. Patrols of sea folk and B'mbaadans crisscrossed the field all night, searching for their own dead and wounded. They carried torches, however, and were easily avoided. When they found the fire-spitter, still conveniently protruding from the river, they tied on to it easily enough, but quickly discovered it was too heavy to drag back to the city. He had decided to push it back, all the way underwater, with the rope still attached. Then they spent the rest of the night groping in the dark, retrieving as much of the carriage as they could find. These parts they cast into the river some distance from where the main part was hidden. Then they hurried to the city before day and the voracious skuggiks arrived.

They didn't return empty-handed, however. They had found one of the chests full of food for the fire-spitter. When night fell again, after the flocks of skuggiks slunk away or lay in bloated torpor, they went forth once more upon the oozing, reeking field. Treading carefully through the already half-eaten host with a much larger force, they retrieved the prize for their new king.

Only a few of that party were ultimately involved in the plan that the king devised. King Alcas himself had seen, during a moment's lull in his own battle against the traitors, what happened when a fire-spitter was fed too much and was offered fire anyway. Surely the force released by such an act would send the invader's iron ship to the bottom of the bay.

With their spines torn from their backs, the cowardly sea folk would never dare campaign against the distant Grik. They certainly wouldn't attack Aryaal in revenge; their weak sensibilities toward killing other People wouldn't let them. No, they would slink away, never to return, and the king could turn his attention to the traitor Rolak and, ultimately, the Orphan Queen across the bay. Everything would be back to normal, and Mank-Lar would be a lord and captain of much renown. The only thing he regretted was that, once again, the Sun couldn't see his deeds.

He thought he heard something stir in the darkness above and he froze. Muffled footsteps sounded on the iron deck, but they were slow and unconcerned. He resumed his task. As much of the bitter-smelling black food as the thing would hold had already been poured down its mouth. On top of that, six of the copper balls were firmly tamped in place and set with wooden wedges and thick red mud. Only the eye was left open at the back of the tube, so it could see the fire that was offered it. Mank-Lar didn't know how the king knew to do these things; perhaps the information came from spies, but it wasn't his concern. All he had to do was finish the job and he would be rewarded beyond his wildest dreams.

He removed the lid from a widemouthed jar. Inside was sap from the gimpra tree; thick and viscous, and quick to take a spark. Once ignited, it would burn with a fierce, hot flame and nothing he knew of could put it out. He smeared the foul-smelling sap all over the front part of the boat, leaving the back clear where he crouched near the mouth of the fire-spitter. He hoped the eye wouldn't see the fire before he and his helpers got away. He removed the remainder of a coil of rope from a perforated copper box at his feet. On one end of the rope glowed a small orange coal. He blew lightly upon it and inched farther back. With a prayer to the Sun, he pitched the smoldering rope onto the sap.

Chief Harvey Donaghey had the deck. He could count on one hand the times he'd had the duty, but everybody was washed out and, he had to admit, the deck-apes were probably more hammered than the snipes for once. Besides, he didn't mind. It was a beautiful, cool, starry night and it was good to be in the open where he could breathe fresh air for a change.

The sound of the blower was reduced to a whisper and the whole ship seemed asleep. Onshore, it was much the same. After the captain came back aboard, everything wrapped up pretty quick. A few fires still glowed by the breastworks, but he imagined that, except for the guards, the whole AEF had knocked out. *Things are gonna start happening soon,* he thought, *and folks are resting up.*

He heard a sound from the amidships deckhouse. Earl Lanier and one of his new monkey-cat mess attendants emerged into the starlight, each carrying a pole. "Not everybody's asleep, I guess," he muttered to himself as the obese cook and his helper neared. "Evening, Earl," he whispered, and nodded at the little black and white 'Cat Earl called Pepper.

"Evenin', P.O.," Lanier grouched. "I'm goin' fishin'," he announced, glancing around. For once, the area was almost clear of sleeping forms. It was cool enough, and after the toil of the storm, nearly everyone wanted the relative comfort of their racks.

"That's fine, Earl. Catch me one too. Just make sure it doesn't eat the ship this time," Harvey warned, absently fingering his pistol. Some of the creatures the cook had dragged aboard from their various anchorages were truly dangerous and most were wildly terrifying. A few had gone . . . on the loose. Earl muttered something under his breath and continued toward the rail. Bored, Donaghey followed him. "Hey," he said, about to ask what Lanier was going to use for bait, when he happened to look over the side and saw a shape on the water below. Earl saw it too and for an instant it looked like a small group of Lemurians sitting in a couple of boats smoking a cigar. Just for an instant.

Before their startled minds could comprehend what they saw, the Lemurian in the bigger boat flicked his "cigar" toward its bow. With a flash of light that seared their eyes the forward part of the boat erupted in flames.

"Bloody hell!" Donaghey shouted and reached for his pistol. The small boat rocked as the arsonist jumped in. One of his accomplices raised something to his shoulder and a crossbow bolt whanged off the rail.

"You little bastards!" Lanier screamed when another bolt appeared, its vaned shaft protruding from his wide, drooping belly. "I'm shot!"

"General quarters! General quarters!" Donaghey yelled at the top of his lungs, firing his pistol at the retreating boat. The slide locked back. Empty. He spun to the startled 'Cat named Pepper. "You speak-ee English?" he demanded, the old China hand. Pepper nodded. "Go, chop-chop, ring-ee bell, wake-ee everybody up! Sabe?"

"Aye, aye, Petty Officer Donaghey!" Pepper replied, and raced forward into the dark. Harvey never even noticed that Pepper's English was clearer than his own.

"What the hell's that?" Lanier demanded, pointing at the boat below. The spreading fire illuminated something lying in it.

"Goddamn! It's a gun! I bet those sneaky bastards filled it full of powder and plugged it up, hoping the fire would cook it off!" He started to run for a fire hose, then stopped dead in his tracks. No time. If he was right, that thing could go off any second. It would take several minutes for the water pressure to build. Without a word, he hopped the rail and began climbing down the rungs.

"Where the hell are you going?" Lanier yelled. "I got an arrow in my gut!"

"I doubt it hit anything vital, you fat tub of lard!" Harvey snarled back. "Don't just stand there. Get the hose!"

Lanier waddled in the direction of the closest hose reel and Donaghey resumed his descent. The initial flash of the conflagration had diminished considerably to a steady blaze in the forward third of the boat. He could hear crackling as the wood began to burn. The heat pushed almost physically against him the lower he went and he wasn't sure he was just imagining his skin beginning to blister.

"Hurry up!" he shouted, unsure if the cook even heard him as he gasped for breath in the acrid smoke. Below him, one rung down, he could see through his slitted, watery eyes that a rope had been tied to the ship. With one hand, he reached into his shirt and retrieved a long-bladed folding knife that always hung around his neck on a braided cord. Called a sausage knife, it had a long, skinny blade that was useful for a variety of things. He opened it with his teeth and leaned down to cut the rope that had already started to burn. He was certain he was blistering now and he cried out in pain. He smelled the hair on his arm begin to singe, mingling with the stench of the smoke. He sawed at the rope like a madman. Suddenly, unexpectedly, it parted under his blade and he would have dropped it in the water but for the cord.

The ship's bell began ringing frantically in the dark, followed moments later by the general alarm. Harvey scrambled back up the side of the ship a few rungs to escape the worst of the heat and looked down at the boat. Slowly, lazily, it drifted with the current. Amid the flames he clearly saw the ruddy shape of the bronze cannon barrel as the fire grew around it. From above he heard shouts and curses and a gurgling stream of seawater trickled on the boat. Other hands had joined or taken over for Lanier and they were finally getting water on the fire. It would still take a while for the pressure to build, but it was better than nothing.

Or was it? Even as he watched he knew with a sinking certainty it would never work. The water was just spreading the flames around. Whatever the saboteur had used as an accelerant was acting like gasoline.

Worse, the boat wasn't drifting away. The incoming tide had served only to press it more firmly against the ship. All it was doing was creeping slowly aft, snug against the hull.

"Cut the water, you're making it worse!" he shouted upward and with only the slightest hesitation he started back down the rungs. The back of the boat was under him now, where the flames had not yet spread, and he jumped down into it. He fell to the floorboards and came up looking directly into the mud-packed muzzle. Lurching to his feet, he snatched one of the sweeps out of its oarlock and pressed against the side of the ship. Gasping with exertion and bellowing in pain, he heaved with all his might. Slowly at first, but then more easily as momentum conquered mass, the boat began to move.

Coughing, he readjusted his grip and heaved again. Through the tears and sweat that ran in his eyes, he saw he had gained a gap about ten yards wide. Clumsily, he dropped the sweep back into its notch and grabbed the other one trailing alongside. Crouching on his knees, and with his hat pulled down low to protect his eyes, he laboriously managed to turn the boat. With a growing sense of urgency that bordered on panic, he rowed as fast as he could. He heard the yells of the men on deck—quite a few now, by the racket they were making—screaming at him to stop, come back, don't be a fool—but there was no choice. He had no choice.

All he knew, as the flesh on his face and hands began to sear and his vision became a red, shimmering fog, was that he had to row. Nothing else in the entire world mattered anymore except for getting that crazy, stupid bomb the hell away from his ship.

He made it almost forty yards.

Captain Reddy paced the deck beside the number two torpedo mount, back and forth, his hands clenched behind his back. Occasionally he ventured near the smoke-blackened rail and stared at the water below. The angry red horizon that preceded the dawn was a singularly appropriate backdrop to the white-hot rage that burned within him. A quiet circle of destroyermen, human and Lemurian, watched him pace, and Sandra and Bradford were nearby as well, conversing in subdued tones. On deck, trussed up like hogs, were two Aryaalans. Dennis Silva towered over them with a pistol in his hand and Earl Lanier, shirt off and with a wide bandage encircling his midsection, menaced the prisoners with his fishing pole.

Harvey Donaghey had hit one of them with a lucky shot from his pistol, causing the 'Cat to lose his oar and slowing their escape. By the time the cannon exploded, the saboteurs were far enough away that they weren't directly injured, but they were so startled by the blast that they dropped the other oar over the side. Thus they were quickly discovered by the vengeful whaleboat, wallowing helplessly back toward their intended victim with the tide. By then, the one Donaghey had shot was dead. Garrett commanded the whaleboat and it was all he could do to bring the others back alive. Even so, their capture hadn't been gentle and the Aryaalans watched Matt pace through puffy, swollen eyes, nervously licking their split, bloody lips.

Mank-Lar had told him everything. Why not? It had been an exploit of warriors and had been commanded by his king. It was the way of things. His dishonor was not what he tried to do, but that he had failed. Rasik-Alcas might kill them for that, but even the sea folk would understand they were bound to obey their king . . . wouldn't they? Mank-Lar vaguely understood that the tail-less sea folk might consider it dishonorable that King Alcas had ordered the attack in the first place, particularly since they were not at war. But that was between them and the king, was it not? He himself was just a tool, and it was pointless to deny his role. Regardless, he couldn't escape a growing concern as he watched the brooding leader of his king's enemy.

Larry Dowden approached his captain with care. He'd seen him this way—this intense—only once before, when *Walker* and *Mahan* made their suicidal charge against *Amagi*, so long ago now. It had worked, somehow, but it had also been a reckless moment and he wondered if the captain was on the verge of another one now. He opened his mouth, but hesitated, daunted by the working jaw and the icy green braziers gazing back.

"Captain," he said quietly, "Radioman Clancy says the radio's up. Lieutenant Mallory requests permission to commence a search for *Revenge*."

Matt looked at his exec for a moment and then nodded slightly. "Very well."

"Aye, aye, sir. Ah, Captain? You said you wanted to begin installing the screw this morning?" Dowden prompted gently. Matt only glanced around for a moment, as if surprised the task wasn't already under way. For the first time he noticed that almost the entire crew was present, grim-faced and angry.

"Right. I guess the men are a little distracted. Have Spanky and the Bosun light a fire under those repair parties." Several of the men held his gaze as it passed across them. "They have their own duties to perform today," he said in a voice that matched his eyes. "I'll take care of this one."

"What should we do with these two, Skipper?" Silva asked, nudging Mank-Lar hard with his shoe. Matt shrugged.

"Don't even need to try them. They've admitted they're enemy saboteurs under orders of their king. But they're without uniforms or even the courtesy of a declaration of war. Hang them."

"I want that little son of a bitch dead!" Matt said in a calm but eerily force-ful tone. The gathering was almost identical to the one the night before, only this time it was convened directly behind the massed block of the Second Marines, flanked by Rolak's expatriate Aryaalans and Queen Maraan's Six Hundred. Another entire regiment of B'mbaadan infantry was added as well. Thirty heavily armed destroyermen—not all human—were in the center, anxious to spearhead the assault with fire. The Orphan Queen stood beside Matt, her eyes gleaming with a feral, joyful light.

"It could break the alliance!" Adar pleaded. "Think of the greater threat!" Sandra stood beside the Lemurian Sky Priest and nodded her agreement, but she seemed deeply troubled.

"Why? I haven't asked any of the Homes or Guard regiments from Baalkpan to contribute to the attack." He wore an ironic expression. "I notice none have offered, either, but if they don't want to be in the assault, that's fine."

"What about the Marines? They are drawn from all our people."

Matt looked coldly at Adar. "The Marines are mine. They're all volun-teers and they've volunteered for this. I ordered Chack to make sure."

"That still does not give you the right to throw them away on this . . . sideshow!"

Matt's mounting fury exploded. "I'm *not* throwing them away! I'm using them for what they're for! We've been attacked! Suddenly and delib-erately and by stealth! Believe me, my people have recent experience with that sort of thing!" His gaze lashed Keje. "We've been attacked!" he re-peated. "And I lost a damn good man who died to save my ship. I thought you said it was 'different' if we were attacked? How is it different? I can't tell yet. I assumed it meant that then you might bring yourselves to fight oth-ers of your kind. Is that it? Or is it only different if *you* are attacked? You'll personally defend yourselves if you're personally attacked? Where would you be today if *Walker* behaved like that?"

Keje met his gaze, but then looked at Adar and blinked furiously with shame and frustration. Matt continued, his voice angry and sarcastic. "Ever since we met, *Walker* has stood up for you and your people, and she's lost a lot of good men—some to save that damn city I'm about to . . . lose *more* good men going into! But now, when it comes time to stand up for *Walker*, she's not 'one of you,' is she? You almost had me fooled. I was ready to leave Rolak's people to fend for themselves—even after they risked everything to come to our aid. We may have helped them first, but at least they know what gratitude is. Still, I was ready to leave them. Now I know there's *no way* we can leave them here with that madman loose be-hind those walls. A madman who tried to *sink my ship* after she saved his *ass* because he thought *that* would break the alliance." He grunted. "I wouldn't have believed it yesterday, but now I think he was right.

"If you still think we can just leave here with that maniac free to threaten our friends and our lines of supply, that's fine. You don't have to soil your delicate sensibilities with a morally questionable fight. I will, though, and I'll tell you something else; after what happened last night, 'greater threat' or not, if I don't make this fight the alliance *will* break. If you're all counting on *Walker* to hold you together, you'd better remember one thing. She may be made of iron, but it takes *men* to hold *her* together. Some of those men aren't even all human anymore, but they're still hers, and the ones who tried to destroy her after the sacrifice she made for them have got to *pay*! That's what *my* people say. If you can't see that, you may be 'People,' but you're not *men* and you're not our friends!"

"But—but what if you're killed?" Adar demanded, putting voice to the concerns of many. His face bore no expression, but his words were anguished. "What if Lieutenant Shinya should fall? What will we do then? I understand your anger, even if it is misplaced, I assure you, but to me the Grik threat is the *only* threat. I have sworn—"

Keje held up his hand, interrupting his old friend. "We know," he growled. "Not to rest. What Captain Reddy asks of us is not a diversion from that struggle. It's a task set before us all. Yet another task we must complete in order to finish the greater one." He turned to the others. "He is right. You all know it is true. The Amer-i-caans are our friends! They are our brothers. They have been attacked by a treacherous foe, a foe that is already the enemy of our brother Lord Rolak, whose people have risked everything to come to our aid." He turned back to Matt. "I am sorry, brother. Sorry and ashamed. I *will* fight with you."

"As will I," growled Ramik-Sa-Ar.

"And I," said Geran-Eras.

Tassat-Ay-Aracca looked bemusedly at his father, Ramik.

"I wanted to all along! I—"

Adar stepped forward as if to shush him but stopped and lowered his head. Finally, he raised his eyes, already blinking furiously with shame. "No, brothers. It is I alone who is without honor." He turned to Matt. "I see nothing but the Grik," he said softly, his silver eyes blinking moistly. "At night my dreams are haunted by the lower deck of *Revenge*. The bones, the smells . . . and the eyes of those still living . . ." He shuddered. "Against the fate that awaits our people, this"—he gestured toward the city—"this is insignificant." He blinked apology. "But you're right. You have been attacked. Lord Rolak has been wronged—as have we all—and many more souls light the heavens because of Rasik's treachery. Souls that would be in this fight yet if not for him. You're right. We cannot just 'leave him here.' He would continue to distract us from our bigger business. Besides, sometimes honor can endure only so much." He drew himself up. "Captain Reddy, you have wronged these chiefs. I alone bear the guilt of perhaps too much zeal for our cause. I made them swear they wouldn't get involved in any Aryaalan . . . adventures. I know now I have been misguided and asked too much of their honor."

Matt wasn't entirely sure if Adar was surrendering because he had to or if he really believed it best. He wasn't certain either if his last statement was an apology or a chastisement. He nodded and grasped Adar's hand. "It's better this way," he assured the priest. "The more we take to the fight, the fewer we will lose." He turned to Keje. Shinya had stepped up beside the Lemurian.

"Thanks. How long before the rest of the forces can be prepared?"

Shinya glanced at Keje and then responded. "An hour, perhaps two, I should think."

Keje nodded. "About that. Not all are ashore, but I doubt we will need all. It will be . . . difficult fighting People instead of animals," he admitted.

"Let's put it this way," Matt answered him grimly. "We saved them from the Grik and yet they threaten to obstruct our war against the common enemy. They've made hostages of their own people and attacked us by surprise—" He stopped and shook his head. "If they'll defend that, then they *are* animals."

Benjamin Mallory hummed to himself through clenched teeth as he struggled to keep the big plane flying in a northerly direction. He'd never flown a PBY in his life before he inherited this one, but for the most part, he had few complaints about its handling—at least from a straight and level perspective. It was no P-40E, or even a P-40B, but it didn't usually take every ounce of his strength to keep it flying in a straight line. Except in a crosswind. As the day wore on and a stiff westerly breeze continued to blow, it was becoming more evident why it had such a big damn rudder. Of course, in some ways the big rudder was part of the problem. It came in real handy if he ever lost an engine—which he knew from personal experience—but it sure put up a hell of a fight in a crosswind. On the other hand, he thought philosophically, if you were born with a big rudder, at least you had a big rudder to make up for it.

"Damn, Tikker," he muttered to his copilot above the droning motors overhead, "I wish your legs were longer. You could give me a hand with this."

"I can give you a hand, boss. Just no feet," Tikker said, looking dubiously down at the distant rudder pedals.

"Smart-ass." Mallory grinned. "You could squirm down there and push 'em with your hands." Tikker blinked at him.

"Your legs are longer than me, my eyes are longer than you. But I can't see through the bottom of the plane. You want me to push pedals or look for ship?"

Ben laughed. He knew that Tikker, like most Lemurians, was extremely literal-minded. He also knew most of the little boogers possessed a highly developed sense of humor and a mischievous streak a mile wide. He didn't know which was in play at the moment. Probably both. "That's okay. I'll go down there and you can fly."

Ed Palmer crawled up between them. "Radio still checks out. But only as long as you don't let the monkey fly . . . sir."

Mallory laughed again. "I swear. You guys ought to trade jobs. I bet you could fly almost as good as Tikker and I *know* he could operate the radio and navigate better than you, Ed."

Ed pushed his clipboard forward so Mallory could look at the charts.

"Where are we?"

"Well, we followed Java west for three hours and we've been flying north-northwest for two. That should put us about here," he said, pointing to a spot just south of Pulau Belitung.

"Okay. That must be it up ahead. That big-assed island with the little white specky ones all around."

Ed squinted through the windscreen. "Damn, you mean we *are* where I thought we are? With all this wind I figured we'd be east."

"Naw, I fudged the headings you gave me." Ben frowned. "Captain said to check these little islands real careful. He figures if the storm drove *Revenge* aground, that's where she'll be."

"What a mess," Ed murmured, looking first at the distant islands and then the chart. "No way she'd have squirmed through, that's for sure."

"Yeah, well," hedged Mallory uncomfortably, "maybe she did. Or maybe she's fine and Rick's still chasing lizards like he was Drake and they were Spaniards."

"Who's Drake?" Ed asked.

"Never mind. British guy."

Tikker leaned forward and squinted until his eyes were tiny slits. "Let me see chart, please," he said, and Ed handed it over. Tikker studied it carefully for a long time and squinted out the windscreen once more. "Very strange," he said and shook his head. "Usually you charts are so good."

"What? Why?"

"I see white islands where chart says should only be water."

Mallory took off his sunglasses and squinted as well. "I don't see anything."

"You push pedals, I look for ship," Tikker said smugly and resumed his study of the horizon. Ed left them and went to the engineer's compartment. One of the few things they'd discovered that still worked in the half-sunken plane when they found it was a thermos. It had been empty at the time, floating in the sandy brown water in the fuselage. Ed rescued it and had used it ever since. The initials "EP" were lightly scratched in the thick aluminum and he was struck by the coincidence since they were the same as his. He often wondered what had become of the original owner. He picked it up and poked his head into the waist gunner's compartment to make sure the other two spotters weren't goofing off. Then he carefully poured a cup of joe into a tin mug and eased his way forward against the jostling motion of the plane.

"Coffee," he announced, slowly extending the cup into Mallory's line of sight.

Ben shook his head. "Can't right now. I need both hands. Thanks, though." Ed only shrugged and took a gentle sip himself. Tikker looked at him and wrinkled his nose. Not very many Lemurians liked real coffee, much less the local brew. Like real coffee, it had a stimulating effect and that's what they used it for: medicine. Not because they liked the taste. The big island was growing larger and many of the smaller ones were easy to distinguish now. Tikker suddenly remembered the binoculars around his neck. He thought they were the neatest things in the world—next to the airplane, of course—but much as he loved them, their technology was still so unfamiliar that he often forgot he had them on. Somewhat embarrassed, he raised them now and adjusted the objective knob. Then he stiffened, and it seemed to Ben every sable hair on his body stood on end.

"What? What do you see?" For a long moment, Tikker couldn't speak. "What is it?" Ben demanded. His copilot's body language had sent a chill of concern down his spine.

"It is not islands where they do not belong," he finally managed. "It is sails. Grik sails."

"Here, give me those," Ben said, taking the binoculars from Tikker's neck. He tried to hold the wheel and the glasses steady at the same time, but found it impossible. He glanced at Tikker, who seemed immobilized by shock. Now wasn't the time for another flying lesson. He handed the binoculars over his shoulder to Ed, who put his cup down on the flight deck in front of him. It immediately began to vibrate violently, "walking" around and sloshing its contents. He raised the glasses to his eyes.

"God a'mighty," he whispered. The entire horizon, from the islands of Pulau Belitung to the distant hint of a smudge that was western Borneo, was dotted with hundreds of dingy pyramid shapes. The water below was still a little foamy and the whitecaps had turned the normally warm, dark blue sea a kind of dirty turquoise, but the hint of red from the enemy hulls made them stand out quite clearly. "God a'mighty," he repeated, a little louder this time and with an edge of panic in his voice.

The intercom crackled and an excited voice reached them from one of the observation blisters. "Ship! Ship! I see ship! Right below! Wake up, you in front! You not see ship?"

Revenge had been through hell. As soon as the size of the storm became apparent, Rick Tolson and Kas-Ra-Ar knew their only hope was to beat north as far as they could and gain as much sea room as possible before the seas grew too large to do anything but run before them. With grim satisfaction, they'd pounded the lone Grik ship with a pair of broadsides as it drew near. Then, leaving the enemy trailing a shattered mainmast and at the mercy of the coming blow, *Revenge* went about. The wind drove out of the west-northwest at first, and the ship shouldered her way through the growing swells far into the Natuna Sea.

For that day and half the night she pounded north, farther than she'd ever been. Past Singapore, in fact, though the chance of anyone seeing her, or caring if they did, was slim. With only her staysails set, she heaved and corkscrewed into the South China Sea as the mounting waves threatened to drive her under with their irresistible force. There were islands in the area too, many islands, but the risk wasn't as great as the almost solid wall that lay to the south. Seams opened and the chain pumps clanked and even the most hard-bitten Lemurian mariners were prostrated with fatigue and seasickness. Finally, when they'd managed as much northeasting as the storm would allow, they wore, and under a bare scrap of her fore-topsail, she ran before the mountainous quartering swell. Rick couldn't believe the height of the sea. It seemed impossible in such shallow water. Occasionally, bits of strange coral and wriggling fish were left in the scuppers when the sea broke over the ship. He half expected her to strike bottom and break her back when in the trough of some of the waves.

The wind and sea whittled her down. Masts and spars and shredded canvas were plucked away bit by bit and the exhausted crew fought like demons to keep the water out. The entire mizzenmast went, along with the maintop, when she was pooped by a mountain of water and several of the crew were lost. The rest of the mainmast, the foretop, and most of the bowsprit were lost the following day when a bolt of lightning struck the ship like a bomb. With only a scrap of the fore course and a single staysail, *Revenge* battled on.

It was in part a testimony, perhaps, to the skill of her hated builders and to the ancient design they'd used. Mostly, however, it was the skill and strength of her officers and crew and their unflagging will to survive and fight that allowed *Revenge* to live to see morning and a calming sea. Just in time. By the end of the final day of the storm's lessening wrath, Pulau Belitung was looming to the south. They dropped both anchors with plenty of scope in the Gaspar Strait, waiting tensely until the ship drug to a stop in the heavy current but lighter swells. There the ship pitched at the end of her cables, waterlogged and shattered, throughout the night and the following day. The crew worked on, repairing what they could with the booming sound of breakers all around.

Rick had worked as tirelessly as any and a close bond was forged between him and the crew. Kas was instrumental, as always, and there was no doubt that if it hadn't been for him, all would have been lost. But it was the symbolism of their Amer-i-caan captain sharing their fate as well as their glory that raised the crew's spirits. Up to that point, Rick had been a popular figure aboard, friendly and competent and raring for a fight. But until then, their greatest challenge had been the Battle of B'mbaado Bay. A great battle and a fine adventure, but *Revenge* had suffered little. Then, throughout their short, successful cruise, *Revenge* had everything her way and their quick, one-sided battles with the Grik had been more play than anything else.

During the storm, however, they'd all suffered deeply. But they'd done it together, as a Home. Captain, crew, and the now strangely less hated ship had worked and fought solely for the common good. None could have survived alone without the others. In spite of everything, *Revenge* was no longer just a ship representing Baalkpan. She'd become a Home. Battered and leaky and in need of much repair, but a real Home nonetheless. And there was no doubt in anyone's mind that Rick Tolson was her High Chief.

That morning, patched and caulked as much as possible, *Revenge* cut her cables and ran down the Gaspar Strait and back into the Java Sea, southeast under as much canvas as she could cram on her reinforced lower foremast. Rick and Kas believed—weather permitting—that they'd limp back into Aryaal in a week or so. Together, they were leaning on the quarterdeck rail, taking turns with Rick's binoculars and studying the nearby islands. The lower, smaller ones had been scoured clean by the storm. Fallen trees and other debris drawn away by the retreating surge floated everywhere, and lizard birds swooped and capered, snatching up dead fish. Rick watched a skuggik, or something similar, standing stoically on a dead tree as it drifted out to sea.

"*Hell* of a storm," he said.

Kas nodded companionably. "I've seen worse, but rarely." The Lemurian grinned and blinked. "And never on anything this small." He pointed at the stranded creature. "Perhaps *he* knows how we feel."

"I wonder if any of the feluccas made it."

Kas's grin quickly faded. "I fear not. They were never designed to ride the Strakka. They are not designed for much at all beyond coastal fishing. We shouldn't have brought them."

"They were a big help. Until we have a larger navy, we may have to use them again." Rick shrugged. "It's war."

Kas looked at him. "I've noticed you Amer-i-caans use that phrase a lot to explain much. You're a war-fighting race. Mine—at least the ones that live upon the sea—is not. Do you find it helps to use the war as an excuse for everything bad that happens?"

Rick returned his stare. "Yeah, I guess so. You like to think that war isn't forever and if it weren't for the war things would be better . . ." He shrugged again. "Besides, it's mostly true—or I hope it is." He shook his head and grinned. "Don't get me wrong, though. I'm having a blast!" Kas looked around them at the devastation and blinked exasperation. Rick chuckled. "Well . . . as Captain Reddy would say"—he screwed his brows into a fair imitation of one of Matt's wry expressions—"'It's been a tough couple of days!'" They both laughed at the understatement.

Rick's face turned thoughtful. "I am having a blast," he repeated. "I have a command of my own and despite her questionable pedigree, she's one of the most powerful warships afloat. When she's in one piece she's fast, well built—thank God!—and weatherly." Glancing past Kas at one of the many work gangs diligently at their labors, he added, "And she's got the best damn crew any ship like her ever had in this messed-up world. A destroyerman couldn't ask for much more." He paused. "Engines would be nice, but then she wouldn't need her sails and that's part of her charm."

He became serious again. "But that's not what you asked." He sighed. "Yeah, the war's to blame. Those fishermen on the feluccas, they wouldn't have been here if not for the war. They'd have been catching flashies and feeding their families instead of fighting for their lives in a storm they couldn't beat. That's the war's fault, not ours. And before you think that if we weren't fighting the war there wouldn't be one, try to remember *why* we fight. It's fight or die and that's not much of a choice. You *might* die if you fight, but you *will* die if you don't. If you look at it like that, the War isn't an excuse but a blessing. A chance for survival." Rick grew silent and thoughtful for a moment.

"You know, now that I think about it, it *is* different here. What I said before is all a bunch of crap. We can shake our heads and say, 'It's war,' because it's easy and it's what my people are used to. At home, it might even be true sometimes. The war we left behind might've been different, but who's to say? The Nazis and the Japs were *very* bad, but most of the time it's not that black and white. Here? It's the lizards. Period. They're the ones to blame. 'The War' is what we're doing to stop the lizards and when you think of it like that, it makes a good explanation." Rick yawned hugely and then smiled at his friend.

"I'm tired, and I may not be making a lot of sense, but whatever else I said, I guess what I mean is, if we lost the feluccas, they didn't die for nothing. They were helping fight the War, and in maybe this one and only instance, war is good."

Kas grinned again. "Before the storm came, you certainly seemed to be enjoying it."

Rick grinned back at him. "Well, when something needs doing, it always helps to be good at doing it, and we were so, so good—"

Kas suddenly tilted his head as if listening intently. Rick heard it too. Within minutes, the entire crew of *Revenge* was jumping up and down and pointing gleefully at the sky as the small dark shape of the PBY grew larger and began a rapid spiraling descent. Soon it was skipping tentatively across the tops of the choppy waves until it splashed to a rather abrupt halt some distance ahead of the ship.

Ordinarily, *Revenge* would heave to and lower a boat. They were going to have to think of something else this time, since all the ship's boats had been either lost or badly damaged. This must've become apparent to the flying boat's crew, because as *Revenge* drew near, a small rubber raft appeared in the water under the plane's left wing. Almost as soon as it did, however, it began to deflate.

"Damn flashies," Rick muttered, realizing the fish must have torn the raft apart. "I wonder what now?"

Eventually a man and a Lemurian appeared out of the top of the pilot's compartment and climbed up onto the wing. Slowly, they made their way to the end and crouched there waiting above the float.

"Dangerous," Kas observed.

Rick nodded and called to the helmsman. "Easy there! Don't so much as scratch that plane. Captain Reddy would never forgive us!"

Slowly, *Revenge* wallowed up to the plane. When she was just a few feet off the wingtip, Tikker leaped lightly across. Ed Palmer followed close behind, but with less self-assurance. Waiting hands grabbed him and kept him from falling backward into the water, and his face was drained of color as he stuck out his hand to Rick.

"Man, are you ever a sight for sore eyes!" Rick said happily as he grasped it. Ed returned the greeting with a small, sickly smile of his own, but he seemed distracted. He was looking around at the ship. In spite of the herculean effort to clean her up, her massive damage was still evident. Her deck stood empty of almost anything but her smiling crew. The jagged stumps of her fallen masts jutted forlornly from the quarterdeck and the waist.

"Uh, Captain Tolson," Palmer said hesitantly, using the honorary but still appropriate title for the commander of any ship. "Can you make this thing go any faster?"

Rick Tolson was taken aback by the abrupt question. "Why?"

"Lizards. Coming this way!"

Rick quickly glanced around. Yeah, she was hammered, but with her guns, she still ought to be able to hold off a couple of enemy ships at once, if she had to.

"No, but we ought to be okay. Guns'll keep them off us." He looked at Kas, smiling. "Oh, well, back to 'the War.' And *you* wanted to throw the guns over the side when we started taking water!" he said. Kas began to reply but Palmer interrupted.

"No, damn it!" he said harshly. "You don't understand!"

They stood at the taffrail, staring aft while the horizon filled with enemy sails.

"Does Captain Reddy know about this?"

"I don't know," Ed confessed. "We've been transmitting, but we're pretty far and the atmospherics are lousy."

"How many can fit in the plane?" Rick asked quietly.

"Uh, maybe twenty or thirty of the little guys. Hell, they don't weigh much. The trick'll be finding a place to cram them all," Ed replied.

"They weigh more than you think. They're all muscle." Rick shook his head. "If you flew due east, you could set them on Borneo. With weapons, many would survive the predators and they could easily evade the lizards if they went ashore looking for them. Three-hour round-trip to get back and pick up another load . . ." He sighed. "Not enough time. I'll get you twenty. I don't know how, draw lots or something, and you get them the hell out."

"Twenty besides you and Gandy Bowles? I'll ask Lieutenant Mallory if we can haul that many."

"No," Rick said. "Gandy should leave, but I'm not going anywhere. If we can't all get out, then I stay. It's *my* ship!"

Ed's mouth dropped open and he just stared. He couldn't help it. "Yeah, but, Captain—Rick—there's *two hundred ships* over there, maybe more! I like cat-monkeys a lot, don't get me wrong. I think they're swell, but we *need* you! There's only about a hundred and thirty humans in the whole wide world, as far as we know!"

Rick smiled. "C'mon, Ed. There's more of us somewhere, even if it's just where we came from." He turned and looked upon the wide-eyed, blinking, but otherwise expressionless faces that stared back at him. The faces of his crew. "*Revenge* needs me more."

Six members of *Revenge*'s crew, those most seriously injured in the storm, were carefully swayed over onto the PBY's wing and gently stowed inside. Mallory remained at the controls throughout, cursing and maneuvering the plane against the swells as best he could. When the six were safely transferred, the *Revenge* crew who'd assisted with the operation all scampered back aboard their ship to await the oncoming horde. Even Gandy Bowles, whom Rick practically ordered to leave, elected to remain behind. Ed crawled out to the wingtip once more and Rick Tolson met him just a few feet away with a leather-bound book in his hand. He had to shout to be heard over the engines as the PBY cruised alongside.

"Here's my log. Give it to Captain Reddy! It's a damned exciting read, if I say so myself!"

Ed grabbed his hat before the wind took it over the side. His eyes were stinging. From the salt spray, he told himself. "I'll give it to him," he managed to reply.

"Kas wrote something in there for Keje. They're cousins, you know." Ed nodded. Rick spared a glance to the north. The mass of enemy ships was close enough now that individual forms could be seen upon them. Their garish banners fluttered ominously in the stiff west wind. In the distance, still beyond the horizon, a dark smudge of smoke was vaguely visible. Maybe one of the damn things has caught fire, Ed hoped bitterly. They'd cut it as close as they dared.

"Tell Captain Reddy . . . thanks," continued Rick, handing the book across. "Thanks for the opportunity. It's been a blast. I always knew I was a pirate at heart!" White teeth shone in his tanned, bearded face. "Now get the hell out of here, Signalman Palmer!"

Ed nodded again, and standing as straight as he dared on the swooping wing, he braced to attention and threw Rick Tolson the best salute he knew how. With that, he turned and made his way carefully back to the space between the engines. Mallory throttled back so as not to blow him into the sea, and Palmer dropped down into the pilot's compartment and disappeared.

Calmly, Captain Tolson, commander of *Revenge,* turned to Kas-Ra-Ar. "Clear for action!" he said, the grin still on his face. "Boy, I get such a kick out of saying that!"

"That's it? *Six?*" Mallory demanded. Ed nodded without a word. "*Shit!*" shouted Ben in frustration. "Now I know what the captain meant when he asked me what I'd do!" Ed had no idea what he was talking about, but given the context of the situation, he could make a pretty good guess. "All right," Mallory said at last. "Strap in. As soon as we're airborne, try to raise *Walker* again. You have ten minutes. Then I want you on the nose gun. Tell those 'Cats in the waist to get ready too." He fiddled with the throttles as he turned the plane into the wind. "Maybe if we strafe 'em a few times we'll scare 'em off," he added doubtfully.

The engines roared and the hull pounded and thundered beneath their feet as the plane tried to increase speed, but instead it just seemed to wallow through the choppy swells.

"C'mon! *C'mon!*" Mallory shouted, and slammed the throttles to their stops.

"What's the matter?" Palmer shouted from behind him. Tikker sat, perfectly still, both eyes clenched shut.

"Oh, ah, nothing, Ed. It's just a little rougher than I'm used to!" His voice was vibrating sympathetically with the airplane.

"I'm gonna be sick!" Palmer moaned when the plane pitched nose-first into a larger wave that seemed to arrest all forward motion. "Airsick and seasick all at once!"

Surprisingly, particularly after the sensation of slowing down, the Catalina suddenly clawed its way out of the water. It clipped the top of another big wave with a resounding boom and a cascade of spray, and then slowly, laboriously, lumbered into the sky.

"Yes!"

At five hundred feet Mallory banked and began a slow turn back toward the crippled ship. The enemy was alarmingly close. Beyond the shock he felt at the sheer number of the things, Ben couldn't imagine how they'd gotten here so quickly. Before the storm, there'd been no evidence such a force even existed—much less was planning to advance. It must have come from somewhere else, close on the heels of the storm, using the very fury of its trailing edge to make them fly. But why now? What was the rush? Ben was certain it was a response to the defeat they'd been handed at Aryaal, but how in blue blazes had the word spread so fast? And how could the enemy have possibly gathered so many ships so quickly? One thing was certain, though; the allied invasion of Singapore was off.

"Get on the horn! We have to tell Captain Reddy!" he cried.

"Maybe that's a little more important than shooting up a few of them?" Ed suggested.

"Sure. But it won't hurt if we do. They don't have anything that can reach us this high, do they?"

"You're asking me? Hell, we're just scouts! We haven't even seen a real battle yet."

"We're about to," Ben muttered. The enemy ships appeared to be making at least eight knots, while *Revenge* was barely making three. Mallory orbited the Catalina above her for several more minutes while Palmer tried to contact the destroyer. The Grik would be in range of *Revenge*'s guns very soon.

"What's the scoop, Ed?"

"I don't know. I think we're transmitting, I don't see why not, but there's a hell of a lot of noise. Probably just out of range." He grunted. "They might be hearing us," he added lamely.

"There's smoke," Tikker said, speaking softly for the first time in a while and pointing at the horizon. "Black smoke. It looks like it's coming from a black island, like a—how you say? Vol-caanno?"

"Volcano," Ben agreed absently. "No shortage of those hereabouts." He continued to crane his neck and stare intently at the drama unfolding below. Never had he felt so helpless, so utterly useless. It was like some horrible nightmare, to stand impotently by while others needed him so desperately and there was absolutely nothing he could do.

Revenge began her fight. Even as he watched, the whole side of the friendly ship disappeared behind a cloud of white smoke. Twelve-pound shot from ten guns shivered the sails of one of the approaching ships, and pieces of debris splashed into the sea around it. It was exhilarating and it felt good to see, but in the face of the descending avalanche, it was nothing. "Give 'em hell, Rick," he whispered. "All right, Ed, get in the nose!" He pressed his microphone. "Waist gunners, I know you haven't had much practice, but you know how to operate your guns. They're packed so tight down there you can't hardly miss, but try to concentrate on killing Grik. You can't do enough damage to enough ships to make a difference. Remember, short, controlled bursts. We might be able to make ammo again someday, but machine-gun barrels are gonna take a while. *Hang on!*"

He banked sharply toward the advancing line and the massive flying-boat thundered over, just three hundred feet above their masts.

"Commence firing!" he shouted. "Just the ones closest to *Revenge*! Damn, what I'd give for a couple of bombs right now!" His last comment was drowned by the staccato bursts of one .30- and two .50-caliber machine guns. The firing in the waist was accompanied by high-pitched squeals of delight. The airframe vibrated more than usual with the recoil of the guns and Ben continued his tight-banking turn to keep his indicated targets in range. Geysers of water marched from ship to ship and then disappeared when the bullets struck wood. Tightly packed Grik warriors were slaughtered in droves.

"Let 'em have it!" Ben screamed. *Revenge* vanished behind another cloud of smoke and this time the foremast of one of the closest ships tottered into the sea. Dragged around by the trailing debris, the ship veered sharply to port and speared into another Grik ship sailing directly alongside. Others slammed into the entangled wrecks from behind and it looked to Ben like a giant chain-reaction pileup on the highway.

"Hell, yes! Outstanding!" he shouted as still more ships added to the catastrophe.

"What are those ones doing?" Tikker asked, pointing. Ben looked. Several ships had broken from the pack and were trying to cut *Revenge* off. If they crossed her bow, the ship's guns wouldn't bear and they'd be free to grapple. Once that happened, it would be all over but the dying.

"New targets!" yelled Ben. "Engage the ships out front! One of them looks different . . . bigger! And the hull's white and gold—not red. I bet it's special somehow. Give it an extra dose!" The nose gun and the port .50 stitched the sea around the unusual ship. Splinters and debris erupted and bodies fell, while others tried to surge away from the impacts. A few even fell into the sea.

"I'm empty!" came a frustrated, keening shriek from aft. So much for controlled bursts. Ben stomped on the right rudder pedal and banked the opposite direction, allowing the starboard gunner a chance.

"Make 'em count!" he snarled. The plane rattled as the other gun resumed fire. Down below, *Revenge* was wreathed in smoke. Bright jets of flame stabbed out at irregular intervals. Several enemy ships were almost upon her and they were being systematically dismantled. Masts crowded with struggling forms fell into the sea and at least one of the enemy was dead in the water, its shattered bow dipping low. So far, none of the enemy had employed their "Grik Fire," however. They seemed intent on coming to grips with *Revenge*, whatever the cost.

"They want her in one piece," Ben surmised aloud. There was nothing he could do about it. Ed's gun had fallen silent in the nose. The PBY wasn't carrying much ammunition—it was never imagined that it would need more than would be necessary to keep a threat at bay while it took off. Much like what had happened right after they discovered it. Now, even as the starboard waist gun continued to stutter, grappling hooks arced through the air, trailing their lines behind them like hundreds of spiders casting their webs.

"Damn it!" Ben exclaimed. His voice cracked. "They want her guns!"

Ed reappeared at his shoulder. "Rick won't let them take her," he said with sad, quiet certainty. Even as they circled, watching with sick fascination, more and more enemy vessels crowded forward like ants upon a stricken comrade. *Revenge* had disappeared entirely within the forest of masts and the only way they could tell her position was by the proximity of the strange white ship and the hazy column of smoke that still rose from the center of the mass. The final waist gun was silent now, but still

Ben orbited above. On the decks of the outer ships, Grik waved their swords at them and made taunting gestures.

There was a brilliant flash of yellow fire and a billowing cloud of smoke. Masts toppled outward from the blast like trees on the slope of a volcano and fiery debris rocketed into the sky. The plane was buffeted by the shock wave of the explosion and Ben fought the wheel to regain control. He quickly banked again to see the results through his suddenly unfocused eyes. Eight or ten ships had been in close contact with *Revenge* when she blew herself up. Two were just gone, and three more were smoldering wrecks. Vigorous fires had taken hold on several more and the smoke added to the vast pall now drifting downwind. Of *Revenge* and the white ship that had been beside her, there was no sign.

"That's the style," muttered Ben. His voice was almost a sob. He gently eased back on the controls and the Catalina began to gain altitude.

"Are we leaving now?" Ed asked.

"I guess," Ben replied. "I just couldn't before. Not while there was anybody down there who could see us." Ed nodded understanding. "Besides, the captain . . . everyone will want to know how it ended." He sighed. "One more thing, too. I want to get a solid count of how many ships they have. We're still the 'eyes' of the fleet."

At three thousand feet, Ben circled again while the others counted the enemy.

"Jesus, there's a lot of them. I've lost count twice," Ed said.

"It doesn't have to be perfect. What do you have, Tikker?"

"Three hundred ten, but that's not all I see, that's all I can count. There's more on the horizon." Tikker squinted again. "There's that Volcaanno still." He shook his head. "It looks closer now."

For the first time, Ben really looked to the north where Tikker had spotted the smoke. Sure enough, a solid black column was slanting away to the east. He blinked and rubbed his eyes. "What the . . . ?" He leveled out and pointed the Catalina north, toward the distant smudge.

"What is it?" asked Ed.

"I dunno. It *looks* like . . . but that's impossible." Frozen mercury poured down his back.

"It *is*!" Ed exclaimed excitedly. He was looking through the binoculars now. "It's a ship! A modern ship! Burning coal, by the look of her. That's why all the black smoke." He hesitated and his face assumed a troubled expression. "But what the hell is she doing running around with a bunch of lizards? Look, they're all around her!"

"Maybe they captured her? She had to have gotten here the same way we did. Hell, they nearly got us, remember?"

Ed was still staring intently through the glasses. "Jeez, that's not just any ship, it's a *warship*! She looks bigger than the goddamn *Arizona*!"

The icy mercury running down Ben's back was suddenly joined in his stomach by molten lead. "Give me those!" he said, snatching the glasses away. "Tikker, take the controls!"

The Lemurian stared, wide-eyed, at the wheel in front of him and then grasped it in both of his clawed hands. The tone in Ben's voice told him that any fooling around wouldn't be acceptable. He clenched his teeth and held the wheel as tight and steady as he could. Ben adjusted the objective until the image became crystal clear. His subconscious mind screamed in protest and he almost dropped the binoculars. Even at twelve or fifteen miles the silhouette was unmistakable. He'd seen it before. The last time had been three-quarters of a year before and he'd been standing on *Walker*'s gun control platform with belts of .30-cal over his shoulders.

"This day just gets worse and worse," he said at last.

"What?" demanded Ed.

"You remember that Jap battle cruiser we fought past to duck into the Squall that brought us here?"

"Yeah . . ." Ed's face went white.

"That's her. *Amagi*."

"Son of a *bitch*!" Ed snarled, "I *knew* it! The lizards are *Japs*! Sneaky sons of bitches!"

"We don't know that. The Japs might be lizards."

"What do you mean?"

"The lizards might've captured her. Learned how to use her. We don't know that they're working together. That's how they got their sailing ships, remember?" He looked through the binoculars again. "Trouble is, I don't think we dare get close enough to find out. If they *are* Japs, they're working with the lizards. They'll blow us out of the sky. If they're lizards, it's clear they got the Japs to show them how to operate the ship. They may not have thought they needed to learn about antiaircraft fire, but we're slow as hell. They might still blow us out of the sky. We've got to warn the captain!"

"How close would we have to get . . . to know?"

"Close enough to see if there's Japs or lizards on her. We'd probably be in range by then."

"What about her flag?" Ed asked. "The lizards have all kinds of flags of their own. If they had the ship, they wouldn't leave the 'meatball.'"

"Good point. We might get close enough to see that before they shoot us down." He shrugged. "It doesn't really matter, though. Whatever flag she's flying, we're screwed."

———

Radioman 1st Class Russell Clancy leaned back in his chair, sipping "monkey joe," in *Walker*'s small, cryptlike radio room underneath the pilothouse. He'd been there all day monitoring the radio and he'd only left once to go to the head. Even then, he'd been reduced to hollering to get somebody to spell him. There was only a skeleton crew aboard. Almost half the human destroyermen were ashore, preparing to attack the city. Most everybody still on the ship was aft, trying to fit the new propeller. His calls to the bridge had been answered, but nobody ever came. That made him mad, since surely they'd heard his yelling—even without the comm. It wasn't like they could have forgotten him. Finally, Reynolds burst into the compartment and told him, "Go! Haul ass!" There was about to be a humongous battle on a shore—they could see everything from the bridge—and he was going to miss it if Clancy didn't hurry up.

That was over an hour ago, and the battle had yet to begin. Occasionally, he stole out the hatch—leaving it open so he could hear—and tried to see up to the north gate of Aryaal, but he wasn't quite high enough. There was a lot of coming and going, though. Troops going ashore from the rest of the fleet. Evidently, the rest of the AEF was pitching in after all. After what had happened, he thought, it was the least they could do. The men were hopping mad over Donaghey's death and the attempt to sink the ship, and Clancy figured that if their friends hadn't come, or worse, tried to stop them, it would have gone down pretty hard.

Clancy was angry as well. He hadn't known Donaghey well—he was a snipe—but he seemed like an all right guy. He wished he was ashore with the others instead of cooped-up waiting for a transmission that never came. That was frustrating too. He *knew* the radio was fine. They'd tested it that morning before the plane flew off. They'd even maintained contact for quite a while as it flew ever farther north. Then, all of a sudden, there was nothing. Just some weird static. It wasn't coming from his end, he was sure, and he doubted that Ed had done anything on his end to cause it. Ed could be a screwball, but he was a pretty good hand with a radio and besides, with the skipper on the warpath, he knew better than to goof around.

A hazy tendril of concern began to creep into Clancy's thoughts. Steve Riggs was in Baalkpan working on a system of communications for the defenses there. With him and Palmer both gone, Clancy would *be* the communications department. Of course, without the radio on the plane, there wouldn't be much need for one. All in all, it had been a pretty nerve-racking day.

"C'mon, Ed," he muttered. "Talk to me."

Suddenly enough to startle him with the irony, he thought he detected something buried in the static. He put his earphones on and began adjusting knobs. There! The unmistakable "beep beeping" began to emerge. Instead of voice, the signal was coming in CW, or Morse code. He snatched up a pencil and began to transcribe the letters as they came.

ZSA ZSA ZSA. (Can you receive?) Over and over again. Clancy quickly tapped back a reply.

ZSB-2. (I can receive. Readability fair.)

ZOE-5-O-J. (I am going to transmit in strings of five-urgent-verify and repeat.)

For an instant Clancy just stared at his key. "What the hell?" he muttered. They'd been transmitting in the clear for so long it didn't make any sense. Why on earth would Ed want to use five-letter code groups?

ZOE-5-O-J, he finally tapped back.

It wouldn't be long now. The bright passion of Matt's rage had ebbed somewhat as the day progressed, and that was probably for the best, he realized. The endless delays of preparing an army for battle had stretched into the midafternoon, and at times he found himself wondering if he really should have waited for the rest of the force to join them. Keje's and even Shinya's estimate of the time it would take to get ready had been overly optimistic. Intellectually, he knew the wait was a small price to pay. Not only would the larger force face less difficulty and take fewer casualties when it stormed the city, but now that it was decided, he believed even more strongly that it was important they all go in together.

The various members of the Allied Expeditionary Force had to learn here and now that they couldn't pick and choose which battles were convenient for them to fight. They were all in this together and if they were going to win this war, they had to share the burden equally. That didn't mean he felt any less frustrated over the delays. Lord Rolak's force and the Marines still constituted the point of the spear, but Queen Maraan's had been pulled back in reserve and replaced by the Third and Fifth Guards. That's what took the most time. It was believed—probably correctly—that the defenders would fight harder if they knew they were facing their ancestral enemies from across the bay. Matt's destroyermen had been redeployed as well— much to their disgust. They'd still go in with the "first wave" but more as heavy-weapons support platoons than front-line shock troops. Their job would be to shoot archers and commanders with the Springfields and Krags and break up enemy concentrations with the Thompsons and BARs. Either way, they'd be in the thick of the fighting, Matt knew, and they'd use an awful lot of ammunition. And there'd be losses. Of that he was certain. But there was no way he could keep his men out of this fight.

He himself was going in, wounded shoulder or not. Sandra hadn't even tried to stop him, knowing it was pointless. Without a word, she'd almost coldly done her best to completely immobilize his left arm while leaving him as much freedom of movement as she could. Then she went to join her medical staff as they prepared for the inevitable wounded. It hurt him to think she disapproved of what he was doing. He recognized the special tragedy of the losses they would endure in this "sideshow" affair. But he was certain to his core that if they didn't fight today, all would eventually be lost. It was more than just a matter of honor—although there was that as well. And it was more than just the danger of leaving a viper at their backs. It would be this event, he hoped, even more than the battle they'd fought against the Grik, that would forge all the fractious forces of the AEF into a single cooperative fighting force. The day had not started out looking like that would be the case, but this new purpose, this goal, had slowly formed throughout the morning as the other commanders came to realize the nature of the test. If it took this "sideshow" to finally weld the Lemurian people—and their American allies—into a united nation of some sort, then so be it.

Lord Rolak was standing beside him, waiting while the final preparations were completed.

"Once more," Matt said. "We'll give them one more chance to lay down their arms and surrender that murdering king. There'll be no time to think about it, no pause for consultations. They'll say yes or no. If they refuse, we attack immediately." Keje nodded solemn agreement. They'd been more than patient. More than fair. Even Adar seemed to have resigned himself to the necessity of the assault. He had embraced the Heavens and blessed the host and most had joined him in the devotional, regardless of denomination. The rites were similar enough, after all, and the bright sun overhead would bear witness to the deeds of B'mbaadans and Aryaalans just as the Heavens would contemplate the actions of the sea folk that day. Now he was as anxious as the others to get on with it. The sooner it was finished, the sooner they could get back to their "bigger business."

Down at the dock, Walker's bell began to ring and her whistle made a sharp exclamation. Matt and his staff turned to look. They saw two men running toward them through the few remaining storm-battered warehouses and the debris of the fishing ghetto. It was half a mile or more, but they were running full out.

"What's that all about?" Matt said aloud. Panting from the unaccustomed exertion, Larry Dowden and Russell Clancy finally lurched to a stop before the captain. Both men saluted, but neither could speak for a moment. "I guess this must be pretty important, Mr. Dowden, for you to leave your posts, run all the way up here, and interrupt our battle," Matt said dryly.

"Yes, sir," Larry gasped, and motioned Clancy forward. "We finally heard from Mallory." Clancy handed over a message form. It was slightly crinkled and blotched with sweat. "I thought you better see that before the fight started," Larry explained.

Matt raised his eyebrows, and then he glanced at the paper in his hand.

REVENGE DAMAGED IN STORM AND BROUGHT TO ACTION BY SUPERIOR ENEMY FLEET X DESTROYED IN BATTLE SOUTH PULAU BELITUNG X SIX SURVIVORS ALL INJURED RETRIEVED BEFORE BATTLE X ENEMY FORCE ESTIMATED 300 REPEAT 300 PLUS SHIPS COURSE SOUTH SOUTHEAST 175 DEGREES EIGHT KNOTS X ENEMY IN COMPANY JAP BATTLE CRUISER BELIEVED AMAGI X NO SHIT X MESSAGE ENDS

For a long, long moment, Captain Reddy stared down at the rumpled sheet. Over and over he read the words, convinced he'd somehow imagined them. As realization began to dawn and disbelief faded into horror, the implications of what he read descended upon him at last. He doubted if any commander in history had ever received such an unexpected and decisively catastrophic dispatch. It was over, hopeless. Everything they'd worked for, the plans and sacrifice, even the victories they'd gained were for nothing. The "Grand Offensive" to destroy the Grik menace forever now smacked of the hubris of a mouse menacing an elephant with a stick. Three hundred enemy ships—that alone made the odds impossible. They represented more than 150,000 warriors. Possibly many more. And if they really had *Amagi* . . .

He looked at his watch. A little after three. They had about five hours of daylight left and *Amagi*, if she was real, was no more than five hundred miles away. At eight knots, she'd be here in just over two days. He turned to Shinya, who was still standing nearby. For a moment he hesitated, studying the Japanese officer he'd come to rely on so much. He shook his head. Time enough later for doubts like that.

"All officers right here, right now. There's not a moment to lose." Shinya saluted, bewildered, and detailed runners to collect the various commanders. Keje looked at Matt. He sensed the change that had come over his friend and he saw that Dowden and Palmer were visibly upset. He gestured at the paper.

"A message from the flying-boat?"

Matt nodded, reading it yet again.

"Bad news?"

Matt glanced at him and then pitched his voice so no one else could hear. "I think we just lost the war."

When the various commanders and chiefs had hastily assembled, Matt regarded them carefully and wondered how to begin. They didn't have time even for this, but if they were to have any chance at all, there could be no lengthy debate. It probably depended most on Queen Maraan and how she reacted. Without her support, all was lost.

"We have no time," he said without preamble. "None." He held up the dispatch so all could see. "*Revenge* has been destroyed. Not in the storm but by the enemy. Right now, more than three hundred of their ships are headed this way. They'll be here in two days."

There were gasps and mumbled protests, but Matt waded through it all. "Even worse, it seems they now have an iron ship of their own. You've all seen what my ship is capable of against the enemy. This ship that has sided with the Grik can destroy *Walker* just as easily."

Now there were shouts of dismay and even an edge of panic. How could it be? Such a ship was surely impossible and if not, how had it come to the Grik? No! It couldn't be. He saw Adar standing as though stricken. His mouth hung open in shock and his eyelids blinked in a furious blur. Forestalling any argument, Matt plowed relentlessly on.

"Imagine a ship newer and more advanced than mine, with more and bigger weapons and almost as large as a Home. That's what we face, combined with the Grik armada. There's *no way* we can stand against it. Not here, not with what we have. Our only hope is to evacuate immediately—everybody—from Aryaal and B'mbaado and retreat to Baalkpan as quickly as possible. The enemy is faster than we are, so we have to leave, all of us, no later than tomorrow. If they catch us at sea we'll all be destroyed." He paused and stared directly at Queen Maraan. The usually self-possessed leader of B'mbaado was caught in an unaccustomed whirlwind of horror and indecision.

"How?" she asked quietly, her large silver eyes wide with shock. "How can I abandon my country, my home?"

"You must, Your Highness," he answered gently. "Land is not important when it comes to the very survival of your people." He shook his head. "No, I didn't mean that. Of course land is important. But it's an asset you can trade for time while you save the people that matter even more. That's something I was just starting to figure out myself a few months back. I didn't like it, and maybe the way we were doing it was screwed up, but it was our only choice. One of these days, we'll get the land back, Your Majesty, but right now your people need you to lead them to safety, and we desperately need you by our side."

"But how will we take them all? The Homes of the battle line were already crowded with troops."

"We'll pack them in like sand, if we have to. Fill the feluccas to over-flowing. We'll leave no one behind."

"But we will!" she insisted bitterly. "We cannot gather them all, not in so little time! Many do not live in the city. B'mbaado is not a bastion in the wilderness where her people skulk behind walls to protect them from the beasts. There are few dangerous animals on the island and many live in the hills and along the coast!"

"Then you'll have to leave some troops to warn them, to help them hide in the interior. The Grik may not even stay here long, or venture far from the city. Maybe we can send fast ships from time to time, like *Walker* or *Mahan,* to take them off." He shrugged. "Together, at Baalkpan, we might even beat them if they follow us there, and then we can retake your kingdom. The defenses of Baalkpan are formidable and there are now many guns. But if you stay here, that'll never happen and all will die."

Finally she nodded, and huge, bright tears welled in the eyes of the Queen Protector of B'mbaado. Matt had never even known Lemurians could cry. Slowly, she turned to Haakar-Faask.

"It must be you," she said in a stricken whisper. "You must gather those we leave behind and protect them." Stiffly, she embraced the old warrior, and just as stiffly, glancing around at those nearby, he embraced her back. Matt could tell there was deep feeling between them but they were also highly conscious that they were on a stage in front of many strangers as well as their own people. He heard a sniff from Sandra's direction, but he was filled with admiration.

Safir Maraan backed away from the embrace and struck a pose before the Allied Expeditionary Force. When she spoke, her voice was shockingly loud for such a small creature, but Matt had grown to expect it by now. All Lemurians were just damn loud when they wanted to be.

"My people! My friends! Events have transpired that will force us to leave our kingdom, our homes, for a time. A Grik host advances that all of us combined"—she gestured at all the allied force—"cannot match. We must fall back upon the stronger defenses and more numerous troops of Baalkpan. When the enemy follows us there, we will destroy him and quickly return to reclaim our sacred land." She paused. "The enemy comes quickly. Perhaps not all can be carried away in the time we have, but we will come back! Haakar-Faask will protect the people we leave behind. He will train them to fight and he will lead them against the Grik if he must until we can return to evict the coming scourge or take all away." She paused, but stood even straighter. "If we cannot return in time . . . he will plan a *great* battle! A battle that will be celebrated until the end of time and that the rest of us will think wistfully of until the day we once more join those who fought and hear their deeds in person!"

A great roar went up and, Safir, her eyes still shining, turned to Matt while Chack translated what she said. All Matt could do was shake his head and wonder. He wasn't about to ask right then.

"What about Aryaal?" she asked, the power gone from her voice. "And there are other cities—Kudraang, Kartaj, Bataava—farther up the coast."

"There's nothing we can do for them," Matt replied somberly. "There's not enough time." He glanced grimly at his watch again and then looked at Rolak. The old warrior was standing, shoulders bowed. He knew that just warning his people wouldn't be enough. Rasik would not believe it and all of his people would stay and perish. He and his warriors couldn't leave them to that, and all would die for nothing.

"No time at all," Matt repeated. "Under the circumstances, Queen Protector, I think your troops would be better employed evacuating B'mbaado immediately. Some of the embedded officers might want to remain, however. They might need the experience."

She nodded gratefully, but blinked surprise. Rolak and many others did the same.

"The way I figure it, we have three hours to take Aryaal."

As expected, a last desperate appeal came to naught. Officially, at least. There was no response to the demand for surrender, but when the guns in the breastworks made ready to fire, the defenders on the walls just vanished. With no apparent opposition, the Second Marines and Rolak's force, now called the First Aryaal, moved forward toward the gate. Matt, Keje, and even Adar fell in behind, and five-member squads of destroyermen interspersed themselves among the troops. Silva's squad remained around its captain.

"You believe this . . . nightmare ship truly exists? That it is coming?" Keje asked. "Perhaps your Mallory made a mistake?"

"A mistake like that . . . wouldn't be possible."

"You never told me there was another ship," Adar said, matching their pace.

"We didn't know."

"Then where did it come from, this ship that has changed everything in an instant?"

Matt sighed. "The same place we did. Through the Squall."

"But you know her?"

Matt nodded. "You remember we once spoke of how *Walker* was damaged so badly? And *Mahan* too? *Amagi* did that, by herself."

Adar shook his head. "Then all is lost."

Matt was silent for a moment as they followed the advance. "If we can get to Baalkpan, perhaps not," he said. "*Amagi* is powerful, more powerful than you can imagine. But she can't move on land. She can blow the hell out of the city, but she can't take it. Only the Grik can do that. If we get there first, with all the forces we have, Baalkpan might be able to hold. *Walker* and *Mahan* will try to deal with *Amagi*."

The Marines were near the gate now. So far there'd been no defensive fire at all.

"How can it be that you people, you Amer-i-caans, help us—and yet others of your kind help the Grik?" Adar asked bitterly. "Are your people truly able to think so differently?"

"Why are we attacking a city we saved from the Grik?" Matt countered. "Can you actually think so differently from them? And the Japanese are as different from us as you are from the Aryaalans. Remember, we were at war with them before we came here."

"But—"

"We'll have to pick it up later," said Matt, hitching his belt as best he could and nodding forward.

"Who was winning?" Adar asked quietly, but Matt didn't answer. Ahead, as the first troops entered the city, the distinctive sound of battle reached them from within. Chack shouted something over the din, but what it was, at first, Matt had no idea. Other shouts echoed back, and when Matt and his companions finally passed through the arch, the cause of the confusion was plain. Battle raged in the courtyard and streets beyond, but as yet the Marines weren't involved. Civil war had come once more to Aryaal.

Word of the final ultimatum, complete with the warning of the Grik, had spread like wildfire throughout the city. It began among the defenders at the gate who fled from the guns. Officer after officer—Rasik's handpicked—tried to stem the tide of desertion and many of them were slain. The palace guard tried to stop them too, but when real fighting began, many who were willing to defend the city joined the mutineers when they saw them being killed by the king's personal troops. It was too much. Most were loyal to their city and their king, no matter who he was. That the loyalists had prevailed in the previous fighting was proof enough of that—even if the purges after the first rebellion had been excessive enough to fire indignation and doubt. But as word of the renewed Grik threat continued to spread, they began to realize that the patient invaders outside the walls weren't the real enemy after all. They knew if it hadn't been for the sea folk, the Grik would have had them already. They could never hold them off a second time. Suddenly, to most of the warriors of Aryaal, the survival of their families transcended nationalism and loyalty to a new king they didn't even like.

By the time Lord Rolak entered the city at the head of his column of native warriors, the uprising in the city—at least the northern half—was already practically over. Marines fanned out and created a perimeter inside the gate, but no one so much as threw a rock at them. Beyond the perimeter there was still fighting, but it flared in fits and spurts. It had degenerated mostly into a grudge match now between the various Aryaalan political houses and the palace guard. None of the combatants from any side seemed to want the Marines to get involved. Lord Rolak paced to the great Fountain of the Sun in the center of the plaza and climbed the stepped circle that surrounded it for a better view. From amid the turmoil of fighting and the growing crowd of townsfolk, someone shouted a cheer at the sight of him. Then another. Within minutes, the dwindling sound of battle was overwhelmed by thunderous cheering that surged and echoed off the walls of the city and the royal palace beyond the plaza. Defenders threw down their weapons and many took up the cheer as well.

Rolak was overcome. Matt mounted the steps beside him, grinning for the first time that day. The sound was overwhelming and it only seemed to build as more and more Aryaalans rushed from other parts of the city. The crowd surged, but the Marines kept them at bay. A phalanx of armed Aryaalans—not palace guards but still a well-turned-out force—made its way through the crowd until it reached the Marines' shield wall. Shinya rushed to the point of contact with Chack by his side and after several moments of hand gestures and shouting, a single figure was let through the wall. Chack hurried to Matt and Rolak, with the individual puffing and almost running to keep up. His flowing embroidered robe threatened to trip him.

"Lord Koratin," Rolak said by way of restrained greeting when the pair drew near. Chack automatically translated for Captain Reddy.

"Lord Rolak," Koratin replied, and bowed.

"I understand you are chief advisor to that murdering coward who has stolen the throne," Rolak said. "We were never friends, but I expected better of you."

"It is true, that was my position, my lord. And that is what I tried to do. But my advice wasn't heeded, or even tolerated. The king is quite mad."

"The attempt to sink the iron ship?"

Koratin nodded. "I told him it was madness when I learned his scheme. I even sent three trusted servants to warn you, but they were caught and killed. The palace guard came for me then, but my retainers held them off." He smiled crookedly. "If not for your timely arrival and the chaos that ensued, I would be dead. How delightfully ironic!"

Rolak barked a laugh. "You always were amazingly skilled at survival, Koratin!"

Koratin bowed. "As you can see, it's a useful skill." His face turned grim. "Is it true? The Grik will return?"

"It is true."

"I feared as much. I feared for my younglings—for all the younglings of our people—but the king would not listen. He does not believe the old stories"—he nodded respectfully at Chack—"that for our salvation the sea folk have preserved!"

"Fear still, Koratin. The danger is greater than you imagine. We must all leave this place and become beggars in the north. The sea folk will succor us, but they need our arms more than our bellies, so all who go must be willing to fight, and provocations won't occur."

Koratin was stunned. "But what of our walls? Can we not hold here if the sea folk come to our aid?"

"No." Rolak nodded toward Matt, who stood listening. "Cap-i-taan Reddy has told me how it must be and I believe him."

Koratin turned to look at Matt for the first time. His stare was an appraising one. "So that is the great tail-less leader of the sea folk," he said. "I suspected as much." He bowed low to the captain.

"Where's Rasik?" Matt demanded, eyes flashing.

"In his palace, lord. Yonder." Koratin pointed at the imposing structure beyond the plaza. "He has almost four hundred guards. Quite fanatical, I'm afraid. It will be difficult and costly to storm."

For a long while, Matt said nothing while those nearby waited for his decision. His expression seemed almost yearning as his eyes bored into the palace walls.

"No, it won't," he said at last. Rolak cocked his head and looked at Matt with a questioning blink. "We're not going to storm it. Oh, don't get me wrong—there's nothing I'd rather do than bring the guns in and blow it down around him, and that's what we'd do if we had the time. We'd *take* our time!" he snarled. Calming, he clasped his hands behind his back. "But we don't have the luxury of time, and I'm not going to waste lives getting the little bastard the old-fashioned way. Chack and his Marines will see that no one gets out while you begin evacuating the city."

Chack was confused and surprised. He was first and foremost a destroyerman, after all, and Donaghey was one of his clan. Surely the captain wouldn't leave his death un-avenged—not after he had been willing to break the alliance that morning to take the city. "But what about the king, Captain?" he prodded. "What are we going to do about him?"

"He doesn't leave his palace. No matter what he says or does. Not until everyone in Aryaal and B'mbaado have been evacuated. In the meantime, you'll remain here with half the Marines and keep him bottled up. The other half, and most of the AEF Guard regiments, will be sent immediately back to Baalkpan in feluccas to help prepare the defense." He put his hand on Chack's shoulder. "You and your Marines will be the last ones out of the city. Make sure we don't leave anyone behind that wants to come, even any of Rasik's guards that manage to wiggle loose."

He looked around, sadly, at the city. It really was quite beautiful in an exotic and unfamiliar way. The Aryaalans seemed to love color as much as any of their cousins, but instead of fabric and tapestries, they applied it to the very stone itself. It was too bad he could see it only now, and for so short a time.

"Burn everything. Don't leave anything for the enemy."

"What about the king?" Chack persisted. Matt's expression went cold.

"Except him," he said. "He doesn't believe the lizards will come back. We'll let them convince him themselves." Chack grinned and almost burst out laughing. That would be satisfactory justice to him.

Koratin watched them wide-eyed and shuddered. *Merciful people,* he thought, *in many ways. But not all.* "I will help all I can," he said, his voice very formal.

The captain waved toward Rolak. "Help him. He's in charge here." He took one more look around the plaza and sighed. "I have a ship to fix."

Matt watched the chaos of the exodus while standing on *Walker's* port bridgewing. It had become the central headquarters for the operation and a steady stream of messengers came and went, bringing news or carrying orders. Lieutenant Mallory joined him there shortly before dark; his plane was alongside *Big Sal* taking on fuel. Now they stood with Adar, Sandra, and Courtney Bradford and stared quietly out upon what looked like the end of the world.

Thousands of terrified refugees, carrying nothing but small parcels of clothing, milled and surged along the waterfront. They were desperate to climb the ramp that led aboard *Humfra-Dar,* and Geran-Eras herself stood at the gangway with a squad of Marines directing the Aryaalan or B'mbaadan passengers toward sections of her ship where they'd be taken in hand by others who would try to accommodate them. Huge bundles of foodstuffs were hoisted aboard and the night was filled with shouts, shrieking infants, anguished cries, and the muffled thunder of countless feet on the wooden dock and deck of the Home. In the distance, flames soared up beyond the walls of Aryaal, as the evacuated portions of the city were put to the torch. Garish flashes pulsed across the bottoms of low clouds that had moved in at dusk, and the light cast an eerie, ruddy glow on the anxious proceedings at the waterfront.

Matt tried to compare the scene to other great national tragedies or evacuations he knew of from history. The sack of Athens, the destruction of

Carthage, or the fall of Rome came to mind, as did the burning of Atlanta and Columbia or the evacuation of Richmond. More recently were the newsreels he'd seen of the devastation of Europe and China by the Nazis and Japanese. Each of those calamities was probably as bad or worse, but he hadn't been there to witness any of them firsthand. He was here now, and everything he could see—the suffering, the devastation, the probable extinction of an entire culture—was happening because he'd ordered it. He knew there was no choice, but the magnitude of the disaster wracked him with guilt. They'd come as naive liberators, bent on saving the people of this world from the depredations of a remorseless foe. They were leaving as destroyers, causing more harm than the Grik had yet managed.

With a surprised thankfulness that he couldn't express, he felt Sandra's hand find his in the darkness and he squeezed it gently before letting go. She'd been more reserved toward him that day than their "agreement" required and he still wondered why. Then he looked at Mallory. The young aviator's face glowed grimly in the reflected light. He'd spoken little since he arrived, only confirming with a nod that the dispatch was entirely accurate. There was no mistake. He stood there now, holding *Revenge*'s log in both hands like a sacred treasure. Matt would read it later, when his attention could be spared from the decisions at hand. Right now it would just be too much. He would share it with Keje when the two of them could quietly mourn their dead alone. He cleared his throat. "So, are they Japs, Mr. Mallory? Did you get close enough to see?"

"I guess they probably are. We saw the flags for sure." He grunted. "And then they started shooting at us. The first air burst we saw, we got the hell out."

Matt nodded, deciding not to chastise the flier for the risk he'd taken. "Lucky they didn't let you get closer before they opened fire. Sounds like they got anxious."

"Yes, sir. They must've been pretty surprised to see *us* too."

Matt rubbed his forehead. "Maybe not. We've been transmitting in the clear all this time. Maybe they've been reading our mail. Any transmission at all would've warned them we were here. If they've been listening in, they may even know where Baalkpan is," he added darkly. "And if that's the case, we won't know until they're almost here whether they're all coming here or they mean to dispatch forces to both places." He ground his teeth. "Damn."

"I'd think *Amagi* would go wherever she thought *Walker* was, Captain," Mallory speculated.

"Maybe. If they know where we are. I wonder if they do?" He paused for a moment and then answered his own question. "Probably. The lizards certainly know we're here." He scratched the stubble on his chin. "But they may not know there are two of us . . . Anyway, that answers my question. We have to assume the Japs know, and the last I heard, they don't like us very much. If they figure we're evacuating for Baalkpan they might try to get between us. Make us come to them." He shook his head. "It'll be tough to do at eight knots. I wonder why they're so slow? *Amagi* used to make over thirty."

"Only as fast as the slowest ship?" Bradford opined.

"Yeah, but the lizards are faster than that . . . unless maybe *Amagi* is the slowest ship! You're sure it was coal smoke you saw?"

"Positive."

"That may be why we haven't seen her till now—they've been converting her boilers. Coal's a lot more efficient than wood, but not as good as oil. Shorter range and a fair cut in speed. Still . . ."

"Damage," Sandra said suddenly. "We've all been thinking of *Amagi* only in terms of firepower. That's a pretty one-sided comparison. But remember, as bad as she roughed us up, *Walker* and *Mahan* got in some pretty good licks. Maybe enough that she nearly *did* sink!"

"Right," Matt breathed. "We know how tough it's been for us to make repairs. Just think of all the problems they'll have had to face! Every piece of that ship is five times bigger than a comparable part of *Walker*. We've been thinking of that only as an advantage to them, but think of the disadvantages! There's no way they could've fixed a lot of the damage we inflicted. I'm still sure *Mahan* put at least two torpedoes into her. It would've been tough to get her out of a real dry dock and a fully equipped yard this fast!"

Bradford looked at Sandra with a growing, affectionate smile. "There you go again, my dear. Leaping directly upon the obvious while we mere males flail helplessly at obscure minutia."

"Well, it's a theory," Matt agreed. "We just have to figure out a way to use it, if it's true." He slapped the rail before him in a release of pent-up frustration. "Damn them to hell! How could even the Japs ally themselves with creatures like the lizards?"

"Because they're Japs!" Mallory answered bitterly. "They're *like* the lizards!"

Adar shook his head sadly. So far, he'd said nothing since joining them on the bridge, besides a subdued greeting. Now he spoke. "Lieutenant Shinya is a 'Jaap,' is he not?" Surprised by the question, Matt nodded. Adar sighed deeply. "I spent a short time with him while the Guard regiments were withdrawn from the city. He is overwhelmed with shame. A shame he cannot show."

"Why?" Sandra asked.

Adar looked at her. "Because he is a 'Jaap.' He's seen the Grik for what they are, as have we all, and he asks himself the same question you do, Captain Reddy. It tortures him that his own people might cavort with such evil. It is much like the shame Lord Rolak feels for the things King Rasik has done, only worse." Adar raised his hands in submission. "I do not pretend to understand you humans, not anymore. But Lieutenant Shinya's clan of humans is more difficult to understand than the rest of you in some ways, but even simpler in others. You Amer-i-caans have a delightfully stark conception of the difference between good and evil. In your case, that conception seems to come from how you have individually decided your society will collectively define good and evil." He gazed for a moment at the fire and tumult of the dying city. "I suppose it is fortunate for us that you've decided my people's enemies are the evil ones in this context." He snorted and shook his head.

"From what he has told me, Lieutenant Shinya's people are the opposite of that. In their society, the few or the one—an emperor, I believe?—decides what all of society will consider good or evil and the individuals are forced to accept that decision." He blinked apologetically. "I may be wrong. Lieutenant Shinya, though, I think has always been an individual with a mind of his own, trapped in that society without a voice. At the same time, he is fiercely loyal to his people. Imagine the conflict he faces. He knows it is wrong for his people to support the Grik, but he also knows the decision will have been made for the many by a few."

He looked Captain Reddy square in the eye. "The same thing happens here, but the decisions you make are supported by the majority of your people. You made that clear today. You couldn't rule long or well without that support." He blinked and clasped his hands behind his back. "It seems your decisions are supported by my people as well," he added in the wry tone he'd been practicing. "But as far as *Amagi* is concerned, that may not be the case. The society from which her people come does not allow them to express their views, or even to have any, if they are not consistent with that of their emperor. Is the warrior who fights for evil still evil himself if his society does not see it as such? Perhaps in that way, the 'Jaaps' are more similar to the Grik than we might think. The problem for Lieutenant Shinya still remains. He is a Jaap. You are the sworn enemy of his emperor, and so, in the collective eyes of his people, you are evil. He knows that is not the case. In your eyes, his people are evil. Not just because they support the Grik, but because they attacked you in the world you came from. I've seen how quick you are to anger in the face of such a thing. But in spite of whether you or I—or even he—believes his people in this world are on the side of evil, he cannot believe that all of them *are* evil."

"What will he do?" Matt asked, alarmed. Not because he believed Shinya would turn on them, but because he had, after all, become such an integral part of *Walker*'s family—not to mention the war effort as a whole—and he was worried about him.

"What will he do, indeed?" Adar blinked rapidly. "In any event, I apologize. I did get horribly sidetracked. I believe your original question was 'why would the Jaaps help the Grik?' not 'how will Lieutenant Shinya deal with his conscience?'" He shook his head. "Until we learn more about the Grik, we may never know. They have obviously communicated with each other—which is something we could never do. Perhaps I was right before and they do have something in common? You said *Walker* and *Mahan* damaged *Amagi* in battle?" Matt nodded. "Well, *Walker* has certainly done a great deal of damage to the Grik." He stopped and looked at the captain with a strange smile on his face. "Perhaps the thing that unites them now is their mutual hatred of you."

Lieutenant Sandison appeared behind them, clambering up the ladder from below. A short, dark-colored Lemurian was with him. A female. She was the liaison from *Humfra-Dar*. Sandison saluted and the little Lemurian imitated the gesture. Matt returned it solemnly.

"Geran-Eras says if she takes on another soul, they'll be standing on each other's heads."

"Very well. She has permission to get under way." Matt had agonized over the decision whether the ships should wait to depart together, or sail independently as soon as they were loaded. He settled on the second alternative. It meant less time they'd be crowded so uncomfortably, but mainly he thought it would actually give them a better chance of escape. If they all headed out together, it increased the possibility that the enemy would catch them together. The mutual protection afforded by numbers would be meaningless against *Amagi*'s guns. Better to split them up. He wasn't worried by the threat posed by any advance scouts. With their big guns, the Homes could repulse even a small squadron of Grik attackers.

"Keje and *Salissa* are next in line," he said. "I want him in Baalkpan as soon as possible to help coordinate the defense. You too, Adar," he added. "Besides, she's the only 'tanker' we have. We'll rig hoses and top off our bunkers while she's taking on passengers. We'll load up on fuel for the PBY while we're at it, just in case. When *Big Sal* gets to Baalkpan, have her fill up again. We might need all the mobile fuel reserve we can get."

A wailing rose from the dock as the ramp to *Humfra-Dar* was blocked. Many might have been separated from their loved ones, or not known there would be other Homes to take them. A panic began to build and several shots were actually fired in an attempt to control the crowd. Adar blinked his distaste.

"It is difficult to believe Amer-i-caans could be as different from the

Jaaps as we are from the land folk," he said. "I cannot imagine my people behaving so."

"Give them a break, Adar. They've just lost everything they had in the world. They're at the mercy of people they've distrusted throughout their history to protect them from creatures that'll eat them if they can. Pray you never find out how your people act in a similar situation." Matt gestured at the seething mob. "Besides, those people are the ones that are going to save yours in the end. After we make an army out of them."

"Land folk females do not fight. Many of their males will not."

"They will when they see what's coming," Mallory interjected quietly.

Matt noticed the female Lemurian was still standing there, holding her salute. "You may dismiss your friend now, Mr. Sandison. She'll miss her boat," he said with a small smile. "Do you have a report for me? About progress with the propeller?"

"Ah, yes, sir. Just a moment, sir." He quickly spoke to the 'Cat, and she darted down the ladder. "Lieutenant McFarlane says, 'It's going,' sir. The flashies started chewing through the sail we rigged so the men could work. We're going to have to rig another one. He thinks it's the lights. They're drawing the fish and making them attack the canvas."

"What about the torpedoes?"

"Yes, sir, sorry, sir," Sandison answered guiltily. "We've started back to work on them too." It had been weeks since anyone had tried to figure out what was wrong with the two condemned torpedoes they'd salvaged from Surabaya so long ago.

Matt nodded. "Not your fault. I've handed you plenty of other chores and it didn't look like we'd need them that bad. Until now. Any problems with our three good torps?"

"No, sir, they're fine. All we have to do is wind 'em up. 'Course, we still have the same problem," he added worriedly. "We don't know why they won't hit anything, or if they do, why they won't go off."

"Figure it out, Mr. Sandison."

"We've been trying. We're fooling around with the dud again and Shinya has a couple of ideas." Sandison shrugged. "It's worth a try." Matt frowned slightly and glanced at Adar.

"Shinya?"

"Yeah. He showed up in the workshop ready to work as soon as he came aboard. Said Chack had command of the Marines around the palace, and"—Bernie shrugged, waving at the pandemonium outside—"there's enough troops on the docks." Sandison looked at the captain and read his mind, or he thought he did. "He's okay, sir. He just needs to sort things out."

"By helping you fix torpedoes to sink his countrymen." Matt muttered darkly.

Bernie's eyes widened. "You don't suppose . . . !"

Matt shook his head. "No, but I don't want you leaving him there by himself right now, either. Let him help if he wants, but remind him that by the terms of his parole he's not required to." He looked at Adar again, impressed as usual by the Sky Priest's sensitivity to matters pertaining to human nature that Matt hadn't even noticed. He took solace in the fact that he had quite a lot on his plate just then, but still . . .

"He say anything to you about *Amagi*?" he asked Sandison.

"Well . . . no, sir. But he knows that's why we're working on the torpedoes again. Why else?"

"And you're absolutely certain he's not pulling your chain?" Matt had to ask.

Sandison shrugged. "I know it sounds strange, but he didn't really say anything. Right now he acts like he doesn't care that there's other Japs on *Amagi*. The only thing that seems to matter to him is that she might help the lizards sink the machine shop." The machine shop had been Shinya's refuge ever since being rescued from the sea.

Matt blinked, and Adar barked a laugh in spite of himself.

"You see, Cap-i-taan Reddy? In some ways, much more simple to understand!"

Matt shook his head. "Adar, a while ago you probably described the differences between us and the Japs to me better than anybody ever has, and then you make a comment like that. I'll tell you right now, whatever Shinya's going through isn't going to be simple to understand at all. Least of all to him." Sandison looked worried. He had grown very fond of the Japanese officer.

"Maybe we should, you know, put a guard on him? Shoot, Skipper, he might . . . hurt himself . . ."

"I'm glad you feel that way, Bernie, because on top of everything else, I want you to stick to Shinya like glue. Don't *let* him 'hurt himself.' Understood?"

"Understood, Skipper."

For a while they all stood quietly, staring at the inferno breeding before them—the seething, dying, shattered fragments of all they'd hoped for when their "crusade" began.

"I guess I can understand the Japs wanting to continue their war with us, no matter where we are. It's stupid, but I understand it. Hell, I even sort of feel the same way. Maybe we've just cut each other too deep." Matt shook his head, amazed. "But there's no way you can get me to understand why they'd help the lizards."

isashi Kurokawa, captain of HIMS *Amagi*, stalked slowly back and forth across the battle cruiser's bridge. His hands were clasped behind his back and the red night-time lighting transformed his round, cherubic features into those of a dark, grimacing Buddha. He paused briefly behind the helmsman, who stiffened nervously under his scrutiny. With a barely audible growl, Kurokawa paced on. If he noticed the tension radiating from each member of the watch as he drew near, he made no sign.

Commander Sato Okada had the watch and he peered warily at the captain as he prowled from station to station. Any minute now he expected *Amagi*'s stocky commander to explode into a fit of rage, triggered by some slight or imagined transgression. Almost twenty minutes had passed since the captain came on the bridge, and lately that seemed to be about the limit. The fits had become so commonplace that they were almost a part of the ship's routine. No one was spared their fury, and Sato himself had probably been on the receiving end of more vitriolic harangues than anyone else on the ship. That was because he often—delicately—told the captain what he actually believed instead of just what he knew the man wanted to hear. More often than not, the disagreements provoked titanic tantrums, and the things the captain said to him in front of other officers and crew were sometimes difficult to bear. But Sato withstood the onslaughts as stoically as he could. The captain believed it was Sato's duty to agree with him, but Sato suspected more and more that his real duty lay in protecting the ship and her crew from the captain.

Right now, for example, he knew Captain Kurokawa was most

displeased about their speed, and Sato couldn't make him understand the engineers were doing all they could. The captain wasn't satisfied. Recently, he'd even gone so far as to charge that there were traitors in the engineering spaces. Sato had done all he could to stanch the loss of morale after that accusation came on top of everything else, but the crew was lost, dispirited and afraid. The fear was feeding on the captain's attitude and spreading like a caustic acid.

The lights of their "allies'" ships were all around them on the broad expanse of the sea, clustered about them as if shepherding them along. That infuriated Kurokawa more than anything else. *Amagi* was the most powerful ship in the world. By rights, she should be leading this task force— not groping along trying to keep up. The Grik had slowed their advance so *Amagi* could remain with the fleet, but "keeping up" wasn't what he wanted to do.

Sato glanced at the captain and noticed with a rush of alarm that he was moving in his direction. He braced himself for the onslaught. To his surprise, the captain's voice was quiet, even mild when he spoke.

"I hope you are feeling better, Commander Okada."

Sato gulped and bowed his head slightly. "Yes, Captain. Much better, thank you. It must have been something I ate."

"Of course. I know you are not timid." The captain's face clouded slightly. "Either in the face of the enemy, or my own."

"It is my duty to advise you, sir."

"It is your duty to obey me!" Kurokawa snapped.

"I have always obeyed."

The captain's face clouded still more but, forcibly, he pushed back the threatening storm. When he spoke again, his voice was controlled once more. "Very well. Since you see it as your duty to advise me, how would you do so now?"

Sato looked at the captain, appalled. It was the first time since Kurokawa assumed command that he'd ever asked anyone what they thought. That might be entirely appropriate under most circumstances, but since the Strange Storm, things had been anything but normal. Still, for Kurokawa to actually ask, let alone care, what Sato thought about their situation was most uncharacteristic. It was probably a trap. Something to get him to commit to a course of insubordination.

"On what subject would you seek my advice?" he asked carefully.

"Ah. Of course. I assumed you would have a differing opinion than I on everything we have done. I was correct. Your reports seethe with discontent! Let us limit our discussion to strategy so I might get some sleep tonight!" His face became grim. "I am frustrated with these barbaric 'allies' of ours, as you know. Dreadful creatures, but useful."

Sato had to suppress a shudder at the thought of the Grik. They'd encountered them first at Singapore when they went there for repairs after their battle with the retreating American force. It was then that they discovered something extraordinary had happened to them. Singapore wasn't there! In its place was only a strange village of some sort with a harbor filled with sailing ships—which had attacked them immediately and as apparently automatically as a disturbed hive of bees. Throughout the day and night they fought, killing thousands of the hideous creatures, which continued the assault even as *Amagi* tried to steam away. But the ship had been too badly damaged by the American destroyers and it couldn't outrun the red-hulled ships.

Finally, after they repelled what seemed like countless assaults, a single ship approached but did not attack. Negotiations were established and a bizarre alliance was struck. *Amagi* would join the creatures that attacked her so fanatically such a short time before. In return, she would be provided with fuel, food, and labor for repairs. At the time, even Sato had seen no other alternative. Since that day, however, not a moment went by when he did not regret the choice.

Communication was still difficult, and rudimentary at best. Neither race could form the sounds to actually speak to one another, but had to rely on written *English,* of all things, in order to converse at all. Not that Sato wanted to talk to them. The Grik were loathsome creatures. Vicious and almost mindless in their obsessive ferocity. As far as he could tell, their one motivation was to conquer the world and kill everything else that lived upon it. In spite of how many his forces had killed, he never got any impression the Grik were afraid of them, or even much cared about those that had fallen. There were no funerals, no ceremonies, no mourning for the dead. He never knew for sure—he didn't want to know—but he suspected that they . . . harvested the carcasses of the slain that were not consumed by the suddenly terrible sea. It was surreal, and it was far too much for many of the crew to accept.

And just as quickly and matter-of-factly as the Grik accepted their losses, they accepted the alliance with *Amagi.* They were appropriately appreciative of her power and recognized her as a useful tool. As promised, they assisted in making what minor repairs they could. Once *Amagi* was relatively seaworthy again, the Grik escorted her to Ceylon for further repairs.

Ceylon was another surprise. Okada remembered the great natural harbor of Colombo on the west coast of the island as a major bastion of British empire. Except for a general geographical resemblance, it was gone. Grik architecture tended toward unimaginative utilitarian slabs, contrasted with occasional terrifyingly rendered art relief, reminiscent of some of the more troubling ancient Mexican art he had seen. He was strangely saddened by the absence of the Galle Face Green, the historic promenade used for horse racing, and one of the most ostentatious manifestations of British colonialism in Ceylon. But most striking of all were the hundreds of Grik ships packed into the huge protected bay. At first sight it had been blindingly obvious that a massive buildup for some monumental offensive was under way. An offensive that *Amagi* was now clearly expected to participate in.

Amagi's stay in Colombo amounted to a strange sort of exile. No one went ashore except the captain and a small entourage, and then only when absolutely necessary. The Grik were extremely terrifying. Powerful, consummate predators that gazed upon you always as if speculating on your flavor. Some visits were unavoidable if repairs were to be coordinated, but nobody ever wanted to go twice, and Okada was convinced that the captain used the detail as a punishment. Why else had he been sent so often? In any event, Sato learned much more about the Grik than anyone else, probably even the captain, and began to realize with sick despair just how cheaply they'd sold their souls. Sato and most of the crew detested the Grik, but his initial hope that they would just steam away from their new "friends" was dashed by the realization that *Amagi* could never outrun them in her present state and there was no doubt they would be attacked if they tried.

Amagi had originally been designed to burn coal, so the reconversion wasn't too difficult. But there was so much damage to the engines and boilers that fully repairing them with the facilities at hand was out of the question. The ship's top speed was gone forever. When they saw the size of the fleet in Ceylon, the impossibility of escaping to make their own way was driven dramatically home. For now, there was nothing to do but repair the ship and, in Sato's mind, wait for an opportunity.

So they joined the Grik in their current war of conquest against strange furry folk that resided at sea on large ships, and in the Dutch East Indies. To make matters even more bizarre, the "tree folk"—he believed that was the best translation—seemed to have allied themselves with one of the American destroyers they'd been fighting when they were swallowed by the Strange Storm. It was that discovery, Sato thought, that finally drove Captain Kurokawa mad. If he'd ever had the intention of slipping away from the Grik, it had now certainly passed.

The captain blamed everything that had happened to them on the two destroyers that so arrogantly charged them right before the Strange Storm brought them here. Sato had been secretly stirred by the courage of their crews, but Kurokawa took their escape and the damage to his mighty ship quite personally. Each wound to the ship was matched by one to the captain's pride. That two such outdated and dilapidated vessels could wreak such destruction on *Amagi* was as if house cats had savaged a tiger. And then, as if in punishment, *Amagi* was taken from the world she knew. That was the Americans' fault too. The fact that one of the badly damaged destroyers still existed in this twisted world struck Kurokawa as a personal insult. He was now obsessed with its destruction in an almost Grik-like way, and if it took alliance with such unpleasant creatures to accomplish that goal, so be it.

"What can we do to increase our prestige among those monsters?" Kurokawa asked, waving toward the endless fleet beyond the glass windows of the bridge and returning Okada's thoughts to the unusual conversation.

"Show ourselves to be even more vicious and contemptible than they are, I suspect," Sato said bitterly. The captain considered his words.

"You may not be mistaken. We must put ourselves forward in battle, Commander Okada. Their commander must see our power for himself!" He clenched his fists at his side in frustration. "Which we cannot do if we are so slow!"

Sato tried to avert his captain's mounting rage by changing the subject. "At least now we know the source of the radio transmissions we detected. Not two ships, but a single ship and a plane. The American flying-boat was unexpected."

"Yes. It did a great deal of damage before it flew away." Kurokawa's features reddened. "If our antiaircraft defenses had been better prepared, we could have shot it down and we would not be having this conversation! The Grik would have certainly seen our worth!"

Sato quickly diverted the captain from attacking another part of the crew. "But the enemy ship did much more damage. I understand one of the Grik commanders was killed and his ship destroyed. The survivors of the raid on Surabaya were right about the cannons."

"So it would seem." Kurokawa hesitated. "The Grik will see *Amagi*'s worth if they face many more of those." He glanced at the clock on the bulkhead. For the first time, Sato thought he saw nervousness behind the captain's eyes. "Soon I must cross to the 'flagship.'"

Sato waited a moment before he spoke. "Must you take Captain Kaufman with you this time? He might be even more valuable to us now, and each time he is in the presence of those creatures, he . . . slips . . . a little more."

Kurokawa regarded him with a hard gaze. "Pity for the enemy, Commander Okada?"

Sato's expression hardened as well. "Empathy for an officer who saw his crew *eaten* by our 'allies,' Captain Kurokawa. Even the Grik spoke highly of his bravery, after a fashion. He did not surrender; he was overwhelmed."

Kurokawa waved his hand dismissively. "I do not care. I can write English," he said distastefully, "as most naval officers once had to. Speak to him, though. Find out why he said nothing about a flying-boat. If he knew of it and did not speak, I want him to regret it deeply!" He smiled. "Perhaps we will return him to his former masters, eh?"

Sato shuddered, and once more changed the subject. He was getting good at maneuvering the conversation to keep his commander's temper in check. "Will you tell the Grik your assumptions based on *all* the radio traffic we intercepted? Before the enemy resumed transmitting in code?"

Kurokawa looked at him. "Of course. It is valuable information and they will see it as such." He smiled. "That we've somehow divined it will surely raise us in their estimation."

Sato took a deep breath and glanced around at the other men on the bridge. He knew they were straining to hear, but doubted they could understand much. In spite of that, he spoke barely above a whisper. "Before we reveal that we can send and receive messages over long distances, let alone where we think the American base might be, would it not be best to speak to the Americans first?"

Kurokawa's eyes bulged and he screamed, "You would *speak* to the enemy?!"

Sato forced his voice to remain calm and low. "Captain, please! Let me speak!" he said. "First, would it not be best to conceal the technology of radio from . . . our 'allies' as long as we can? Once they know of its existence, we will have irretrievably lost an advantage. They will want its secrets and we will have difficulty withholding them."

Taken aback, Kurokawa lowered his voice. "But what good is it to keep the secret? *We* have no one to talk to!"

"That may not always be the case! Besides, we have two aircraft of our own. The spotting planes! They have radios!"

Amagi had lost one of her spotting planes in the battle that brought her here—ironically when a Japanese dive-bomber went out of control and crashed directly atop her amidships ten-inch turret, destroying it as well as the plane and catapult on top of it. But she still had two planes left. Both were obsolete, short-range biplanes. Nakajima Type 95 E8Ns, to be precise. They were single-engine affairs and carried one huge float under the fuselage and a couple of smaller ones under the wings. They were good, reliable, low-maintenance airplanes with all-metal structures covered by fabric. The two-man crew sat in individual open cockpits where they would never have to worry about being too comfortable to keep their eyes open. Perfect for observation planes. Probably the best kind of planes they could have right now, since they were so simple. But they were certainly not fighters.

Kurokawa still seethed constantly over the loss of their much more capable plane, the Aichi Type Zero E13A1 that had been turned into flaming confetti along with quite a lot of other very useful equipment, weapons, ammunition, and fuel—Kurokawa didn't consider the men—when the crippled plane smashed into his ship. Okada mourned every scratch *Amagi* suffered and every life she lost, but practically speaking, under the circumstances, he'd trade the Type Zero for the Type 95s any day.

"True, but we have hardly any fuel for them," the captain snapped bitterly. He waved his hand. "Enough for a few short flights. Most of our reserve was destroyed by the Americans' cowardly torpedo attack . . . And That Imbecile Who Crashed Into My Ship!" The entire bridge watch tensed for a moment, waiting to see if the captain's loud imprecations toward the dead pilot would manage to snare anyone else. Remarkably, they sometimes did.

"But the Americans obviously *do* have aviation fuel—and probably fuel oil as well!" Okada interjected. "It should have been easy for them to get. Is that not why we were intent on conquering the Dutch East Indies in the first place?"

"We shall still!" roared the captain and Sato recoiled. "What would you have me do? *Beg* the Americans for *fuel*?!" Kurokawa seethed. "The situation may have changed somewhat, but I still have my orders! To assist in the capture of the Emperor's objective!"

Sato couldn't stop himself. "But, Captain, the Emperor is not *here*! Assisting the Grik in *their* objective would not, I think, please His Majesty! They are . . . hideous barbarians! Inhuman monsters! The Americans at least are people!" He lowered his voice, hoping the captain wouldn't explode. He desperately wanted to crack Kurokawa's apparently maniacal shell.

"I think we should speak to them—before we help the Grik wipe them out! I must tell you, Captain, I fear this course we've embarked upon is without honor! It's not of the Way! I implore you, sir, let us detach ourselves from this unwholesome alliance! We could tell the Grik we've had another breakdown—they would surely believe that—and when we have only a few escorts, we could easily break away!"

Sato braced himself for the hurricane of rage that was sure to follow his outburst. Instead, Kurokawa only stared at him, his expression cold as ice. "Commander Okada. Your suggestion regarding the radio is well taken. I will endeavor to relate our suspicions about the enemy base without disclosing that secret. But hear me! The Empire of Japan is *at war* with the United States of America, and that war will be prosecuted whenever and wherever our forces meet! I have no illusions that the Grik are our friends, but they are not our enemies either. I will use their assistance to achieve our ultimate objective, and that objective is the destruction of any American or allied force within the Malay Barrier. Is that understood?" Sato could only nod. "Good," continued Kurokawa in a mounting voice, "because according to this Kaufman, the Grik have already destroyed one of the destroyers that crippled my ship and that leaves only one for me! I *will have that ship* if I have to chase it around the *world*! Is that understood? I will capture it or send it to the bottom. It makes no difference to me. That is what my orders prescribe and *my* honor demands! And if you utter one more suggestion that I should treat with the enemies of the Emperor, I will have you executed for treason!"

With that, Captain Kurokawa spun on his heel and exited the bridge. Sato Okada could only stare after him, shaking with frustration and terror.

Captain David Kaufman, U.S. Army Air Corps, sat on an inverted bucket in a darkened compartment somewhere deep in the Japanese ship. He had nothing to read, nothing to do with his hands. Nothing at all to divert his mind during the endless hours of solitude between the infrequent visits of his captors. It was dank and stuffy and smelled of old paint and oily machinery. The deck beneath his feet vibrated slightly and there was a dull roar from the engines, although he didn't know if he was forward or aft of the engineering spaces. If he hadn't already been out of his mind, the sensory deprivation and boredom would certainly have done the trick. All he could do was sit on the bucket, alone, and relive the horrible memories of the events that brought him to this place.

If only he'd left well enough alone. It was clear from his most recent interrogation that *Walker* was still afloat. If he hadn't seized control of *Mahan*, she'd have rejoined her sister and he would be safe among his own kind. Safe for a while, at least, he corrected. He'd seen the size of the Grik armada when the Japanese "rescued" him from the Grik commander. Even without *Amagi*, there was no hope for *Walker* now. He must have been totally out of his mind when the Japanese came. Hunger, terror, and the shock of his circumstances had left him a jibbering wreck. He'd been feverish when he arrived in Colombo and he'd almost thought he imagined *Amagi* in the bay, but when he saw the Japanese officers from where he was chained, naked, at the base of Tsalka's throne, he was sure the madness had entirely overwhelmed him. After everything else that had happened to him, to see *Japs* there too . . . He fought like an animal, slashing with his teeth, his fingernails—anything he could use. Either they'd kill him or he'd wake up from his nightmare at last. Knocked unconscious, he was brought aboard *Amagi*.

As his senses returned, he was given clothes and fed, and for a brief time he clung to his Japanese guards like saviors. They kicked him and cuffed him and treated him worse than an animal, but he didn't think they'd eat him. For a while, that was enough. Then the questions started. In spite of the fact that they had rescued him from the Grik, a distant sense of propriety made him try to reveal only his name, rank, and serial number. After all, his saviors were still the enemy, weren't they? His questioners beat him. He was so far gone physically and mentally, and so glad they'd saved him from the Grik, he almost felt that he deserved the torment—felt almost guilty that he wanted to keep things from them. His resistance was short-lived and he told them everything he knew.

Mahan was lost. She must be. Most of her crew had been with him, and then the other Grik ships went after her. Shorthanded as she was, and in her condition, there was no way she could have repelled the thousands that rounded the southern point of Nias and headed toward the anchorage where he left her. Everyone who'd been aboard her was now certainly dead and it was all his fault. His only slight consolation was that *Mahan* had apparently burned and sunk. At least the lizards hadn't gotten their hands on her.

He told them everything he knew about *Walker* too, but he didn't know enough to satisfy them, so the beatings resumed with even greater vigor than before. He must have almost died. He remembered little of what happened, only that the torture suddenly stopped and there was an officer in the compartment. He passed out. Later, he remembered being carried to his cell and he was even visited by a doctor. Slowly, he healed. The days passed without notice and he managed to keep some idea of the time only by the meals they brought him. Therefore he knew that about a week had passed before he had his first visit by the officer.

Since then the officer had appeared several times, never giving his name, only his rank—commander. But he was solicitous and kind and he was someone to talk to. Twice when he came, they'd blindfolded him and taken him to the Grik. He was terrified that they were giving him back to them, but they only used him to translate messages that the Grik and the Japanese captain passed to one another. He'd learned quite a lot about the situation that way, not that it would do him any good. Besides, he'd been so relieved when they returned him to his cell that he found he forgot much of what he'd translated. Even in spite of his fear, however, Kaufman yearned for the man to come.

With a rasp of gears and a metallic *clunk,* the hatch swung wide and the compartment was bathed in the light of the passageway. It hurt his eyes and he squinted as a man stepped inside. Another light came on, from a single bulb overhead. A switch in the passageway activated it. The officer said something in Japanese and the hatch was closed and secured. As always, now that they were alone, the officer wrinkled his nose at the stench from the other bucket, in the corner. Kaufman didn't even notice the smell anymore. Still squinting, he hastily stood.

"Good morning, Captain Kaufman," said the man in pleasant, if badly accented, English.

"Is it morning?" Kaufman asked eagerly.

"Yes. Just dawn." Sato paused, watching the nervous twitch that had taken control of the prisoner's pale, waxy face. That was new. "I have not come to take you to the Grik," he hastily assured him. "You are well?"

Much of Kaufman's tension ebbed, but the twitch remained. "I am, thank God. I mean, thank God . . ." He shuddered, and Sato nodded understanding.

"I too am glad," he muttered. "But I have to ask you a question."

Kaufman nodded and straightened his shoulders. "Of course."

"Yesterday, our . . . the fleet we are a part of was involved in action with an enemy ship . . ." Kaufman tensed again and his expression was one of anguish. "It wasn't the American destroyer," Sato mercifully assured him. "It was a captured Grik vessel that the enemy had supplied with cannons. They were most effective. Many Grik ships were destroyed." He paused and watched to see how Kaufman reacted to that. He wasn't surprised to see a fragile smile and he had to struggle not to match it. "Regrettably, from an intelligence standpoint, the ship was destroyed. Nothing was recovered, but there is testimony from the survivors on nearby ships that there was one human, perhaps two, on board the enemy ship. We can only conclude they were countrymen of yours." Sato hesitated when he saw the prisoner's stricken look. "For that, you have my condolences. What I must ask you, however, is whether or not you were aware of the existence of an American flying-boat?"

Kaufman's eyes went wide and, if anything, his twitch became more violent. He began scratching the left side of his face unconsciously. "Well, yes, I am . . . I mean, I was. You mean you've seen it?" Sato nodded and Captain Kaufman closed his eyes and smiled with genuine relief. "My God. So Mallory made it after all!" He stopped and looked at Commander Okada. "We found it on the beach. The plane, that is. It was shot up and half sunk, but Mallory and a couple other fellas got it flying. The Grik nearly got them! Anyway, I sent it on to Ceylon to bring out an escort for *Mahan*." He stopped and his face was stricken. "But he couldn't have gone to Ceylon . . . could he?"

"Why did you never mention the plane before?"

Kaufman glanced vacantly around. "Nobody asked. I just figured it was lost. The Griks that got after it saw it that day." He looked imploringly at Sato. "I'm sorry. I would have told you, I swear! I just never thought it was still around!" He sat back down on his bucket and rubbed his twitching face, staring at Sato through his fingers with red-rimmed eyes. "Please," he whispered. "Don't beat me anymore."

Sato stared down at the prisoner, sickened. As much with Kaufman as with himself. "You won't be beaten," he said. He glanced back at the hatch to make sure it was still dogged. "This plane," he said, "has a radio." It wasn't a question, but a statement of fact. "So too does the American destroyer. If I could arrange it so you had access to a radio yourself, could you contact either of them?"

Kaufman looked down at the floor. "I don't have a code-book," he said quietly.

"That doesn't matter. If I am able to arrange a radio, you would be able to speak in the clear."

"What would you want me to say?"

Sato shook his head. "I do not know yet. That would depend on a number of things . . . What I want to know now is can you do it? Do you think they would listen to you?"

"I doubt Reddy would," he said grimly, and Okada recognized the name of the destroyer's commander. "I doubt he trusts me. I know he doesn't like me. Mallory, though . . ."

"Mallory is the pilot of the flying-boat?"

"Yes. At least he was. I think I could talk to him. Maybe he'd talk to Reddy . . ." Kaufman looked up at Sato. "Why?"

"Perhaps no reason. But let us keep this between ourselves." He waited until he saw Kaufman nod. "In the meantime, is there anything I can do for you?"

For a long moment, the aviator didn't reply. He just stared at Sato with astonished eyes. Finally, he spoke.

"Light. Leave the light on, please."

Sato nodded. "Anything else?"

Kaufman blinked and looked vaguely around the compartment. "Something to read," he pleaded. "I don't care what it is."

Big Sal left at dawn. Slowly, majestically, the giant wings spread and the sweeps were stowed. Matt watched her go with tired eyes and decidedly mixed emotions. *Big Sal* or Keje had always been there, somewhere nearby, almost since they came to this world, and he knew he'd miss them and worry about their safety. *Aracca* Home was being loaded now, and in the distance he saw the first smoke of the fires that would consume B'mbaado City. He realized with regret that he'd never even visited the Orphan Queen's palace, and now it was being destroyed. At least not all of it would be lost. Several feluccas had been detailed to take away B'mbaado's greatest treasures. He wished the same could have been done for Aryaal, but Rasik still hoarded them to himself, locked in the royal palace. Matt realized that the vengeance he'd chosen had contributed to that loss, but lives were more important. His conscience wouldn't suffer much when all was said and done.

His coffee cup was empty and Juan was nowhere in sight. Garrett had the watch and so he decided to try and find some, and maybe grab something to eat. That reminded him he'd been too busy to check on Earl Lanier and he grimaced at the thought. Sandra had told him the cook would be fine. The shaft hadn't penetrated beyond his impressive layer of fat. But Matt should have checked.

Thinking of injuries . . . Experimentally, he tensed a muscle in his shoulder to see what he could get away with. To his surprise, it seemed considerably better. Time to pester Sandra again about getting the dressings removed. He was sick of running around trying to do everything with one hand. He knew Sandra was asleep, though. For now, he'd leave her alone.

First get something to eat, and then go aft. He figured it wouldn't hurt to see for himself how the work on the propeller was shaping up. Progress there had him more worried than he cared to admit. They'd finally been forced to lay off work last night when the flashies tore through a second sail. Spanky himself was in the water and they nearly got him. Hopefully they'd make up for lost time in the light of day. He didn't like the idea of the world falling on top of them when they had a half-installed screw. With two engines, three boilers, and a full bunker of fuel, he would feel a lot more confident in the face of what was coming.

For the moment at least, everything was well in hand onshore, and the evacuation had taken on a more orderly atmosphere. The panic of the night before had subsided, despite the fact that time was increasingly short. Perhaps it was the daylight that eased people's fears. *Walker*'s crew was making preparations for getting under way and, except for the propeller, there were no difficulties in that regard. For the first time in longer than he could remember he faced no pressing decisions that he alone could make. They'd all been made already, and now there was nothing left to do but watch while others carried them out and hope it wasn't all for nothing. It left him somewhat at a loss. He couldn't shake the feeling there was something left undone. Pondering his unease, he descended to the wardroom. There he found Courtney Bradford, alone and sleeping in a chair at the table. His head was tilted back and his mouth was open. Loud snores filled the compartment.

There was a coffee cup on the table, but by the smell of the room, coffee hadn't been in it. Matt sighed and poured some lukewarm coffee for himself from a carafe. Then he opened the portholes on either side of the wardroom to let the warm morning air circulate within. Bradford's snore caught in his throat and he opened his eyes and blinked. Matt sat across from him and emptied the carafe into the Australian's cup. Then he gestured at it.

"That's got to stop, Courtney," he scolded him gently. "It sets a bad example."

"'m not in the Navy," Bradford grumbled. "And even if I was, it would be the Royal Australian Navy, which, I might remind you, certainly does not persecute the occasional tot."

"Your 'tots' are no longer occasional. Alcohol's not allowed on U.S. Navy ships, but so far I've turned a blind eye because of your . . . unusual status . . . and because, until lately, you've been discreet." He rubbed his eyes and cleared his throat. "I need you sober, Mr. Bradford. I need you sober and clearheaded all the time. We're all going to need our wits to survive." He smiled slightly. "And I've come to rely heavily on yours."

Bradford snorted and sipped from his cup. Grimacing, he set it aside. "I'm not much good to anyone, I'm afraid." He spoke with a still muzzy voice. "Sometimes I think there is really not much point. No matter what we do, we are continually faced with ever greater obstacles." He covered his face with his hands. "I grow so weary and . . . I miss my son quite dreadfully, you know."

Matt leaned back. Bradford had never spoken of a son. Like most of them, he hadn't said much at all about what he'd left behind. Bradford shook his head and sat up straighter. "Oh, he's alive, for all I know. Flying Hurricanes for the RAAF, in England." He frowned. "For all I know. The trouble is, I don't know for sure and I never, ever will." He glared at Matt. "We Australians still have somewhat closer ties to the mother country than you Yanks, and even though we were considerably farther away, the threat posed by Hitler struck a little closer to home. My son volunteered to fight against him almost a year and a half ago." He glanced down at his cup and took another reluctant sip. "Adar always talks about the 'greater threat'—we all do, and we've certainly been proved right in this instance. But while my son and most of the rest of the world were confronting the Nazis, you Yanks were busy antagonizing the Japs."

He paused, and turned visibly inward. Then he held up his hand. "I apologize," he said at last. "That was unfair. I was about to ask why you should care a damn what the Japs did in China when I recognized my own hypocrisy. Why should England? Or why should anyone care about Poland, you could say. Perhaps I am a bigot, after all, although I've always loved the Malays. And now the Lemurians . . . God help me, I do love the little buggers . . ." He stifled a hiccup and coughed.

"I suppose I have at times resented you Yanks for not helping my son fight the Nazis. That made it all very personal, don't you see? Of course you do. But the Japs are just as bad and they are physically much closer to home. What they did in Nanking . . . They actually bombed Australia, did you know?" Matt nodded patiently. One of *Walker*'s sisters, the *Peary*, had been sunk by the Japanese in Port Darwin. "So I suppose it makes little difference," Bradford mumbled. "You Yanks are fighting Hitler now—or were—whatever. My point is, the reason that's the case is that the Jappos and the Nazis are allies. You said you couldn't understand why the Japs would help the Grik? If they are on the same side as Hitler, there's no telling what they might do."

"That's a good point, Mr. Bradford, although war can certainly force you to make some awfully unusual friends. Uncle Joe's no saint."

"True, but Stalin shared with us the dubious distinction of being one of the Attacked, not the Attacker. In this instance at least. I won't belabor Poland, or mention Finland for the moment." He crossed his arms on the table and laid his head down. He wore no hat, and a long wisp of thinning hair trailed down almost into his cup. "I just miss my boy," he said at last.

"I understand," Matt said around a lump that had formed in his own throat. "I miss my folks. I wonder sometimes how they are and what they're doing. As far as they know, *we're* dead. It's pretty tough sometimes." Bradford raised his head and looked at him with red-rimmed eyes. "Everyone aboard must feel the same way," Matt continued. He gestured at the cup, and by inference, what had been in it before. "But we can't find solace in that. If we do, we lose." He shrugged. "We might lose anyway, but we owe it to our people here on *Walker,* as well as our new friends, to do our very best, and wallowing in booze and self-pity's not the way." Bradford's eyes flared with anger, but Matt continued on. "The war back home will be won or lost—there's nothing we can do about that. I hope your son survives, but if he doesn't, he'll have died for a good cause that he actually chose. In the meantime, we have our own war to fight, against an enemy that's just as bad as Hitler—maybe worse in a way—and our odds of survival are even worse as well. But we have to go on—not only for ourselves but for the people who trust us. Human and Lemurian."

Bradford's anger had disappeared and he sat staring at his hands. "What do you want from me?" he asked quietly.

"Ease off on your 'tots,'" Matt replied. "Other than that, what I want you to do—what I need you to do—is to keep on being the same cheerful, irreverent, awkward—brilliant—pain in the ass you've been since the day you came aboard. The men—our allies too—like you, Courtney, and they count on you in ways you can't imagine. I do too. If they think you've lost hope, then they might too." He stood.

"I came down here wondering what I was forgetting, what I've neglected to do with everything else that's been going on. I just realized what it was. Sometimes, even when we're in a group, people get to feeling like they're all alone. It's like you're sitting on the track and there's a freight train headed your way and there's nothing you can do to stop it. All you can do is look around and hope *somebody* knows what the hell they're doing. Even while the train's bearing down, you gain strength from your comrades, not only from their courage but from the realization that you're not the only one that's scared to death. At the same time, you need to believe that the one person you hope and pray has all the answers, really, really does." He smiled. "And so, I'm going to take a leisurely stroll. Walk around the ship and look at parts of it I haven't seen with my own eyes in weeks—and I'm going to *act* like I've got a pair of aces up my sleeve."

Bradford stood as well. His face was apologetic, and he toyed with the cup on the table, not meeting Matt's eyes. "What can I do?"

Matt shrugged. "Like I said, pretty much the same. Be seen. Do an autopsy on a skuggik on top of one of the torpedo mounts, for all I care. Just talk strange and say weird stuff." He grinned. "Be yourself."

"If you really think it'll help . . ."

Matt nodded. "If Jim Ellis were here, he'd be doing much the same thing. It's kind of the executive officer's job. But he's not and I don't think Larry Dowden can pull it off."

"Why not? He seems a capable young officer."

"Oh, he's that, but he's way too honest." Matt's grin began to fade. "Spanky and the Bosun'll keep things from falling apart, but if we have to tangle with *Amagi* again, they'll need all the help they can get. In more ways than one."

Walking slowly aft, Matt offered smiles and encouragement to the busy, hardworking destroyermen. As he passed under the amidships gun platform, he noticed Silva putting some of the Lemurian crew through gunnery drill on one of the four-inch-fifties overhead. The 'Cats bent themselves to the task with a will, enthusiastically traversing the gun and chittering to one another in their own tongue—as well as a broken English. Silva's bellowed instructions and threats sounded apoplectic, but there was a satisfied grin on his face. Passing by the galley, Matt snatched up the last sandwich from a platter full of crumbs just as Ray Mertz turned with a tray heaped with fresh ones he'd just made. He set it down hastily and wiped his hands on his shirt.

"Morning, Mertz. How's Lanier today?"

A chair groaned inside the galley as a great weight lifted from it. "Sufferin' sore, Captain," Lanier said around a mouthful of food as he appeared in the window. "Sufferin' sore." He gestured at the greasy bandage around his middle that could be seen through his open shirt.

"But not too sore to feed the men, I see," Matt observed.

Lanier took on a pious look. "No, sir. Never. Ravenous bastards, too, sir—beggin' your pardon. Never a word of thanks neither, but I toil away regardless." He gave a murderous look to Mertz. "Whaddaya mean, givin' that stale damn thing to the captain? Especially after Rodriguez . . ." He paused, catching himself. Matt was already chewing a bite.

"What did Rodriguez do to it?" he finally asked when he swallowed. Lanier looked stricken.

"He, uh, knocked it off onto the deck." He cringed. Matt looked down for a moment where the sandwich had probably lain and let the tension build. Then he chuckled.

"Must not have been there long, or the roaches would have carried it off." He took another bite.

"Uh, no, sir, Captain! Not long," Lanier said with evident relief. He speared Mertz with another seething glare. Then he turned back to Matt and proudly beckoned him to behold the glorious pile of newly constructed sandwiches as though he was displaying a work of art. "There you go, Captain. Take your pick! Eat two! You're too skinny as it is, if you don't mind me sayin', sir."

"Don't mind if I do," Matt said, selecting another sandwich from the pile. Earl beamed. Unhurried, Matt transferred it to his still-immobilized left hand and, munching on the first one, he continued aft.

"You idiot!" Earl cursed quietly and slapped Mertz on the side of the head. "It's a good thing the captain likes my cookin' or you'd be in a hell of a mess."

"But you *told* me to pick it up!" Ray protested.

"I didn't tell you to give it to the captain!"

Matt heard the exchange and a genuine smile replaced the false one he had worn. *In spite of everything,* he thought again, *some things never change.* He passed the number one torpedo mount, where some 'Cat and human torpedomen were checking the pressure in the air flasks and accumulators. The flasks had been empty for the last few months—which was customary when the torpedoes weren't needed. Now they were full. Sandison had asked him that morning if he could perform quarterly maintenance on the operable fish and Matt agreed, so long as all three would be ready when *Walker* got under way. By the time he reached the number four mount, he could already hear Spanky's curses from the fantail. The engineer and the Bosun were supervising their respective divisions in—hopefully—the final process of installing the propeller. Gray's men were trying to keep the sail tight against the hull so no flashies could get past and Spanky's snipes were controlling the now submerged screw with taglines. A heavy cable descended into the water from a makeshift boom, down between the supports for the propeller guard, and Dean Laney was reluctantly preparing to go back into the water. Astern, a far more orderly procession than the night before was mounting the ramp onto *Aracca*'s deck and a smoky haze had descended from the nearby burning city.

It was already warming up and Spanky wiped sweat from his brow. He was vigorously chewing a quid of something that caused a distinct bulge in his cheek. "What's that in your mouth?" Matt asked.

Surprised, Spanky turned and saw the captain. "Good morning, Skipper," he said and saluted with a grimy hand. He shifted his chaw speculatively. "I'm not rightly sure. Something Chack came up with. He said it was 'courtesy of King Rasik.' They use it for some kind of holy stink-weed or something hereabouts. It looks like a yellow tomato leaf, but it sorta tastes like tobacco." He shrugged. "Anyway, some of his boys were poking around near the palace and found a warehouse full of the stuff. They sent down what must be a ton of it last night."

"Has it made anybody sick?"

"Silva's been chewing it steady, ever since it came aboard, and he's okay so far."

Matt chuckled. "I'm surprised Silva would chew anything Chack recommended—after last time."

Spanky joined him in a laugh. "So you knew about that?"

"Of course." Matt grinned.

Chack had Silva chewing every dead leaf he could find, trying to find some replacement for his precious tobacco. The process left Dennis ill enough to waste a shell on an easy shot against a Grik ship. Silva did not endure ridicule gladly, and Matt was certain that was when the scheme between Risa and Silva—to embarrass Chack—had been hatched.

"Maybe with a real, good-faith tobacco substitute, Silva will forgive Chack and quit pretending to carry on with his sister. I need Chack sharp, and I know that drives him nuts."

Spanky nodded vigorously. It drove him nuts too and he was almost sure Silva *wasn't* pretending. "Order 'em to stay away from each other," he urged.

"Can't. Other than Chack, the 'Cats don't think it's a big deal even if they are . . ." He shuddered. "And I can't start giving orders against frater-nization between our people. We need each other too much." Matt fumed. "Besides, then that bastard Silva would have won. He would've forced me to call his bluff. No. He can put more significance and meaning in an arched eyebrow—" He snorted a laugh, his face red, and shook his head.

He gestured at the work with his second sandwich in his hand. "How's it going?"

"Slower than I'd hoped," Spanky replied, glad to change the subject. "But we'll have it shipped by this afternoon. The screw is almost in position. Once it's there, we slide it on the shaft and bolt it down. Easy as pie in dry dock, but a little more involved under the circumstances."

"That's cutting it pretty close. If the enemy scout ahead, some of them could be here by tonight."

Spanky's expression grew solemn. "Yes, sir. We're going as fast as we can."

Matt patted him on the arm. "Of course you are." He looked ashore, at the teeming mass of Lemurians waiting to board *Aracca*. The haze was thicker toward Aryaal, although the massive fires of the night before had dwindled. To the northeast, B'mbaado City was engulfed in flames. It looked like hell, and it was all so very familiar. Less than a year ago, they'd steamed out of what the maps showed as this very bay in the face of an overwhelming invasion. Of course, somehow that happened in an entirely different world. Regardless, the sense of impending doom was very much the same. Also, fantastically, it was once again the Japanese they were running from. It was as though *Walker* was condemned to repeat the same event in increasingly warped realities, over and over until the end of time. Or until fate finally caught up with her.

Spanky followed his gaze and then spoke more quietly so those nearby couldn't hear. "Would we be running if it weren't for the Japs?" he asked, reading Matt's mind. His voice was bitter. "The boys are tired of running. They were used to winning for a change."

Matt nodded. "I know. It was a good feeling, wasn't it?" He sighed. "Yeah, we'd still have to run. There's too many of them this time, even without *Amagi*. If we make it back to Baalkpan we'll have a chance." He raised his voice. "Keep up the good work. When you get finished, this old bucket'll be the fastest thing in the world again. The Japs are down to eight knots, after the last time they tangled with us. If they want a rematch, we'll run rings around 'em!"

There were tired but determined growls of approval, and Matt grinned at the men's spirit. Inside, he was sick with dread.

A little after noon, Matt watched *Aracca* fade into the haze to the east. They were cutting it close indeed. *Nerracca* was now alongside the pier and was quickly filling with the increasingly nervous refugees. They would have to pack them in tighter than ever before, but Tassat-Ay-Aracca assured him they'd find a place for everyone. When last he checked, Spanky'd said the screw was finally in place. Now all that remained was to bolt it down—a laborious and dangerous underwater procedure, but one that wouldn't take much longer. All the feluccas were gone and the last company of Chack's Marines was marching down the harbor road. They would come aboard *Walker*.

Alone in his palace now, except for his most fanatical followers, Rasik-Alcas, king of Aryaal, continued to rave and threaten and occasionally even plead for his people not to leave him. None of the few who remained on the pier could hear him, but it wouldn't have made any difference if they had.

Ben Mallory was up, scouting the enemy approach. He'd sent a warning a few minutes earlier that advance elements of the enemy fleet, a dozen ships, were less than fifty miles away. The rest seemed to be coming on hard not too far behind. Hundreds of ships could be seen in the distance, more spread out than before since they were no longer confined between Belitung and Borneo.

Matt ordered Mallory to fly back in the direction of Aryaal until he was out of sight of the lizards, and then proceed toward Baalkpan. Nakja-Mur's city would need constant reports, and Matt wanted to resume direct communications with Baalkpan. In case the Japanese were able to find their direction by radio, however, he forbade any further transmissions by the PBY except in an emergency. Once home, they could monitor *Walker*'s transmissions. If the enemy still didn't know about Baalkpan, Matt didn't want to tell them now.

Every day they had to prepare was precious. He even toyed with the idea of broadcasting continuously from *Walker* while steaming away down the Lesser Sunda Islands. Then they could go silent and run up around Celebes and down to Baalkpan from the northeast. It would lengthen the enemy's lines of supply and leave them no idea where their quarry was, but it was an awfully long way and Matt wasn't sure he even had the fuel to do it. Besides, they'd have no way of knowing if the enemy took the bait. Better to stick with the original plan and just try to get around them undetected. That was going to be hard. Even if she left right now, *Nerracca* would risk discovery by the advance force. The greatest danger of that would come after dark, however, and maybe then the massive ship could avoid being seen.

"Marines are coming aboard now, Skipper," Lieutenant Garrett reported, "and *Nerracca* says she'll be ready to shove off within the hour."

"Anything new from Spanky?"

"At least another hour, maybe more. They had to pull Laney out. He was nearly unconscious. The flashies must've figured out something's in the sail and they're beating the hell out of it."

Matt nodded and winced. He remembered Laney's bruises from the last time. "Very well. Have *Nerracca* get under way as soon as she's able. Don't wait for us. We'll catch up. We can move faster than she can even with only one engine if we have to."

Garrett shifted uncomfortably. "We'll risk losing the screw if it's not bolted on tight, Skipper."

"I'm aware of that, Mr. Garrett. I'm sure Spanky is too. But we aren't going to bug him anymore. If it comes down to it and we have to move before he's ready, then we will. I'd rather risk losing the screw than the ship."

Dennis Silva had made some dumb choices in his life, but this one took the cake. He'd volunteered to go in the water and finish the job after Laney was hauled back aboard, but even then he was less than enthusiastic. Laney looked like they'd dragged him out of a Shanghai bar after he told a dozen Royal Marines the king was queer. He was black and blue with bruises again, and at first he could barely move. It was obvious that swimming with the flashies, even with the sail as protection, wasn't going to be a walk in the park. There was nothing for it, though. When Laney finally opened his eyes, they settled challengingly on Silva. Not a word was spoken, but the implication was clear. The snipes had done their part. Now it was the deck-ape's turn. As one of the only said "apes" qualified in a suit, Silva had to pick up the slack. There was *no way* the mighty Dennis Silva would admit he was afraid to do anything a damn snipe would do, and as soon as the helmet sealed out the smoky air of the harbor, over the side he went. That was less than half an hour ago and already he was beginning to think that a fight with a dozen Marines would have been a good trade.

Even over the sound of the bubbles and his breathing, he could *hear* the bony-headed flashies thumping the canvas around him. Occasionally, when he strayed too close to the sail, one struck close enough to hit him. It felt like a pile driver. It was like being hit by a dud torpedo, he imagined, except the flashies didn't weigh as much. After two or three such blows, he thought he had a broken rib. One blow struck him on the elbow and he dropped one of the precious baseball-sized nuts. He had to go down into the bottom of the sail to retrieve it, and it took forever because every time he reached for the damn thing, a fish would strike nearby and launch it. He finally got it only because it was literally bounced into his left hand by a strike. His right arm was still numb from his shoulder to his fingertips.

"Funny bone, my ass," he grumbled. Raising himself back up on a level with the screw, he began threading the nut onto the final remaining stud. Nearby in the murk hung a giant wrench suspended by a rope from above. With the nut screwed down as far as he could turn it with the clumsy gloves of the diving suit, he reached up for the wrench. A blow from directly behind drove him facefirst into the screw. He grunted from the pain that spread between his shoulder blades and he had to blink to clear the tears that sprang to his eyes. He was also nearly deafened by the bell-like *clang* of the helmet striking the bronze propeller. "Son of a bitch!" he muttered through clenched teeth. "I think it was a Buick, officer!"

He grabbed the wrench again and began to tighten the nut. Another off-center hit in his back drove the wind out of him for a moment, but he doggedly continued his task. The fish were becoming more aggressive. They'd been doing this long enough—the flashies had to be convinced there was something in the sail. Something good to eat. Or maybe the sound or the bubbles stirred them up. Whatever the case, Silva was ready to get out of the water.

The nut was tight at last and he grabbed the wrench with both hands and heaved down as hard as he could. "Done, dammit!" he gasped.

Suddenly, a bright, silvery-shape about four feet long ricocheted off the side of his helmet and drove headfirst into one of the propeller blades with a distinctive muffled *gong*. For an instant, the hideous thing just hung there, stunned by the impact with the ship. Silva was just as stunned with shock and terror that one of the things was in there with him. Then it began to recover. Quickly, he grabbed it by the tail and yanked it toward him. Catching it by the head, he sank his fingers into its eyes on each side of its skull and held on for dear life when it began to thrash. It was incredibly powerful and it took all his strength to keep its gnashing jaws away from him. He didn't dare turn it loose. Instead, he grasped his hose and yanked it frantically as hard as he could. That was the signal to pull him up. Even as he began to rise, it dawned on him with a flash of terror that if one of the damn things had gotten in, so could others. The seconds between that realization and the instant his head broke water were the most viscerally frightening of his life.

He clenched his eyes shut until he was hauled entirely out of the water and he lay crouching on the fantail beside the depth charge rack. Slowly his breathing returned to normal and he began to wonder why no one had cracked his helmet. The fish thrashed spastically in his grasp. Oh. With some difficulty, he stood and took two steps over to the little three-inch antiaircraft gun and, with all his might, he bashed the fish against the barrel again and again. Finally, when its thrashing had been reduced to a faint twitch, Silva threw it hard against the deck. Only then did someone venture close enough to help him remove the helmet.

He looked at the shocked, wide-eyed expressions all around him. Some began to edge closer. Spanky was above him, leaning on the aft deckhouse rail, chew in his mouth. He just shook his head. Then Silva saw that Laney had retreated as far aft as he possibly could, until he stood wedged between the depth charge racks where they angled together near the jackstaff. He still had a blanket draped across his bruised shoulders and his jaw hung slack.

"There you go, Laney!" Silva bellowed, managing to leer at the machinist mate and gesturing grandly at the fish. "I brung you a present!"

By the time the sail was jettisoned and *Walker* was ready to get under way, *Nerracca* was a blur in the smoke as she worked downwind across the bay. Black puffs of smoke rose from *Walker*'s numbers three and four stacks and joined the baleful pall drifting eastward from the two gutted cities. The pier was almost empty except for the line handlers, and even they quickly deserted it when their chores were done. Only Chack and Safir Maraan, Queen Protector of B'mbaado, remained behind. She'd insisted on being the last of those leaving to set foot on this land, even if she now stood on Aryaalan soil. It was the symbolism of the act, Matt knew, as he watched the pair staring across the bay toward the flames that roared above B'mbaado City. Rolak had wanted to stay, but the bulk of his troops had embarked on *Big Sal* and Matt wanted him with them. He and Queen Maraan had become very close, but she had a functioning staff to ride herd on her people. Rolak didn't. He would have to create one on the fly. And so the Orphan Queen remained behind, the last representative of both their peoples. Gently, Chack touched her arm and with him in the lead so she could, in fact, be the last, they finally came aboard. Once behind the railing, she leaned against it, arms outstretched, as if reaching for her island home. In an almost singsong chant that hushed all chatter around her, she spoke:

"I shall not forget you, Haakar-Faask, or those whom you shall lead. No matter how long it takes, even if it costs my life, this I swear to you: I shall return!"

Slowly, the breeze and the ebbing tide moved the ship into the bay. The new propeller got an immediate trial when Matt gave the order: "Port engine, ahead one-third. Right ten degrees rudder." The deck began to vibrate under their feet, and everyone noticed immediately that the vibration was slightly different than it had ever been before. Not bad, just different. An uncertain smile crossed Dowden's face and he looked at Matt with his eyebrows raised. It was as if the propeller had brought a little of *Mahan*'s personality along with it and *Walker*'s distant sister was somehow helping her escape the relentless enemy.

"All ahead one-third," Matt commanded when *Walker*'s nose swung around to point away from the smoke-dimmed sun approaching the distant peaks of Java.

"Recommend course zero eight zero," Larry Dowden said.

"Very well. Make your course zero eight zero. Increase speed slowly to two-thirds." Matt was still testing the "feel" of the new screw. The blower noise began to increase. Unseen, Sandra Tucker had climbed the ladder behind him.

"Request permission to come on the bridge," she inquired as softly as she could and still be heard. Ever since she'd helped Matt prepare to storm Aryaal, she'd been somewhat distant. More proper, but cool.

"Permission granted," he said and she walked to the starboard bridgewing not far from where he stood. She leaned on the rail, staring aft. After a moment Matt joined her.

"I'll take care of Queen Maraan," she volunteered. "God, did you see them just now? I thought I would bawl."

"I was hoping you would," Matt said quietly. "With Rick dead, and Alan and Steve in Baalkpan, she can have their quarters. How many attendants did she bring aboard?"

"Only three. She understood the accommodations on *Walker* are less opulent than she's accustomed to." A ghost of a smile touched Sandra's lips.

"Well, I guess they can hot-bunk, or maybe we can cram a cot in there."

Sandra nodded. "I'll figure something out," she said in a low, sad voice. She stared down at the water for a long moment as it swished by below. "I feel like somebody I was trying to save just died on my operating table."

"I know what you mean," Matt agreed.

She sighed. "Maybe you really do." She was quiet again as he stood there beside her. "I'm sorry for the way I acted before you went into the city," she said at last.

"Nothing to apologize for."

"Yes, there is. I acted very badly and there's no excuse at all. I understood why you had to go into Aryaal—why everyone did—but I was mad because you were going to risk your life. And like any idiot girl, I took my anger out on you—the person I was most concerned about." She coughed a little from the smoke. "Not very professional, or even very adult. But I couldn't help myself. I nursed you back to health after your terrible wounds, and there you were, about to run yourself through the meat grinder all over again." She managed a slight smile. "It all seemed so ungrateful. Thank God it wasn't a meat grinder . . . this time."

"I'm not ungrateful," he murmured. Sandra shook her head.

"I know that. That's not the point." She glanced quickly over her shoulder at the bridge watch and lowered her voice even further. "Look, I know we had a deal, that we wouldn't let our feelings show—and I know, deep down, it's the right thing to do. But sometimes it's so hard. Particularly when I've seen you shattered and had to put you back together. I didn't know what I'd do if you got hurt again. Or worse. I didn't think I could take it. I was being selfish and I'm sorry."

He wanted to hold her then, to console her. To tell her everything would be all right, even as the smoke of defeat stung their eyes. But he couldn't. Not here. Not now.

"Do we have any chance at all?" she asked finally in an almost plaintive tone. Matt could see there were tears in her eyes. He wondered what she meant by that. Did she mean love? Or survival?

"Yes," he finally answered, hoping his voice sounded more sure than he felt. "Yesterday I wouldn't have given odds, but today? Yes. We've managed to evacuate thousands of people from two cities, something I thought we'd never pull off. And *Walker* has her legs back under her again. That by itself has sure improved my frame of mind. Yesterday, when I read Ben's dispatch, all I could focus on was *Amagi* and how powerful she is. I was in shock, I guess. Part of it was losing *Revenge*, but mainly I just couldn't believe *Amagi* had somehow followed us here. It was too damn much. Then, when we were talking about it last night, you reminded me of *Amagi*'s vulnerabilities. You gave me hope, Sandra. Since then I've been thinking about *our* advantages for a change. There aren't very many, I'll be honest, but we do have a few. With luck, they'll be enough and someday we'll come back to this place and the people who live here will return."

Sandra was shaking her head. "I think you do know how I feel. You fought just as hard to save this place and its people as I've fought to save the wounded those battles have sent me. You thought you had it done, but then . . . the patient took a turn for the worse." She looked at him. "I feel like we're caught in a nightmare that never ends. It just seems that, no matter what . . ." She stopped. "These Lemurians, these people—they're *good* people, aren't they?"

Matt nodded. "For the most part, I think they are. Just like most of the folks back home are good. There're always exceptions."

"So we just have to keep on trying, don't we? No matter what."

He looked at her for a moment and smiled. "Like you said, the patient has taken a turn for the worse, but he's not dead yet. We can't ever give up as long as there's hope." Affectionately, and fully aware of the irony, he slapped the railing under his hand. His gaze swept aft, where he saw the distinctly satisfying wide, churning wake that only two engines could make. "And as long as we have this tired, worn-out heap of rusty baling wire . . . hope will survive." Matt started to turn back to his chair. The new screw was behaving itself and he wanted to increase speed. He stopped and looked at the nurse. "Speaking of hope and baling wire, don't you think it's time to unstrap my wing? It itches something fierce."

Unseen by the captain and the nurse, in the deepening evening gloom of the pilothouse, the members of the bridge watch surreptitiously glanced at one another and tried to hide their grins. With everything else that was going on, at least the captain and his girl had made up.

Walker caught *Nerracca* long before the giant ship drew abreast of the Sapudi Islands and she slowed her exuberant sprint to a crawl. There were no lights showing on either vessel. The only illumination came from the stars and the tiniest sliver of moon in the clearing sky. Far astern, above the two destroyed cities, a faint ruddy glow remained. *Walker*'s Lemurian lookout spotted *Nerracca*'s darkened shape with his keen eyes as they came alongside. A human might have missed her. Together, the last two ships to leave B'mbaado/Aryaal Bay worked east into the Bali Sea until they made their turn north, past the Kangean group. It took all night to get that far, and it was in the first gray light of morning that Matt studied the charts with Larry Dowden, who'd just resumed his watch.

Matt had slept little—again—and his eyes felt like gritty balls of lead. He'd been on edge all night, poised for battle because he half expected to encounter enemy pickets in the dark waters of the Bali Sea. If the enemy had pushed very hard, using the brisk west wind that still prevailed, the twelve ships of the advance force could have slanted down between the Sapudis and Kangean. If the entire invasion fleet was indeed headed for Aryaal, that would have been its only chance to stop them before they got into the Java Sea.

The wind had been good to *Nerracca* too, though, and as heavily loaded as she was, she managed a solid five knots throughout the night. Even so, at five knots it was an awful long way to the Makassar Strait. Matt didn't like to think about what might happen if part of the Grik armada was headed for Baalkpan instead. If that was the case, by the time *Nerracca* and *Walker* reached the strait, they might find themselves caught *behind* the enemy fleet. There wasn't much they could do about that but plod slowly onward and hope for the best.

Juan arrived in the pilothouse with the morning coffee and Matt gratefully accepted a refill. He reflected idly for a moment on how accustomed he'd grown to that particular ritual. Like all the routine activities that somehow carried on aboard his ship in spite of everything, it was a comforting taste of normalcy. The weird part was, ever since they ran completely out of "real" coffee and Juan was forced to make do with the local stuff, the morning brew had actually improved. In some corner of his mind, Matt still remembered the taste and smell of the coffee his mother used to make, and there was no comparison between that nostalgic ideal and what he was drinking now. But Juan's new coffee was unquestionably better than it had been when he had the "real" stuff to ruin. Matt's tired mind attempted to grasp the significance of that even while he tried to concentrate on the chart, but all he could come up with at the moment was that either he was actually beginning to get used to "monkey joe" or Juan's coffee had been even worse than he realized. He straightened, shaking his head.

"I'm going to stretch out for a while, Mr. Dowden. Continue 'steaming as before.' Your course is zero two zero. Wake me if . . ." He shrugged and addressed the pilothouse at large. "Mr. Dowden has the deck and the conn."

"Aye, aye, sir," Dowden replied. He turned to the helmsman. "This is Mr. Dowden. I have the deck and the conn . . ."

Even as Larry spoke, Matt was descending the ladder. Down the companionway and into his quarters, he had no conscious memory of how he arrived, sitting on his bunk and taking off his shoes. It had been a particularly grueling couple of days, physically as well as emotionally. The bad thing was, despite what he'd said to Sandra, it was only liable to get much worse.

"Captain to the bridge!"

Matt's eyes opened with a start and he rolled over and looked at the speaker on the bulkhead. Had the summons really come or had he only imagined it? His brain was still foggy with the unpleasant and, as usual, quickly receding remnants of the elusive dream. It was uncomfortably hot and stuffy in the compartment and his shirt was soaked with sweat. He'd been so tired when he finally turned in that he hadn't even clicked on the little fan. The light was still on too, and he wondered how long he'd slept. Rolling to a sitting position, he pressed the comm stud.

"Bridge. This is the captain . . . Did you just call me?" His voice was rough and his mouth was dry.

"Yes, sir. This is Mr. Garrett. You're needed on the bridge."

Surprised that it wasn't Larry Dowden's voice, Matt quickly looked at his watch. 1700. Somehow, he must have been asleep for almost nine hours and Dowden was probably in his own rack by now. As the Lemurian recruits were trained to the point they could competently exercise the duties of those they'd lost, *Walker* had finally been able to return to a normal watch rotation. So had her bridge officers, now they no longer had to wear so many other hats as well. Matt pressed the stud again.

"On my way."

He pulled his shoes back on and quickly ran a comb through his hair. Dampening a towel in his tiny basin, he wiped the sleep from his eyes and moistened his face. Contemplating his razor for just a moment, he decided it could wait until he knew what the situation was. With the exception of Courtney Bradford, himself—and Sandra Tucker of course—virtually the entire crew now sported beards. The quality of each beard varied with the men's individual ability to grow one, however, and a few were a little sparse. The razors on the ship would last only so long and he wasn't going to force the men to shave, but he did require they keep themselves trimmed. His own determination was to remain clean-shaven as long as he possibly could and he disliked appearing with stubble. It was his little ritualistic way of showing daily defiance toward the adversity they faced.

Sensing it was important somehow, he picked up the razor after all. His officers knew he preferred to take the few extra minutes to make himself presentable. It never hurt for the men to see, no matter how desperate the situation, their skipper was always calm enough to hold a razor to his face. If time was critical enough to prevent him from doing so now, Garrett would have made that clear. He did hurry, though, and in just a few minutes he was climbing the ladder at the rear of the pilothouse. As he did so, he was surprised how rested and vigorous he felt. The long sleep had done him a world of good, but in spite of that he couldn't ignore the growing dread that welled inside him. He always felt apprehensive when called to the bridge unexpectedly, but the fact that they were in the middle of the Java Sea, in broad daylight, only made his concern more acute. He knew his officers had probably conspired to let him sleep as long as he could and it would have taken something fairly serious to disturb him. In their current situation, things went from "fairly serious" to "catastrophic" pretty damn quick.

"Captain on the bridge!" Garrett called. He was waiting for him by the chart table.

"As you were. What's up, Mr. Garrett?"

"Surface contact, Captain," he said. "You can see it better from the fire-control platform." The gunnery officer led him up the next ladder to the platform above the bridge. Matt followed slowly, still hampered by the use of only one arm. His plea the evening before had come to naught, but Sandra had promised to take another look at his shoulder today. Then she would make her decision. He hadn't seen her yet today, having been asleep for most of it. Slightly winded, he gained the platform and joined the lieutenant beside the useless range finder.

"Port bow," Garrett suggested, and pointed. "On the horizon. *Nerracca* saw them first and signaled. Her lookouts are a lot higher than ours. It didn't take long for us to see them, though."

Matt raised his binoculars and peered through them for a moment, adjusting the objective. *Walker* and *Nerracca* were in one of those rare parts of the Java Sea in which absolutely no land could be seen in any direction. They would soon raise the islands off the southern coast of Borneo, but for now there was nothing. The afternoon was bright and almost completely clear. A few high clouds scudded hastily overhead in the direction of Borneo. Evidently the wind had finally shifted back out of the south.

Matt focused carefully at the point where the sea met the sky and as he stared, he began to discern towering, dirty-white sails outlined against the light blue background. There was no doubt about it. Even as he concentrated on holding the binoculars steady, more and more of the ominous shapes resolved themselves in the distance. It wasn't just the advance element of the enemy fleet they'd been avoiding either. There were far too many. In spite of the heat, icy tendrils clutched his heart and radiated outward, across his chest and down his back. Far in the distance, beyond the ever more crowded horizon, Matt thought he could see a hazy column of black-gray smoke drifting away to the north and up toward Borneo and the Makassar Strait. He lowered the binoculars until they hung suspended from the strap around his neck.

"They must've seen us," he observed. "At least *Nerracca*. Her masts are twice as tall as theirs."

"Yes, sir. It's hard to tell, but it looks like they've altered course since I first saw them. Right before I called you. Should I sound general quarters?"

Matt shook his head. "Not yet. But please do have Mr. McFarlane, Mr. Dowden, and the Bosun report to the bridge immediately."

"Aye, aye, Captain."

Ten minutes later, Matt gently tapped the chart with his index finger. "We're here," he said to the small group that had quickly gathered on the bridge. Then the same finger stabbed down a little to the northwest of their position. "The enemy is there. There's no longer any question in my mind that they know where Baalkpan is. There's no other reason for them to come this way." His lips formed a rueful smirk. "Just like we feared, the Japs must've been 'reading our mail.' Monitoring our transmissions." The smirk changed to a snarl. "And they ratted us out to the lizards. Regardless whatever other 'inducements' the Grik might have used to get the Japs to help them, they told them about Baalkpan because they wanted to." He shook his head, genuinely amazed. The Japanese were the enemy and when it came to *Amagi*, he had to admit it was even kind of personal. But he still found it hard to believe they would actively, voluntarily, help the Grik. Fleetingly, he wondered how *Amagi*'s more junior personnel felt about that. Pointless to speculate. He looked at each of those present. "Whether this force represents the bulk of the enemy fleet or not is impossible to say just yet, but it's certainly a sizable fraction of it. *Nerracca*'s lookouts have counted upwards of a hundred ships so far." He paused and took a deep breath. "And there's definitely a column of dark smoke rising from somewhere within or beyond the enemy force. We have to assume that smoke represents *Amagi*."

"But . . . when Lieutenant Mallory reported the advance force nearing Surabaya, he also sighted a significant number of enemy ships on an identical course less than thirty miles behind them," Dowden stressed.

"Yeah, but as I've been concerned all along, if they really have more than three hundred ships, they have more than enough to send a 'significant number' in two directions at once. It seems that's what they've done."

"We gotta warn Baalkpan!" Spanky said, around a mouthful of the yellow leaves.

"That's happening right now. I just hope they can hear us. We're still pretty far away." He frowned. "I told Clancy to ask for confirmation when he gets through. Radio silence is pointless at this stage. They clearly know where we're going."

Dowden's face suddenly went white with dreadful realization. "What are we going to do about *Nerracca*?"

Matt nodded slowly. "Precisely. What *are* we going to do? *Walker* can easily outrun the enemy, but obviously *Nerracca* can't. She's gained almost a knot, with this good wind on her starboard quarter. For her, that's really moving. Right now the lizards are beating into the wind, but once they turn north after passing these islands here"—he pointed again at the chart—"she won't have a chance. She might not anyway." He nodded toward the distant ships. "As you can see, they have the angle on us."

"Damn it, Skipper!" Gray growled with frustration. "What can we do? There's seven or eight thousand people on that ship!"

Matt glared at him. "That's what I was going to ask you!" He rubbed his eyes and looked at the others. "Gentlemen, we've *got* to come up with something, and we've got to do it now!" McFarlane's face wore a thoughtful expression. "Spit it out, Spanky!"

"Well, you said *Nerracca's* making six knots."

"Thereabouts."

"If we light off the number two boiler, *Walker* can make thirty for a while. Hell, we could sustain twenty-eight if nothing pops." He glanced around at the expectant faces. "That's a hell of a lot of horsepower."

"You mean, rig a *tow*?" Matt breathed. Spanky nodded.

"But will it be enough?" Garrett asked skeptically. "I know *Nerracca's* mostly wood, but her hull is incredibly thick and she's . . . *huge*! Especially with all those people on board, I bet she weighs twenty thousand tons!"

"Probably more," Spanky said.

"Could we add enough to her speed to make it worth the effort?" Matt asked, but Spanky shook his head.

"Skipper, I got no idea. I don't know what else we can do."

"I'm all in favor of giving it a try," said Gray, "but we don't even have a cable big enough. What are we gonna pull her with, kite string?"

"*Nerracca* has heavy cable," Garrett said, thinking aloud. "Hell, her anchor cable is three feet thick."

"Right," said Gray, "and what are we gonna secure it to? There's not a cleat on the ship that would stand strain like that!"

Spanky glared at the Chief. "Then figure it out, Fitz! You're in charge of the deck divisions. You're always reminding us of that! Rigging the tow is something you're going to have to solve! Distribute the load to more than one cleat—you can come up with something!"

Gray nodded. "That might work," he said. "I'll see what I can do."

"There's going to be other problems, Captain," Larry Dowden warned.

Matt sighed. "I know, Mr. Dowden. We'll just have to solve them, won't we?" For a moment he watched the distant armada creeping slowly but inexorably closer to the point far ahead that he'd calculated *Walker* and *Nerracca* must reach before the enemy did. "We don't have any choice."

Pete Alden stood on one of the many balconies surrounding Nakja-Mur's Great Hall. The branches of the mighty tree that soared from the top of the impressive structure provided some much-appreciated shade. Still, it was hot and humid and it had been a long, grueling day. He wiped sweat from his eyes and took a sip of some sour-sweet nectar that had been offered him by a member of the High Chief's expanded staff. Pete grimaced at the taste, as well as the situation. In the distance, down at the pier, he made out *Mahan*'s disheveled form. Still wounded by all she'd been through and badly battered by the storm, she'd crept painfully into Baalkpan Bay just two days before. She looked muddy with rust and her missing 'stack and searchlight tower gave her a gap-toothed appearance. Her steering had been repaired before she left Aryaal and her bridge was a bridge again, but there sure weren't any bells and whistles.

Jim Ellis had made his report and it still felt sort of weird having an officer come to him. Letts had administrative command—after Nakja-Mur, of course—but he'd been off inspecting the wellhead and retrieving the launch from upriver when *Mahan* arrived. It had finally been determined that Tony Scott must have fallen prey to a "super lizard," an ambush hunting descendant of Allosaurus, according to Bradford. The things were rare and Pete had never seen one, but by all accounts they were one of the few "dinosaurs" of this region that weren't stunted. The Lemurian scouts had discovered tracks and blood on the pipeline. The monster must have been lying in wait for passing prey, hunkered slightly back in the dense foliage along the trail when Scott came ambling by. It was a terrible loss and Pete shuddered to think about how it must have been. Even so, the irony of the coxswain's death wasn't lost on him.

Anyway, since Pete had operational command of Baalkpan's defenses, Jim cheerfully reported to him when he arrived. There wasn't even the tiniest hint that Mr. Ellis considered it inappropriate and Pete was grateful for that. The irony of a naval lieutenant in command of a destroyer reporting to Mrs. Alden's son was even more bizarre, to him at least, than the way poor Scott had gotten it. Ever since then, though, Jim had been down at the dock working night and day, with hundreds of Lemurian "yard-apes" crawling all over his ship. By Nakja-Mur's command, every possible assistance, regardless of expense, was placed at the disposal of the young lieutenant and his wounded destroyer.

Nakja-Mur had certainly stepped up to the plate; Alden had no complaints about that. He no longer questioned what things cost. The High Chief had finally completely grasped the concept of total war, and everything else had dimmed to insignificance. Nothing was as important to him as saving his city and its people and he'd do whatever it took. With Letts's help, the High Chief of Baalkpan had blossomed into a kind of bureaucratic prodigy. In a government like that of the United States, Nakja-Mur would have been performing all the duties usually associated with the secretaries of state, commerce, agriculture, public works, and war. He didn't really know doodly-squat about any of those things, but he was smart enough to know it, and he delegated all the hands-on work to people who did. He just made sure the wheels were greased and he arbitrated disputes. He was also a genius at sorting out priorities and making sure the most important projects got the assets they needed the quickest. He relied heavily on Alden and Letts to advise him as to which projects those were, but since Baalkpan's defense and the support of the AEF were almost everybody's top priority, there was rarely any disagreement between them.

The exception to this unity of purpose was still represented by what Letts called the Run Away Party, which was enjoying a resurgence that began with *Fristar's* return and was reinforced by the terrible news that the offensive was turning into a desperate retreat. The "Run-Aways" were still a minority since most of them had, of course, already run away. But Alden figured that as soon as the new scope of the threat they faced became known, the Run-Aways would gain many converts. There was no Lemurian president, or anything of the sort, to rule the collection of independent Homes and peoples from other "land" Homes that had gathered at Baalkpan. The leadership was more like some sort of screwy legislature of equal representatives. Kind of like the city-state setup of ancient Greece, Alden thought. Unlike the captain, Pete didn't know much about history—beyond that of the Marine Corps—but he'd heard of the Spartans and he knew about Thermopylae. He hoped they weren't facing a similar situation. He knew one of the problems the Greeks had faced was an inability to work together. But Nakja-Mur chaired all the meetings since he was High Chief of the "Host" Home. Hell, throw in speaker of the house while you're at it, Alden thought. So far he'd managed to keep everybody's eye on the ball.

Pete gazed out across the city below and wondered yet again at the ingenuity of the people here. Instead of walls to protect them from predators, like the Aryaalans used, they had opted for a raised-platform architecture that allowed them to sleep safely at night, when those predators were most likely to visit. The problem with that type of defense, however, was it was useless in the face of an invading army. That was a threat Baalkpan had never had to contend with before, and Alden could sympathize with the growing panic felt by those who heard the news brought by the flying-boat the evening before.

A brief attempt was made, at first, to control the news of *Revenge's* loss and the forced evacuation of Aryaal and B'mbaado in the face of an exponentially increased threat. That effort didn't last long. Nakja-Mur felt compelled to share the information with the other chiefs and the news leaked out as quickly as that. When Steve Riggs came to Pete and said a fishmonger near the pier told him less than an hour after the meeting of the chiefs that the entire AEF had been destroyed, Pete knew something had to be done. He and Steve immediately went to Nakja-Mur and told him they had to make an announcement *now* and tell the people *everything*—not just that the AEF was in retreat but that they were bringing thousands of new allies to defend Baalkpan. Otherwise, by morning there wouldn't be a single Home in Baalkpan Bay and half the city would be empty. Nakja-Mur made the announcement. Soon the hysteria began to subside, but in its place remained a deep anxiety.

Baalkpan did have more allies now, besides the B'mbaadans and Aryaalans. Several more Homes had arrived since the AEF set out and word of the Grik menace was spreading fast. It was generally agreed they were facing a repeat of the prehistoric, almost mythical conflict that drove the People from paradise. Those who knew of the Great War in the west believed Baalkpan and the Homes that answered her call were doing great work on behalf of all the People to stamp out this terrible scourge. It was known and appreciated that Baalkpan had split its own defenses in order to take the fight to the enemy. But few foreign warriors came to Baalkpan's aid.

A few hundred came from across the Makassar Strait on Celebes, from a small colony city called Sular. The Sularans were nervous from the start about the ambitious battle plan and had sent no representatives to the conference. Once the offensive began, they were convinced it would meet disaster, and their entire population evacuated to—of all places, Pete thought—Manila. That was where many of Baalkpan's people had gone as well. But the Sularan warriors who remained behind were among the most fanatical converts to the tactics Alden taught. There weren't enough of them to defend Sular but, possibly ashamed of the rest of their people, they were determined to fight the Grik. They had, in fact, been preparing to move to Aryaal with the next transport.

Manila was the largest known land outpost of the Lemurian People, in terms of numbers, and it shared a religion and heritage with the people of Baalkpan. Led by a High Chief named San-Kakja, the Manilos sent food and promised workers and warriors to bolster the defenses of their sister city to the south. The warriors would also learn the new ways of war being taught there. San-Kakja dared not send too many troops because he feared that if the war went poorly and Baalkpan fell, it would be only a matter of time before the enemy came to Manila, and he had his own defenses to prepare. His city was open to any and all refugees, however, and it was to Manila that all of Baalkpan would eventually retreat if they were forced to—and if they were able. Pete hoped the promised troops would arrive in time.

The people of the seagoing Homes had been helpful as well, serving as transports for goods and refugees. It was a dangerous passage, since they risked the attention of the mountain fish, a few of which were known to dwell in the deeper parts of the Celebes Sea. Normally, these creatures weren't a threat to a Home—that was one of the reasons the ships were so large in the first place. Mountain fish were certainly *capable* of destroying a Home, but they only rarely ever tried. Perhaps it was because the Homes of the People were almost as big as they were and they just didn't think of them as food, or maybe they thought the Homes were other mountain fish. Whatever the reason, the only time they seemed aggressive toward them was, unfortunately, at this time of year. It was mating season for the mountain fish and instinctual urges triggered aggressive and possibly territorial reactions toward the Homes precisely because they thought they were other mountain fish. Of course, no one knew for certain. In any event, even though the Homes that plied back and forth between Baalkpan and Manila provided no troops for Baalkpan's defense, the aid they delivered was doubly appreciated because of the risk involved.

Pete harbored no illusions that the Homes would help defend Baalkpan if the Grik came this way. They'd definitely been a help, but like

Fristar, few of the Homes' people or High Chiefs could understand why the people of Baalkpan—or any land Home, for that matter—would choose to defend, well, *land* in the first place. They considered it regrettable and inconvenient that the Ancient Enemy had found them again and some boasted that if they'd been aware of the offensive against the Grik they might have been willing to participate. But if the Grik learned where Baalkpan was and came to threaten it directly, they would undoubtedly flee. Why not? Unlike their ancestors, the sea folk weren't tied to the land. They could just move on whenever the Grik became a threat. Nakja-Mur tried to convince them it was different this time. The Grik now had ships that could follow, wherever they went. What would they do when they faced the Great Eastern Ocean? Would they continue to flee until they fell off the world? In this instance at least, his pleading was to no avail.

Alden didn't really much care. He wanted only dedicated soldiers under his command. Maybe it was the Marine in him, but he wasn't interested in using troops to keep an eye on other troops that didn't want to fight. Besides, if the Grik did come, the Homes would be needed to evacuate the last of Baalkpan's noncombatants—though there weren't many of those left. Most who hadn't already fled or been sent away had been training to become soldiers and Marines even while they worked on the city's defenses.

As he'd reported to the captain, those defenses were impressive. Much of the works were visible from where he stood on Nakja-Mur's balcony. Baalkpan had a wall now, ten feet high and made of hard-packed dirt. Reinforced with timbers from the surrounding jungle, it completely surrounded the city. A wide, deep moat was at its base and beyond that was an impressive killing ground full of sharpened stakes and entanglements. Heavy guns like those they'd armed the Homes with faced the bay, where they could bear on enemy ships. Dozens of the smaller twelve-pounder guns, like those that had been aboard *Revenge,* protected the approaches from the land. Behind them were the mortar emplacements. All the guns had overhead protection from plunging crossbow bolts and nowhere could the enemy get close enough to the walls to use their firebomb throwers without coming under direct artillery fire. There were multiple magazines for ammunition storage and extra wells had been dug to improve their water supply—not just for drinking but for fighting fires. Tons of food had been prepared and preserved and, even if most was fish, there should be enough for many months.

On the promontory overlooking the mouth of the bay, Lieutenant Brister had overseen the construction of a fort in the shape of a pentagon, much like those that proved so effective in the eighteenth and nineteenth centuries. Like its predecessors, this one was festooned with heavy guns that covered the harbor entrance and there were defenses around it similar to those that encircled the city. There were also sufficient provisions within that it could hold for quite a while if it was ever cut off from Baalkpan. Brister had named it Fort Atkinson, after *Mahan*'s captain who'd been killed in the battle with *Amagi*. Brister had admired Captain Atkinson very much. He was proud of the fort and Pete was too. He was proud of everything they'd done to prepare for a possible attack. Now, as he stood waiting for Nakja-Mur to join him for their afternoon bull session, he fervently prayed that all the defenses he'd helped design and build and all the citizen-soldiers he'd trained would never face the test they'd been preparing for.

A tapestry separating the balcony from the Great Hall parted, and Nakja-Mur strode through to join Sergeant Alden with his own goblet of nectar in his hand. His face was expressionless, as usual, beyond a small, clipped frown that didn't reveal his teeth. His shoulders sagged and his tail drooped and it was clear he was exhausted.

"Good afternoon, Gener-aal Aalden," he said by way of greeting.

Pete grimaced. He hated it when Nakja-Mur called him that, especially in front of others. "Good afternoon, Nakja-Mur, U-Amaki Ay Baalkpan."

"Preparations continue to proceed well?" Nakja-Mur asked.

Pete shrugged. "Well enough. We started building up the overhead protection for the batteries today, now that we know about *Amagi*." He shook his head. "Not that it'll do much good against ten-inch guns. That's one thing we never planned for. I've also started working on more shelters for troops and medical facilities. It's mostly revetments to protect from fragments, but it's better than nothing."

"These ten-inch guns are very bad?"

Pete nodded. "They're more than twice as big as *Walker*'s."

"But the guns you helped build for my people are as well."

"True," Alden agreed, "but as we've discussed many times, those guns, as powerful as they are, are still no match for *Walker*'s in range, power, or accuracy. I wish they were, but we just don't have the facilities to make anything like that yet. As for *Amagi*, her guns are bigger still than the best we've been able to make and they can shoot ten times as far."

Nakja-Mur nodded solemnly. "You're saying we have no real defense against this *Amagi*? Not even now that there are two of your fast iron ships?"

"No. As you can surely see for yourself, *Mahan*'s in no shape for a fight. Jim's killing himself trying to get her ready and hopefully he'll have time. But even if *Walker* and *Mahan* were brand spanking new, they'd be no match for that damn thing. We'll think of something. We have to. But right now I sure don't know what it'll be. Pray, I guess."

Nakja-Mur nodded. "I will certainly do that," he said. "I will pray that it never comes. It may not, you know," he added hopefully.

Just then, Ed Palmer was escorted onto the balcony by a pair of Nakja-Mur's guardsmen, who paused and waited to be summoned close. Ed accompanied them and Pete's heart sank when he saw the signalman's ashen face.

"My guess is," Pete said before Ed spoke a word, "we should have been praying already."

A skeptical but willing Tassat-Ay-Aracca supervised the passage of a fat, looped hawser to *Walker*'s fantail as the destroyer lay hove-to in the massive ship's lee. The heaviest cables that could be secured were attached to four mooring stanchions, two on each side of *Walker*'s aft deckhouse. The cables were rigged aft, outboard, and draped across the top of the propeller guards. Once they were secured to *Nerracca*'s cable, the connection point was allowed to trail fifty yards astern. Hundreds of hopeful faces lined the Home's catwalk railing and watched while the work was completed. A party of Marines under Chack's direction accomplished much of the labor. Now that he was back aboard ship, he'd quickly reverted to his position of bosun's mate. When completed, Gray reluctantly gave his approval to the unorthodox rig. The strain on *Walker*'s hull would be immense, but it was all they could manage in the time they had.

Slowly, with hot exhaust gases rippling above three of her stacks, *Walker* surged ahead to take up the slack. The cable rose, dripping, from the depths, and with a nerve-racking, trembling groan the old four-stacker added her thrust to *Nerracca*'s sails. Gray was on the aft deckhouse scrutinizing the cables as the strain began to build and Spanky was below, monitoring the engines and the boilers. Matt paced back and forth between the port wing and the aft bridge rail. From that position he could see *Nerracca*, the length of his ship, and the enemy as well. He called a slight course correction to Larry Dowden, who stood at the helmsman's side. It had been carefully stressed to Tassat that *Nerracca* must follow exactly in *Walker*'s wide wake. The frothing violence of that wake was unprecedented as the RPMs of the twin screws rapidly built.

Garrett appeared at Matt's side. "Thank God the sea's not running very high, Captain," he said. "We could break her back if it was."

Sandra and Queen Maraan stepped out onto the weather deck below. The queen looked up at him with her wide silver eyes.

"Thank you, Cap-i-taan Reddy, for what you are trying to do. Many of my people are aboard that ship."

Matt shifted uncomfortably and nodded. The queen had spoken in almost perfect English. He knew Chack was still teaching her, but Sandra might have told her what to say. Regardless, it was obvious she'd wanted to say it. "We'll do our best, Your Highness," he replied. "We're doing all we can."

"Seven knots!" came the cry from the wheelhouse. "We're starting to gain a little!"

Slowly, agonizingly, the speed mounted while *Walker* bucked and heaved like a greyhound dragging an elephant. Triumphantly, they passed eight knots. Then nine. The enemy force grew closer, but they were still on a slower tack. *Amagi* wasn't, however. As slow as she was, she still wasn't dependent on the wind, and she shouldered her way forward through the temporarily slower ships. The column of dark smoke grew ever more distinct and the lookout had reported her pagoda-like superstructure on the distant horizon.

Ten knots seemed to be it, for once they reached that speed, no amount of labor on *Walker*'s part was able to increase it. The sun was beginning to set, but the Grik were much closer now. Soon they'd know if it would be a stern chase or a fight. Matt tried to estimate how fast the enemy could sail with the wind directly astern. He'd seen them make at least twelve knots once before, but that was with the wind slightly abaft the beam, a square-rigger's best point of sailing. If *Walker* could somehow manage to keep this speed all the way to Baalkpan, and if they could squeeze past the foremost ships that were straining to cut them off, Matt didn't think the Grik could catch them. On the other hand, *Amagi* would soon be in range of her big guns. With darkness falling, she wouldn't have a target, though, would she? Once she got behind them, she'd never catch up either. Not if eight knots was all she had.

A couple of Grik ships, either because of better seamanship or cleaner hulls, were drawing ahead of the pack. Matt had a good eye for geometry and there was no way *Walker* would drag *Nerracca* past those two, at least.

"Sound general quarters," he ordered at last. The raucous "gong, gong, gong" reverberated throughout the ship and hats were exchanged for helmets. Matt knew the consensus was that no one wanted to go in the water with a life jacket on, but he ordered them worn regardless. Sandra suggested that the possibility a crewman might be eaten was more than offset by the protection against crossbow bolts and flying debris that the jackets afforded them. The Lemurian destroyermen hated the jackets even more than the humans did. In their case it was because, for the most part, they were way too big. They wore them nonetheless.

Bernard Sandison was the last to report, as usual. He had the farthest to go from where he was supervising the preparation of the torpedoes. He plugged in his headset, turned to the talker, and gave a thumbs-up sign.

"All stations manned and ready, Captain," Reynolds said aloud.

"Very well. Who's in the crow's nest?"

"Bosun's Mate Chack, sir."

Matt nodded. Early on, Lieutenant Garrett had worked very closely with the burly young Lemurian. He'd picked up ranges well. Matt didn't have the perspective of the lookout, but those two lead ships were obviously in range. He wanted to knock them out before they got dead ahead, when only the number one gun would bear. "Inform Mr. Garrett he may commence firing when ready," he said.

On the fire-control platform, Garrett listened to Chack's report as it came through his earpiece. He echoed it to Sandy Newman, who was operating the mechanical fire-control computer. "Load one, two, and four. Range to target four O double O. Angle is zero six zero, speed seven knots."

"On target!" chorused the director and the pointer.

Garrett knew they didn't have the ammunition to waste on an "up ladder." Since there was still some visibility, he would fire a single salvo and hope they could correct from there. Chack had good eyes; he should spot the fall of shot.

"One round each, salvo fire. Commence firing!"

The salvo buzzer alerted the bridge crew and a moment later the ship shook perceptibly with the booming roar of three four-inch guns. In the deepening twilight the tracers quickly converged on the target. A bright, rippling flash erupted amidships of the first enemy ship and a chorus of exultant shouts rose up. Matt was excited as well. Chack was right on the money.

"Silence!" bellowed Chief Gray on the fo'c'sle, right behind number one. "Grab that damn shell, Davis, before it goes over the side!" His yell was loud enough that half the ship must have heard.

Still grinning, Matt turned to the talker. "By all means let's have some quiet so the men can do it again."

The next ship in line was destroyed almost as quickly, but it took two salvos instead of one. It must have maneuvered to avoid the sinking, burning hulk in front of it. More ships were cracking on, though. It was as though the destruction of the first two only spurred the rest to greater effort. Reynolds spoke up. "Captain, Mr. Garrett recommends we go to single shots, alternating the guns. We may not sink 'em every time but we ought to slow them down."

"Agreed," Matt said. "We don't have enough shells to fire even once at every ship out there." For the next several minutes there was a steady booming, going from forward, aft, and then forward again. In the deepening gloom, the sea off the port bow was littered with burning ships they'd hit. Garrett was judiciously targeting only the ones that might cut them off and it looked like the strategy was working. Matt scanned the sea to port to see if he could tell how close *Amagi* was, but it was impossible to say. The sun had set behind the Grik fleet and *Amagi's* pagoda was lost in the hundreds of silhouetted sails. But at that very instant, a bright flash of light erupted a little farther to the north than he'd been looking. It seemed closer than he expected, too.

"Captain!" cried Reynolds. "Lookout reports *Amagi* has opened fire!"

"I saw it!" Matt answered. "Right full—" He stopped. "Belay that! Keep your rudder amidships! Maintain current heading!" *Walker* couldn't make any evasive maneuvers at all. Not while she had *Nerracca* in tow.

"My God," Dowden muttered. "We're a sitting duck!"

Matt turned to him. "Mr. Dowden. I believe your action station is the auxiliary conn, aft. Why don't you get there as quickly as you can?"

"Aye, aye, Captain! Sorry!" Dowden muttered, and without another word, he bolted for the ladder. Before he even reached it, eight enormous waterspouts marched across the sea, the closest about fifteen hundred yards off the port quarter. The impacts were widely spaced, across a square mile of ocean. They must be near *Amagi's* maximum range.

Matt turned to the talker, judging the wind. "Make smoke! Signal *Nerracca*; no lights at all!" Another enemy salvo rained down, a little closer than the first but no less scattered. Thick columns of black smoke gushed from *Walker's* stacks and drifted northward, toward the enemy. The light was failing fast, but what little there was would be right on *Walker* and *Nerracca*. The smoke might help a little, but all by herself, there was no way the old destroyer could pump out enough to cover something the size of a small island. He hollered up at Garrett on the fire-control platform. "What's it look like ahead?" Matt could no longer see any Grik ships other than those that were afire. Unlike the ones that invested Aryaal, these were not lit from stem to stern with lanterns. "Do you think we can get clear if we cease firing? Our gun flashes will give them a target."

"No, sir," Garrett replied. "There's a couple more of the bastards that might get close. If they throw a firebomb on us or *Nerracca*, the Jap'll really have a target!"

"Very well. Try not to shoot unless you have to, though." He glanced aft. Even through the smoke and the darkness, the massive white sails of the Home seemed painfully bright. Another salvo from *Amagi* lit the night. A few moments later he watched as the bright underwater flashes sent more geysers into the air. The pressure of the explosions pounded his ears and seemed to suck the air from his lungs. Closer still, and they weren't using armor-piercing shells this time. They wouldn't need them; high explosive would be far more devastating. He looked down and caught a glimpse of Queen Maraan, Bradford, and Sandra on the weather deck looking up at him. Sandra must have been trying to keep the other two out from underfoot. Otherwise, he imagined she'd be on the bridge. Suddenly he realized he wanted her there. "Come on up!" he shouted over the roar of the blower. "Just stay on the wing, if you please." The three quickly scrambled up the ladder and stood beside him.

"Well done, Captain!" Courtney cried, grasping his hand and shaking it. "You've been giving those lizards quite a thrashing! And those Jappos are just killing fish!"

"I would never have believed the power of the Jaap's guns, if I hadn't seen it for myself!" Safir Maraan breathed. "Are we safe from them here?"

Another salvo rumbled in. This time they were going to be close. Even over the sound of the blower, the heavy, ripping-canvas sound could be heard. The majority of the salvo sent spume into the air less than a hundred yards to port. One was inside of thirty and the terrible force of the blast sent heavy pieces of shrapnel crashing into the side of the ship as a high-pitched shriek rent the air. One went ridiculously long and exploded without effect two hundred yards off *Walker's* starboard quarter.

One hit *Nerracca* in the port bow at the base of the forward tower and tripod mast. It detonated with a tremendous explosion and a roiling ball of flame. Splinters and shell fragments rained into the sea for hundreds of yards and splintered wood sprayed the destroyer. Wood, and pieces of God knew how many refugees. The queen held her hand over her open mouth in a very human gesture of horror and Courtney Bradford clasped her protectively to his side. Matt realized he'd done the same with Sandra and he immediately released her and spun back inside the wheelhouse.

"Damage report!" he demanded.

A few moments later Reynolds recited the litany. "Minor flooding in the aft engine room! Half a dozen holes in the port side, anywhere from the size of a quarter to one that looks like a boot. Only a couple are on the waterline and they think they can get them plugged pretty quick." Reynolds listened for a moment. "The number four torpedo mount looks like Swiss cheese and one of the 'Cats bought it. Three wounded are on their way to the wardroom." Matt looked out where Sandra had been standing, but she was already gone. The salvo buzzer rang and the numbers one and two guns fired almost simultaneously at a pair of Grik ships that were edging too close. The express-train rumble of another Japanese salvo neared and Matt dashed back onto the bridgewing. Mountainous splashes straddled *Nerracca* and one erupted near *Walker's* fantail but evidently didn't explode. Sheets of water cascaded down on the men on the aft deckhouse and the crew of number four. Another explosion on *Nerracca* lit the night not far from where the first one hit. The enormous forward sail began to burn.

"All ahead flank!" Matt yelled. The bridge watch exchanged nervous looks, but the order was relayed. *Walker*'s stern crouched even lower and the thrashing wake threatened to swamp the fantail. If *Walker* hadn't been constrained, she would have been kicking up a rooster tail six feet over the stern. The terrible vibration they'd almost gotten used to suddenly tripled, and the old destroyer wheezed in agony as she loyally strained to do what was asked of her.

"Captain!" Reynolds called, "Lieutenant McFarlane says we don't have the fuel for this—to make it to Baalkpan—even if she doesn't tear her guts out. His words, sir."

"We don't have to do this all the way to Baalkpan! We just have to get away from *that*!" Another forest of splashes appeared close by the struggling ships. *Nerracca*'s forward sail was fully engulfed now. Flaming debris and clouds of sparks drifted downwind. Some fell on *Walker*'s deck and men and Lemurians scurried about, kicking the burning fragments over the side. Even over all the noise and turmoil, a great, high-pitched, moaning wail arose from the stricken Home as the suffering and terror there passed endurance.

Chief Gray appeared on the port bridgewing. He cast a fixed, stony glance where Bradford was trying to console the weeping queen. The sight of Safir Maraan—usually so stoic and strong—in such a state almost broke his resolve. But he steeled himself for what he had to do and stepped before the captain. "It's no use, Skipper," he said quietly.

"No!" Matt snarled, just as quiet but from within a furious rage. "We can't leave them here! There's *thousands* . . . !" Suddenly, his mind's eye saw a bright, sunny day with high, drifting clouds overhead—and *Exeter*'s barnacle-encrusted bottom rolling toward the sky while shells fell on the men struggling in the water. Then, all over again, it was *Encounter*'s turn, and he watched as the gallant British destroyer disappeared under a marching haze of foam. At last there was *Pope*, mortally wounded and low by the stern while the white-painted buzzards with red spots on their wings circled overhead. *Pope*, like all the others, was in *Walker*'s wake, but *Walker* wasn't the one who'd left her. It was Matt who had done that. Finally, in the midst of all this horror, the nightmare he could never remember came to his waking eyes. He knew it was the thing that had driven him all this time to save all that he could. It pushed him to crusade against the Grik and it fueled his hatred of them once he came to know what they were. They were the physical personification, in this twisted alien place, of the remorselessly inhuman juggernaut that had hounded *Walker* here in the first place. The Grik had become the Japanese. And now *Amagi*, the arch-villain of the nightmares that tortured his sleep, had chased them into hell itself to finally finish the job.

His eyes had taken on a cold inner light when he refocused them on the Chief and spoke in a soft, but almost manically precise tone. "We Are Not Leaving Anyone Else Behind." Gray took a step back. Even given the situation, he was surprised by the captain's intensity. Matt's eyes still didn't leave him. Finally he called over his shoulder. "Speed?"

"We almost had eleven knots there for a minute, Skipper, but now we're down to nine—and falling." Another salvo plummeted down and multiple explosions convulsed *Nerracca*. Her forward tripod teetered and fell, taking with it much of the pagoda tower it straddled. Fire was spreading toward the center sail. *Walker* shook from end to end like a giant hand had slapped her. Shell fragments rattled the amidships gun platform and the two stacks forward of it. They sounded like heavy hail on a tin roof.

"Lieutenant McFarlane says we have to back it down, Captain!" Reynolds pleaded. His voice was almost a squeak. He was hearing constant reports now from all over the ship, detailing all the things that were breaking. And yet, right there in front of him was the captain, who seemed set on a course of action that would only redouble those reports. Reynolds was caught in the middle. He felt like he was the only person on the entire ship that was getting information from every perspective, because he wasn't entirely sure the captain was even listening anymore. He was terrified. Regardless, he dutifully passed the rest of Spanky's urgent message. "He says pressure's dropping on the number four boiler. He thinks the feedwater pump is crapping out. He also thinks that last near miss might've shaken something loose inside it."

"We're down to six knots!" shouted Norman Kutas, who was monitoring their speed. In addition to losing a third of her own propulsion, *Nerracca* was getting heavier as tons of seawater poured inside her through gaping holes and opened seams. As tough as the Homes of the People were, they were never designed to absorb the type of punishment *Amagi* was inflicting.

For a long, torturous moment, Matt said nothing. He just continued to stare at Gray with a look of inexorable determination. The salvo buzzer rang again and the number one gun fired into the night. Then . . . he blinked. It was as though the nightmare that had surged from his subconscious mind was suddenly subverted by the one he was living now.

"Secure from flank," he said in a subdued voice.

"Captain!" shouted Sandison from the starboard bridgewing, "Small craft are coming alongside!" Matt raced to join him and peered over the rail. A shoal of small double-ended sailing craft, about thirty feet long, were struggling to catch up with the destroyer. Matt immediately recognized them as boats the People used to hunt the gri-kakka. Much like human whaleboats of the past, they carried the hunters close enough to strike their prey with a lance. Most Homes carried dozens of the extremely fast things and launched them from the large internal bays Matt had first seen on *Big Sal*. The gri-kakka boats were packed to overflowing.

"Get boarding nets over the side!" Matt shouted. "Slow to two-thirds!"

Immediately, as soon as the nets were rigged, boat after boat thumped alongside and terrified Lemurians swarmed up to the deck. Most were younglings.

"What the hell are they doing?" Gray demanded.

"They're trying to get as many off as they can!" Matt shouted. "Get down there and start packing them in!"

Gray was stunned. "But how many can we hold?"

"As many as they send us! Now get your ass down there and get them below! We have to keep the ship trimmed and you're the only one that can do it. Use all the help you need!" The Bosun dashed toward the ladder. Matt realized Queen Maraan had joined him. With her black fur and clothing she was almost invisible in the dark. Only her silver eyes and the tears matting the fur around them were visible, reflecting the light of the fire that raged aboard *Nerracca*. More shells shrieked down and churned the sea.

"You risk much," she said in a soft, sad voice.

"I'm risking everything," he told her truthfully. Even he realized it now. One lucky hit and *Walker* and everyone aboard her would be blown into quickly sinking fragments. A few would survive in the water long enough to know they were being eaten. And then *Amagi* and the Grik armada would continue remorselessly toward Baalkpan with little more than poor, crippled *Mahan* to stand in the way. *Nerracca* was doomed no matter what. Probably the only reason *Amagi* was still shooting at her was that her fires gave the Japanese gunners a target in the distant dark. There was always the chance they would hit the American destroyer. "Sometimes you just don't have any choice."

The gri-kakka boats scurried back and forth, ferrying people as fast as they could while *Walker* still heaved on the cable. It made the transfer more difficult, but they had to remain under way to keep as much distance as possible between themselves and *Amagi*, as well as the approaching Grik. Also, if *Nerracca* went dead in the water, she would be a sitting duck and the Japanese gunners would finish her in a matter of minutes. As it was, Matt began gently altering course as radically as possible, trying to throw some errors into the enemy fire control. It was very subtle because they couldn't do much, but the number of hits *Amagi* scored began to decline. Still, the shells continued to rain down and Matt had to wonder why the enemy was expending so much of their limited ordnance. Evidently, whoever was in command over there wasn't willing to risk any possibility that his prey would escape. Even temporarily.

Another nearby salvo tossed *Walker* like a cork. So far, she'd taken no direct hits, but the damage from near misses and shell fragments was becoming critical. The wardroom was filling with wounded but, miraculously, no more of her crew had been killed. That luck didn't extend to the refugees. Almost a dozen had been scythed down on *Walker*'s deck, and many more died when two of the gri-kakka boats were pulverized by a direct hit alongside. Refugees filled *Walker*'s lower decks and every crevice and compartment was packed to overflowing. Even the sweltering engineering spaces were full of panting Lemurians and the air was filled with a desolate, terrified keening sound and the smell of soggy fur and voided bowels.

"Keep packing them in," Matt ordered the Bosun when he came to report.

"It's turning into hell down there, Captain," Gray replied.

Matt nodded grimly. "Just put them wherever you can. It sure beats the alternative."

Gray nodded. "If they fill up the main deck, she'll capsize," he warned. "We're already so low in the water with all the extra weight that we're taking water through holes above the waterline. Damage control can't even get to them with all the bodies down there."

"I know. Are the pumps keeping up?"

"So far—" Gray was interrupted by the bark of the number three gun. The Grik were closing on them now and all guns were in local control, firing at nearby targets of opportunity. The sea to port was scattered with burning hulks. *Amagi* had slipped aft somewhat, until now she was off *Nerracca*'s port quarter. She was closing, though, since their own speed had diminished so much. She had advanced through most of the Grik that accompanied her until, by the flashes of her guns, they saw few lizard ships remaining between them. Most of the main Grik force had caught the favorable wind and were closing on the port bow. Matt realized bitterly that if it hadn't been for those early hits, their scheme to pull the Home clear of danger would probably have worked.

Both the ships were heavier now. Behind them Matt saw that *Nerracca* was horrifyingly low in the water. All of her masts and sails were aflame, as was virtually everything on or above her main deck from stem to stern. The only people escaping now came from the bays low on her hull. Even that couldn't last much longer. Soon they would be underwater.

"Four knots!" Kutas yelled shrilly over the roar of the tortured blower and the rattling cacophony of the exhausted ship. Several falling shells struck *Nerracca* simultaneously and rocked the hulk with what seemed like a single massive detonation. One shell went long and exploded just off *Walker*'s starboard bow. Matt, Safir, and Bernie Sandison were all knocked off their feet by the concussion, and fragments sleeted into the side of the bridge and the splinter shield on the number one gun. Leo Davis went sprawling and two of the Lemurian loaders were swept away.

Then, as those on the bridge gained their feet, they were hurled backward against the chart house and *Walker* erupted forward like a racehorse from the gate. Matt staggered up, climbing the conduits on the bulkhead. Reynolds was down, but conscious, and he was scrambling to put his headset back on. His helmet was nowhere to be seen.

"Report!"

"The cable parted!" Reynolds cried.

"Did it burn through?"

"No, sir. Mr. Dowden says it was cut! One of those whaleboats of theirs did it!"

Matt's shoulders sagged. "Come about. Right full rudder. Get me the crow's nest."

"Chack's on the line, Captain."

"Ask him how many boats are in the water with people in them." There was a momentary pause while *Walker* churned back toward the burning Home.

"Chack says the one that cut the cable is the only one under way. All the others have unloaded and been cast adrift."

"Rudder amidships. Slow to one-third," Matt ordered the helmsman. "We'll pick up the people in that last boat."

"Aye, aye, sir."

The final gri-kakka boat came alongside while Matt stared ahead at the burning, wallowing wreck. *Nerracca* was so low in the water now that there was no way anyone else could have escaped through her launch bays. Whoever cut the cable must have been on the last boat out. He had no idea how many Lemurians *Walker* had taken aboard, but surely there were still thousands left behind, trapped between the inferno above and the rising water below.

"All aboard, Captain," Reynolds reported quietly. "They've jettisoned the boat and are securing the nets now." The darkness to the south-southwest lit up again with another mighty salvo. The bastards were *still* shooting at *Nerracca!*

"Helm, make your course one six zero, all ahead full," Matt ordered.

Sandison looked at him hesitantly. "Captain . . . Baalkpan's almost due north."

"I'm well aware of that, and so is the enemy. They'll expect us to hightail it there as fast as we can because that's probably what we ought to do. There's no moon and once we're out of *Nerracca's* glare, no one will ever see us." As if to punctuate his point, *Amagi's* latest salvo erupted in the sea behind them, on and around the helpless Home. None of the shells came close to the destroyer and Matt didn't even flinch when they detonated.

"That's not what we're going to do?" Sandison asked. His eyes were wide. In spite of the rage that threatened to engulf him, Matt almost laughed at the young officer's expression.

"No, Bernie, we're not. We'll use this excellent moonless night to our advantage for another purpose. We're going to steam south until we arrive off *Amagi*'s starboard beam and then we're going to turn directly toward her. At that point you, Mr. Sandison, are going to slam our last three working torpedoes into her goddamn side."

Bernie gulped. "Aye, aye, sir."

"The enemy ship is destroyed, Captain," Sato Okada said quietly but urgently. He was standing beside Kurokawa on *Amagi*'s bridge. The middle distance was awash with flames, both from their allies' ships and from the giant Tree Folk vessel. "I recommend we cease firing and conserve ammunition." Kurokawa turned to him and regarded him intently. His eyes reflected the flames of the burning ships like little mirrors, and Sato suspected with a shudder that that's what they were. Mirrors to his soul.

"The American destroyer? Do you think we got it?"

"Impossible to say. As soon as it began to tow the bigger ship directly away from us, it was lost to view." Sato almost shrugged. "There were many explosions. Perhaps she was hit. Right now, however, we are wasting ammunition."

"Oh, very well, Commander," Kurokawa growled. "You may cease firing. We will steer toward the wreckage and see for ourselves. If we did not sink the American ship, we almost certainly damaged it. She will fly as fast as she can to her lair and we will catch her soon." He paced the length of the bridge as though lost in thought while Sato gave the order to stop the bombardment of the burning, sinking hulk. A moment later he returned to Sato's side. Strangely, there was a smile on his face. "A most impressive display for our allies, I should think," he said. "None of them could stop the enemy ship, and yet we did it with contemptuous ease. I expect a greater say in matters after this!"

Sato bowed, but he cleared his throat. When he spoke, his voice was brittle. "Before it grew too dark, the lookout reported that the enemy ship seemed to be packed with refugees. Civilians."

"So? It was to be expected. They have evacuated Surabaya." The captain's gaze grew intent once more. "They are the enemy, Commander Okada. You would do well to remember that." His expression became coldly philosophical. "Besides, we gave them a quicker and more honorable death than the Grik would have afforded them."

Sato turned away to conceal his disgust. "Honorable," he whispered.

"We've outpaced our escorts for once," Kurokawa said with satisfaction as he glanced astern. "I expect the flagship will signal us shortly, as soon as it catches up. When it does so, you will inform me at once. I will be in my quarters."

Sato bowed and, to his immense relief, the captain left the bridge. Staring at the distant glare, he wondered about what he had seen. When the report came that the American destroyer was actually *towing* the enormous enemy ship, once again something stirred within him. Rather than make an easy escape, the destroyer had done everything she could to aid her slower consort. *That* was honor. They may be the enemy, but Sato could still find it within himself to respect them for what they'd done. He wondered why Kurokawa could not. His hatred had blinded him to every-thing but revenge. Something was fundamentally wrong with this entire situation, but he had no idea what to do about it.

Effectively invisible, *Walker* steamed south at twenty-five knots with a bone in her teeth and blood in her eye. Chack remained in the crow's nest, occasionally calling out a range and bearing to the target whenever *Amagi* fired her guns, but that didn't last much longer. Finally, she wearied of wasting ammunition and her salvos at last ceased. Chack's reports grew farther apart and less certain as he tried to pick the battle cruiser from among the stars she obscured. *Nerracca* was still an inferno behind them, but it was clear by now, even to the enemy, that no one could possibly sur-vive aboard her. Matt was staring at her with a profound sense of loss and failure. He wondered if she would never sink and end the agony at last.

His reverie was interrupted when Chief Gray escorted a young Lemu-rian female onto the bridge. Her fur was scorched and it was impossible to tell what color it had been. She was also entirely naked except for a towel someone had given her to replace her lost kilt. In spite of her disheveled appearance, she looked vaguely familiar. As soon as she saw him, she threw herself upon the wooden strakes of the wheelhouse and clasped his leg below the knee. Matt looked at Gray for an explanation.

"That's Tassat's daughter, Tassana," the Bosun said, his rough voice almost cracking. "I bet she's about thirteen." Matt looked back down at her. Now he remembered. She'd been present at some meeting or other, there to attend her father, Tassat-Ay-Aracca, *Nerracca*'s High Chief. She began to shake with sobs as she clutched him. "She was on the last boat out," Gray continued. "She helped cut the cable herself, with an axe. Her dad told her to."

"Tassat?" Matt asked quietly.

Gray shook his head. "He didn't make it."

Of course he didn't. The ebullient Lemurian would never have abandoned his Home while there was anyone left aboard. He might not have even then. A further wave of sadness swept over Matt and he knelt beside Tassana. Queen Maraan joined him there and embraced her.

"You save so many, at such great risk," Tassana murmured through her tears. "My father bade me honor you with his final words to me. Honor all *Walkers* for their courage. *Nerracca* Clan . . ." Her voice caught with a shudder. What few of *Nerracca's* people that still lived no longer had a Home. ". . . *Nerracca* Clan never forget," she finally managed. Queen Maraan gently rocked her back and forth as Tassana began to cry again. She soothed her while Matt continued to kneel beside them, unable to speak. To him it seemed so terribly wrong for anyone to be grateful to him. So many had died. He stood and Safir helped Tassana to her feet. The Bosun started to lead her away.

"How many did we save?" Matt asked him. Gray shook his head.

"I have no idea. They're packed away below like those damn Vienna scum weenies. Eight hundred? Maybe more." He looked Matt in the eye. "We couldn't have taken many more anyway, Skipper. Not and stayed afloat." Matt said nothing and Gray gently led Tassana toward the ladder. Matt turned and found Queen Maraan's shining eyes fixed upon him.

"B'mbaado will never forget what you've done for us either, Cap-i-taan Reddy," she said. She motioned at the night. "You go now to try and strike a blow against *Nerracca's* murderers and I would be a part of that." She shook her head. "But I am of no use to you here." She paused. "My people believe that the God of the Great Light that burns during the day does not see the deeds that take place when he is not above. I do not know if that is true or not. But the souls of *Nerracca's* dead have already been carried skyward by the pyre. They know what has happened and they will watch what is yet to be. Whether the Sun sees them or not, He will hear of *Walker's* deeds and He will honor you as well." She smiled at him then. "I am shamed by my inaction. With your permission, I will go where I may be of help. I will join your mate in the wardroom and see if I may assist with the wounded."

"Of course," he said. "I'm sure that—" He stopped. What had she just said? "Lieutenant Tucker would appreciate the help, and the company. Please ask her to make a quick report as soon as it's convenient." Bowing her head, Queen Maraan left the bridge.

"Captain, lookout reports a surface contact bearing one one zero degrees. Range about eighteen thousand. He's not completely sure, sir, but he thinks it's her."

"Very well. Helm, make your course one four zero. Reduce speed to two-thirds." He caught a couple of raised eyebrows at that. "Don't worry, gentlemen. That bastard doesn't have a clue we're here. We're going to get in as close as we can and I don't want him to spot our wake. We'll keep the steam up in case we have to jump."

Sandison was double-double-checking his headset connection to Randal Hale, who was the captain of the number one torpedo mount behind the amidships deckhouse on the starboard side. Hale's station was directly atop the mount. Beneath him, nestled in their tubes, the final three operating MK-15, twenty-one-inch torpedoes in the entire world patiently waited, their safety pins removed. There had probably never been any more lovingly treated and carefully maintained torpedoes in the history of the Asiatic Fleet and they'd been painstakingly tested for every conceivable defect. Each of the three weapons was a marvel of technology and precise engineering and was, pound for pound, the most complicated piece of machinery aboard the entire ship. Not to mention the fact they'd cost the War Department of the United States more than ten thousand dollars apiece.

And nobody really trusted them to work.

There were many theories as to why the American torpedoes had performed so dismally. Much of the problem was undoubtedly due to the fact that prior to the war, destroyer and submarine crews were allowed very little practice in their use. They were fantastically expensive and the budget for the Asiatic Fleet in particular was extremely tight. Bernie Sandison, however, as well as his division, was convinced the problem was far more insidious. At Balikpapan, they'd *seen* the foaming wake of one of their torpedoes end directly amidships of a Japanese transport at the height of that confusing fight. To their amazement, it didn't explode. On other occasions they'd been positive that the weapons ran true, but in spite of their certainty, their efforts and risks weren't rewarded. Destroyermen on other ships, not to mention submariners, complained bitterly about similar experiences. It was obvious there was something fundamentally wrong with the MK-15 and -14 torpedoes. There were really only two possible mechanical explanations. Either the torpedoes were running too deep or something was wrong with their magnetic detonators. Maybe both.

With the captain's permission, Bernie had set the last three fish to run about half as deep as the manual prescribed. The worst thing that could happen, theoretically, was that they'd explode against *Amagi*'s side instead of underneath her like they were designed to do. The damage wouldn't be as great, but at least they should hit the target. That left only the problem of the MK-6 magnetic exploders. The MK-14 submarine torpedo they'd salvaged in Surabaya had actually struck a ship and failed to go off and *Walker*'s torpedomen were highly suspicious that it had to do with the MK-6. Bernie and his men, as well as Shinya, had been all over the damn things. The best they could figure was since the weapons were designed to explode magnetically, not enough thought had gone into what was essentially the backup contact detonator. Shinya was accustomed to the evidently far superior Japanese torpedoes and he'd seen it first. The contact detonators on the American torpedoes weren't robust enough to operate properly when they struck the side of a ship at close to fifty knots.

If that was indeed the case, the torpedoes America had taken to war were hamstrung by a no-win situation. If they went too deep, which Bernie was positive they did, the magnetic exploder failed to operate. If they actually hit the target, they wouldn't explode because the contact detonator often malfunctioned. That would explain a lot and, if true, it was a miracle that any U.S. torpedoes had gone off since the war began. Sandison had taken his case to the captain late the night before and he'd agreed to let them try to beef up the contact exploder on one of the fish. It was a risk, because they might only ensure it wouldn't go off, but nobody wanted to fire the last fish they had and just trust to luck, as they had in the past. They had to try something.

Lieutenant Sandison continued to worry as he made his final preparations. Self-doubt constantly warred with his conviction that he'd been right to make the modifications. He knew his division had done everything humanly possible to ensure that the attack would succeed. But if he was wrong . . .

Chack finally reported that he was certain the target was *Amagi* and there were no Grik between them and the enemy. The range had dwindled to less than four miles—well within the range of the torpedoes—and so far there was no indication the Japanese even suspected they were there. A hush fell over the crew. Creeping up on a battle cruiser in the dark wasn't a tactic they'd ever trained for or ever dreamed they'd use. The normal procedure was to race in at top speed and fire torpedoes from the maximum range of about eight miles. This method was . . . surreal.

Walker continued her leisurely approach, her bow-on aspect presenting the smallest possible target in the pitch-dark night. The tubes were rigged out at a thirty-degree angle and awaiting the command. Now that Chack was sure, he was calling constant corrections. Bernie didn't need them now. Even he could see the massive ship looming ahead, a malignant black outline against a wash of stars beyond. He tracked the target with his torpedo director. Nine thousand, eight thousand, seven thousand yards, and still they narrowed the gap. *Amagi* was making barely eight knots and her course was constant. She was a sitting duck. The range was becoming almost ridiculously close when Captain Reddy finally spoke.

"Mr. Reynolds, remind Mr. Garrett not to open fire unless I give the command, but be ready if I do." He looked at Bernie Sandison and, even in the darkness, Bernie thought he detected a ferocious, predatory gleam in the captain's eye. "Fire your torpedoes, Mr. Sandison."

"Aye, aye, Captain." Bernie addressed Randal Hale in a brisk, nervous voice. "Mount one: Fire one! Fire three! Fire five!"

With each new command, there was a *thump-chuff!* and a sharp flash of yellow light aft as the small black-powder charge within each tube expelled the torpedo. The brightly polished weapons shone only as long dull shadows as they arced into the sea and entered the water amid a gray, concave splash.

"Helm, left full rudder. Come about to course one zero zero."

"Aye, aye, sir. Left full rudder," confirmed the helmsman. "Making my course one zero zero!"

As the destroyer heeled to starboard, Matt went out on the port bridgewing and waited for the stern to come around. This would be the most critical moment. If anyone on *Amagi* saw the impulse charges go off and looked hard in their direction, they'd probably see the ship as she turned broadside-on for a moment. Soon *Walker* steadied and Matt heard the helmsman announce he'd achieved his course. He raised his binoculars to watch the enemy ship. He couldn't see the torpedoes and he felt strangely cheated, even though he knew it was for the best. If it was too dark for him to see the telltale trails of bubbles, then the Japs couldn't see them either. Uh-oh, something was happening. Even as Matt stared at *Amagi,* a searchlight flared to life. Then another.

"All ahead flank!" Matt shouted into the pilothouse. The launch must have been seen after all. The searchlights stabbed at the darkness in their general direction, but for the moment they concentrated on an area to port. Then another light came on and almost instantly, *Walker* was seared by the harsh, bright glare.

"Commence firing!" Matt yelled. "Target their searchlights!" Garrett must have heard him because the salvo buzzer rang even before Reynolds relayed the order. Number two and number four fired together and the tracers lanced into the night. Another salvo left the guns before the first was halfway there.

"Come left ten degrees!" Matt said and raised his glasses again, trying to see through the blinding light. He knew the course change would make *Walker* a larger target, but he wanted the number one gun in the fight. When the next salvo fired, it joined the others. The other two lights had found them now, and then yet a fourth. One suddenly winked out, however, and Matt supposed they must have gotten a hit. "How long on the torpedoes, Mr. Sandison?" he demanded.

"Another minute, Captain." The torpedo officer had taken station on the port torpedo director—not that there was anything left to direct. He just had to see . . .

Other lights lit the battle cruiser, gun flashes from her secondary armament. The first splashes fell about two hundred yards to starboard and a little aft. The second group of enemy shells raised geysers just off the port beam and shell fragments peppered *Walker*. *Amagi*'s secondaries weren't nearly as large as her main battery, but they were bigger than anything *Walker* had. The ship staggered under the force of a direct hit aft, and the sound of the explosion and the screams of refugees were deafening. The ship recovered herself, however, and continued her frantic sprint. Another blast, farther aft, and *Walker* shuddered in agony.

"Torpedoes?!"

Sandison's eyes flicked to the stopwatch in his hand.

"Now!"

The lights went out.

Matt snapped the binoculars to his eyes in time to see a bright, slashing pulse of fire rising from *Amagi*'s waterline, just aft of amidships. A jet of sparks vomited from her stack and illuminated the rising cloud of smoke caused by the blast. The searchlights that just moments ago had been so remorselessly fixed on the destroyer were now askew, throwing eerie, smoke-dense beams in all directions.

"*Yes!*" shouted Bernie as his relief surged forth. Not what they'd hoped for, but one hit out of three was better than their average to date. He was pretty sure he knew which one it had been. Cheers erupted all over the ship. Cheers of relief and vindication.

"Secure from flank! Come right ten degrees. Let's get some distance while she decides whether or not to sink. If she doesn't, I'd just as soon we were out of range when they get their priorities straightened out. Cease firing main battery."

A few more desultory shells landed in *Walker*'s wake, but without the searchlights to guide them the Japanese gunners fired blind. However much damage they'd caused, the torpedo attack had taken them completely by surprise. By the time the searchlights began scanning for *Walker* again, she had disappeared completely into the dark.

Matt slowly let out a breath. "Damage report?"

"That last hit tore hell out of the guinea pullman," Reynolds said, referring to the crew's berthing space situated above the propellers. "Lots of refugee casualties in there." He paused. "There's some flooding in aft general storage and the steering engine room . . . There's people in there too."

Matt was staring aft at the amidships deckhouse. He couldn't see much in the darkness except for the occasional white T-shirt and hat dashing through the smoke that still poured from under it. "What about the hit amidships?" he asked.

The talker nodded. "The Chief says there were a lot of 'Cats hunkered under the deckhouse. He has no idea how many bought it. The galley's a wreck, but Lanier made it okay." Reynolds blinked. "He was in the head. Mertz and the cat-monkey mess attendant are both wounded." The talker paused again, listening. "Oh, goddamn!" he exclaimed in an indignant voice. "Beggin' your pardon, Captain."

"What else?"

"Those Jap bastards got the Coke machine!"

Matt almost laughed. The last of their Cokes had been gone for weeks—all except one that was stashed in his own quarters. He doubted he'd ever drink it. The machine itself had remained a source of pride to the crew, in a strange, black-humor sort of way. They may have been lost on a hostile, alien—other—earth, but by God, the Coke machine still worked. The men would take that news disproportionately hard. Compared to the other sacrifices he'd seen that night, the destruction of the Coke machine seemed pretty ridiculous. He had to maintain appearances, however.

"Well, let's just hope it was worth it. I think the Japs would trade a dozen Coke machines for the hole we put in their guts."

He looked back at the distant ship. There was a fire aboard her now and it might have been his imagination or even just wishful thinking, but it seemed she was listing to starboard. He wanted more than anything to stay, to see for sure if they'd banished this particular demon once and for all. But deep down in his heart, he couldn't bring himself to believe it. One more fish would have done the job. He was certain of that. He should have let Sandison alter them all. He shook his head. Another mistake. One thing was sure, however. Whether *Amagi* sank or not, *Walker* had hurt her badly. The sparks from her stack had come from a boiler, one that was burning coal, so they were bound to have slowed her down, at least. And maybe, just maybe, they had managed to kill whoever it was who was responsible for what she'd done to *Nerracca*.

"Take that, you son of a bitch," he muttered under his breath. Then he raised his voice. "Helm. Make your course zero two zero. We've still got to get through the lizards and I'd just as soon we didn't run into any if you don't mind." He turned to Reynolds. "We'll have the searchlights on just as soon as we're sure we're out of *Amagi*'s range. The main battery won't fire on any lizards we see unless they give us no choice. We have to conserve ammunition." He finally walked over and sat in his chair. "Besides," he added quietly, "we've got a lot of shook-up folks on board. It's probably time we gave them a break."

He rubbed his eyes and spoke once more: "Help Clancy compose a full report of tonight's action, Mr. Reynolds, and transmit it to Baalkpan. Then tell Lieutenant Mallory I want him in the air as soon as it's light enough to fly. Give *Amagi*'s current position and tell Ben to see if she's still afloat or not, and what she's doing if she is. But whatever he does, he *will* stay out of range of her antiaircraft weapons. Make sure he understands that's an order."

At almost dawn, but long before Matt would have personally considered it "light enough to fly," the loud engines of the big flying-boat droned by overhead in the darkness. He had Radioman Clancy send Ben the additional instruction to check on *Aracca*. *Walker* had steamed past her a little before three in the morning and flashed a brief account of the battle. *Aracca*'s High Chief, Ramik-Sa-Ar, was Tassat's father and most of the people on the two Homes were related. Matt hated to break the news like that, but he had little choice. With her heavy load of survivors aboard, *Walker* was taking more water than her pumps could keep up with. *Aracca* was far enough ahead of the Grik that she should be safe from pursuit, but Matt wanted Ben to make sure.

Tsalka glared across the water as Kurokawa's launch returned to his ship. "You know, General, I grow increasingly weary of that creature."

General Esshk hissed agreement. "I begin to understand why those who joined us in the Great Hunt in the past have ultimately fallen prey themselves. If they were as grasping and unpleasant as that one"—he gestured at the retreating boat—"it is no wonder the Hij of old turned them out and hunted them to extinction." Tsalka agreed, but he knew there was more to it than that. Despite the Ancient Way, that whoever hunts together may partake of the meal, he knew it was difficult for any predator to share its prey. The tail-less, almost toothless Hij he had just endured was not one he would care to dine beside.

"Their iron ship is damaged again and it will move even slower now," Tsalka mused. "But it is still wondrously powerful. I heard the tales of how it destroyed our Uul before it joined the hunt. Last night, I saw how it did so. Magnificent!"

"Most impressive," Esshk hedged. "But to strike from such a distance! Where is the challenge . . . the sport in that? It is the hunt that counts. The harvest is secondary."

Tsalka looked at him with his slitted yellow eyes. "Indeed. But it is not very sporting when the prey consumes the hunter. This prey has teeth! I do not desire another catastrophe such as befell our hunters at the walled city. Such a thing has never happened before and it will not happen again. The Celestial Mother would not be pleased and neither would I." He gazed at the lumbering iron monstrosity. Black smoke belched from its middle as it burned the coal that somehow pushed it along. There was other smoke still, from the wound it suffered last night, and Tsalka perceived a slight list. Despite its amazing power, the Tree Prey had friends who could damage it. The thought gave him pause. They had damaged a thing that multiple vigorous assaults by his own race did not scratch. Insufferable as the Hij leader of the iron ship folk might be, Tsalka was beginning to suspect that he was right about one thing: the Grik needed them, and might need them very much if the Grand Swarm was to meet with success. The thought rankled, and yet it might be true. The Tree Prey had grown into Worthy Prey in their own right, but with friends such as they had . . . the slow iron ship of the new hunters might have to make the difference.

Initially, as was customary, the new hunters had been treated with proper disdain. That was appropriate, since they were the newest hunters in the pack. But things had changed. The prey fought well. They had flying things to help them, as well as an iron ship of their own. Much as he disliked the idea, Tsalka admitted it was probably wise to heed the council of a creature—however distasteful—who knew how to counter such things. For the first time, that morning he had actually paid attention to what the iron ship leader had to write.

"You and I are Hij, General Esshk," he said. "We can look back upon the Uul-life with fondness and nostalgia. That was our time for the hunt to be sport. That time is past. I joined the Swarm because I was bored and there has not been a Grand Swarm in my lifetime. I wanted to see it for myself. Although I appreciate your courtesy, command is yours, of course. But I flatter myself that my advice may have some value."

General Esshk bowed low and hissed respectfully. "Your wisdom is renowned, Lord Regent. As always, I crave your counsel."

"Very well then. We must look to the welfare of our Uul. They are our children, General, and they will do what we ask of them. But we may need to protect them from their own exuberance. I do not think there has ever been a hunt quite like this before, and to avoid learning too much about what the Tree Prey and their friends know about thwarting the hunter, I would not hesitate to strike them from farther than I can see, if I could. We must use the iron ship to our utmost advantage because I suspect there will be very little sport to this hunt in the end."

"We both already agree on that, so what is your counsel?"

"Only this: that we postpone this hunt. We should return to the Walled City—Aryaal, I believe? There we should repair the iron ship and summon more Uul. We will gather our strength and when we advance it will be with all our might, at the head of a Swarm such as the world has never seen!"

Captain Hisashi Kurokawa was in a towering rage when he returned from his visit aboard the painfully bright, white-painted ship, and he was seething when he stormed onto the bridge. For quite some time, as much as possible, the bridge watch stood silent, fearing that any sound or voice would draw the captain's wrath. He had already had last night's lookouts arrested and put in irons. They should have seen the American destroyer and had their searchlights on her sooner. Now his ship was even further crippled. With the flooding of another fireroom and the certain destruction of two more boilers, *Amagi* would be even slower than before. He tried to explain to the stupid lizards that his ship *had* to have proper repairs, that she couldn't continue to steam all over the place with half her insides open to the sea. If he could just *fix* her, she would be faster than any ship afloat.

But they just stood there and stared at him as he wrote his demands. Acted as if the inconvenience of his ship's damage was *his* fault! He had suggested that if some of the red ships of their lower class had been screening him, the torpedo wouldn't have gotten through, but that got a stony response. Finally he left, half convinced that he would open fire on the Grik leader's ship as soon as he returned to his own. He still yearned to do so, but there were more than two hundred other Grik ships close by. If he gave in to the impulse to destroy their leaders, surely the others would swarm his ship. Not only would that ruin all his plans, but he would certainly be killed. No, the time would come. For now, he would content himself with finding fault with those who were at his mercy. Commander Okada had the watch, just as he did last night when they were damaged. He would start with him.

"Captain?" came a tentative voice from the bridgewing lookout's position.

"Yes, what is it?" he snapped.

"A signal from the Grik flagship." Like all their technical writing, the Grik used English for their signal flags. Kurokawa assumed there was some connection to the ships they built, since they looked very eighteenth-century British. Regardless, using English to communicate with the monsters was convenient, even if it rankled.

"Well, what does it say?" he snarled impatiently.

"Ah . . . the fleet will come about and join our 'brethren' who have already surely taken the Walled City. There, we will refit and repair all our ships and wait for more hunters to join the Swarm."

"So," grumped Kurokawa, "they listened after all." His mood brightened perceptibly. "Helmsman, bring us about." He smirked. "And do be careful not to smash any of our 'allies.'"

The next hour was awkward for Okada because the captain never left the bridge. He almost never stayed that long, and most of the watch was nervous to the point of distraction—particularly when Kurokawa stepped near their station. But the entire fleet had changed its course, and despite the fact that the damage to *Amagi* was probably responsible, the captain acted like he had achieved some sort of victory.

"Captain!" a talker suddenly blurted nervously. "The lookout reports sighting the American flying-boat, almost directly overhead!"

Kurokawa and Okada both raced out onto the bridgewing with their binoculars. Sure enough, floating lazily above, droning motors lost in the cacophony of *Amagi*'s abused machinery, was the PBY Catalina.

"Damn them!" shouted Kurokawa. He looked around. "Why isn't anyone shooting at them?"

"They are out of range. If you want to waste ammunition to no effect—for all to see—we certainly can."

Kurokawa's gaze slashed at Okada. Then he raised his binoculars toward the Grik flagship. Some of the "officers" were clearly staring at the plane—the damn things had phenomenal eyes—and some were looking right back at him.

"Commander Okada," he said in a menacing tone, "we must destroy that plane."

Okada was incredulous. "But . . . how?"

"We will use one of our planes, of course."

"But, Captain! Those planes are some of our most precious assets and we only have enough fuel for a couple of flights. Also, as you yourself pointed out, they are not fighters, they are spotting planes. They are lightly armed, and I'm not even sure they are fast enough to *catch* the American plane."

Kurokawa's round face regarded Okada without expression. "You, Commander, will choose a flight crew for the fastest of the two planes, if there is any difference. You will have it only half filled with fuel since it needn't go far. That should improve its speed and will save fuel as well. You will then tell the crew that they will destroy the American plane or they need not return. Finally, if they are not in the air in ten minutes, they will be shot." He snorted. "Remember, our 'allies' are watching."

All Okada could do as he raced aft was mutter, "Madness!" under his breath.

"There they are!" Tikker shouted excitedly long before Ben Mallory could see anything but water and sky. By the time the leading edge of the enemy armada was visible to the pilot, Tikker already had an answer to one of their questions. The Grik had turned around. "They go home!" he shouted with glee.

"I doubt it." Mallory sighed. "I bet they're headed for Aryaal. They'll set up a base there and hit us when they're ready. Question is, why aren't they ready now? Do you see any sign of *Amagi*?"

"I'm afraid so," said Tikker with disappointment. "There is a large, dark shape farther ahead with smoke rising above it. It seems smoky all over, so maybe it is badly damaged. But we are still too far to tell."

"There's nothing for it then. We have to take a closer look."

"Sure," said Ed Palmer, standing in his usual place at the rear of the flight deck, "but I'm relieved for *Aracca*'s sake."

"You and me both," sighed Ben. "She might have made it, but if they'd still been coming on even at eight knots . . . Well, *Walker*'s report about what happened to *Nerracca* . . ." Everyone nodded. There was no reason to go on.

It was convenient that the PBY had full tanks of oxygen when they found it and Ben had them use some now, so they could get above the antiaircraft weapons. The seals on the masks didn't work too well because even Ben and Ed had fur on their faces now, but there was plenty of oxygen for the few minutes they would need it. They would barely scratch the surface. There was almost a ten-hour supply. Ben pulled back on the wheel and slightly advanced the throttles. Before long, they were cruising at 18,000 feet—the big plane's maximum service ceiling. Now the Japanese could shoot at them all they wanted, but the chances they'd hit anything were infinitesimal. Ben was betting they knew that too and wouldn't want to waste ammo in front of their "friends."

Ed was back in one of the observation blisters, staring straight down with his binoculars. At over three miles, the visibility wasn't what he would have liked, but it was good enough. *Amagi* had been hard hit and she had a distinct list to starboard. Gray smoke from extinguished fires still rose to join the black smoke from her stack. Unfortunately, she was still clearly under way and in no apparent danger of sinking. They'd done all they could and she was still afloat. Ed didn't think they'd get another "surprise" chance like the one last night, and they were out of torpedoes anyway, weren't they? There was no way *Walker* and *Mahan*, even together, could stop her in a stand-up gunnery duel. They would have to think of something else.

Fortunately, it looked like they were going to have time to do that. *Walker* had clearly pounded the Grik fleet the night before. Several ships could be seen under tow, while more than a dozen had apparently been abandoned as beyond repair, or unable to make the voyage to Aryaal. A couple didn't look too bad to Ed. He'd mark their positions. Maybe they could come out and tow them in. There was no telling how many ships *Walker* sent to the bottom. Regardless, however many Grik ships the old destroyer sank or damaged the night before, it was an insignificant percentage of the whole. If the Grik had wanted to, they could have come straight on. They would be mauled, but they would probably win. But they weren't coming on. Just like what they had originally taken to be the "leading edge" of the Grik fleet, *Amagi* had reversed her course. Like those of the hundreds of sailing ships around her, the battle cruiser's rather jagged, uneven wake proved she was headed back in the direction of Aryaal.

Perhaps *Amagi* was the reason they'd stopped! After last night, they might think they had to have her and if that was the case, they might attempt major repairs! That could take a long, long time. There was no question the Grik threat would only grow during that period, but if *Walker's* desperate torpedo attack hadn't destroyed *Amagi,* it had certainly bought them some time. Time they desperately needed.

Ed relinquished his vantage point to the Lemurian waist gunner and made his way forward. After he relayed his observations and deductions to Ben, he returned to his post at the radio and began signaling *Walker* with the news. Ben flew on a while longer, taking in the scope of the enemy fleet, then banked the plane until it pointed in an almost due-northerly direction. Once the battle cruiser was safely behind them, he began a slow descent. At 7,000 feet, the Catalina's most efficient cruising altitude, he leveled off and asked Ed for some coffee. They'd already secured the oxygen masks.

Ed poked his head up between the two seats on the flight deck. "Sure thing. I'll have some too." He looked at the sable-furred Lemurian. "How 'bout you?" Tikker just grimaced and shook his head.

"Just give it a chance," urged Ben. "It'll grow on you."

"Like a great, hideous tumor, I suspect," retorted the 'Cat. They all laughed. Suddenly there was a sound like heavy gravel being thrown hard against the plane's aft fuselage, followed by a high-pitched shriek.

"What the *hell!*"

"Plane! Plane! Behind us shooting!" came the panicked cry from one of the Lemurians in the waist.

"Shoot back at him!" Mallory bellowed as he instinctively shoved the oval wheel forward to the stop. With the nose pointed at the sea—too close—he slammed the throttles forward and began banking right. He had no idea what was on their tail except it must have come from *Amagi.* That meant it was an observation plane of some sort and had to be dragging floats. The thing was, the Japanese had seaplane versions of almost all their first-line fighters—including the notorious Zeke. If that was what was after them . . . All he could do was what he'd done. The dope coming out of China and the Philippines was that the Zeke couldn't dive, and if it did it had a hard time turning right against the torque of its radial engine.

"Ed," he shouted over the roar of engines, the rattling moan of the stressed airframe and the screech of terrified Lemurians, "get an eyeball on that guy and see what we're up against!"

Palmer dragged himself aft and upward. It seemed like forever before he reached the waist gunner's compartment, but when he did, he was greeted by a dreadful sight. Daylight streamed through a dozen bullet holes in the ceiling of the compartment and he knew there were probably many more aft. The Plexiglas in the starboard observation blister was shattered and a hurricane of wind swirled around him. There were brains spattered all over the forward bulkhead and the deck, and blood seemed to have been smeared over every surface with a mop. The dead Lemurian was sprawled in the middle of the aisle, his partner curled in a fetal position on the port side of the bulkhead, rocking back and forth and emitting a keening moan. Ed barely controlled his reflex to retch and snatched the headset off the live Lemurian. "Snap out of it!" he yelled, somewhat shakily. He leaned into the intact blister. First he looked down—he couldn't help it—at the rapidly approaching water. He was no pilot, but *he* damn sure would have been pulling up by now. He took a deep breath and faced aft. Nothing but sky. Their maneuver should have caused their pursuer to overshoot and dump some speed before trying to match their turn. He should have been able to see it.

More "gravel" slammed into the plane. Many of the impacts were quieter that the first and he felt them more than heard them. They must have been in the wings. A final burst sounded directly overhead and it ended with an explosion of sound up forward.

"Goddamn it! What the hell is he?" Mallory screamed.

Ed lunged to the shattered blister, his hat instantly disappearing in the slipstream. Through squinted and watering eyes, he caught a glimpse of a winged shape swerving from starboard to port. He leaped back across the dead Lemurian and finally caught a good view of their tormentor. "It's a *biplane*," he cried into his borrowed microphone, incredulously. "Radial engine and three floats. One big one under the fuselage and two smaller ones under the wings. I swear to God it looks like a Stearman with floats! Two crew—pilot and spotter. The spotter has a gun too." Ed grabbed hold of the .50-caliber machine gun in its pintle mount and prepared to open fire. There were flashes of light from the Japanese spotter's gun before the plane began to bank toward them for another run. The PBY had the lead in their race to the deck, but the biplane was almost as fast and much more agile. Ed looked behind him for an instant, checking to see if the gun in the damaged blister was okay. He blinked. "Uh, Ben . . . I see smoke. Are we on fire?"

Even as Ben's mind absorbed Ed's report and he realized they were under attack by a lowly "Dave" or, to be more specific, a Nakajima Type

95, at present he was too busy to respond with anything more than "Shoot him!" He was trying to pull the big plane out of the dive he'd put it in while listening to the starboard engine, almost directly over Tikker's head, tear itself apart.

"Help me with the stick, Tikker! We've gotta get her nose back up!"

"Yes, yes!" agreed the copilot. "But the engine!" Everything Ben had taught him flew in the face of what they were doing right now.

"I know," Ben yelled to be heard over the calamitous uproar, "but we can't pull out with only one engine." He motioned over his head while he pulled back on the wheel. "I think the Japs must've knocked a jug off her—a cylinder. That's what that god-awful racket is, a piston flailing around, on the loose, banging the crap out of the jugs on either side." He shook his head and snorted, an almost rueful expression joining his clenched-teeth concentration. "I wouldn't have thought a Dave would have the firepower to do that."

"That kill engine?" Tikker asked nervously, looking up at the clattering monstrosity mere feet above his head. Oil was leaking everywhere, running back along the wing, spraying from the cowling, pouring a growing stream of gray-white smoke.

"Maybe," Ben replied. "Right now I just hope it has enough horsepower to keep us from getting wet!" From behind them, they heard the staccato and felt the vibration of one of the .50s opening up. He glanced nervously up at the engine and then at the gauges. Temperature was through the roof, oil pressure was nonexistent. RPMs were dropping . . . He looked at the altimeter and saw it was no longer spinning. With a sigh, he realized they'd begun to level off. Now, if they could shake or shoot down the enemy plane, they'd be all right. He began to give the order to shut down the starboard engine when it suddenly erupted in a bright fireball of greasy yellow flames.

"Shit!" screamed Tikker. "Fire! Fire! We on fire! We burn! Goddamn!"

"Cut the fuel!" yelled Ben. "Activate the fire extinguisher and feather the prop!"

Tikker quickly obeyed. He closed the valve that allowed fuel to flow to the burning engine and hit the extinguisher, but in growing panic he scanned the control panel.

"I cut fuel and use extinguisher like you tell me—like you *show* me! But you never show me feathers for prop!"

If Ben hadn't been so terrified, he would have laughed. As it was, he simply reached over and feathered the prop himself and watched while the blades turned edge-on, somewhat reducing the drag of the now dead engine. Thankfully, the flames had almost entirely flickered out as well. A fuel line must have been hit too, and as fuel and oil sprayed on the increasingly hot engine ... Ben and Tikker both sighed with relief when the last ten-drils of flame disappeared. One disaster averted. Now what? Throughout the battle in the cockpit, they'd heard intermittent firing from aft and Ben wondered how Ed's battle was going. So far, the enemy had scored no further hits, but they were still on the defensive. That didn't sit well with Mallory's personality or fighter training. The question was, what else could they do? He glanced at the airspeed indicator; with the port engine at full throttle, they were barely hovering around ninety knots. He thought a Type 95 could do about a hundred and fifty, so they weren't going to outrun him.

He berated himself. That's exactly what he should have done from the start, if he'd known what was after them. The Japanese pilot must have used their leisurely exploration of the enemy fleet to work himself into what he thought was a one-chance attack. If Ben had thrown the throttles to the stops and slowly *climbed,* they would have had a forty-knot and ten-thousand-foot advantage. As it was, he, Lieutenant Benjamin Mallory, trained fighter pilot, had been bested in his first aerial combat by what was essentially an obsolete trainer with floats. It didn't matter that he'd assumed the enemy was far more capable. He shouldn't have assumed anything. Hindsight could hurt.

"Ed," he called over the intercom.

"Thanks for remembering me," came the sarcastic reply. "I see you have at least stopped our uncontrolled plummet to the sea and the smoke's not quite as bad."

"Sorry about that," Ben replied in his best upper-crust British accent. "One of our engines developed a bit of a ... stitch and we thought it best to let it rest a while. We only have one other one, you know." His voice turned serious. "What's our troublesome little friend been up to?"

"He's been coming in on our flanks, trying to get an angle on our engines, I guess. His last few tries have been to port. I guess he knows the other one's out."

"How are things back there?"

"One of the gunners is dead. I've been alone back here most of the time. I finally got the other one to snap out of it and he's doing okay. I think he got a piece of the bastard on his last attack. He's on the port side. Starboard's a little unpleasant."

"Understood."

"Other than that, things are about the same. We're a long way from home and almost out of ammo."

"Can the gunner back there handle things for now?"

"Well ... I guess."

"Good. Then I want you in the nose turret."

"The *nose* turret! Ben, this guy hasn't come anywhere near the nose since he started."

"That's about to change. Give all your bullets to the port gunner and tell him to hammer away the next time that Jap gets in range. He's got all the bullets in the world, got it?"

"Sure, but . . ."

"That's when I'm going to lower the wing floats."

"What! Damn, Ben! That'll just slow us down even further. We'll be sitting ducks!"

"No, listen! If he thinks we're about to set down, he'll pull out all the stops. He has to *shoot* this plane down to destroy it. Once we're down, he can shoot at it till he runs out of fuel or bullets—which he has to be getting low on—and not do any appreciable damage unless he gets another lucky hit on an engine. Besides, he's bound to know our marksmanship would improve dramatically. Hitting a moving target from a stationary one is a lot easier than moving versus moving."

"Are we going to land on the water?"

"Not unless we have to," Ben confessed.

"Why not? It sounds like the perfect plan. We'd have all the advantages. If we don't shoot him down, we just wait till he flies away." Ben cleared his throat.

"We set down only if we have to. Honest to God, I don't think I can get this crate off the water with one engine. Half the time I don't know how I do it with two. You keep forgetting—I'm not a seaplane pilot. I'm still making most of this up as I go."

Ed groaned. "Okay, Ben. I'm with you. And here comes our little friend, right on cue."

"Get in the nose, Ed. As soon as he starts shooting, I'm lowering the floats. Anything could happen after that."

Ed rushed forward. When he arrived, he was reminded just how much he hated the nose turret. It was built for guys a lot smaller than he was and it seemed like a stupid design. He had actually given it a lot of thought and believed he could have come up with something better. The first change would have been the emplacement of something more powerful than a measly .30-cal. It might have been a little cramped with a .50, but they could get a smaller guy. If they got a smaller guy to work the plane's radios and help with navigation, that would be fine too. He put on the headset and racked the bolt, chambering a round.

"Aaaa-eeesh!" cried the gunner in the waist. "I chop him up good that time! Shoot up tail! Maybe kill gunner. Get even for my friend!"

"Where'd he go?" questioned Ben.

"Straight out, away. Direction . . . nine . . . nine clocks?"

"You get that, Ed? I think it's working. Keep your eyes peeled."

"I got it." Palmer strained his eyes through the cloudy Plexiglas. The plane and all its components had been through so much, looking for a plane through the turret was like looking for a minnow in four feet of murky water.

In any event, it took much longer than any of them expected for the Dave to get around in front of them. Maybe it was being careful, or maybe it truly was damaged and had lost some speed. Whatever the reason, when Ed first saw the enemy plane, it was already closer than they'd hoped to spot it, but it was doing exactly what they'd expected: going for the PBY's remaining engine from the front.

"There he is," Ed announced, more calmly than he felt. "I can't judge distance through this crummy glass, though. You're going to have to tell me when he's in range."

"Uh, he's already shooting at us, so whenever you're ready . . ."

"Have you seen this can of ammo down here?" he demanded hotly. "This *one* can of ammo? I need him closer!" A few bullets began to strike the plane.

"He's getting closer!"

"Just a few more seconds!" Ed could see the plane clearly now. If it was damaged aft, he couldn't tell, but it was coming straight in, yellow flashing from its single forward firing machine gun. More bullets were hitting the PBY and Ben's voice grew more insistent. Even Tikker's voice rose in an indignant shriek. Ed paid no attention—even when one bullet grazed the curved Plexiglas mere inches in front of his face. He was concentrating on the sights. They were crude and pretty much limited to known ranges, but he aimed carefully at the steady target of the biplane's round engine, raised the sights a little, and started to fire. He wasn't using short bursts like he ought to have; he was trying to hose out a solid wall of lead that the seemingly flimsy biplane couldn't survive. Evidently, by the sounds of impact, that's what the enemy hoped as well.

Finally, exultantly, he saw a flash and a gout of smoke erupt from the Dave's engine, and the plane seemed to wobble as if the pilot was struggling for control. Ed let out a whoop, but an instant later the firing pin in the .30-cal snapped on an empty chamber. "I'm out!" he yelled over the comm.

"Relax," shouted Ben in return. It sounded like he was talking over a hurricane. "He must be empty too, or you wrecked his gun."

Ed studied the oncoming plane. Sure enough, the shooting had stopped . . . but why was he still coming on? The Japanese pilot was clearly having trouble keeping the plane in the air. He ought to have been headed for the deck where he could set down on the water and call for help. The last thing in the world he should be doing was struggling to maintain altitude and trying to keep his nose pointed right at the PBY as the distance between them closed . . . Ice water poured down Ed Palmer's back. "He's gonna ram us!" he shouted. "The crazy bastard's gonna ram us with his plane!"

"Where is he?" Ben's voice sounded almost as panicked as his own. "The windscreen is gone! All I've got is my sunglasses, but blood keeps getting in my eyes. Tikker doesn't even have sunglasses! You have to tell me, Ed!"

"Oh, God! . . . Okay! He's eleven o'clock low, so I doubt you'd see him over my turret anyway. We're closing pretty fast, so whatever you do, do it *now!*"

In the space of an instant, Ben Mallory made up his mind. Up and away would make them a bigger, slower target. Up and toward might do the same thing, but it was better. Down and away was probably the worst choice he could make. It would give the enemy time to fine-tune his aim. No, down and toward would surprise the enemy and he'd have no time to adjust. "Hold on!" he screamed.

Ed watched it all from the confines of the turret, almost removed somehow from the trauma of the moment. When Ben actually turned *toward* the suicide plane, his panic reached a point of almost surrealistic calm. Analytical. He thought he knew what Ben was trying to do and whether it was inspired by madness or brilliance he didn't know, but it seemed to be working. Suddenly, the Type 95 was clearly visible trailing smoke and angling for the spot the PBY would have been in just a few seconds. The big bright red circles clearly contrasted with the dark green paint. Ed almost thought he could see the pilot's face. It looked like they were clear. Then, with a tight, rolling maneuver that the big flying-boat could never match, the agile biplane flipped on its back, the light gray bottom of its big central float flashing in the sun, and slanted toward them again. Even if he'd had time to warn Mallory, he wouldn't have known what to say.

Someone must have warned him, or maybe he saw it himself, because the Catalina suddenly banked right as hard as he'd ever felt it—back toward the enemy again—but this time it was too little, too late. Ed closed his eyes when he felt the jarring impact and saw the first flash of the fireball.

It was midafternoon when *Walker* steamed into Baalkpan Bay and the usual midday squall had just passed. By the time they gazed upon the city in the steamy light, they could clearly see the many changes that had been made since they'd left. Fort Atkinson loomed above them at the harbor entrance; its big guns with their gaping mouths would be a formidable deterrent to a rational enemy. But the Grik weren't rational. They would be slaughtered, but chances were they'd get past the fort.

Around the city, they saw a high earthen rampart, reinforced with heavy timbers and faced by obstacles and entanglements on both sides of a wide moat. More heavy guns poked from embrasures and there was good killing ground before them. While they watched, work was under way to reinforce the overhead protection beyond the rampart—particularly over the guns. Pointless against *Amagi*'s main battery, of course, but it might help against secondaries or fragments. Beyond the fortifications, Matt saw little change to the city he'd come to think of almost as home, but the fortifications themselves made a profound difference.

In the distance, tied to the old fitting-out pier, was *Mahan*. A wisp of smoke coiled from her number one stack and she seemed to be nearly half covered by Chief Gray's new light gray paint scheme. Matt knew Jim wouldn't be goofing around with paint if a lot of his ship's other issues hadn't already been resolved.

By contrast, if the city and its surroundings looked different now than they had when *Walker* led the Allied Expeditionary Force to raise the siege of Aryaal, the destroyer had changed just as much. Gone was her own dazzling light gray paint. Instead, the elderly ship was almost a uniform orange color, with heavy, darker streaks down her sides. Harsh red rust shone through the smoke-blackened sections, and the large numbers, 163, that had stood so tall and proud at her bow were nearly obliterated. Clusters of splinter wounds and a few larger holes were visible in her flanks, and streams of water coursed over the side as beleaguered pumps struggled to force it out of the overloaded, battered hull. Alone she would have been a dismal, dispiriting sight, but the hundreds of hollow-eyed, bedraggled Lemurians packing her top-heavy deck gave testimony to the greater tragedy.

Because of her arrival, even with all the preparations under way, thousands of people were on hand to witness her slow approach to the dock. The contents of the radio message detailing the events of the night had rapidly spread. There was no reason to conceal the fact that *Nerracca* and most of the people aboard her were lost. It would have been a greater shock to the morale of the defenders if they'd known nothing until *Walker* came in alone. The one thing that mitigated against total despair was the obvious fact that *Walker* had put up a hell of a fight and had saved as many as she could. So strong was the Lemurian faith in the old destroyer's power, they felt sure if *Walker* looked this bad, surely *Amagi* was in much worse condition—if she had in fact survived. Most of them couldn't conceive of the difference between the two ships' relative size and power, and

Walker's daring, vengeful counterattack had been duly reported as well. It was still a somber crowd that waited to greet the survivors.

Finally, a sharp, congratulatory *toot! toot!* and a cloud of steam issued from *Mahan*'s repaired whistle and the trancelike immobility of the crowd was broken. Dockworkers shouldered their way through and positioned themselves to catch lines thrown by destroyermen on the ship. Up close, *Walker* looked even worse and the smoke and steam that rose from her aft stacks resembled nothing so much as an exhausted gasp. Gangplanks were rigged and the stunned survivors began to disembark. Some were met by family or acquaintances who had already arrived on *Humfra-Dar*. *Big Sal* was in the bay but hadn't yet reached the dock. No one aboard her would have any idea what had taken place. *Walker* flew only a cryptic signal as she churned past her lumbering old friend. "Glad to see you. Must off-load passengers before we sink."

Most of the survivors weren't met by anyone. They just wandered around in small, confused groups as though in a daze. Most were females or younglings who'd lost everything they ever knew. They'd suffered the trauma of leaving their homes and had nearly been killed at sea. Many of their loved ones were dead. Now they were cast on the shores of an unknown, alien land. Fortunately, someone in a position of authority had their wits about them, and squads of troops were detailed to gently take the refugees in hand. With as little fuss as possible, they were led away. At the urging of officers, the crowd began to disperse and return to their now even more insistent chores. When a lane was cleared, the wounded were carried ashore. There were quite a few.

Matt watched from the port bridgewing while Sandra supervised below. Beside her still was Queen Maraan, giving support and encouragement to the injured—no matter where they were from. Matt's admiration for the Orphan Queen had grown even greater than before. He knew she was a strong and respected leader to the people of B'mbaado, but she'd also shown herself to be wise and compassionate to her former Aryaalan enemies and strangers as well. He was certain she'd be a major unifying figure and a force to be reckoned with in the events that were to come. Beside him stood Chack, watching as well. The young Lemurian was tired but surprisingly alert after spending virtually the entire night in the crow's nest. Matt nodded toward the queen.

"Go give them a hand if you want," he said with a small smile. "Or you can hit the rack. It's your choice."

"If it makes no difference to you, Cap-i-taan, I will help the ladies." He grinned.

"That's fine, but be back aboard by the first watch. We've got a hell of a mess and the Chief's going to need your help. Try to get some sleep between now and then. It's going to be a busy night."

"Aye, aye, Cap-i-taan." Chack saluted him and bailed down the ladder. Matt shook his head. Very carefully, he tried to stretch. Not long before they opened Baalkpan Bay, he'd finally convinced Sandra to remove the rigid strapping that held his arm immobilized. He felt no pain at all from his ribs and the wound through his shoulder had healed remarkably well. That seemed to be the case with every patient treated with the infection-fighting goo. Sandra knew where it came from now—fermented polta fruit that was further processed in some seemingly mystical way—but she still didn't know what made it work and she yearned for a microscope to study it with. Matt didn't care what the stuff was so long as it worked and he was eager to get his considerably atrophied arm back in service. He stretched a little farther, tensing the muscles, and tried to raise the arm from his side. Salvos of pain shot in all directions, and with a wince he let the arm drop. The pain lingered, throbbing with heat, but as it began to subside, he tried again.

"Ahh!"

Deciding to delay his therapy a little longer, he looked back down at the dock. A procession of Guardsmen dressed in the colors of Nakja-Mur's clan had arrived and Nakja-Mur himself was ascending the gangway with Alan Letts and Jim Ellis. Despite the mess and the chaos on deck, Chief Gray managed to assemble a side party to receive them and the sound of his bosun's pipe twittered from below. A few moments later, the two men and the rotund Lemurian leader were admitted to the bridge. Out in the open air, salutes were exchanged and Jim and Alan extended their hands in heartfelt relief. To Matt's surprise, Nakja-Mur enveloped him in a crushing embrace.

"Ah!" Matt said again, clenching his eyes shut.

"I am so glad you and your ship did not die!" the High Chief exclaimed in much improved English. He was oblivious to the pain he'd accidentally caused.

"Me too," Matt agreed, once he could trust his voice. "*Nerracca* wasn't so lucky."

Nakja-Mur nodded grimly. "A terrible thing. I am deeply grieved and angered by its loss. As I am for *Revenge*." Matt remembered that almost the entire crew of *Revenge* had come from Baalkpan.

"*Revenge* died well, Nakja-Mur," he said quietly. "She destroyed hundreds of the enemy. The families of her people can be proud."

"They are," the High Chief confirmed. "As am I. But pride is mixed with sorrow."

"Of course."

Nakja-Mur gestured at the pier where the last of the wounded were being taken away. "You saved many from *Nerracca*."

"As many as we could. Tassat is a hero. He's the one that made it possible, by sending them over in the gri-kakka boats. When all was lost, it was his daughter herself who cut the cable that doomed her father but saved everyone else. A hell of a thing."

Nakja-Mur nodded. "Indeed. She and all her people will be welcome in my clan if they desire. They will probably go back to *Aracca*, but . . . they are welcome." He stopped for a moment but then looked up into Matt's eyes. It was time to get to the point. "Do you think you destroyed the iron ship of the enemy?" he asked urgently. Of course, by asking the question, Nakja-Mur confirmed Matt's fear as he looked again at the empty pier where the PBY should have been tied several hours before. So it hadn't just been moved ashore for repairs.

"Well, in that respect, it seems we have good news and bad," Matt hedged.

"I must know." The Lemurian pressed him. "Did you destroy that terrible ship?"

Matt finally exhaled and shook his head. "No," he said at last and watched the humans' faces fall. Nakja-Mur only blinked. "We got in a damn good lick and she wasn't in good shape to start with—but Ben's last report had her listing but afloat and under way."

Letts shook his head. "And it's not just the Japs. There's still tens of thousands of those damn lizards coming right at us. It's going to be tough with or without the Japs."

"We must have a council tonight," Nakja-Mur declared distractedly. "By then, with your Maall-orry's help, we will know exactly what we face, as well as when the blow will fall."

"No," Matt said. "That's more of the bad news—as well as the good." He gestured toward the empty pier. "It looks like the plane didn't make it. The last word we had was that *Amagi,* as well as the entire enemy fleet, has turned around and is headed for Aryaal. Signalman Palmer speculated it was damage to *Amagi* that influenced them to delay their attack, so at least we bought a little time. How much is anybody's guess." His voice became even grimmer. "Without the plane, it'll be harder to figure out." He looked at Jim and offered a brittle smile. "Right back where we started. Outnumbered, and no air cover."

"How can you be sure the plane is lost?" whispered Nakja-Mur, devastated.

"It should have beaten us here by two or three hours at least, and there hasn't been any radio contact since right after what I told you." He paused. "If you still want a meeting tonight, that's fine, but"—he gestured around at the ship—"I've got a lot of work to do between now and then. I'll see you tonight, Nakja-Mur."

"And I respectfully recommend," added Jim Ellis, "that we continue to prepare as if, as far as we know, they're coming straight on."

The High Chief blinked agreement. "We all have much to prepare." He turned to go, but then looked back at Matt. "I am *very* glad you did not die, Cap-i-taan Reddy."

"I think he kind of missed you, Skipper," Letts said when Nakja-Mur had gone. "I know I sure as hell did!"

They all glanced down the ladder to see Lieutenant Sandison clomping up the rungs. His clothes and hands were covered with grease and he'd smeared some across his nose. When he looked up and saw the officers gathered above him, his expression became apprehensive.

"What is it, Mr. Sandison?" Matt asked, his eyebrow arched at Bernie's apparent mood.

"Uh, final report on the condemned torpedoes, Captain."

"So soon?" Matt wasn't being sarcastic. He was genuinely surprised that the torpedo officer had come up with an answer so fast now that he was working on it again. Bernie visibly flinched. He did think the captain was being sarcastic. What's more, he thought he had every right to be.

"Well, sir, you may remember there were two of them," he temporized. Matt nodded.

"I believe I remember that number being mentioned," he said.

"And that they were submarine torpedoes . . ."

Matt nodded again, making a "come on" gesture with his hand. The fact they were submarine torpedoes didn't really matter. The MK-14s were virtually identical to the MK-15s designed for destroyer use, except they were shorter and had a shorter range. They were even identical down to the fact that they had all the exact same problems. They could still be used in *Walker*'s launchers, however. "Get on with it, Mr. Sandison."

"Uh, yes, sir. Well, one of them is totally wrecked. The one they pulled out of the side of that Dutch freighter. That's the one that had me looking at the exploders. Maybe we can use it for a pattern someday, for parts, but it's done for. It's just too badly damaged to repair."

"That's pretty much what you told me before," said Matt a little impatiently. "I assume you have news about the other torpedo?" Sandison nodded his head, looking miserable. "Well? What's the matter with it?"

"Nothing." He took half a step back.

"*Nothing?!*"

"Yes, sir. Nothing, as far as Lieutenant Shinya and I can tell. We've been all over that thing and we just can't find anything wrong with it." He held up his greasy hands.

"If there's nothing wrong with it, why would it have been condemned? Especially the way everybody was screaming for torpedoes?"

"Well, Captain, I got to thinking . . . maybe it wasn't really condemned."

"What the hell are you talking about?" Ellis interrupted. "Of course it was condemned! I was there when we swiped them, remember? They both had tags—"

Sandison shook his head. "No, sir, they *didn't* both have tags. This one didn't. That's why we never could figure out where to start looking for a problem."

"But—" Ellis stopped. "Then why was it in there *with* a bunch of condemned torpedoes?"

Sandison took a deep breath and then let it out. "Because it's old. It's not a MK-14 submarine torpedo; it's an MK-10!"

"What diff—" Alan Letts slapped his forehead. "Of *course!*" He turned to Captain Reddy. "The MK-10 is an S-Boat torpedo—an *old* S-Boat torpedo! The newer fish won't fit in the oldest subs we have—" He corrected himself, "I mean *had*. So they gathered up all the MK-10s to save them just for the older boats. They probably wound up with one running loose in Surabaya and stuck it with the rejects!"

Sandison was nodding. "That's what I was thinking."

Matt looked at him. "There's *nothing* wrong with it?"

"No, sir."

"We can use it?"

"Yes, sir. MK-10s are slow, but they bloody well *work*. They don't have any damn MK-6 exploders!"

Matt shook his head and closed his eyes, then opened them again and looked at nothing in particular. "We sure could've used it last night!"

"Yes, sir," Sandison agreed, miserable.

Matt patted him on the shoulder. "Not your fault." He glanced aft. "Thank Lieutenant Shinya for his assistance, but ask him to report to Mr. Alden to resume his primary duty of helping train Lemurian troops. We're going to need all we can get." He maneuvered Sandison slightly aside. "Please do discuss our . . . concerns about Mr. Shinya with Mr. Alden."

"Certainly, Captain."

After everyone returned to their duties, Matt found himself alone on the starboard bridgewing, staring out across the busy bay. He glanced at his watch. He'd tried not to allow himself to hope the PBY might still make it. If it lost an engine and Ben was flying very carefully it could conceivably arrive hours late. But no matter how he stacked it, he just couldn't justify the amount of time that had passed.

"Don't give up," came a soft voice beside him. He turned to see Sandra standing there, folding her bloody apron. She looked exhausted.

"On the plane? I'm afraid there's not much choice."

"I wouldn't write them off just yet, but that's not what I mean. I mean don't give up on what you've started here; this 'crusade' of yours to save the Lemurians—and, incidentally, us—from the creatures of whatever species that could do what was done to *Nerracca* last night." She sighed and looked at him almost apologetically. "I admit, at first I was skeptical we could accomplish much and afraid that we'd bitten off more than we could chew—especially after the Battle of Aryaal. But then I saw something happen. In spite of all the blood and suffering, or maybe even because of it, all these disparate peoples began to come together, to fight for a common cause. And all that happened because of you." She shrugged. "So we won a few battles by the skin of our teeth. So we lost a campaign. So we got kicked out and thousands of people died! Think about it: we saved many thousands more people than we lost—than would have been saved if we'd never acted." She paused, looking at him. Searching. "Eventually, the Grik and *Amagi* will come here. We will have prepared as best we can and the biggest, most horrifying battle ever waged on this entire planet will take place. And you know what? We're going to *win*! We'll win because we'll have an army of many cultures fighting for a common ideal, an army that's been trained to win. We'll win because of the memory of Aryaal and Baalkpan burning on the horizon, and we know the alternative to victory. And we'll win because of what happened to *Nerracca*. People, Lemurians, will remember, and they'll rally to that!" She glanced around and saw no one looking, then raised both hands and put them on his shoulders. "And we'll win because you'll be leading us." Her voice was intent. "You have to believe that!"

He smiled at her wistfully. "I believe almost every single thing you just said, except for one thing: I'm not as sure as you are that we'll win." Sandra seemed thoughtful for a moment, as if considering his words, then looked at him with a strange expression.

"The same 'not sure' the PBY will return? More? Less?"

"I'm a little more sure than that." His voice lowered. "Sandra, the plane is lost."

"Sure?"

He was becoming a little annoyed, and was about to say, "Sure," when he saw the impish look on her face. Then his gunnery-damaged hearing caught it too—about the same time the other human destroyermen did, and he realized that even Sandra had been relying on the excited reactions of Lemurian crewfolk on the fo'c'sle. The bells on both ships began to ring and the whistles blew. What had been rather somber destroyermen and dockworkers now leaned on the rails and shouted or waved their hats in the air. They could see the plane now, out over the bay. It was running on only one engine, but they'd seen that the day it first arrived. Something was different this time, though.

"Pipe down!" bellowed the Bosun loud enough for the crews of both ships to hear. He leaned over the side. "Stow that crap and get some men in Scott's launch!" Gray caught himself and looked up at the captain. Matt nodded, making it official. From now on, the big launch would be named after *Walker*'s former coxswain. Everyone had learned of his death as soon as they tied up and many were deeply saddened by the loss. The news came as yet another blow after the last few days they'd endured. Sandra took it hard; he'd saved her life. But, oddly, Silva seemed the most affected. Everyone knew the two men were friends, but as soon as Nurse Cross was seen telling him the news, he disappeared entirely.

The PBY labored as close to its usual landing area near the pier as it could get, but apparently exhausted, it seemed to give up. The plane's nose was a little high, and the tail of the boat-hull dragged on the water until the plane just stalled, and with a thundering boom, pancaked almost to a stop on the mercifully calm water. It was as close to a controlled crash as the plane and its crew could probably survive. The exuberance of a moment before turned to a collective horror at the condition of the plane, and dread over the condition of the crew.

The starboard propeller was feathered and the cowling was riddled with holes and black with smoke. Virtually the entire plane was full of holes, for that matter, and even if they weren't very big, they seemed to concentrate in critical areas—where people had been. The cockpit windscreen was shot away, as were both the observation blisters. A few holes even crazed the nose turret. As for the rest of the plane, the wings had taken enough hits for fuel to be dripping from numerous places, in spite of the self-sealing tanks. Exotic colors dappled the water where the drops fell. The canvas control surfaces, particularly on the port side of the tail, were ravaged, and the aluminum skin around them seemed riddled by shrapnel. Most terrifying, and frankly amazing, of all was that beyond the port wing float, three or four feet of the wingtip were missing, as was the entire port aileron, as if they'd been bitten off by a shark. The float itself was unsupported, but just by hanging there it kept the wing out of the water. At least here, in the calm.

"My God," murmured Sandra, her smile fading away. "How did they ever make it?" Matt was wondering to himself how many actually had. Scott's launch throttled up and headed for the plane even as its remaining engine wound down. It wasn't even going to attempt an approach to the pier. One of *Mahan*'s launches raced to assist. While they watched, three bloody forms were removed from the plane and loaded in Scott's launch. One was clearly human. They were joined by a human and a 'Cat and when they were aboard, the launch throttled up and headed for the pier, where an ambulance cart awaited. Nurse Karen Theimer, whom they'd left in Baalkpan, had taken to heart her directive to continue working to establish an efficient hospital and ambulance corps.

Three of the launch's passengers were whisked away on the 'Cat-drawn cart, while the others painfully scrambled across *Walker*'s gangplank. A few moments later, they both stood before Matt, Sandra, and a growing number of officers from both ships. Probably only Chief Gray's imposing presence could have kept the rest of the crew at a respectful distance.

Ed Palmer saluted and Jis-Tikkar nervously copied the gesture. He'd never met Captain Reddy before. Ed's voice was exhausted and full of delayed stress when he spoke.

"Captain Reddy, I must report the successful completion of our mission to observe the enemy fleet and report their course and disposition." He sighed. "I must also report that Lieutenant Mallory was badly wounded in the head and shoulder and both of our waist gunners were killed." The Lemurian elbowed him sharply and Palmer rolled his eyes. "Acting copilot trainee Jis-Tikkar was also bravely wounded during the action." Tikker proudly tugged on his right ear, displaying the neat, round 7.7-millimeter hole. Matt nodded in appreciation of the Lemurian's sacrifice, then returned his attention to Ed.

"What happened?"

"We got jumped by a plane." Palmer continued his tale in the face of astonished expressions, detailing everything from the first shot to the last. When it came time to describe the final act, his own expression turned to one of incomprehension.

"He just rammed into us, Skipper. Deliberately. The fight was over. There was nothing either of us could do to the other, but despite everything Ben could do—he almost got us clear—that Jap still managed to hit us. As he tore into our wing, though, the wing must've ripped open his fuel tank. He was already on fire and he just blew up. That's where all the damage on the port side came from and that's when our other waist gunner bought it."

"Is that when Mr. Mallory was incapacitated?"

"Well, no, sir, he was already wounded. Bad scalp wound and shot through the shoulder. But he was still flying until about an hour ago. He was getting woozy from blood loss, so I got him out of the chair and patched him up. He . . . sorta told us what to do after that." Matt blinked.

"Am I to understand that you, Signalman Palmer, flew and landed that plane?"

"No, sir," answered Ed distinctly. That left only one other possibility. Matt looked incredulously at the Lemurian standing as tall and straight as he could—and coming up to Ed's shoulder. "He sat on two parachute packs and I worked the rudder. It was . . . a little uncoordinated at first, but we got the hang of it." Matt grinned at what had to have been a monumental understatement.

"Very well, and well done. Now, both of you get some rest. With Mr. Mallory laid up, you two will have your jobs cut out for you coordinating repairs to the plane." He paused. "By the way, you're both promoted. I just have to figure out what to. Carry on."

"Aye, aye, Skipper," replied Ed with a tired grin of his own. He pointed at the plane. "We'll get some rest, but I recommend you get somebody to drag that thing up on the beach before it sinks."

When everyone had returned to their duties, or in Ed and Tikker's case, gone ashore to their berths, Matt found himself almost alone with Sandra again. Almost, because they'd been joined by Courtney Bradford. Together they watched while hundreds of Lemurians heaved on ropes, dragging the battered plane ashore. The exotic city of elevated pagoda-like structures with their slightly eastern flair was now strangely familiar and certainly a welcome sight.

"Remarkable!" Courtney exclaimed.

"Indeed," agreed Matt. "Remarkable in every way." He looked at Sandra and smiled. "Everything that's happened since we got to this world. Remarkable deeds accomplished by remarkable people, both humans and 'Cats." He shook his head, looking back at the plane. "And that's why I won't give up and why, eventually, we'll win." He snorted. "We may not live to see it, and this city will probably look worse than that plane, but if the enemy comes here, we'll beat them here and then wherever else we have to because, in the end, we have no choice—and it's the right thing to do."

*I*sak Rueben, Gilbert Yager, and Tab-At emerged into the light. They'd gone to their berthing space only to discover their racks were wrecked, along with most of the others, and so, on a whim, they decided to expose themselves to the outside world for the first time in several days. They resembled disoriented, grimy moles, squinting and sniffing at the unaccustomed evening sunlight. Gradually, their eyes began to adjust. All around was frantic activity. Rapid repairs were under way, being performed by the ship's crew and dozens of Lemurian yard workers. The Mice had a lot of work as well, but they'd just stood eight consecutive watches and Spanky ordered them to take one off and get some sleep. That order was going to be difficult to follow. Everywhere they looked they saw extremely noisy activity.

Right in front of them, the perforated number four torpedo mount was being disassembled. It was destroyed beyond repair, but they could salvage the steel. An incessant staccato clanging came from everywhere as tortured plates were beaten back into shape, and arcs of fire soared in all directions as the welders went to work. Air hoses and torch lines snaked underfoot and the smell of hot steel and burning paint filled the air along with bilingual curses. To Isak, the scene looked more like the scrapyards of hell than the deck of a ship that might ever fight again.

Slowly, they worked their way forward through the jostling workers, trying to avoid being knocked down, burnt, or crushed. They made it under the shade of the amidships gun platform, but things were just as hectic there. Lanier was sitting on a stool, watching protectively while repairs were made to the galley. The shredded Coke machine lay in state on its back off to one side. For a wreath, somebody had decorated the dead machine with a silk lei they'd brought from Pearl when they joined the Asiatic Fleet. The compressor and tubing had already been removed. Lanier was guarding a platter of sandwiches on his lap. By the crumbs around his mouth, an undetermined number no longer required his protection.

"Here," he said, offering the plate as the Mice squeezed past. His voice held little of its usual acerbic impatience. It just sounded . . . sad. "Nothin' but sammiches for a while, till the galley's fixed. Thank God they didn't get the refrigerator! No fresh bread—you better eat one of these!" he insisted. When all three Mice accepted one, Lanier continued talking, shaking his head mournfully. "Made these with the last of the bread. Now we're gonna be tryin' to choke down that local shit until I get my oven back."

"It could'a been worse," Yager said, taking a bite. "How's Mertz?"

Lanier waved his hand. "Got a piece of shrapnel in his ass, and a couple more in the back of his leg. Lost a finger too, and he thinks it's a big deal. Hell, he's got nine more. No, the worst part is, besides the Coke machine, the damn Japs got my spice locker! The last black pepper in the whole wide world's just . . . gone! Sneakiest stunt they've pulled since Pearl Harbor!" Lanier's tone began to return to normal as he seethed. "Bastards!"

Tabby was surprised by the cook's priorities, but Isak and Gilbert both nodded solemnly. "It's a hell of a thing," Isak agreed. "How's your gut feelin', Earl?" Lanier glared up at him.

"None of your goddamn business, snipe!" He straightened up on the stool as best he could and pulled his shirt closed over his grimy bandage. "Now you've stolen the best sammiches I had left, why don't you quit goofin' off and get back to work! I can't fix the whole ship by myself!"

They crossed the deck and ducked under the bridge beside the radio shack. Clancy was inside with the hatch open. His earphones were on his head and he nodded as they passed. Who knew what he was listening for. Going through the hatchway that led onto the foredeck, they emerged into sunlight again. Finally they'd found a place that hadn't been damaged the night before—beyond a few dents and scratches from shell fragments—and so, for now at least, it was probably the quietest place on the ship. They crawled up under the splinter shield of the number one gun and stretched out in the sparse shade beneath it.

"Laan-yeer is a strange man," Tabby observed at length. "He think whole ship—just so he have galley."

"Yeah," Isak agreed from beneath his right arm, which rested across his eyes. "But we're sort of the same way, I guess. Nothin' really matters except our boilers. Spanky has it tough. He has to worry about the boilers *and* the engines. Other stuff too. Chief Gray's like that with the topsides. But that's just the way it is. Everybody has a particular part of the ship that it's their job to take care of. Nobody could do it all."

"Except the cap-i-taan," Tabby said thoughtfully. "He have to worry about everything. Not just all ship, but *everything*."

They lay quietly for a moment, listening to the racket from aft.

"Yeah," Yager breathed at last. "I sure wouldn't want his job."

MEET THE AUTHOR

Photo: © Jim Goodrich

TAYLOR ANDERSON is a gunmaker and a forensic ballistic archaeologist who has been a technical and dialogue consultant for movies and documentaries. He is also a member of the National Historical Honor Society and of the United States Field Artillery Association, which awarded him with the Honorable Order of St. Barbara. He has a master's degree in history and teaches that subject at Tarleton State University in Stephenville, Texas. He lives in nearby Granbury with his family.